Generally regarded as America's most distinguished modern novelist, William Faulkner garnered most of the literary honors available, including the Nobel Prize, the Pulitzer Prize, and the National Book Award. In his own lifetime, he moved from relative obscurity to international prominence. Born in New Albany, Mississippi, on September 25, 1897, he lived in nearby Oxford until his death, on July 6, 1962. His parents were members of old and respected Southern families, and his schooling was concentrated but informal. He read extensively on his own and attended high school and the University of Mississippi, although he was never graduated from either. He served in the British Royal Air Force during the First World War, then worked at odd jobs and drifted to New Orleans, where he began writing for a "little magazine." His early novels, *Soldiers' Pay, Mosquitoes, Sartoris,* and *The Sound and the Fury,* attracted favorable attention, but with the publication of *Sanctuary* he finally achieved financial as well as critical success. Despite the honors his writings earned, Faulkner preferred farming, hunting, and fishing in Oxford to the literary haunts of New York or California. A nonconformist as a person and as a writer, acutely sensitive and a dedicated artist, William Faulkner was an authentic and powerful storyteller who never deserted his vision, "to create out of the materials of the human spirit, something which did not exist before."

Sartoris

WILLIAM FAULKNER

FOREWORD BY
ROBERT CANTWELL

AFTERWORD BY
LAWRANCE THOMPSON

 A SIGNET CLASSIC

Published by
THE NEW AMERICAN LIBRARY, NEW YORK AND TORONTO

SIGNET TRADEMARK REG. U.S. PAT. OFF. AND FOREIGN COUNTRIES
REGISTERED TRADEMARK—MARCA REGISTRADA
HECHO EN CHICAGO, U.S.A.

SIGNET CLASSICS are published *in the United States* by
The New American Library, Inc.,
1301 Avenue of the Americas, New York, New York 10019,
in Canada, by The New American Library of Canada Limited,
295 King Street East, Toronto 2, Ontario

PRINTED IN THE UNITED STATES OF AMERICA

TO SHERWOOD ANDERSON

through whose kindness I was first published,
with the belief that this book will give him
no reason to regret that fact

FOREWORD *

William Faulkner's third novel, *Sartoris,* first published in 1929, is in many respects a key volume in his works, the one that sets the pattern for them all. *Sartoris* introduces the two great families who figure directly or indirectly throughout his cycle of novels—the Sartoris family and the Snopes family. In *Sartoris* Faulkner first outlined the town of Jefferson, which is the center of his fiction. And, finally, *Sartoris* marked a decisive change in his attitude toward his own work. His first two books, *Soldiers' Pay* and *Mosquitoes,* were bright and sardonic, and sometimes brilliant novels, but they were characterized by a casual and indifferent air, whereas with *Sartoris* his purpose became serious and remained so.

The change, which can almost be felt in the prose as the novel proceeds, is one of the most dramatic and unusual developments in literary history. Faulkner has told how he began to write fiction under the influence of Sherwood Anderson, to whom *Sartoris* is dedicated: he noticed that Anderson had a pretty good life, only working in the morning, and he thought that he would like to be a writer himself. Mrs. Anderson told him that if he wrote a novel she would get Sherwood to read it, and if Sherwood liked it he would get his publisher, Liveright, to publish it.

Faulkner wrote *Soldiers' Pay* in six weeks and took the manuscript to Mrs. Anderson. She returned it the next day, saying, "Sherwood says if he isn't required to read this he'll get Liveright to publish it." And so Faulkner became a novelist, Liveright giving him advances of $200 apiece on his next

* Here reprinted in abbreviated form.

two novels. "And then," he said, "I liked that money. It seemed to me a mighty easy way to earn money."

In his book *William Faulkner*, the critic Irving Howe has suggested that Faulkner was pulling the public's leg with this story. But he has so concluded by leaving out the most important part of it. What Faulkner was saying was that the same attitude toward his writing lasted until he wrote *Sartoris*. He was halfway through *Sartoris* when suddenly "I discovered that writing was a mighty fine thing," he said. "You could make people stand on their hind legs and cast a shadow. I felt that I had all these people, and as soon as I discovered it I wanted to bring them all back."

His story is confirmed by the lift in the quality of his writing in *Sartoris*. And after *Sartoris* Faulkner turned out in a few months, in an unbroken surge of creative activity, the great books on which his standing as a novelist depends: *The Sound and the Fury, As I Lay Dying, Sanctuary* (though it is not generally listed with them, and he has written disparagingly of it), *Light in August*. When he turned away from the Sartoris theme and the locale of Jefferson, as in *Pylon* and *The Wild Palms*, the result was a sense of strain in the books; he seems to be trying to recapture his earlier inspiration in them rather than to actually possess it. When he returned to the Sartoris story and setting with *The Hamlet*, in 1940, he wrote one of his best novels.

The dividing line in his work between its arty and frivolous earlier phase, and the power of its great period, is in *Sartoris*. More specifically, it is in something in *Sartoris* that reached beyond the novel itself and gave Faulkner the vision of his work as a whole. His first two novels were satires, but the basis of their satire is uneven, so that they often seem an expression of personal irritation and nervous rejection. Turning from them to *Sartoris*, we find ourselves at once in the concrete reality of the town of Jefferson, seventy-five miles from Memphis, a town in upland country, lying in tilted slopes against the unbroken blue of the hills, in the midst of good broad fields richly somnolent. As the novel proceeds we become aware of a mysterious sense of excitement and intensity, communicated by the sensuous images of the town, the country, and the woods rather than (as is customary in Faulkner's books) the violent action or the violent imagery.

There are the landmarks so often found in Faulkner's novels, the brick courthouse with stone arches rising among the elms, the monument of the Confederate soldier under the trees, shading his carved eyes with his stone hand, and the courthouse square, with its unbroken low skyline of old weathered brick. Four miles from the square, beyond the streets arched with trees, is the Sartoris house, white and simple, with a curving drive and iron gates, set among oaks and locust trees, with wisteria and roses at one end of the veranda, and inside a curving stairway of white spindles and red carpet, an expanse of shuttered sunlight broken by the crystal chandelier and the tall mirror. . . .

The quality that adds intensity to *Sartoris* is inspiration, and the sources of inspiration are always beyond the reach of critical analysis. About all we can say is that continued effort along probably fruitful lines ensures a greater likelihood of inspiration finding an outlet when, if ever, it occurs. Faulkner had been writing for a considerable period on *Soldiers' Pay* and *Mosquitoes* when he was inspired with the concept of Colonel Sartoris that came with this book. . . . Colonel Sartoris is modeled on Colonel William C. Falkner, his great-grandfather. . . .

Colonel Falkner was born in Knox County in eastern Tennessee in 1825 (though the authorities differ as to the exact time and place), and was taken to Ste. Genevieve, Missouri. His father died when William was still a child. As an orphan he walked from Middleton, Tennessee, to Ripley, Mississippi, to make his home with an uncle, some time between the ages of ten and fourteen—an epic journey of which he wrote a brilliant, if romanticized, account in his novel *The White Rose of Memphis*. For four years, while he went to school, he worked in the Ripley jail, employed by the sheriff—another experience of which he made good use in *The White Rose*.

In 1845 an emigrant family named Adcock, moving from Tennessee to the West, stopped for the night at the camping grounds north of Ripley. A man named McCannon killed all the members of the family with an ax, stole the slaves, and started back to Tennessee. McCannon was caught near the Tennessee line, and a mob prepared to lynch him. Young Falkner started out at midnight with the posse after McCannon, rode twenty miles, and helped rescue the murderer from the mob, despite guns drawn against him. McCannon was taken back to Ripley to stand trial. There, however, another mob got him away from the authorities. Again at the point of being hanged, McCannon gained some time by promising to tell the full story of the crime. He confessed, and in the period before his execution told the story of his life to young Falkner, who wrote it up and had it printed as a pamphlet, on credit, at the press of the Ripley *Advertiser*.

He offered the pamphlet for sale on the day of McCannon's execution. It was a terrific success, and after paying the newspaper, Falkner cleared $1,250, the first money he had ever earned. His enemies later pictured him hawking the pamphlet to the crowd while McCannon's body was still spinning from the limb of a tree in the yard before the Ripley courthouse—some townspeople continued to do so, in fact, in William Faulkner's lifetime. But there is no contemporary evidence for such a grisly scene, nor any indication in Falkner's character of a tendency to work in that fashion.

There is abundant contemporary evidence, however, that Falkner's pamphlet aroused intense hostility from prominent people in nearby communities—Tuscumbia, Alabama, and Holly Springs, Mississippi, among others—who were mentioned in McCannon's narrative as his friends and the companions of his drinking bouts. These threatened to horsewhip Falkner, or worse. The Ripley *Advertiser* came to Falkner's defense. It stated that there was no young man in the community who stood higher in terms of moral integrity and courage. These comments were exchanged early in 1846. In May of that year, when the Mexican War began, Falkner was elected first lieutenant of the Tippah Volunteers, his commission being dated June 1, 1846. The company was attached to the Second Regiment, Second Mississippi Infantry, and saw service in Mexico, where Falkner was wounded on April 14, 1847.

The second lieutenant of the company was Robert Hindman, whose brother, Thomas Hindman, was a private in the ranks.* These were the sons of a prominent and long-estab-

---

* According to *Biographical Sketches of Gen. Pat Cleburne, and Gen. T. C. Hindman,* by Charles Edward Nash, a kinsman of Hindman by marriage, Hindman, who had "a wonderful talent for getting into fusses" and was "ambitious and overbearing," was promoted to first lieutenant in Mexico for valorous conduct.

lished family, the father a hero of the War of 1812, who lived in a new mansion two and a half miles from Ripley. Young Falkner and the Hindmans were friends. After the war they returned to Ripley, where Falkner married Miss Holland Pearce, of Knoxville, Tennessee, and began to practice law in his uncle's law office.

On May 8, 1849, Falkner met Robert Hindman, apparently beside the Hindman house. To his astonishment, Hindman violently attacked him. He stated that he knew of no reason for Hindman's fury, and his account is altogether convincing. Hindman drew a pistol. Falkner grabbed his arm. Hindman, who was stronger, threw Falkner back against the wall of the house. (Both Hindman brothers were large, powerful men, locally remembered as "brave, fearless, high-strung," or even aggressive in the extreme, inclined to be reckless, but "no braver men ever lived than those two brothers.") Hindman placed his pistol at Falkner's breast and pulled the trigger.

The gun failed to fire. Falkner drew his knife. Hindman cocked the gun again and fired again. The pistol again failed to fire. Subsequent examination revealed that the bullets did not exactly fit; the hammer did not quite strike the cap. As Hindman tried to fire the third time, Falkner stabbed and killed him.

Falkner was arrested, charged with murder. The case split the town. The trial was not held until February, 1851, the next regular term of the court. In the meantime, Falkner's wife died, after bearing him a son, William Faulkner's grandfather. Thomas Hindman, who had just been admitted to the bar, made his first speech as the prosecuting attorney, "pregnant with bitter denunciation." But the evidence made out a clear case of self-defense, and Falkner was acquitted.

As he stepped from the courtroom into the Ripley street, Thomas Hindman attacked him. In the struggle, Falkner killed a man named Morris, a Hindman partisan in the feud that was dividing the town.

Falkner was immediately rearrested and tried for the murder of Morris and again acquitted.

On this occasion, as he stepped forth free, he met Thomas Hindman in the dining room of the Ripley hotel. Hindman drew his pistol, but dropped it, and it fired as it hit the floor, the bullet striking the ceiling above Falkner's head.

Hindman challenged Falkner to a duel. Falkner did not believe in dueling as a matter of principle, but he accepted the challenge and prepared to meet Hindman at 6 A.M. on April 1, 1851, at the dueling ground 400 feet from the Arkansas bank of the Mississippi River, opposite the foot of Jefferson Street in Memphis. There were to be no seconds or surgeons present, and only one witness, who was to do nothing but keep out of the way. Both men were to be armed with two pistols at fifty paces, and at the word were to advance on each other, firing as often as they wished or were able.

Before the duel, Falkner and a friend, Dr. De Soto, met Hindman. De Soto drew his pistol and started to shoot Hindman, but Falkner grabbed the gun, and the hammer struck his hand.

The witness chosen was Colonel Galloway, an editor of the Memphis *Appeal,* who had a reputation as a peacemaker. He learned that Falkner knew of no reason for the Hindmans' animosity and succeeded in preventing the duel; Hindman subsequently moved to Arkansas.

Falkner remained in Ripley, where he became a leader of the Know-Nothing party and the editor of its paper, *Uncle Sam,* which held it together.* When the Civil War began,

---

* The Know-Nothing party was an attempt to substitute anti-Catholic and antiforeign agitation for the issue of slavery, which was dividing the country. At the height of its influence, in 1855, the Know-Nothings elected governors and legislatures in New Hampshire, Massachusetts, Rhode Island, Connecticut, New York, Kentucky, and California, and nearly carried Texas, Virginia, Georgia, Alabama, Mississippi, and Louisiana. It was a secret, fraternal order, organized in lodges like the Masons, and only members who reached the higher degrees knew its full name ("The Sons of '76, or Order of the Star-Spangled Banner") or its precise objectives. They answered questions about it by saying "I don't know," which resulted in its popular name.

After leaving Mississippi, Hindman as a young lawyer and politician conducted a whirlwind campaign against the Know-Nothings, who were at the point of dissolution nationally, and became famous for having destroyed the Know-Nothings forever in Arkansas. He fought, or barely avoided by the action of peacemakers, a number of duels. At a political rally, Colonel Falkner strangely spoke in his favor.

In 1858 Hindman accused a politician named Rice of selling out to the Know-Nothings. Rice left town, Helena, Arkansas, and returned with his brother. Saying that he feared he would not have a fair chance, Hindman asked the help of Pat Cleburne, a young drug clerk, formerly a British Army officer and later one of the finest officers in the Confederate Army. As the two men walked past

Falkner raised his own company, the Magnolia Rifles of Tippah County, and was elected captain on February 23, 1861. The Magnolia Rifles became part of the Second Infantry of the Confederate States Army, of which Falkner was elected colonel. He had in the meantime, in 1850, married a second time, his second wife bearing him four children: three daughters and a son. The Second Infantry under his command played an important part at the Battle of Bull Run, after which it went into winter quarters at Harpers Ferry. There Mrs. Falkner and the children joined the Colonel, one son and a newborn daughter, christened Elizabeth Manassas, having died in Ripley in Colonel Falkner's absence. In the elections in the spring of 1862, John M. Stone, a former station agent at Iuka on the Memphis and Charleston Railroad, was elected colonel of the Second Mississippi, and Colonel Falkner returned to Ripley. He bore a commission from Jefferson Davis to raise a cavalry regiment.

Some local sources in Ripley imply that Colonel Falkner's Civil War record was "nothing to be proud of." Actually, no such interpretation need be made of his return. The time was after the Confederate disaster in Grant's capture of Fort Donelson and Island No. 10, and the need for cavalry in the vast country, now wide open for invasion, was evident

---

Moore's dry-goods store on the streets of Helena, a shot from behind the door, at a distance of three feet, missed Hindman. A second shot struck Cleburne in the back. A physician, a cousin of the Rice brothers, standing across the street, shot Hindman in the breast, and was killed, as both Cleburne and Hindman, before falling, shot him in the bowels. Cleburne hovered between life and death for ten days. Hindman was not seriously wounded.

Dr. Nash, in whose drugstore Cleburne worked, and who wrote his recollections of both men, feared to remove the bullet from Cleburne's back. It was later removed by Hindman's brother-in-law.

Hindman became a power in Arkansas politics, built a mansion in Helena (later a Catholic school), and resigned his seat in Congress as secession got under way. He enlisted as a private in Yell's Rifles, was elected captain, became a Confederate major general, and fled to Mexico, where he operated a coffee plantation, after the Civil War. His wife's parents had objected to his courtship of her. They sent her to a Catholic school, St. Agnes, in Memphis, to get her away from him. Posing as her uncle, Hindman managed to see her at the school, and they were subsequently married. In Mexico Hindman seems to have prospered, but Mrs. Hindman objected to the children being brought up under Catholic influence, and they returned to Helena during Reconstruction. At a political meeting, Hindman objected to statements made by Clayton Powell at a Negro meeting and was killed.

even before Shiloh, only forty-odd miles away. Also, the strange local situation in northern Mississippi, always exceptional in the course of American history, warranted the presence of an experienced officer who knew the country. Falkner organized the Seventh Mississippi Cavalry, sometimes called the First Partisan Rangers. He had his regiment up to full strength in the spring, but in the fall of that year it was completely disorganized. In March, 1863, we find him reporting to the head of the Confederate Secret Service in the Middle West that the men were leaving the regular army to enroll in the irregular state units, where they were not subject to discipline and were able to live at home. He reported that they were foraging off the people, stealing all the horses (a forecast of Ab Snopes), terrorizing the women, and confiscating the property of those they called Tories. He reported that robberies and the murders of unarmed citizens were a daily occurrence, that the independent squads were growing rich by speculation and trading with the enemy, and that the people would not be able to make a crop unless some protection was afforded them. He added a note that "the Genl"—meaning Forrest—"need have no fears of my being surprised or overpowered, because I know every creek, road and path in these northern counties."

A Northern expedition that set out for Ripley in May, 1864, from Memphis reported that for forty miles the country was completely devastated. In July of that year Ripley itself was destroyed. The circumstances were strange. When Sherman started for Atlanta, he ordered a movement of 8,000 troops from Memphis to distract Forrest and to prevent Forrest striking his lines of communication. When this force reached Ripley, a Northern officer, Colonel De Witt Thomas, asked Colonel Falkner's wife (who he said was a very intelligent woman) where General Forrest was and how many men he had. Mrs. Falkner laughed and said that Forrest had left the region to go after Sherman, but had now returned and would attack in a few days. She said that Forrest had 28,000 men.

The Northern commander stopped in Ripley and held a council of his senior officers. He said that he wanted to turn back because Forrest had probably concentrated an overwhelming force against him. His officers were inclined to agree with him, but since a previous expedition had turned

back only a short time before, they felt the blow to morale
would be disastrous.

The decision was therefore reached to continue. On the
morning of June 10, 1864, the two armies met at Guntown,
or Brice's Cross Roads, on Tishmingo Creek. From its physical description, the town is probably the original of Faulkner's legendary town of Frenchman's Bend. The result was
a Northern debacle. The Northern losses were 2,240 men
killed, wounded, or missing, 22 guns, 250 six-horse wagons,
a thousand rounds of artillery ammunition and 300,000
rounds of small-arms ammunition, and great stores of medical and quartermaster supplies. Forrest, who had about
8,000 rather than 28,000 men, lost 96 men killed. At dawn
the next day, the fleeing Northern officers reached Ripley.
Mrs. Falkner had breakfast prepared and invited Colonel
Thomas to eat with her. "She wanted to know," he said, "if
I did not find her words very nearly correct." *

After the Civil War, as is told in *Sartoris,* Colonel Falkner
built the Ripley, Ship Island and Kentucky Railroad. At the
height of his prosperity he operated a plantation of 1,200
acres, managed a hundred tenants, and ran a gristmill, cotton mill, and sawmill. He started a college, Stonewall College, and wrote and produced a play about the Civil War,
The Lost Diamond. In 1880 the plant of the Ripley *Advertiser* burned and Colonel Falkner advanced the money to
get the paper started again, also writing *The White Rose of
Memphis* as a serial to help the paper along. With its background as the inside story of something comparable to the
Falkner-Hindman feud, *The White Rose* was a sensation and
doubled the circulation of the paper before it was reprinted
as a book. (It went into thirty-five editions and sold 160,000
copies before it went out of print, in 1909.) He then wrote
a historical novel, *The Little Brick Church,* and a book about
his travels in Europe.

In *Sartoris* Colonel Sartoris is described as having been
elected to the legislature after a hard fight. In life, Colonel
Falkner was nominated to the Mississippi legislature while
he was absent in New York. At five o'clock on the day of
his election he walked into the public square at Ripley. Ac-

* Colonel Thomas' report of his conversations with Mrs. Falkner are
included in *The Official Records of the War of the Rebellion,*
volume 77.

cording to contemporary newspaper accounts, he stopped to talk with an old friend, Thomas Rucker, about sawing some timber.

The two men were approached by a Ripley businessman, J. H. Thurmond, Falkner's partner in the building of the railroad and now his business rival and personal enemy. According to the Memphis *Appeal*, Thurmond drew a pistol without speaking and pointed it at the colonel.

"What do you mean, Dick?" Falkner said. "Don't shoot!"

Thurmond fired, and the bullet, a .44-caliber, entered Falkner's mouth, passed under his tongue, breaking the jawbone, and lodged in the right side of his neck under his ear. The shot was at such close range that Thomas Rucker's face was powder-burned. Colonel Falkner fell to the pavement. His son-in-law, Dr. Carter, wiped the blood from his face. Sitting on the pavement, Falkner turned to Thurmond, who remained standing nearby, and said, "Dick, what did you do it for?"

He died at eleven o'clock that night, November 5, 1889. Thurmond was tried and acquitted in one of the most sensational trials in the history of northern Mississippi. He moved to North Carolina, where he established another fortune in the textile industry, and the Falkners, after selling the railroad, began the moves that resulted in their settling in Oxford, Mississippi, where William Faulkner lived across the street from the old home of Jacob Thompson, the top secret agent of the Confederacy.

"Great God," says one of Faulkner's Negro characters after a comparable tragedy. "White folks." It is an appropriate comment for so strange and violent a career. The legend of Colonel Falkner was alive throughout the years of Faulkner's youth. The manner of Colonel Falkner's death was not a topic of casual conversation. It is still a delicate subject in the region. When William Faulkner was writing his great novels Colonel Falkner was still a living reality to people who lived around Ripley. They spoke of him as if he were still alive, up in the hills somewhere, and might come in at any time. As late as 1938, when I asked about Colonel Falkner there, I encountered the sensation described in the opening sentences of *Sartoris*, that of a living presence in the room, summoned up by the intensity of feeling that the colonel's life and death had aroused.

Ordinarily I do not take much stock in supernatural visitations, but I must admit that I felt uneasy at the response when I inquired about Colonel Falkner, and I felt that the people of whom I inquired were even more uneasy than I was. In 1952, in gathering some additional facts in Ripley, I encountered an even deeper sense of disquiet, as if the people who supplied the information feared that by doing so they ran the risk of arousing the spirits of Colonel Falkner and those of his former opponents to resume their quarrels. In retrospect the opening sentences of *Sartoris* are an extremely unusual beginning for a novel. What is that specific description again? The banker and the pauper sitting silently in the presence of a dead man who is more real than they are? A strange beginning for *Sartoris,* but an even stranger beginning for the cycle of novels that it inspired. The discovery that William Faulkner made when he was halfway through *Sartoris,* that writing was a mighty fine thing, was a potent revelation. It led to the creation of a picture of a whole society, a whole area, through three generations, the visualization of a kind of life previously unsuspected. It formed a vision of the South and of Southern small-town life that has profoundly modified American thought and influenced American literature so deeply that much contemporary writing scarcely reflects anything else. It led to the thirty years of labor to which Faulkner referred in his speech accepting the Nobel Prize.

A powerful visitation. In my own case, in asking about Colonel Falkner, I did not get quite the same impression of benignity in the spectral invocation that is ascribed to Colonel Sartoris' return in *Sartoris.* Fear would be a better word. But it is true that the ghost itself seemed benign, the fear being associated with something other than the recollection of Colonel Falkner personally. In any event, the legend of Colonel Falkner is so real that the opening scene of *Sartoris* is simply an acute description of a social fact in the region around Ripley. And this leads to an observation that must strike every reader who tries to relate Faulkner's fiction to the Mississippi countryside.

It is commonly asserted that the strength of Faulkner's novels comes from the depth of his absorption with the life of his own region. Most critics would agree that a prevailing weakness in modern American literature is the lack of a comparable sense of identification in most writers. Faulkner has consequently always been a central figure to the regionalists. He has been their proof of the advantage to the author of remaining in his own hometown, close to his origins, among people he knows, with traditions he understands, and away from the vast anonymous crowds of the cities, with whom he can have at best only a formal kinship. I am in agreement with their argument in general, but *Sartoris* and, still more, the legend of Colonel Falkner seem to me to prove that the writer must choose most carefully the small town he is to remain in. Faulkner's achievement was not that he chose to live in a provincial community, but that he selected this particular one. The life of northern Mississippi, on which he focused his imagination, needed an interpreter in the way that desert regions need irrigation. The immense influence of his work stands as a renewed affirmation of what one man can do. . . .

ROBERT CANTWELL

PART ONE

As USUAL, old man Falls had brought John Sartoris into the room with him, had walked the three miles in from the county Poor Farm, fetching, like an odor, like the clean dusty smell of his faded overalls, the spirit of the dead man into that room where the dead man's son sat and where the two of them, pauper and banker, would sit for a half an hour in the company of him who had passed beyond death and then returned.

Freed as he was of time and flesh, he was a far more palpable presence than either of the two old men who sat shouting periodically into one another's deafness while the business of the bank went forward in the next room and people in the adjoining stores on either side listened to the indistinguishable uproar of their voices coming through the walls. He was far more palpable than the two old men cemented by a common deafness to a dead period and so drawn thin by the slow attenuation of days; even now, although old man Falls had departed to tramp the three miles back to that which he now called home, John Sartoris seemed to loom still in the room, above and about his son, with his bearded, hawklike face, so that as old Bayard sat with his crossed feet propped against the corner of the cold hearth, holding the pipe in his hand, it seemed to him that he could hear his father's breathing even, as though that other were so much more palpable than mere transiently articulated clay as to even penetrate into the uttermost citadel of silence in which his son lived.

The bowl of the pipe was ornately carved, and it was charred with much usage, and on the bit were the prints of his father's teeth, where he had left the very print of his ineradicable bones as though in enduring stone, like the creatures of that prehistoric day that were too grandly conceived and executed either to exist very long or to vanish utterly when dead from an earth shaped and furnished for punier things. Old Bayard sat holding the pipe in his hand.

"What are you giving it to me for, after all this time?" he had asked.

"Well, I reckon I've kept it long as Cunnel aimed for me to," old man Falls answered. "A po'house ain't no fitten place for anything of his'n, Bayard. And I'm gwine on ninety-fo' year old."

Later he gathered up his small parcels and left, but still old Bayard sat for some time, the pipe in his hand, rubbing the bowl slowly with his thumb. After a while John Sartoris departed also, withdrawn rather to that place where the peaceful dead contemplate their glamorous frustrations, and old Bayard rose and thrust the pipe into his pocket and took a cigar from the humidor on the mantel. As he struck the match the door across the room opened and a man wearing a green eyeshade entered and approached.

"Simon's here, Colonel," he said in a voice utterly without inflection.

"What?" old Bayard said across the match.

"Simon's come."

"Oh. All right."

The other turned and went out. Old Bayard flung the match into the grate and put the cigar in his pocket and closed his desk and took his black felt hat from the top of it and followed the other from the room. The man in the eyeshade and the cashier were busy beyond the grille. Old Bayard stalked on through the lobby and passed through the door with its drawn green shade and emerged upon the street, where Simon in a linen duster and an ancient top hat held the matched geldings glittering in the spring afternoon, at the curb. There was a hitching-post there, which old Bayard retained with a testy disregard of industrial progress, but Simon never used it. Until the door opened and Bayard emerged from behind the drawn shades bearing the words "Bank Closed" in cracked gold leaf Simon retained his seat, the reins in his left hand and the thong of the whip caught smartly back in his right and usually the unvarying and seemingly incombustible fragment of a cigar at a swaggering angle in his black face, talking to the shining team in a steady, loverlike flow. He spoiled horses. He admired Sartorises and he had for them a warmly protective tenderness, but he loved horses and beneath his hands the sorriest beast bloomed and acquired comeliness like a caressed woman, temperament like an opera star.

Old Bayard closed the door behind him and crossed to the carriage with that stiff erectness which, as a countryman once remarked, if he ever stumbled, would meet itself falling down. One or two passers and a merchant or so in the adjacent doorways saluted him with a sort of florid servility.

Nor did Simon dismount even then. With his race's fine feeling for potential theatrics he drew himself up and arranged the limp folds of the duster, communicating by some means the histrionic moment to the horses so that they too flicked their glittering coats and tossed their leashed heads, and into Simon's wizened black face there came an expression indescribably majestical as he touched his whiphand to his hat-brim. Bayard got into the carriage and Simon clucked to the horses, and the onlookers, halted to admire the momentary drama of the departure, fell behind.

There was something different in Simon's air today, in the very shape of his back and the angle of his hat; he appeared to be bursting with something momentous and ill-contained. But he withheld it for the time being and at a dashing, restrained pace he drove among the tethered wagons about the square and swung into a broad street where what Bayard called paupers sped back and forth in automobiles; withheld it until the town was behind and they trotted on across burgeoning countryside cluttered still with gasoline-propelled paupers but at greater intervals, and his employer had settled back for the changing and peaceful monotony of the four-mile drive. Then Simon checked the team to a more sedate pace and turned his head.

His voice was not particularly robust nor resonant, yet somehow he could talk to old Bayard without difficulty. Others must shout in order to penetrate that wall of deafness within which Bayard lived, yet Simon could and did hold long, rambling conversations with him in that monotonous, rather high singsong of his, particularly while in the carriage, the vibration of which helped Bayard's hearing a little.

"Mist' Bayard done got home," Simon remarked in a conversational tone.

Old Bayard sat perfectly and furiously still for a moment while his heart went on, a little too fast and a little too lightly, cursing his grandson for a furious moment; sat so still that Simon looked back and found him gazing quietly out across the land. Simon raised his voice a little.

"He got offen de two o'clock train," he continued. "Jumped off de wrong side and lit out th'ough de woods. Section han' seed 'im. Only he ain't never come out home yit when I lef'. I thought he wuz wid you, maybe." Dust spun beneath the horses' feet and moiled in a sluggish cloud behind. Against the thickening hedgerows their shadow rushed in failing surges, with twinkling spokes and high-stepping legs in a futility of motion without progress. "Wouldn't even git off at de dee-po," Simon continued, with a kind of fretted exasperation, "de dee-po his own folks built. Jumpin' off de bline side like a hobo. He never even had on no sojer-clothes. Jes' a suit, like a drummer er somethin'. And when I 'members dem shiny boots and dem light yaller pants and dat 'ere double-jinted backin'-up strop he wo' home las' year . . ." He turned and looked back again. "Cunnel, you reckon dem foreign folks is done somethin' ter him?"

"What do you mean?" Bayard demanded. "Is he lame?"

"I mean, him sneakin' into his own town. Sneakin' into town on de ve'y railroad his own gran-pappy built, jes' like he wuz trash. Dem foreign folks done done somethin' ter him, er dey done sot dey po-lice atter him. I kep' a-tellin' him when he fust went off to dat 'ere foreign war him and Mr. Johnny neither never had no business at——"

"Drive on!" Bayard said. "Drive on, damn your black hide."

Simon clucked to the horses and shook them into a swifter gait. The road went on between hedgerows paralleling them with the terrific antics of their shadow. Beyond the bordering gums and locusts and massed vines fields new-broken or being broken spread on toward patches of woodland newly green and splashed with dogwood and judas trees. Behind laborious plows viscid shards of new-turned earth glinted damply in the sun.

This was upland country, lying in tilted slopes against the unbroken blue of the hills, but soon the road descended sheerly into a valley of good broad fields richly somnolent in the leveling afternoon, and presently they drove upon Bayard's own land and from time to time a plowman lifted his hand to the passing carriage. Then the road approached the railway and crossed it, and at last the house John Sartoris had built stood among locusts and oaks and Simon swung between iron gates and into a curving drive.

There was a bed of salvia where a Yankee patrol had halted on a day long ago. Simon brought up here with a flourish and Bayard descended and Simon clucked to the team again and rolled his cigar to a freer angle and took the road back to town.

Bayard stood for a while before his house. The white simplicity of it dreamed unbroken among ancient sunshot trees. Wistaria mounting one end of the veranda had bloomed and fallen, and a faint drift of shattered petals lay palely about the dark roots of it and about the roots of a rose trained on to the same frame. The rose was slowly but steadily choking the other vine. It bloomed now thickly with buds no bigger than a thumbnail and blown flowers no larger than silver dollars, myriad, odorless and unpickable.

But the house itself was still and serenely benignant and he mounted to the empty colonnaded veranda and crossed it and entered the hall. The house was silent, richly desolate of motion or any sound. He stopped in the middle of the hall.

"Bayard."

The stairway with its white spindles and red carpet mounted in a tall slender curve into upper gloom. From the center of the ceiling hung a chandelier of crystal prisms and shades, fitted originally for candles but since wired for electricity. To the right of the entrance, beside folding doors rolled back upon a dim room emanating an atmosphere of solemn and seldom violated stateliness and known as the parlor, stood a tall mirror filled with grave obscurity like a still pool of evening water. At the opposite end of the hall checkered sunlight fell in a long slant across the door, and from somewhere beyond the bar of sunlight a voice rose and fell in a steady preoccupied minor, like a chant. The words were not distinguishable, but Bayard could not hear them at all. He raised his voice again.

"Jenny."

The chanting ceased, and as he turned toward the stairs a tall mulatto woman appeared in the slanting sunlight at the back door and came sibilantly into the house. Her faded blue garment was pinned up about her knees and it was darkly and irregularly blotched with moisture. Beneath it her shanks were straight and lean as the legs of a tall bird, and her bare feet were pale coffee-splashes on the dark polished floor.

"Wuz you callin' somebody, Cunnel?" she said, raising her voice to penetrate his deafness. Bayard paused with his hand on the walnut newel post and looked down at the woman's pleasant yellow face.

"Has anybody come out here this afternoon?" he asked.

"Why, naw, suh," Elnora answered. "Dey ain't nobody here a-tall, dat I knows about. Miss Jenny done gone to her club-meetin' in town dis evenin'," she added. Bayard stood with his foot raised to the step, glowering at her.

"Why in hell can't you niggers tell me the truth about things?" he raged suddenly. "Or not tell me anything at all?"

"Lawd, Cunnel, who'd be comin' out here, lessen you er Miss Jenny sont 'um?" But he had gone on, tramping furiously up the stairs. The woman looked after him, then she raised her voice: "Does you want Isom, er anything?" He did not look back. Perhaps he had not heard her, and she stood and watched him out of sight. "He's gittin' old," she said to herself quietly, and she turned on her sibilant bare feet and returned down the hall whence she had come.

Bayard stopped again in the upper hall. The western windows were closed with lattice blinds, through which sunlight seeped in yellow dissolving bars that but served to increase the gloom. At the opposite end a tall door opened upon a shallow grilled balcony which offered the valley and the cradling semicircle of the eastern hills in panorama. On either side of this door was a narrow window set with leaded panes of vari-colored glass that, with the bearer of them, constituted John Sartoris' mother's deathbed legacy to him, which his youngest sister had brought from Carolina in a straw-filled hamper in '69.

This was Virginia Du Pre, who came to them two years
a wife and seven years a widow at thirty—a slender woman
with a delicate replica of the Sartoris nose and that expression of indomitable and utter weariness which all Southern
women had learned to wear, bringing with her the clothing
in which she stood and a wicker hamper filled with colored
glass. It was she who told them of the manner of Bayard
Sartoris' death prior to the second battle of Manassas. She
had told the story many times since (at eighty she still told it,
on occasions usually inopportune) and as she grew older the
tale itself grew richer and richer, taking on a mellow splendor
like wine; until what had been a harebrained prank of two
heedless and reckless boys wild with their own youth had
become a gallant and finely tragical focal point to which the
history of the race had been raised from out the old miasmic
swamps of spiritual sloth by two angels valiantly fallen and
strayed, altering the course of human events and purging the
souls of men.

That Carolina Bayard had been rather a handful even for
Sartorises. Not so much a black sheep as a nuisance, all of
whose qualities were positive and unpredictable. His were
merry blue eyes, and his rather long hair fell in tawny curls
about his temples. His high-colored face wore that expression
of frank and high-hearted dullness which you imagine
Richard First as wearing before he went Crusading, and
once he hunted a pack of fox hounds through a rustic taber-
nacle in which a Methodist revival was being held; and thirty
minutes later (having caught the fox) he returned alone and
rode his horse into the ensuing indignation meeting. In a
spirit of fun, purely: he believed too firmly in Providence,
as all his actions clearly showed, to have any religious convictions whatever. So when Fort Moultrie fell and the gover-
nor refused to surrender it, the Sartorises were privately a
little glad, for now Bayard would have something to do.

In Virginia, as an A.D.C. of Jeb Stuart's, he found plenty
to do. As the A.D.C. rather, for though Stuart had a large
military family, they were soldiers trying to win a war and
needing sleep occasionally: Bayard Sartoris alone was willing, nay eager, to defer sleep to that time when monotony
should return to the world. But this was a holiday.

The war was a godsend to Jeb Stuart also, and shortly
thereafter, against the dark and bloody obscurity of the

northern Virginia campaigns, Stuart at thirty and Bayard
Sartoris at twenty-three stood briefly like two flaming stars
garlanded with Fame's burgeoning laurel and the myrtle
and roses of Death, [incalculable and sudden as meteors in
General Pope's troubled military sky;] thrusting upon him like
an unwilling garment that notoriety which his skill as a
soldier could never have won him. And still in a spirit of
pure fun: [neither Jeb Stuart nor Bayard Sartoris, as their
actions clearly showed, had any political convictions involved
at all.

Aunt Jenny told the story first shortly after she came to
them. It was Christmas time and they sat before a hickory
fire in the rebuilt library—Aunt Jenny with her sad resolute
face and John Sartoris bearded and hawklike, and his three
children and a guest, a Scottish engineer whom John Sartoris
had met in Mexico in '45 and who was now helping him to
build his railroad.

Work on the railroad had ceased for the holiday season
and John Sartoris and his engineer had ridden in at dusk
from the suspended railhead in the hills to the north, and
they now sat after supper in the firelight. The sun had set
ruddily, leaving the air brittle as thin glass with frost, and
presently Joby came in with an armful of firewood. He put
a fresh billet on the fire, and in the dry air the flames crackled
and snapped, popping in fading embers outward upon the
hearth.

"Chris'mus!" Joby exclaimed, with the grave and simple
pleasure of his race, prodding at the blazing logs with the
Yankee musket barrel which stood in the chimney corner
until sparks swirled upward into the dark maw of the chimney in wild golden veils. "Y'ear dat, chilluns?" John Sartoris'
eldest daughter was twenty-two and would be married in
June, Bayard was twenty, and the younger girl seventeen;
and so Aunt Jenny, for all her widowhood, was one of the
chilluns too, to Joby. Then he replaced the musket barrel in
its niche and fired a long pine sliver at the hearth in order
to light the candles. But Aunt Jenny stopped him, and he was
gone—a shambling figure in an old formal coat too large
for him, stooped and gray with age; and Aunt Jenny, speaking always of Jeb Stuart as Mister Stuart, told her story.

It had to do with an April evening, and coffee. Or the
lack of it, rather; and Stuart's military family sat in the

scented darkness beneath a new moon, talking of ladies and dead pleasures and thinking of home. Away in the darkness horses moved invisibly with restful sounds, and bivouac fires sank to glowing points like spent fireflies, and somewhere neither near nor far, the General's body servant touched a guitar in lingering, random chords. Thus they sat in the poignance of spring and youth's immemorial sadness, forgetting travail and glory, remembering instead other Virginian evenings with fiddles among the myriad candles and slender grave measures picked out with light laughter and lighter feet, thinking "When will this be again? Shall I make one?" —until they had talked themselves into a state of savage nostalgia and words grew shorter and shorter and less and less frequent. Then the General roused himself and brought them back by speaking of coffee, or its lack.

This talk of coffee began to end a short time later with a ride along midnight roads and then through woods black as pitch, where horses went at a walk and riders rode with saber or musket at arm's length before them lest they be swept from saddle by invisible boughs, and continued until the forest thinned with dawn-ghosts and the party of twenty was well inside the Federal lines. Then the dawn accomplished itself yet more and all efforts toward concealment were discarded and they galloped again and crashed through astonished picket parties returning peacefully to camp, and fatigue parties setting forth with picks and axes and shovels in the golden sunrise, and swept yelling up the knoll where General Pope and his staff sat at breakfast *al fresco*.

Two men captured a fat staff-major. The others pursued the fleeing breakfasters for a short distance into the sanctuary of the woods, but most of them rushed on to the General's private commissary tent and emerged presently from the cyclonic demolition of it, bearing plunder. Stuart and the three officers with him halted their dancing mounts at the table and one of them swept up a huge blackened coffee-pot and tendered it to the General, and while the enemy shouted and fired muskets among the trees, they toasted one another in sugarless and creamless scalding coffee, as with a loving-cup.

"General Pope, sir," Stuart said, bowing to the captured officer. He drank and extended the pot.

"I'll drink it, sir," the major replied. "And thank God he is not here to respond in person."

"I had remarked that he appeared to leave hurriedly," Stuart said. "A prior engagement, perhaps?"

"Yes, sir. With General Halleck," the major agreed drily. "I am sorry we have him for an opponent instead of Lee."

"So am I, sir," Stuart answered. "I like General Pope in a war." Bugles were shrilling among the trees far and near, sending the alarm in flying echoes from brigade to brigade lying about the forest, and drums were beating wildly to arms and erratic bursts of musketry surged and trickled along the scattered outposts like the dry clatter of an opening fan, for the name Stuart speeding from picket to picket had peopled the blossoming peaceful woods with gray phantoms.

Stuart turned in his saddle and his men came up and sat their horses and watched him alertly, their spare eager faces like mirrors reflecting their leader's constant consuming flame. Then from the flank there came something like a concerted volley, striking the coffee-pot from Bayard Sartoris' hand and clipping and snapping viciously among the dappled branches above their heads.

"Be pleased to mount, sir," Stuart said to the captive major, and though his tone was exquisitely courteous, all levity was gone from it. "Captain Wylie, you have the heaviest mount: will you——?" The Captain freed his stirrup and hauled the prisoner up behind him. "Forward," the General said and whirled, roweling his bay, and with the thunderous coördination of a single centaur they swept down the knoll and crashed into the forest at the point from which the volley had come, before it could be repeated. Blue-clad shapes plunged scattering before and beneath them, and they rushed on among trees vicious with Miniés like wasps. Stuart now carried his plumed hat in his hand, and his long tawny locks, tossing to the rhythm of his speed, appeared as gallant flames smoking with the wild and self-consuming splendor of his daring.

Behind them and on one flank muskets still banged and popped at their flashing phantoms, and from brigade to brigade lying spaced about the jocund forest bugles shrilled their importunate alarms. Stuart bore gradually to the left, bringing all the uproar into his rear. The country became

more open and they swung into column at the gallop. The
captured major bounced and jolted behind Captain Wylie,
and the General reined back beside the gallant black thundering along beneath its double load.

"I am distressed to inconvenience you thus, sir," he began
with his exquisite courtesy. "If you will indicate the general
location of your nearest horse picket, I shall be most happy
to capture a mount for you."

"Thank you, General," the major replied. "But majors
can be replaced much easier than horses. I shall not trouble you."

"Just as you wish, sir," Stuart agreed stiffly. He spurred
on to the head of the column again. They now galloped
along a faint trace that was once a road. It wound on between vernal palisades of undergrowth and they followed it
at a rapid but controlled gait and debouched suddenly into a
glade, and a squadron of Yankee cavalry reined back in
amazement, then hurled forward again.

Without faltering Stuart whirled his party and plunged
back into the forest. Pistol balls were thinly about their
heads, and the flat tossing reports were trivial as snapping
twigs above the converging thunder of hooves. Stuart swerved
from the road and they crashed headlong through undergrowth. The Federal horse came yelling behind them and
Stuart led his party in a tight circle and halted it panting in
a dense swampy copse, and they heard the pursuit sweep
past.

They pushed on and regained the road and retraced their
former course, silently and utterly alert. To the left the sound
of the immediate pursuit crashed on, dying away. Then they
cantered again. Presently the woods thickened and forced
them to a trot, then a walk. Although there was no more
firing and the bugles too had ceased, into the silence, above
the strong and rapid breathing of the horses and the sound of
their own hearts in their ears, was a nameless something—a
tenseness seeping from tree to tree like an invisible mist,
filling the dewy morning woods with portent although birds
flashed swooping from tree to tree, unaware or disregardful
of it.

A gleam of white through the trees ahead; Stuart raised
his hand and they halted and sat their horses, watching him
quietly and holding their breath with listening. Then he ad-

vanced again and broke through the undergrowth into another glade. They followed, and before them stood the knoll with the deserted breakfast table and the rifled commissary tent. They trotted warily across and halted at the table while the General scribbled hastily upon a scrap of paper. The glade lay quiet and empty of threat beneath the mounting golden day; laked in it lay a deep and abiding peace like golden wine, yet beneath this solitude and permeating it, was that nameless and waiting portent, patient and brooding and sinister.

"Your sword, sir," Stuart commanded. The prisoner removed his weapon and Stuart took it and pinned his scribbled note to the table top. The note read: "General Stuart's compliments to General Pope, and he is sorry to have missed him again. He will call again tomorrow."

Stuart gathered up his reins. "Forward," he said.

They descended the knoll and crossed the empty glade and at an easy canter they took the road they had traversed that dawn; the road that led home. Stuart glanced back at his captive, at the gallant black with its double burden. "If you will direct us to your nearest cavalry picket, I will provide you with a proper mount," he offered again.

"Will General Stuart, cavalry leader and General Lee's eyes, jeopardize his safety and that of his men and his cause in order to provide for the temporary comfort of a minor prisoner to his sword?" the major said. "This is not bravery: it is the rashness of a heedless and headstrong boy. There are fifteen thousand men within a radius of two miles of this point; even General Stuart cannot conquer that many, though they are Yankees, single-handed."

"Not for the prisoner, sir," Stuart replied haughtily, "but for the officer suffering the fortune of war. No gentleman would do less."

"No gentleman has any business in this war," the major retorted. "There is no place for him here. He is an anachronism, like anchovies. At least General Stuart did not capture our anchovies," he added tauntingly. "Perhaps he will send Lee for them in person."

"Anchovies," repeated Bayard Sartoris, who galloped near by, and he whirled his horse. Stuart shouted at him, but Sartoris lifted his reckless stubborn hand and flashed on; and as the General would have turned to follow, a Yankee

picket fired his piece from the roadside and dashed into the
woods, shouting the alarm. Immediately other muskets exploded on all sides, and from the forest to the right came
the sound of a considerable body put suddenly into motion,
and behind them in the direction of the invisible knoll a
volley crashed. A third officer spurred up and caught Stuart's
bridle.

"Sir, sir!" he exclaimed. "What would you do?"

Stuart held his mount rearing, and another volley rang
behind them, dribbling off into single scattered reports,
crashed again, and the noise to the right swelled nearer. "Let
go, Alan," Stuart said. "He is my friend."

But the other clung to the bridle. "It is too late," he
cried. "Sartoris can only be killed; you would be captured."

"Forward, sir, I beg," the captive major added. "What is
one man to a renewed belief in mankind?"

"Think of Lee, for God's sake, General!" the aide implored. "Forward!" he shouted to the troop, spurring his
own mount and dragging the General's onward as a body of
Federal horse broke from the woods behind them.

"And so," Aunt Jenny finished, "Mister Stuart went on
and Bayard rode back after those anchovies, with all
Pope's army shooting at him. He rode yelling, 'Yaaaiiiih,
Yaaaiiiih, come on, boys!' right up the knoll and jumped his
horse over the breakfast table and rode it into the wrecked
commissary tent, and a cook who was hidden under the
mess stuck his arm out and shot Bayard in the back with a
derringer.

"Mister Stuart fought his way out and got back home
without losing but two men. He always spoke well of Bayard.
He said he was a good officer and a fine cavalryman, but
that he was too reckless."

They sat quietly for a time in the firelight. The flames
leaped and popped on the hearth and sparks soared in wild
swirling plumes up the chimney, and Bayard Sartoris' brief
career swept like a shooting star across the dark plain of their
mutual remembering and suffering, lighting it with a transient
glare like a soundless thunder-clap, leaving a sort of radiance
when it died. The guest, the Scottish engineer, had sat
quietly, listening. After a time he spoke.

"When he rode back, he was no actually certain there
were anchovies, was he?"

"The Yankee major said there were," Aunt Jenny replied.

"Ay." The Scotsman pondered again. "And did Muster Stuart return next day, as he said in's note?"

"He went back that afternoon," Aunt Jenny answered, "looking for Bayard." Ashes soft as rosy feathers shaled glowing on to the hearth and faded to the softest gray. John Sartoris leaned forward into the firelight and punched at the blazing logs with the Yankee musket barrel.

"That was the goddamnedest army the world ever saw, I reckon," he said.

"Yes," Aunt Jenny agreed. "And Bayard was the goddamnedest man in it."

"Yes," John Sartoris admitted soberly, "Bayard was wild."

The Scotsman spoke again. "This Muster Stuart, who said your brother was reckless—who was he?"

"He was the cavalry general Jeb Stuart," Aunt Jenny answered. She brooded for a while upon the fire; her pale indomitable face held for a moment a tranquil tenderness. "He had a strange sense of humor," she said. "Nothing ever seemed quite so diverting to him as General Pope in his night-shirt." She dreamed once more on some far-away place beyond the rosy battlements of the embers. "Poor man," she said; then she said quietly, "I danced a valse with him in Baltimore in '58," and her voice was proud and still as banners in the dust.

But the door was closed now, and what light passed through the colored panes was richly solemn. To Bayard's left was his grandson's room, the room in which his grandson's wife and her child had died last October. He stood beside this door for a moment, then he opened it quietly. The blinds were closed and the room had that breathless tranquillity of unoccupation, and he closed the door and tramped on with that heavy-footed obliviousness of the deaf and entered his own bedroom and crashed the door behind him, as was his way of shutting a door.

He sat down and removed his shoes, the shoes that were made to his measure twice a year by a St. Louis house, and in his stockings he went to the window and looked down upon his saddled mare tethered to a mulberry tree in the back yard and a Negro lad lean as a hound, richly static beside it. From the kitchen, invisible from this window, Elnora's endless minor ebbed and flowed, unheard by Bayard, upon the lazy scene.

He crossed to the closet and drew out a pair of scarred riding-boots and stamped into them and took a cigar from the humidor on his night table, and he stood for a time with the cold cigar between his teeth. Through the cloth of his pocket his hand had touched the pipe there, and he took it out and looked at it again, and it seemed to him that he could still hear old man Fall's voice in roaring recapitulation: "Cunnel was settin' thar in a cheer, his sock feet propped on the po'ch railin', smokin' this hyer very pipe. Old Louvinia was settin' on the steps, shellin' a bowl of peas fer supper. And a feller was glad to git even peas sometimes, in them days. And you was settin' back again' the post. They wa'n't nobody else thar 'cep' you' aunt, the one 'fo' Miss Jenny come. Cunnel had sont them two gals to Memphis to yo' gran'pappy when he fust went to Virginny with that 'ere regiment that turnt right around and voted him outen the colonelcy. Voted 'im out because he wouldn't be Tom, Dick and Harry with ever' skulkin' camp-robber that come along with a salvaged muskit and claimed to be a sojer. You was about half-grown then, I reckon. How old was you then, Bayard?"

"Fourteen."

"Hey?"

"Fourteen. Do I have to tell you that every time you tell me this damn story?"

"And thar you was a-settin' when they turned in at the gate and come trottin' up the carriage drive.

"Old Louvinia drapped the bowl of peas and let out one squawk, but Cunnel shet her up and told her to run and git his boots and pistols and have 'em ready at the back do', and you lit out ter the barn to saddle that stallion. And when them Yankees rid up and stopped—they stopped right whar that flower bed is now—they wa'n't nobody in sight but Cunnel, a-settin' thar like he never even heerd tell of no Yankees.

"The Yankees they sot thar on the hosses, talkin' 'mongst theyselves if this was the right house or not, and Cunnel settin' thar with his sock feet on the railin', gawkin' at 'em like a hill-billy. The Yankee officer he tole one man to

ride back to the barn and look fer that 'ere stallion, then
he says to Cunnel:

" 'Say, Johnny, whar do the rebel John Sartoris live?'

" 'Lives down the road a piece,' Cunnel says, not bat-
tin' a eye even. ' 'Bout two mile,' he says. 'But you won't
find 'im now. He's away fightin' the Yanks agin.'

" 'Well, I reckon you better come and show us the way,
anyhow,' the Yankee officer says.

"So Cunnel he got up slow and tole 'em to let 'im git
his shoes and walkin'-stick, and limped into the house,
leavin' 'em settin' thar waitin'.

"Soon's he was out of sight he run. Old Louvinia was
waitin' at the back do' with his coat and boots and pistols
and a snack of cawn bread. That 'ere other Yankee had rid
into the barn, and Cunnel taken the things from Louvinia
and wropped 'em up in the coat and started acrost the back
yard like he was jest takin' a walk. 'Bout that time the Yankee
come to the barn do'.

" 'They ain't no stock hyer a-tall,' the Yank says.

" 'I reckon not,' Cunnel says. 'Cap'm says fer you to come
on back,' he says, goin' on. He could feel that 'ere Yank
a-watchin' him, lookin' right 'twixt his shoulder blades whar
the bullet would hit. Cunnel says that was the hardest thing
he ever done in his life, walkin' on thar acrost that lot with
his back to'a'ds that Yankee without breakin' into a run. He
was aimin' to'a'ds the corner of the barn, where he could
put the house between 'em, and Cunnel says hit seemed like
he'd been walkin' a year without gittin' no closer and not
darin' to look back. Cunnel says he wa'n't even thinkin' of
nothin' 'cep' he was glad the gals wa'n't at home. He says he
never give a thought to you' aunt back thar in the house,
because he says she was a fullblood Sartoris and she was a
match fer any jest a dozen Yankees.

"Then the Yank hollered at him, but Cunnel kep' right
on, not lookin' back nor nothin'. Then the Yank hollered
agin and Cunnel says he could hyear the hoss movin'
and he decided hit was time to stir his shanks. He made
the corner of the barn jest as the Yank shot the fust time, and
by the time the Yank got to the corner, he was in the hawg-
lot, tearin' through the jimson weeds to'a'ds the creek
whar you was waitin' with the stallion hid in the willers.

"And thar you was a-standin', holdin' the hoss, and that

'ere Yankee patrol yellin' up behind, until Cunnel got his boots on. And then he tole you to tell yo' aunt he wouldn't be home fer supper."

"But what are you giving it to me for, after all this time?" he had asked, fingering the pipe, and old man Falls had said a poorhouse was no fit place for it.

"A thing he toted in his pocket and got enjoyment outen, in them days. Hit 'ud be different, I reckon, while we was a-buildin' the railroad. He said often enough in them days we was all goin' to be in the po'house by Sat'd'y night. Only I beat him, thar. I got thar fo' he did. Or the cemetery he meant mo' likely, him ridin' up and down the survey with a saddle-bag of money night and day, keepin' jest one cross tie ahead of the po'house, like he said. That 'us when hit changed. When he had to start killin' folks. Them two cyarpet-baggers stirrin' up niggers, that he walked right into the room whar they was a-settin' behind a table with they pistols layin' on the table, and that robber and that other feller he kilt, all with the same dang der'nger. When a feller has to start killin' folks, he 'most always has to keep on killin' 'em. And when he does, he's already dead hisself."

It showed on John Sartoris' brow, the dark shadow of fatality and doom, that night when he sat beneath the candles in the dining-room and turned a wineglass in his fingers while he talked to his son. The railroad was finished, and that day he had been elected to the state legislature after a hard and bitter fight, and doom lay on his brow, and weariness.

"And so," he said, "Redlaw'll kill me tomorrow, for I shall be unarmed. I'm tired of killing men. . . . Pass the wine, Bayard."

And the next day he was dead, whereupon, as though he had but waited for that to release him of the clumsy cluttering of bones and breath, by losing the frustration of his own flesh he could now stiffen and shape that which sprang from him into the fatal semblance of his dream; to be evoked like a genie or a deity by an illiterate old man's tedious reminiscing or by a charred pipe from which even the rank smell of burnt tobacco had long since faded away.

Old Bayard roused himself and went and laid the pipe on his chest of drawers. Then he quitted the room and

tramped heavily down the stairs and out through the
back.

The Negro lad waked easily and untethered the mare and
held the stirrup. Old Bayard mounted and remembered the
cigar at last and fired it. The Negro opened the gate into
the lot and trotted on ahead and opened the second gate
and let the rider into the field beyond. Bayard rode on,
trailing his pungent smoke. From somewhere a ticked setter
came up and fell in at the mare's heels.

Elnora stood barelegged on the kitchen floor and soused
her mop into the pail and thumped it on the floor again.

> Sinner riz fum de moaner's bench,
> Sinner jump to de penance bench;
> When de preacher ax 'im whut de reason why,
> Say, "Preacher got de women jes' de same ez I."
>   Oh, Lawd, oh, Lawd!
> Dat's whut de matter wid de church today.

2

Simon's destination was a huge brick house set well up to
the street. The lot had been the site of a fine old colonial
house which stood among magnolias and oaks and flowering
shrubs. But the house had burned, and some of the trees had
been felled to make room for an architectural garbling so
imposingly terrific as to possess a kind of majesty. It was
a monument to the frugality (and the mausoleum of the
social aspirations of his women) of a hill-man who had
moved in from a small settlement called Frenchman's Bend
and who, as Miss Jenny Du Pre put it, had built the hand-
somest house in Frenchman's Bend on the most beautiful lot in Jefferson. The hill-man had stuck it out for two
years, during which his womenfolk sat on the veranda all
morning in lace-trimmed "boudoir caps" and spent the afternoons in colored silk, riding about town in a rubber-tired
surrey; then the hill-man sold his house to a newcomer
to the town and took his women back to the country and
doubtless set them to work again.

A number of motor cars ranked along the curb lent a formally festive air to the place, and Simon with his tilted cigar stub wheeled up and drew rein and indulged in a brief, colorful altercation with a Negro sitting at the wheel of a car parked before the hitching-block. "Don't block off no Sartoris ca'iage, black boy," Simon concluded, when the other had moved the motor and permitted him access to the post. "Block off de commonality, ef you wants, but don't intervoke no equipage waitin' on Cunnel er Miss Jenny. Dey won't stan' fer it."

He descended and tethered the horses, and his spirit mollified by the rebuke administered and laved with the beatitude of having gained his own way, Simon paused and examined the motor car with curiosity and no little superciliousness tinged faintly with respectful envy, and spoke affably with its conductor. But not for long, for Simon had sisters in the Lord in this kitchen, and presently he let himself into the yard and followed the gravel driveway around to the back. He could hear the party going on as he passed beneath the windows—that sustained, unintelligible gabbling with which white ladies could surround themselves without effort and which they seemed to consider a necessary (or unavoidable) adjunct to having a good time. The fact that it was a card-party would have seemed neither paradoxical nor astonishing to Simon, for time and much absorbing experience had taught him a fine tolerance of white folks' vagaries and for those of ladies of any color.

The hill-man had built his house so close to the street that the greater part of the original lawn with its fine old trees lay behind it. There were once crape myrtle and syringa and lilac and jasmine bushes without order, and massed honeysuckle on fences and tree trunks; and after the first house had burned, these had taken the place and made of its shaggy informality a mazed and scented jungle loved of mocking-birds and thrushes, where boys and girls lingered on spring and summer nights among drifting fireflies and choiring whippoorwills and usually the liquid tremolo of a screech owl. Then the hill-man had bought it and cut some of the trees in order to build his house near the street after the country fashion, and chopped out the jungle and whitewashed the remaining trees and ran his barn- and hog- and

chicken-lot fences between their ghostly trunks. He hadn't
remained long enough to learn of garages.

Some of the antiseptic desolation of his tenancy had
faded now, and its present owner had set out more shrub-
bery—jasmine and mock-orange and verbena—with green
iron tables and chairs beneath them, and a pool and a
tennis court; and Simon went on with discreet assurance,
and on a consonantless drone of female voices he rode into
the kitchen, where a thin woman in a funereal purple
turban, poising a beaten biscuit heaped with mayonnaise,
and a mountainous one in the stained apron of her calling drinking melted ice cream from a saucer, rolled their
eyes at him.

"I seed him on de street, and he looked bad; he jes'
don't favor hisself," the visitor was saying as Simon entered, but they dropped the theme of the conversation and
made him welcome.

"Ef it ain't Brother Strother," they said in unison. "Come
in, Brother Strother. How is you?"

"Po'ly, ladies; po'ly," Simon replied. He doffed his hat
and unclamped his cigar stub and stowed it away in the
hat. "I'se had a right smart mis'ry in de back. Is y'all kep'
well?"

"Right well, I thank you, Brother Strother," the visitor
replied. Simon drew a chair to the table, as he was bidden.

"Whut you gwine eat, Brother Strother?" the cook demanded hospitably. "Dey's party fixin's, en dey's some col'
greens en a little sof' ice cream lef' fum dinner."

"I reckon I'll have a little ice cream en some of dem
greens, Sis' Rachel," Simon replied. "My teef ain't so much
on party doin's no mo'." The cook rose with majestic deliberation and waddled across to a pantry and reached
down a platter. She was one of the best cooks in Jefferson;
no mistress dared protest against the social amenities of
Rachel's kitchen.

"Ef you ain't de beatin'es' man!" the first guest exclaimed.
"Eatin' ice cream at yo' age!"

"I been eatin' ice cream sixty years," Simon said. "Whut
reason I got fer quittin' now?"

"Dat's right, Brother Strother," the cook agreed, placing
the dish before him. "Eat yo' ice cream when you kin git
it. Jes' a minute en I'll—— Here, Meloney," she interrupted

herself as a young light Negress in a smart white apron and
cap entered, bearing a tray of plates containing remnants of
edible edifices copied from pictures in ladies' magazines and
possessing neither volume nor nourishment, with which the
party had been dulling its palates against supper, "git Brother
Strother a bowl of dat 'ere ice cream, honey."

The girl clashed the tray into the sink and rinsed a bowl
at the water tap while Simon watched her with his still
little eyes. She whipped the bowl through a towel with a
fine show of derogatory carelessness, and with her chin at
a supercilious angle she clattered on her high heels across
the kitchen, still under Simon's unwinking regard, and
slammed a door behind her. Then Simon turned his head.

"Yes, ma'am," he repeated, "I been eatin' ice cream too
long ter quit at my age."

"Dey won't no vittles hurt you ez long ez you kin stomach
'um," the cook agreed, raising her saucer to her lips again.
The girl returned and with her head still averted she set the
bowl of viscid liquid before Simon, who, under cover of this
movement, dropped his hand on her thigh. The girl smacked
him sharply on the back of his gray head with her flat palm.

"Miss Rachel, can't you make him keep his hands to hisself?" she said.

"Ain't you 'shamed," Rachel demanded, but without rancor,
"a ole gray-head man like you, wid a fam'ly of grown chillen
and one foot in de graveyard?"

"Hush yo' mouf, woman," Simon said placidly, spoon-
ing spinach into his melted ice cream. "Ain't dey erbout
breakin' up in yonder yit?"

"I reckon dey's erbout to," the other guest answered, putting another laden biscuit into her mouth with a gesture of
elegant gentility; "seems like dey' talkin' louder."

"Den dey's started playin' again," Simon corrected. "Talkin' jes' eased off whiles dey et. Yes, suh, dey's started playin' again. Dat's white folks. Nigger ain't got sense ernough
ter play cards wid all dat racket gwine on."

But they were breaking up. Miss Jenny Du Pre had just
finished a story which left the three at her table avoiding
one another's eyes a little self-consciously, as was her way.
Miss Jenny traveled very little, and in Pullman smoking-
rooms not at all, and people wondered where she got her

stories, who had told them to her. And she repeated them anywhere and at any time, choosing the wrong moment and the wrong audience with a cold and cheerful audacity. Young people liked her, and she was much in demand as a chaperone for picnic parties.

She now spoke across the room to the hostess. "I'm going home, Belle," she stated. "I think we are all tired of your party. I know I am." The hostess was a plump, youngish woman and her cleverly-rouged face showed now a hysterical immersion that was almost repose, but when Miss Jenny broke into her consciousness with the imminence of departure, this faded quickly and her face resumed its familiar expression of strained and vague dissatisfaction and she protested conventionally but with a petulant sincerity, as a well-bred child might.

But Miss Jenny was adamant. She rose and her slender wrinkled hand brushed invisible crumbs from the bosom of her black silk dress. "If I stay any longer, I'll miss Bayard's toddy-time," she explained with her usual forthrightness. "Come on, Narcissa, and I'll drive you home."

"I have my car, thank you, Miss Jenny," the young woman to whom she spoke replied in a grave contralto, rising also; and the others got up with sibilant gathering motions above the petulant modulation of the hostess' protests, and they drifted slowly into the hall and clotted again before various mirrors, colorful and shrill. Miss Jenny pushed steadily toward the door.

"Come along, come along," she repeated. "Harry Mitchell won't want to run into all this gabble when he comes home from work."

"Then he can sit in the car out in the garage," the hostess rejoined sharply. "I do wish you wouldn't go, Miss Jenny; I don't think I'll ask you again."

But Miss Jenny only said "Good-bye, good-bye" with cold affability, and with her delicate replica of the Sartoris nose and that straight, grenadier's back of hers which gave the *pas* for erectness to only one back in town—that of her nephew Bayard—she stood at the steps, where Narcissa Benbow joined her, bringing with her like an odor that aura of grave and serene repose in which she dwelt. "Belle meant that, too," Miss Jenny said.

"Meant what, Miss Jenny?"

"About Harry. . . . Now, where do you suppose that damn nigger went to?" They descended the steps and from the parked motors along the curb came muffled starting explosions, and the two women traversed the brief flower-bordered walk to the street. "Did you see which way my driver went?" Miss Jenny asked of the Negro in the nearest car.

"He went to'ds de back, ma'am." The Negro opened the door and slid his legs, clad in army O.D. and a pair of linoleum putties, to the ground. "I'll go git 'im."

"Thank you. Well, thank the Lord, that's over," she added. "It's too bad folks haven't the sense or courage to send out invitations, then shut up the house and go away. All the fun of parties is in dressing up and getting there." Ladies came steadily in shrill groups down the walk and got into cars or departed on foot with bright, not quite musical calls to one another. The sun was down behind Belle's house, and when the women passed from the shadow into the level bar of sunlight beyond, they became delicately brilliant as paroquets. Narcissa Benbow wore gray, and her eyes were violet, and in her face was that tranquil repose of lilies.

"Not children's parties," she protested.

"I'm talking about parties, not about having fun," Miss Jenny said. "Speaking of children—what's the news from Horace?"

"Oh, hadn't I told you?" the other said quickly. "I had a wire yesterday. He landed in New York Wednesday. It was such a mixed-up sort of message, I never could understand what he was trying to tell me, except that he would have to stay in New York for a week or so. It was over fifty words long."

"Was it a straight message?" Miss Jenny asked. The other said yes and she added: "Horace must have got rich, like the soldiers say all the Y.M.C.A. did. Well, if it has taught a man like Horace to make money, the war was a pretty good thing, after all."

"Miss Jenny! How can you talk that way, after John's —after . . ."

"Fiddlesticks," Miss Jenny said. "The war just gave John a good excuse to get himself killed. If it hadn't been that,

it would have been some other way that would have been a
bother to everybody around."

"Miss Jenny!"

"I know, my dear. I've lived with these bullheaded Sartorises for eighty years, and I'll never give a single ghost of
'em the satisfaction of shedding a tear over him. What did
Horace's message say?"

"It was about something he was bringing home with him,"
the other answered, and her serene face filled with a sort
of fond exasperation. "It was such an incoherent message.
. . . Horace never could say anything clearly from a distance."
She mused again, gazing down the street with its tunnel of
oaks and elms, between which sunlight fell in spaced tiger
bars. "Do you suppose he could have adopted a war-orphan?"

"War-orphan," Miss Jenny repeated. "More likely it's some
war-orphan's mamma."

Simon appeared at the corner of the house, wiping his
mouth on the back of his hand, and crossed the lawn with
shuffling celerity. His cigar was not visible.

"No," the other said quickly, with grave concern. "You
don't believe he would have done that? No, no, he wouldn't
have; Horace wouldn't have done that. He never does anything without telling me about it first. He would have written;
I know he would. You really don't think that sounds like
Horace, do you? A thing like that?"

"Hmph," Miss Jenny said through her high-bridged Norman nose. "An innocent like Horace straying with that trusting air of his among all those man-starved European women?
He wouldn't know it himself, until it was too late; especially
in a foreign language. I bet in every town he was in over
seven days, his landlady or somebody was keeping his supper on the stove when he was late, or holding out sugar on
the other men to sweeten his coffee with. Some men are
born to always have a woman making a doormat of herself for him, just as some men are born cuckolded. . . .
How old are you?"

"I'm still twenty-six, Miss Jenny," the younger woman
replied equably. Simon unhitched the horses and he stood
now beside the carriage in his Miss Jenny attitude. It
differed from the bank one; there was now in it a gallant
and protective deference. Miss Jenny examined the still
serenity of the other's face.

"Why don't you get married, and let that baby look after himself for a while? Mark my words, it won't be six months before some other woman will be falling all over herself for the privilege of keeping his feet dry, and he won't even miss you."

"I promised mother," the other replied quietly and without offense. . . . "I don't see why he couldn't have sent an intelligible message."

"Well . . ." Miss Jenny turned to her carriage. "Maybe it's only an orphan, after all," she said with comfortless reassurance.

"I'll know soon, anyway," the other agreed, and she crossed to a small car at the curb and opened the door.

Miss Jenny got in her carriage and Simon mounted and gathered up the reins. "Let me know when you hear again," she called as the carriage moved forward. "Drive out and get some more flowers when you want 'em."

"Thank you. Good-bye."

"All right, Simon." The carriage moved on again, and again Simon withheld his news until they were out of town.

"Mist' Bayard done got home," he remarked, in his former conversational tone.

"Where is he?" Miss Jenny demanded immediately.

"He ain't come out to de place yit," Simon answered. "I speck he went to de graveyard."

"Nonsense," Miss Jenny snapped. "No Sartoris ever goes to the cemetery but once. . . . Does Colonel know he's home?"

"Yessum. I tole him, but he don't ack like he believed I wuz tellin' him de troof."

"You mean nobody's seen him but you?"

"I ain't seed 'im neither," Simon disclaimed. "Section han' seed 'im jump off de train and tole me——"

"You damn fool nigger!" Miss Jenny stormed. "And you went and blurted a fool thing like that to Bayard? Haven't you got any more sense than that?"

"Section han' seed 'im," Simon repeated stubbornly. "I reckon he knowed Mist' Bayard when he seed 'im."

"Well, where is he, then?"

"He mought have gone to de graveyard," Simon suggested. "Drive on!"

Miss Jenny found her nephew with two bird dogs in his office. The room was lined with bookcases containing rows of heavy legal tomes bound in dun calf and emanating an atmosphere of dusty and undisturbed meditation, and a miscellany of fiction of the historical-romantic school (all Dumas was there, and the steady progression of the volumes now constituted Bayard's entire reading, and one volume lay always on the night table beside his bed) and a collection of indiscriminate objects—small packets of seed, old rusted spurs and bits and harness buckles, brochures on animal and vegetable diseases, ornate tobacco containers which people had given him on various occasions and anniversaries and which he had never used, inexplicable bits of rock and desiccated roots and grain pods—all collected one at a time and for reasons which had long since escaped his memory, yet preserved just the same. The room contained an enormous closet with a padlocked door, and a big table littered with yet more casual objects, and a locked roll-top desk (keys and locks were an obsession with him), and a sofa and three big leather chairs. This room was always referred to as the office, and Bayard now sat here with his hat on and still in his riding boots, transferring bourbon whisky from a small rotund keg to a silver-stoppered decanter, while the two dogs watched him with majestic gravity.

One of the dogs was quite old and nearly blind. It spent most of the day lying in the sun in the back yard or, during the hot summer day, in the cool dusty obscurity beneath the kitchen. But toward the middle of the afternoon it went around to the front and waited there quietly and gravely until the carriage came up the drive; and when Bayard had descended and entered the house it returned to the back and waited again until Isom led the mare up and Bayard came out and mounted. Then together they spent the afternoon going quietly and unhurriedly about the meadows and fields and woods in their seasonal mutations—the man on his horse and the ticked setter gravely beside him, while the descending evening of their lives drew toward its peaceful close upon the kind land that had bred them both.

The young dog was not yet two years old; his net was too hasty for the sedateness of their society overlong, and though at times he set forth with them or came quartering up, splashed and eager, from somewhere to join them in

midfield, it was not for long, and soon he must dash away
with his tongue flapping and the tense, delicate feathering
of his tail in pursuit of the maddening elusive smells with
which the world surrounded him and tempted him from
every thicket and copse and ravine.

Bayard's boots were wet to the tops and the soles were
caked with mud, and he bent with intent preoccupation
over his keg and the bottle under the sober curiosity of the
dogs. The keg was propped bung-upward in a second chair
and he was siphoning the rich brown liquor delicately into
the decanter by means of a rubber tube. Miss Jenny entered
with her black bonnet still perched on the exact top of her
trim white head and the dogs looked up at her, the older
with grave dignity, the younger more quickly, tapping his
tail on the floor with fawning diffidence. But Bayard didn't
raise his head. Miss Jenny closed the door and stared coldly
at his boots.

"Your feet are wet," she stated. Still he didn't look up,
but held the tube delicately in the bottle-neck while the
liquor mounted steadily in the decanter. At times his deafness was very convenient, more convenient than actual, perhaps; but who could know certainly? "You go upstairs and
get those boots off," Miss Jenny commanded, raising her
voice; "I'll fill the decanter."

But within the serene walled tower of his deafness his
imperturbability did not falter until the decanter was full
and he pinched the tube and raised it and drained it back
into the keg. The older dog had not moved, but the younger
one had retreated beyond Bayard, where it lay motionless
and alert, its head on its crossed forepaws, watching Miss
Jenny with one melting, unwinking eye. Bayard drew the tube
from the keg and looked at her for the first time. "What did
you say?"

But Miss Jenny returned to the door and opened it and
shouted into the hall, eliciting an alarmed response from
the kitchen, followed presently by Simon in the flesh. "Go
up and get Colonel's slippers," she directed. When she turned
into the room again neither Bayard nor the keg was visible,
but from the open closet door there protruded the young
dog's interested hindquarters and the tense feathering of his
barometric tail; then Bayard thrust the dog out of the closet

with his foot and emerged himself and locked the door behind him.

"Has Simon come in yet?" he asked.

"He's coming now," she answered; "I just called him. Sit down and get those wet boots off." At that moment Simon entered with the slippers, and Bayard sat obediently and Simon knelt and drew his boots off under Miss Jenny's martinet eye. "Are his socks dry?" she asked.

"No'm, dey ain't wet," Simon answered. But she bent and felt them herself.

"Here," Bayard said testily, but Miss Jenny ran her hand over both his feet with brusque imperturbability.

"Precious little fault of his if they ain't," she said across the topless wall of his deafness. "And then you have to come along with that fool yarn of yours."

"Section han' seed 'im," Simon repeated stubbornly, thrusting the slippers on Bayard's feet; "I ain't never said I seed him." He stood up and rubbed his hands on his thighs.

Bayard stamped into the slippers. "Bring the toddy fixings, Simon." Then to his aunt, in a tone which he contrived to make casual: "Simon says Bayard got off the train this afternoon." But Miss Jenny was storming at Simon again.

"Come back here and get these boots and set 'em behind the stove," she said. Simon returned and sidled swiftly to the hearth and gathered up the boots. "And take these dogs out of here, too," she added. "Thank the Lord he hasn't thought about bringing his horse in with him." Immediately the old dog came to his feet, and followed by the younger one's diffident alacrity, departed with that same assumed deliberation with which both Bayard and Simon obeyed Miss Jenny's brisk implacability.

"Simon says——" Bayard repeated.

"Simon says fiddlesticks," Miss Jenny snapped. "Have you lived with Simon sixty years without learning that he don't know the truth when he sees it?" And she followed Simon from the room and on to the kitchen, and while Simon's tall yellow daughter bent over her biscuit board and Simon filled a glass pitcher with fresh water and sliced lemons and set them and a sugar bowl and two tall glasses on a tray, Miss Jenny stood in the doorway and curled Simon's grizzled remaining hair into tighter kinks yet. She had a fine command

of language at all times, but when her ire was aroused she
soared without effort to sublime heights. Hers was a force-
ful clarity and a colorful simplicity and a bold use of
metaphor that Demosthenes would have envied and which
even mules comprehended and of whose intent the most
obtuse persons remained not long in doubt; and beneath it
Simon's head bobbed lower and lower and the fine assumption of detached preoccupation moulted like feathers
from about him, until he caught up the tray and ducked from
the room. Miss Jenny's voice followed him, descending easily
with a sweeping comprehensiveness that included a warning
and a suggestion for future conduct for Simon and Elnora
and all their descendants, actual and problematical, for some
years.

"And the next time," she concluded, "you, or any section
hand, or brakeman, or delivery boy either, sees or hears
anything you think will be of interest to Colonel, you tell
me about it first; I'll do all the telling after that." She gave
Elnora another glare for good measure and returned to the
office, where her nephew was stirring sugar and water carefully in the two glasses.

Simon in a white jacket officiated as butler—doubled in
brass, you might say. Only it was not brass, but silver so
fine and soft that some of the spoons were worn now almost
to paper thinness where fingers in their generations had held
them; silver which Simon's grandfather Joby had buried on
a time beneath the ammoniac barn floor while Simon, aged
three, in a single filthy garment, had looked on with a
child's grave interest in the curious game.

An effluvium of his primary calling clung about him always, however, even when he was swept and garnished for
church and a little shapeless in a discarded Prince Albert
coat of Bayard's; and his every advent into the dining-room
with dishes brought with him, and the easy attitudes into
which he fell near the sideboard while answering Miss Jenny's abrupt questions or while pursuing some fragmentary
conversation which he and Bayard had been engaged in
earlier in the day, disseminated, and his exits left behind
him, a faint nostalgia of the stables. But tonight he brought
the dishes in and set them down and scuttled immediately

back to the kitchen: Simon realized that again he had talked
too much.

Miss Jenny, with a shawl of white wool about her shoulders against the evening's coolness, was doing the talking tonight, immersing herself and her nephew in a wealth of
trivialities—petty doings and sayings and gossip—a behavior
which was not like Miss Jenny at all. She had opinions, and
a pithy, savagely humorous way of stating them, but it was
very seldom that she descended to gossip. Meanwhile Bayard had shut himself up in that walled tower of his deafness
and raised the drawbridge and clashed the portcullis to, where
you never knew whether he heard you or not, while his
corporeal self ate its supper steadily. Presently they had
done, and Miss Jenny rang the little silver bell at her hand
and Simon opened the pantry door and received again the
cold broadside of her displeasure, and shut the door and
lurked behind it until they had left the room.

Bayard lit his cigar in the office and Miss Jenny followed
him there and drew her chair to the table beneath the lamp
and opened the daily Memphis newspaper. She enjoyed humanity in its more colorful mutations, preferring lively romance to the most impeccable of dun fact, so she took in
the more lurid afternoon paper, even though it was yesterday's when it reached her, and read with cold avidity accounts of arson and murder and violent dissolution and
adultery; in good time and soon the American scene was to
furnish her with diversion in the form of bootleggers' wars,
but this was not yet. Her nephew sat beyond the mellow
downward pool of the lamp, his feet braced against the
corner of the hearth, from which his boot-soles and the boot-
soles of John Sartoris before him had long since worn the
varnish away, puffing his cigar. He was not reading, and at
intervals Miss Jenny glanced above her glasses and across
the top of the paper at him. Then she read again, and there
was no sound in the room save the sporadic rustling of the
page.

After a time he rose, with one of his characteristic plunging movements, and she watched him as he crossed the room
and passed through the door and banged it behind him. She
read on for a while longer, but her attention had followed
the heavy tramp of his feet up the hall, and when this

ceased she rose and laid the paper aside and followed him to the front door.

The moon had got up beyond the dark eastern wall of hills and it lay without emphasis upon the valley, mounting like a child's balloon behind the oaks and locusts along the drive. Bayard sat with his feet on the veranda rail, in the moonlight. His cigar glowed at special intervals, and a shrill monotone of crickets rose from the immediate grass, and further away, from among the trees, a fairylike piping of young frogs like endless silver small bubbles rising. A thin, sourceless odor of locust drifted up, intangible as fading tobacco-wraiths, and from the rear of the house, up the dark hall, Elnora's voice floated in meaningless minor suspense.

Miss Jenny groped in the darkness beside the door, and from beside the yawning lesser obscurity of the mirror she took Bayard's hat from the hook and carried it out to him and put it in his hand. "Don't sit out here too long, now. It ain't summer yet."

He grunted indistinguishably, but he put the hat on and she turned and went back to the office, and finished the paper and folded it and laid it on the table. She snapped the light off and mounted the dark stairs to her room. The moon shone above the trees at this height and fell in broad silver bars through the eastern windows.

Before turning on the light she crossed to the southern wall and raised a window there, upon the crickets and frogs and somewhere a mocking-bird. Outside the window was a magnolia tree, but it was not in bloom yet, nor had the honeysuckle massed along the garden fence flowered. But this would be soon, and from here she could overlook the garden, could look down upon Cape jasmine and syringa and callacanthus where the moon lay upon their bronze and yet unflowered sleep, and upon other shoots and graftings from the far-away Carolina gardens she had known as a girl.

Just beyond the corner, from the invisible kitchen, Elnora's voice welled in mellow, falling suspense. "All folks talkin' 'bout heaven ain't gwine dar," Elnora sang, and presently she and Simon emerged into the moonlight and took the path to Simon's cabin below the barn. Simon had fired his cigar at last, and the evil smoke of it trailed behind him, fading. But when they had gone the rank pungency of it seemed still to

linger within the sound of the crickets and of the frogs upon
the silver air, mingled and blended inextricably with the
dying fall of Elnora's voice: "All folks talkin' 'bout heaven
ain't gwine dar."

His cigar was cold, and he moved and dug a match
from his waistcoat and relit it and braced his feet again
upon the railing, and again the drifting sharpness of tobacco lay along the windless currents of the silver air, straying and fading slowly with locust-breaths and the ceaseless
fairy reiteration of crickets and frogs. There was a mocking-
bird somewhere down the valley, and after a while another
sang from the magnolia at the corner of the garden fence.
An automobile passed along the smooth valley road, slowed
for the railway crossing, then sped on. Before the sound
of it had died away the whistle of the nine-thirty train drifted
down from the hills.

Two long blasts with dissolving echoes, two short following ones, but before it came in sight his cigar was
cold again and he sat holding it in his fingers and watched
the locomotive drag its string of yellow windows up the
valley and into the hills once more, where after a time it
whistled again, arrogant and resonant and sad. John Sartoris
had sat so on this veranda and watched his two daily trains
emerge from the hills and cross the valley into the hills, with
lights and smoke and a noisy simulation of speed. But now
the railway belonged to a syndicate and there were more
than two trains on it that ran from Lake Michigan to the Gulf
of Mexico, completing his dream, while John Sartoris slept
among martial cherubim and the useless vainglory of whatever God he did not scorn to recognize.

Old Bayard's cigar was cold again. He sat with it dead
in his fingers and watched a tall shape emerge from the
lilac bushes beside the garden fence and cross the patchy
moonlight toward the veranda. His grandson wore no hat
and he came on and mounted the steps and stood with the
moonlight bringing the hawklike planes of his face into high
relief while his grandfather sat with his dead cigar and
looked at him.

"Bayard, son?" old Bayard said. Young Bayard stood in
the moonlight. His eyesockets were cavernous shadows.

"I tried to keep him from going up there on that goddam

little popgun," he said at last with brooding savageness. Then he moved again and old Bayard lowered his feet, but his grandson only dragged a chair violently up beside him and flung himself into it. His motions were abrupt also, like his grandfather's, but controlled and flowing for all their violence.

"Why in hell didn't you let me know you were coming?" old Bayard demanded. "What do you mean, straggling in here like this?"

"I didn't let anybody know." Young Bayard dug a cigarette from his pocket and raked a match on his shoe.

"What?"

"I didn't tell anybody I was coming," he repeated above the cupped match, raising his voice.

"Simon knew it. Do you inform nigger servants of your movements instead of your own granddaddy?"

"Damn Simon, sir," young Bayard shouted. "Who set him to watching me?"

"Don't yell at me, boy," old Bayard shouted in turn. His grandson flung the match away and drew at the cigarette in deep, troubled draughts. "Don't wake Jenny," old Bayard added more mildly, striking a match to his cold cigar. "All right, are you?"

"Here," young Bayard said, extending his hand, "let me hold it. You're going to set your mustache on fire." But old Bayard repulsed him sharply and sucked stubbornly and impotently at the match in his unsteady fingers.

"I said, are you all right?" he repeated.

"Why not?" young Bayard snapped. "Takes damn near as big a fool to get hurt in a war as it does in peacetime. Damn fool, that's what it is." He drew at the cigarette again, then he hurled it, not half consumed, after the match. "There was one I had to lay for four days to catch. Had to get Sibleigh in an old crate of an Ak. W. to suck him in for me. Wouldn't look at anything but cold meat, him and his skull and bones. Well, he got it. Stayed on him for six thousand feet, put a whole belt right into his cockpit. You could 'a' covered 'em all with your hat. But the bastard just wouldn't burn." His voice rose again as he talked on. Locust drifted up in sweet gusts, and the crickets and frogs were clear and monotonous as pipes blown drowsily by an idiot boy. From her silver casement the moon looked down upon the valley dissolving in opaline tranquillity into the serene mysterious infinitude of the hills, and young Bayard's voice went on and on, recounting violence and speed and death.

"Hush," old Bayard said again. "You'll wake Jenny." And his grandson's voice sank obediently, but soon it rose again, and after a time Miss Jenny emerged with the white woolen shawl over her night-dress and came and kissed him.

"I reckon you're all right," she said, "or you wouldn't be in such a bad humor. Tell us about Johnny."

"He was drunk," young Bayard answered harshly, "or a fool. I tried to keep him from going up there, on that damn Camel. You couldn't see your hand that morning. Air all full of hunks of cloud, and any fool could 'a' known that on their side it'd be full of Fokkers that could reach twenty-five thousand, and him on a damn Camel. But he was hell-bent on going up there, damn near to Lille. I couldn't keep him from it. He shot at me," young Bayard said; "I tried to drive him back but he gave me a burst. He was already high as he could get, but they must have been five thousand feet above us. They flew all over him. Hemmed him up like a damn calf in a pen while one of them sat right on his tail until he took fire and jumped. Then they streaked for home." Locust drifted and drifted on the still air, and the silver rippling of the frogs. In the magnolia at the corner of the house the mocking-bird sang; down the valley the other one replied.

"Streaked for home, with the rest of his gang," young Bayard said, "him and his skull and bones. It was Ploeckner," he added, and for the moment his voice was still and untroubled with vindicated pride. "He was one of the best they had. Pupil of Richthofen's."

"Well, that's something," Miss Jenny agreed, stroking his head.

Young Bayard brooded for a time.

"I tried to keep him from going up there on that goddam little popgun," he burst out again.

"What did you expect, after the way you raised him?" Miss Jenny asked. "You're the oldest. . . . You've been to the cemetery, haven't you?"

"Yessum," he answered quietly.

"What's that?" old Bayard demanded.

"That old fool Simon said that's where you were. . . . You come on and eat your supper," she said briskly and firmly, entering his life again without a by-your-leave, taking up the snarled threads of it after her brisk and capable fashion, and he rose obediently.

"What's that?" old Bayard repeated.

"And you come on in, too." Miss Jenny swept him also into the orbit of her will as you gather a garment from a chair in passing. "Time you were in bed." They followed her to the kitchen and stood while she delved into the ice-box and set food on the table, and a pitcher of milk, and drew up a chair.

"Fix him a toddy, Jenny," old Bayard suggested. But Miss Jenny vetoed this immediately.

"Milk's what he wants. I reckon he had to drink enough whisky during that war to last him for a while. Bayard used to never come home from his without wanting to ride his horse up the front steps and into the house. Come on, now," and she drove old Bayard firmly out of the kitchen and up the stairs. "You go on to bed, you hear? Let him alone for a while." She saw his door shut and entered young Bayard's room and prepared his bed, and after a while from her own room she heard him mount the stairs.

His room was treacherously illumined by the moon, and without turning on the light he went and sat on the bed. Outside the windows the interminable crickets and frogs, as though the moon's rays were thin glass impacting among the trees and shrubs and shattering in brittle musical rain upon the ground; and above this and with a deep, timbrous quality, the measured respirations of the pump in the electric plant beyond the barn.

He dug another cigarette from his pocket and lit it. But he took only two draughts before he flung it away. And then he sat quietly in the room which he and John had shared in the young masculine violence of their twinship, on the bed where he and his wife had lain the last night of his leave, the night before he went back to England and out to the Front again, where John already was. Beside him on the pillow the wild bronze swirling of her hair was hushed now in the darkness, and she lay holding his arm with both hands against her breast while they talked quietly, soberly at last.

But he had not been thinking of her then. When he thought of her who lay rigid in the dark beside him, holding his arm tightly to her breast, it was only to be a little savagely ashamed of the heedless thing he had done to her. He was thinking of his brother whom he had not seen in over a year, thinking that in a month they would see one another again.

Nor was he thinking of her now, although the walls held, like a withered flower in a casket, something of that magical chaos in which they had lived for two months, tragic and transient as a blooming of honeysuckle and sharp as the odor of mint. He was thinking of his dead brother; the spirit of their violent complementing days lay like dust everywhere in the room, obliterating that other presence, stopping his breathing, and he went to the window and flung the sash crashing upward and leaned there, gulping air into his lungs like a man who has been submerged and who still cannot believe that he has reached the surface again.

Later, lying naked between the sheets, he waked himself with his own groaning. The room was filled now with a gray light, sourceless and chill, and he turned his head and saw Miss Jenny, the woolen shawl about her shoulders, sitting in a chair beside the bed.

"What's the matter?" he said.

"That's what I want to know," Miss Jenny answered. "You make more noise than that water pump."

"I want a drink."

Miss Jenny leaned over and raised a glass from the floor beside her. Bayard had risen to his elbow and he took the glass. His hand stopped before the glass reached his mouth and he hunched on his elbow, the glass beneath his nose.

"Hell," he said, "I said a drink."

"You drink that milk, boy," Miss Jenny commanded. "You think I'm going to sit up all night just to feed you whisky? Drink it, now."

He emptied the glass obediently and lay back. Miss Jenny set the glass on the floor.

"What time is it?"

"Hush," she said. She laid her hand on his brow. "Go to sleep."

He rolled his head on the pillow, but he could not evade her hand.

"Get away," he said. "Let me alone."

"Hush," Miss Jenny said. "Go to sleep."

PART TWO

castration

Simon said: "You ain't never yit planted nothin' whar hit ought ter be planted." He sat on the bottom step, whetting the blade of a hoe with a file. Miss Jenny stood with her caller at the edge of the veranda above him, in a man's felt hat and heavy gloves. A pair of shears dangled below her waist, glinting in the morning sunlight.

"And whose business is that?" she demanded. "Yours, or Colonel's? Either one of you can loaf on this porch and tell me where a plant will grow best or look best, but if either of you ever grew as much as a weed out of the ground yourselves, I've never seen it. I don't give two whoops in the bad place where you or Colonel, either, thinks a flower ought to be planted: I plant my flowers just exactly where I want 'em to be planted."

"And den dares 'um not ter come up," Simon added. "Dat's de way you en Isom gyardens. Thank de Lawd Isom ain't got to make his livin' wid de sort of gyardenin' he learns in dat place." Still whetting at the hoe blade he jerked his head toward the corner of the house.

He wore a disreputable hat, of a fabric these many years anonymous. Miss Jenny stared coldly down upon this hat.

"Isom made his living by being born black," Miss Jenny snapped. "Suppose you quit scraping at that hoe and see if you can't dare some of the weeds in that salvia bed to come up."

"I got to git a aidge on dis curry-comb," Simon said. "You go'n out dar to yo' gyarden: I'll git dis bed cleaned up." He scraped steadily at the hoe blade.

"You've been at that long enough to find out you can't possibly wear that blade down to the handle with just a file,"

56

Miss Jenny said. "You've been at it ever since breakfast. I heard you. You get on out there where folks passing will think you're working, anyhow."

Simon groaned dismally and spent a half minute laying the file aside. He laid it on a step, then he picked it up and moved it to another step. Then he laid it against the step behind him. He ran his thumb along the blade, examining it with morose hopefulness.

"Hit mought do now," he said. "But hit'll be jes' like weedin' wid a curry-c——"

"You try it, anyway," Miss Jenny said. "Maybe the weeds'll think it's a hoe. You go give 'em a chance to, anyhow."

"Ise gwine, Ise gwine," Simon answered pettishly, rising and hobbling away. "You go'n see erbout dat place o' yo'n; I'll 'tend ter dis."

Miss Jenny and the caller descended the steps and went on toward the corner of the house.

"Why he'd rather sit there and rasp at that new hoe with a file instead of grubbing up a dozen blades of grass in that salvia bed, I can't see," Miss Jenny said. "But he'll do it. He'd sit there and scrape at that hoe until it looked like a saw blade, if I'd let him. Bayard bought a lawn mower three or four years ago—God knows what for—and turned it over to Simon. The folks that made it guaranteed it for a year. They didn't know Simon, though. I often thought, reading about those devastations and things in the paper last year, what a good time Simon would have had in the war. He could have shown 'em things about devastation they never thought of. Isom!" she shouted.

They entered the garden and Miss Jenny paused at the gate. "You, Isom!"

This time there was a reply, and Miss Jenny went on with her caller and Isom lounged up from somewhere and clicked the gate after him.

"Why didn't you——" Miss Jenny looked back over her shoulder, then she stopped and regarded Isom's suddenly military figure with brief and cold astonishment. He now wore khaki, with a divisional emblem on the shoulder and a tarnished service stripe on his cuff. His lean sixteen-year-old neck rose from the slovenly collar's limp, overlarge embrace and a surprising amount of wrist was visible below

the cuffs. The breeches bagged hopelessly into the unskill-
ful wrapping of the putties which, with either a fine
sense for the unique or a bland disregard of military usage,
he had donned prior to his shoes, and the soiled overseas
cap came down regrettably on his bullet head.

"Where did you get those clothes?" The sunlight glinted
on Miss Jenny's shears, and Miss Benbow in her white
dress and soft straw hat turned also and looked at him
with a strange expression.

"Dey's Caspey's," Isom answered. "I jes' bor'd 'um."

"Caspey?" Miss Jenny repeated. "Is he home?"

"Yessum. He got in las' night on de nine-thirty."

"Last night, did he? Where is he now? Asleep, I reckon?"

"Yessum. Dat's whar he wuz when I lef' home."

"And I reckon that's how you borrowed his uniform,"
Miss Jenny said tartly. "Well, let him sleep this morning.
Give him one day to get over the war. But if it made a
fool out of him like it did out of Bayard, he'd better put
that thing on again and go back to it. I'll declare, men
can't seem to stand anything." She went on, the guest in her
straight white dress following.

"You are awfully hard on men, not to have a husband
to bother with, Miss Jenny," she said. "Besides, you're judging all men by your Sartorises."

"They ain't my Sartorises," Miss Jenny disclaimed promptly; "I just inherited 'em. But you just wait: you'll have one
of your own to bother with soon; you just wait until Horace
gets home, then see how long it takes him to get over it.
Men can't stand anything," she repeated. "Can't even stand
helling around with no worry and no responsibility and no
limit to all the meanness they can think about wanting to do.
Do you think a man could sit day after day and month
after month in a house miles from nowhere and spend the
time between casualty lists tearing up bedclothes and window curtains and table linen to make lint, and watching
sugar and flour and meat dwindling away, and using pine
knots for light because there aren't any candles and no
candlesticks to put 'em in if there were, and hiding in
nigger cabins while drunken Yankee generals set fire to the
house your great-great-grandfather built and you and all
your folks were born in? Don't talk to me about men suffering in war." Miss Jenny snipped larkspur savagely. "Just

you wait until Horace comes home; then you'll see. Just a good excuse for 'em to make nuisances of themselves and stay in the way while the womenfolks are trying to clean up the mess they left with their fighting. John at least had consideration enough, after he'd gone and gotten himself into something where he had no business, not to come back and worry everybody to distraction. But Bayard now, coming back in the middle of it and having everybody thinking he was settled down at last, teaching at that Memphis flying school, and then marrying that fool girl."

(ie, not fighting)

"Miss Jenny!"

"Well, I don't mean that, but she'd ought've been spanked, hard. I know: didn't I do the same thing, myself? It was all that harness that Bayard wore. Talk about men being taken in by a uniform!" She clipped larkspur. "Dragging me up there to the wedding, mind you, with a church full of rented swords and some of Bayard's pupils trying to drop roses on 'em when they came out. I reckon some of 'em were not his pupils, because one of 'em finally did drop a handful that missed everything and fell in the street." She snipped larkspur savagely. "I had dinner with 'em one night. Sat in the hotel an hour until they remembered to come for me. Then we stopped at a delicatessen and Bayard and Caroline got out and went in and came back with about a bushel of packages and dumped 'em into the car, where they leaked grease on my new stockings. That was the dinner I'd been invited to, mind you; there wasn't a sign of anything that looked or smelled like a stove in the whole place. I didn't offer to help 'em. I told Caroline I didn't know anything about that sort of housekeeping because my folks were old-fashioned enough to cook food.

"Then the others came in—some of Bayard's soldier friends, and a drove of other folks' wives, near as I could gather. Young women that ought to've been at home, seeing about supper, gabbling and screeching in that silly way young married women have when they're doing something they hope their husbands won't like. They were all unwrapping bottles—about two dozen, I reckon, and Bayard and Caroline came in with that silver I gave 'em and monogrammed napkins and that delicatessen fodder that tasted like swampgrass, on paper plates. We ate it there, sitting on the floor or standing up or just wherever you happened to be.

"That was Caroline's idea of keeping house. She said they'd settle down when they got old, if the war was over by then. About thirty-five, I suppose she meant. Thin as a rail; there wouldn't have been much to spank. But she'd ought to have had it, just the same. Soon as she found out about the baby, she named it. Named it nine months before it was born and told everybody about it. Used to talk about it like it was her grandfather or something. Always saying Bayard won't let me do this or that or the other."

Miss Jenny continued to clip larkspur, the caller tall in a white dress beside her. The fine and huge simplicity of the house rose among thickening trees, the garden lay in sunlight bright with bloom, myriad with scent and with a drowsy humming of bees—a steady golden sound, as of sunlight become audible—all the impalpable veil of the immediate, the familiar; just beyond it a girl with a bronze swirling of hair and a small, supple body in a constant epicene unrepose, a dynamic fixation like that of carven sexless figures caught in moments of action, striving, a mechanism all of whose members must move in performing the most trivial action, her wild hands not accusing but passionate still beyond the veil impalpable but sufficient.

Miss Jenny stooped above the flower bed, her narrow back, though stooping, erect still, indomitable. A thrush flashed modestly across the bright air and into the magnolia tree in a dying parabola. "And then, when he had to go back to the war, of course he brought her out here and left her on my hands." The caller stood motionless in her white dress, and Miss Jenny said, "No, I don't mean that." She snipped larkspur.

"Poor women," she said, "I reckon we do have to take our revenge wherever and whenever we can get it. Only she ought to've taken it out on Bayard."

"When she died," Narcissa said, "and he couldn't know about it; couldn't have come to her if he had? And you can say that?"

"Bayard love anybody, that cold devil?" Miss Jenny clipped larkspur. "He never cared a snap of his fingers for anybody in his life except John." She snipped larkspur savagely. "Swelling around here like it was our fault, like we made 'em go to that war. And now he's got to have an automobile, got to go all the way to Memphis to buy one. An

automobile in Bayard Sartoris' barn, mind you; him that
won't even lend the bank's money to a man that owns one.
. . . Do you want some sweet peas?"

"Yes, please," Narcissa answered. Miss Jenny straightened
up, then she stopped utterly still.

"Just look yonder, will you?" She pointed with the shears.
"That's how they suffer from war, poor things." Beyond a
frame of sweet peas Isom in his khaki strode solemnly back
and forth. Upon his right shoulder was a hoe and on his face
an expression of rapt absorption, and as he reversed at the
end of his beat he murmured to himself in measured singsong.

"You, Isom!" Miss Jenny shouted.

He halted in mid-stride, still at shoulder arms. "Ma'am?"
he said mildly. Miss Jenny continued to glare at him, and
his military bearing faded and he lowered his piece and
executed a sort of effacing movement within his martial
shroud.

"Put that hoe down and bring that basket over here. That's
the first time in your life you ever picked up a garden tool
of your own free will. I wish I could discover the kind of
uniform that would make you dig in the ground with it; I'd
certainly buy you one."

"Yessum."

"If you want to play soldier, you go off somewhere with
Bayard and do it. I can raise flowers without any help
from the army," she added, turning to the guest with her
handful of larkspur. "And what are you laughing at?" she
demanded.

"You both look so funny," the younger woman explained.
"You looked so much more like a soldier than poor Isom,
for all his uniform." She touched her eyes with her finger
tips. "I'm sorry: please forgive me for laughing."

"Hmph," Miss Jenny sniffed. She put the larkspur into the
basket and went on to the sweet peas and snipped again,
viciously. The guest followed, as did Isom with the basket;
and presently Miss Jenny had done with sweet peas and she
moved on again with her train, pausing to cut a rose here
and there, and stopped before a bed where tulips lifted their
bright inverted bells. She and Isom had guessed happily this
time; the various colors formed an orderly pattern.

"When we dug 'em up last fall," she told her guest, "I'd

put a red one in Isom's right hand and a yellow one in his left. Then I'd say, 'All right, Isom, give me the red one.' He'd never fail to hold out his left hand, and if I just looked at him long enough, he'd hold out both hands. 'Didn't I tell you to hold that red one in your right hand?' I'd say. 'Yessum, here 'tis,' and out would come his left hand again. 'That ain't your right hand, stupid,' I'd say. 'Dat's de one you said wuz my right hand a while ago,' Isom says. Ain't that so, nigger?" Miss Jenny glared at Isom, who again performed his deprecatory effacing movement behind the slow equanimity of his grin.

"Yessum, I 'speck it is."

"You'd better," Miss Jenny rejoined warningly. "Now, how can anybody have a decent garden, with a fool like that? I expect every spring to find corn or lespedeza coming up in the hyacinth beds or something." She examined the tulips again, weighing the balanced colors one against the other in her mind. "No, you don't want any tulips," she decided, moving on.

"No, Miss Jenny," the guest agreed demurely. They went on to the gate, and Miss Jenny stopped and took the basket from Isom.

"And you go home and take that thing off, you hear?"

"Yessum."

"And I want to look out that window in a few minutes and see you in the garden with that hoe again," she added. "And I want to see both of your hands on it this time, and I want to see it moving, too. You hear me?"

"Yessum."

"And tell Caspey to be ready to go to work in the morning. Even niggers that eat here have got to work some." But Isom was gone, and they went on and mounted to the veranda. "Don't he sound like that's exactly what he's going to do?" she confided as they entered the hall. "He knows as well as I do that I won't dare look out that window, after what I said. Come in," she added, opening the parlor doors.

This room was open but seldom now, though in John Sartoris' day it had been constantly in use. He was always giving dinners, and balls too on occasion, with the folding doors between it and the dining-room thrown open and three Negroes with stringed instruments on the stairway and all the candles burning, surrounding himself with a pageantry of color and scent and music against which he moved with his bluff and jovial arrogance. [He lay also overnight in this room in his gray regimentals and so brought to a conclusion the colorful, if not always untarnished, pageant of his own career, contemplating for the last time his own apotheosis from the jocund mellowness of his generous hearth.

But during his son's time it fell less and less into use, and slowly and imperceptibly [it lost its jovial but stately masculinity,] becoming by mutual agreement a place for his wife and his son John's wife and Miss Jenny to clean thoroughly twice a year and in which, preceded by a ritualistic unswaddling of brown holland, they entertained their more formal callers. This was its status at the birth of his grandsons and it continued thus until the death of their parents, and later, to that of his wife. After that Miss Jenny bothered with formal callers but little and with the parlor not at all. [She said it gave her the creeps.]

And so it stayed closed nearly all the time, and slowly acquired an atmosphere of solemn and macabre fustiness. Occasionally young Bayard or John would open the door and peer into the solemn obscurity in which the shrouded furniture loomed with a sort of ghostly benignance, like albino mastodons. [But they did not enter; already in their minds the room was associated with death, an idea which even the holly and tinsel of Christmastide could not completely obscure.] They were away at school by the time they reached party age, but even during vacations, though they had filled the house with the polite bedlam of their contemporaries, the room would be opened only on Christmas Eve, when the tree was set up and a fire lighted, and a bowl of eggnog on the table in the center of the hearth. And after they went to England in '16 it was opened twice a year to be cleaned after the ancient ritual that even Simon had inherited from his forefathers, and to have the piano tuned, or when Miss Jenny and Narcissa spent a forenoon or afternoon there, but formally not at all.

The furniture loomed shapelessly in its dun shrouds. The piano alone was uncovered, and Narcissa drew the bench out and removed her hat and dropped it beside her. Miss Jenny set the basket down and from the gloom back of the instrument she drew a straight, hard chair, uncovered also, and sat down and removed her felt hat from her trim white head. Light came through the open door, but the windows were shuttered behind heavy maroon curtains, and it served only to enhance the obscurity and to render more shapeless the hooded anonymous furniture.

But behind these dun bulks and in all the corners of the room there waited, as actors stand within the wings beside the waiting stage, figures in crinoline and hooped muslin and silk; in stocks and flowing coats, in gray too, with crimson sashes and sabers in gallant, sheathed repose; Jeb Stuart himself, perhaps, on his glittering garlanded bay or with his sunny hair falling upon fine broadcloth beneath the mistletoe and holly boughs of Baltimore in '58. Miss Jenny sat with her uncompromising grenadier's back and held her hat upon her knees and fixed herself to look on as her guest touched chords from the keyboard and wove them together, and rolled the curtain back upon the scene.

In the kitchen Caspey was having breakfast while Simon his father, and Elnora his sister, and Isom his nephew (in uniform) watched him. He had been Simon's understudy in the stables, and general handy man about the place, doing all the work that Simon managed, through the specious excuse of decrepitude and filial gratitude, to slough on to his shoulders and that Miss Jenny could devise for him and he could not evade. Old Bayard also employed him in the fields occasionally. Then the draft had got him and bore him to France and the Saint Sulpice docks as one of a labor battalion, where he did what work corporals and sergeants managed to slough on to his unmilitary shoulders, and that white officers could devise for him and he could not evade.

Thus all the labor about the place devolved on Simon and Isom. But Miss Jenny kept Isom piddling about the house so much of the time that Simon was soon as bitter against the War Lords as any professional Democrat. Meanwhile Caspey was working a little and trifling with continental life in its martial phases rather to his future detriment, for at last the tumult died and the captains departed and left a vacuum filled with the usual bitter bickerings of Armageddon's heirs-at-law; and Caspey returned to his native land a total loss, sociologically speaking, with a definite disinclination toward labor, honest or otherwise, and two honorable wounds incurred in a razor-hedged crap game.

But return he did, to his father's querulous satisfaction and Elnora's and Isom's admiration, and he now sat in the kitchen, telling them about the war.

"I don't take nothin' fum no white folks no mo'," he was saying. "War done changed all dat. If us cullud folks is good enough ter save France fum de Germans, den us is good enough ter have de same rights de Germans is. French folks think so, anyhow, and ef America don't, dey's ways of learnin' 'um. Yes, suh, it wuz de cullud soldier saved France and America bofe. Black regiments kilt mo' Germans dan all de white armies put together, let 'lone unloadin' steamboats all day long fer a dollar a day."

"War ain't hurt dat big mouf o' yo'n, anyhow," Simon said.

"War unloosed de black man's mouf," Caspey corrected. "Give him de right to talk. Kill Germans, den do yo' oratin', dey tole us. Well, us done it."

"How many you kilt, Unc' Caspey?" Isom asked deferentially.

"I ain't never bothered to count 'um up. Been times I kilt mo' in one mawnin' dan dey's folks on dis whole place. One time we wuz down in de cellar of a steamboat tied up to de bank, and one of these submareems come up and stopped, and all de white officers run up on de bank and hid. Us boys downstairs didn't know dey wuz anything wrong 'twell folks started clambin' down de ladder. We never had no guns wid us at de time, so when we seed dem green legs comin' down de ladder, we crope up behin' 'um, and ez dey come down one of de boys would hit 'um over de haid wid a piece of scantlin' and another would drag 'um outen de way and cut dey th'oat wid a meat-plow. Dey wuz about thirty of 'em. . . . Elnora, is dey any mo' of dat coffee lef'?"

"Sho'," Simon murmured. Isom's eyes popped quietly and Elnora lifted the coffee-pot from the stove and refilled Caspey's cup.

Caspey drank coffee for a while.

"And another time me and a boy wuz gwine along a road. We got tired unloadin' dem steamboats all day long, so one day de Captain's dog-robber foun' whar he kep' dese here unloaded passes and he tuck a han'ful of 'em, and me and him wuz on de road to town when a truck come along and de boy axed us did us want a lif'. He wuz a school boy, so he writ on three of de passes whenever we come to a place dat mought be M.P. infested, and we got along fine, ridin' about de country on dat private truck, 'twell one mawnin' we looked out whar de truck wuz and dey wuz a M.P. settin' on it whilst de truck boy wuz tryin' to explain to him. So we turned de other way and lit out walkin'. After dat we had to dodge de M.P. towns, 'case me and de other boy couldn't write on de passes.

"One day we wuz gwine along a road. It wuz a busted-up road and it didn't look like no M.P. country. But dey wuz some of 'em in de las' town we dodged, so we didn't know we wuz so close to whar de fightin' wuz gwine on 'twell we walked on to a bridge and come right on a whole regiment of Germans, swimmin' in de river. Dey seed us about de same time we seed dem and div under de water, and me and de other boy grabbed up two machine guns settin' dar and we sot on de bridge rail, and ev'y time a German stuck his haid up fer a new breaf, us shot 'im. It wuz jes' like shootin' turkles in a slough. I reckon dey wuz close to a hund'ed us kilt 'fo' de machine guns run dry. Dat's whut dey gimme dis fer." He drew from his pocket a florid, plated medal of Porto Rican origin, and Isom came quietly up to see.

"Umumuh," Simon said. He sat with his hands on his knees, watching his son with rapt astonishment. Elnora came up also, her arms daubed with flour.

"Whut does dey look like?" she asked. "Like folks?"

"Dey's big," Caspey answered. "Sort of pink lookin' and about eight foot tall. Only folks in de whole American war dat could handle 'um wuz de cullud regiments."

Isom returned to his corner beside the woodbox.

"Ain't you got some gyardenin' to do, boy?" Simon asked him.

"Naw, suh," Isom answered, his enraptured gaze still on his uncle. "Miss Jenny say us done caught up dis mawnin'."

"Well, don't you come whinin' ter me when she jumps on you," Simon warned him. "Whar'd you kill de nex' lot?" he asked his son.

"Us didn't kill no mo' after dat," Caspey said. "We decided dat wuz enough and dat we better leave de rest of 'um fer de boys dat wuz gittin' paid fer killin' 'um. We went on 'twell de road played out in a field. Dey wuz some ditches and ole wire fences and holes in de field, wid folks livin' in 'um. De folks wuz white American soldiers and dey egvised us to pick out a hole and stay dar fer a while, ef us wanted de peace and comfort of de war. So we picked us out a dry hole and moved in. Dey wasn't nothin' to do all day long but lay in de shade and watch de air balloons and listen to de shootin' about fo' miles up de road. De boy wid me claimed it wuz rabbit hunters, but I knowed better. De white boys could write, so dey fixed up de passes and we tuck time about gwine to whar de army wuz and gittin' grub. When de passes give out we foun' whar a French army wid some cannons wuz livin' over in de woods a ways, so we went over whar dey wuz and et.

"Dat went on fer a long time, 'twell one day de balloons wuz gone and de white boys says it wuz time to move again. But me and de other boy didn't see no use in gwine nowhar else, so us stayed. Dat evenin' we went over to whar de French army wuz fer some grub, but dey wuz gone too. De boy wid me says de Germans done caught 'um, but we didn't know; hadn't heard no big racket since yistiddy. So we went back to de hole. Dey wuzn't no grub, so we crawled in and went to bed and slep' dat night, and early de nex' mawnin' somebody come in de hole and tromped on us and woke us up. It wuz one of dese army upliftin' ladies huntin' German bayonets and belt-buckles. She say, 'Who dat in here?' and de other boy says, 'Us shock troops.' So we got out, but we hadn't gone no piece 'fo' here come a wagginload of M.P.'s. And de passes had done give out."

"Whut you do den?" Simon asked. Isom's eyes bulged quietly in the gloom behind the woodbox.

"Dey tuck us and shut us up in de jail-house fer a while. But de war wuz mos' th'ough and dey needed hands to load dem steamboats back up, so dey sont us to a town name' Bres'. . . . I don't take nothin' offen no white man, M.P. er not," Caspey stated again. "Us boys wuz in a room one night, shootin' dice. De bugle had done already played de lights out tune, but we wuz in de army, whar a man kin do whut he wants to es long es dey'll let 'im, so when de M.P. come along and says, 'Put out dat light,' one of de boys says, 'Come in here, and we'll put yo'n out.' Dey wuz two of de M.P.'s and dey kicked de do' in and started shootin', and somebody knocked de light over and we run. Dey foun' one of de M.P.'s de nex' mawnin' widout nothin' to hole his collar on, and two of de boys wuz daid, too. But dey couldn't fin' who de res' of us wuz. And den we come home."

Caspey emptied his cup. "I don't take nothin' offen no white man no mo', lootenant ner captain ner M.P. War showed de white folks dey can't git along widout de cullud man. Tromple him in de dus', but when de trouble bust loose, hit's 'Please, suh, Mr. Cullud Man; right dis way whar de bugle blowin', Mr. Cullud Man; you is de savior of de country.' And now de cullud race gwine reap de benefits of de war, and dat soon."

"Sho," murmured Simon.

"Yes, suh. And de women, too. I got my white in France, and I'm gwine git it here, too."

"Lemme tell you somethin', nigger," Simon said. "De good Lawd done took keer of you fer a long time, now, but He ain't gwine bother wid you always."

"Den I reckon I'll git along widout Him," Caspey retorted. He rose and stretched. "Reckon I'll go down to de big road and ketch a ride to town. Gimme dem clothes, Isom."

Miss Jenny and her guest stood on the veranda when he passed along beside the house and crossed toward the drive.

"There goes your gardener," Narcissa said. Miss Jenny looked.

"That's Caspey," she corrected. "Now, where do you reckon he's headed? Town, I'll bet a dollar," she added, watching his lounging khaki back, by means of which he contrived to disseminate in some way a sort of lazy insolence. "You, Caspey!" she called.

He slowed in passing Narcissa's small car and examined it with a disparagement too lazy to sneer even, then he slouched on.

"You, Caspey!" Miss Jenny repeated, raising her voice. But he went steadily on down the drive, insolent and slouching and unhurried. "He heard me," she said ominously. "We'll see about this when he comes back. Who was the fool anyway, who thought of putting niggers into the same uniform with white men? Mr. Vardaman knew better; he told those fools at Washington at the time it wouldn't do. But politicians!" She invested the innocent word with an utter and blasting derogation. "If I ever get tired of as-

sociating with gentlefolks, I know what I'll do: I'll run for
Congress. . . . Listen at me!—tiradin' again. I declare, at
times I believe these Sartorises and all their possessions just
set out to plague and worry me. Thank the Lord, I won't
have to associate with 'em after I'm dead. I don't know
where they'll be, but no Sartoris is going to stay in heaven
any longer than he can help."

The other laughed. "You seem very sure of your own
destination, Miss Jenny."

"Why shouldn't I be? Haven't I been laying up crowns and
harps for a long time?" She shaded her eyes with her hand
and gazed down the drive. Caspey had reached the gate and
he now stood beside the road, waiting for a wagon to pass.
"Don't you stop for him, you hear?" she said suddenly. . . .
"Why won't you stay for dinner?"

"No," the other answered, "I must get on home. Aunt
Sally's not well today." She stood for a moment in the sunlight, her hat and her basket of flowers on her arm, musing.
Then with a sudden decision she drew a folded paper from
the front of her dress.

"Got another one, did you?" Miss Jenny asked, watching
her. "Lemme see it." She took the paper and opened it and
stepped back out of the sun. Her nose glasses hung on a
slender silk cord that rolled on to a spring in a small gold
case pinned to her bosom. She snapped the cord out and
set the glasses on her high-bridged nose. Behind them her
eyes were cold and piercing as a surgeon's.

The paper was a single sheet of foolscap; it bore writing in a frank, open script that at first glance divulged no
individuality whatever; a hand youthful, yet at the same
time so blandly and neatly unsecretive that presently you
wondered a little:

"You did not answer mine of 25th. I did not expect you
answer it yet. You will answer soon I can wait. I will not
harm you I am square and honest you will lern when our
ways come to gether. I do not expect you answer yet but
you know where you make a sign."

Miss Jenny refolded the paper with a gesture of fine and
delicate distaste. "I'd burn this thing, if it wasn't the only

thing we have to catch him with. I'll give it to Bayard to-night."

"No, no," the other protested quickly, extending her hand, "please don't. Let me have it and tear it up."

"It's the only evidence, child—this and the other one. We'll get a detective."

"No, no; please! I don't want anybody else to know about it. Please, Miss Jenny." She reached her hand again.

"You want to keep it," Miss Jenny accused coldly. "Just like a young fool woman, to be flattered by a thing like this."

"I'll tear it up," the other repeated. "I would have sooner, but I wanted to tell somebody. It—it—I thought I wouldn't feel so filthy, after I had shown it to somebody else. Let me have it, please."

"Fiddlesticks. Why should you feel filthy? You haven't encouraged it, have you?"

"Please, Miss Jenny."

But Miss Jenny still held on to it. "Don't be a fool," she snapped. "How can this thing make you feel filthy? Any young woman is liable to get an anonymous letter. And a lot of 'em like it. We are all convinced that men feel that way about us, and we can't help but admire the one that's got the courage to tell us, no matter who he is."

"If he'd just signed his name. I wouldn't mind who it was. But like this . . . Please, Miss Jenny."

"Don't be a fool," Miss Jenny repeated. "How can we find who it is if you destroy the evidence?"

"I don't want to know." Miss Jenny released the paper and Narcissa tore it to bits and cast them over the rail and rubbed her hands on her dress. "I don't want to know. I want to forget all about it."

"Nonsense. You're dying to know, right now. I bet you look at every man you pass and wonder if it's him. And as long as you don't do something about it, it'll go on. Get worse, probably. You better let me tell Bayard."

"No, no. I'd hate for him to know, to think that I would —might have . . . It's all right: I'll just burn them up after this, without opening them. . . . I really must go."

"Of course: you'll throw 'em right into the stove," Miss Jenny agreed with cold irony. Narcissa descended the steps and Miss Jenny came forward into the sunlight again, letting her glasses whip back into the case. "It's your business, of course. But I'd not stand for it, if 'twas me. But then, I ain't twenty-six years old. . . . Well, come out again when you get another one, or you want some more flowers."

"Yes, I will. Thank you for these."

"And let me know what you hear from Horace. Thank the Lord, it's just a glass-blowing machine and not a war-widow."

"Yes, I will. Good-bye." She went on through the dappled shade in her straight white dress and her basket of flowers stippled upon it, and got in her car. The top was back and she put her hat on and started the engine. She looked back again and waved her hand. "Good-bye."

The Negro had moved down the road, slowly, and stopped again, and he was watching her covertly as she approached. As she passed he looked full at her and she knew he was about to hail her. She opened the throttle and passed him with increasing speed and drove swiftly on to town, where she lived in a brick house among cedars on a hill.

She was arranging the larkspur in a dull lemon urn on the piano. Aunt Sally Wyatt rocked steadily in her chair beside the window, clapping her feet flatly on the floor at each stroke. Her work-basket sat on the window ledge between the gentle billowing of the curtains, her ebony walking-stick leaned beside it.

"And you were out there two hours," she said, "and never saw him at all?"

"He wasn't there," Narcissa answered. "He's gone to Memphis."

Aunt Sally rocked steadily. "If I was them, I'd make him stay there. I wouldn't have that boy around me, blood or no blood. . . . What did he go to Memphis for? I thought that aeroplane what-do-you-call-it was broke up."

"He went on business, I suppose."

"What business has he got in Memphis? Bayard Sartoris has got more sense than to turn over any business to that harebrained fool."

"I don't know," Narcissa answered, arranging the larkspur. "He'll be back soon, I suppose. You can ask him then."

"Me ask him? I never said two words to him in his life.

And I don't intend to. I been used to associating with gentle-folks."

Narcissa broke some of the stems, arranging the blooms in a pattern. "What's he done that a gentleman doesn't do, Aunt Sally?"

"Why, jumping off water tanks and going up in balloons just to scare folks. You think I'd have that boy around me? I'd have him locked up in the insane asylum, if I was Bayard and Jenny."

"He didn't jump off the tank. He just swung off of it on a rope and dived into the swimming-pool. And it was John that went up in the balloon."

"That wasn't what I heard. I heard he jumped off that tank, across a whole row of freight cars and lumber piles, and didn't miss the edge of the pool an inch."

"No, he didn't. He swung on a rope from the top of a house and then dived into the pool. The rope was tied to the tank."

"Well, didn't he have to jump over a lot of lumber and freight cars? And couldn't he have broken his neck just as easy that way as jumping off the tank?"

"Yes," Narcissa answered.

"There! What'd I tell you? And what was the use of it?"

"I don't know."

"Of course you don't. That was the reason he did it." Aunt Sally rocked triumphantly for a while. Narcissa put the last touches to the blue pattern of the larkspur. A tortoise-shell cat bunched suddenly and silently on the window be-side the work-basket, with an effect as of sleight-of-hand. Still crouching, it blinked into the room for a moment, then it sank to its belly and with arched neck fell to grooming its shoulder with a narrow pink tongue. Narcissa moved to the window and laid her hand on the creature's sleek back.

"And then, going up in that balloon, when——"

"That wasn't Bayard," Narcissa repeated. "That was John."

"That wasn't what I heard. I heard it was the other one and that Bayard and Jenny were both begging him with tears in their eyes not to do it. I heard——"

"Neither of them were there. Bayard wasn't even there. It was John did it. He did it because the man that came with the balloon got sick. John went up in it so the country people wouldn't be disappointed. I was there."

"Stood there and let him do it, did you, when you could 'a' telephoned Jenny or walked across the square to the bank and got Bayard? You stood there and never opened your mouth, did you?"

"Yes," Narcissa answered. Stood there beside Horace in the slow, intent ring of country people, watching the globe swelling and tugging at its ropes, watched John Sartoris in a faded flannel shirt and corduroy breeches while the carnival man explained the rip-cord and the parachute to him; stood there feeling her breath going out faster than she could draw it in again, and watched the thing lurch into the air with John sitting on a frail trapeze bar swinging beneath it, with eyes she could not close; saw the balloon and people and all swirl slowly upward and then found herself clinging to Horace behind the shelter of a wagon, trying to get her breath.

He landed three miles away in a brier thicket and disengaged the parachute and regained the road and hailed a passing Negro in a wagon. A mile from town they met old Bayard driving furiously in the carriage, and the two vehicles stopped side by side in the road while old Bayard in the one exhausted the accumulate fury of his rage and in the other his grandson sat in his shredded clothes, and on his scratched face that look of one who had gained for an instant a desire so fine that its escape was a purification, not a loss.

The next day, as she was passing a store, he emerged with that abrupt violence which he had in common with his brother, pulling short up to avoid a collision with her.

"Oh, ex—— Why, hello," he said. Beneath the crisscrosses of tape his face was merry and bold and wild, and he wore no hat. For a moment she gazed at him with wide, hopeless eyes, then she clapped her hand to her mouth and went swiftly on, almost running.

Then he was gone, with his brother, shut away by the war as two noisy dogs are penned in a kennel far away. Miss Jenny gave her news of them, of the dull, dutiful letters they sent home at sparse intervals; then he was dead—but away beyond the seas, and there was no body to be returned clumsily to earth, and so to her he seemed still to be laughing at that word as he had laughed at all the other mouth-sounds that stood for repose, who had not waited for Time and its furniture to teach him that the end of wisdom is to dream high enough not to lose the dream in the seeking of it.

Aunt Sally rocked steadily in her chair.

"Well, it don't matter which one it was. One's bad as the other. But I reckon it ain't their fault, raised like they were. Rotten spoiled, both of 'em. Lucy Sartoris wouldn't let anybody control 'em while she lived. If they'd been mine, now . . ." She rocked on. "Beat it out of 'em, I would. Raising two wild Indians like that. But those folks, thinking there wasn't anybody quite as good as a Sartoris. Even Lucy Cranston, come of as good people as there are in the state, acting like it was divine providence that let her marry one Sartoris and be the mother of two more. Pride, false pride."

She rocked steadily in her chair. Beneath Narcissa's hand the cat purred with lazy arrogance.

"It was a judgment on 'em, taking John instead of that other one. John at least tipped his hat to a lady on the street, but that other boy . . ." She rocked monotonously, clapping her feet flatly against the floor. "You better stay away from that boy. He'll be killing you same as he did that poor little wife of his."

"At least, give me benefit of clergy first, Aunt Sally," Narcissa said. Beneath her hand, beneath the cat's sleek hide, muscles flowed suddenly into tight knots, like wire, and the animal's body seemed to elongate like rubber as it whipped from beneath her hand and flashed out of sight across the veranda.

"Oh!" Narcissa cried. Then she whirled and caught up Aunt Sally's stick and ran from the room.

"What——" Aunt Sally said. "You bring my stick back here," she said. She sat staring at the door, hearing the swift clatter of the other's heels in the hall and then on the veranda. She rose and leaned in the window. "You bring my stick back here," she shouted.

Narcissa sped on across the porch and to the ground. In the canna bed beside the veranda the cat, crouching, jerked its head around and its yellow unwinking eyes. Narcissa rushed at it, the stick raised.

"Put it down!" she cried. "Drop it!" For another second the yellow eyes glared at her, then the animal ducked its

head and leaped away in a long fluid bound, the bird between its jaws.

"Oh-h-h, damn you!" she cried. "Damn you! You—you
Sartoris!" And she hurled the stick after the final tortoise
flash as the cat flicked around the corner of the house.

"You get my stick and bring it right back this minute!"
Aunt Sally shouted from the window.

She and Miss Jenny were sitting in the dim parlor. The
doors were ajar as usual, and young Bayard appeared suddenly between them and stood looking at her.

"It's Bayard," Miss Jenny said. "Come in here and speak
to Narcissa, sonny."

He said "Hello" vaguely and she turned on the piano
bench and shrank a little against the instrument.

"Who is it?" he said. He came in, bringing with him that
leashed cold violence which she remembered.

"It's Narcissa," Miss Jenny said testily. "Go on and speak
to her and stop acting like you don't know who she is."

Narcissa gave him her hand and he stood holding it
loosely, but he was not looking at her. She withdrew her
hand. He looked at her again, then away, and he loomed
above them and stood rubbing his hand through his hair.

"I want a drink," he said. "I can't find the key to the
desk."

"Stop and talk to us a few minutes and you can have one."

He stood for a moment above them, then he moved abruptly and before Miss Jenny could speak he had dragged the
envelope from another chair.

"Let that alone, you Indian!" Miss Jenny exclaimed. She
rose. "Here, take my chair, if you're too weak to stand up.
I'll be back in a minute," she added to Narcissa; "I'll have
to get my keys."

He sat laxly in the chair, rubbing his hand over his head,
his gaze brooding somewhere about his booted feet. Narcissa sat utterly quiet, shrunk back against the piano. She
spoke at last.

"I am so sorry about your wife . . . John. I asked Miss
Jenny to tell you when she . . ."

He sat rubbing his head slowly, in the brooding violence of
his temporary repose.

"You aren't married yourself, are you?" he asked. She sat

perfectly still. "Ought to try it," he added. "Everybody ought to get married once, like everybody ought to go to one war."

Miss Jenny returned with the keys, and he got his long abrupt body erect and left them.

"You can go on, now," she said. "He won't bother us again."

"No, I must go." Narcissa rose quickly and took her hat from the top of the piano.

"Why, you haven't been here any time, yet."

"I must go," Narcissa repeated. Miss Jenny rose.

"Well, if you must. I'll cut you some flowers. Won't take a minute."

"No, some other time; I—I have—I'll come out soon and get some. Good-bye." At the door she glanced swiftly down the hall; then she went on. Miss Jenny followed to the veranda. The other had descended the steps and she now went swiftly on toward her car.

"Come back again soon," Miss Jenny called.

"Yes. Soon," Narcissa answered. "Good-bye."

2

Young Bayard came back from Memphis in his car. Memphis was seventy-five miles away and the trip had taken an hour and forty minutes because some of the road was clay country road. The car was long and low and gray. The four-cylinder engine had sixteen valves and eight spark-plugs, and the people had guaranteed that it would run eighty miles an hour, although there was a strip of paper pasted to the windshield, to which he paid no attention whatever, asking him in red letters not to do so for the first five hundred miles.

He came up the drive and stopped before the house, where his grandfather sat with his feet on the veranda railing and Miss Jenny stood trim in her black dress beside a post. She descended the steps and examined it, and opened the door and got in to try the seat. Simon came to the door and gave it a brief, derogatory look and retired, and Isom appeared around the corner and circled the car quietly with an utter and yearning admiration. But old Bayard just looked down at the long, dusty thing, his cigar in his fingers, and grunted.

"Why, it's as comfortable as a rocking-chair," Miss Jenny said. "Come here and try it," she called to him. But he grunted again, and sat with his feet on the rail and watched young Bayard slide in under the wheel. The engine raced experimentally, ceased. Isom stood like a leashed hound beside it. Young Bayard glanced at him.

"You can go next time," he said.

"Why can't he go now?" Miss Jenny said. "Jump in, Isom."

Isom jumped in, and old Bayard watched them move soundlessly down the drive and watched the car pass from sight down the valley. Presently above the trees a cloud of dust rose into the azure afternoon and hung rosily fading in the sun, and a sound as of remote thunder died muttering behind it. Old Bayard puffed his cigar again. Simon appeared again in the door and stood there.

"Now whar you reckon dey gwine right here at suppertime?" he said. Bayard grunted, and Simon stood in the door, mumbling to himself.

Twenty minutes later the car slid up the drive and came to a halt almost in its former tracks. In the back seat Isom's face was like an open piano. Miss Jenny had worn no hat, and she held her hair with both hands, and when the car stopped she sat for a moment so. Then she drew a long breath.

"I wish I smoked cigarettes," she said, and then: "Is that as fast as it'll go?"

Isom got out and opened the door for her. She descended a little stiffly, but her eyes were shining and her dry old cheeks were flushed.

"How fer y'all been?" Simon asked from the door.

"We've been to town," she answered proudly, and her voice was clear as a girl's. Town was four miles away.

One day a week later old man Falls came in to town and found old Bayard in his office. The office was also the directors' room. It was a large room containing a long table lined with chairs, and a tall cabinet where blank banking forms were kept, and old Bayard's roll-top desk and swivel chair and a sofa on which he napped for an hour each noon.

The desk, like the one at home, was cluttered with a

variety of objects which bore no relation whatever to the
banking business, and the mantel above the fireplace bore
still more objects of an agricultural nature, as well as a
dusty assortment of pipes and three or four jars of tobacco
which furnished solace for the entire banking force from
president to janitor and for a respectable portion of the
bank's clientele. Weather permitting, old Bayard spent most
of the day in a tilted chair in the street door, and when
these patrons found him there, they went on back to the
office and filled their pipes from the jars. It was a sort of
unspoken convention not to take more than a pipeful at a
time. Here old man Falls and old Bayard retired on the old
man's monthly visits and shouted at one another (they
were both deaf) for a half hour or so. You could hear them
plainly from the street and in the adjoining store on either
side.

Old man Falls' eyes were blue and innocent as a boy's
and his first act was to open the parcel which old Bayard
had for him and take out a plug of chewing-tobacco, cut
off a chew and put it in his mouth, replace the plug and
tie the parcel neatly again. Twice a year the parcel contained an entire outfit of clothing, on the other occasions
tobacco and a small sack of peppermint candy. He would
never cut the string, but always untied it with his stiff,
gnarled fingers and tied it back again. He would not accept money.

He sat now in his clean, faded overalls, with the parcel on
his knees, telling Bayard about the automobile that had
passed him on the road that morning. Old Bayard sat quite
still, watching him with his fierce old eyes until he had
finished.

"Are you sure who it was?" he asked.

"Hit passed me too fast fer me to tell whether they was
anybody in hit a-tall or not. I asked when I fetched town
who 'twas. Seems like ever'body but you knows how fast
he runs hit."

Old Bayard sat quietly for a time. Then he raised his voice.
"Byron."

The door opened and the bookkeeper entered.

"Yes, sir, Colonel," he said without inflection.

" 'Phone out to my house and tell my grandson not to
touch that car until I come home."

"Yes, sir, Colonel." And he was gone as silently as he appeared.

Bayard slammed around in his swivel chair again and old man Falls leaned forward, peering at his face.

"What's that 'ere wen you got on yo' face, Bayard?" he asked.

"What?" Bayard demanded, then he raised his hand to a small spot which the suffusion of his face had brought into relief. "Here? I don't know what it is. It's been there about a week. Why?"

"Is it gittin' bigger?" the other asked. He rose and laid his parcel down and extended his hand. Old Bayard drew his head back.

"It's nothing," he said testily. "Let it alone." But old man Falls put the other's hand aside and touched the spot with his fingers.

"H'm," he said. "Hard's a rock. Hit'll git bigger, too. I'll watch hit, and when hit's right, I'll take it off. 'Tain't ripe, yit." The bookkeeper appeared suddenly and without noise beside them.

"Yo' cook says him and Miss Jenny is off car-ridin' some-wheres. I left yo' message."

"Jenny's with him, you say?" old Bayard asked.

"That's what yo' cook says," the bookkeeper repeated in his inflectionless voice.

"Well. All right."

The bookkeeper withdrew and old man Falls picked up his parcel. "I'll be gittin' on too," he said. "I'll come in next week and take a look at it. You better let hit alone till I git back." He followed the bookkeeper from the room, and presently old Bayard rose and stalked through the lobby and tilted his chair in the door.

That afternoon when he arrived home, the car was not in sight nor did his aunt answer his call. He mounted to his room and put on his riding-boots and lit a cigar, but when he looked down from his window into the back yard, neither Isom nor the saddled mare was visible. The old setter sat looking up at his window. When old Bayard's head appeared there the dog rose and went to the kitchen door and stood there; then it looked up at his window again. Old Bayard tramped down the stairs and on through the house and entered the kitchen, where Caspey sat at the table, eating and talking to Isom and Elnora.

"And one mo' time me and another boy——" Caspey was saying. Then Isom saw Bayard, and rose from his seat in the woodbox corner, and his eyes rolled whitely in his bullet head. Elnora paused also with her broom, but Caspey turned his head without rising, and still chewing steadily, he blinked his eyes at old Bayard in the door.

"I sent you word a week ago to come on out here at once, or not to come at all," Bayard said. "Did you get it?" Caspey mumbled something, still chewing, and old Bayard came into the room. "Get up from there and saddle my horse."

Caspey turned his back deliberately and raised his glass of buttermilk. "Git on, Caspey!" Elnora hissed at him.

"I ain't workin' here," he answered, just beneath Bayard's deafness. He turned to Isom. "Whyn't you go'n git his hoss fer him? Ain't you workin' here?"

"Caspey, fer Lawd's sake!" Elnora implored. "Yes, suh, Cunnel; he's gwine," she said loudly.

"Who, me?" Caspey said. "Does I look like it?" He raised the glass steadily to his mouth; then Bayard moved again and Caspey lost his nerve and rose quickly before the other reached him, and crossed the kitchen toward the door, but with sullen insolence in the very shape of his back. As he fumbled with the door Bayard overtook him.

"Are you going to saddle that mare?" he demanded.

"Ain't gwine skip it, big boy," Caspey answered, just below Bayard's deafness.

"What?"

"Oh, Lawd, Caspey!" Elnora moaned. Isom crouched into his corner. Caspey raised his eyes swiftly to Bayard's face and opened the screen door.

"I says, I ain't gwine skip it," he repeated, raising his voice. Simon stood at the foot of the steps beside the setter, gaping his toothless mouth at them, and old Bayard reached a stick of stove wood from the box at his hand and knocked Caspey through the opening door and down the steps at his father's feet.

"Now, you go saddle that mare," he said.

Simon helped his son to rise and led him away toward the barn while the setter looked after them, gravely in-

terested. "I kep' tellin' you dem new-fangled war notions of
yo'n wa'n't gwine ter work on dis place," he said angrily.
"And you better thank de good Lawd fer makin' yo' haid
hard ez hit is. You go'n git dat mare, and save dat nigger
freedom talk fer townfolks: dey mought stomach it. Whut
us niggers want ter be free fer, anyhow? Ain't we got ez many
white folks now ez we kin suppo't?"

That night at supper, old Bayard looked at his grandson
across the roast of mutton. "Will Falls told me you passed
him on the poorhouse hill today running forty miles an
hour."

"Forty fiddlesticks," Miss Jenny answered promptly. "It
was fifty-four. I was watching the—what do you call it,
Bayard?—speedometer."

Old Bayard sat with his head bent a little, watching his
hands trembling on the carving knife and fork; hearing beneath the napkin tucked into his waistcoat, his heart a little
too light and a little too fast; feeling Miss Jenny's eyes upon
his face.

"Bayard," she said sharply, "what's that on your cheek?"
He rose so suddenly that his chair tipped over backward
with a crash, and he tramped blindly from the room.

3

"I know what you want me to do," Miss Jenny told old
Bayard across her newspaper. "You want me to let my housekeeping go to the dogs and spend all my time in that car,
that's what you want. Well, I'm not going to do it. I don't
mind riding with him now and then, but I've got too much to
do with my time to spend it keeping him from running that
car too fast. Neck, too," she added. She rattled the paper
crisply.

She said: "Besides, you ain't foolish enough to believe he'll
drive slow just because there's somebody with him, are you?
If you do think so, you'd better send Simon along. Lord
knows Simon can spare the time. Since you quit using the car-

riage, if he does anything at all, I don't know it." She read the paper again.

Old Bayard's cigar smoked in his still hand.

"I might send Isom," he said.

Miss Jenny's paper rattled sharply and she stared at her nephew for a long moment. "God in heaven, man, why don't you put a block and chain on him and have done with it?"

"Well, didn't you suggest sending Simon with him, yourself? Simon has his work to do, but all Isom ever does is saddle my horse once a day, and I can do that myself."

"I was trying to be ironical," Miss Jenny said. "God knows, I should have learned better by this time. But if you've got to invent something new for the niggers to do, you let it be Simon. I need Isom to keep a roof over your head and something to eat on the table." She rattled the paper. "Why don't you come right out and tell him not to drive fast? A man that has to spend eight hours a day sitting in a chair in that bank door ought not to have to spend the rest of the afternoon helling around the country in an automobile if he don't want to."

"Do you think it would do any good to ask him? There never was a damned one of 'em yet ever paid any attention to my wishes."

"Ask, the devil," Miss Jenny said. "Who said anything about ask? Tell him not to. Tell him that if you hear again of his going fast in it, that you'll frail the life out of him. I believe anyway that you like to ride in that car, only you won't admit it, and you just don't want him to ride in it when you can't go too." But old Bayard had slammed his feet to the floor and risen, and he tramped from the room.

Instead of mounting the stairs, however, Miss Jenny heard his footsteps die away down the hall, and presently she rose and followed to the back porch, where he stood in the darkness there. The night was dark, myriad with drifting odors of the spring, and with insects. Dark upon lesser dark, the barn loomed against the sky.

"He hasn't come in yet," she said impatiently, touching his arm. "I could have told you. Go on up and go to bed, now; don't you know he'll let you know when he comes in? You're going to think him into a ditch somewhere, with these fool notions of yours." Then, more gently: "You're too childish about that car. It's no more dangerous at night than it is in daytime. Come on, now."

He shook her hand off, but he turned obediently and entered the house. This time he mounted the stairs and she could hear him in his bedroom, thumping about. Presently he ceased slamming doors and drawers and lay beneath the reading-lamp with his Dumas. After a time the door opened and young Bayard entered and came into the radius of the light with his bleak eyes.

His grandfather did not remark his presence and he touched his arm. Old Bayard looked up, and when he did so young Bayard turned and quitted the room.

After the shades on the bank windows were drawn at three o'clock old Bayard retired to the office. Inside the grille the cashier and the bookkeeper could hear him clattering and banging around beyond the door. The cashier paused, a stack of silver clipped neatly in his fingers.

"Hear 'im?" he said. "Something on his mind here, lately. Used to be he was quiet as a mouse back there until they come for him, but last few days he tromples and thumps around back there like he was fighting hornets."

The bookkeeper said nothing. The cashier set the stack of silver aside, built up another one.

"Something on his mind lately. That examiner must 'a' put a bug in his ear, I reckon."

The bookkeeper said nothing. He swung the adding-machine to his desk and clicked the lever over. In the back room old Bayard moved audibly about. The cashier stacked the remaining silver neatly and rolled a cigarette. The bookkeeper bent above the steady clicking of the machine, and the cashier sealed his cigarette and lit it and waddled to the window and lifted the curtain.

"Simon's brought the carriage, today," he said. "That boy finally wrecked that car, I reckon. Better call Colonel."

The bookkeeper slid from his stool and went back to the door and opened it. Old Bayard glanced up from his desk, with his hat on.

"All right, Byron," he said. The bookkeeper returned to his desk.

Old Bayard stalked through the bank and opened the street door and stopped utterly, the doorknob in his hand.

"Where's Bayard?" he said.

"He ain't comin'," Simon answered. Old Bayard crossed to the carriage.

"What? Where is he?"

"Him en Isom off somewhar in dat cyar," Simon said. "Lawd knows whar dey is by now. Takin' dat boy away fum his work in de middle of de day, cyar-ridin'." Old Bayard laid his hand on the stanchion, the spot on his face coming again into white relief. "Atter all de time I spent tryin' to git some sense inter Isom's haid," Simon continued. He held the horses' heads up, waiting for his employer to enter. "Cyar-ridin'," he said. "Cyar-ridin'."

Old Bayard got in and sank heavily into the seat.

"I'll be damned," he said, "if I haven't got the triflingest set of folks to make a living for God ever made. There's one thing about it: when I finally have to go to the poorhouse, every damned one of you'll be there when I come."

"Now, here you quoilin' too," Simon said, "Miss Jenny yellin' at me 'twell I wuz plum out de gate, and now you already started at dis en'. But ef Mist' Bayard don't leave dat boy alone, he ain't gwine ter be no better'n a town nigger spite of all I kin do."

"Jenny's already ruined him," old Bayard said. "Even Bayard can't hurt him much."

"You sho' tole de troof den," Simon agreed. He shook the reins. "Come up, dar."

"Here, Simon," old Bayard said. "Hold up a minute."

Simon reined the horses back. "Whut you want now?"

The spot on old Bayard's cheek had resumed its normal appearance.

"Go back to my office and get me a cigar out of that jar on the mantel," he said.

Two days later, as he and Simon tooled sedately homeward through the afternoon, simultaneously almost with the warning thunder of it, the car burst upon him on a curve, slewed into the ditch and on to the road again and rushed on, and in the flashing instant he and Simon saw the whites of Isom's eyes and the ivory cropping of his teeth behind the steering-wheel. When the car returned home that afternoon Simon conducted Isom to the barn and whipped him with a harness strap.

That night they sat in the office after supper. Old Bayard

held his cigar unlighted in his fingers. Miss Jenny read the
paper. Faint airs blew in, laden with spring.

Suddenly old Bayard said, "Maybe he'll get tired of it
after a while."

Miss Jenny raised her head. "And when he does, don't
you know what he'll get then?—when he finds that car
won't go fast enough?" she demanded, staring at him across
the paper. He sat with his unlighted cigar, his head bent a
little, not looking at her. "He'll buy an aeroplane." She
rattled the paper, turned the page. "He ought to have a wife,"
she added, reading again. "Let him get a son, then he can
break his neck as soon and as often as he pleases. Providence doesn't seem to have any judgment at all," she said,
thinking of the two of them, of his dead brother. She said:
"But Lord knows, I'd hate to see any girl I was fond of married to him." She rattled the paper again, turned another
page. "I don't know what else you expect of him. Of any
Sartoris. You don't waste your afternoons riding with him
just because you think it'll keep him from turning that car
over. You go because when it does happen, you want to
be in it, too. So do you think you've got any more consideration for folks than he has?"

He held his cigar, his face still averted. Miss Jenny was
watching him again across the paper.

"I'm coming down town in the morning and we're going
and have the doctor look at that bump on your face, you
hear?"

In his room, as he removed his collar and tie before his
chest of drawers, his eye fell upon the pipe which he had
laid there four weeks ago, and he put the collar and tie
down and picked up the pipe and held it in his hand, rubbing the charred bowl slowly with his thumb.

Then with sudden decision he quitted the room and
tramped down the hall, at the end of which a stair mounted
into the darkness. He fumbled the light switch beside it and
mounted, following the cramped turnings cautiously in the
dark, to a door set at a difficult angle, and opened it upon a
broad, low room with a pitched ceiling, smelling of dust and
silence and ancient disused things.

The room was cluttered with indiscriminate furniture—
chairs and sofas like patient ghosts holding lightly in

dry and rigid embrace yet other ghosts—a fitting place for
dead Sartorises to gather and speak among themselves of
glamorous and old disastrous days. The unshaded light swung
on a single cord from the center of the ceiling. He unknotted
it and drew it across to a nail in the wall above a cedar chest
and fastened it here, and drew a chair to the chest and sat
down.

The chest had not been opened since 1901, when his son
John had succumbed to yellow fever and an old Spanish
bullet-wound. There had been two occasions since, in July
and in October of last year, but the other grandson still possessed quickness and all the incalculable portent of his heritage. So he had forborne for the time being, expecting to be
able to kill two birds with one stone, as it were.

The lock was stiff, and he struggled patiently with it for
some time. Rust shaled off, rubbed off onto his hands, and he
desisted and rose and rummaged about and returned to the
chest with a heavy, cast-iron candlestick and hammered the
lock free and removed it and raised the lid. From the chest
there rose a thin exhilarating odor of cedar, and something
else: a scent drily and muskily nostalgic, as of old ashes.
The first object was a garment. The brocade was richly
hushed, and the fall of fine Mechlin was dustily yellow, pale
and textureless as February sunlight. He lifted the garment
carefully out. The lace cascaded mellow and pale as spilled
wine upon his hands, and he laid it aside and lifted out next
a rapier. It was a Toledo, a blade delicate and fine as the prolonged stroke of a violin bow, in a velvet sheath. The
sheath was elegant and flamboyant and soiled, and the
seams had cracked drily.

Old Bayard held the rapier upon his hands for a while,
feeling the balance of it. It was just such an implement
as a Sartoris would consider the proper equipment for raising
tobacco in a virgin wilderness, it and the scarlet heels and
the ruffled wristbands in which he broke the earth and fought
his stealthy and simple neighbors.

He laid it aside. Next came a heavy cavalry saber, and
a rosewood case containing two dueling pistols with silver
mountings and the lean, deceptive delicacy of race-horses,
and what old man Falls had called "that 'ere dang der'nger."
It was a stubby, evil-looking thing with its three barrels,
viciously and coldly utilitarian, and between the other two

weapons it lay like a cold and deadly insect between two flowers.

He removed next the blue army forage-cap of the 'forties and a small pottery vessel and a Mexican machete, and a long-necked oil-can such as locomotive drivers use. It was of silver, and engraved upon it was the picture of a locomotive with a huge bell-shaped funnel and surrounded by an ornate wreath. Beneath it, the name "Virginia" and the date "August 9, 1873."

He put these aside and with sudden purposefulness he removed the other objects—a frogged and braided coat of Confederate gray and a gown of sprigged muslin scented faintly of lavender and evocative of old formal minuets and drifting honeysuckle among steady candle-flames—and came upon a conglomeration of yellowed papers neatly bound in packets, and at last upon a huge, brass-bound Bible. He lifted this to the edge of the chest and opened it. The paper was brown and mellow with years, and it had a texture like that of slightly moist wood-ashes, as though each page were held intact by its archaic and fading print. He turned the pages carefully back to the fly-leaves. Beginning near the bottom of the final blank page a column of names and dates rose in stark and fading simplicity, growing fainter and fainter where time had lain upon them. At the top they were still legible, as they were at the foot of the preceding page. But halfway up this page they ceased, and from there on the sheet was blank save for the faint, soft mottlings of time and an occasional brownish pen-stroke.

Old Bayard sat for a long time, regarding the stark dissolving apotheosis of his name. Sartorises had derided Time, but Time was not vindictive, being longer than Sartorises. And probably unaware of them. But it was a good gesture, anyway.

"In the nineteenth century," John Sartoris said, "genealogy is poppycock. Particularly in America, where only what a man takes and keeps has any significance and where all of us have a common ancestry and the only house from which we can claim descent with any assurance is the Old Bailey. Yet the man who professes to care nothing about his forebears is only a little less vain than the man who bases all his actions on blood precedent. And I reckon a Sartoris can have a little vanity and poppycock, if he wants it."

Yes, it was a good gesture, and old Bayard sat and mused quietly on the tense he had unwittingly used. Was. Fatality; the augury of a man's destiny peeping out at him from the roadside hedge, if he but recognize it, and again he ran panting through undergrowth while the fading thunder of the smoke-colored stallion swept on in the dusk and the Yankee patrol crashed behind him, crashed fainter and fainter until he crouched with spent, laboring lungs in a brier thicket and heard the pursuit rush on. Then he crawled forth and went to a spring he knew that flowed from the roots of a beech, and as he leaned down to it the final light of day was reflected on to his face, bringing into sharp relief forehead and nose above the cavernous sockets of his eyes and the panting snarl of his teeth, and from the still water there stared back at him, for a sudden moment, a skull.

The unturned corners of man's destiny. Well, heaven, that crowded place, lay just beyond one of them, they claimed; heaven filled with every man's illusion of himself and with the conflicting illusions of him that parade through the minds of other illusions. . . . He stirred and sighed quietly, and took out his fountain pen. At the foot of the column he wrote:

"John Sartoris. July 5, 1918."

and beneath that:

"Caroline White Sartoris and son. October 27, 1918."

When the ink was dry he closed the book and replaced it and took the pipe from his pocket and put it in the rosewood case with the dueling pistols and the derringer and replaced the other things and closed the chest and locked it.

Miss Jenny found old Bayard in his tilted chair in the bank door. He looked up at her with a fine assumption of surprise and his deafness seemed more pronounced than usual. But she got him up with cold implacability and led him, still grumbling, down the street where merchants and others spoke to her as to a martial queen, old Bayard stalking along beside her with sullen reluctance.

They turned presently and mounted a narrow stairway

debouching between two stores, beneath an array of dingy professional signs. At the top was a dark corridor with doors, the nearest of pine, its gray paint scarred at the bottom as though it had been kicked repeatedly at the same height and with the same force. In the door itself two holes an inch apart bore mute witness to the missing hasp, and from a staple in the jamb depended the hasp itself, fixed there by a huge, rusty lock of an ancient pattern. Bayard offered to stop here, but Miss Jenny led him firmly on to a door across the hall.

This door was freshly painted and grained to represent walnut. Into the top half of it was let a pane of thick, opaque glass bearing a name in raised gilt letters, and two embracing office hours. Miss Jenny opened this door and Bayard followed her into a small cubbyhole of a room of Spartan but suave asepsis. The walls were an immaculate new gray, with a reproduction of a Corot and two spidery dry-points in narrow frames, and it contained a new rug in warm buff tones and a bare table and four chairs in fumed oak—all impersonal and clean and inexpensive, but revealing at a glance the proprietor's soul; a soul hampered now by material strictures, but destined and determined some day to function amid Persian rugs and mahogany or teak, and a single irreproachable print on the chaste walls. A young woman in a starched white dress rose from a smaller table on which a telephone sat, and patted her hair.

"Good morning, Myrtle," Miss Jenny said. "Tell Dr. Alford we'd like to see him, please."

"You have an appointment?" the girl asked in a voice without any inflection at all.

"We'll make one now, then," Miss Jenny replied. "You don't mean to say Dr. Alford don't come to work before ten o'clock, do you?"

"Dr. Alford don't—doesn't see any one without an appointment," the girl parroted, gazing at a point above Miss Jenny's head. "If you have no appointment, you'll have to have an ap——"

"Tut, tut," Miss Jenny interrupted briskly. "You run and tell Dr. Alford Colonel Sartoris wants to see him, there's a good girl."

"Yessum, Miss Jenny," the girl said obediently and she crossed the room, but at the other door she paused again, and again her voice became parrotlike. "Won't you sit down? I'll see if the doctor is engaged."

"You go and tell Dr. Alford we're here," Miss Jenny repeated affably. "Tell him I've got some shopping to do this morning and I haven't got time to wait."

"Yessum, Miss Jenny," the girl agreed, and disappeared, and after a dignified interval she returned, once more clothed faultlessly in her professional manner. "The doctor will see you now. Come in, please." She held the door open and stood aside.

"Thank you, honey," Miss Jenny replied. "Is your mamma still in bed?"

"No'm, she's sitting up now, thank you."

"That's good," Miss Jenny agreed. "Come on, Bayard."

This room was smaller than the other, and brutally carbolized. There was a white enameled cabinet filled with vicious nickel gleams, and a metal operating-table and an array of electric furnaces and ovens and sterilizers. The doctor in a white linen jacket bent over a small desk, and for a while he proffered them his sleek oblivious head. Then he glanced up, and rose.

He was in the youthful indeterminate thirties, a newcomer to the town and nephew of an old resident. He had made a fine record in medical school and was of a personable exterior, but there was a sort of preoccupied dignity, a sort of erudite and cold unillusion regarding mankind, about him that precluded the easy intimacy of the small town and caused even those who remembered him as a visiting boy to address him as Doctor or Mister. He had a small mustache and a face like a mask—a comforting face, but cold; and while old Bayard sat restively the doctor probed delicately with dry, scrubbed fingers at the wen on his face. Miss Jenny asked him a question, but he continued his exploration raptly, as though he had not heard, as though she had not even spoken; inserting a small electric bulb, which he first sterilized, into Bayard's mouth and snapping its ruby glow on and off within his cheek. Then he removed it and sterilized it again and returned it to the cabinet.

"Well?" Miss Jenny said impatiently. The doctor shut the cabinet carefully and washed and dried his hands and came and stood above them, and with his thumbs hooked in his jacket pockets he became solemnly and unctuously technical,

rolling the harsh words upon his tongue with epicurean deliberation.

"It should be removed at once," he concluded. "It should
be removed while in its early stage; that is why I advise an
immediate operation."

"You mean, it might develop into cancer?" Miss Jenny
asked.

"No question about it at all, madam. Course of time.
Neglect it, and I can promise you nothing; have it out now,
and he need never worry about it again." He looked at old
Bayard again with lingering and chill contemplation. "It will
be very simple. I'll remove it as easily as that." And he made
a short gesture with his hand.

"What's that?" Bayard demanded.

"I say, I can take that growth off so easily you won't know
it, Colonel Sartoris."

"I'll be damned if you do!" Bayard rose with one of his
characteristic plunging movements.

"Sit down, Bayard," Miss Jenny ordered. "Nobody's
going to cut on you without your knowing it.—Should it
be done right away?" she asked.

"Yes, ma'am. I wouldn't have that thing on my face overnight. Otherwise, it is only fair to warn you that no doctor
can assume responsibility for what might ensue. . . . I could
remove it in two minutes," he added, looking at Bayard's
face again with cold speculation. Then he half turned his
head and stood in a listening attitude, and beyond the thin
walls a voice in the other room boomed in rich, rolling waves.

"Mawnin', sister," it said. "Didn't I hear Bayard Sartoris
cussin' in here?" The doctor and Miss Jenny held their arrested attitudes; then the door opened and the fattest man in
the whole county filled it. He wore a shiny alpaca coat over
waistcoat and trousers of baggy black broadcloth; above a
plaited shirt the fatty rolls of his dewlap practically hid his
low collar and a black string tie. His Roman senator's head
was thatched with a vigorous curling of silvery hair. "What
the devil's the matter with you?" he boomed; then he sidled
into the room, filling it completely, dwarfing its occupants and
its furnishings.

This was Dr. Lucius Quintus Peabody, eighty-seven years
old and weighing three hundred and ten pounds and possessing a digestive tract like a horse. He had practiced medicine

in the county when a doctor's equipment consisted of a saw
and a gallon of whisky and a satchel of calomel; he had been
John Sartoris' regimental surgeon, and up to the day of the
automobile he would start out at any hour of the twenty-
four in any weather and for any distance, over practically
impassable roads in a lopsided buckboard, to visit any one,
white or black, who sent for him, accepting for fee usually a
meal of corn pone and coffee, or perhaps a small measure
of corn or fruit, or a few flower bulbs or graftings.

When he was young and hasty he had kept a daybook,
kept it meticulously until these hypothetical assets totaled
$10,000. But that was forty years ago, and since then he
hadn't bothered with a record at all; and now from time to
time a countryman enters his shabby office and discharges
an obligation, commemorating sometimes the payer's entry
into the world, incurred by his father or grandfather, which
Dr. Peabody himself had long since forgotten about. Every
one in the county knew him and sent him hams and wild
game at Christmas, and it was said that he could spend the
balance of his days driving about the county in the buckboard he still used, with never a thought for board and lodg-
ing and without the expenditure of a penny for either. He
filled the room with his bluff and homely humanity, and as
he crossed the floor and patted Miss Jenny's back with one
flail-like hand, the whole building trembled to his tread.

"Mawnin', Jenny," he said. "Havin' Bayard measured for
insurance?"

"This damn butcher wants to cut on me," old Bayard said
querulously. "You come on and make 'em let me alone,
Loosh."

"Ten A.M.'s mighty early in the day to start carvin' white
folks," Dr. Peabody boomed. "Nigger's different. Chop up a
nigger any time after midnight. What's the matter with him,
son?" he asked Dr. Alford.

"I don't believe it's anything but a wart," Miss Jenny said,
"but I'm tired of looking at it."

"It's no wart," Dr. Alford corrected stiffly. He recapitu-
lated his diagnosis in technical terms while Dr. Peabody
enveloped them all in the rubicund benevolence of his presence.

"Sounds pretty bad, don't it?" he agreed, and he shook
the floor again and pushed Bayard firmly into his chair with

one huge hand, and with the other he dragged his face up
to the light. Then he dug a pair of iron-bowed spectacles
from the pocket of his coat and examined Bayard's face.
"Think it ought to come off, do you?"

"I do," Dr. Alford answered coldly. "I think it is im-
perative that it be removed. Unnecessary there. Cancer."

"Folks got along with cancer a long time befo' they invented knives," Dr. Peabody said drily. "Hold still, Bayard."

And people like you are one of the reasons, was on the
tip of the younger man's tongue. But he forbore and said
instead, "I can remove that growth in two minutes, Colonel
Sartoris."

"Damned if you do," Bayard rejoined violently, trying to
rise. "Get away, Loosh."

"Sit still," Dr. Peabody said equably, holding him down
while he probed at the wen. "Does it hurt any?"

"No. I never said it did. And I'll be damned——"

"You'll probably be damned anyway," Dr. Peabody told
him. "You'd be about as well off dead, anyhow. I don't
know anybody that gets less fun out of living than you do."

"You told the truth for once," Miss Jenny agreed. "He's
the oldest person I ever knew in my life."

"And so," Dr. Peabody continued blandly, "I wouldn't
worry about it. Let it stay there. Nobody cares what your
face looks like. If you were a young fellow, now, out sparkin'
the gals every night——"

"If Dr. Peabody is permitted to interfere with impu-
nity——" Dr. Alford began.

"Will Falls says he can cure it," Bayard said.

"With that salve of his?" Dr. Peabody asked quickly.

"Salve?" Dr. Alford repeated. "Colonel Sartoris, if you
permit any quack that comes along to treat that growth
with home-made or patent remedies, you'll be dead in six
months. Dr. Peabody even will bear me out," he added with
fine irony.

"I don't know," Dr. Peabody replied slowly. "Will has done
some curious things with that salve of his."

"I must protest against this," Dr. Alford said. "Mrs. Du
Pre, I protest against a member of my profession sanction-
ing, even negatively, such a procedure."

"Pshaw, boy," Dr. Peabody answered, "we ain't goin' to
let Will put his dope on Bayard's wart. It's all right for

niggers and livestock, but Bayard don't need it. We'll just let this thing alone, long as it don't hurt him."

"If that growth is not removed immediately, I wash my hands of all responsibility," Dr. Alford stated. "To neglect it will be as fatal as Mr. Falls' salve. Mrs. Du Pre, I ask you to witness that this consulation has taken this un-ethical turn through no fault of mine and over my protest."

"Pshaw, boy," Dr. Peabody said again, "this ain't hardly worth the trouble of cuttin' out. We'll save you an arm or a leg as soon as that fool grandson of his turns that automo-bile over with 'em. Come on with me, Bayard."

"Mrs. Du Pre——" Dr. Alford essayed.

"Bayard can come back, if he wants to," Dr. Peabody patted the younger man's shoulder with his heavy hand. "I'm going to take him to my office and talk to him a while. Jenny can bring him back, if she wants to. Come on, Bayard." And he led old Bayard from the room. Miss Jenny rose also.

"That Loosh Peabody is as big a fogy as old Will Falls," she said. "Old people just fret me to death. You wait: I'll bring him right back here, and we'll finish this business." Dr. Alford held the door open for her and she sailed in a stiff, silk-clad rage from the room and followed her nephew across the corridor and through the scarred door with its rusty lock, and into a room resembling a miniature cyclonic devas-tation mellowed peacefully over with dust ancient and un-disturbed.

"You, Loosh Peabody," Miss Jenny said.

"Sit down, Jenny," Dr. Peabody told her. "And be quiet. Unfasten your shirt, Bayard."

"What?" old Bayard said belligerently. The other thrust him into a chair.

"Want to see your chest," he explained. He crossed to an ancient roll-top desk and rummaged through the dusty litter upon it. There was litter and dust everywhere in the huge room. Its four windows gave upon the square, but the elms and sycamores ranged along the sides of the square shaded these first floor offices, so that light entered them, but tempered, like light beneath water. In the corners of the ceiling were spider webs thick and heavy as Spanish moss and dingy as old lace, and the once-white walls were an even and unemphatic drab save for a paler rectangle here and

there where an outdated calendar had hung and been removed. Besides the desk, the room contained three or four
miscellaneous chairs in various stages of decrepitude, a
rusty stove in a sawdust-filled box, and a leather sofa holding mutely amid its broken springs the outline of Dr. Peabody's recumbent shape; beside it and slowly gathering suc-
cessive layers of dust, was a stack of lurid, paper-covered
nickel novels. This was Dr. Peabody's library, and on this
sofa he passed his office hours, reading them over and over.
Other books there were none.

But the waste-basket beside the desk and the desk itself
and the mantel above the trash-filled fireplace, and the window ledges too, were cluttered with circular mail matter and
mail-order catalogues and government bulletins of all kinds.
In one corner, on an up-ended packing-box, sat a water cooler
of stained oxidized glass, in another corner leaned a clump
of cane fishing-poles warping slowly of their own weight;
and on every horizontal surface rested a collection of objects
not to be found outside of a second-hand store—old garments, bottles, a kerosene lamp, a wooden box of tins of
axle grease, lacking one; a clock in the shape of a bland
china morning-glory supported by four garlanded maidens
who had suffered sundry astonishing anatomical mishaps,
and here and there among the dusty indiscrimination, various
instruments pertaining to the occupant's profession. It was
one of these that Dr. Peabody sought now in the littered
desk on which sat a single photograph in a wooden frame,
and though Miss Jenny said again, "You, Loosh Peabody,
you listen to me," he continued to seek it with bland and
unhurried equanimity.

"You fasten your clothes and we'll go back to that doctor," Miss Jenny ordered her nephew. "Neither you nor I
can waste any more time with a doddering old fool."

"Sit down, Jenny," Dr. Peabody repeated, and he drew out
a drawer and removed from it a box of cigars and a handful
of faded artificial trout flies and a soiled collar, and lastly a
stethoscope; then he tumbled the other things back into the
drawer and shut it with his knee.

Miss Jenny sat trim and outraged, fuming while he listened to old Bayard's heart.

"Well," she snapped, "does it tell you how to take that

wart off his face? Will Falls didn't need any telephone to
find that out."

"It tells more than that," Dr. Peabody answered. "It tells
how Bayard'll get rid of all his troubles, if he keeps on riding
in that hellion's automobile."

"Fiddlesticks," Miss Jenny said, "Bayard's a good driver.
I never rode with a better one."

"It'll take more'n a good driver to keep this"—he tapped
Bayard's chest with his blunt finger—"goin', time that boy
whirls that thing around another curve or two like I've seen
him do."

"Did you ever hear of a Sartoris dying from a natural
cause, like anybody else?" Miss Jenny demanded. "Don't
you know that heart ain't going to take Bayard off before his
time? You get up from there, and come on with me," she
added to her nephew. Bayard buttoned his shirt. Dr. Peabody sat on the sofa and watched him quietly.

"Bayard," he said suddenly, "why don't you stay out of
that damn thing?"

"What?"

"If you don't stay out of that car, you ain't goin' to need
me nor Will Falls, nor that boy in yonder with all his hand-
boiled razors, neither."

"What business is it of yours?" old Bayard demanded.
"By God, can't I break my neck in peace if I want to?" He
rose. He was trembling, fumbling at his waistcoat buttons,
and Miss Jenny rose also and made to help him, but he put
her roughly aside. Dr. Peabody sat quietly, thumping his fat
fingers on one fat knee. "I have already outlived my time,"
old Bayard continued more mildly. "I am the first of my
name to see sixty years that I know of. I reckon Old Marster
is keeping me for a reliable witness to the extinction of it."

"Now," Miss Jenny said icily, "you've made your speech,
and Loosh Peabody has wasted the morning for you, so I
reckon we can leave now and let Loosh go out and doctor
mules for a while, and you can sit around the rest of the
day, being a Sartoris and feeling sorry for yourself. Good
morning, Loosh."

"Make him let that place alone, Jenny," Dr. Peabody said.

"Ain't you and Will Falls going to cure it for him?"

"You keep him from letting Will Falls put anything on it,"

Dr. Peabody repeated equably. "It's all right. Just leave it alone."

"We're going to a doctor, that's what we're going to do," Miss Jenny replied. "Come on here."

When the door had closed, he sat motionless and heard them quarreling beyond it. Then the sound of their voices moved on down the corridor toward the stairs, and still quarreling loudly and, on old Bayard's part, with profane emphasis, the voices died away. Then Dr. Peabody lay back on the sofa shaped already to the bulk of him, and with random deliberation he reached a nickel thriller blindly from the stack at the head of the couch.

4

As they neared the bank Narcissa Benbow came along from the opposite direction, and they met at the door, where he made her a ponderous compliment on her appearance while she stood in her pale dress and shouted her grave voice into his deafness. Then he took his tilted chair, and Miss Jenny followed her into the bank and to the teller's window. There was no one behind the grille at the moment save the book-keeper. He looked at them briefly and covertly across his shoulder, then slid from his stool and crossed to the window, but without raising his eyes again.

He took Narcissa's check, and while she listened to Miss Jenny's recapitulation of Bayard's and Loosh Peabody's stubborn masculine stupidity she remarked the reddish hair which clothed his arms down to the second joints of his fingers, and remarked with a faint yet distinct distaste, and a little curiosity since it was not particularly warm, the fact that his hands and arms were beaded with perspiration.

Then she made her eyes blank again and took the notes which he pushed under the grille to her and opened her bag. From its blue satin maw the corner of an envelope and some of its superscription peeped suddenly, but she crumpled it quickly from sight and put the money in and closed the bag. They turned away, Miss Jenny still talking, and she paused at the door again, clothed in her still aura of quietness, while old Bayard twitted her heavily on imaginary affairs of the heart which furnished the sole theme of conversation between them, shouting serenely at him in return. Then she went on, surrounded by tranquillity like a visible presence or an odor or a sound.

As long as she was in sight the bookkeeper stood at the window. His head was bent and his hand made a series of neat, meaningless figures on the pad beneath it. Then she went on and passed from sight. He moved, and in doing so he found that the pad had adhered to his damp wrist, so that when he moved his arm it came also. Then its own weight freed it and it fell to the floor.

After the bank closed that afternoon Snopes crossed the square and entered a street and approached a square frame building with a double veranda, from which the mournful cacophony of a cheap talking-machine came upon the afternoon. He entered. The music came from the room to the right and as he passed the door he saw a man in a collarless shirt sitting in a chair with his sock feet on another chair, smoking a pipe, the evil reek of which followed him down the hall. The hall smelled of damp, harsh soap, and the linoleum carpet gleamed, still wet. He followed it and approached a sound of steady, savage activity, and came upon a woman in a shapeless gray garment, who ceased mopping and looked at him across her gray shoulder, sweeping her lank hair from her brow with a reddened forearm.

"Evenin', Miz Beard," Snopes said. "Virgil come home yet?"

"He was through here a minute ago," she answered. "If he ain't out front, I reckon his paw sent him on a arr'nd. Mr. Beard's takin' one of his spells in the hip agin. He might 'a' sent Virgil on a arr'nd." Her hair fell lankly across her face again. Again she brushed it aside with a harsh gesture. "You got some mo' work fer him?"

"Yessum. You don't know which-a-way he went?"

"Ef Mr. Beard ain't sont him nowheres he mought be in the back yard. He don't usually go fur away." Again she dragged her lank hair aside; shaped so long to labor, her muscles were restive under inaction. She grasped the mop again.

Snopes went on and stood on the kitchen steps above an

enclosed space barren of grass and containing a chicken
pen, also grassless, in which a few fowls huddled or moved
about in forlorn distraction in the dust. On one hand was a
small kitchen garden of orderly, tended rows. In the corner
of the yard was an outhouse of some sort, of weathered
boards.

"Virgil," he said. The yard was desolate with ghosts;
ghosts of discouraged weeds, of food in the shape of empty
tins, broken boxes and barrels; a pile of stove wood and a
chopping-block across which lay an ax whose helve had been
mended with rusty wire amateurishly wound. He descended
the steps and the chickens raised a discordant clamor, anticipating food.

"Virgil."

Sparrows found sustenance of some sort in the dust among
the fowls, but the fowls themselves, perhaps with a foreknowledge of frustration and of doom, huddled back and
forth along the wire, discordant and distracted, watching
him with predatory, importunate eyes. He was about to
turn and reënter the kitchen when the boy appeared silently
and innocently from the outhouse, with his straw-colored
hair and his bland eyes. His mouth was pale and almost
sweet, but secretive at the corners. His chin was negligible.

"Hi, Mr. Snopes. You calling me?"

"Yes. If you ain't doing anything special," Snopes answered.

"I ain't," the boy said. They entered the house and passed
the room where the woman labored with drab fury. The
reek of the pipe, the lugubrious reiteration of the phono-
graph, filled the hall, and they mounted stairs carpeted also
with linoleum fastened to each step by a treacherous sheet-
iron strip treated to resemble brass and scuffed and scarred
by heavy feet. The upper hall was lined by two identical
rows of doors. They entered one of these.

The room contained a bed, a chair, a dressing-table, and
a wash-stand with a slop-jar beside it. The floor was covered
with straw matting, frayed in places. The single light hung
unshaded on a greenish-brown cord. Upon the wall above the
paper-filled fireplace a framed lithograph of an Indian maiden
in immaculate buckskin leaned her naked bosom above a
formal moonlit pool of Italian marble. She held a guitar

and a rose, and dusty sparrows sat on the window ledge and watched them brightly through the dusty screen.

The boy entered politely. His pale eyes took in the room and its contents at a comprehensive glance. He said, "That air gun ain't come yet, has it, Mr. Snopes?"

"No, it ain't," Snopes answered. "It'll be here soon, though."

"You ordered off after it a long time, now."

"That's right. But it'll be here soon. Maybe they haven't got one in stock, right now." He crossed to the dresser and took from a drawer a few sheets of foolscap and laid them on the dresser top and drew a chair up and dragged his suitcase from beneath the bed and set it on the chair. Then he took his fountain pen from his pocket and uncapped it and laid it beside the paper. "It ought to be here any day, now."

The boy seated himself on the suitcase and took up the pen. "They got 'em at Watts' hardware store," he suggested.

"If the one we ordered don't come soon, we'll git one there," Snopes said. "When did we order it, anyway?"

"Week ago Tuesday," the boy answered glibly. "I wrote it down."

"Well, it'll be here soon. You ready?"

The boy squared himself before the paper. "Yes, sir." Snopes took a folded paper from the top pocket of his trousers and spread it open.

"Code number forty-eight. Mister Joe Butler, Saint Louis, Missouri," he read, then he leaned over the boy's shoulder, watching the pen. "That's right: up close to the top," he commended. "Now." The boy dropped down the page about two inches, and as Snopes read, he transcribed in his neat, copy-book hand, pausing only occasionally to inquire as to the spelling of a word.

"'I thought once I would try to forget you. But I cannot forget you because you cannot forget me. I saw my letter in your hand satchel today. Every day I can put my hand out and touch you you do not know it. Just to see you walk down the street To know what I know what you know. Some day we will both know to gether when you got use to it. You kept my letter but you do not anser. That is a good sign you do——'" The boy had reached the foot of the page. Snopes removed it, leaving the next sheet ready. He continued to read in his droning, inflectionless voice:

" '——not forget me you would not keep it. I think of you at night the way you walk down the street like I was dirt. I can tell you something you will be surprised I know more than watch you walk down the street with cloths. I will some day you will not be surprised then. You pass me you do not know it I know it. You will know it some day. Be cause I will tell you.' Now," he said, and the boy dropped on to the foot of the page. " 'Yours truly Hal Wagner. Code number twenty-four.' " Again he looked over the boy's shoulder. "That's right." He blotted the final sheet and gathered it up also. The boy recapped the pen and thrust the chair back, and Snopes produced a small paper bag from his coat.

The boy took it soberly. "Much obliged, Mr. Snopes," he said. He opened it and squinted into it. "It's funny that air gun don't come on."

"It sure is," Snopes agreed. "I don't know why it don't come."

"Maybe it got lost in the post office," the boy suggested.

"It may have. I reckon that's about what happened to it. I'll write 'em again, tomorrow."

The boy rose, but he stood yet with his straw-colored hair and his bland, innocent face. He took a piece of candy from the sack and ate it without enthusiasm. "I reckon I better tell papa to go to the post office and ask 'em if it got lost."

"No, I wouldn't do that," Snopes said quickly. "You wait; I'll 'tend to it. We'll get it, all right."

"Papa wouldn't mind. He could go over there soon's he comes home and see about it. I could find him right now, and ask him to do it, I bet."

"He couldn't do no good," Snopes answered. "You leave it to me. I'll get that gun, all right."

"I could tell him I been working for you," the boy pursued. "I remember them letters."

"No, no, you wait and let me 'tend to it. I'll see about it first thing tomorrow."

"All right, Mr. Snopes." He ate another piece of candy, without enthusiasm. He moved toward the door. "I remember ever' one of them letters. I bet I could sit down and write 'em all again. I bet I could. Say, Mr. Snopes, who is Hal Wagner? Does he live in Jefferson?"

"No, no. You never seen him. He don't hardly never

come to town. That's the reason I'm 'tending to his business for him. I'll see about that air gun, all right."

The boy opened the door, then he paused again. "They got 'em at Watts' hardware store. Good ones. I'd sure like to have one of 'em. Yes, sir, I sure would."

"Sure, sure," Snopes repeated. "Ourn'll be here tomorrow. You just wait; I'll see you git that gun."

The boy departed. Snopes locked the door, and for a while he stood beside it with his head bent, his hands slowly knotting and writhing together. Then he took up the folded sheet and burned it over the hearth and ground the carbonized ash to dust under his heel. With his knife he cut the address from the top of the first sheet and the signature from the bottom of the second, and folded them and inserted them in a cheap envelope. He sealed this and stamped it, and took out his pen and with his left hand he addressed the envelope in labored printed characters. That night he took it to the station and mailed it on the train.

The next afternoon Virgil Beard killed a mocking-bird. It was singing in the peach tree that grew in the corner of the chicken-yard.

5

At times, as Simon puttered about the place during the day, he could look out across the lot and into the pasture and see the carriage horses growing daily shabbier and less prideful with idleness and lack of their daily grooming, or he would pass the carriage motionless in its shed, its tongue propped at an accusing angle, and in the harness room the duster and the top hat gathered slow dust on the nail in the wall, holding too in their mute waiting a patient and questioning uncomplaint. And at times, when he stood shabby and stooped a little with stubborn bewilderment and age, on the veranda with its ancient roses and wistaria and all its spacious and steadfast serenity, and watched Sartorises come and go in a machine a gentleman of his day would have scorned and which any pauper could own and any fool would ride in, it seemed to him that John Sartoris stood beside him, with his bearded and hawklike face and an expression of haughty and fine contempt.

And as he stood so, with afternoon slanting athwart the southern end of the porch and the heady and myriad odors of the waxing spring and the drowsy humming of insects and the singing of birds steady upon it, Isom within the cool doorway or at the corner of the house would hear his grandfather mumbling in a monotonous singsong in which was incomprehension and petulance and querulousness; and Isom would withdraw to the kitchen where his mother with her placid yellow face and her endless crooning labored steadily.

"Pappy out dar talkin' to Ole Marster again," Isom told her. "Gimme dem cole 'taters, mammy."

"Ain't Miss Jenny got some work fer you dis evenin'?" Elnora demanded, giving him the potatoes.

"No'm. She gone off in de cyar again."

"Hit's de Lawd's blessin' you and her ain't bofe gone in it, like you is whenever Mist' Bayard'll let you. You git on outen my kitchen, now. I got dis flo' mopped and I don't want it tracked up."

Quite often these days Isom could hear his grandfather talking to John Sartoris as he labored about the stable or the flower beds or the lawn, mumbling away to that arrogant shade which dominated the house and the life that went on there and the whole scene itself, across which the railroad he had built ran punily with distance. But distinct with miniature verisimilitude, as though it were a stage set for the diversion of him whose stubborn dream, flouting him so deviously and cunningly while the dream was impure, had shaped itself fine and clear, now that the dreamer was purged of the grossness of pride with that of flesh.

"Gent'mun equipage," Simon mumbled. He was busy again with his hoe in the salvia bed at the top of the drive. "Ridin' in dat thing, wid a gent'mun's proper equipage goin' ter rack en ruin in de barn." He wasn't thinking of Miss Jenny. It didn't make much difference what women rode in, their menfolks permitting. They only showed off a gentleman's equipage, anyhow; they were but the barometers of his establishment, the glass of his gentility: horses themselves knew it. "Yo' own son, yo' own twin grandson, ridin' right up in yo' face in a contraption like dat," he continued, "and you lettin' 'um do it. You bad ez dey is. You jes' got ter lay down de law ter 'um, Marse John; wid all dese foreign wars en sich de young folks is growed away fum de correck behavior; dey don't know how ter conduck deyselfs in de gent'mun way. Whut you reckon folks gwine think when dey sees yo' own folks ridin' in de same kine o' rig trash rides in? You jes' got ter resert yo'self, Marse John. Ain't Sartorises sot de quality in dis country since befo' de War? And now jes' look at 'um."

He leaned on his hoe and watched the car swing up the drive and stop before the house. Miss Jenny and young Bayard got out and mounted to the veranda. The engine was still running; a faint shimmer of exhaust drifted upon the bright forenoon, and Simon came up with his hoe and peered at the array of dials and knobs on the dash. Bayard turned in the door and spoke his name.

"Cut the switch off, Simon," he ordered.

"Cut de which whut off?" Simon said.

"That little bright lever by the steering-wheel there. Turn it down."

"Naw, suh," Simon answered, backing away, "I ain't gwine tech it. I ain't gwine have it blowin' up in my face."

"It won't hurt you," Bayard said impatiently. "Just put your hand on it and pull it down. That little bright jigger there."

Simon peered doubtfully at the gadgets and things, but without coming any nearer; then he craned his neck further and stared over into the car. "I don't see nothin' but dis yere big lever stickin' up thoo de flo'. Dat ain't de one you mentionin', is hit?"

Bayard said "Hell." He descended in two strides and leaned across the door and cut the switch under Simon's curious blinking regard. The purr of the engine ceased.

"Well, now," Simon said, "is dat de one you wuz talkin' erbout?" He stared at the switch for a time, then he straightened up and stared at the hood. "She's quit b'ilin' under dar, ain't she? Is dat de way you stops her?" But Bayard had mounted the steps again and entered the house.

Simon lingered a while longer, examining the gleaming long thing, touching it lightly with his hand, then rubbing his hand on his thigh. He walked slowly around it and touched the tires, mumbling to himself and shaking his head.

Then he returned to the salvia bed, where Bayard, emerging presently, found him.

"Want to take a ride, Simon?" he said.

Simon's hoe ceased and he straightened up. "Who, me?"

"Sure. Come on. We'll go up the road a piece."

Simon stood with his static hoe, rubbing his head slowly.

"Come on," Bayard said, "we'll just go up the road a piece. It won't hurt you."

"Naw, suh," Simon agreed, "I don't reckon hit's gwine ter hurt me."

He allowed himself to be drawn gradually toward the car, gazing at its various members with slow, blinking speculation, now that it was about to become an actual quantity in his life. At the door and with one foot raised to the running-board, he made a final stand against the subtle powers of evil judgment. "You ain't gwine run it th'ough de bushes like you en Isom done dat day, is you?"

Bayard reassured him, and he got in slowly, with mumbled sounds of anticipatory concern, and he sat well forward on the seat with his feet drawn under him, clutching the door with one hand and a lump of shirt on his chest with the other as the car moved down the drive. They passed through the gates and on to the road, and still he sat hunched forward on the seat. The car gained speed, and with a sudden convulsive motion he caught his hat just as it blew off his head.

"I 'speck dis is fur enough, ain't it?" he suggested, raising his voice. He pulled his hat down on his head, but when he released it he had to clutch wildly at it again, and he removed it and clasped it beneath his arm, and again his hand fumbled at his breast and clutched something beneath his shirt. "I got to weed dat bed dis mawnin'," he said, louder still. "Please, suh, Mist' Bayard," he added, and his wizened old body sat yet further forward on the seat and he cast quick, covert glances at the steadily increasing rush of the roadside growth.

Then Bayard leaned forward and Simon watched his forearm tauten, and then they shot forward on a roar of sound like blurred thunder. Earth, the unbelievable ribbon of the road, crashed beneath them and away behind into mad dust, and the roadside greenery was a tunnel rigid and streaming and unbroken. But he said no word, made no other sound,

and when Bayard glanced the cruel derision of his teeth at
him presently, Simon knelt on the floor, his old disreputable
hat under his arm and his hand clutching a fold of his shirt
on his breast. Later Bayard glanced at him again, and Simon
was watching him and the blurred irises of his eyes were
no longer a melting, pupilless brown: they were red, and in
the blast of wind they were unwinking and in them was
that mindless phosphorescence of an animal's. Bayard
jammed the throttle down to the floor.

The wagon was moving drowsily and peacefully along
the road. It was drawn by two mules and was filled with
Negro women asleep in chairs. Some of them wore drawers. The mules themselves didn't wake at all, but ambled
sedately on with the empty wagon and the overturned chairs,
even when the car crashed into the shallow ditch and surged
back on to the road again and thundered on without slowing.
The thunder ceased, but the car rushed on under its own
momentum, and it began to sway from side to side as
Bayard tried to drag Simon's hands from the switch. But
Simon knelt in the floor with his eyes shut tightly and the
air-blast toying with the grizzled remnant of his hair, holding the switch with both hands.

"Turn it loose!" Bayard shouted.

"Dat's de way you stops it, Lawd! Dat's de way you stops
it, Lawd!" Simon chanted, keeping the switch covered with
his hands while Bayard hammered at them with his fist.
And he clung to it until the car slowed and stopped. Then
he fumbled the door open and climbed out. Bayard called to
him, but he went on back down the road at a rapid limping
shuffle.

"Simon!" Bayard called again. But Simon went on stiffly,
like a man who has been deprived of the use of his legs
for a long time. "Simon!" But he neither slowed nor looked
back, and Bayard started the car again and drove on until he
could turn it. Simon now stood in the ditch beside the road,
his head bent above his hands, when Bayard overtook him
and stopped.

"Come on here and get in," he commanded.

"Naw, suh. I'll walk."

"Jump in, now," Bayard ordered sharply. He opened the
door, but Simon stood in the ditch with his hand thrust inside his shirt, and Bayard could see that he was shaking as

with an ague. "Come on, you old fool; I'm not going to hurt you."

"I'll walk home," Simon repeated stubbornly, but without heat. "You git on wid dat thing."

"Ah, get in, Simon. I didn't know I'd scare you that bad. I'll drive slow. Come on."

"You git on home," Simon said again. "Dey'll be worried erbout you. You kin tell 'um whar I'm at."

Bayard watched him for a moment, but Simon was not looking at him, and presently he slammed the door and drove on. Nor did Simon look up even then, even when the car burst once more into thunder and a soundless dun crash of fading dust. After a while the wagon emerged from the dust, the mules now at a high, flop-eared trot, and jingled past him, leaving behind it upon the dusty, insect-rasped air a woman's voice in a quavering wordless hysteria. This faded slowly down the shimmering reaches of the valley, and Simon removed from the breast of his shirt an object slung by a greasy cord about his neck. It was small and of no particular shape and it was covered with soiled, napped fur—the first joint of the hind leg of a rabbit, caught supposedly in a graveyard in the dark of the moon, and Simon rubbed it through the sweat on his forehead and on the back of his neck; then he returned it to his bosom. His hands were still trembling, and he put his hat on and got back into the road and turned homeward through the dusty noon.

Bayard drove on down the valley toward town, passing the iron gates and the serene white house among its trees, and went on at speed. The sound of the unmuffled engine crashed into the dust and swirled it into lethargic bursting shapes and faded across the planted land. Just outside of town he came upon another wagon and he held the car upon it until the mules reared, tilting the wagon; then he swerved and whipped past with not an inch to spare, so close that the yelling Negro in the wagon could see the lipless and savage derision of his teeth.

He went on. In a mounting swoop like a niggard zoom the cemetery with his great-grandfather in pompous effigy flashed past, and he thought of old Simon trudging along the dusty road toward home, clutching his rabbit's foot, and he felt savage and ashamed.

Town among its trees, its shady streets like green tunnels, along which tight lives accomplished their peaceful tragedies. He closed the muffler and at a sedate pace he approached the square. The clock on the courthouse lifted its four faces above the trees, in glimpses seen between arching vistas of trees. Ten minutes to twelve. At twelve exactly his grandfather would repair to the office in the rear of the bank and drink the pint of buttermilk which he brought in with him in a vacuum bottle every morning, and then sleep for an hour on the sofa there. When Bayard turned on to the square the tilted chair in the bank door was already vacant. He slowed the car and eased it in to the curb before a propped sandwich-board.

Fresh Catfish Today the board stated in letters of liquefied chalk, and through the screen doors beyond it came a smell of refrigerated food—cheese and pickle and such—with a faint overtone of fried grease.

He stood for a while on the sidewalk, while the noon throng parted and flowed about him—Negroes slow and aimless as figures of a dark, placid dream, with an animal odor, murmuring and laughing among themselves; there was in their consonantless murmuring something ready with mirth, in their laughter something grave and sad—country people, men in overalls or corduroy or khaki and without neckties, women in shapeless calico and sunbonnets and snuff-sticks—groups of young girls in stiff mail-order finery, the young heritage of their bodies' grace dulled already by self-consciousness and labor and unaccustomed high heels, and soon to be obscured forever by childbearing—youths and young men in cheap, tasteless suits and shirts and caps, weather-tanned and clean-limbed as race-horses and a little belligerently blatant. Against the wall, squatting, a blind Negro beggar, with a guitar and a wire frame holding a mouth-organ to his lips, patterned the background of smells and sounds with a plaintive reiteration of rich, monotonous chords, rhythmic as a mathematical formula, but without music. He was a man of at least forty and his was that patient resignation of many sightless years; yet he too wore filthy khaki with a corporal's stripes on one sleeve and a crookedly-sewn Boy Scout emblem on the other, and on his breast a button commemorating the fourth Liberty Loan and a small metal brooch bearing two gold stars, obviously intended for female adornment. His weathered derby was encircled by an officer's hat-cord, and on the pavement between his feet sat a tin cup containing a dime and three pennies.

Bayard sought a coin in his pocket, and the beggar sensed his approach and his tune became a single repeated chord, but without a break in the rhythm, until the coin rang into the cup, and still without a break in the rhythm and the meaningless strains of the mouth-organ, his left hand dropped groping a little, to the cup and read the coin in a single motion; then once more guitar and mouth-organ resumed their monotonous pattern. As Bayard turned away some one spoke at his side—a broad, squat man with a keen weathered face and gray temples. He wore corduroys and boots, and his body was the supple body of a horseman, and his brown still hands were the hands that horses love. MacCallum his name, one of a family of six brothers who lived eighteen miles away in the hills and with whom Bayard and John hunted foxes and 'coons during their vacations.

"Been hearing about that car of yourn," MacCallum said. "That's her, is it?" He stepped down from the curb and moved easily about the car, examining it, his hands on his hips. "Too much barrel," he said, "and she looks heavy in the withers. Clumsy. Have to use a curb on her, I reckon?"

"I don't," Bayard answered. "Jump in, and I'll show you what she'll do."

"No, much obliged," the other answered. He stepped on to the pavement again, among the Negroes gathered to stare at the car. The clock on the courthouse struck twelve, and already along the street there came in small groups children going home from school for the noon recess—little girls with colored boxes and skipping ropes, talking sibilantly among themselves of intense feminine affairs, and boys in various stages of deshabille, shouting and scuffling and jostling the little girls, who shrank together and gave the little boys cold reverted glares. "Going to eat a snack," MacCallum explained. He crossed the pavement and opened the screen door. "You ate yet?" he asked, looking back. "Come on in a minute, anyway," and he patted his hip significantly.

The store was half grocery and confectionery, and half

restaurant. A number of customers stood about the cluttered but clean front, with sandwiches and bottles of soda-water, and the proprietor bobbed his head at them with flurried, slightly distrait affability above the counter. The rear half was filled with tables at which a number of men and a woman or so, mostly country people, sat eating with awkward and solemn decorum. Next to this was the kitchen, filled with frying odors and the brittle hissing of it, where two Negroes moved like wraiths in a blue lethargy of smoke. They crossed this room and MacCallum opened a door set in an outthrust angle of the wall, and they entered a. smaller room, or rather a large closet. There was a small window high in the wall, and a bare table and three or four chairs, and presently the younger of the two Negroes followed them.

"Yes, suh, Mr. MacCallum and Mr. Sartoris." He set two freshly rinsed glasses, to which water yet adhered in sliding beads, on the table, and stood drying his hands on his apron. He had a broad, untroubled face, a reliable sort of face.

"Lemons and sugar and ice," MacCallum said. "You don't want none of that soda-pop, do you?" The Negro paused with his hand on the door.

"No," Bayard answered. "Rather have a toddy myself."

"Yes, suh," the Negro agreed. "Y'all wants a toddy." And he bowed again with grave approval, and turned again and stepped aside as the proprietor in a fresh apron entered at his customary distracted trot and stood rubbing his hands on his thighs.

"Morning, morning," he said. "How're you, Rafe? Bayard, I saw Miss Jenny and the old Colonel going up to Doc Peabody's office the other day. Ain't nothing wrong, is there?" His head was like an inverted egg; his hair curled meticulously away from the part in the center into two careful reddish-brown wings, like a toupee, and his eyes were a melting, passionate brown.

"Come in here and shut that door," MacCallum ordered, drawing the other into the room. He produced from beneath his coat a bottle of astonishing proportions and set it on the table. It contained a delicate amber liquid, and the proprietor rubbed his hands on his thighs, and his hot mild gaze gloated upon it.

"Great Savior," he said, "where'd you have that demijohn hid? In your pants leg?" MacCallum uncorked the bottle and extended it and the proprietor leaned forward and sniffed it, his eyes closed. He sighed.

"Henry's," MacCallum said. "Best run he's made in six months. Reckon you'd take a drink if Bayard and me was to hold you?" The other cackled loudly, unctuously.

"Ain't he a comical feller, now?" he asked Bayard. "Some joker, ain't he?" He glanced at the table. "You ain't got but two gl——" Some one tapped at the door; the proprietor leaned his conical head to it and waggled his hand at them. MacCallum concealed the bottle without haste as the other opened the door. It was the Negro, with another glass and lemons and sugar and ice in a cracked bowl. The proprietor admitted him.

"If they want me up front, tell 'em I've stepped out but I'll be back in a minute, Houston."

"Yes, suh," the Negro replied, setting his burden on the table. MacCallum produced the bottle again.

"What do you keep on telling your customers that old lie for?" he asked. "Everybody knows what you are doing."

The proprietor cackled again, gloating upon the bottle. "Yes, sir," he repeated, "he's sure some joker. Well, you boys have got plenty of time, but I got to get on back and keep things running."

"Go ahead," MacCallum told him, and the proprietor made himself a toddy. He raised the glass, stirring it and sniffing it alternately, while the others followed suit. Then he removed his spoon and laid it on the table.

"Well, I hate to hurry a good thing mighty bad," he said, "but business don't wait on pleasure, you know."

"Work does interfere with a man's drinking," MacCallum agreed.

"Yes, sir, it sure does," the other replied. He raised his glass. "Your father's good health," he said and drank. "I don't see the old gentleman in town much, nowadays."

"No," MacCallum answered, "he ain't never got over Buddy being in the Yankee army. Claims he ain't coming to town again until the Democratic party denies Woodrow Wilson."

"It'll be the best thing they ever done, if they was to recall him and elect a man like Debs or Senator Vardaman president," the proprietor agreed sagely. "Well, that sure was fine. Henry's sure a wonder, ain't he?" He set his glass down and turned to the door. "Well, you boys make yourselves at home. If you want anything, just call Houston." And he bustled out at his distracted trot.

"Sit down," MacCallum said. He drew up a chair, and Bayard drew another up opposite across the table. "Deacon sure ought to know good whisky. He's drunk enough of it to float his counters right out the front door." He filled his glass and pushed the bottle across to Bayard, and they drank again, quietly.

"You look bad, son," MacCallum said suddenly, and Bayard raised his head and found the other examining him with his keen, steady eyes. "Overtrained," he added. Bayard made an abrupt gesture of negation and raised his glass, but he could still feel the other watching him steadily. "Well, you haven't forgot how to drink good whisky, anyhow. . . . Why don't you come out and take a hunt with us? Got an old red we been saving for you. Been running him off and on for two years, now, with the young dogs. Ain't put old General on him yet, because the old feller'll nose him out, and we wanted to save him for you boys. John would have enjoyed that fox. You remember that night Johnny cut across down to Samson's bridge ahead of the dogs, and when we got there, here come him and the fox floating down the river on that drift log, the fox on one end and Johnny on the other, singing that fool song as loud as he could yell? John would have enjoyed this fox. He outsmarts them young dogs every time. But old General'll get him."

Bayard sat turning his glass in his hand. He reached a packet of cigarettes from his jacket and shook a few of them on to the table at his hand and flipped the packet across to the other. MacCallum drank his toddy steadily and refilled his glass. Bayard lit a cigarette and emptied his glass and reached for the bottle.

"You look like hell, boy," MacCallum repeated.

"Dry, I reckon," Bayard answered in a voice as level as the other's. He made himself another toddy, his cigarette smoking on the table edge. He raised the glass, but instead of drinking, he held it for a moment beneath his nose while the muscles at the base of his nostrils tautened whitely, then he swung the glass from him and with a steady hand he emp-

tied it on the floor. The other watched him quietly while he
poured his glass half full of raw liquor and sloshed a little
water into it and tilted it down his throat. "I've been good
too damn long," he said aloud, and he fell to talking of
the war. Not of combat, but rather of a life peopled by
young men like fallen angels, and of a meteoric violence
like that of fallen angels, beyond heaven or hell and partaking of both: doomed immortality and immortal doom.

MacCallum sat and listened quietly, drinking his whisky
steadily and slowly and without appreciable effect, as
though it were milk he drank, and Bayard talked on and presently found himself without surprise eating food. The bottle
was now less than half full. The Negro Houston had brought
the food in and had his drink, taking it neat and without
batting an eye. "Ef I had a cow dat give dat, de calf
wouldn't git no milk a-tall," he said, "and I wouldn't never
churn. Thanky, Mr. MacCallum, suh."

Then he was out, and Bayard's voice went on, filling the
cubbyhole of a room, surmounting the odor of cheap
food too quickly cooked and of sharp, spilt whisky with
ghosts of a thing high-pitched as a hysteria, like a glare of
fallen meteors on the dark retina of the world. Again a
light tap at the door, and the proprietor's egg-shaped head
and his hot, diffident eyes.

"You gentlemen got everything you want?" he asked, rubbing his hands on his thighs.

"Come and get it," MacCallum said, jerking his head toward the bottle, and the other made himself a toddy in his
stale glass and drank it, while Bayard finished his tale of
himself and an Australian major and two ladies in the
Leicester lounge one evening (the Leicester lounge being out
of bounds, and the Anzac lost two teeth and his girl, and
Bayard himself got a black eye), watching the narrator with
round, melting astonishment.

"Great Savior," he said, "them av'aytors was sure some
hell-raisers, wasn't they? Well, I reckon they're wanting me
up front again. You got to keep on the jump to make a
living, these days." And he scuttled out again.

"I've been good too goddam long," Bayard repeated harshly,
watching MacCallum fill the two glasses. "That's the only
thing Johnny was ever good for. Kept me from getting in a
rut. Bloody rut, with a couple of old women nagging at

me and nothing to do except scare niggers." He drank his whisky and set the glass down, still clutching it. "Damn ham-handed Hun," he said. "He never could fly, anyway. I kept trying to keep him from going up there on that goddam pop-gun," and he cursed his dead brother savagely. Then he raised his glass again, but halted it halfway to his mouth. "Where in hell did my drink go?"

MacCallum emptied the bottle into Bayard's glass, and he drank again and banged the thick tumbler on the table and rose and lurched back against the wall. His chair crashed over backward, and he braced himself, staring at the other. "I kept on trying to keep him from going up there, with that Camel. But he gave me a burst. Right across my nose."

MacCallum rose also. "Come on here," he said quietly, and he offered to take Bayard's arm, but Bayard evaded him and they passed through the kitchen and traversed the long tunnel of the store. Bayard walked steadily enough, and the proprietor bobbed his head at them across the counter.

"Call again, gentlemen," he said, "call again."

"All right, Deacon," MacCallum answered. Bayard strode on. As they passed the soda-fountain a young lawyer standing beside a stranger addressed him.

"Captain Sartoris, shake hands with Mr. Gratton here. Gratton was up on the British front last spring." The stranger turned and extended his hand, but Bayard stared at him bleakly and strode so steadily on that the other involuntarily gave back in order not to be overborne.

"Why, God damn his soul," he said to Bayard's back. The lawyer grasped his arm.

"He's drunk," he whispered quickly, "he's drunk."

"I don't give a damn," the other exclaimed loudly. "Because he was a goddam shave-tail he thinks——"

"Shhhhh, shhhhhh," the lawyer hissed. The proprietor came to the corner of his candy case and peered out with hot, round alarm.

"Gentlemen, gentlemen!" he exclaimed. The stranger made another violent movement, and Bayard stopped.

"Wait a minute while I bash his face in," he told Mac-Callum, turning. The stranger thrust the lawyer aside and stepped forward.

"You never saw the day——" he began. MacCallum took Bayard's arm firmly and easily.

"Come on here, boy."

"I'll bash his bloody face in," Bayard stated, looking bleakly
t the angry stranger. The lawyer grasped his companion's
rm again.

"Get away," the stranger said, flinging him off. "Just let
im try it. Come on, you limey——"

"Gentlemen! Gentlemen!" the proprietor wailed.

"Come on here, boy," MacCallum said. "I've got to look
t a horse."

"A horse?" Bayard repeated. He turned obediently. Then
ne stopped and looked back. "Can't bash your face in now,"
he told the stranger. "Sorry. Got to look at a horse. Call for
you later at the hotel." But the stranger's back was turned,
and behind it the lawyer grimaced and waggled his hand at
MacCallum.

"Get him away, MacCallum, for God's sake."

"Bash his face in later," Bayard repeated. "Can't bash yours,
though, Eustace," he told the lawyer. "Taught us in ground-
school never seduce a fool nor hit a cripple."

"Come on, here," MacCallum repeated, leading him on. At
the door Bayard must stop again to light a cigarette; then
they went on. It was three o'clock and again they walked
among school children in released surges. Bayard strode
steadily enough, and a little belligerently, and soon Mac-
Callum turned into a side street and they went on, passing
Negro stores, and between a busy grist mill and a silent
cotton gin they turned into a lane filled with tethered horses
and mules. From the end of the lane an anvil clanged.
They passed the ruby glow of it and a patient horse standing on three legs in the blacksmith's doorway and the squatting overalled men along the shady wall, and came then to a
high-barred gate backing a long, dun-colored brick tunnel
smelling of ammonia. A few men sat on the top of the
gate; others leaned their crossed arms upon it. From the
paddock itself came voices, then through the slatted gate
gleamed a haughty, motionless shape of burnished flame.

The stallion stood against the yawning cavern of the livery
stable door like a motionless bronze flame, and along its
burnished coat ran at intervals little tremors of paler flame,
little tongues of nervousness and pride. But its eye was
quiet and arrogant, and occasionally and with a kingly air,
its gaze swept along the group at the gate with a fine dis-

dain, without seeing them as individuals at all, and again
little tongues of paler flame rippled flicking along its coat.
About its head was a rope hackamore; it was tethered to a
door post, and in the background a white man moved about
at a respectful distance with a proprietorial air, beside him
a Negro hostler with a tow-sack tied about his waist with a
string. MacCallum and Bayard halted at the gate, and the
white man circled the stallion's haughty immobility and
crossed to them. The Negro hostler came forth also, with a
soft, dirty cloth and chanting in a mellow singsong. The stallion permitted him to approach and suffered him to erase
with his rag the licking nervous little flames that ran in renewed ripples under its skin.

"Ain't he a picture, now?" the white man demanded of
MacCallum, leaning his elbow on the gate. A cheap nickel
watch was attached to his suspender loop by a length of raw-
hide lace leather worn black and soft with age, and his
shaven beard was heaviest from the corners of his mouth
to his chin: he looked always as though he were chewing
tobacco with his mouth open. He was a horse-trader by
profession, and he was constantly engaged in litigation with
the railroad company over the violent demise of his stock by
its agency. "Look at that nigger, now," he added. "He'll let
Tobe handle him like a baby. I wouldn't git within ten foot
of him, myself. Dam'f I know how Tobe does it. Must be
some kin between a nigger and a animal, I always claim."

"I reckon he's afraid you'll be crossing the railroad with
him some day about the time Thirty-nine is due," Mac-
Cullum said drily.

"Yes, I reckon I have the hardest luck of any feller in the
county," the other agreed. "But they got to settle this time:
I got 'em dead to rights, this time."

"Yes," MacCallum said, "the railroad company ought to
furnish that stock of yourn with time tables." The other onlookers guffawed.

"Ah, the company's got plenty of money," the trader rejoined. Then he said: "You talk like I might have druv them
mules in front of that train. Lemme tell you how it come
about——"

"I reckon you won't never drive him in front of no train."
MacCallum jerked his head toward the stallion. The Negro

burnished its shimmering coat, crooning to it in a monotonous singsong. The trader laughed.

"I reckon not," he admitted, "not less'n Tobe goes too. Just look at him now. I wouldn't no more walk up to that animal than I'd fly."

"I'm going to ride that horse," Bayard said suddenly.

"What hoss?" the trader demanded, and the other onlookers watched Bayard climb the gate and vault over into the lot.

"You let that hoss alone, young feller," the trader said. But Bayard paid him no heed. He went on; the stallion swept its regal regard upon him and away.

"You let that hoss alone," the trader shouted, "or I'll have the law on you."

"Let him be," MacCullum said.

"And let him damage a fifteen-hundred-dollar stallion? That hoss'll kill him. You, Sartoris!"

From his hip pocket MacCallum drew a wad of bills enclosed by a rubber band. "Let him be," he repeated. "That's what he wants."

The trader glanced at the roll of money with quick calculation. "I take you gentlemen to witness——" he began loudly; then he ceased, and they watched tensely as Bayard approached the stallion. The beast swept its haughty, glowing eye upon him again and lifted its head without alarm and snorted. The Negro glanced over his shoulder and crouched against the animal, and his crooning chant rose to a swifter beat. "Go back, white folks," he said.

The beast snorted again and swept its head up, snapping the rope like a gossamer thread, and the Negro grasped at the flying rope-end. "Git away, white folks," he cried. "Git away, quick."

But the stallion eluded his hand. It cropped its teeth in a vicious arc and the Negro leaped sprawling as the animal soared like a bronze explosion. Bayard had dodged beneath the sabring hooves, and as the horse swirled in a myriad flickering like fire, the spectators saw that the man had contrived to take a turn with the rope-end about its jaws; then they saw the animal rear again, dragging the man from the ground and whipping his body like a rag upon its flashing arc. Then it stopped, trembling, as Bayard closed its nostrils with the twisted rope, and suddenly he was upon its back while it stood with lowered head and rolling eyes, rippling its coat into quivering tongues before exploding again.

The beast burst like bronze unfolding wings; the onlookers tumbled away from the gate and hurled themselves to safety as the gate splintered to matchwood beneath its soaring volcanic thunder. Bayard crouched on its shoulders and dragged its mad head around and they swept down the lane, spreading pandemonium among the horses and mules tethered and patient about the blacksmith shop and among the wagons there. Where the lane debouched into the street a group of Negroes scattered before them, and without a break in its stride the stallion soared over a small Negro child clutching a stick of striped candy directly in its path. A wagon drawn by mules was just turning into the lane: these reared madly before the wild, slack-jawed face of the white man in the wagon, and again Bayard sawed his thunderbolt around and headed it away from the square. Down the lane behind him the spectators ran shouting through the dust, the trader among them, and Rafe MacCallum still clutching his roll of money.

The stallion moved beneath him like a tremendous mad music, uncontrolled, splendidly uncontrollable. The rope served only to curb its direction, not its speed, and among shouts from the pavement on either hand he swung the animal into another street. This was a quieter street; soon they would be in the country, where the stallion could exhaust its rage without the added hazards of motors and pedestrians. Voices faded behind him in his own thunder: "Runaway! Runaway!" But the street was deserted save for a small automobile going in the same direction, and further along beneath the green tunnel, bright small spots of color scuttled out of the street. Children. "Hope they stay there," he said to himself. His eyes were streaming a little; beneath him the surging lift and fall; in his nostrils a sharpness of rage and energy and violated pride like smoke from the animal's body, and he swept past the motor-car, remarking in a flashing second a woman's face and a mouth partly open and two eyes round with tranquil astonishment. But the face flashed away without registering on his mind and he saw the children huddled on one side of the street, and on the opposite side a Negro playing a hose on the sidewalk and beside him a second Negro with a pitchfork.

Some one screamed from a veranda, and the huddle of children broke, shrieking. A small figure in a white shirt and diminutive pale blue pants darted into the street and Bayard leaned downward and wrapped the rope about his hand and swerved the beast toward the opposite sidewalk where the two Negroes stood, gape-mouthed. The small figure came on, flashed safely behind; then a narrow band of rushing green, a tree trunk like a wheel spoke in reverse, and the stallion struck clashing fire from wet concrete. It slid, clashed, fighting for balance, lunged and crashed down, and for Bayard a red shock, then blackness.

The horse scrambled up and whirled and poised and struck viciously at the prone man with its hooves, but the Negro with the pitchfork drove it away and it trotted stiffly and with tossing head up the street and passed the halted motor-car. At the end of the street it stood trembling and snorting and permitted the Negro hostler to touch it. Rafe MacCallum still clutched his roll of bills.

6

They gathered him up and brought him to town in a commandeered motor-car and roused Dr. Peabody from slumber, and Dr. Peabody profanely bandaged Bayard's head and gave him a drink from the bottle which resided in the cluttered waste-basket, and threatened to telephone Miss Jenny if he didn't go straight home. Rafe MacCallum promised to see that he did so, and the owner of the impressed automobile offered to drive him out. It was a Ford body with, in place of a tonneau, a miniature one-room cabin of sheet iron, no larger than a dog kennel, in each painted window of which a painted housewife simpered across a painted sewing-machine; in it an actual sewing-machine neatly fitted, borne thus about the countryside by the agent. The agent's name was V. K. Suratt and he now sat, with his shrewd, plausible face, behind the wheel. Bayard with his humming head sat beside him, and to the fender clung a youth with brown forearms and a slanted extremely new straw hat, who let his

limber body absorb the jolts with negligent ease as they
rattled sedately out of town on the valley road.

The drink Dr. Peabody had given him, instead of quieting
his jangled nerves, rolled sluggishly and hotly in his stomach
and served only to nauseate him a little, and against his
closed eyelids red antic shapes coiled in throbbing and
tedious cycles. He watched them dully and without astonishment as they emerged from blackness and swirled sluggishly
and consumed themselves and reappeared, each time a little
fainter as his mind cleared. And yet, somewhere blended with
them and at the same time apart and beyond them with a
tranquil aloofness and steadfast among their senseless
convolutions, was a face. It seemed to have some relation
to the instant itself as it culminated in crashing blackness;
at the same time it seemed, for all its aloofness, to be a part
of the whirling ensuing chaos; a part of it, yet bringing into
the red vortex a sort of constant coolness like that of a
faint, shady breeze. So it remained, aloof, not quite distinct,
while the coiling shapes faded into a dull unease of physical
pain from the jolting of the car, leaving about him like an
echo that cool serenity and something else—a sense of shrinking, yet fascinated distaste of which he or something he
had done was the object.

Evening was coming. On either hand cotton and corn
thrust green spears above the rich, dark soil, and in the
patches of woodland where the sun slanted among violet
shadows, doves called moodily. After a time Suratt turned
from the highway into a faint, rutted wagon road between
a field and a patch of woods, and they drove straight into
the sun and Bayard removed his hat and held it before his
face.

"Sun hurt yo' haid?" Suratt asked. " 'Tain't long, now."
The road wound presently into the woods, where the sun
was intermittent, and it rose to a gradual, sandy crest. Beyond this the land fell away in ragged, ill-tended fields and
beyond them, in a clump of sorry fruit trees and a stunted
grove of silver poplar shrubs pale as absinthe and twinkling
ceaselessly with no wind, a small weathered house squatted.
Beyond it and much larger, loomed a barn gray and gaunt
with age. The road forked here. One faint arm curved sandily
away toward the house; the other went on between rank weed

toward the barn. The youth on the fender leaned his head
into the car. "Drive on to the barn," he directed.

Suratt obeyed. Beyond the bordering weeds a fence strag-
gled in limp dilapidation, and from the weeds beside it the
handles of a plow stood at a gaunt angle while its share
rusted peacefully in the undergrowth, and other implements
rusted half concealed there—skeletons of labor healed over by
the earth they were to have violated, kinder than they. The
fence turned at an angle and Suratt stopped the car and the
youth stepped down and opened the warped wooden gate
and Suratt drove on into the barnyard where stood a wagon
with drunken wheels and a home-made bed, and the rusting
skeleton of a Ford car. Low down upon its domed and bald
radiator the two lamps gave it an expression of beetling and
patient astonishment and a lean cow ruminated and
watched them with moody eyes.

The barn doors sagged drunkenly from broken hinges, held
to the posts with twists of rusty wire; beyond, the cavern of
the hallway yawned in a stale desolation—a travesty of
earth's garnered fullness and its rich inferences. Bayard sat
on the fender and leaned his bandaged head against the
side of the car and watched Suratt and the youth enter the
barn and mount slowly on invisible ladder-rungs. The cow
chewed in slow dejection, and upon the yellow surface of
a pond enclosed by banks of trodden and sun-cracked clay,
geese drifted like small muddy clouds. The sun fell in a
long slant upon their rumps and upon their suave necks, and
upon the cow's gaunt, rhythmically twitching flank, ridging
her visible ribs with dingy gold. Presently Suratt's legs
fumbled into view, followed by his cautious body, and
after him the youth slid easily down the ladder in one-
handed swoops.

He emerged carrying an earthen jug close against his leg.
Suratt followed in his neat, tieless blue shirt and jerked
his head at Bayard, and they turned the corner of the barn
among waist-high jimson weeds. Bayard overtook them as
the youth with his jug slid with a single motion between two
lax strands of barbed wire. Suratt stooped through more
sedately, and he held the top strand taut and set his foot on
the lower one until Bayard was through. Behind the barn
the ground descended into shadow, toward a junglish growth
of willow and elder, against which a huge beech and a clump

of saplings stood like mottled ghosts and from which a cool dankness rose like a breath to meet them. The spring welled from the roots of the beech, into a wooden frame sunk to its top in white sand that quivered ceaselessly and delicately beneath the water's limpid unrest, and went on into the willow and elder growth.

The earth about the spring was trampled smooth and packed as an earthen floor. Near the spring a blackened iron pot sat on four bricks; beneath it was a heap of pale woodashes and a litter of extinct brands and charred fagot-ends. Against the pot leaned a scrubbing-board with a ridged metal face, and a rusty tin cup hung from a nail in the tree above the spring. The youth set the jug down and he and Suratt squatted beside it.

"I don't know if we ain't a-goin' to git in trouble, givin' Mr. Bayard whisky, Hub," Suratt said. "Still, Doc Peabody give him one dram hisself; so I reckon we kin give him one mo'. Ain't that right, Mr. Bayard?" Squatting, he looked up at Bayard with his shrewd affable face. Hub twisted the corn-cob stopper from the jug and passed it to Suratt, who tendered it to Bayard. "I been knowin' Mr. Bayard ever since he was a chap in knee pants," Suratt confided to Hub. "But this is the first time me and him ever taken a drink together. Ain't that so, Mr. Bayard? . . . I reckon you'll want a drinkin'-cup, won't you?" But Bayard was already drinking, with the jug tilted across his horizontal forearm and the mouth held to his lips by the same hand, as it should be done. "He knows how to drink outen a jug, don't he?" Suratt added. "I knowed he was all right," he said in a tone of confidential vindication. Bayard lowered the jug and returned it to Suratt, who tendered it formally to Hub.

"Go ahead," Hub said. "Hit it." Suratt did so, with measured pistonings of his Adam's apple. Above the stream gnats whirled and spun in a leveling ray of sunlight, like erratic golden chaff. Suratt lowered the jug and passed it to Hub and wiped his mouth on the back of his hand.

"How you feel now, Mr. Bayard?" he asked. Then he said heavily: "You'll have to excuse me. I reckon I ought to said Cap'm Sartoris, oughtn't I?"

"What for?" Bayard asked. He squatted also on his heels against the bole of the beech tree. The rising slope of ground behind them hid the barn and the house, and the

three of them squatted in a small bowl of peacefulness remote from the world and time, and filled with the cool and
limpid breathing of the spring and a seeping of sunlight
among the elders and willows like a thinly diffused wine.
On the surface of the spring the sky lay reflected, strippled
over with windless beech leaves. Hub squatted leanly, his
brown forearms clasped about his knees, smoking a cigarette
beneath the tilt of his hat. Suratt was across the spring
from him. He wore a faded blue shirt, and in contrast to it
his hands and face were a rich, even brown, like mahogany.
The jug sat rotund and benignant between them.

"Yes, sir," Suratt repeated, "I always find the best cure fer
a wound is plenty of whisky. Doctors, these here fancy young
doctors'll tell a feller different, but old Doc Peabody hisself cut off my granpappy's laig while granpappy laid back
on the kitchen table with a demijohn in his hand and a mattress and a cheer acrost his laigs and fo' men a-holdin'
him down, and him cussin' and singin' so scandalous the
womenfolks and the chillen went down to the pasture behind the barn and waited. Take some mo'," he said, and he
passed the jug across the spring and Bayard drank again.
"Reckon you're beginnin' to feel pretty fair, ain't you?"

"Damned if I know," Bayard answered. "It's dynamite,
boys."

Suratt poised the jug and guffawed, then he lipped it and
his Adam's apple pumped again, in relief against the wall
of elder and willow. The elder would soon flower, with
pale clumps of tiny bloom. Miss Jenny made a little wine
of it every year. Good wine, if you knew how and had the
patience. Elder-flower wine. Like a ritual for a children's
game; a game played by little girls in small pale dresses, between supper and twilight. Above the bowl where sunlight
yet came in a leveling beam, gnats whirled and spun like
dust-motes in a still, disused room. Suratt's voice went on
affably, ceaselessly recapitulant, in polite admiration of the
hardness of Bayard's head and the fact that this was the
first time he and Bayard had ever taken a drink together.

They drank again, and Hub began to borrow cigarettes
of Bayard and he too became a little profanely and ro-
bustly anecdotal in his country idiom, about whisky and
girls and dice; and presently he and Suratt were arguing
amicably about work. They appeared to be able to sit tire-

lessly and without discomfort on their heels, but Bayard's legs had soon grown numb and he straightened them, tingling with released blood, and he now sat with his back against the tree and his long legs straight before him, hearing Suratt's voice without listening to it.

His head was now no more than a sort of taut discomfort; at times it seemed to float away from his shoulders and hang against the green wall like a transparent balloon, within which or beyond which that face that would neither emerge completely nor yet fade completely away, lingered with shadowy exasperation—two eyes round with grave, shocked astonishment, two lifted hands flashing behind little white shirt and blue pants swerving into a lifting rush plunging clatter crash blackness. . . .

Suratt's slow, plausible voice went on steadily, but without any irritant quality. It seemed to fit easily into the still scene, speaking of earthy things. "Way I learnt to chop cotton," he was saying, "my oldest brother taken and put me in the row ahead of him. Started me off, and soon's I taken a lick or two, here he come behind me. And ever' time my hoe chopped once, I could hear hisn chop twice. I never had no shoes in them days, neither," he added drily. "So I had to learn to chop fast, with that 'ere hoe of hisn cuttin' at my bare heels. But I swo' then, come what mought, I wouldn't never plant nothin' in the ground, soon's I could he'p myself. It's all right fer folks that owns the land, but folks like my folks was don't never own no land, and ever' time we made a furrow, we was scratchin' dirt fer somebody else." The gnats danced and whirled more madly yet in the sun, above the secret places of the stream, and the sun's light was taking on a rich copper tinge. Suratt rose. "Well, boys, I got to git on back to'rds town, myself." He looked at Bayard again with his shrewd, kind face. "I reckon Mr. Bayard's clean fergot about that knock he taken, ain't he?"

"Dammit," Bayard said, "quit calling me Mr. Bayard."

Suratt picked up the jug. "I knowed he was all right, when you got to know him," he told Hub. "I been knowin' him since he was knee-high to a grasshopper, but me and him jest ain't been throwed together like this. I was raised a pore boy, fellers, while Mr. Bayard's folks has lived on that 'ere big place with plenty of money in the bank and niggers to wait on 'em. But he's all right," he repeated. "He ain't goin' to say nothin' about who give him this here whisky."

"Let him tell if he wants to," Hub answered. "I don't give a damn."

They drank again. The sun was almost gone, and from the secret marshy places of the stream came a fairylike piping of young frogs. The gaunt invisible cow lowed barnward, and Hub replaced the corn cob in the jug and drove it home with a blow of his palm, and they mounted the hill and crawled through the fence. The cow stood in the barn door and watched them approach and lowed again, moody and mournful. The geese had left the pond and they now paraded sedately across the barnyard towards the house, in the door of which, framed by two crape myrtle bushes, a woman stood.

"Hub," she said in a flat, country voice.

"Goin' to town," Hub answered shortly. "Sue'll have to milk."

The woman stood quietly in the door. Hub carried the jug into the barn and the cow followed him, and he heard her and turned and gave her a resounding kick in her gaunt ribs and cursed her without heat. Presently he reappeared and went on to the gate and opened it, and Suratt drove through. Then he closed it and wired it to again and swung on to the fender. Bayard moved over and prevailed on Hub to get inside. The woman stood yet in the door, watching them quietly. About the doorstep the geese surged erratically with discordant cries, their necks undulant and suave as formal gestures in a pantomime.

The shadow of the fruit trees fell long across the untidy fields, and the car pushed its elongated shadow before it like the shadow of a huge, hump-shouldered bird. They mounted the sandy hill in the last of the sun and dropped downward out of the sunlight and into violet dusk. The road was soundless with sand, and the car lurched in the worn and shifting ruts and on to the highroad again.

The waxing moon stood overhead. As yet it gave off no light, though, and they drove on toward town, passing an occasional country wagon homeward bound. These Suratt, who knew nearly every soul in the county, greeted with a grave gesture of his brown hand, and presently where the road crossed a wooden bridge among more willows and elder and where dusk was denser and more palpable, Suratt stopped the car and climbed out over the door.

"You fellers set still," he said. "I won't be but a minute. Got to fill that 'ere radiator." They heard him at the rear of the car; then he reappeared with a tin bucket and let himself gingerly down the roadside bank beside the bridge. Water chuckled and murmured beneath the bridge, invisible in the twilight, its murmur burdened with the voice of cricket and frog. Above the willows that marked the course of the stream gnats still spun and whirled, for bull bats appeared from nowhere in long swoops, in mid-swoop vanished, then appeared again swooping against the serene sky, silent as drops of water on a window-pane; swift and noiseless and intent as though their wings were feathered with twilight and with silence.

Suratt scrambled up the bank with his pail and removed the cap and tilted the bucket above the radiator. The moon stood without emphasis overhead; yet a faint shadow of Suratt's head and shoulders fell upon the hood of the car, and upon the pallid planking of the bridge the leaning willow fronds were faintly and delicately penciled in shadow. The last of the water gurgled with faint rumblings into the engine's interior and Suratt replaced the pail and climbed over the blind door. The lights were operated from a generator; he switched these on now. While the car was in low speed, the lights glared to crescendo, but when he let the clutch in they dropped to a wavering glow no more than a luminous shadow.

Night was fully come when they reached town. Across the land the lights on the courthouse clock were like yellow beads above the trees, and upon the green afterglow a column of smoke stood like a balanced plume. Suratt put them out at the restaurant and drove on, and they entered and the proprietor raised his conical head and his round, melting eyes from behind the soda-fountain.

"Great Savior, boy," he exclaimed, "ain't you gone home yet? Doc Peabody's been huntin' you ever since four o'clock, and Miss Jenny drove to town in the carriage, looking for you. You'll kill yourself."

"Get to hell on back yonder, Deacon," Bayard answered, "and bring me and Hub about two dollars' worth of ham and eggs."

Later they returned for the jug in Bayard's car, Bayard
and Hub and a third young man, freight agent at the railway station, with three Negroes and a bull fiddle in the rear
seat. But they drove no farther than the edge of the field
above the house and stopped there while Hub went on afoot
down the sandy road toward the barn. The moon stood pale
and cold overhead, and on all sides insects shrilled in the
dusty undergrowth. In the rear seat the Negroes murmured
among themselves.

"Fine night," Mitch, the freight agent, suggested. Bayard
made no reply. He smoked moodily, his head closely helmeted
in its white bandage. Moon and insects were one, audible
and visible, dimensionless and without source.

After a while Hub materialized against the dissolving
vagueness of the road, crowned by the silver slant of his hat,
and he came up and swung the jug on to the door and removed the stopper. Mitch passed it to Bayard.

"Drink," Bayard said, and Mitch did so. The others drank.

"We ain't got nothin' for the niggers to drink out of,"
Hub said.

"That's so," Mitch agreed. He turned in his seat. "Ain't
one of you boys got a cup or something?" The Negroes
murmured again, questioning one another in mellow consternation.

"Wait," Bayard said. He got out and lifted the hood and
removed the cap from the breather-pipe. "It'll taste a little
like oil for a drink or two. But you boys won't notice it after
that."

"Naw, suh," the Negroes agreed in chorus. One took the
cup and wiped it out with the corner of his coat, and they
too drank in turn, with smacking expulsions of breath. Bayard replaced the cap and got in the car.

"Anybody want another right now?" Hub asked, poising
the corn cob.

"Give Mitch another," Bayard directed. "He'll have to
catch up."

Mitch drank again. Then Bayard took the jug and tilted
it. The others watched him respectfully.

"Dam'f he don't drink it," Mitch murmured. "I'd be afraid
to hit it so often, if I was you."

"It's my damned head." Bayard lowered the jug and

passed it to Hub. "I keep thinking another drink will ease it off some."

"Doc put that bandage on too tight," Hub said. "Want it loosened some?"

"I don't know." Bayard lit another cigarette and threw the match away. "I believe I'll take it off. It's been on there long enough." He raised his hands and fumbled at the bandage.

"You better let it alone," Mitch warned him. But he continued to fumble at the fastening; then he slid his fingers beneath a turn of the cloth and tugged at it savagely. One of the Negroes leaned forward with a pocket knife and severed it, and they watched him as he stripped it off and flung it away.

"You ought not to done that," Mitch told him.

"Ah, let him take it off if he wants," Hub said. "He's all right." He got in and stowed the jug away between his knees, and Bayard turned the car about. The sandy road hissed beneath the broad tires of it and rose shaling into the woods again where the dappled moonlight was intermittent, treacherous with dissolving vistas. Invisible and sourceless among the shifting patterns of light and shade, whippoorwills were like flutes tongued liquidly. The road passed out of the woods and descended, with sand in shifting and silent lurches, and they turned on to the valley road and away from town.

The car went on, on the dry hissing of the closed muffler. The Negroes murmured among themselves with mellow snatches of laughter whipped like scraps of torn paper away behind. They passed the iron gates and Bayard's home serenely in the moonlight among its trees, and the silent, box-like flag station and the metal-roofed cotton gin on the railroad siding.

The road rose at last into hills. It was smooth and empty and winding, and the Negroes fell silent as Bayard increased speed. But still it was not anything like what they had anticipated of him. Twice more they stopped and drank, and then from an ultimate hilltop they looked down upon another cluster of lights like a clotting of beads upon the pale gash where the railroad ran. Hub produced the breather-cap and they drank again.

Through streets identical with those at home they moved slowly, toward an identical square. People on the square turned and looked curiously after them. They crossed the square and followed another street and went on between broad lawns and shaded windows, and presently beyond an iron fence and well back among black-and-silver trees, lighted windows hung in ordered tiers like rectangular lanterns strung among the branches.

They stopped here, in shadow. The Negroes descended and lifted the bass viol out, and a guitar. The third one held a slender tube frosted over with keys upon which the intermittent moon glinted in pale points, and they stood with their heads together, murmuring among themselves and touching plaintive muted chords from the strings. Then the one with the clarinet raised it to his lips.

The tunes were old tunes. Some of them were sophisticated tunes and formally intricate, but in the rendition this was lost, and all of them were imbued instead with a plaintive similarity, a slurred and rhythmic simplicity; and they drifted in rich, plaintive chords upon the silver air, fading, dying in minor reiterations along the treacherous vistas of the moon. They played again, an old waltz. The college Cerberus came across the dappled lawn to the fence and leaned his arms upon it, a lumped listening shadow among other shadows. Across the street, in the shadows there, other listeners stood. A car approached and slowed to the curb and shut off engine and lights, and in the tiered windows heads leaned, aureoled against the lighted rooms behind, without individuality, feminine, distant, delicately and divinely young.

They played "Home, Sweet Home," and when the rich minor died away, across to them came a soft clapping of slender palms. Then Mitch sang "Good Night, Ladies" in his true, oversweet tenor, and the young hands were more importunate, and as they drove away the slender heads leaned aureoled with bright hair in the lighted windows and the soft clapping drifted after them for a long while, fainter and fainter in the silver silence and the moon's infinitude.

At the top of the first hill out of town they stopped and Hub removed the breather-cap. Behind them random lights shone among the trees, and it was as though there still came to them across the hushed world that sound of young palms like flung delicate flowers before their masculinity and their youth, and they drank without speaking, lapped still in the fading magic of that lost moment. Mitch sang to himself softly; the car slid purring on again. The road dropped curving smoothly, empty and blanched. Bayard spoke, his voice harsh, abrupt.

"Cut-out, Hub," he said. Hub bent forward and reached his hand under the dash, and the car swept on with a steady, leashed muttering like waking thunderous wings; then the road flattened in a long swoop toward another rise and the muttering leaped to crescendo and the car shot forward with neck-snapping violence. The Negroes had stopped talking; one of them raised a wailing shout.

"Reno lost his hat," Hub said, looking back.

"He don't need it," Bayard replied. The car roared up this hill and rushed across the crest of it and flashed around a tight curve.

"Oh, Lawd," the Negro wailed. "Mr. Bayard!" The air-blast stripped his words away like leaves. "Lemme out, Mr. Bayard!"

"Jump out, then," Bayard answered. The road fell from beneath them like a tilting floor, and away across a valley, straight now as a string. The Negroes clutched their instruments and held to one another. The speedometer showed fifty-five and sixty and turned gradually on. Sparse houses flashed slumbering away, and fields and patches of woodland like tunnels.

The road went on across the black-and-silver land. Whippoorwills called on either side, one to another inquiring, liquid reiterations; now and then as the headlights swept in the road's abrupt windings, two spots of pale fire blinked in the dust before them as the bird blundered awkwardly somewhere beneath the radiator. The ridge rose steadily, with wooded slopes falling away on either hand. Sparse Negro cabins squatted on the slopes or beside the road.

The road dipped, then rose again in a long slant broken by another dip; then it stood directly before them like a wall. The car shot upward and over the dip and left the road completely, then swooped dreadfully on, and the Negroes' concerted wail whipped forlornly away. Then the ridge attained its crest and the car's thunder ceased and it rolled to a stop. The Negroes now sat in the bottom of the tonneau.

"Is dis heaven?" one murmured after a time.

"Dey wouldn't let you in heaven, wid likker on yo' breaf and no hat, feller," another said.

"Ef de Lawd don't take no better keer of me dan He done of dat hat, I don't wanter go dar, noways," the first rejoined.

"Mmmmmmm," the second agreed, "when us come down dat 'ere las' hill, dis yere cla'inet almos' blowed clean outen my han', let 'lone my hat."

"And when us jumped over dat 'ere lawg er whutever it wuz back dar," the third one added, "I thought fer a minute dis whole auto'bile done blowed outen my han'."

They drank again. It was high here, and the air moved with grave coolness. On either hand lay a valley filled with silver mist and with whippoorwills; beyond these valleys the silver earth rolled on into the sky. Across it, mournful and far, a dog howled. Bayard's head was as cool and clear as a clapperless bell. Within it that face emerged clearly at last: those two eyes round with grave astonishment, winged serenely by two dark wings of hair. It was that Benbow girl, he said to himself, and he sat for a while, gazing into the sky. The lights on the town clock were steadfast and yellow and unwinking in the dissolving distance, but in all other directions the world rolled away in slumbrous ridges, milkily opaline.

Her appetite was gone at supper, and Aunt Sally Wyatt mouthed her soft prepared food and mumbled querulously at her because she wouldn't eat.

"My mother saw to it that I drank a good cup of bark tea when I come sulking to the table and wouldn't eat," Aunt Sally stated, "but folks nowadays think the good Lord's going to keep 'em well and them lifting no finger."

"I'm all right," Narcissa insisted. "I just don't want any supper."

"That's what you say. Let yourself get down, and Lord knows, I ain't strong enough to wait on you. In my day young folks had more consideration for their elders." She mouthed her food unprettily, querulously and monotonously retrospective, while Narcissa toyed restively with the food she could not eat. Later Aunt Sally continued her monologue while she rocked with her interminable fancy-work on her lap. She would never divulge what it was to be when com-

pleted, nor for whom, and she had been working on it for
fifteen years, carrying about with her a shapeless bag of
dingy, threadbare brocade containing odds and ends of
colored fabric in all possible shapes. She could never bring
herself to trim them to any pattern; so she shifted and fitted
and mused and fitted and shifted them like pieces of a patient puzzle-picture, trying to fit them to a pattern or create
a pattern about them without using her scissors; smoothing
her colored scraps with flaccid, putty-colored fingers, shifting
and shifting them. From the bosom of her dress the needle
Narcissa had threaded for her dangled its spidery skein.

Across the room Narcissa sat with a book. Aunt Sally's
voice droned on with querulous interminability while Narcissa read. Suddenly she rose and laid the book down and
crossed the room and entered the alcove where her piano
sat. But she had not played four bars before her hands
crashed in discord, and she shut the piano and went to the
telephone.

Miss Jenny thanked her tartly for her solicitude, and dared
to say that Bayard was all right: still an active member of the
so-called human race, that is, since they had received no official word from the coroner. No, she had heard nothing of
him since Loosh Peabody 'phoned her at four o'clock that
Bayard was on his way home with a broken head. The
broken head she readily believed, but the other part of the
message she had put no credence in whatever, having lived
with those damn Sartorises eighty years and knowing that
home would be the last place in the world a Sartoris with a
broken head would ever consider going. No, she was not even
interested in his present whereabouts, and she hoped he hadn't
injured the horse. Horses were valuable animals.

Narcissa returned to the living-room and explained to Aunt
Sally whom she had been talking to and why, and drew a
low chair to the lamp and took up her book.

"Well," Aunt Sally said after a time, "if you ain't going
to talk any . . ." She fumbled her scraps together and
crammed them into the bag. "I thank the Lord sometimes
you and Horace ain't any blood of mine, the way you all
go on. But if you'd drink it, I don't know who's to get
sassafras for you: I ain't able to, and you wouldn't know
it from dog fennel or mullein, yourself."

"I'm all right," Narcissa protested.

"Go ahead," Aunt Sally repeated, "get flat on your back, with me and that trifling nigger to take care of you. She ain't wiped off a picture frame in six months, to my certain knowledge. And I've done everything but beg and pray." She rose and said good night and hobbled from the room. Narcissa sat and turned the pages on, hearing the other mount the stairs with measured, laborious tappings of her stick, and for a while longer she sat and turned the pages of her book.

But presently she flung the book away and went to the piano again, but Aunt Sally thumped on the floor overhead with her stick, and she desisted and returned to her book. So it was with actual pleasure that she greeted Dr. Alford a moment later.

"I was passing and heard your piano," he explained. "You haven't stopped?"

She explained that Aunt Sally had gone to bed, and he sat formally and talked to her in his stiff, pedantic way on cold and erudite subjects for two hours. Then he departed and she stood in the door and watched him down the drive. The moon stood overhead; along the drive the cedars in a rigid curve were pointed against the pale, faintly spangled sky.

She returned to the living-room and got her book and turned out the lights and mounted the stairs. Across the hall Aunt Sally snored with genteel placidity, and Narcissa stood for a moment, listening to the homely noise. "I will be glad when Horry gets home," she thought, going on.

She turned on her light and undressed and took her book to bed, where she again held her consciousness submerged deliberately, as you hold a puppy under water until its struggles cease. And after a time her mind surrendered to the book and she read on, pausing from time to time to think warmly of sleep, reading again. And so when the Negroes first blended their instruments beneath the window she paid them only the most perfunctory notice. "Why in the world are those jellybeans serenading me?" she thought with faint amusement, visioning immediately Aunt Sally in her nightcap leaning from a window and shouting them away. And she lay with the book open, seeing upon the spread page the picture she had created while the plaintive rhythm of the strings and clarinet drifted into the open window.

Then she sat bolt upright, with a sharp and utter certainty, and clapped the book shut and slipped from bed. From the adjoining room she looked down.

The Negroes were grouped on the lawn; the frosted clarinet, the guitar, the sober, comical bulk of the bass fiddle. At the street entrance to the drive a motor-car stood in shadow. The musicians played once; then a voice called from the car, and they retreated across the lawn and the car moved away, without lights. She was certain, then: no one else would play one tune beneath a lady's window, just enough to waken her from sleep, then go away.

She returned to her room. The book lay face down upon the bed, but she went to the window and stood there, between the parted curtains, looking out upon the black-and-silver world and the peaceful night. The air moved upon her face and amid the dark, fallen wings of her hair with grave coolness. "The beast, the beast," she whispered to herself. She let the curtains fall and on her silent feet she descended the stairs again and found the telephone in the darkness, muffling its bell when she rang.

Miss Jenny's voice came out of the night with its usual brisk and cold asperity, and without surprise or curiosity. No, he had not returned home, for he was by now safely locked up in jail, she believed, unless the city officers were too corrupt to obey a lady's request. Serenading? Fiddlesticks. What would he want to go serenading for? He couldn't injure himself serenading, unless some one killed him with a flatiron or an alarm clock. And why was she concerned about him?

Narcissa hung up, and for a moment she stood in the darkness, beating her fists on the telephone's unresponsive box. The beast, the beast.

She received three callers that night. One came formally; the second came informally; the third came anonymously.

The garage which sheltered her car was a small brick building surrounded by evergreens. One side of it was a continuation of the garden wall. Beyond the wall a grass-grown lane led back to another street. The garage was about fifteen yards from the house and its roof rose to the level of the first-floor windows: Narcissa's bedroom windows looked out upon the slate roof of it.

This third caller entered by the lane and mounted on to the wall and thence to the garage roof, where he now lay in the shadow of a cedar, sheltered so from the moon. He had lain there for a long time. The room facing him was dark when he arrived, but he had lain in his fastness quiet as an animal and with an animal's patience, without movement save to occasionally raise his head and reconnoiter the immediate scene with covert dartings of his eyes.

But the room facing him remained dark while an hour passed. In the meantime a car entered the drive (he recognized it; he knew every car in town) and a man entered the house. The second hour passed and the room was still dark, and the car stood yet in the drive. Then the man emerged and drove away, and a moment later the lights downstairs went out, and then the window facing him glowed, and through the sheer curtains he saw her moving about the room, watched the shadowy motions of her disrobing. Then she passed out of his vision. But the light still burned and he lay with still and infinite patience; lay so while another hour passed and another car stopped before the house and three men carrying an awkwardly-shaped burden came up the drive and stood in the moonlight beneath the window; lay so until they played once and went away. When they had gone, she came to the window and parted the curtains and stood for a while in the dark fallen wings of her hair, looking directly into his hidden eyes.

Then the curtains fell again, and once more she was a shadowy movement beyond them. Then the light went off, and he lay face downward upon the steep pitch of the roof, utterly motionless for a long time, darting from beneath his hidden face covert, ceaseless glances, quick and darting, all-embracing as those of an animal.

To Narcissa's home they came finally. They had visited the dark homes of all the other unmarried girls one by one and sat in the car while the Negroes stood on the lawn with their blended instruments. Heads had appeared at darkened windows, sometimes lights went up; once they were invited in, but Hub and Mitch hung diffidently back; once refreshment was sent out to them; once they were heartily cursed by a young man who happened to be sitting with the young lady on the dark veranda. In the meantime they had lost the breather-cap, and as they moved from house to house, all six of them drank fraternally from the jug, turn and turn about. At last they reached the Benbows' and played once beneath the cedars. There was a light yet in one window, but none came to it.

The moon stood well down the sky. Its light was now a cold silver on things, spent and a little wearied, and the world was empty as they rolled without lights along a street lifeless and fixed in black and silver as any street in the moon itself. Beneath stippled intermittent shadows they went, passed quiet intersections dissolving away, occasionally a car motionless at the curb before a house. A dog crossed the street ahead of them trotting, and went on across a lawn and so from sight, but saving this there was no movement anywhere.

The square opened spaciously about the absinthe-cloudy mass of elms that surrounded the courthouse. Among them the round spaced globes were more like huge, pallid grapes than ever. Above the exposed vault in each bank burned a single bulb; inside the hotel lobby, before which a row of cars was aligned, another burned. Other lights there were none.

They circled the courthouse, and a shadow moved near the hotel door and detached itself from shadow and came to the curb, a white shirt glinting within a spread coat; and as the car swung slowly toward another street, the man hailed them. Bayard stopped and the man came through the blanched dust and laid his hand on the door.

"Hi, Buck," Mitch said. "You're up pretty late, ain't you?"

The man had a sober, good-natured horse's face. He wore a metal star on his unbuttoned waistcoat. His coat humped slightly over his hip. "What you boys doin'?" he asked. "Been to a dance?"

"Serenading," Bayard answered. "Want a drink, Buck?"

"No, much obliged." He stood with his hand on the door, gravely and good-naturedly serious. "Ain't you fellers out kind of late, yo'selves?"

"It is gettin' on," Mitch agreed. The marshal lifted his foot to the running-board. Beneath his hat his eyes were in shadow. "We're going home now," Mitch said. The other pondered quietly, and Bayard added:

"Sure; we're on our way home now."

The marshal moved his head slightly and spoke to the Negroes. "I reckon you boys are about ready to turn in, ain't you?"

"Yes, suh," the Negroes answered, and they got out and lifted the viol out. Bayard gave Reno a bill and they thanked him and said good night and picked up the viol and departed quietly down a side street. The marshal turned his head again.

"Ain't that yo' car in front of Rogers' café, Mitch?" he asked.

"Reckon so. That's where I left it."

"Well, suppose you run Hub out home, lessen he's goin' to stay in town tonight. Bayard better come with me."

"Aw, hell, Buck," Mitch protested.

"What for?" Bayard demanded.

"His folks are worried about him," the other answered. "They ain't seen hide nor hair of him since that stallion throwed him. Where's yo' bandage, Bayard?"

"Took it off," he answered shortly. "See here, Buck, we're going to put Mitch out and then Hub and me are going straight home."

"You been on yo' way home ever since fo' o'clock, Bayard," the marshal replied soberly, "but you don't seem to git no nearer there. I reckon you better come with me tonight, like yo' aunt said."

"Did Aunt Jenny tell you to arrest me?"

"They was worried about you, son. Miss Jenny just phoned and asked me to kind of see if you was all right until mawnin'. So I reckon we better. You ought to went on home this evenin'."

"Aw, have a heart, Buck," Mitch protested.

"I ruther make Bayard mad than Miss Jenny," the other answered patiently. "You boys go on, and Bayard better come with me."

Mitch and Hub got out and Hub lifted out his jug and they said good night and went on to where Mitch's car stood before the restaurant. The marshal got in beside Bayard. The jail was not far. It loomed presently above its walled court, square and implacable, its slitted upper windows brutal as saber-blows. They turned into an alley, and the marshal descended and opened a gate, and Bayard drove into the grass-less and littered compound and stopped while the other went on ahead to a small garage in which stood a Ford. He backed this out and motioned Bayard forward. The garage was built to the Ford's dimensions and about a third of Bayard's car stuck out the door of it.

"Better'n nothin', though," the marshal said. "Come on." They entered through the kitchen, into the jail-keeper's living-quarters, and Bayard waited in a dark passage until the other found a light. Then he entered a bleak, neat room, containing spare conglomerate furnishings and a few scattered articles of masculine apparel.

"Say," Bayard objected, "aren't you giving me your bed?"

"Won't need it befo' mawnin'," the other answered. "You'll be gone, then. Want me to he'p you off with yo' clothes?"

"No. I'm all right." Then, more graciously: "Good night, Buck. And much obliged."

"Good night," the marshal answered.

He closed the door behind him and Bayard removed his coat and shoes and his tie and snapped the light off and lay on the bed. Moonlight seeped into the room impalpably, refracted and sourceless; the night was without any sound. Beyond the window a cornice rose in a succession of shallow steps against the opaline and dimensionless sky. His head was clear and cold; the whisky he had drunk was completely dead. Or rather, it was as though his head were one Bayard who lay on a strange bed and whose alcohol-dulled nerves radiated like threads of ice through that body which he must drag forever about a bleak and barren world with him. "Hell," he said, lying on his back, staring out the window where nothing was to be seen, waiting for sleep, not knowing if it would come or not, not caring a particular damn either way. Nothing to be seen, and the long, long span of a man's natural life. Three score and ten years to drag a stubborn body about the world and cozen its insistent demands. Three score and ten, the Bible said. Seventy years. And he was only twenty-six. Not much more than a third through it. Hell.

PART THREE

HORACE BENBOW in his clean, wretchedly-fitting khaki which but served to accentuate his air of fine and delicate futility, and laden with an astonishing impedimenta of knapsacks and kit bags and paper-wrapped parcels, got off the two-thirty train. Across the tight clotting of descending and ascending passengers the sound of his spoken name reached him, and he roved his distraught gaze, like a somnambulist rousing to avoid traffic, about the agglomerate faces. "Hello, hello," he said; then he thrust himself clear and laid his bags and parcels on the edge of the platform and moved with intent haste up the train toward the baggage car.

"Horace!" his sister called again, running after him. The station agent emerged from his office and stopped him and held him like a finely-bred restive horse and shook his hand, and thus his sister overtook him. He turned at her voice and came completely from out his distraction and swept her up in his arms until her feet were off the ground, and kissed her on the mouth.

"Dear old Narcy," he said, kissing her again. Then he set her down and stroked his hands on her face, as a child would. "Dear old Narcy," he repeated, touching her face with his fine spatulate hands, gazing at her as though he were drinking that constant serenity of hers through his eyes. He continued to say "Dear old Narcy," stroking his hands on her face, utterly oblivious of his surroundings until she recalled him.

"Where in the world are you going, up this way?"

Then he remembered, and released her and rushed on, she following, and stopped again at the door of the baggage car, from which the station porter and a train hand were taking trunks and boxes as the baggage clerk tilted them out.

"Can't you send down for it?" she asked. But he stood peering into the car, oblivious of her again. The two Negroes returned and he stepped aside, still looking into the car with peering, birdlike motions of his head. "Let's send back for it," his sister said again.

"What? Oh. I've seen it every time I changed cars," he told her, completely forgetting the sense of her words. "It'd be rotten luck to have it go astray right at my doorstep, wouldn't it?" Again the Negroes moved away with a trunk, and he stepped forward again and peered into the car. "That's just about what happened to it; some clerk forgot to put it on the train at M——there it is," he interrupted himself. "Easy now, Cap," he called in the country idiom, in a fever of alarm as the clerk slammed into the doorway a box of foreign shape stenciled with a military address; "she's got glass in her."

"All right, Colonel," the baggage clerk agreed. "We ain't hurt her none, I reckon. If we have, all you got to do is sue us." The two Negroes backed up to the door and Horace laid his hands on the box as the clerk tilted it outward.

"Easy now, boys," he repeated nervously, and he trotted beside them as they crossed to the platform. "Set it down easy, now. Here, sis, lend a hand, will you?"

"We got it all right, Cap'm," the station porter said; "we ain't gwine drop it." But Horace continued to dab at it with his hands, and when they set it down he leaned his ear to it.

"She's all right, ain't she?" the station porter asked.

"It's all right," the train porter assured him. He turned away. "Let's go," he called.

"I think it's all right," Horace agreed, his ear against the box. "I don't hear anything. It's packed pretty well." The engine whistled and Horace sprang erect, and digging into his pocket he ran toward the moving cars. The porter was closing the vestibule, but he leaned down to Horace's hand, then straightened up and touched his cap. Horace returned to his box and gave another coin to the second Negro. "Put it in the house for me, careful, now," he directed. "I'll be back for it in a few minutes."

"Yes, suh, Mr. Benbow. I'll look out fer it."

"I thought it was lost, once," Horace confided, slipping his arm within his sister's, and they moved toward her car.

"It was delayed at Brest and didn't come until the next boat. I had the first outfit I bought—a small one—with me, and I pretty near lost that one, too. I was blowing a small one in my cabin on the boat one day, when the whole thing, cabin and all, took fire. The captain decided that I'd better not try it again until we got ashore, what with all the men on board. The vase turned out pretty well, though," he babbled, "lovely little thing. I'm catching on; I really am. Venice. A voluptuous dream, a little sinister. Must take you there some day." Then he squeezed her arm and fell to repeating "Dear old Narcy," as though the homely sound of the nickname on his tongue was a taste he loved and had not forgotten. A few people still lingered about the station. Some of them spoke to him and he stopped to shake their hands, and a marine private with the Second Division Indian head on his shoulder, remarked the triangle on Horace's sleeve and made a vulgar sound of derogation through his pursed lips.

"Howdy, buddy," Horace said, turning upon him his shy startled gaze.

"Evenin', General," the marine answered. He spat, not exactly at Horace's feet, and not exactly anywhere else. Narcissa clasped her brother's arm against her side.

"Do come on home and get into some decent clothes," she said in a lower tone, hurrying him along.

"Get out of uniform?" he said. "I rather fancied myself in khaki," he added, a little hurt. "You really think I am ridiculous in this?"

"Of course not," she answered immediately, squeezing his hand. "Of course not. I'm sorry I said that. You wear your uniform just as long as you want to."

"It's a good uniform," he said soberly. "I don't mean this," he said, gesturing toward the symbol on his arm. They went on. "People will realize that in about ten years, when noncombatants' hysteria has worn itself out and the individual soldiers realize that the A.E.F. didn't invent disillusion."

"What did it invent?" she asked, holding his arm against her, surrounding him with the fond, inattentive serenity of her affection.

"God knows. . . . Dear old Narcy," he said again, and they crossed the platform toward her car. "So you have dulled your palate for khaki."

"Of course not," she repeated, shaking his arm a little

as she released it. "You wear it just as long as you want to." She opened the car door. Some one called after them and they looked back and saw the porter trotting after them with Horace's hand-luggage, which he had walked off and left lying on the platform.

"Oh, Lord," he exclaimed, "I worry with it for four thousand miles, then lose it on my own doorstep. Much obliged, Sol." The porter stowed the things in the car. "That's the first outfit I got," Horace added to his sister, "and the vase I blew on shipboard. I'll show it to you when we get home."

His sister got in under the wheel. "Where are your clothes? In the box?"

"Haven't any. Had to throw most of 'em away to make room for the other things. No room for anything else." Narcissa sat and looked at him for a moment with fond exasperation. "What's the matter?" he asked innocently. "Forgot something yourself?"

"No. Get in. Aunt Sally's waiting to see you."

They drove on and mounted the shady gradual hill toward the square, and Horace looked about happily on familiar scenes. Sidings with freight cars; the platform which in the fall would be laden with cotton bales in serried rotund ranks; the town power plant, a brick building from which there came a steady, unbroken humming and about which in the spring gnarled heaven-trees swung ragged lilac bloom against the harsh ocher and Indian red of a clay cut-bank. Then a street of lesser residences, mostly new. Same tight little houses with a minimum of lawn, homes built by country-bred people and set close to the street after the country fashion; occasionally a house going up on a lot which had been vacant sixteen months ago when he went away. Then other streets opened away beneath arcades of green, shadier, with houses a little older and more imposing as they got away from the station's vicinity; and pedestrians, usually dawdling Negro boys at this hour or old men bound townward after their naps, to spend the afternoon in sober, futile absorptions.

The hill flattened away into the plateau on which the town proper had been built these hundred years and more ago, and the street became definitely urban presently with garages and small shops with merchants in shirt sleeves, and customers; the picture show with its lobby plastered with life, episodic in colored lithographed mutations. Then the square, with its unbroken low skyline of old weathered brick and fading dead names stubborn yet beneath scaling paint, and drifting Negroes in casual and careless O.D. garments worn by both sexes, and country people in occasional khaki too; and the brisker urbanites weaving among their placid chewing unhaste and among the men in tilted chairs before the stores.

The courthouse was of brick too, with stone arches rising amid elms, and among the trees the monument of the Confederate soldier stood, his musket at order arms, shading his carven eyes with his stone hand. Beneath the porticoes of the courthouse and on benches about the green, the city fathers sat and talked and drowsed, in uniform too, here and there. But it was the gray of Old Jack and Beauregard and Joe Johnston, and they sat in a grave sedateness of minor political sinecures, smoking and spitting, about checkerboards. When the weather was bad they moved inside to the circuit clerk's office.

It was here that the young men loafed also, pitching dollars or tossing baseballs back and forth or lying on the grass until the young girls in their little colored dresses and cheap nostalgic perfume should come trooping down town through the late afternoon, to the drug store. When the weather was bad these young men loafed in the drug stores or in the barbershop.

"Lots of uniforms yet," Horace remarked. "All be home by June. Have the Sartoris boys come home yet?"

"John is dead," his sister answered. "Didn't you know?"

"No," he answered quickly, with swift concern. "Poor old Bayard. Rotten luck they have. Funny family. Always going to wars, and always getting killed. And young Bayard's wife died, you wrote me."

"Yes. But he's here. He's got a racing automobile and he spends all his time tearing around the country in it. We are expecting every day to hear he's killed himself in it."

"Poor devil," Horace said, and again: "Poor old Colonel. He used to hate an automobile like a snake. Wonder what he thinks about it."

"He goes with him."

"What? Old Bayard in a motor-car?"

"Yes. Miss Jenny says it's to keep Bayard from turning

it over. But she says Colonel Sartoris doesn't know it, but that Bayard would just as soon break both their necks; that he probably will before he's done." She drove on across the square, among tethered wagons, and cars parked casually and without order. "I hate Bayard Sartoris," she said with sudden vehemence; "I hate all men." Horace looked at her quickly.

"What's the matter? What's Bayard done to you? No, that's backward: what have you done to Bayard?" But she didn't answer. She turned into another street bordered by Negro stores of one story and shaded by metal awnings beneath which Negroes lounged, skinning bananas or small florid cartons of sweet biscuits; and then a grist mill driven by a spasmodic gasoline engine. It oozed chaff and a sifting dust, motelike in the sun, and above the door a tediously hand-lettered sign: W. D. BEARDS MILL. Between it and a shuttered and silent gin draped with feathery soiled festoons of lint, an anvil clanged at the end of a short lane filled with wagons and horses and mules and shaded by mulberry trees beneath which countrymen in overalls squatted.

"He ought to have more consideration for the old fellow than that," Horace said fretfully. "Still, they've just gone through with an experience that pretty well shook the verities and the humanities, and whether they know it or not, they've got another one ahead of 'em that'll pretty well finish the business. Give him a little time. . . . But personally I can't see why he shouldn't be allowed to kill himself, if that's what he thinks he wants. Sorry for Miss Jenny, though."

"Yes," his sister agreed, quietly again. "They're worried about Colonel Sartoris' heart, too. Everybody is except him and Bayard, that is. I'm glad I have you instead of one of those Sartorises, Horry." She laid her hand quickly and lightly on his thin knee.

"Dear old Narcy," he said. Then his face clouded again. "Damn scoundrel," he said. "Well, it's their trouble. How's Aunt Sally been?"

"All right." And then: "I *am* glad you're home, Horry."

The shabby small shops were behind and now the street opened away between old shady lawns, spacious and quiet. These homes were quite old, in appearance at least, and set well back from the street and its dust, they emanated a gracious and benign peace, steadfast as a windless afternoon in a world without motion or sound. Horace looked about him and drew a long breath.

"Perhaps this is the reason for wars," he said. "The meaning of peace."

They turned into an intersecting street, narrower but more shady and even quieter, with a golden Arcadian drowse, and turned through a gate in a honeysuckle-covered fence of iron pickets. From the gate the cinder-packed drive rose in a grave curve between cedars. The cedars had been set out by an English architect of the '40's, who had built the house (with the minor concession of a veranda) in the funereal light Tudor which the young Victoria had sanctioned; and beneath and among them, even on the brightest days, lay a resinous exhilarating gloom. Mocking-birds loved them, and catbirds, and thrushes demurely mellifluous in the late afternoon; but the grass beneath them was sparse or nonexistent, and there were no insects save fireflies in the dusk.

The drive ascended to the house and curved before it and descended again to the street in an unbroken arc of cedars. Within the arc rose a lone oak, broad and huge and low; around its trunk ran a wooden bench. About this half-moon of lawn and without the arc of the drive were bridal wreath and crape myrtle bushes old as time and huge as age would make them. Big as trees they were, and in one fence corner was an astonishing clump of stunted banana palms and in the other a lantana with its clotted wounds, which Francis Benbow had brought home from Barbados in a top-hat box in '71.

About the oak and from the funereal scimitar of the drive descending, lawn flowed streetward with good sward broken by random clumps of jonquils and narcissi and gladioli. Originally the lawn was in terraces and the flowers a formal bed on the first terrace. Then Will Benbow, Horace's and Narcissa's father, had had the terraces obliterated. It was done with plows and scrapers and seeded anew with grass, and he had supposed the flower bed destroyed. But the next spring the scattered bulbs sprouted again, and now every year the lawn was stippled with bloom in yellow, white, and pink without order. A certain few young girls asked and received permission to pick some of them each spring, and neighbors' children played quietly among them and beneath the cedars.

At the top of the drive, where it curved away descending again, sat the brick doll's house in which Horace and Narcissa lived, surrounded always by that cool, faintly astringent odor of cedar trees.

It was trimmed with white and it had mullioned casements brought out from England; along the veranda eaves and above the door grew a wistaria vine like heavy tarred rope and thicker than a man's wrist. The lower casements stood open on gently billowing curtains; on the sill you expected to see a scrubbed wooden bowl, or at least an immaculate and supercilious cat. But the window sill held only a wicker work-basket from which, like a drooping poinsettia, spilled an end of patchwork in crimson and white; and in the doorway Aunt Sally, a potty little woman in a lace cap, leaned on a gold-headed ebony walking-stick.

Just as it should be, and Horace turned and looked back at his sister crossing the drive with the parcels he had forgotten again.

He banged and splashed happily in his bathroom, shouting through the door to his sister where she sat on his bed. His discarded khaki lay on a chair, holding yet through long association, in its harsh drab folds, something of that taut and delicate futility of his. On the marble-topped dresser lay the crucible and tubes of his glass-blowing outfit, the first one he had bought, and beside it the vase he had blown on shipboard—a small chaste shape in clear glass, not four inches tall, fragile as a silver lily and incomplete.

"They work in caves," he was shouting through the door, "down flights of stairs underground. You feel water seeping under your foot while you're reaching for the next step; and when you put your hand out to steady yourself against the wall, it's wet when you take it away. It feels just like blood."

"Horace!"

"Yes, magnificent. And 'way ahead you see the glow. All of a sudden the tunnel comes glimmering out of nothing; then you see the furnace, with things rising and falling before it, shutting off the light, and the walls go glimmering again. At first they're just shapeless things hunching about. Antic, with shadows on the bloody walls, red shadows. A glare, and black shapes like paper dolls weaving and rising and falling in front of it, like a magic-lantern shutter. And then a face comes out, blowing, and other faces sort of swell out of the red dark like painted balloons.

"And the things themselves. Sheerly and tragically beautiful. Like preserved flowers, you know. Macabre and inviolate; purged and purified as bronze, yet fragile as soap bubbles. Sound of pipes crystallized. Flutes and oboes, but mostly reeds. Oaten reeds. Damn it, they bloom like flowers right before your eyes. Midsummer Night's Dream to a salamander." His voice became unintelligible, soaring into measured phrases which she did not recognize, but which from the pitch of his voice she knew to be Milton's archangels in their sonorous plunging ruin.

He emerged at last, in a white shirt and serge trousers, but still borne aloft on his flaming verbal wings, and while his voice chanted in measured syllables she fetched a pair of shoes from the closet, and while she stood holding the shoes in her hands he ceased chanting and touched her face again with his hands after that fashion of a child.

At supper Aunt Sally broke into his staccato babbling: "Did you bring your Snopes back with you?" she asked. This Snopes was a young man, member of a seemingly inexhaustible family which for the last ten years had been moving to town in driblets from a small settlement known as Frenchman's Bend. Flem, the first Snopes, had appeared unheralded one day behind the counter of a small restaurant on a side street, patronized by country folk. With this foothold and like Abraham of old, he brought his blood and legal kin household by household, individual by individual, into town, and established them where they could gain money. Flem himself was presently manager of the city light and water plant, and for the following few years he was a sort of handy man to the municipal government; and three years ago, to old Bayard's profane astonishment and unconcealed annoyance, he became vice president of the Sartoris bank, where already a relation of his was a bookkeeper.

He still retained the restaurant, and the canvas tent in the rear of it, in which he and his wife and baby had passed the first few months of their residence in town; and it served as an alighting-place for incoming Snopeses, from which they spread to small third-rate businesses of various kinds—grocery stores, barbershops (there was one, an invalid of some sort, who operated a second-hand peanut roaster)—

where they multiplied and flourished. The older residents from their Jeffersonian houses and genteel stores and offices, looked on with amusement at first. But this was long since become something like consternation.

The Snopes to which Aunt Sally referred was named Montgomery Ward, and just before the draft law went into operation in '17 he applied to a recruiting officer in Memphis and was turned down for military service because of his heart. Later, to every one's surprise, particularly that of Horace Benbow's friends, he departed with Horace to a position in the Y.M.C.A. Later still, it was told of him that he had traveled all the way to Memphis on that day when he had offered for service, with a plug of chewing tobacco beneath his left armpit. But he and his patron were already departed when that story got out.

"Did you bring your Snopes back with you?" Aunt Sally asked.

"No," he answered, and his thin, nerve-sick face clouded over with a fine cold distaste. "I was very much disappointed in him. I don't even care to talk about it."

"Anybody could have told you that when you left." Aunt Sally chewed slowly and steadily above her plate. Horace brooded for a moment; his thin hand tightened slowly upon his fork.

"It's individuals like that, parasites——" he began, but his sister interrupted.

"Who cares about an old Snopes, anyway? Besides, it's too late at night to talk about the horrors of war."

Aunt Sally made a moist sound through her food, a sound of vindicated superiority.

"It's the generals they have nowadays," she said. "General Johnston or General Forrest wouldn't have took a Snopes in his army at all." Aunt Sally was no relation whatever. She lived next door but one with two maiden sisters, one younger and one older than she. She had been in and out of the house ever since Horace and Narcissa could remember, having arrogated to herself certain rights in their lives before they could walk; privileges which were never definitely expressed and of which she never availed herself, yet the mutual admission of whose existence she never permitted to fall into abeyance. She would walk into any room in the house unannounced, and she liked to talk tediously and a little tactlessly of Horace's and Narcissa's infantile ailments. It was said that she had once "made eyes" at Will Benbow, although she was a woman of thirty-four or -five when Will married; and she still spoke of him with a faintly disparaging possessiveness, and of his wife she always spoke pleasantly too. "Julia was a right sweet-natured girl," she would say.

So when Horace went off to the war Aunt Sally moved over to keep Narcissa company: no other arrangement had ever occurred to any of the three of them; the fact that Narcissa must have Aunt Sally in the house for an indefinite year or two or three appeared as unavoidable as the fact that Horace must go to the war. Aunt Sally was a good old soul, but she lived much in the past, shutting her mind with a bland finality to anything which had occurred since 1901. For her, time had gone out drawn by horses, and into her stubborn and placid vacuum the squealing of automobile brakes had never penetrated. She had a lot of the crudities which old people are entitled to. She liked the sound of her own voice and she didn't like to be alone at any time, and as she had never got accustomed to the false teeth which she had bought twelve years ago and so never touched them other than to change weekly the water in which they reposed, she ate unprettily of unprepossessing but easily malleable foods.

Narcissa reached her hand beneath the table and touched her brother's knee again. "I *am* glad you're home, Horry."

He looked at her quickly, and the cloud faded from his face as suddenly as it had come, and his spirit slipped, like a swimmer into a tideless sea, into the serene constancy of her affection again.

He was a lawyer, principally through a sense of duty to the family tradition, and though he had no particular affinity to it other than a love for printed words, for the dwelling-places of books, he contemplated returning to his musty office with a glow of . . . not eagerness, no: of deep and abiding unreluctance, almost of pleasure. The meaning of peace. Old unchanging days; unwinged perhaps, but undisastrous, too. You don't see it, feel it, save with perspective. Fireflies had not yet come, and the cedars flowed unbroken on either hand down to the street, like a curving ebony wave with rigid unbreaking crests pointed on the sky. Light fell outward from the window, across the porch and on a bed of cannas, hardy, bronzelike—none of your flowerlike fragility, theirs; and within the room Aunt Sally's quavering monotone. Narcissa was there too, beside the lamp with a book, filling the room with her still and constant presence like the odor of jasmine, watching the door through which he had passed; and Horace stood on the veranda with his cold pipe, surrounded by that cool astringency of cedars like another presence. "The meaning of peace," he said to himself once more, releasing the grave words one by one within the cool bell of silence into which he had come at last again, hearing them linger with a dying fall pure as silver and crystal struck lightly together.

"How's Belle?" he asked on the evening of his arrival.

"They're all right," his sister answered. "They have a new car."

"Dare say," Horace agreed with detachment. "The war should certainly have accomplished that much."

Aunt Sally had left them at last and tapped her slow bedward way. Horace stretched his serge legs luxuriously, and for a while he ceased striking matches to his stubborn pipe and sat watching his sister's dark head bent above the magazine upon her knees, lost from lesser and inconstant things. Her hair was smoother than any reposing wings, sweeping with burnished unrebellion to a simple knot low in her neck.

"Belle's a rotten correspondent," he said. "Like all women."

She turned a page, without looking up.

"Did you write to her often?"

"It's because they realize that letters are only good to bridge intervals between actions, like the interludes in Shakespeare's plays," he went on, oblivious. "And did you ever know a woman who read Shakespeare without skipping the interludes? Shakespeare himself knew that, so he didn't put any women in the interludes. Let the men bombast to one another's echoes while the ladies are backstage washing the dinner dishes or putting the children to bed."

"I never knew a woman that read Shakespeare at all," Narcissa corrected. "He talks too much."

Horace rose and stood above her and patted her dark head.

"O profundity," he said, "you have reduced all wisdom to a phrase, and measured your sex by the stature of a star."

"Well, they don't," she repeated, raising her face.

"No? Why don't they?" He struck another match to his pipe, watching her across his cupped hands as gravely and with poised eagerness, like a striking bird. "Your Arlens and Sabatinis talk a lot, and nobody ever had more to say and more trouble saying it than old Dreiser."

"But they have secrets," she explained. "Shakespeare doesn't have any secrets. He tells everything."

"I see. Shakespeare had no sense of discrimination and no instinct for reticence. In other words, he wasn't a gentleman," he suggested.

"Yes. . . . That's what I mean."

"And so, to be a gentleman, you must have secrets."

"Oh, you make me tired." She returned to her magazine and he sat beside her on the couch and took her hand in his and stroked it upon his cheek and upon his wild hair.

"It's like walking through a twilit garden," he said. "The flowers you know are all there, in their shifts and with their hair combed out for the night, but you know all of them. So you don't bother 'em, you just walk on and sort of stop and turn over a leaf occasionally, a leaf you hadn't noticed before; perhaps you find a violet under it, or a blue-bell or a lightning bug; perhaps only another leaf or a blade of grass. But there's always a drop of dew on it." He continued to stroke her hand upon his face. With her other hand she turned the magazine slowly on, listening to him with fond and serene detachment.

"Did you write to Belle often?" she repeated. "What did you say to her?"

"I wrote what she wanted to read. What all women want in letters. People are really entitled to half of what they think they should have."

"What did you tell her?" Narcissa persisted, turning the pages slowly, her passive hand in his, following the stroking movement of his.

"I told her I was unhappy. Perhaps I was," he added. His sister freed her hand quietly and laid it on the page. He said:

"I admire Belle. She's so cannily stupid. Once I feared her. Perhaps . . . No, I don't. I am immune to destruction: I have a magic. Which is a good sign that I am due for it, say the sages," he added. "But then, acquired wisdom is a dry thing; it has a way of crumbling to dust where a sheer and blind coursing of stupid sap is impervious." He sat without touching her, in rapt and instantaneous repose. "Not like yours, O Serene," he said, waking again. Then he fell to saying "Dear old Narcy," and again he took her hand. It did not withdraw; neither did it wholly surrender.

"I don't think you ought to say I'm dull so often, Horry," she said.

"Neither do I," he agreed. "But I must take some sort of revenge on perfection."

Later she lay in her dark room. Across the corridor Aunt Sally snored with placid regularity; in the adjoining room Horace lay while that wild, fantastic futility of his voyaged in lonely regions of its own beyond the moon, about meadows nailed with firmamented stars to the ultimate roof of things, where unicorns filled the neighing air with galloping, or grazed or lay supine in golden-hoofed repose.

Horace was seven when she was born. In the background of her sober babyhood were three beings—a lad with a wild, thin face and an unflagging aptitude for tribulation; a darkly gallant shape romantic with smuggled edibles, with strong, hard hands that smelled always of a certain thrilling carbolic soap—a being something like Omnipotence but without awesomeness; and lastly a gentle figure without legs or any inference of locomotion whatever, like a minor shrine, surrounded always by an aura of gentle melancholy and an endless and delicate manipulation of colored silken thread. This last figure was constant with gentle and melancholy unassertion; the second revolved in an orbit which bore it at regular intervals into outer space, then returned it with its strong and jolly virility into her intense world again. But the first she had made her own by a sober and maternal perseverance, and so by the time she was five or six people coerced Horace by threatening to tell Narcissa on him.

Julia Benbow died genteelly when Narcissa was seven, had been removed from their lives as a small sachet of lavender might be removed from a chest of linen, leaving a delicate lingering impalpability, and through the intense maturity of seven and eight and nine she cajoled and commanded the other two. Then Horace was in school at Sewanee and later at Oxford, from which he returned just in time to see Will Benbow join his wife among pointed cedars and carven doves and other serene marble shapes; later Horace was separated from her again by a stupid mischancing of human affairs.

But now he lay in the adjoining room, voyaging in safe and glittering regions beyond the moon, and she lay in her dark bed, quiet, peaceful, a little too peaceful to sleep.

2

He was settled soon and easily into the routine of days between his office and his home. The musty, solemn familiarity of calf-bound and never-violated volumes, on whose dusty bindings prints of Will Benbow's dead fingers might probably yet be found; a little tennis in the afternoons, usually on Harry Mitchell's fine court; cards in the evenings, also with Belle and Harry as a general thing, or again and better still, with the ever-accessible and never-failing magic of printed pages, while his sister sat across the table from him or played softly to herself in the darkened room across the hall. Occasionally men called on her; Horace received them with unfailing courtesy and a little exasperation, and departed soon to tramp about the streets or to read in bed. Dr. Alford came stiffly once or twice a week, and Horace, being somewhat of an amateur casuist, amused himself by blunting delicately feathered metaphysical darts upon the doctor's bland scientific hide for an hour or so; it would not be until then that they realized that Narcissa had not spoken a word for sixty or seventy or eighty minutes. "That's why they come to see you," Horace told her—"for an emotional mudbath."

Aunt Sally had returned home, with her bag of colored scraps and her false teeth, leaving behind her a fixed impalpability of a nebulous but definite obligation discharged at some personal sacrifice, and a faint odor of old female flesh which faded slowly from the premises, lingering yet in unexpected places so that at times Narcissa, waking and lying for a while in the darkness, in the sensuous pleasure of having Horace home again, imagined that she could hear yet, in the dark myriad silence of the house, Aunt Sally's genteel and placid snores.

At times it would be so distinct that she would pause suddenly and speak Aunt Sally's name into an empty room. And sometimes Aunt Sally replied, having availed herself again of her prerogative of coming in at any hour the notion took her, unannounced, to see how they were getting along and to complain querulously of her own household. She was old, too old to react easily to change, and it was hard for her to re-adjust herself to her sisters' ways again after her long sojourn in a household where every one gave in to her regarding all domestic affairs. At home her elder sister ran things in a capable, shrewish fashion; she and the third sister persisted in treating Aunt Sally like the child she had been sixty-five years ago, whose diet and clothing and hours must be rigor-ously and pettishly supervised.

"I can't even go to the bathroom in peace," she complained querulously. "I'm a good mind to pack up and move back over here and let 'em get along the best they can." She rocked fretfully in the chair which by unspoken agreement was never disputed her, looking about the room with bleared, pro-testing old eyes. "That nigger don't half clean up, since I left. That furniture, now . . . a damp cloth . . ."

"I wish you would take her back," Miss Sophia, the elder sister, told Narcissa. "She's got so crochety since she's been with you that there's no living with her. What's this I hear Horace has taken up—making glassware?"

His proper crucibles and retorts had arrived intact. At first he had insisted on using the cellar, clearing out the lawn mower and the garden tools and all the accumulate im-pedimenta, and walling up the windows so as to make a dungeon of it. But Narcissa had finally persuaded him upon the upper floor of the garage and here he had set up his furnace and had set fire to the building once and had had four mishaps and produced one almost perfect vase of clear amber, larger, more richly and chastely serene, which he kept always on his night table and called by his sister's name in the intervals of apostrophizing both of them impartially in his moments of rhapsody over the realization of the meaning of peace and the unblemished attainment of it, as "Thou still unravished bride of quietness."

Bareheaded, in flannels and a blue jacket with his Oxford club insignia embroidered on the pocket and his racket under his arm, Horace passed on around the house, and the court came into view with its two occupants in fluid violent action. Beneath an arcade of white pilasters and vine-hung beams, Belle, surrounded by the fragile, harmonious impedimenta of the moment, was like a butterfly. Two sat with her, in bright relief against the dark foliage of a crape myrtle not yet in flower. The other woman (the third member of the group was a young girl in white, with a grave molasses bang, and a tennis racket across her knees) spoke to him, and Belle greeted him with a sort of languid possessive desolation. Her hand was warm, prehensile, like mercury in his palm exploring softly, with delicate bones and petulant scented flesh. Her eyes were like hothouse grapes and her mouth was redly mobile, rich with discontent.

She had lost Meloney, she told him.

"Meloney saw through your gentility," Horace said. "You grew careless, probably. Your elegance is much inferior to Meloney's. You surely didn't expect to always deceive any one who can lend as much rigid discomfort to the function of eating and drinking as Meloney could, did you? Or has she got married some more?"

"She's gone in business," Belle answered fretfully. "A beauty shop. And why, I can't for the life of me see. Those things never do last, here. Can you imagine Jefferson women supporting a beauty shop, with the exception of us three? Mrs. Marders and I might; I'm sure we need it, but what use has Frankie for one?"

"What seems curious to me," the other woman said, "is where the money came from. People thought that perhaps you had given it to her, Belle."

"Since when have I been a public benefactor?" Belle said coldly. Horace grinned faintly. Mrs. Marders said:

"Now, Belle, we all know how kind-hearted you are; don't be modest."

"I said a public benefactor," Belle repeated. Horace said quickly:

"Well, Harry would swap a handmaiden for an ox, any day. At least, he can save a lot of wear and tear on his cellar, not having to counteract your tea in a lot of casual masculine tummies. I suppose there'll be no more tea out here, will there?" he added.

"Don't be silly," Belle said.

Horace said: "I realize now that it is not tennis that I

come here for, but for the incalculable amount of uncomfortable superiority I always feel when Meloney serves me tea. . . . I saw your daughter as I came along."

"She's around somewhere, I suppose," Belle agreed indifferently. "You haven't had your hair cut yet," she stated. "Why is it that men have no sense about barbers?" she said generally. The older woman watched Belle and Horace brightly, coldly, across her two flaccid chins. The young girl sat quietly in her simple, virginal white, her racket on her lap and one brown hand lying upon it like a sleeping tan puppy. She was watching Horace with sober interest but without rudeness, as children do. "They either won't go to the barber at all, or they insist on having their heads all gummed up with pomade and things," Belle added.

"Horace is a poet," the other woman said. Her flesh draped loosely from her cheekbones like rich, slightly soiled velvet; her eyes were like the eyes of an old turkey, predatory, unwinking; a little obscene. "Poets must be excused for what they do. You should remember that, Belle."

Horace bowed toward her. "Your race never fails in tact, Belle," he said. "Mrs. Marders is one of the few people I know who give the law profession its true evaluation."

"It's like any other business, I suppose," Belle said. "You're late today. Why didn't Narcissa come?"

"I mean, dubbing me a poet," Horace explained. "The law, like poetry, is the final resort of the lame, the halt, the imbecile, and the blind. I dare say Caesar invented the law business to protect himself against poets."

"You're so clever," Belle said.

The young girl spoke suddenly: "Why do you bother about what men put on their hair, Miss Belle? Mr. Mitchell's bald."

The other woman laughed, unctuously, steadily, watching them with her lidless unlaughing eyes. She watched Belle and Horace and still laughed steadily, brightly and cold. " 'Out of the mouths of babes——' " she said. The young girl glanced from one to another with her clear, sober eyes. She rose.

"I guess I'll see if I can get a set now," she said.

Horace moved also. "Let's you and I——" he began. Without turning her head Belle touched him with her hand.

"Sit down, Frankie," she commanded. "They haven't finished the game yet. You shouldn't laugh so much on an empty stomach," she told Mrs. Marders. "Do sit down, Horace."

The girl stood yet with slim and awkward grace, holding her racket. She looked at Belle a moment, then she turned her face to the court again. Horace took the chair beyond Belle. Her hand dropped hidden into his, with that secret movement; then it grew passive; it was as though she had turned a current off somewhere—like one entering a dark room in search of something, finding it and pressing the light off again.

"Don't you like poets?" Horace spoke across Belle's body. The girl did not turn her head.

"They can't dance," she answered. "I guess they are all right, though. They went to the war, the good ones did. There was one was a good tennis player, that got killed. I've seen his picture, but I don't remember his name."

"Oh, don't start talking about the war, for heaven's sake," Belle said. Her hand stirred in Horace's. "I had to listen to Harry for two years. Explaining why he couldn't go. As if I cared whether he did or not."

"He had a family to support," Mrs. Marders suggested brightly. Belle half reclined, her head against the chairback, her hidden hand moving slowly in Horace's, exploring, turning ceaselessly, like a separate volition curious but without warmth.

"Some of them were aviators," the girl continued. She stood with one little unemphatic hip braced against the table, her racket clasped beneath her arm, turning the pages of a magazine. Then she closed the magazine and again she watched the two figures leanly antic upon the court. "I danced with one of those Sartoris boys once. I was too scared to know which one it was. I wasn't anything but a baby, then."

"Were they poets?" Horace asked. "I mean, the one that got back? I know the other one, the dead one, was."

"He sure can drive that car of his," she answered, still watching the players, her straight hair (hers was the first bobbed head in town) not brown, not gold, her brief nose in profile, her brown, still hand clasping her racket. Belle stirred and freed her hand.

"Do go and play, you all," she said. "You make me nervous, both of you."

Horace rose with alacrity. "Come on, Frankie. Let's you and I take 'em on for a set."

They took the court, matched against the two youths. Horace was an exceptional player, erratic and brilliant. One who knew tennis and who had a cool head could have defeated him out of hand by letting him beat himself. But not these. His partner overreached herself frequently, but Horace managed to retrieve the point with stroking or strategy so audacious as to obscure the faultiness of his tactics.

Just as Horace made the final point Harry Mitchell appeared, in tight flannels and a white silk shirt and new ornate sport shoes that cost twenty dollars. With a new racket in a patent case and press, he stood with his squat legs and his bald bullet head and his undershot jaw of rotting teeth beside the studied picture of his wife. Presently, when he had been made to drink a cup of tea, he would gather up all the men present and lead them through the house to his bathroom and give them whisky, pouring a glass and bringing it down to Rachel in the kitchen on the way back. He would give you the shirt off of his back. He was a cotton speculator and a good one; he was ugly as sin and kind-hearted and dogmatic and talkative, and he called Belle "little mother" until she broke him of it.

Horace and his partner left the court together and approached the group.

Mrs. Marders sat now with her slack chins in a raised teacup.

The girl turned to him with polite finality. "Thanks for playing with me," she said. "I'll be better some day, I hope. We beat 'em," she said generally.

"You and the little lady gave 'em the works, hey, big boy?" Harry Mitchell said, showing his discolored teeth. His heavy prognathous jaw narrowed delicately down, then nipped abruptly off into bewildered pugnacity.

"Mr. Benbow did," the girl corrected in her clear voice. She took the chair next Belle. "I kept on letting 'em get my alley."

"Horace," Belle said, "your tea is getting cold."

It had been fetched out by the combination gardener-stableman-chauffeur, temporarily impressed in a white jacket and smelling of vulcanized rubber and ammonia. Mrs. Marders removed her chins from her cup.

"Horace plays too well," she said, "really too well. The other men can't compare with him. You were lucky to have him for a partner, child."

"Yessum," the girl agreed. "I guess he won't risk me again."

"Nonsense," Mrs. Marders rejoined. "Horace enjoyed playing with you, with a young, fresh girl. Didn't you notice it, Belle?"

Belle made no reply. She poured Horace's tea, and at this moment her daughter came across the lawn in her crocus-yellow dress. Her eyes were like stars, more soft and melting than any deer's, and she gave Horace a swift shining glance.

"Well, Titania?" he said.

Belle half turned her head, with the teapot poised above the cup, and Harry set his cup on the table and went and knelt on one knee in her path, as though he were cajoling a puppy. The child came up, still watching Horace with radiant and melting diffidence, and permitted her father to embrace her and fondle her with his short, heavy hands.

"Daddy's gal," Harry said. She submitted to having her prim little dress mussed, pleasurably but a little restively. Her eyes flew shining again.

"Don't muss your dress, sister," Belle said. The child evaded her father's hands with a prim movement. "What is it now?" Belle asked. "Why aren't you playing?"

"Nothing. I just came home." She came and stood diffidently beside her mother's chair.

"Speak to the company," Belle said. "Don't you know better than to come where older people are without speaking to them?" The little girl did so, shyly and faultlessly, greeting them in rotation, and her mother turned and pulled and patted at her straight, soft hair. "Now, go on and play. Why do you always want to come around where grown people are? You're not interested in what we're doing."

"Ah, let her stay, mother," Harry said. "She wants to watch her daddy and Horace play tennis."

"Run along, now," Belle repeated, with a final pat. "And do keep your dress clean."

"Yessum," the child agreed, and she turned obediently, giving Horace another quick shining look. He watched her and saw Rachel open the kitchen door and speak to her as she passed, saw her turn and mount the steps into the kitchen.

"What a beautifully mannered child," Mrs. Marders said.

"They're so hard to do anything with," Belle said. "She has some of her father's traits. Drink your tea, Harry."

Harry took his cup from the table and sucked its lukewarm contents into himself noisily and dutifully. "Well, big boy, how about a set? These squirrels think they can beat us."

"Frankie wants to play again," Belle interposed. "Let the child have the court for a little while, Harry." Harry was busy uncasing his racket. He paused and raised his savage undershot face and his dull kind eyes.

"No, no," the girl protested quickly. "I've had enough. I'd rather look on a while."

"Don't be silly," Belle said. "They can play any time. Make them let her play, Harry."

"Sure the little lady can play," Harry said. "Help yourself; play as long as you want to." He bent again and returned his racket to its intricate casing, twisting nuts here and there; his back was sullen, with a boy's sullenness.

"Please, Mr. Mitchell," the girl said.

"Go ahead," Harry repeated. "Here, you jelly beans, how about fixing up a set with the little lady?"

"Don't mind him," Belle told the girl. "He and Horace can play some other time. He'll have to make a fourth, anyway."

The two players stood now, politely waiting.

"Sure, Mr. Harry, come on. Me and Frankie'll play you and Joe," one of them said.

"You folks go ahead and play a set," Harry repeated. "I've got a little business to talk over with Horace. You all go ahead." He overrode their polite protests, and they took the court. Then he jerked his head significantly at Horace.

"Go on with him," Belle said. "The baby!" Without looking at him, without touching him, she enveloped him with rich and smoldering promise. Mrs. Marders sat across the table from them, curious and bright and cold with her teacup. "Unless you want to play with that silly child again."

"Silly?" Horace repeated. "She's too young to be unconsciously silly yet."

"Run along," Belle told him, "and hurry back. Mrs. Marders and I are tired of one another."

Horace followed his host into the house, followed his short, rolling gait and the bald indomitability of his head. From the kitchen as they passed little Belle's voice came steadily, recounting some astonishment of the day, with an occasional mellow ejaculation from Rachel for antistrophe. In the bathroom Harry got a bottle from a cabinet, and preceded by labored, heavy footsteps mounting, Rachel entered without knocking, bearing a pitcher of ice water.

"Why'n't y'all go'n and play, ef you wants?" she demanded. "Whut you let that 'oman treat you and that baby like she do, anyhow?" she demanded of Harry. "You ought to take and lay her out wid a stick of wood. Messin' up my kitchen at fo' o'clock in de evenin'. And you ain't helpin' none, neither," she told Horace. "Gimme a dram, Mr. Harry, please, suh."

She held her glass out and Harry filled it, and she waddled heavily from the room. They heard her descend the stairs slowly and heavily on her fallen arches. "Belle couldn't get along without Rachel," Harry said. He rinsed two glasses with ice water and set them on the lavatory. "She talks too much, like all niggers." He poured into the two tumblers, set the bottle down. "To listen to her you'd think Belle was some kind of a wild animal. A damn tiger or something. But Belle and I understand each other. You've got to make allowances for women, anyhow. Different from men. Born contrary; complain when you don't please 'em and complain when you do." He added a little water to his glass; then he said, with astonishing irrelevance: "I'd kill the man that tried to wreck my home like I would a damn snake. Well, let's take one, big boy."

Presently he sloshed water into his empty glass and gulped that, too, and he reverted to his former grievance.

"Can't get to play on my own damn court," he said. "Belle gets all these damn people here every day. What I want is a court where I can come home from work and get in a couple of fast sets every afternoon. Appetizer before supper. But every damn day I get home from work and find a bunch of young girls and jelly beans, using it like it was a public court in a damn park." Horace drank his more moderately. Harry lit a cigarette and threw the match on to the floor and swung his leg across the lavatory. "I reckon I'll have to build another court for my own use and put a hog-

wire fence around it with a Yale lock, so Belle can't give
picnics on it. There's plenty of room down there by the lot
fence. No trees, too. Put it out in the damn sun, and I
reckon Belle'll let me use it now and then. Well, suppose we
get on back."

He led the way through his bedroom and stopped to show
Horace a new repeating rifle he had just bought and to press
upon him a package of cigarettes which he imported from
South America, and they descended and emerged into afternoon become later. The sun was level now across the court
where three players leaped and sped with soft quick slap-
pings of rubber soles, following the fleeting impact of the
ball. Mrs. Marders sat yet with her ceaseless chins, although
she was speaking of departure when they came up. Belle
turned her head against the chair-back, but Harry led Horace
on.

"We're going to look over a location for a tennis court.
I think I'll take up tennis, myself," he told Mrs. Marders
with heavy irony. It was later still when they returned. Mrs.
Marders was gone and Belle sat alone, with a magazine. A
youth in a battered Ford had called for the girl Frankie, but
another young man had dropped in, and when Horace and
Harry came up the three youths clamored politely for Harry
to join them.

"Take Horace here," Harry said, obviously pleased. "He'll
give you a run for your money." But Horace demurred and
the three continued to importune Harry.

"Lemme get my racket, then," he said finally, and Horace
followed the heavy scuttling of his backside across the court.
Belle looked briefly up.

"Did you find a place?"

"Yes," Harry answered, uncasing his racket again; "where
I can play myself, sometimes. A place too far from the
street for everybody that comes along to see it and stop."
But Belle was reading again. Harry unscrewed his racket
press and removed it.

"I'll go in one set; then you and I can get in a fast one
before dark," he told Horace.

"Yes," Horace agreed. He sat down and watched Harry
stride heavily on to the court and take his position, watched
the first serve. Then Belle's magazine rustled and slapped on
to the table.

"Come," she said, rising. Horace rose, and Belle preceded him and they crossed the lawn and entered the house. Rachel moved about in the kitchen, and they went on through the house, where all noises were remote and the furniture gleamed peacefully indistinct in the dying evening light. Belle slid her hand into his, clutching his hand against her silken thigh, and led him on through a dusky passage and into her music room. This room was quiet too and empty and she stopped against him half turning, and they kissed. But she freed her mouth presently and moved again, and he drew the piano bench out and they sat on opposite sides of it and kissed again. "You haven't told me you love me," Belle said, touching his face with her finger tips, and the fine devastation of his hair, "not in a long time."

"Not since yesterday," Horace agreed, but he told her, she leaning her breast against him and listening with a sort of rapt, voluptuous inattention, like a great, still cat; and when he had done and sat touching her face and her hair with his delicate wild hands, she removed her breast and opened the piano and touched the keys. Saccharine melodies she played, from memory and in the current mode, that you might hear on any vaudeville stage, and with a shallow skill, a feeling for their oversweet nuances. They sat thus for some time while the light faded, Belle in another temporary vacuum of discontent, building for herself a world in which she moved romantically, finely, and a little tragically, with Horace sitting beside her and watching both Belle in her self-imposed and tragic rôle, and himself performing his part like the old actor whose hair is thin and whose profile is escaping him via his chin, but who can play to any cue at a moment's notice while the younger men chew their bitter thumbs in the wings.

Presently the rapid heavy concussions of Harry's feet thumped again on the stairs mounting, and the harsh wordless uproar of his voice as he led some one else in the back way and up to his bathroom. Belle stopped her hands and leaned against him and kissed him again, clinging. "This is intolerable," she said, freeing her mouth with a movement of her head. For a moment she resisted against his arm, then her hands crashed discordantly upon the keys and slid through Horace's hair and down his cheeks tightening. She freed her mouth again. "Now, sit over there."

He obeyed; she on the piano bench was in half shadow.
Twilight was almost accomplished; only the line of her bent
head and her back, tragic and still, making him feel young
again. We do turn corners upon ourselves, like suspicious old
ladies spying on servants, Horace thought. No, like boys
trying to head off a parade. "There's always divorce," he said.

"To marry again?" Her hands trailed off into chords;
merged, faded again into a minor in one hand. Overhead
Harry moved with his heavy staccato tread, shaking the
house. "You'd make a rotten husband."

"I won't as long as I'm not married," Horace answered.

She said, "Come here," and he went to her, and in the
dusk she was again tragic and young and familiar with a
haunting sense of loss, and he knew the sad fecundity of the
world and time's hopeful unillusion that fools itself. "I want
to have your child, Horace," she said, and then her own
child came up the hall and stood diffidently in the door.

For a moment Belle was an animal awkward and mad
with fear. She surged away from him in a mad, spurning
movement; her hands crashed on the keys as she controlled
her instinctive violent escape that left in the dusk a mindless
protective antagonism, pervading, in steady cumulate waves,
directed at Horace as well.

"Come in, Titania," Horace said.

The little girl stood diffidently in silhouette. Belle's voice
was sharp with relief. "Well, what do you want? Sit over
there," she hissed at Horace. "What do you want, Belle?"
Horace drew away a little, but without rising.

"I've got a new story to tell you, soon," he said. But little
Belle stood yet, as though she had not heard, and her mother
said:

"Go on and play, Belle. Why did you come in the house?
It isn't suppertime yet."

"Everybody's gone home," she answered. "I haven't got
anybody to play with."

"Go to the kitchen and talk to Rachel, then," Belle said.
She struck the keys again, harshly. "You worry me to death,
hanging around the house." The little girl stood for a moment longer; then she turned obediently and went away.
"Sit over there," Belle repeated. Horace resumed his chair
and Belle played again, loudly and swiftly, with cold hysterical skill. Overhead Harry thumped again across the floor;

they descended the stairs. Harry was still talking; the voices passed on toward the rear, ceased. Belle continued to play; still about him in the darkening room that blind protective antagonism, like a muscular contraction that remains after the impulse of fright has died. Without turning her head she said, "Are you going to stay to supper?"

He was not, he answered, waking suddenly. She did not rise with him, did not turn her head, and he let himself out the front door and into the late spring twilight, where was already a faint star above the windless trees. On the drive just without the garage, Harry's new car stood. At the moment he was doing something to the engine of it while the house-yard-stable-boy held a patent trouble-lamp above the beetling crag of his head, and his daughter and Rachel, holding tools or detached sections of the car's vitals, leaned their intent dissimilar faces across his bent back and into the soft bluish glare of the light. Horace went on homeward. Twilight, evening, came swiftly. Before he reached the corner where he turned, the street lamps sputtered and failed, then glared above the intersections, beneath the arching trees.

3

It was the evening of little Belle's recital, the climacteric of her musical year. During the whole evening Belle had not looked at him, had said no word to him, even when, in the departing crush at the door and while Harry was trying to persuade him upstairs for a night-cap, he felt her beside him for an instant, smelled the heavy scent she used. But she said no word to him even then, and he put Harry aside at last and the door closed on little Belle and on Harry's glazed dome, and Horace turned into the darkness and found that Narcissa hadn't waited. She was halfway to the street.

"If you're going my way, I'll walk along with you," he called to her. She made no reply, neither did she slacken her pace nor increase it when he joined her.

"Why is it," he began, "that grown people will go to so much trouble to make children do ridiculous things, do you suppose? Belle had a houseful of people she doesn't care anything about and most of whom don't approve of her, and kept little Belle up three hours past her bedtime; and the result is, Harry's about half tight, and Belle is in a bad humor, and little Belle is too excited to go to sleep, and you and I wish we were home and are sorry we didn't stay there."

"Why do you go there, then?" Narcissa asked. Horace was suddenly stilled. They walked on through the darkness, toward the next street light. Against it branches hung like black coral in a yellow sea.

"Oh," Horace said. Then: "I saw that old cat talking with you."

"Why do you call Mrs. Marders an old cat? Because she told me something that concerns me and that everybody else seems to know already?"

"So that's who told you, is it? I wondered. . . ." He slid his arm within her unresponsive one. "Dear old Narcy." They passed through the dappled shadows beneath the light, went on into darkness again.

"Is it true?" she asked.

"You forget that lying is a struggle for survival," he said, "little puny man's way of dragging circumstance about to fit his preconception of himself as a figure in the world. Revenge on the sinister gods."

"Is it true?" she persisted. They walked on, arm in arm, she gravely insistent and waiting, he shaping and discarding phrases in his mind, finding time to be amused at his own fantastic impotence in the presence of her constancy.

"People don't usually lie about things that don't concern them," he answered wearily. "They are impervious to the world, even if they aren't to life. Not when the actuality is so much more diverting than their imaginings could be," he added. She freed her arm with grave finality.

"Narcy——"

"Don't," she said. "Don't call me that." The next corner, beneath the next light, was theirs; they would turn there. Above the arched canyon of the street the sinister gods stared down with pale unwinking eyes. Horace thrust his hands into his jacket and for a space he was stilled again while his fingers learned the unfamiliar object they had found in his pocket. Then he drew it forth: a sheet of heavy note-paper, folded twice and impregnated with a fading heavy scent. A familiar scent, yet baffling for the moment, like a face watching him from an arras. He knew the face would emerge in a moment, but as he held the note in his fingers and sought the face through the corridors of his present distraction, his sister spoke suddenly and hard at his side.

"You've got the smell of her all over you. Oh, Horry, she's dirty!"

"I know," he answered unhappily. "I know."

It was now well into June, and the scent of Miss Jenny's transplanted jasmine drifted steadily into the house and filled it with constant cumulate waves like a fading resonance of viols. The earlier flowers were gone, and the birds had finished eating the strawberries and now sat about the fig bushes all day, waiting for them to ripen; zinnia and delphinium bloomed without any assistance from Isom, who, since Caspey had more or less returned to normalcy and laying-by time was yet a while away, might be found on the shady side of the privet hedge along the garden fence, trimming the leaves one by one from a single twig with a pair of mule shears until Miss Jenny returned to the house; whereupon he retreated himself and lay on the creek-bank for the rest of the afternoon, his hat over his eyes and a cane fishing-pole propped between his toes.

Simon pottered querulously about the place. His linen duster and top hat gathered chaff and dust on the nail in the harness room, and the horses waxed fat and lazy and insolent in the pasture. The duster and hat came down from the nail and the horses were harnessed to the carriage but once a week now—on Sundays, to drive in to town to church. Miss Jenny said she was too far along to jeopardize salvation by driving to church at fifty miles an hour; that she had as many sins as her ordinary behavior could take care of, particularly as she had old Bayard's soul to get into heaven somehow also, what with him and young Bayard tearing around the country every afternoon at the imminent risk of their necks. About young Bayard's soul Miss Jenny did not alarm herself at all: he had no soul.

Meanwhile he rode about the farm and harried the Negro tenants in his cold fashion, and in two-dollar khaki breeches and a pair of field boots that had cost fourteen guineas he tinkered with farming machinery and with the tractor he had persuaded old Bayard to buy: for the time being he had become almost civilized again. He went to town only occasionally now, and often on horseback, and all in all his days had become so usefully innocuous that both his aunt and his grandfather were growing a little nervously anticipatory.

"Mark my words," Miss Jenny told Narcissa on the day she drove out again, "he's storing up devilment that's going to burst loose all at once, some day. And then there'll be hell to pay. Lord knows what it'll be—maybe he and Isom will take his car and that tractor and hold a steeple-chase with 'em. . . . What did you come out for? Got another letter?"

"I've got several more," Narcissa answered lightly. "I'm saving them until I get enough for a book; then I'll bring them all out for you to read." Miss Jenny sat opposite her, erect as a crack guardsman, with that cold briskness of hers that caused agents and strangers to stumble through their errands with premonitions of failure before they began. The guest sat motionless, her limp straw hat on her knees. "I just came to see you," she added, and for a moment her face held such grave and still despair that Miss Jenny sat more erect yet and stared at her guest with her piercing gray eyes.

"Why, what is it, child? Did the man walk into your house?"

"No, no." The look was gone, but still Miss Jenny watched her with those keen old eyes that seemed to see so much more than you thought—or wished. "Shall I play a while? It's been a long time, hasn't it?"

"Well," Miss Jenny agreed, "if you want to."

There was dust on the piano. Narcissa opened it with a fine gesture. "If you'll let me get a cloth——"

"Here, lemme dust it," Miss Jenny said, and she caught up her skirt by the hem and mopped the keyboard violently. "There, that'll do." Then she drew her chair from behind the instrument and seated herself. She still watched the other's profile with speculation and a little curiosity, but presently the old tunes stirred her memory again, and in a while her eyes softened, and the other and the trouble that had shown momentarily in her face were lost in Miss Jenny's own vanquished and abiding dead days, and it was some time before she realized that Narcissa was weeping quietly while she played.

Miss Jenny leaned forward and touched her arm. "Now, you tell me what it is," she commanded. And Narcissa told her in her grave contralto, still weeping quietly.

"Humph," Miss Jenny said. "That's to be expected of a man that hasn't any more to do than Horace has. I don't see why you are so upset over it."

"But that woman," Narcissa wailed suddenly, like a little girl, burying her face in her hands. "She's so dirty!"

Miss Jenny dug a man's handkerchief from the pocket of her skirt and gave it to the other. "What do you mean?" she asked. "Don't she wash often enough?"

"Not that way. I m-mean she's—she's——" Narcissa turned suddenly and laid her head on the piano.

"Oh," Miss Jenny said. "All women are, if that's what you mean." She sat stiffly indomitable, contemplating the other's shrinking shoulders. "Hmph," she said again, "Horace has spent so much time being educated that he never has learned anything. . . . Why didn't you break it up in time? Didn't you see it coming?"

The other wept more quietly now. She sat up and dried her eyes on Miss Jenny's handkerchief. "It started before he went away. Don't you remember?"

"That's so. I do sort of remember a lot of women's gabble. Who told you about it, anyway? Horace?"

"Mrs. Marders did. And then Horace did. But I never thought that he'd—— I never thought——" Again her head dropped to the piano, hidden in her arms. "I wouldn't have treated Horace that way," she wailed.

"Sarah Marders, was it? I might have known. . . . I admire strong character, even if it is bad," Miss Jenny stated. "Well, crying won't help any." She rose briskly. "We'll think what to do about it. Only I'd let him go ahead: it'll do him good if she'll just turn around and make a doormat of him. . . . Too bad Harry hasn't got the spunk to . . . But I reckon he'll be glad; I know I would. . . . There, there," she said, at the other's movement of alarm, "I don't reckon Harry'll hurt him. Dry your face, now. You better go to the bathroom and fix up. Bayard'll be coming in soon, and you don't want him to see you've been crying, you know." Narcissa glanced swiftly at the door and dabbed at her face with Miss Jenny's handkerchief.

Then he would seek her through the house, and cross the drive and descend the lawn in the sunny afternoon to where she sat in the white dresses he loved beneath the oak, into which a mocking-bird came each afternoon to sing, bringing her the result of his latest venture in glass-blowing. He had five now, in different colors and all nearly perfect, and each of them had a name. And as he finished them and while they were scarce cooled, he must bring them across the lawn to where she sat with a book or with a startled caller perhaps—in his stained disheveled clothes and his sooty hands in which the vase lay demure and fragile as a bubble, and with his face blackened too with smoke and a little mad, passionate and fine and austere.

4

For a time the earth held him in a hiatus that might have been called contentment. He was up at sunrise, planting things in the ground and watching them grow and tending them; he cursed and harried niggers and mules into motion and kept them there, and put the grist mill into running shape and taught Caspey to drive the tractor, and came in at mealtimes and at night smelling of machine oil and of stables and of the earth, and went to bed with grateful muscles and with the sober rhythms of the earth in his body and so to sleep. But he still waked at times in the peaceful darkness of his room and without previous warning, tense and sweating with old terror. Then, momentarily, the world was laid away and he was a trapped beast in the high blue, mad for life, trapped in the very cunning fabric that had betrayed him who had dared chance too much, and he thought again if, when the bullet found you, you could only crash upward, burst; anything but earth. Not death, no: it was the crash you had to live through so many times before you struck that filled your throat with vomit.

But his days were filled, at least, and he discovered pride again. Nowadays he drove the car into town to fetch his grandfather from habit alone, and though he still considered forty-five miles an hour merely cruising speed, he no longer

took cold and fiendish pleasure in turning curves on two
wheels or detaching mules from wagons by striking the whif-
fletrees with his bumper in passing. Old Bayard still insisted
on riding with him when he must ride, but with freer breath,
and once he aired to Miss Jenny his growing belief that at
last young Bayard had outworn his seeking for violent destruction.

Miss Jenny, being a true optimist—that is, expecting the
worst at all times and so being daily agreeably surprised—
promptly disillusioned him. Meanwhile she made young Bayard drink plenty of milk and otherwise superintended his
diet and hours in her martinetish way, and at times she entered his room at night and sat for a while beside the bed
where he slept.

Nevertheless young Bayard improved in his ways. Without
being aware of the progress of it he had become submerged
in a monotony of days, had been snared by a rhythm of
activities repeated and repeated until his muscles grew so familiar with them as to get his body through the days without
assistance from him at all. He had been so neatly tricked by
earth, that ancient Delilah, that he was not aware that his
locks were shorn, was not aware that Miss Jenny and old
Bayard were wondering how long it would be before they
grew out again. "He needs a wife," was Miss Jenny's
thought; "then maybe he'll stay sheared. A young person
to worry with him," she said to herself; "Bayard's too old,
and I've got too much to do to worry with the long devil."

He saw Narcissa about the house now and then, sometimes at the table these days, and he still felt her shrinking
and her distaste, and at times Miss Jenny sat watching
the two of them with a sort of speculation and an exasperation with their seeming obliviousness of one another.
"He treats her like a dog would treat a cut-glass pitcher,
and she looks at him like a cut-glass pitcher would look at a
dog," she told herself.

Then sowing-time was over and it was summer, and he
found himself with nothing to do. It was like coming dazed
out of sleep, out of the warm, sunny valleys where people
lived into a region where cold peaks of savage despair stood
bleakly above the lost valleys, among black and savage stars.

The road descended in a quiet red curve between pines

through which the hot July winds swelled with a long sound like a far-away passing of trains, descended to a mass of lighter green of willows, where a creek ran beneath a stone bridge. At the top of the grade the scrubby, rabbitlike mules stopped, and the younger Negro got down and lifted a gnawed white-oak sapling from the wagon and locked the off rear wheel by wedging the pole between the warped, wire-bound spokes of it and across the axletree. Then he climbed back into the crazy wagon, where the other Negro sat motionless with the rope-spliced reins in his hand and his head tilted creekward. "Whut 'uz dat?" he said.

"Whut wuz whut?" the other asked. His father sat in his attitude of arrested attention, and the young Negro listened also. But there was no further sound save the long sough of the wind among the sober pines and the liquid whistling of a quail somewhere among the green fastnesses of them. "Whut you hear, pappy?" he repeated.

"Somethin' busted down dar. Tree fell, maybe." He jerked the reins. "Hwup, mules." The mules flapped their jack-rabbit ears and lurched the wagon into motion and they descended among cool, dappled shadows, on the jarring scrape of the locked wheel that left behind it a glazed bluish ribbon in the soft red dust. At the foot of the hill the road crossed the bridge and went on mounting again; beneath the bridge the creek rippled and flashed brownly among willows, and beside the bridge and bottom up in the water, a motor-car lay. Its front wheels were still spinning and the engine ran at idling speed, trailing a faint shimmer of exhaust. The older Negro drove on to the bridge and stopped, and the two of them sat and stared statically down upon the car's long belly. The young Negro spoke suddenly.

"Dar he is! He in de water under hit. I kin see his foots stickin' out."

"He liable ter drown, dar," the other said, with interest and disapproval, and they descended from the wagon. The young Negro slid down the creek-bank. The other wrapped the reins deliberately about one of the stakes that held the bed on the frame and thrust his peeled hickory goad beneath the seat, and went around and dragged the pole free of the locked wheel and put it in the wagon. Then he also slid gingerly down the bank to where his son squatted, peering at Bayard's submerged legs.

"Don't you git too clost ter dat thing, boy," he commanded. "Hit mought blow up. Don't you hear it still grindin' in dar?"

"We got to git dat man out," the young one replied. "He gwine drown."

"Don't you tech 'im. White folks be sayin' we done it. We gwine wait right here 'twell some white man comes erlong."

"He'll drown 'fo' dat," the other said, "layin' in dat water." He was barefoot, and he stepped into the water and stood again with brown flashing wings of water stemming about his lean black calves.

"You, John Henry!" his father said. "You come 'way fum dat thing."

"We got to git 'im outen dar," the boy repeated, and the one in the water and the other on the bank, they wrangled amicably while the water rippled about Bayard's boot toes. Then the young Negro approached warily and caught Bayard's leg and tugged at it. The body responded, shifted, stopped again, and grunting querulously, the older Negro sat and removed his shoes and stepped into the water also. "He hung again," John Henry said, squatting in the water with his arms beneath the car. "He hung under de guidin'-wheel. His haid ain't quite under water, dough. Lemme git de pole."

He mounted the bank and got the sapling from the wagon and returned and joined his father where the other stood in sober, curious disapproval above Bayard's legs, and with the pole they lifted the car enough to drag Bayard out. They lifted him on to the bank and he sprawled there in the sun, with his calm, wet face and his matted hair, while water drained out of his boots, and they stood above him on alternate legs and wrung out their overalls.

"Hit's Cunnel Sartoris's boy, ain't it?" the elder said at last, and he lowered himself stiffly to the sand, groaning and grunting, and donned his shoes.

"Yessuh," the other answered. "Is he daid, pappy?"

"Co'se he is," the elder answered pettishly. "Atter dat otto'bile jumped offen dat bridge wid 'im en den trompled 'im in de creek? Whut you reckon he is ef he ain't daid? And whut you gwine say when de law axes you how come you de onliest one dat foun' 'im daid? Tell me dat."

"Tell 'um you holp me."

"Hit ain't none of my business. I never run dat thing

offen dat bridge. Listen at it dar, mumblin' and grindin' yit. You git on 'fo' hit blows up."

"We better git 'im into town," John Henry said. "Dey mought not nobody else be comin' 'long today." He stooped and lifted Bayard's shoulders and tugged him to a sitting position. "He'p me git 'im up de bank, pappy."

"Hit ain't none o' my business," the other repeated. But he stooped and picked up Bayard's legs and they lifted him, and he groaned without waking.

"Dar, now," John Henry exclaimed. "Hear dat? He ain't daid." But he might well have been, with his long, inert body and his head wrung excruciatingly against John Henry's shoulder. They shifted their grip and turned toward the road. "Hah!" John Henry exclaimed. "Le's go!"

They struggled up the shaling bank with him and on to the road, where the elder let his end of the burden slip to the ground. "Whuf." He expelled his breath sharply. "He heavy ez a flou' bar'l."

"Come on, pappy," John Henry said, "le's git 'im in de waggin." The other stooped again, and they raised Bayard with dust caked redly on his wet thighs and heaved him by grunting stages into the wagon. "He look like a daid man," John Henry added, "and he sho' do ack like one. I'll ride back here wid 'im and keep his haid fum bumpin'."

"Git dat brakin' pole you lef' in de creek," his father ordered, and John Henry descended and retrieved the sapling and got in the wagon again and lifted Bayard's head on to his knees. His father unwrapped the reins and mounted to the sagging seat and picked up his peeled wand.

"I don't like dis kin' o' traffickin'," he repeated. "Hwup, mules." The mules lurched the wagon into motion once more, and they went on. Behind them the car lay on its back in the creek, its engine still muttering at idling speed.

Its owner lay in the springless wagon, lax and inert with the jolting of it. Thus for some miles, while John Henry held his battered straw hat between the white man's face and the sun. Then the jolting penetrated into that region where Bayard lay, and he groaned again.

"Drive slower, pappy," John Henry said. "De joltin's wakin' 'im up."

"I can't help dat," the elder replied; "I never run dat

otto'bile offen de bridge. I got to git on into town en git on back home. Git on dar, mules."

John Henry made to ease him to the jolting, and Bayard groaned again and raised his hand to his chest. He moved and opened his eyes. But he closed them immediately against the sun, and he lay with his head on John Henry's knees, cursing. Then he moved again, trying to sit up. John Henry held him down, and he opened his eyes again, struggling.

"Let go, God damn you!" he said. "I'm hurt."

"Yessuh, Captain, ef you'll jes' lay still——"

Bayard heaved himself violently, clutching his side; his teeth glared between his drawn lips and he gripped John Henry's shoulder with a clutch like steel hooks. "Stop!" he shouted, glaring wildly at the back of the older Negro's head. "Stop him; make him stop! He's driving my damn ribs right through me." He cursed again, trying to get on to his knees, gripping John Henry's shoulder, clutching his side with the other hand. The older Negro turned and looked back at him. "Hit him with something!" Bayard shouted. "Make him stop. I'm hurt, God damn it!"

The wagon stopped. Bayard was now on all fours, his head hanging and swaying from side to side like a wounded beast's. The two Negroes watched him quietly, and still clutching his side, he moved and essayed to climb out of the wagon. John Henry jumped down and helped him, and he got slowly out and leaned against the wheel, with his sweating, bloodless face and his clenched grin.

"Git back into de waggin, Captain," John Henry said, "and le's git to town to de doctor."

The color seemed to have drained from his eyes too. He leaned against the wagon, moistening his lips with his tongue. He moved again and sat down at the roadside, fumbling at the buttons of his shirt. The two Negroes watched him.

"Got a knife, son?" he asked.

"Yessuh." John Henry produced it, and by Bayard's direction he slit the shirt off. Then with the Negro's help Bayard bound it tightly about his body. He got to his feet.

"Got a cigarette?"

John Henry had not. "Pappy got some chewin'-terbacker," he suggested.

"Gimme a chew, then." They gave him a chew and helped him back into the wagon and on to the seat. The other

Negro took up the lines. They jingled and rattled interminably on in the red dust, from shadow to sunlight, uphill and down. Bayard clutched his chest with his arms and chewed and cursed steadily. On and on, and at every jolt, with every breath, his broken ribs stabbed and probed into his flesh; on and on from shadow to sunlight and into shadow again.

A final hill, and the road emerged from the shade and crossed the flat, treeless valley and joined the highway. Here they stopped, the sun blazing downward on his naked shoulders and bare head, while he and the old Negro wrangled as to whether they should take Bayard home or not. Bayard raged and swore, but the other was querulously adamant, whereupon Bayard took the reins from his hand and swung the mules up the valley and with the end of the reins lashed the astonished creatures into mad motion.

This last mile was the worst of all. On all sides of them cultivated fields spread away to the shimmering hills. Earth was saturated with heat and broken and turned and saturated again and drunken with it, exuding heat like an alcoholic's breath. The trees along the road were sparse and but half grown, and the mules slowed to a maddening walk in their own dust. He surrendered the reins again, and in a red doze he clung to the seat, conscious only of dreadful thirst, knowing that he was becoming lightheaded. The Negroes too realized that he was going out of his head, and the young one removed his frayed hat and Bayard put it on.

The mules with their comical, overlarge ears assumed fantastic shapes, merged into other shapes without significance; shifted and merged again. At times it seemed that they were traveling backward, that they would crawl terrifically past the same tree or telephone pole time after time; and it seemed to him that the three of them and the rattling wagon and the two beasts were caught in a senseless treadmill: a motion without progress, forever and to no escape.

But at last and without his being aware of it, the wagon turned in between the iron gates. Shadow fell upon his naked shoulders and he opened his eyes, and his home swam and floated in a pale mirage. The jolting stopped and the two Negroes helped him down and the young one followed him to the steps, holding his arm. But he flung him off and mounted and crossed the veranda. In the hallway, after the outer glare, he could see nothing for a moment, and he stood swaying and a little nauseated, blinking. Then Simon's eyeballs rolled out of the obscurity.

"Whut in de Lawd's name," Simon said, "is you been into now?"

"Simon?" he said. He swayed, staggered a little for balance, and blundered into something. "Simon."

Simon moved quickly and touched him. "I kep' tellin' you dat car 'uz gwine kill you; I kep' tellin' you!" Simon slid his arm around Bayard and led him on toward the stairs. But he would not turn here, and they went on down the hall and Simon helped him into the office and he stopped, leaning on a chair.

"Keys," he said thickly, "Aunt Jenny. Get drink."

"Miss Jenny done gone to town wid Miss Benbow," Simon answered. "Dey ain't nobody here, ain't nobody here a-tall 'cep' de niggers. I kep' tellin' you!" he moaned again, pawing at Bayard. "Dey ain't no blood, dough. Come to de sofa and lay down, Mist' Bayard."

Bayard moved again. Simon supported him and he lurched around the chair and slumped into it, clutching his chest. "Dey ain't no blood," Simon babbled.

"Keys," Bayard repeated. "Get the keys."

"Yessuh, I'll git 'um." But he continued to flap his distracted hands about Bayard until Bayard swore at him and flung him violently off. Still moaning "Dey ain't no blood," Simon turned and scuttled from the room. Bayard sat forward, clutching his chest. He heard Simon mount the stairs and cross the floor overhead. Then he was back, and Bayard watched him open the desk and extract the silver-stoppered decanter. He set it down and scuttled out again and returned with a glass, to find Bayard beside the desk, drinking from the decanter. Simon helped him back to the chair and poured him a drink into the glass. Then he fetched him a cigarette and hovered futilely and distractedly about him. "Lemme git de doctuh, Mist' Bayard."

"No. Gimme another drink."

Simon obeyed. "Dat's three already. Lemme go git Miss Jenny en de doctuh, Mist' Bayard, please, suh."

"No. Leave me alone. Get out of here."

He drank that one. The nausea, the mirage shapes, were gone, and he felt better. At every breath his side stabbed

him with hot needles, so he was careful to breathe shallowly. If he could only remember that . . . Yes, he felt much
better; so he rose carefully and went to the desk and had
another drink. Yes, that was the stuff for a wound, like
Suratt had said. Like that time he got that tracer in his
belly and nothing would stay on his stomach except gin-
and-milk. And this, this wasn't anything: just a few caved
slats. Patch up his fuselage with a little piano wire in ten
minutes. Not like Johnny. They were all going right into
his thighs. Damn butcher wouldn't even raise his sights a
little. He must remember to breathe shallowly.

He crossed the room slowly. Simon flitted in the dim
hall before him, and he mounted the stairs slowly, holding
to the rail, while Simon flapped his hands and watched him.
He entered his room, the room that had been his and John's,
and he stood for a while against the wall until he could
breathe shallowly again. Then he crossed to the closet and
opened it, and kneeling carefully, with his hand against his
side, he opened the chest which was there.

There was not much in it: a garment, a small leather-
bound book, a shotgun shell to which was attached by a
bit of wire a withered bear's paw. It was John's first bear,
and the shell with which he had killed it in the river bottom near MacCallum's when he was twelve years old. The
book was a New Testament; on the flyleaf in faded brown,
"To my son, John, on his seventh birthday, March 16, 1900,
from his Mother." He had one exactly like it; that was the
year Grandfather had arranged for the morning local freight
to stop and pick them up and take them in to town to start
school. The garment was a canvas hunting-coat, stained and
splotched with what had once been blood, and scuffed and
torn by briers and smelling yet faintly of saltpeter.

Still kneeling, he lifted the objects out one by one and
laid them on the floor. He picked up the coat again, and
its fading, stale acridity drifted in his nostrils with an intimation of life and of warmth. "Johnny," he whispered,
"Johnny." Suddenly he raised the garment toward his face
but halted it as sharply, and with the coat half raised he
looked swiftly over his shoulder. But immediately he recovered himself and turned his head and lifted the garment
and laid his face against it, defiantly and deliberately, and
knelt so for a time.

Then he rose and gathered up the book and the trophy and the coat and crossed to his chest of drawers and took from it a photograph. It was a picture of John's Princeton eating-club group, and he gathered this also under his arm and descended the stairs and passed on out the back door. As he emerged, Simon was just crossing the yard with the carriage, and as he passed the kitchen Elnora was crooning one of her mellow, endless songs.

Behind the smoke-house squatted the black pot and the wooden tubs where Elnora did her washing in fair weather. She had been washing today; the clothesline swung with its damp, limp burden, and beneath the pot smoke yet curled from the soft ashes. He thrust the pot over with his foot and rolled it aside, and from the woodshed he fetched an armful of rich pine and laid it on the ashes. Soon a blaze, pale in the sunny air, and when the wood was burning strongly he laid the coat and the Testament and the trophy and the photograph on the flames and prodded and turned them until they were consumed. In the kitchen Elnora crooned mellowly as she labored. Her voice came rich and plaintful and sad along the sunny reaches of the air. He must remember to breathe shallowly.

Simon drove rapidly to town, but he had been forestalled. The two Negroes had told a merchant about finding Bayard on the roadside, and the news had reached the bank, and old Bayard sent for Dr. Peabody. But Dr. Peabody had gone fishing, so he took Dr. Alford instead, and the two of them in Dr. Alford's car passed Simon just on the edge of town. He turned about and followed them, but when he arrived home they had young Bayard anesthetized and temporarily incapable of further harm; and when Miss Jenny and Narcissa drove unsuspectingly up the drive an hour later, he was bandaged and conscious again. They had not heard of it. Miss Jenny did not recognize Dr. Alford's car standing in the drive, but she had one look at the strange motor.

"That fool has killed himself at last," she said, and she got out of Narcissa's machine and sailed into the house and up the stairs.

Bayard lay white and still and a little sheepish in his bed. Old Bayard and the doctor were just leaving, and Miss Jenny waited until they were out of the room. Then she raged and stormed at him and stroked his hair while Simon bobbed and mowed in the corner between bed and wall. "Dasso, Miss Jenny, dasso! I kep' a-tellin' 'im!"

She left him then and descended to the veranda where Dr. Alford stood in impeccable departure. Old Bayard sat in the car waiting for him, and on Miss Jenny's appearance he became his stiff self again and completed his departing, and he and old Bayard drove away.

Miss Jenny also looked up and down the veranda, then into the hall. "Where—" she said; then she called, "Narcissa." A reply. "Where are you?" she added. The reply came again, and Miss Jenny reëntered the house and saw Narcissa's white dress in the gloom where she sat on the piano bench. "He's awake," Miss Jenny said. "You can come up and see him." The other rose and turned her face to the light. "Why, what's the matter?" Miss Jenny demanded. "You look lots worse than he does. You're white as a sheet."

"Nothing," the other answered. "I——" She stared at Miss Jenny a moment, clenching her hands at her sides. "I must go," she said, and she emerged into the hall. "It's late, and Horace . . ."

"You can come up and speak to him, can't you?" Miss Jenny asked, curiously. "There's not any blood, if that's what you are afraid of."

"It isn't that," Narcissa answered. "I'm not afraid."

Miss Jenny approached her, piercing and curious. "Why, all right," she said kindly, "if you'd rather not. I just thought perhaps you'd like to see he's all right, as long as you're here. But don't if you don't feel like it."

"Yes. Yes. I feel like it. I want to." She passed Miss Jenny and went on. At the foot of the stairs she paused until Miss Jenny came up behind her; then she went on, mounting swiftly and with her face averted.

"What's the matter with you?" Miss Jenny demanded, trying to see the other's face. "What's happened to you? Have you gone and fallen in love with him?"

"In love . . . him? Bayard?" She paused, then hurried on, clutching the rail. She began to laugh thinly, and put her other hand to her mouth. Miss Jenny mounted beside her, piercing and curious and cold. Narcissa hurried on. At the stairhead she stopped again, still with her face averted, and let Miss Jenny pass her, and just without the door she stopped and leaned against it, throttling her laughter and her trembling. Then she entered the room, where Miss Jenny stood beside the bed, watching her.

There was a sickish-sweet lingering of ether in the room, and she approached the bed blindly and stood beside it with her hidden clenched hands. Bayard's head was pallid and calm, like a chiseled mask brushed lightly over with his spent violence, and he was watching her, and for a while she gazed at him; and Miss Jenny and the room and all, swam away.

"You beast, you beast," she cried thinly, "why must you always do these things where I've got to see you?"

"I didn't know you were there," Bayard answered mildly, with weak astonishment.

Every few days, by Miss Jenny's request, she came out and sat beside his bed and read to him. He cared nothing at all about books; it is doubtful if he had ever read a book on his own initiative, but he would lie motionless in his cast while her grave contralto voice went on and on in the quiet room. Sometimes he tried to talk to her, but she ignored his attempts and read on; if he persisted, she went away and left him. So he soon learned to lie, usually with his eyes closed, voyaging alone in the bleak and barren regions of his despair, while her voice flowed on and on above the remoter sounds that came up to them —Miss Jenny scolding Isom or Simon downstairs or in the garden, the twittering of birds in the tree just beyond the window, the ceaseless groaning of the water pump below the barn. At times she would cease and look at him and find that he was peacefully sleeping.

5

Old man Falls came through the lush green of early June, came into town through the yet horizontal sunlight of morning, and in his dusty, neat overalls he now sat opposite old Bayard in immaculate linen and a geranium like a merry wound. The room was cool and still, with the clear morning light and the casual dust of the Negro janitor's infrequent disturbing. Now that old Bayard was aging and what with the deaf tenor of his stiffening ways, he was showing more and more a preference for surrounding himself with things of a like nature; showing an incredible aptitude for choosing servants who shaped their days to his in a sort of pottering and hopeless futility. The janitor, who dubbed old Bayard General, and whom old Bayard, and the other clients for whom he performed seemingly interminable duties of a slovenly and minor nature, addressed as Doctor Jones, was one of these. He was black and stooped with querulousness and age, and he took advantage of every one who would permit him, and old Bayard swore at him all the time he was around and allowed him to steal his tobacco and the bank's winter supply of coal by the scuttleful and peddle it to other Negroes.

The window behind which old Bayard and his caller sat gave upon a vacant lot of rubbish and dusty weeds. It was bounded by weathered rears of sundry one-story board buildings in which small businesses—repair- and junk-shops and such—had their lowly and ofttimes anonymous being. The lot itself was used by day by country people as a depot for their teams. Already some of these were tethered somnolent and ruminant there, and about the stale ammoniac droppings of their patient generations sparrows swirled in garrulous clouds, or pigeons slanted with sounds like rusty shutters and strode and preened in burnished and predatory pomposity, crooning among themselves with guttural unemphasis.

Old man Falls sat on the opposite side of the trash-filled fireplace, mopping his face with a clean blue bandana.

"It's my damned old legs," he roared, faintly apologetic. "Used to be I'd walk twelve-fifteen mile to a picnic or a singin' with less study than what that 'ere little old three mile into town gives me now." He mopped the handkerchief about that face of his, browned and cheerful these many years with the simple and abounding earth. "Looks like they're fixin' to give out on me, and I ain't but ninety-three, neither." He held his parcel in his other hand, but he continued to mop his face, making no motion to open it.

"Why didn't you wait on the road until a wagon came along?" Old Bayard shouted. "Always some damn feller with a fieldful of weeds coming to town."

"I reckon I mought," the other agreed. "But gittin' here so quick would sp'ile my holiday. I ain't like you town folks. I ain't got so much time I kin hurry it." He stowed the handkerchief away and rose and laid his parcel carefully on the mantel, and from his shirt pocket he produced a small object wrapped in a clean, frayed rag. Beneath his tedious and unhurried fingers there emerged a tin snuff-box polished long since to the dull, soft sheen of silver by handling and age. Old Bayard sat and watched, watched quietly as the other removed the cap of the box and put this, too, carefully aside.

"Now, turn yo' face up to the light," old man Falls directed.

"Loosh Peabody says that stuff will give me blood-poisoning, Will."

The other continued his slow preparations, his blue innocent eyes raptly preoccupied. "Loosh Peabody never said that," he corrected quietly. "One of them young doctors told you that, Bayard. Lean yo' face to the light." Old Bayard sat tautly back in his chair, his hands on the arms of it, watching the other with his piercing old eyes soberly, a little wistfully; eyes filled with unnamable things, like the eyes of old lions, and intent.

Old man Falls poised a dark gob of his ointment on one finger and set the box carefully on his vacated chair, and put his hand on old Bayard's face. But old Bayard still resisted, though passively, watching him with unutterable things in his eyes. Old man Falls drew his face firmly and gently into the light from the window.

"Come on here. I ain't young enough to waste time hurtin' folks. Hold still, now, so I won't spot yo' face up. My hand ain't steady enough to lift a rifle-ball offen a hot stove-led no mo'."

Bayard submitted then, and old man Falls patted the salve on to the spot with small deft touches. Then he took the bit of cloth and removed the surplus from Bayard's face and wiped his fingers and dropped the rag onto the hearth and knelt stiffly and touched a match to it. "We allus do that," he explained. "My granny got that 'ere from a Choctow woman nigh a hundred and thutty year ago. Ain't none of us never told what hit air, nor left no after-trace." He rose stiffly and dusted his knees. He recapped the box

with the same unhurried care and put it away, and picked
up his parcel from the mantel and resumed his chair.

"Hit'll turn black tomorrer, and long's hit's black, hit's
workin'. Don't put no water on yo' face befo' mawnin', and
I'll come in again in ten days and dose hit again, and on
the"—he mused a moment, counting slowly on his gnarled
fingers; his lips moved, but with no sound—"the ninth day of
July, hit'll drap off. And don't you let Miss Jenny nor none of
them doctors worry you about hit."

He sat with his knees together. The parcel lay on his
knees and he now opened it after the ancient laborious ritual,
picking patiently at the pink knot until a younger person
would have screamed at him. Old Bayard merely lit a cigar
and propped his feet against the fireplace, and in good time
old man Falls solved the knot and removed the string and
laid it across his chair-arm. It fell to the floor and he bent
and fumbled it into his blunt fingers and laid it again across
the chair-arm and watched it a moment lest it fall again; then
he opened the parcel. First was his carton of tobacco, and
he removed a plug and sniffed it, turned it in his hand and
sniffed it again. But without biting into it he laid it and its
fellows aside and delved yet further. He spread open the
throat of the resulting paper bag, and his innocent boy's
eyes gloated soberly into it.

"I'll declare," he said, "sometimes I'm right ashamed for
havin' sech a consarned sweet tooth. Hit don't give me no
rest a-tall." Still carefully guarding the other objects on his
knees, he tilted the sack and shook two or three of the
striped, shrimplike things into his palm, and returned all but
one, which he put in his mouth. "I'm a-feard now I'll be
losin' my teeth some day and I'll have to start gummin' 'em
or eatin' soft ones. I never did relish soft candy." His leathery
cheek bulged slightly with slow regularity like a respira-
tion. He peered into the sack again, and he sat weighing it
in his hand.

"They was times back in sixty-three and -fo' when a feller
could 'a' bought a section of land and a couple of niggers
with this here bag of candy. Lots of times I mind, with
ever'thing goin' agin us like, and sugar and cawfee gone
and food sca'ce, eatin' stole cawn when they was any to
steal, and ditch weeds ef they wa'n't; bivouackin' at night
in the rain, more'n like . . ." His voice trailed away among

ancient phantoms of the soul's and body's fortitudes, in those regions of glamorous and useless striving where such ghosts abide. He chuckled and mouthed his peppermint again.

"I mind that day we was a-dodgin' around Grant's army, headin' nawth. Grant was at Grenada then, and Cunnel had rousted us boys out and we taken hoss and jined Van Dorn down that-a-way. That was when Cunnel had that 'ere silver stallion. Grant was still at Grenada, but Van Dorn lit out one day, headin' nawth. Why, us boys didn't know. Cunnel mought have knowed, but he never told us. Not that we keered much, long's we was headin' to'a'ds home.

"So our boys was ridin' along to ourselves, goin' to jine up with the balance of 'em later. Leastways the rest of 'em thought we was goin' to jine 'em. But Cunnel never had no idea of doin' that; his cawn hadn't been laid by yit, and he was goin' home fer a spell. We wa'n't runnin' away," he explained. "We knowed Van Dorn could handle 'em all right fer a week or two. He usually done it. He was a putty good man," old man Falls said, "a putty good man."

"They were all pretty good men in those days," old Bayard agreed. "But you damn fellers quit fighting and went home too often."

"Well," old man Falls rejoined defensively, "even ef the hull country's overrun with bears, a feller can't hunt bears all the time. He's got to quit once in a while, ef hit's only to rest up the dawgs and hosses. But I reckon them dawgs and hosses could stay on the trail long as any," he added with sober pride. " 'Course ever'body couldn't keep up with that 'ere mist-colored stallion. They wasn't but one animal in the Confedrit army could tech him—that last hoss Zeb Fothergill fotch back outen one of Sherman's cavalry pickets on his last trip into Tennessee.

"Nobody never did know what Zeb done on them trips of hisn. Cunnel claimed hit was jest to steal hosses. But he never got back with less 'en one. One time he come back with seven of the orneriest critters that ever walked, I reckon. He tried to swap 'em fer meat and cawn-meal, but wouldn't nobody have 'em. Then he tried to give 'em to the army, but even the army wouldn't have 'em. So he finally turned 'em loose and requisitioned to Joe Johnston's haidquarters fer ten hosses sold to Forrest's cavalry. I don't know ef he ever got air answer. Nate Forrest wouldn't 'a' had them hosses. I

doubt ef they'd even 'a' et 'em in Vicksburg. . . . I never did
put no big reliability in Zeb Fothergill, him comin' and
goin' by hisself like he done. But he knowed hosses, and he
usually fotch a good 'un home ever' time he went away to'a'ds
the war. But he never got another'n like this befo'."

The bulge was gone from his cheek, and he produced his
pocket knife and cut a neat segment from his plug of tobacco and lipped it from the knife-blade. Then he rewrapped
his parcel and tied the string about it. The ash of old
Bayard's cigar trembled delicately about its glowing heart,
but did not yet fall.

Old man Falls spat neatly and brownly into the cold
fireplace. "That day we was in Calhoun county," he continued. "Hit was as putty a summer mawnin' as you ever
see; men and hosses rested and fed and feelin' peart,
trottin' along the road through the woods and fields whar
birds was a-singin' and young rabbits lopin' acrost the road.
Cunnel and Zeb was ridin' along side by side on them two
hosses, Cunnel on Jupiter and Zeb on that sorrel two-year-
old, and they was a-braggin' as usual. We all knowed Cunnel's
Jupiter, but Zeb kep' a-contendin' that he wouldn't take no
man's dust. The road was putty straight across the bottom
to'a'ds the river and Zeb kep' a-aggin' the Cunnel fer a race,
until Cunnel says 'All right.' He told the boys to come on
and him and Zeb would wait fer us at the river bridge 'bout
fo' mile ahead, and him and Zeb lined up and lit out.

"Them hosses was the puttiest livin' things I ever see.
They went off together like two hawks, neck and neck. They
was outen sight in no time, with dust swirlin' behind, but we
could foller 'em fer a ways by the dust they left, watchin'
it kind of suckin' on down the road like one of these here
ottomobiles was in the middle of it. When they come to whar
the road drapped down to the river, Cunnel had Zeb beat by
about three hundred yards. Thar was a spring-branch jest
under the ridge, and when Cunnel sailed over the rise, thar
was a comp'ny of Yankee cavalry with their hosses picketed
and their muskets stacked, eatin' dinner by the spring. Cunnel
says they was a-settin' thar gapin' at the rise when he come
over hit, holdin' cups of cawfee and hunks of bread in
their hands and their muskets stacked about fo'ty foot away,
buggin' their eyes at him.

"It was too late fer him to turn back, anyhow, but I don't

reckon he would have ef they'd been time. He jest spurred
down the ridge and rid in amongst 'em, scatterin' cook-fires
and guns and men, shoutin', 'Surround 'em, boys! Ef you
move, you air dead men.' One or two of 'em made to break
away, but Cunnel drawed his pistols and let 'em off, and they
come back and scrouged in amongst the others, and thar they
set, still a-holdin' their dinner, when Zeb come up. And that
was the way we found 'em when we got thar ten minutes
later." Old man Falls spat again, neatly and brownly, and he
chuckled. His eyes shone like periwinkles. "That cawfee was
sho' mighty fine," he added.

"And thar we was, with a passel of prisoners we didn't
have no use fer. We held 'em all that day and et their
grub; and when night come we taken and throwed their
muskets into the branch and taken their ammunition and the
rest of the grub and put a gyard on their hosses; then the rest
of us laid down. And all that night we laid thar in them fine
Yankee blankets, listenin' to them prisoners sneakin' away
one at a time, slippin' down the bank into the branch and
wading off. Time to time one would slip er make a splash
er somethin'; then they'd all git right still fer a spell. But
putty soon we'd hear 'em at it again, crawlin' through the
bushes to'a'ds the water, and us layin' thar with blanket-
aidges held agin our faces. Hit was nigh dawn 'fore the
last one had snuck off in a way that suited 'em.

"Then Cunnel from whar he was a-layin' let out a yell
them pore critters could hear fer a mile.

"'Go it, Yank,' he says, 'and look out fer moccasins!'

"Next mawnin' we saddled up and loaded our plunder and
ever' man taken him a hoss and lit out fer home. We'd been
home two weeks and Cunnel had his cawn laid by, when
we heard 'bout Van Dorn ridin' into Holly Springs and burnin'
Grant's sto's. Seems like he never needed no help from us,
noways." He chewed his tobacco for a time, quietly retrospective, reliving, in the company of men now dust with
the dust for which they had, unwittingly perhaps, fought,
those gallant, pinch-bellied days into which few who now
trod that earth could enter with him.

Old Bayard shook the ash from his cigar. "Will," he said,
"what the devil were you folks fighting about, anyhow?"

"Bayard," old man Falls answered, "be damned ef I ever
did know."

After old man Falls had departed with his small parcel
and his innocently bulging cheek, old Bayard sat and smoked
his cigar. Presently he raised his hand and touched the wen
on his face, but lightly, remembering old man Falls' parting
stricture; and recalling this, the thought that it might not yet
be too late, that he might yet remove the paste with water,
followed.

He rose and crossed to the lavatory in the corner of the
room. Above it was fixed a small cabinet with a mirror in the
door, and in it he examined the black spot on his cheek,
touching it again with his fingers, then examining his
hand. Yes, it might still come off. . . . But be damned if he
would; be damned to a man who didn't know his own mind.
He flung his cigar away and quitted the room and tramped
through the lobby toward the door where his chair sat. But
before he reached the door he turned about and came up to
the cashier's window, behind which the cashier sat in a green
eyeshade.

"Res," he said.

The cashier looked up. "Yes, Colonel?"

"Who is that damn boy that hangs around here, looking
through that window all day?" Old Bayard lowered his voice
within a pitch or so of an ordinary conversational tone.

"What boy, Colonel?"

Old Bayard pointed, and the cashier raised himself on
his stool and peered over the partition and saw, beyond the
indicated window, a boy of ten or twelve watching him
with an innocent and casual air. "Oh. That's Will Beard's
boy, from up at the boarding-house," he shouted. "Friend
of Byron's, I think."

"What's he doing around here? Every time I walk through
here, there he is looking in that window. What does he
want?"

"Maybe he's a bank robber," the cashier suggested.

"What?" Old Bayard cupped his ear fiercely in his palm.

"Maybe he's a bank robber," the other shouted, leaning
forward on his stool. Old Bayard snorted and tramped
violently on and slammed his chair back against the door. The
cashier sat lumped and shapeless on his stool, rumbling
deep within his gross body. He said without turning his
head: "Colonel's let Will Falls treat him with that salve."
Snopes at his desk made no reply; did not raise his head.

After a time the boy moved, and drifted casually and innocently away.

Virgil Beard now possessed a pistol that projected a stream of ammoniac water excruciatingly painful to the eyes, a small magic lantern, and an ex-candy showcase in which he kept birds' eggs and an assortment of insects that had died slowly on pins, and a modest hoard of nickels and dimes.

In July Snopes had changed his domicile. He avoided Virgil on the street and so for two weeks he had not seen the boy at all, until one evening after supper he emerged from the front door of his new abode and found Virgil sitting blandly and politely on the front steps.

"Hi, Mr. Snopes," Virgil said.

6

Miss Jenny's exasperation and rage when old Bayard arrived home that afternoon was unbounded. "You stubborn old fool," she stormed, "can't Bayard kill you fast enough that you've got to let that old quack of a Will Falls give you blood poisoning? After what Dr. Alford told you, when even Loosh Peabody, who thinks a course of quinine or calomel will cure anything from a broken neck to chilblains, agreed with him? I'll declare, sometimes I just lose patience with you folks; wonder what crime I seem to be expiating by having to live with you. Soon as Bayard sort of quiets down and I can quit jumping every time the 'phone rings, you have to go and let that old pauper daub your face up with axle grease and lampblack. I'm a good mind to pack up and get out, and start life over in some place where they never heard of a Sartoris." She raged and stormed on; old Bayard raged in reply, with violent words and profane, and their voices swelled and surged through the house until Elnora and Simon in the kitchen moved furtively, with cocked ears. Finally old Bayard tramped from the house and mounted his horse and rode away, leaving Miss Jenny to wear her rage out upon the empty air, and then there was peace for a time.

But at supper the storm brewed and burst again. Behind the swing door of the butler's pantry Simon could hear them, and young Bayard too, trying to shout them down. "Let up, let up," he howled, "for God's sake. I can't hear myself chew, even."

"And you're another one." Miss Jenny turned promptly upon him. "You're just as trying as he is. You and your stiff-necked, sullen ways. Helling around the country in that car just because you think there may be somebody who cares a whoop whether or not you break your worthless neck, and then coming in to the supper-table smelling like a stable hand! Just because you went to a war. Do you think you're the only person in the world that ever went to a war? Do you reckon that when my Bayard came back from The War that he made a nuisance of himself to everybody that had to live with him? But he was a gentleman: he raised the devil like a gentleman, not like you Mississippi country people. Clod-hoppers. Look what he did with just a horse," she added. "He didn't need any flying-machine."

"Look at the little two-bit war he went to," young Bayard rejoined, "a war that was so sorry that grandfather wouldn't even stay up there in Virginia where it was."

"And nobody wanted him at it," Miss Jenny retorted, "a man that would get mad just because his men deposed him and elected a better colonel in his place. Got mad and came back to the country to lead a bunch of red-neck brigands."

"Little two-bit war," young Bayard repeated, "and on a horse. Anybody can go to a war on a horse. No chance for him to do much of anything."

"At least he got himself decently killed," Miss Jenny snapped. "He did more with a horse than you could do with that aeroplane."

"Sho'," Simon breathed against the pantry door. "Ain't dey gwine it? Takes white folks to sho' 'nough quoil."

And so it surged and ebbed through the succeeding days; wore itself out, then surged again when old Bayard returned home with another application of salve. But by this time Simon was having troubles of his own, troubles on which he finally consulted old Bayard one afternoon. Young

Bayard was laid up in bed with his crushed ribs, with Miss Jenny mothering him with savage and cherishing affection and Miss Benbow to visit with him and read aloud to him, and Simon had come into his own again. The top hat and the duster came down from the nail, and old Bayard's cigars depleted daily by one, and the fat matched horses spent their accumulated laziness between home and the bank, before which Simon swung them to a halt each afternoon as of old, with his clamped cigar and smartly-furled whip and all the theatrics of the fine moment. "De ottomobile," Simon philosophized, "is all right fer pleasure en excitement, but fer de genu-wine gentlemun tone, dey ain't but one thing: dat's hosses."

Thus Simon's opportunity came ready to his hand, and once they were clear of town and the team had settled into its gait, he took advantage of it.

"Well, Cunnel," he began, "looks like me en you's got to make some financial 'rangements."

"What?" Old Bayard brought his attention back from where it wandered about the familiar planted fields and the blue, shining hills beyond.

"I says it looks like me en you's got to arrange erbout a little cash money."

"Much obliged, Simon," old Bayard answered, "but I don't need any money right now. Much obliged, though."

Simon laughed heartily. "I declare, Cunnel, you sho' is comical. Rich man like you needin' money!" Again he laughed, with unctuous and abortive heartiness. "Yes, suh, you sho' is comical." Then he ceased laughing and became engrossed with the horses for a moment. Twins they were: Roosevelt and Taft, with sleek hides and broad, comfortable buttocks. "You, Taf', lean on dat collar! Laziness gwine go in on you some day en kill you, sho'." Old Bayard sat watching his apelike head and the swaggering tilt of the top hat. Simon turned his wizened, plausible face over his shoulder again. "But sho' 'nough, now, we is got to quiet dem niggers somehow."

"What have they done? Can't they find anybody to take their money?"

"Well, suh, hit's like dis," Simon explained. "Hit's kind of all 'round cu'i's. You see, dey been collectin' buildin' money fer dat church whut burnt down, en ez dey got de money up, dey turnt hit over ter me, whut wid my 'ficial position on de church boa'd en bein' I wuz a member of de bes' fambly round here. Dat 'uz erbout las' Chris'mus time, en now dey wants de money back."

"That's strange," old Bayard said.

"Yessuh," Simon agreed readily. "Hit struck me jes' 'zackly dat way."

"Well, if they insist, I reckon you'd better give it back to 'em."

"Now, you's gittin' to it." Simon turned his head again; his manner was confidential, and he exploded his bomb in a hushed, melodramatic tone: "De money's gone."

"Dammit, I know that," old Bayard answered, his levity suddenly gone. "Where is it?"

"I went and put it out," Simon told him, and his tone was still confidential, with a little pained astonishment at the world's obtuseness. "And now dem niggers 'cusin' me of stealin' it."

"Do you mean to tell me you took charge of money belonging to other people, and then went and loaned it to somebody else?"

"You does de same thing ev'ry day," Simon answered. "Ain't lendin' money yo' main business?"

Old Bayard snorted violently. "You get that money back and give it to those niggers, or you'll be in jail, you hear?"

"You talks jes' like dem uppity town niggers," Simon told him in a pained tone. "Dat money done been put out, now," he reminded his patron.

"Get it back. Haven't you got collateral for it?"

"Is I got which?"

"Something worth the money, to keep until the money is paid back."

"Yessuh, I got dat." Simon chuckled again, unctuously, a satyrish chuckle rich with complacent innuendo. "Yessuh, I got dat, all right. Only I never heard hit called collateral befo'. Naw, suh, not dat."

"Did you give that money to some nigger wench?" old Bayard demanded.

"Well, suh, hit's like dis—" Simon began. But the other interrupted him.

"Ah, the devil. And now you expect me to pay it back, do you? How much was it?"

"I don't rightly ricollick. Dem niggers claims hit wuz sevumty er ninety dollars er somethin'. But don't you pay 'um no mind; you jes' give 'um whutever you think is right: dey'll take it."

"I'm damned if I will. They can take it out of your worthless hide, or send you to jail—whichever they want to, but I'm damned if I'll pay one cent of it."

"Now, Cunnel," Simon said, "you ain't gwine let dem town niggers 'cuse a member of yo' fambly of stealin', is you?"

"Drive on!" old Bayard shouted. Simon turned on the seat and clucked to the horses and drove on, his cigar tilted toward his hat-brim, his elbows out and the whip caught smartly back in his hand, glancing now and then with tolerant and easy scorn at the field niggers laboring among the cotton-rows.

Old man Falls replaced the cap on his tin of salve, wiped the tin carefully with the bit of rag, then knelt on the cold hearth and held a match to the rag.

"I reckon them doctors air still a-tellin' you hit's gwine to kill you, ain't they?" he asked.

Old Bayard propped his feet against the hearth, cupping a match to his cigar, cupping two tiny match-flames in his eyes. He flung the match away and grunted.

Old man Falls watched the rag take fire sluggishly, with a pungent pencil of yellowish smoke that broke curling in the still air. "Ever' now and then a feller has to walk up and spit in deestruction's face, sort of, fer his own good. He has to kind of put a aidge on hisself, like he'd hold his ax to the grindstone," he said, squatting before the pungent curling of the smoke as though in a pagan ritual in miniature. "Ef a feller'll show his face to deestruction ever' now and then, deestruction'll leave 'im be 'twell his time comes. Deestruction likes to take a feller in the back."

"What?" old Bayard said.

Old man Falls rose and dusted his knees carefully.

"Deestruction's like airy other coward," he roared. "Hit won't strike a feller that's a-lookin' hit in the eye lessen he pushes hit too clost. Your paw knowed that. Stood in the do' of that sto' the day them two cyarpetbaggers brung them niggers in to vote 'em that day in '72. Stood thar in his

Prince Albert coat and beaver hat, with his arms folded, when ever'body else had left, and watched them two Missouri fellers herdin' them niggers up the road to'ds the sto'; stood right in the middle of the do' while them two cyarpetbaggers begun backin' off with their hands in their pockets until they was cl'ar of the niggers, and cussed him. And him standin' thar jest like this." He crossed his arms on his breast, his hands in sight, and for a moment old Bayard saw, as through a cloudy glass, that arrogant and familiar shape which the old man in shabby overalls had contrived in some way to immolate and preserve in the vacuum of his own abnegated self.

"Then, when they was gone on back down the road, Cunnel reached around inside the do' and taken out the ballot-box and sot hit between his feet.

" 'You niggers come hyer to vote, did you?' he says. 'All right, come up hyer and vote.'

"When they had broke and scattered he let off that 'ere dang der'nger over their heads a couple of times; then he loaded hit agin and marched down the road to Miz Winterbottom's, whar them two fellers boa'ded.

" 'Madam,' he says, liftin' his beaver, 'I have a small matter of business to discuss with yo' lodgers. Permit me,' he says, and he put his hat back on and marched up the stairs steady as a parade, with Miz Winterbottom gapin' after him with her mouth open. He walked right into the room whar they was a-settin' behind a table facin' the do', with their pistols layin' on the table.

"When us boys outside heard the three shots we run in. Thar wuz Miz Winterbottom standin' thar, gapin' up the stairs, and in a minute hyer come Cunnel with his hat cocked over his eye, marchin' down steady as a co't jury, breshin' the front of his coat with his hank'cher. And us standin' thar, a-watchin' him. He stopped in front of Miz Winterbottom and lifted his hat agin.

" 'Madam,' he says, 'I was fo'ced to muss up yo' guest-room right considerable. Pray accept my apologies, and have yo' nigger clean it up and send the bill to me. My apologies again, madam, fer havin' been put to the necessity of exterminatin' vermin on yo' premises. Gentlemen,' he says to us, 'good mawnin'.' And he cocked that 'ere beaver on his head and walked out.

"And, Bayard," old man Falls said, "I sort of envied them two Nawthuners, be damned ef I didn't. A feller kin take a wife and live with her fer a long time, but after all they ain't no kin. But the feller that brings you into the world or sends you outen hit . . ."

Where he lurked behind the pantry door Simon could hear the steady storming of Miss Jenny's and old Bayard's voices; later when they had removed to the office and Elnora and Caspey and Isom sat about the table in the kitchen waiting for him, the concussion of Miss Jenny's raging and old Bayard's rocklike stubbornness came in muffled surges, as of far-away surf.

"What de quoilin' erbout now?" Caspey asked. "Is you been and done somethin'?" he demanded of his nephew.

Isom rolled his eyes quietly above his steady jaws. "Naw, suh," he mumbled. "I ain't done nuthin'."

"Seems like dey'd git wo' out, after a while. What's pappy doin', Elnora?"

"Up dar in de hall, listenin'. Go tell 'im to come on and git his supper, so I kin git done, Isom."

Isom slid from his chair, still chewing, and left the kitchen. The steady raging of the two voices increased; where the shapeless figure of his grandfather stood like a disreputable and ancient bird in the dark hallway, Isom could distinguish words: poison . . . blood . . . think you can cut your head off and cure it . . . fool put it on your foot but . . . face head . . . dead and good riddance . . . fool of you dying because of your own bullheaded folly . . . you first lying on your back though . . .

"You and that damn doctor are going to worry me to death." Old Bayard's voice drowned the other temporarily. "Will Falls won't have a chance to kill me. I can't sit in my chair in town without that damn squirt sidling around me and looking disappointed because I'm still alive on my feet. And when I get home, get away from him, you can't even let me eat supper in peace. Have to show me a lot of damn colored pictures of what some fool thinks a man's insides look like."

"Who gwine die, pappy?" Isom whispered.

Simon turned his head. "Whut you hangin' eround here fer, boy? Go'n back to dat kitchen, whar you belongs."

"Supper waitin'," Isom said. "Who dyin', pappy?"

"Ain't nobody dyin'. Does anybody soun' dead? You git on outen de house, now."

Together they returned down the hall and entered the kitchen. Behind them the voices raged and stormed, blurred a little by walls, but dominant and unequivocal.

"Whut dey fightin' erbout now?" Caspey, chewing, asked.

"Dat's white folks' bizness," Simon told him. "You tend to yo'n, and dey'll git erlong all right." He sat down and Elnora rose and filled a cup from the coffee-pot on the stove and brought it to him. "White folks got dey troubles same as niggers is. Gimme dat dish o' meat, boy."

In the house the storm ran its nightly course, ceased as though by mutual consent, both parties still firmly entrenched; resumed at the supper table the next evening. And so on, day after day, until in the second week in July and six days after young Bayard had been fetched home with his chest crushed, Miss Jenny and old Bayard and Dr. Alford went to Memphis to consult a well-known authority on blood and glandular diseases with whom Dr. Alford, with some difficulty, had made a formal engagement. Young Bayard lay upstairs in his cast, but Narcissa Benbow had promised to come out and keep him company during the day.

Between the two of them they got old Bayard on the early train, still protesting profanely, like a stubborn and bewildered ox. There were others who knew them in the car and who remarked Dr. Alford's juxtaposition and became curious and solicitous. Old Bayard took these opportunities to assert himself again, with violent rumblings which Miss Jenny ignored.

They took him, like a sullen small boy, to the clinic where the specialist was to meet them, and in a room resembling an easy and informal summer hotel lobby they sat among quiet, waiting people talking in whispers, and an untidy clutter of papers and magazines, waiting for the specialist to arrive. They waited a long time.

Meanwhile from time to time, Dr. Alford assaulted the impregnable affability of the woman at the switchboard, was repulsed, and returned and sat stiffly beside his patient, aware that with every minute he was losing ground in Miss Jenny's opinion of him. Old Bayard was cowed too, by now, though occasionally he rumbled hopefully at Miss Jenny.

"Oh, stop swearing at me," she interrupted him at last. "You can't walk out now. Here, here's the morning paper—take it, and be quiet."

Then the specialist entered briskly and went to the switchboard woman, where Dr. Alford saw him and rose and went to him. The specialist turned—a brisk, dapper man, who moved with arrogant, jerky motions, as though he were exercising with a smallsword, and who in turning almost stepped on Dr. Alford. He gave Dr. Alford a glassy, impatient stare; then he shook his hand and broke into a high, desiccated burst of words. "On the dot, I see. Promptness. Promptness. That's good. Patient here? Stood the trip all right, did she?"

"Yes, Doctor, he's——"

"Good; good. Undressed and all ready, eh?"

"The patient is a m——"

"Just a moment." The specialist turned. "Oh, Mrs. Smith."

"Yes, Doctor." The woman at the switchboard did not raise her head, and at that moment another specialist of some kind, a large one, with a majestic, surreptitious air like a royal undertaker, entered and stopped Dr. Alford, and for a while the two of them rumbled and rattled at one another while Dr. Alford stood ignored near by, fuming stiffly and politely, feeling himself sinking lower and lower in Miss Jenny's opinion of his professional status. Then the two specialists had done, and Dr. Alford led his man toward the patient.

"Got the patient all ready, you say? Good; good; save time. Lunching down town today. Had lunch yourself?"

"No, Doctor. But the patient is a——"

"Dare say not," the specialist agreed. "Plenty of time, though." He turned briskly toward a curtained exit, but Dr. Alford took his arm firmly but courteously and halted him. Old Bayard was reading the paper. Miss Jenny was watching them frigidly, her bonnet on the exact top of her head.

"Mrs. Du Pre; Colonel Sartoris," Dr. Alford said, "this is Dr. Brandt. Colonel Sartoris is your p——"

"How d'ye do? How d'ye do? Come along with the patient, eh? Daughter? Granddaughter?" Old Bayard looked up.

"What?" he said, cupping his ear, and found the specialist staring at his face.

"What's that on your face?" he demanded, jerking his

hand forth and touching the blackened excrescence. When
he did so the thing came off in his fingers, leaving on old
Bayard's withered but unblemished cheek a round spot of
skin rosy and fair as any baby's.

On the train that evening old Bayard, who had sat for a
long time in deep thought, spoke suddenly.

"Jenny, what day of the month is this?"

"The ninth," Miss Jenny answered. "Why?"

Old Bayard sat for a while longer. Then he rose. "Think
I'll go up and smoke a cigar," he said. "I reckon a little
tobacco won't hurt me, will it, Doctor?"

Three weeks later they got a bill from the specialist for
fifty dollars. "Now I know why he's so well known," Miss
Jenny said acidly. Then to her nephew: "You better thank
your stars it wasn't your hat he lifted off."

Toward Dr. Alford her manner is fiercely and belligerently
protective; to old man Falls she gives the briefest and coldest
of nods and sails on with her nose in air; but to Loosh Peabody she does not speak at all.

7

She passed from the fresh, hot morning into the cool hall,
where Simon, uselessly and importantly proprietorial with
a duster, bobbed his head to her. "Dey done gone to Memphis today," he told her. "But Mist' Bayard waitin' fer you.
Walk right up, Missy."

"Thank you," she answered, and she went on and
mounted the stairs and left him busily wafting dust from one
surface to another and then back again. She mounted into
a steady draft of air that blew through the open doors
at the end of the hall. Through these doors she could see
a segment of blue hills and salt-colored sky. At Bayard's
door she stopped and stood there for a time, clasping the
book to her breast.

The house, despite Simon's activity in the hall below,
was a little portentously quiet without the reassurance of
Miss Jenny's bustling presence. Faint sounds reached her from
far away—out-of-door sounds whose final drowsy rever-

berations drifted into the house on the vivid July air; sounds too somnolent and remote to die away.

But from the room before her no sound came at all. Perhaps he was asleep, and the initial impulse—her passed word, and the fortitude of her desperate heart which had enabled her to come out despite Miss Jenny's absence —having served its purpose and deserted her, she stood just without the door, hoping that he was asleep, that he would sleep all day.

But she would have to enter the room in order to find if he slept, so she touched her hands to her face, as though by that she would restore to it its wonted serene repose for him to see, and entered.

"Simon?" Bayard said. He lay on his back, his hands beneath his head, gazing out the window across the room, and she paused again just within the door. At last, roused by her silence, he turned his head and his bleak gaze. "Well, I'm damned. I didn't believe you'd come out today."

"Yes," she answered. "How do you feel?"

"Not after the way you sit with one foot in the hall all the time Aunt Jenny's out of the room," he continued. "Did she make you come anyway?"

"She asked me to come out. She doesn't want you to be alone all day, with just Simon in the house. Do you feel better today?"

"So?" he drawled. "Won't you sit down, then?" She crossed to where her customary chair had been moved into a corner and drew it across the floor. He was watching her as she turned the chair about and seated herself. "What do you think about it?"

"About what?"

"About coming out to keep me company."

"I've brought a new book," she said. "One H— one I just got. I hope you'll like this one."

"I hope so," he agreed, but without conviction. "Seems like I'd like one after a while, don't it? But what do you think about coming out here today?"

"I don't think a sick person should be left alone with just Negroes around," she said, her face lowered over the book. "The name of this one is——"

"Why not send a nurse out, then? No use your coming way out here." She met his gaze at last, with her grave, desperate eyes. "Why do you come when you don't want to?" he persisted.

"I don't mind," she answered. She opened the book. "The name of this one——"

"Don't," he interrupted. "I'll have to listen to that damn thing all day. Let's talk a while." But her head was bent and her hands were still on the open book. "What makes you afraid to talk to me?"

"Afraid?" she repeated. "Had you rather I'd go?"

"What? No, damn it. I want you to be human for one time and talk to me. Come over here." She would not look at him, and she raised her hands between them as though he did not lie helpless on his back two yards away. "Come over here closer," he commanded. She rose, clutching the book.

"I'm going," she said. "I'll tell Simon to stay where he can hear you call. Good-bye."

"Here," he exclaimed. She went swiftly to the door. "Good-bye."

"After what you just said, about leaving me alone with just niggers on the place?" She paused at the door, and he added with cold cunning: "After what Aunt Jenny told you —what'll I tell her, tonight? Why are you afraid of a man flat on his back, in a damn cast-iron strait-jacket, anyway?" But she only looked at him with her sober hopeless eyes. "All right, damn it," he said violently. "Go, then." And he jerked his head on the pillow and stared again out the window while she returned to her chair. He said, mildly, "What's the name of this one?" She told him. "Let her go, then. I reckon I'll be asleep soon, anyway."

She opened the book and began to read, swiftly, as though she were crouching behind the screen of words her voice raised between them. She read steadily on for some time, while he on the bed made no movement, her head bent over the book, aware of time passing, as though she were in a contest with time. She finished a sentence and ceased, without raising her head, but almost immediately he spoke.

"Go on; I'm still here. Better luck next time."

The forenoon passed on. Somewhere a clock rang the quarter hours, but saving this there was no other sound in the house. Simon's activity below stairs had ceased long since, but a murmur of voices reached her at intervals

from somewhere, murmurously indistinguishable. The leaves
on the branch beyond the window did not stir, and upon
the hot air myriad noises blended in a drowsy monotone—
the Negroes' voices, sounds of animals in the barnyard, the
rhythmic groaning of the water pump, a sudden cacophony
of fowls in the garden beneath the window, interspersed with
Isom's meaningless cries as he drove them out.

Bayard was asleep now, and as she realized this she
realized also that she did not know just when she had
stopped reading. And she sat with the page open on her
knees, a page whose words left no echoes whatever in her
mind, looking at his calm face. It was again like a bronze
mask, purged by illness of the heat of its violence, yet with
the violence still slumbering there and only refined a little.
. . . She looked away and sat with the book open, her hands
lying motionless on the page, gazing out the window. The
curtains hung without motion. On the branch athwart the
window the leaves hung motionless beneath the intermittent
fingers of the sun, and she sat also without life, the fabric
of her dress unstirred by her imperceptible breathing, thinking that there would be peace for her only in a world
where there were no men at all.

The clock rang twelve times. Immediately after, preceded
by stertorous breathing and surreptitious sounds as of a
huge rat, and yet other furtive ratlike sounds in the hall,
Simon thrust his head around the door, like the grandfather
of all apes.

"Is he 'sleep yit?" he said in a rasping whisper.

"Shhhhhh," Narcissa said, lifting her hand. Simon entered
on tiptoe, breathing heavily, scraping his feet on the floor.
"Hush," Narcissa said quickly, "you'll wake him."

"Dinner ready," Simon said, still in that rasping whisper.

"You can keep his warm until he wakes up, can't you?"
Narcissa whispered. "Simon!" she whispered. She rose, but he
had already crossed to the table, where he fumbled clumsily at
the stack of books and contrived at last to topple it to the
floor in a random crash. Bayard opened his eyes.

"Good God," he said, "are you here again?"

"Well, now," Simon exclaimed with ready dismay, "ef
me en Miss Benbow ain't waked him up."

"Why you can't bear to see anybody lying on their back

with their eyes closed, I can't see," Bayard said. "Thank God you were not born in a drove, like mosquitoes."

"Jes lissen at 'im," Simon said. "Go to sleep quoilin' en wake up quoilin'. Elnora got dinner ready fer y'all."

"Why didn't you bring it up, then?" Bayard said. "Miss Benbow's too. Unless you'd rather go down?" he added.

In all his movements Simon was a caricature of himself. He now assumed an attitude of shocked reproof. "Dinin'-room de place fer comp'ny," he said.

"No," Narcissa said, "I'll go down. I won't put Simon to that trouble."

"'Taint no trouble," Simon disclaimed. "Only hit ain't no——"

"I'll come down," Narcissa said. "You go on and see to Mr. Bayard's tray."

"Yes'm," Simon said. He moved toward the door. "You kin walk right down. Elnora have hit on de table time you git dar." He went out.

"I tried to keep——" Narcissa began.

"I know," Bayard interrupted, "he won't let anybody sleep through mealtime. And you'd better go and have yours, or he'll carry everything back to the kitchen. And you don't have to hurry back just on my account," he added.

"Don't have to hurry back?" She paused at the door and looked back at him. "What do you mean?"

"I thought you might be tired of reading."

"Oh," she said, and looked away and stood for a moment clothed in her grave despair.

"Look here," he said suddenly. "Are you sick or anything? Had you rather go home?"

"No," she answered. She moved again. "I'll be back soon."

She had her meal in lonely state in the somber dining-room while Simon, having dispatched Bayard's tray by Isom, moved about the table and pressed dishes upon her with bland insistence or leaned against the sideboard and conducted a rambling monologue that seemed to have had no beginning and held no prospect of any end. It still flowed easily behind her as she went up the hall; when she stood in the front door it was still going on, volitionless, as though entranced with its own existence and feeding on its own momentum.

Beyond the porch the salvia bed lay in an unbearable

glare of white light, in clamorous splashes. Beyond it the drive shimmered with heat until, arched over with locust and oak, it descended in a cool green tunnel to the gates and the sultry ribbon of the highroad. Beyond the road fields spread away shimmering, broken here and there by motionless clumps of wood, on to the hills dissolving bluely in the July haze.

She leaned for a while against the door, in her white dress, her cheek against the cool, smooth plane of the jamb, in a faint draft that came steadily from somewhere though no leaf stirred. Simon had finished in the dining-room and a drowsy murmur of voices came up the hall from the kitchen, borne upon that thin stirring of air too warm to be called a breeze.

At last she heard a movement from above stairs and she remembered Isom with Bayard's tray, and she turned and slid the parlor doors ajar and entered. The shades were drawn closely, and the crack of light that followed her but deepened the gloom. She found the piano and stood beside it for a while, touching its dusty surface, thinking of Miss Jenny erect and indomitable in her chair beside it. She heard Isom descend the stairs; soon his footsteps died away down the hall, and she drew out the bench and sat down and laid her arms along the closed lid.

Simon entered the dining-room again, mumbling to himself and followed presently by Elnora, and they clashed dishes and talked with a mellow rise and fall of consonant-less and indistinguishable words. Then they went away, but still she sat with her arms along the cool wood, in the dark, quiet room where even time stagnated a little.

The clock rang again and she moved. "I've been crying," she thought. "I've been crying," she said in a sad whisper that savored its own loneliness and its sorrow. At the tall mirror beside the parlor door she stood and peered at her dim reflection, touching her eyes with her finger tips. Then she went on, but paused again at the stairs, listening. Then she mounted briskly and entered Miss Jenny's room and went on to her bathroom and bathed her face.

Bayard lay as she had left him. He was smoking a cigarette now. Between puffs he dabbed it casually at a saucer on the bed beside him. "Well?" he said.

"You're going to set the house on fire, that way," she

told him, removing the saucer. "You know Miss Jenny wouldn't let you do that."

"I know it," he agreed, a little sheepishly, and she dragged the table up and set the saucer upon it.

"Can you reach it now?"

"Yes, thanks. Did they give you enough to eat?"

"Oh, yes. Simon's very insistent, you know. Shall I read some more, or had you rather sleep?"

"Read, if you don't mind. I think I'll stay awake, this time."

"Is that a threat?"

He looked at her quickly as she seated herself and picked up the book. "Say, what happened to you?" he demanded. "You acted like you were all in, before dinner. Simon give you a drink, or what?"

"No, not that bad." And she laughed, a little wildly, and opened the book. "I forgot to mark the place," she said, turning the leaves swiftly. "Do you remember—— No, you were asleep, weren't you? Shall I go back to where you stopped listening?"

"No. Just read anywhere. It's all about alike, I guess. If you'll move a little nearer, I believe I can stay awake."

"Sleep if you want to. I don't mind."

"Meaning you won't come any nearer?" he asked, watching her with his bleak gaze. She moved her chair nearer and opened the book again and turned the pages on.

"I think it was about here," she said, with indecision. "Yes." She read to herself for a line or two, then she began aloud, read to the end of the page, where her voice trailed off in grave consternation. She turned the next page, then flipped it back. "I read this once; I remember it now." She turned the leaves on, her serene brow puckered a little. "I must have been asleep too," she said, and she glanced at him with friendly bewilderment. "I seem to have read pages and pages . . ."

"Oh, begin anywhere," he repeated.

"No: wait; here it is." She read again and picked up the thread of the story. Once or twice she raised her eyes swiftly and found him watching her, bleakly but quietly. After a time he was no longer watching her, and at last, finding that his eyes were closed, she thought he slept. She finished the chapter and stopped.

"No," he said drowsily, "not yet." Then, when she failed

to resume, he opened his eyes and asked for a cigarette. She laid the book aside and struck the match for him, and picked up the book again.

The afternoon wore away. The Negroes had gone, and there was no sound about the house save her voice, and the clock at quarter-hour intervals; outside, the shadows slanted more and more, peaceful harbingers of evening. He was asleep now, despite his contrary conviction, and after a while she stopped and laid the book away. The long shape of him lay stiffly in its cast beneath the sheet, and she sat and looked at his bold, still face and the broken travesty of him and her tranquil sorrow overflowed in pity for him. He was so utterly without any affection for anything at all; so— so . . . hard . . . No, that's not the word. But "cold" eluded her; she could comprehend hardness, but not coldness. . . .

Afternoon drew on; evening was finding itself. She sat musing and still and quiet, gazing out of the window where no wind yet stirred the leaves, as though she were waiting for some one to tell her what to do next, and she had lost all account of time other than as a dark unhurrying stream into which she gazed until the mesmerism of water conjured the water itself away.

He made an indescribable sound, and she turned her head quickly and saw his body straining terrifically in its cast and his clenched hands and his teeth beneath his lifted lip, and as she sat blanched and incapable of further movement he made the sound again. His breath hissed between his teeth and he screamed, a wordless sound that merged into a rush of profanity, and when she rose at last and stood over him with her hands against her mouth, his body relaxed and from beneath his sweating brow he watched her with wide intent eyes in which terror lurked, and mad, cold fury, and despair.

"He damn near got me, then," he said in a dry, light voice, still watching her from beyond the fading agony in his wide eyes. "There was a sort of loop of 'em around my chest, and every time he fired, he twisted the loop a little tighter. . . ." He fumbled at the sheet and tried to draw it up to his face. "Can you get me a handkerchief? Some in that top drawer there."

"Yes," she said, "yes," and she went to the chest of drawers and held her shaking body upright by clinging to it,

and found a handkerchief and brought it to him. She tried
to dry his brow and face, but at last he took the handkerchief from her and did it himself. "You scared me," she
moaned. "You scared me so bad. I thought . . ."

"Sorry," he answered shortly. "I don't do that on purpose.
I want a cigarette."

She gave it to him and struck the match, and again he
had to grasp her hand to hold the flame steady, and still
holding her wrist, he drew deeply several times. She tried
to free her wrist, but his fingers were like steel, and her
trembling body betrayed her and she sank into her chair
again, staring at him with terror and dread. He consumed the
cigarette in deep swift draughts, and still holding her wrist
he began to talk of his dead brother, without preamble,
brutally. It was a brutal tale, without beginning, and crassly
and uselessly violent and at times profane and gross, though
its very wildness robbed it of offensiveness, just as its grossness kept it from obscenity. And beneath it all, the bitter
struggling of his false and stubborn pride, and she sitting
with her arm taut in his grasp and her other hand pressed
against her mouth, watching him with terrified fascination.

"He was zigzagging: that was why I couldn't get on the
Hun. Every time I got my sights on the Hun, John'd barge in
between us again, and then I'd have to hoick away before
one of the others got on me. Then he quit zigzagging. Soon
as I saw him sideslip I knew it was all over. Then I saw the
fire streaking out along his wing, and he was looking back.
He wasn't looking at the Hun at all; he was looking at me.
The Hun stopped shooting then, and all of us sort of just
sat there for a while. I couldn't tell what John was up to
until I saw him swing his feet out. Then he thumbed his
nose at me like he was always doing and flipped his hand
at the Hun and kicked his machine out of the way and
jumped. He jumped feet first. You can't fall far feet first,
you know, and pretty soon he sprawled out flat. There was
a bunch of cloud right under us and he smacked on it
right on his belly, like what we used to call gut-busters in
swimming. But I never could pick him up below the cloud.
I know I got down before he could have come out, because after I was down there his machine came diving out
right at me, burning good. I pulled away from it, but the
damn thing zoomed past and did a split-turn and came at

me again, and I had to dodge. And so I never could pick
him up when he came out of the cloud. I went down fast,
until I knew I was below him, and looked again. But I
couldn't find him and then I thought that maybe I hadn't
gone far enough, so I dived again. I saw the machine crash
about three miles away, but I never could pick John up
again. And then they started shooting at me from the
ground——"

He talked on and her hand came away from her mouth
and slid down her other arm and tugged at his fingers.

"Please," she whispered. "Please!" He ceased then and
looked at her and his fingers shifted, and just as she thought
she was free they clamped again, and now both of her
wrists were prisoners. She struggled, staring at him dreadfully, but he grinned his teeth at her and pressed her
crossed arms down upon the bed beside him.

"Please, please," she implored, struggling; she could feel
the flesh of her wrists, feel the bones turn in it as a loose
garment, could see his bleak eyes and the fixed derision of
his teeth, and suddenly she swayed forward in her chair
and her head dropped between her prisoned arms and she
wept with hopeless and dreadful hysteria.

After a while there was no sound in the room again,
and he moved his head and looked at the dark crown of
her head. He lifted his hand and saw the bruised discolora-
tions where he had gripped her wrists. But she did not stir
even then, and he dropped his hand upon her wrists again
and lay quietly, and after a while even her shuddering and
trembling had ceased.

"I'm sorry," he said. "I won't do it again."

He could see only the top of her dark head, and her hands
lay passive beneath his.

"I'm sorry," he repeated. "I won't do it any more."

"You won't drive that car fast any more?" she asked,
without moving; her voice was muffled.

"What?"

She made no answer, and with infinite small pains and
slowly he turned himself, cast and all, by degrees on to his
side, chewing his lip and swearing under his breath, and laid
his other hand on her hair.

"What are you doing?" she asked, still without raising her head. "You'll break your ribs again."

"Yes," he agreed, stroking her hair awkwardly.

"That's the trouble, right there," she said. "That's the way you act: doing things that—that—— You do things to hurt yourself just to worry people. You don't get any fun out of doing them."

"No," he agreed, and he lay with his chest full of hot needles, stroking her dark head with his hard, awkward hand. Far above him now the peak among the black and savage stars, and about him the valleys of tranquillity and of peace. It was later still; already shadows were growing in the room and losing themselves in shadow, and beyond the window sunlight was a diffused radiance, sourceless yet palpable. From somewhere cows lowed one to another, moody and mournful. At last she sat up, touching her face and her hair.

"You're all twisted. You'll never get well if you don't behave yourself. Turn on your back, now." He obeyed, slowly and painfully, his lip between his teeth and faint beads on his forehead, while she watched him with grave anxiety. "Does it hurt?"

"No," he answered, and his hand shut again on her wrists that made no effort to withdraw. The sun was gone, and twilight, foster dam of quietude and peace, filled the fading room, and evening had found itself.

"And you won't drive that car fast any more?" she persisted from the dusk.

"No," he answered.

8

Meanwhile she had received another letter from her anonymous correspondent. Horace, when he came in one night, had brought it in to her as she lay in bed with a book; tapped at her door and opened it and stood for a moment diffidently, and for a while they looked at one another across the barrier of their estrangement and their stubborn pride.

"Excuse me for disturbing you," he said stiffly. She lay

beneath the shaded light, with the dark splash of her hair on the pillow, and only her eyes moved as he crossed the room and stood above her where she lay with her lowered book, watching him with sober interrogation.

"What are you reading?" he asked. For reply she shut the book on her finger, with the jacket and its colored legend upward. But he did not look at it. His shirt was open beneath his silk dressing-gown and his thin hand moved among the objects on the table beside the bed; picked up another book. "I never knew you to read so much."

"I have more time for reading, now," she answered.

"Yes." His hand still moved about the table, touching things here and there.

She lay waiting for him to speak. But he did not, and she said, "What is it, Horace?"

He came and sat on the edge of the bed. But still her eyes were antagonistic and interrogatory and the shadow of her mouth was stubbornly cold. "Narcy?" he said. She lowered her eyes to the book, and he added: "First, I want to apologize for leaving you alone so often at night."

"Yes?"

He laid his hand on her knee. "Look at me." She raised her face, and the antagonism of her eyes. "I want to apologize for leaving you alone at night," he repeated.

"Does that mean you aren't going to do it any more, or that you're not coming in at all?"

For a while he sat brooding on the wild repose of his hand lying on her covered knee. Then he rose and stood beside the table again, touching the objects there; then he returned and sat on the bed. She was reading again, and he tried to take the book from her hand. She resisted.

"What do you want, Horace?" she asked impatiently.

He mused again while she watched his face. He looked up. "Belle and I are going to be married," he blurted.

"Why tell me? Harry is the one to tell. Unless you and Belle are going to dispense with the formality of divorce."

"Yes," he said. "He knows it." He laid his hand on her knee again, stroking it through the cover. "You aren't even surprised, are you?"

"I'm surprised at you, but not at Belle. Belle has a backstairs nature."

"Yes," he agreed; then: "Who said that to you? You didn't

think of that yourself." She lay with her book half raised, watching him. He took her hand roughly; she tried to free it, but vainly. "Who was it?" he demanded.

"Nobody told me. Don't, Horace."

He released her hand. "I know who it was. It was Mrs. Du Pre."

"It wasn't anybody," she repeated. "Go away and leave me alone, Horace." And behind the antagonism her eyes were hopeless and desperate. "Don't you see that talking doesn't help any?"

"Yes," he said wearily, but he sat for a while yet, stroking her knee. Then he rose and thrust his hands into his gown, but turning he paused again and drew forth an envelope from his pocket. "Here's a letter for you. I forgot it this afternoon. Sorry."

She was reading again. "Put it on the table," she said, without raising her eyes. He laid the letter on the table and quitted the room. At the door he looked back, but her head was bent over her book.

As he removed his clothes it did seem that that heavy fading odor of Belle's body clung to them, and to his hands even after he was in bed; and clinging, shaped in the darkness beside him Belle's rich voluptuousness until within that warm, not-yet-sleeping region where dwells the mother of dreams, Belle grew palpable in ratio as his own body slipped away from him. And Harry too, with his dogged inarticulateness and his hurt groping which was partly damaged vanity and shock, yet mostly a boy's sincere bewilderment that freed itself terrifically in the form of movie subtitles. Just before he slept, his mind, with the mind's uncanny attribute for irrelevant recapitulation, reproduced with the startling ghostliness of a dictaphone an incident which at the time he had considered trivial. Belle had freed her mouth, and for a moment, her body still against his, she held his face in her two hands and stared at him with intent, questioning eyes. "Have you plenty of money, Horace?" And "Yes," he had answered immediately, "of course I have." And then Belle again, enveloping him like a rich and fatal drug, like a motionless and cloying sea in which he watched himself drown.

The letter lay on the table that night, forgotten; it was

not until the next morning that she discovered it and opened it.

"I am trying to forget you I cannot forget you Your big eyes your black hair how white your black hair make you look. And how you walk I am watching you a smell you give off like a flowr. Your eyes shine with mistry and how you walk makes me sick like a fevver all night thinking how you walk. I could touch you you would not know it. Every day But I can not I must pore out on paper must talk You do not know who. Your lips like cupids bow when the day comes when I press it to mine. Like I dreamed in a fevver from heaven to Hell. I know what you do I know more than you think I see men visit you with bitter twangs. Be care full I am a desprate man Nothing any more to me now If you unholy love a man I will kill him.

"You do not anser. I know you got it I saw one in your hand bag. You better anser soon I am desprate man eat up with fevver I can not sleep for. I will not hurt you but I am desprate. Do not forget I will not hurt you but I am a desprate man."

Meanwhile the days accumulated. Not sad days nor lonely: they were too feverish to be sorrowful, what with her nature torn in two directions and the walls of her serene garden cast down and she herself like a night animal or bird caught in a beam of light and trying vainly to escape. Horace had definitely gone his way, and like two strangers they followed the routine of their physical days, in an unbending estrangement of long affection and similar pride beneath a shallow veneer of trivialities. She sat with Bayard almost every day now, but at a discreet distance of two yards.

At first he had tried to override her with bluster, then with cajolery. But she was firm, and at last he desisted and lay gazing quietly out the window or sleeping while she read. From time to time Miss Jenny would come to the door and look in at them and go away. Her shrinking, her sense of anticipation and dread while with him, was gone now, and at times instead of reading they talked, quietly and impersonally, with the ghost of that other afternoon between them, though neither ever referred to it. Miss Jenny had been a little curious about that day, but Narcissa was gravely and demurely noncommittal about it, nor had Bayard ever talked of it. And so there was another bond between them, but unirksome. Miss Jenny had heard gossip about Horace and Belle, but on this subject also Narcissa had nothing to say.

"Have it your own way," Miss Jenny said tartly; "I can draw my own conclusions. I imagine Belle and Horace can produce quite a mess together. And I'm glad of it. That man is making an old maid out of you. It isn't too late now, but if he'd waited five years later to play the fool, there wouldn't have been anything left for you except to give music lessons. But you can get married, now."

"Would you advise me to marry?" Narcissa asked.

"I wouldn't advise anybody to marry. You won't be happy, but then, women haven't got civilized enough yet to be happy unmarried, so you might as well try it. We can stand anything, anyhow. And change is good for folks. They say it is, at least."

But Narcissa didn't believe that. "I shall never marry," she told herself. Men . . . that was where unhappiness lay, getting men into your life. "And if I couldn't keep Horace, loving him as I did . . ." Bayard slept. She picked up the book and read on to herself, about antic people in an antic world where things happened as they should happen. The shadows lengthened eastward. She read on, lost from mutable things.

After a while Bayard waked, and she fetched him a cigarette and a match. "You won't have to do this any more," he said. "I reckon you're sorry."

His cast would come off tomorrow, he meant, and he lay smoking his cigarette and talking of what he would do when he was about again. He would see about getting his car repaired first thing; have to take it in to Memphis, probably. And he planned a trip for the three of them—Miss Jenny, Narcissa and himself—while the car was in the shop. "It'll take about a week," he added. "She must be in pretty bad shape. Hope I didn't hurt her guts any."

"But you aren't going to drive it fast any more," she reminded him. He lay still, his cigarette burning in his fingers. "You promised," she insisted.

"When did I promise?"

"Don't you remember? That . . . afternoon, when they were . . ."

"When I scared you?" She sat watching him with her

grave, troubled eyes. "Come here," he said. She rose and went to the bed and he took her hand.

"You won't drive it fast again?" she persisted.

"No," he answered, "I promise." And they were still so, her hand in his. The curtains stirred in the breeze, and the leaves on the branch beyond the window twinkled and turned and lisped against one another. Sunset was not far away. The breeze would cease then. He moved.

"Narcissa," he said. She looked at him. "Lean your face down here."

She looked away, and for a while there was no movement, no sound between them.

"I must go," she said at last, quietly, and he released her hand.

His cast was gone, and he was up and about again, moving a little gingerly, to be sure, but already Miss Jenny was beginning to contemplate him a little anxiously. "If we could just arrange to have one of his minor bones broken every month or so, just enough to keep him in the house . . ."

"That won't be necessary," Narcissa told her. "He's going to behave from now on."

"How do you know?" Miss Jenny demanded. "What in the world makes you think that?"

"He promised he would."

"He'll promise anything when he's flat on his back," Miss Jenny retorted. "They all will; always have. But what makes you think he'll keep it?"

"He promised me he would," Narcissa replied serenely.

His first act was to see about his car. It had been pulled into town and patched up after a fashion until it would run under its own power, but it would be necessary to take it to Memphis to have the frame straightened and the body repaired. Bayard was all for doing this himself, fresh-knit ribs and all, but Miss Jenny put her foot down, and after a furious half hour he was vanquished. And so the car was driven in to Memphis by a youth who hung around one of the garages in town. "Narcissa'll take you driving in her car, if you must ride," Miss Jenny told him.

"In that little peanut-parcher?" Bayard said derisively. "It won't do better than twenty-one miles."

"No, thank God," Miss Jenny answered. "And I've written to Memphis and asked 'em to fix yours so it'll run just like that, too."

Bayard stared at her with humorless bleakness. "Did you do any such damn thing as that?"

"Oh, take him away, Narcissa," Miss Jenny exclaimed. "Get him out of my sight. I'm so tired looking at you."

But he wouldn't ride in Narcissa's car at first. He missed no opportunity to speak of it with heavy, facetious disparagement, but he wouldn't ride in it. Dr. Alford had evolved a tight elastic bandage for his chest so that he could ride his horse, but he had developed an astonishing propensity for lounging about the house when Narcissa was there. And Narcissa came quite often. Miss Jenny thought it was on Bayard's account and pinned the guest down in her forthright way; whereupon Narcissa told her about Horace and Belle while Miss Jenny sat indomitably erect on her straight chair beside the piano.

"Poor child," she said, and: "Lord, ain't they fools?" And then: "Well, you're right; I wouldn't marry one of 'em either."

"I'm not," Narcissa answered. "I wish there weren't any of them in the world."

Miss Jenny said "Hmph."

And then one afternoon they were in Narcissa's car and Bayard was driving, over her protest at first. But he was behaving himself quite sensibly, and at last she relaxed. They drove down the valley road and turned into the hills and she asked where they were going, but his answer was vague. So she sat quietly beside him and the road mounted presently in long curves among dark pines in the slanting afternoon. The road wound on, with changing sun-shot vistas of the valley and the opposite hills at every turn, and always the somber pines and their faint, exhilarating odor. After a time they topped a hill and Bayard slowed the car. Beneath them the road sank, then flattened away toward a line of willows, crossed a stone bridge, and rose again, curving redly from sight among the dark trees.

"There's the place," he said.

"The place?" she repeated dreamily; then as the car rolled forward again, gaining speed, she roused herself and understood what he meant. "You promised!" she cried, but he

jerked the throttle down the ratchet, and she clutched him
and tried to scream. But she could make no sound, nor could
she close her eyes as the narrow bridge hurtled dancing toward them. And then her breath stopped and her heart as
they flashed, with a sharp reverberation like hail on a tin
roof, between willows and a crashing glint of water and shot
on up the next hill. The small car swayed on the curve,
lost its footing and went into the ditch, bounded out and
hurled across the road. Then Bayard straightened it out and
with diminishing speed it rocked on up the hill, and stopped.
She sat beside him, her bloodless mouth open, beseeching
him with her wide, hopeless eyes. Then she caught her
breath, wailing.

"I didn't mean——" he began awkwardly. "I just wanted
to see if I could do it," and he put his arms around her and
she clung to him, moving her hands crazily about his shoulders. "I didn't mean——" he essayed again, and then her
crazed hands were on his face and she was sobbing wildly
against his mouth.

9

All the forenoon he bent over his ledgers, watching his hand
pen the neat figures into the ruled columns with a sort of
astonishment. After his sleepless night he labored in a kind
of stupor, his mind too spent even to contemplate the coiling
images of his lust, thwarted now for all time, save with a dull
astonishment that the images no longer filled his blood with
fury and despair, so that it was some time before his dulled
nerves reacted to a fresh threat and caused him to raise his
head. Virgil Beard was just entering the door.

He slid hurriedly from his stool and slipped around the
corner and darted through the door of old Bayard's office.
He crouched within the door, heard the boy ask politely
for him, heard the cashier say that he was there a minute
ago but that he reckoned he had stepped out; heard the boy
say, well, he reckoned he'd wait for him. And he crouched
within the door, wiping his drooling mouth with his handkerchief.

After a while he opened the door cautiously. The boy

squatted patiently and blandly on his heels against the wall, and Snopes stood again with his clenched and trembling hands. He did not curse: his desperate fury was beyond words, but his breath came and went with a swift ah-ah-ah sound in his throat and it seemed to him that his eyeballs were being drawn back into his skull, turning further and further until the cords that drew them reached the snapping point. He opened the door.

"Hi, Mr. Snopes," the boy said genially, rising. Snopes strode on and entered the grille and approached the cashier.

"Res," he said in a voice scarcely articulate, "gimme five dollars."

"What?"

"Gimme five dollars," he repeated hoarsely. The cashier did so, and scribbled a notation and speared it on the file beside him. The boy had come up to the window, but Snopes went on and he followed the man back to the office, his bare feet hissing on the linoleum floor.

"I tried to find you last night," he explained. "But you wasn't to home." Then he looked up and saw Snopes' face, and after a moment he screamed and broke his trance and turned to flee. But the man caught him by his overalls, and he writhed and twisted, screaming with utter terror as the man dragged him across the office and opened the door that gave upon the vacant lot. Snopes was trying to say something in his mad, shaking voice, but the boy screamed steadily, hanging limp from the other's hand as he tried to thrust the bill into his pocket. At last he succeeded and released the boy, who staggered away, found his legs and fled.

"What were you whuppin' that boy, for?" the cashier asked curiously, when Snopes returned to his desk.

"For not minding his own business," he snapped, opening his ledger again.

As he crossed the now empty square he looked up at the lighted face of the clock. It was ten minutes past eleven. There was no sign of life save the lonely figure of the night marshal in the door of the lighted post-office lobby.

He left the square and entered a street and went steadily beneath the arc lights, having the street to himself and the regular recapitulation of his striding shadow dogging him out of the darkness, through the pool of the light and into

darkness again. He turned a corner and followed a yet quieter
street and turned presently from it into a lane between
massed banks of honeysuckle higher than his head and sweet
on the night air. The lane was dark and he increased his pace.
On either hand the upper stories of houses rose above the
honeysuckle, with now and then a lighted window among
the dark trees. He kept close to the wall and went swiftly
on, passing now between back premises. After a while another
house loomed, and a serried row of cedars against the paler
sky, and he stole beside a stone wall and so came opposite the
garage. He stopped here and sought in the lush grass beneath the wall and stooped and picked up a pole, which he
leaned against the wall. With the aid of the pole he mounted
on to the wall and thence to the garage roof.

The house was dark, and presently he slid to the ground
and stole across the lawn and stopped beneath a window.
There was a light somewhere toward the front, but no sound,
no movement; and he stood for a time listening, darting his
eyes this way and that, covert and ceaseless as a cornered
animal.

The screen responded easily to his knife, and he raised
it and listened again. Then with a single scrambling motion
he was in the room, crouching. Still no sound save the thudding of his heart, and the whole house gave off that unmistakable emanation of temporary desertion. He drew out his
handkerchief and wiped his mouth.

The light was in the next room, and he went on. The
stairs rose from the end of this room and he scuttled silently
across it and mounted swiftly into the upper darkness and
groped forward until he touched a wall, then a door. The
knob turned in his fingers.

It was the right room; he knew that at once. Her presence
was all about him, and for a time his heart thudded and
thudded in his throat and fury and lust and despair shook
him. He pulled himself together; he must get out quickly, and
he groped his way across to the bed and lay face down on it,
his head buried in the pillows, writhing and making smothered, animal-like moanings. But he must get out, and he got
up and groped across the room again. What little light there
was was behind him now, and instead of finding the door,
he blundered into a chest of drawers, and stood there a moment, learning its shape with his hands. Then he opened one

of the drawers and fumbled in it. It was filled with a faint-ly-scented fragility of garments, but he could not distinguish one from another with his hands.

He found a match in his pocket and struck it beneath the shelter of his palm, and by its light he chose one of the soft garments, discovering as the match died a packet of letters in the corner of the drawer. He recognized them at once, dropped the dead match to the floor and took the packet from the drawer and put it in his pocket, and placed the letter he had just written in the drawer, and he stood for a time with the garment crushed against his face; remained so for some time before a sound caused him to jerk his head up, listening. A car was entering the drive, and as he sprang to the window its lights swept beneath him and fell full upon the open garage, and he crouched at the window in a panic. Then he sped to the door and stopped again, crouching, panting and snarling with indecision.

He ran back to the window. The garage was dark, and two dark figures were approaching the house, and he crouched beside the window until they had passed from sight. Then, still clutching the garment, he climbed out the window and swung from the sill a moment by his hands, and closed his eyes and dropped.

A crash of glass, and he sprawled numbed by shock amid lesser crashes and a burst of stale, dry dust. He had fallen into a shallow flower-pit and he scrambled out and tried to stand and fell again, while nausea swirled in him. It was his knee, and he lay sick and with drawn, gasping lips while his trouser leg sopped slowly and warmly, clutching the garment and staring at the dark sky with wide, mad eyes. He heard voices in the house, and a light came on behind the window above him and he turned crawling, and at a scrambling hobble he crossed the lawn and plunged into the shadow of the cedars beside the garage, where he lay watching the window in which a man leaned, peering out; and he moaned a little while his blood ran between his clasped fingers. He drove himself onward again and dragged his bleeding leg up on to the wall, and dropped into the lane and cast the pole down. A hundred yards further he stopped and drew his torn trousers aside and tried to bandage the gash in his leg. But the handkerchief stained over almost at once and still blood ran and ran down his leg and into his shoe.

Once in the back room of the bank he rolled his trouser leg up and removed the handkerchief and bathed the gash at the lavatory. It still bled, and the sight of his own blood sickened him, and he swayed against the wall, watching his blood. Then he removed his shirt and bound it as tightly as he could about his leg. He still felt nausea, and he drank long of the tepid water from the tap. Immediately it welled salinely within him and he clung to the lavatory, sweating, trying not to vomit, until the spell passed. His leg felt numb and dead, and he was weak and he wished to lie down, but he dared not.

He entered the grille, his left heel showing a red print at each step. The vault door opened soundlessly; without a light he found the key to the cash box and opened it. He took only bank notes, but he took all he could find. Then he closed the vault and locked it, returned to the lavatory and wetted a towel and removed his heel prints from the linoleum floor. Then he passed out the back door, threw the latch so it would lock behind him. The clock on the courthouse rang midnight.

In an alley between two Negro stores a Negro man sat in a battered Ford, waiting. He gave the Negro a bill and the Negro cranked the engine and came and stared curiously at the bloody cloth beneath his torn trousers. "Whut happened, boss? Y'ain't hurt, is you?"

"Run into some wire," he answered shortly. "She's got plenty gas, ain't she?" The Negro said yes, and he drove on. As he crossed the square the marshal, Buck, stood beneath the light before the post office, and Snopes cursed him with silent and bitter derision. He drove on and entered another street and passed from view, and presently the sound of his going had died away.

PART FOUR

IT WAS A SUNNY SUNDAY afternoon in October. Narcissa and Bayard had driven off soon after dinner and Miss Jenny and old Bayard were sitting on the sunny end of the veranda when, preceded by Simon, the deputation came solemnly around the corner of the house from the rear. It consisted of six Negroes in a catholic variety of Sunday raiment and it was headed by a huge, bull-necked Negro in a hind-side-before collar and a Prince Albert coat, with an orotund air and a wild, compelling eye.

"Yere dey is, Cunnel," Simon said, and without pausing he mounted the steps and turned about, leaving no doubt in any one's mind as to which side he considered himself aligned with. The deputation halted and milled a little, solemnly decorous.

"What's this?" Miss Jenny asked. "That you, Uncle Bird?"

"Yessum, Miss Jenny." One of the committee uncovered his grizzled wool and bowed. "How you gittin' on?" The others shuffled their feet, and one by one they removed their hats. The leader clasped his across his chest like a Congressman being photographed.

"Here, Simon," old Bayard demanded, "what's this? What did you bring these niggers around here for?"

"Dey come fer dey money," Simon explained.

"What?"

"Money?" Miss Jenny repeated with interest. "What money, Simon?"

"Dey come fer dat money you promised 'um," Simon shouted.

"I told you I wasn't going to pay that money," old Bayard

220

said. "Did Simon tell you I was going to pay it?" he demanded of the deputation.

"What money?" Miss Jenny repeated. "What are you talking about, Simon?" The leader of the committee was shaping
his face for words, but Simon forestalled him.

"Why, Cunnel, you tole me yo'self to tell dem niggers
you wuz gwine pay 'um."

"I didn't do any such thing," old Bayard answered
violently. "I told you that if they wanted to put you in jail,
to go ahead and do it. That's what I told you."

"Why, Cunnel. You said it jes' ez plain. You jes' fergot
erbout it. I kin prove it by Miss Jenny you tole me——"

"Not by me," Miss Jenny interrupted. "This is the first I
heard about it. Whose money is it, Simon?"

Simon gave her a pained, reproachful look. "He tole me
to tell 'um he wuz gwine pay it."

"I'm damned if I did," old Bayard shouted. "I told you
I wouldn't pay a damn cent of it. And I told you that if you
let 'em worry me about it, I'd skin you alive, sir."

"I ain't gwine let 'um worry you," Simon answered, sooth-
ingly. "Dat's whut I'm fixin' now. You jes' give 'um dey
money, en me en you kin fix it up later."

"I'll be eternally damned if I will; if I let a lazy nigger that
ain't worth his keep——"

"But somebody got to pay 'um," Simon pointed out patiently. "Ain't dat right, Miss Jenny?"

"That's right," Miss Jenny agreed. "But I ain't the one."

"Yessuh, dey ain't no argument dat somebody got to pay
'um. Ef somebody don't quiet 'um down, dey'll put me in
de jail. And den whut'll y'all do, widout nobody to keep dem
hosses fed en clean, en to clean de house en wait on de
table? Co'se I don't mine gwine to jail, even ef dem stone flo's
ain't gwine do my mis'ry no good." And he drew a long and
affecting picture, of high, grail-like principles and of patient
abnegation. Old Bayard slammed his feet to the floor.

"How much is it?"

The leader swelled within his Prince Albert. "Brudder Mo',"
he said, "will you read out de total emoluments owed to de
pupposed Secon' Baptis' Church by de late Deacon Strother
in his capacity ez treasurer of de church boa'd?"

Brother Moore created a mild disturbance in the rear of
the group, emerging presently by the agency of sundry will-

ing hands—a small, reluctant ebon Negro in somber, over-large black—where the parson majestically made room for him, contriving by some means to focus attention on him. He laid his hat on the ground at his feet and from the right-hand pocket of his coat he produced in order a red bandana handkerchief, a shoe-horn, a plug of chewing-tobacco, and holding these in his free hand he delved again, with an expression of mildly conscientious alarm. Then he replaced the objects, and from his left pocket he produced a pocket knife, a stick on which was wound a length of soiled twine, a short piece of leather strap attached to a rusty and apparently idle buckle, and lastly a greasy, dog-eared note-book. He crammed the other things back into his pocket, drop-ping the strap, which he stooped and recovered; then he and the parson held a brief whispered conversation. He opened the notebook and fumbled at the leaves, fumbled at them until the parson leaned over his shoulder and found the proper page and laid his finger on it.

"How much is it, reverend?" old Bayard asked impatiently.

"Brudder Mo' will now read out de amount," the parson intoned. Brother Moore looked at the page with his tranced gaze and mumbled something in a practically indistinguishable voice.

"What?" old Bayard demanded, cupping his ear.

"Make 'im talk out," Simon said. "Can't nobody tell whut he sayin'."

"Louder," the parson rumbled, with just a trace of impatience.

"Sixty-sevum dollars en fawty cents," Brother Moore enunciated at last. Old Bayard slammed back in his chair and swore for a long minute while Simon watched him with covert anxiety. Then he rose and tramped up the veranda and into the house, still swearing. Simon sighed and relaxed. The deputation milled again, and Brother Moore faded briskly into the rear of it. The parson, however, still retained his former attitude of fateful and impressive profundity.

"What became of that money, Simon?" Miss Jenny asked curiously. "You had it, didn't you?"

"Dat's whut dey claims," Simon answered.

"What did you do with it?"

"Hit's all right," Simon assured her. "I jes' put it out, sort of."

"I bet you did," she agreed drily. "I bet it never even got cool while you had it. They deserve to lose it for ever giving it to you in the first place. Who did you put it out to?"

"Oh, me en Cunnel done fix dat up," Simon said easily, "long time ago." Old Bayard tramped in the hall again and emerged, flapping a check in his hand.

"Here," he commanded, and the parson approached the railing and took it and folded it away in his pocket. "And if you folks are fools enough to turn any more money over to him, don't come to me for it, you hear?" He glared at the deputation a moment; then he glared at Simon. "And the next time you steal money and come to me to pay it back, I'm going to have you arrested and prosecute you myself. Get those niggers out of here."

The deputation had already stirred with a concerted movement, but the parson halted them with a commanding hand. He faced Simon again. "Deacon Strother," he said, "ez awdained minister of de late Fust Baptis' Church, en recalled minister of de pupposed Secon' Baptis' Church, en chairman of dis committee, I hereby reinfests you wid yo' fawmer capacities of deacon in de said pupposed Secon' Baptis' Church. Amen. Cunnel Sartoris and ma'am, good day." Then he turned and herded his committee from the scene.

"Thank de Lawd, we got dat offen our mind," Simon said, and he came and lowered himself to the top step, groaning pleasurably.

"And you remember what I said," old Bayard warned him. "One more time, now——"

But Simon was craning his head in the direction the church board had taken. "Dar, now," he said, "whut you reckon dey wants now?" For the committee had returned and it now peered diffidently around the corner of the house.

"Well?" old Bayard demanded. "What is it now?"

They were trying to thrust Brother Moore forward again, but he won, this time. At last the parson spoke.

"You fergot de fawty cents, white folks."

"What?"

"He says, you lef' out de extry fawty cents," Simon shouted. Old Bayard exploded; Miss Jenny clapped her hands to her ears and the committee rolled its eyes in fearsome admiration while he soared to magnificent heights, alighting finally on Simon.

"You give him that forty cents, and get 'em out of here," old Bayard stormed. "And if you ever let 'em come back here again, I'll take a horsewhip to the whole passel of you!"

"Lawd, Cunnel, I ain't got no fawty cents, en you knows it. Can't dey do widout dat, after gittin' de balance of it?"

"Yes, you have, Simon," Miss Jenny said. "You had a half a dollar left after I ordered those shoes for you last night." Again Simon looked at her with pained astonishment.

"Give it to 'em," old Bayard commanded. Slowly Simon reached into his pocket and produced a half dollar and turned it slowly in his palm.

"I mought need dis money, Cunnel," he protested. "Seems like dey mought leave me dis."

"Give 'em that money!" old Bayard thundered. "I reckon you can pay forty cents of it, at least." Simon rose reluctantly, and the parson approached.

"Whar's my dime change?" Simon demanded, nor would he surrender the coin until two nickels were in his hand. Then the committee departed.

"Now," old Bayard said, "I want to know what you did with that money."

"Well, suh," Simon began readily, "it wuz like dis. I put dat money out." Miss Jenny rose.

"My Lord, are you all going over that again?" And she left them. In her room, where she sat in a sunny window, she could still hear them—old Bayard's stormy rage and Simon's bland and plausible evasion, rising and falling on the drowsy Sabbath air.

There was a rose, a single remaining rose. Through the sad, dead days of late summer it had continued to bloom, and now though persimmons had long swung their miniature suns among the caterpillar-festooned branches, and gum and maple and hickory had flaunted two gold and scarlet weeks, and the grass, where grandfathers of grasshoppers squatted sluggishly like sullen octogenarians, had been penciled twice delicately with frost, and the sunny noons were scented with sassafras, it still bloomed—overripe now, and a little gallantly blowsy, like a fading burlesque star.

Miss Jenny worked in a sweater these days, and her trowel glinted in her earthy glove.

"It's like some women I've known," she said. "It just don't know how to give up gracefully and be a grandmamma."

"Let it have the summer out," Narcissa in her dark woolen dress protested. She had a trowel too, and she pottered serenely after Miss Jenny's scolding and brisk impatience, accomplishing nothing. Worse than nothing, worse than Isom even, because she demoralized Isom, who had immediately given his unspoken allegiance to the left, or passive, wing. "It's entitled to its summer."

"Some folks don't know when summer's over," Miss Jenny rejoined. "Indian summer's no excuse for senile adolescence."

"It isn't senility, either."

"All right. You'll see, some day."

"Oh, some day. I'm not quite prepared to be a grandmother, yet."

"You're doing pretty well." Miss Jenny troweled a tulip bulb carefully and expertly up and removed the clotted earth from its roots. "We seem to have pretty well worn out Bayard, for the time being," she continued. "I reckon we'd better name him John this time."

"Yes?"

"Yes," Miss Jenny repeated. "We'll name him John. You, Isom!"

The gin had been running steadily for a month, now, what with the Sartoris cotton and that of other planters further up the valley, and of smaller croppers with their tilted fields among the hills. The Sartoris place was farmed on shares. Most of the tenants had picked their cotton, and gathered the late corn; and of late afternoons, with Indian summer on the land and an ancient sadness sharp as wood-smoke on the windless air, Bayard and Narcissa would drive out where, beside a spring on the edge of the woods, the Negroes brought their cane and made their communal winter sorghum molasses. One of the Negroes, a sort of patriarch among the tenants, owned the mill and the mule that furnished the motive power. He did the grinding and superintended the cooking of the sap for a tithe, and when Bayard and Narcissa arrived the mule would be plodding in its monotonous and patient circle, its feet rustling in the dried cane-pith, while one of the patriarch's grandsons fed the cane into the crusher.

Round and round the mule went, setting its narrow, deer-like feet delicately down in the hissing cane-pith, its neck bobbing limber as a section of rubber hose in the collar, with its trace-galled flanks and flopping, lifeless ears and its half-closed eyes drowsing venomously behind pale lids, apparently asleep with the monotony of its own motion. Some Homer of the cotton fields should sing the saga of the mule and of his place in the South. He it was, more than any other one creature or thing, who, steadfast to the land when all else faltered before the hopeless juggernaut of circumstance, impervious to conditions that broke men's hearts because of his venomous and patient preoccupation with the immediate present, won the prone South from beneath the iron heel of Reconstruction and taught it pride again through humility, and courage through adversity overcome; who accomplished the well-nigh impossible despite hopeless odds, by sheer and vindictive patience. Father and mother he does not resemble, sons and daughters he will never have; vindictive and patient (it is a known fact that he will labor ten years willingly and patiently for you, for the privilege of kicking you once); solitary but without pride, self-sufficient but without vanity; his voice is his own derision. Outcast and pariah, he has neither friend, wife, mistress, nor sweetheart; celibate, he is unscarred, possesses neither pillar nor desert cave, he is not assaulted by temptations nor flagellated by dreams nor assuaged by vision; faith, hope and charity are not his. Misanthropic, he labors six days without reward for one creature whom he hates, bound with chains to another whom he despises, and spends the seventh day kicking or being kicked by his fellows. Misunderstood even by that creature, the nigger who drives him, whose impulses and mental processes most closely resemble his, he performs alien actions in alien surroundings; he finds bread not only for a race, but for an entire form of behavior; meek, his inheritance is cooked away from him along with his soul in a glue factory. Ugly, untiring and perverse, he can be moved neither by reason, flattery, nor promise of reward; he performs his humble monotonous duties without complaint, and his meed is blows. Alive, he is haled through the world, an object of general derision; unwept, unhonored and unsung, he bleaches his awkward accusing bones among rusting cans and broken crockery and worn-out automobile tires on lonely hillsides while his flesh soars unawares against the blue in the craws of buzzards.

As they approached, the groaning and creaking of the mill would be the first intimation, unless the wind happened to blow toward them; then it would be the sharp, subtly exciting odor of fermentation and of boiling molasses. Bayard liked the smell of it and they would drive up and stop for a time while the boy rolled his eyes covertly at them as he fed cane into the mill, while they watched the patient mule and the old man stooped over the simmering pot. Sometimes Bayard got out and went over and talked to him, leaving Narcissa in the car, lapped in the ripe odors of the failing year and all its rich, vague sadness, her gaze brooding on Bayard and the old Negro—the one lean and tall and fatally young and the other stooped with time, and her spirit went out in serene and steady waves, surrounding him unawares.

Then he would return and get in beside her and she would touch his rough clothing, but so lightly that he was not conscious of it, and they would drive back along the faint, uneven road, beside the flaunting woods, and soon, above turning locusts and oaks, the white house simple and huge and steadfast, and the orange disk of the harvest moon getting above the ultimate hills, ripe as cheese.

Sometimes they went back after dark. The mill was still then, its long arm motionless across the firelit scene. The mule was munching in stable, or stamping and nuzzling its empty manger, or asleep standing, boding not of tomorrow; and against the firelight many shadows moved. The Negroes had gathered now: old men and women sitting on crackling cushions of cane about the blaze which one of their number fed with pressed stalks until its incense-laden fury swirled licking at the boughs overhead, making more golden still the twinkling golden leaves; and young men and girls, and children squatting and still as animals, staring into the fire. Sometimes they sang—quavering, wordless chords in which plaintive minors blent with mellow bass in immemorial and sad suspense, their grave dark faces bent to the flames and with no motion of lips.

But when the white folks arrived the singing ceased, and

they sat or lay about the fire on which the blackened pot simmered, talking in broken, murmurous overtones ready with sorrowful mirth, while in shadowy beds among the dry whispering cane-stalks youths and girls murmured and giggled.

Always one of them, and sometimes both, stopped in the office where old Bayard and Miss Jenny were. There was a fire of logs on the hearth now and they would sit in the glow of it—Miss Jenny beneath the light with her lurid daily paper; old Bayard with his slippered feet propped against the fireplace, his head wreathed in smoke and the old setter dreaming fitfully beside his chair, reliving proud and ancient stands perhaps, or further back still, the lean, gawky days of his young doghood, when the world was full of scents that maddened the blood in him and pride had not taught him self-restraint; Narcissa and Bayard between them—Narcissa dreaming too in the firelight, grave and tranquil, and young Bayard smoking his cigarettes in his leashed and moody repose.

At last old Bayard would throw his cigar into the fire and drop his feet to the floor, and the dog would wake and raise its head and blink and yawn with such gaping deliberation that Narcissa, watching him, invariably yawned also.

"Well, Jenny?"

Miss Jenny would lay her paper aside and rise. "Let me," Narcissa would say. "Let me go." But Miss Jenny never would, and presently she would return with a tray and three glasses, and old Bayard would unlock his desk and fetch the silver-stoppered decanter and compound three toddies with ritualistic care.

Once Bayard persuaded her into khaki and boots and carried her 'possum-hunting. Caspey with a streaked lantern and a cow's horn slung over his shoulder, and Isom with a gunny sack and an ax and four shadowy, restless hounds waited for them at the lot gate and they set off among ghostly shocks of corn, where every day Bayard kicked up a covey of quail, toward the woods.

"Where we going to start tonight, Caspey?" Bayard asked.

"Back of Unc' Henry's. Dey's one in dat grapevine behine de cotton house. Blue treed 'im down dar las' night."

"How do you know he's there tonight, Caspey?" Narcissa asked.

"He be back," Caspey answered confidently. "He right dar now, watchin' dis lantern wid his eyes scrooched up, listenin' to hear ef de dawgs wid us."

They climbed through a fence and Caspey stooped and set the lantern down. The dogs moiled and tugged about his legs with sniffings and throaty growls at one another as he unleashed them. "You, Ruby! Stan' still, dar. Hole up here, you potlickin' fool." They whimpered and surged, their eyes melting in fluid brief gleams; then they faded soundlessly and swiftly into the darkness. "Give 'um a little time," Caspey said; "let 'um see ef he dar yit." From the darkness ahead a dog yapped three times on a high note. "Dat's dat young dog," Caspey said. "Jes' showin' off. He ain't smelt nothin'."

Overhead the stars swam vaguely in the hazy sky; the air was not yet chill, the earth still warm to the touch. They stood in a steady oasis of lantern light in a world of but one dimension, a vague cistern of darkness filled with meager light and topped with an edgeless canopy of ragged stars. The lantern was smoking and emanating a faint odor of heat. Caspey raised it and turned the wick down and set it at his feet again. Then from the darkness there came a single note, resonant and low and grave.

"Dar he," Isom said.

"Hit's Ruby," Caspey agreed, picking up the lantern. "She got 'im." The young dog yapped again, with fierce hysteria; then the single low cry chimed. Narcissa slid her arm through Bayard's. "'Tain't no rush," Caspey told her. "Dey ain't treed yit. Whooy. H'mawn, dawg." The young dog had ceased its yapping, but still at intervals the other one bayed her single timbrous note, and they followed it. "H'mawn, dawg!"

They stumbled a little over fading plow scars, after Caspey's bobbing lantern, and the darkness went suddenly crescendo with short, steady cries in four keys. "Dey got 'im," Isom said.

"Dat's right," Caspey agreed. "Le's go. Hold 'im, dawg!" They trotted now, Narcissa clinging to Bayard's arm, and plunged through rank grass and over another fence and so among trees. Eyes gleamed fleetingly from the darkness ahead; another gust of barking interspersed with tense,

eager whimperings, and among stumbling half-lit shadows
dogs surged about them. "He up dar," Caspey said. "Ole
Blue sees 'im."

"Dar Unc' Henry's dawg, too," Isom said.

Caspey grunted. "I knowed he'd be here. He can't keep
up wid a 'possum no mo', but jes let a dawg tree whar he
kin hear 'im . . ." He set the lantern on his head and peered
up into the vine-matted sapling, and Bayard drew a flash
light from his pocket and turned its beam into the tree. The
three older hounds and Uncle Henry's ancient, moth-eaten
beast sat in a tense circle about the tree, whimpering or
barking in short spaced gusts, but the young one yapped
steadily in mad, hysterical rushes. "Kick dat puppy still,"
Caspey commanded.

"You, Ginger, hush yo' mouf," Isom shouted. He laid his
ax and sack down and caught the puppy and held it between
his knees. Caspey and Bayard moved slowly about the tree,
among the eager dogs. Narcissa followed them.

"Dem vines is so thick up dar . . ." Caspey said.

"Here he is," Bayard said suddenly. "I've got 'im." He
steadied his light and Caspey moved behind him and looked
over his shoulder.

"Where?" Narcissa asked. "Can you see it?"

"Dat's right," Caspey agreed. "Dar he is. Ruby don't lie.
When she say he dar, he dar."

"Where is he, Bayard?" Narcissa repeated. He drew her
before him and trained the light over her head, into the
tree, and presently from the massed vines two reddish points
of fire not a match-breadth apart gleamed at her, winked out,
then shone again.

"He movin'," Caspey said. "Young 'possum. Git up dar
and shake 'im out, Isom." Bayard held his light on the
creature's eyes and Caspey set his lantern down and herded
the dogs together at his knees. Isom scrambled up into the
tree and vanished in the mass of vine, but they could follow
his progress by the shaking branches and his panting
ejaculations as he threatened the animal with a mixture of
cajolery and adjuration.

"Hah," he grunted, "ain't gwine hurt you. Ain't gwine
do nothin' ter you but th'ow you in de cook-pot. Look out,
mister, I'se comin' up dar." More commotion; it ceased, they

could hear him moving the branches cautiously. "Here he," he called suddenly. "Hole dem dawgs, now."

"Little 'un, ain't he?" Caspey asked.

"Can't tell. Can't see nothin' but his face. Watch dem dawgs." The upper part of the sapling burst into violent and sustained fury; Isom whooped louder and louder as he shook the branches. "Whooy, here he comes," he shouted, and something dropped sluggishly and reluctantly from branch to invisible branch, stopped; and the dogs set up a straining clamor. The thing fell again, and Bayard's light followed a lumpy object that plumped with a resounding thud to the ground and vanished immediately beneath a swirl of hounds.

Caspey and Bayard leaped among them with shouts and at last succeeded in dragging them clear, and Narcissa saw the creature in the pool of the flash light, lying on its side in a grinning curve, its eyes closed and its pink, babylike hands doubled against its breast. She looked at the motionless thing with pity and distinct loathing—such a paradox, its vulpine, skull-like grin and those tiny, human-looking hands, and the long ratlike tail of it. Isom dropped from the tree and Caspey turned the three straining clamorous dogs he held over to his nephew and picked up the ax, and while Narcissa watched in shrinking curiosity, he laid the ax across the thing's neck and put his foot on either end of the helve, and grasped the animal's tail. . . . She turned and fled, her hand to her mouth.

But the wall of darkness stopped her and she stood trembling and a little sick, watching them as they moved about the lantern. Then Caspey drove the dogs away, giving Uncle Henry's octogenarian a hearty and resounding kick that sent him homeward with blood-curdling and astonished wails, and Isom swung the lumpy sack to his shoulder and Bayard turned and looked for her. "Narcissa?"

"Here," she answered. He came to her.

"That's one. We ought to get a dozen, tonight."

"Oh, no," she shuddered. "No." He peered at her; then he snapped his flash light full on her face. She lifted her hand and put it aside.

"What's the matter? Not tired already, are you?"

"No." She went on, "I just . . . Come on: they're leaving us."

Caspey led them on into the woods. They walked now in a dry sibilance of leaves and crackling undergrowth. Trees loomed into the lantern light; above them, among the thinning branches, stars swam in the hushed, vague sky. The dogs were on ahead, and they went on among the looming tree trunks, sliding down into ditches where sand gleamed in the lantern's pool and where the scissoring shadow of Caspey's legs was enormous, struggled through snatching briers and up the other bank.

"We better head away fum de creek bottom," Caspey suggested. "Dey mought strike a 'coon, and den dey won't git home 'fo' day." He bore away toward the open again; they emerged from the woods and crossed a field of sedge, odorous of sun and dust, in which the lantern was lightly nimbused. "H'mawn, dawg."

They entered the woods again. Narcissa was beginning to tire, but Bayard strode on with a fine obliviousness of that possibility, and she followed without complaint. At last, from some distance away, came that single ringing cry. Caspey stopped. "Le's see which way he gwine." They stood in the darkness, in the sad, faintly chill decline of the year, among the dying trees, listening. "Whooy," Caspey shouted mellowly. "Go git 'im."

The dog replied, and they moved again, slowly, pausing at intervals to listen again. The hound bayed; there were two voices now, and they seemed to be moving in a circle across their path. "Whooy," Caspey called, his voice ebbing in falling echoes among the trees. They went on. Again the dogs gave tongue, half the circle away from where the first cry had come. "He ca'yin' 'um right back whar he come fum," Caspey said. "We better wait 'twell dey gits 'im straightened out." He set the lantern down and squatted beside it, and Isom sloughed his burden and squatted also, and Bayard sat against a tree trunk and drew Narcissa down beside him. The dogs bayed again, nearer. Caspey stared off into the darkness toward the sound.

"I believe hit's a 'coon dey got," Isom said.

"Mought be. Hill 'coon."

"Headin' fer dat holler tree, ain't he?"

"Soun' like it." They listened, motionless. "We have a job, den," Caspey added. "Whooy." There was a faint chill in the air now, as the day's sunlight cooled from the ground, and Narcissa moved closer to Bayard. He took a packet of cigarettes from his jacket and gave Caspey one and lit one for himself. Isom squatted on his heels, his eyes rolling whitely in the lantern light.

"Gimme one, please, suh," he said.

"You ain't got no business smokin', boy," Caspey told him. But Bayard gave him one, and he squatted leanly on his haunches, holding the white tube in his black diffident hand. There was a scurrying noise in the leaves behind them and a tense whimpering, and the young dog came into the light and slid with squeaking whimpers, and the diffident, fleeting phosphorus of its eyes against Caspey's leg. "Whut you want?" Caspey said, dropping his hand on its head. "Somethin' skeer you out dar?" The puppy genuflected its gawky young body and nuzzled whimpering at Caspey's hand. "He mus' 'a' foun' a bear down yonder," Caspey said. "Wouldn't dem other dawgs he'p you ketch 'im?"

"Poor little fellow," Narcissa said. "Did he really get scared, Caspey? Come here, puppy."

"De other dawgs jes' went off and lef' 'im," Caspey answered. The puppy moiled diffidently about Caspey's knees; then it scrambled up and licked his face.

"Git down fum here!" Caspey exclaimed, and he flung the puppy away. It flopped awkwardly in the dry leaves and scrambled to its feet, and at that moment the hounds bayed again, mellow and chiming and timbrous in the darkness, and the puppy whirled and sped yapping shrilly toward the sound. The dogs bayed again; Isom and Caspey listened. "Yes, suh," Caspey repeated, "he headin' fer dat down tree."

"You know this country like you do the back yard, don't you, Caspey?" Narcissa said.

"Yessum, I ought to. I been over it a hund'ed times since I wuz bawn. Mist' Bayard knows hit, too. He been huntin' it long ez I is, pretty near. Him and Mist' Johnny bofe. Miss Jenny send me wid 'um when dey had dey fust gun; me and dat 'ere single bar'l gun I use ter have ter tie together wid a string. You 'member dat ole single bar'l, Mist' Bayard? But hit would shoot. Many's de fox squir'l we shot in dese woods. Rabbits, too." Bayard was leaning back against the tree. He was gazing off into the treetops and the soft sky beyond, his cigarette burning slowly in his hand. She looked at his bleak profile against the lantern glow and moved closer against him. But he did not respond, and she slid her hand in his. But it too was cold, and again he had left her for the lonely heights of his despair. Caspey was speaking again, in his slow, consonantless voice with its overtones of mellow sadness. "Mist' Johnny, now, he sho' could shoot. You 'member dat time me and you and him wuz——"

Bayard rose. He dropped his cigarette and crushed it carefully with his heel. "Let's go," he said. "They ain't going to tree." He drew Narcissa to her feet and turned and went on. Caspey got up and unslung his horn and put it to his lips. The sound swelled about them, grave and clear and prolonged; then it died into echoes and so into silence again, leaving no ripple in the still darkness.

It was near midnight when they left Caspey and Isom at their cabin and followed the lane toward the house. The barn loomed presently beside them, and the house among its thinning trees, against the hazy sky. He opened the gate and she passed through and he followed and closed it, and turning he found her beside him, and stopped. "Bayard?" she whispered, leaning against him, and he put his arms around her and stood so, gazing above her head into the sky. She took his face between her palms and drew it down, but his lips were cold and upon them she tasted fatality and doom, and she clung to him for a time, her head bowed against his chest.

After that she would not go with him again. So he went alone, returning anywhere between midnight and dawn, ripping his clothing off quietly in the darkness and sliding cautiously into bed. But when he was still she would touch him and speak his name in the dark beside him, and turn to him warm and soft with sleep. And they would lie so, holding to one another in the darkness and the temporary abeyance of his despair and the isolation of that doom he could not escape.

2

"Well," Miss Jenny said briskly, above the soup, "your girl's gone and left you, and now you can find time to come out and see your kinfolks, can't you?"

Horace grinned a little. "To tell the truth, I came out to get something to eat. I don't think that one woman in ten has any aptitude for housekeeping, but my place is certainly not in the home."

"You mean," Miss Jenny corrected, "that not one man in ten has sense enough to marry a decent cook."

"Maybe they have more sense and consideration for others than to spoil decent cooks," he suggested.

"Yes," young Bayard said, "even a cook'll quit work when she gets married."

"Dat's de troof," Simon, propped in a slightly florid attitude against the sideboard, in a collarless boiled shirt and his Sunday pants (it is Thanksgiving Day) and reeking a little of whisky in addition to his normal odors, agreed. "I had to fin' Euphrony fo' new cookin' places de fust two mont' we wuz ma'ied."

Dr. Peabody said, "Simon must have married somebody else's cook."

"I'd rather marry somebody else's cook than somebody else's wife," Miss Jenny snapped.

"Miss Jenny!" Narcissa reproved. "You hush."

"I'm sorry," Miss Jenny said immediately. "I wasn't saying that at you, Horace; it just popped into my head. I was talking to you, Loosh Peabody. You think, just because you've eaten off of us Thanksgiving and Christmas for sixty years, that you can come into my own house and laugh at me, don't you?"

"Hush, Miss Jenny!" Narcissa repeated. Horace put down his spoon, and Narcissa's hand found his beneath the table.

"What's that?" Old Bayard, his napkin tucked into his waistcoat, lowered his spoon and cupped his hand to his ear.

"Nothing," young Bayard told him. "Aunt Jenny and Doc fighting again. Come alive, Simon." Simon stirred and removed the soup plates, but laggardly, still giving his interested attention to the altercation.

"Yes," Miss Jenny rushed on, "just because that old fool of a Will Falls put axle grease on a little bump on his face without killing him, you have to go around swelled up like a poisoned dog. What did you have to do with it? You certainly didn't take it off. Maybe you conjured it on his face to begin with?"

"Haven't you got a piece of bread or something Miss Jenny can put in her mouth, Simon?" Dr. Peabody asked mildly. Miss Jenny glared at him a moment; then she flopped back in her chair.

"You, Simon! Are you dead?" Simon removed the plates and bore them out, and the guests sat avoiding one another's eyes a little while Miss Jenny, behind her barricade of cups and urns and jugs and things, continued to breathe fire and brimstone.

"Will Falls," old Bayard repeated. "Jenny, tell Simon, when he fixes that basket, to come to my office; I've got something to go in it." This was the pint flask of whisky which he included in old man Falls' Thanksgiving and Christmas basket and which the old fellow divided out by spoonfuls as far as it would go among his ancient and homeless cronies on those days; and invariably old Bayard reminded her to tell Simon of something which neither of them had overlooked.

"All right," she returned. Simon reappeared, with a huge silver coffee-urn, set it beside Miss Jenny, and retreated to the kitchen.

"How many of you want coffee now?" she asked generally. "Bayard will no more sit down to a meal without his coffee than he'd fly. Will you, Horace?" He declined, and without looking at Dr. Peabody she said, "I reckon you'll have to have some, won't you?"

"If it's no trouble," he answered mildly. He winked at Narcissa and assumed an expression of lugubrious diffidence. Miss Jenny drew two cups, and Simon appeared with a huge platter borne gallantly and precariously aloft and set it before old Bayard with a magnificent flourish.

"My God, Simon," young Bayard said, "where did you get a whale this time of year?"

"Dat's a fish in dis worl', mon," Simon agreed. And it was a fish. It was a yard long and broad as a saddle blanket; it was a jolly red color and it lay gaping on the platter with an air of dashing and rollicking joviality.

"Dammit, Jenny," old Bayard said pettishly, "what did you want to have this thing for? Who wants to clutter his stomach up with fish in November, with a kitchen full of 'possum and turkey and squirrel?"

"There are other people to eat here besides you," she retorted. "If you don't want any, don't eat it. We always had a fish course at home," she added. "But you can't wean these Mississippi country folks away from bread and meat to save your life. Here, Simon." Simon set a stack of plates before old Bayard and he now came with his tray and Miss Jenny put two coffee cups on it and he served them to old Bayard and Dr. Peabody. Miss Jenny drew a cup for herself, and Simon passed sugar and cream. Old Bayard, still grumbling heavily, carved the fish.

"I ain't ever found anything wrong with fish at any time of year," Dr. Peabody said.

"You wouldn't," Miss Jenny snapped. Again he winked heavily at Narcissa.

"Only," he continued, "I like to catch my own, out of my own pond. Mine have mo' food value."

"Still got your pond, Doc?" young Bayard asked.

"Yes. But the fishin' ain't been so good, this year. Abe had the flu last winter, and ever since he's been goin' to sleep on me, and I have to sit there and wait until he wakes up to take the fish off and bait the hook again. But finally I thought about tyin' a cord to his leg and the other end of it to the bench, and now when I get a bite, I just reach around and give the string a yank and wake 'im up. You'll have to bring yo' wife out some day, Bayard. She ain't never seen my pond."

"You haven't?" Bayard asked Narcissa. She had not. "He's got benches all around it, with footrests, and a railing just high enough to prop your pole on, and a nigger to every fisherman to bait his hook and take the fish off. I don't see why you feed all those niggers, Doc."

"Well, I've had 'em around so long I don't know how to get shut of 'em, 'less I drown 'em. Feedin' 'em is the main trouble, though. Takes everything I can make. If it wasn't for them, I'd 'a' quit practicin' long ago. That's the reason I dine out whenever I can: every time I get a free meal, it's the same as a half holiday to a workin' man."

"How many have you got, Doctor?" Narcissa asked.

"I don't rightly know," he answered. "I got six or seven registered ones, but I don't know how many scrubs I have. I see a new yearlin' every day or so." Simon was watching him with rapt interest.

"You ain't got no extry room out dar, is you, Doctuh?" he asked. "Here I slaves all de livelong day, keepin' 'um in vittles en sech."

"Can you eat cold fish and greens every day?" Dr. Peabody asked him solemnly.

"Well, suh," Simon answered doubtfully, "I ain't so sho' erbout dat. I burnt out on fish once, when I wuz a young man, en I ain't had no right stomach fer it since."

"Well, that's all we have to eat, out home."

"All right, Simon," Miss Jenny said. Simon was propped statically against the sideboard, watching Dr. Peabody with musing astonishment.

"En you keeps yo' size on cole fish en greens? Gentlemun, I'd be a bone-rack on dem kine o' vittles in two weeks, I sholy would."

"Simon!" Miss Jenny raised her voice sharply. "Why won't you let him alone, Loosh, so he can 'tend to his business?" Simon came abruptly untranced and removed the fish. Beneath the table Narcissa slipped her hand in Horace's again.

"Lay off of Doc, Aunt Jenny," young Bayard said. He touched his grandfather's arm. "Can't you make her let Doc alone?"

"What's he doing, Jenny?" old Bayard asked. "Won't he eat his dinner?"

"None of us'll get anything to eat if he sits there and talks to Simon about cold fish and turnip greens," Miss Jenny replied.

"I think you're mean, to treat him like you do, Miss Jenny," Narcissa said.

"Well, it gives me something to be thankful for," Dr. Peabody answered, "that you never took me when you had the chance. I went and proposed to Jenny once," he told them.

"You old gray-headed liar," Miss Jenny said, "you never did any such a thing!"

"Oh, yes, I did. Only I did it on John Sartoris' account. He said he was havin' mo' trouble than he could stand with politics outside his home. And, do you know——"

"Loosh Peabody, you're the biggest liar in the world!"

"—I pretty near had her persuaded for a while? It was that first spring them weeds she brought out here from Ca'lina bloomed, and there was a moon and we were in the garden and there was a mockin'-bird——"

"No such thing!" Miss Jenny shouted. "There never was——"

"Look at her face, if you believe I'm lyin'," Dr. Peabody said.

"Look at her face," young Bayard echoed rudely. "She's blushing!"

And she was blushing, but her cheeks were like banners, and her head was still high amid the gibing laughter. Narcissa rose and came to her and laid her arm about her trim erect shoulders. "You all hush this minute," she said. "You'd better consider yourselves lucky that any of us ever marry you, and flattered even when we refuse."

"I am flattered," Dr. Peabody rejoined, "or I wouldn't be a widower now."

"Who wouldn't be a widower, the size of a hogshead and living on cold fish and turnip greens?" Miss Jenny said. "Sit down, honey. I ain't scared of any man alive."

Narcissa resumed her seat, and Simon appeared again, with Isom in procession now, and for the next few minutes they moved steadily between kitchen and dining-room with a roast turkey and a smoked ham and a dish of quail and another of squirrels, and a baked 'possum in a bed of sweet potatoes and squash and pickled beets, and sweet potatoes and Irish potatoes, and rice and hominy, and hot biscuit and beaten biscuit and delicate long sticks of cornbread, and strawberry and pear preserves, and quince and apple jelly, and stewed cranberries and pickled peaches.

Then they ceased talking for a while and really ate, glancing now and then across the table at one another in a rosy glow of amicability and steamy odors. From time to time Isom entered with hot bread, while Simon stood overlooking the field somewhat as Caesar must have stood looking down into Gaul, once it was well in hand, or the Lord God Him-

self when He contemplated his latest chemical experiment
and saw that it was good.

"After this, Simon," Dr. Peabody said, and he sighed a
little, "I reckon I can take you on and find you a little
side meat now and then."

"I 'speck you kin," Simon agreed, watching them like an
eagle-eyed general who rushes reserves to the threatened
points, pressing more food upon them as they faltered. But
even Dr. Peabody allowed himself vanquished after a time,
and then Simon brought in pies of three kinds, and a small,
deadly plum pudding, and a cake baked cunningly with
whisky and nuts and fruits and ravishing as odors of heaven
and treacherous and fatal as sin; and at last, with an air
sibylline and solemnly profound, a bottle of port. The sun lay
hazily in the glowing west, falling levelly through the windows and on the silver arrayed on the sideboard, dreaming in mellow gleams among its placid rotundities and on the
colored panes in the fanlight high in the western wall.

But that was November, the season of hazy, languorous
days, when the first flush of autumn is over and winter
beneath the sere horizon breathes yet a spell—November,
when like a shawled matron among her children, the year
dies peacefully, without pain and of no disease. Early in
December the rains set in and the year turned gray beneath
the season of dissolution and of death. All night long and
all day it whispered on the roof and along the eaves. The
trees shed their final stubborn leaves in it and gestured their
black and sorrowful branches against ceaseless vistas; only a
lone hickory at the foot of the park kept its leaves, gleaming like a sodden flame on the eternal azure, and beyond
the valley the hills were hidden by a swaddling of rain.

Almost daily, despite Miss Jenny's strictures and commands
and the grave protest in Narcissa's eyes, Bayard went forth
with a shotgun and the two dogs, to return just before
dark, wet to the skin. And cold; his lips would be chill on
hers and his eyes bleak and haunted, and in the yellow
firelight of their room she would cling to him, or lie crying
quietly in the darkness beside his rigid body, with a ghost between them.

"Look here," Miss Jenny said, coming on her as she sat
brooding before the fire in old Bayard's den, "you spend

too much time this way; you're getting moony. Stop worrying about him; he's spent half his life soaking wet, yet neither one of 'em ever had a cold even, that I can remember."

"Hasn't he?" she answered listlessly. Miss Jenny stood beside her chair, watching her keenly. Then she laid her hand on Narcissa's head, quite gently for a Sartoris.

"Are you worrying because maybe he don't love you like you think he ought to?"

"It isn't that," she answered. "He doesn't love anybody. He won't even love the baby. He doesn't seem to be glad, or sorry, or anything."

"No," Miss Jenny agreed. The fire crackled and leaped among the resinous logs. Beyond the gray window the day dissolved endlessly. "Listen," Miss Jenny said abruptly. "Don't you ride in that car with him any more. You hear?"

"No. It won't make him drive slowly. Nothing will."

"Of course not. Nobody believes it will, not even his grandfather. He goes along for the same reason that boy himself does. Sartoris. It's in the blood. Savages, every one of 'em. No earthly use to anybody." Together they gazed into the leaping flames, Miss Jenny's hand still lying on Narcissa's head. "I'm sorry I got you into this."

"You didn't do it. Nobody got me into it. I did it myself."

"H'm," Miss Jenny said. And then: "Would you do it over again?" The other did not reply, and she repeated the question. "Would you?"

"Yes," Narcissa answered. "Don't you know I would?" Again there was silence between them, in which without words they sealed their hopeless pact with that fine and passive courage of women. Narcissa rose.

"I believe I'll go in and spend the day with Horace, if you don't mind," she said.

"All right," Miss Jenny agreed. "I believe I would, too. Horace probably needs a little looking after, by now. He looked sort of gaunt when he was out here last week. Like he wasn't getting proper food."

When she entered the kitchen door Eunice, the cook, turned from the bread board and lifted her hands in a soft, dark gesture. "Well, Miss Narcy," she said, "we ain't seed you in a mont'. Is you come all de way in de rain?"

"I came in the carriage. It was too wet for the car." She

came into the room. Eunice watched her with grave pleasure. "How are you all getting along?"

"He gits enough to eat," Eunice answered; "I sees to dat. But I has to make him eat it. He needs you back here."

"I'm here, for the day, anyhow. What have you got for dinner?" Together they lifted lids and peered into the simmering vessels on the stove and in the oven. "Oh, chocolate pie!"

"I has to toll 'im wid dat," Eunice explained. "He'll eat anything, ef I jes' makes 'im a chocolate pie," she added proudly.

"I bet he does," Narcissa agreed. "Nobody can make chocolate pies like yours."

"Dis one ain't turnt out so well," Eunice said, deprecatory. "I ain't so pleased wid it."

"Why, Eunice! It's perfect."

"No'm, it ain't up to de mark," Eunice insisted. But she beamed, gravely diffident, and for a few minutes the two of them talked amicably while Narcissa pried into cupboards and boxes.

Then she returned to the house and mounted to her room. The dressing-table was bare of its intimate silver and crystal, and the drawers were empty, and the entire room, with its air of still and fading desolation, reproached her. Chill too; there had been no fire in the grate since last spring, and on the table beside the bed, forgotten and withered and dead, was a small bunch of flowers in a blue vase. Touching them, they crumbled in her fingers, leaving a stain, and the water in the vase smelled of rank decay. She opened the window and threw them out.

The room was too chill to stop in long, and she decided to ask Eunice to build a fire on the hearth for the comfort of that part of her which still lingered here, soberly and a little sorrowful in the chill and reproachful desolation. At her chest of drawers she paused again and remembered those letters, fretfully and with a little musing alarm, deprecating anew her carelessness in not destroying them. But maybe she had, and so she entered again into the closed circle of her bewilderment and first fear, trying to remember what she had done with them. But she was certain that she had left them in the drawer with her under things, positive that she had put them there. Yet she had never been able to find them, nor had Eunice nor Horace seen them. The day she had missed them was the day before her wedding, when she had packed her things. That day she had missed them, finding in their stead one in a different handwriting, which she did not remember having received. The gist of it was plain enough, although she had not understood some of it literally. But on that day she had read it with tranquil detachment: it and all it brought to mind was definitely behind her now. And lacking even this, she would not have been shocked if she had comprehended it. Curious a little, perhaps, at some of the words, but that is all.

But what she had done with those other letters she could not remember, and not being able to gave her moments of definite fear when she considered the possibility that people might learn that some one had had such thoughts about her and put them into words. Well, they were gone; there was nothing to do save hope that she had destroyed them as she had the last one, or if she had not, to trust that they would never be found. Yet that brought back the original distaste and dread: the possibility that the intactness of her deep and heretofore inviolate serenity might be the sport of circumstance; that she must trust to chance against the eventuality of a stranger casually picking a stray bit of paper from the ground. . . .

But she would put this firmly aside, for the time being, at least. This should be Horace's day, and her own too— a surcease from that ghost-ridden dream to which she clung, waking. She descended the stairs. There was a fire in the living-room. It had burned down to embers, however, and she put coal on it and punched it to a blaze. That would be the first thing he'd see when he entered; perhaps he'd wonder, perhaps he'd know before he entered, having sensed her presence. She considered telephoning him, and she mused indecisively for a moment before the fire, then decided to let it be a surprise. But supposing he didn't come home to dinner because of the rain. She considered this, and pictured him walking along a street in the rain, and immediately and with instinctive foreknowledge, she went to the closet beneath the stairs and opened the door. It was as she had known; his overcoat and his raincoat both hung there, and the chances were he didn't even have an umbrella; and again irritation and exasperation and untroubled affection welled within her and it was as it had been of old again, and all that had since come between them rolled away like clouds.

Heretofore her piano had always been rolled into the living-room when cold weather came. But now it stood yet in the smaller alcove. There was a fireplace here, but no fire had been lighted yet, and the room was chilly. Beneath her hands the cold keys gave forth a sluggish chord, accusing, reproving too, and she returned to the fire and stood where she could see, through the window, the drive beneath its somber, dripping cedars. The small clock on the mantel behind her chimed twelve, and she went to the window and stood with her nose touching the chill glass and her breath frosting it over. Soon, now: he was erratic in his hours, but never tardy, and every time an umbrella came into sight her heart leaped a little. But it was not he, and she followed the bearer's plodding passage until he shifted the umbrella enough for her to recognize him, and so she did not see Horace until he was halfway up the drive. His hat was turned down about his face and his coat collar was hunched to his ears, and as she had known, he didn't even have an umbrella.

"Oh, you idiot," she said and ran to the door and through the curtained glass she saw his shadowy shape come leaping up the steps. He flung the door open and entered, whipping his sodden hat against his leg, and so did not see her until she stepped forth. "You idiot," she said, "where's your raincoat?"

For a moment he stared at her with his wild and diffident unrepose; then he said "Narcy!" and his face lighted and he swept her into his wet arms.

"Don't," she cried. "You're wet!" But he swung her from the floor, against his sopping chest, repeating "Narcy, Narcy"; then his cold nose was against her face and she tasted rain.

"Narcy," he said again, hugging her, and she ceased resisting and clung to him. Then abruptly he released her and jerked his head up and stared at her with sober intensity. "Narcy," he said, still staring at her, "has that surly blackguard——"

"No, of course not," she answered sharply. "Have you gone crazy?" Then she clung to him again, wet clothes and all, as though she would never let him go. "Oh, Horry," she said, "I've been a beast to you!"

3

This time it was a Ford car, and Bayard saw its wild skid as the driver tried to jerk it across the treacherous, thawing road, and in the flashing moment and with swift amusement, he saw, between the driver's cravatless collar and the woman's stocking bound around his head beneath his hat and tied under his chin, his Adam's apple like a scared puppy in a tow sack. This flashed on and behind, and Bayard wrenched the wheel. The stalled Ford swam sickeningly into view again as the big car slewed on the greasy surface, its declutched engine roaring. Then the Ford swam from sight again as he wrenched the wheel over and slammed the clutch in for more stability; and once more that sickening, unhurried rush as the car refused to regain its feet and the frosty December world swept laterally across his vision. Old Bayard lurched against him; from the corner of his eye he could see the old fellow's hand clutching the top of the door. Now they were facing the bluff on which the cemetery lay; directly above them John Sartoris' effigy lifted its florid stone gesture and from amid motionless cedars gazed out on the valley where for two miles the railroad he had built ran beneath his carven eyes. Bayard wrenched the wheel once more.

On the other side of the road a precipice dropped sheer away, among scrub cedars and corroded ridges skeletoned brittlely with frost and muddy ice where the sun had not yet reached. The rear end of the car hung timelessly over this before it swung again, with the power full on, swung on until its nose pointed downhill again, with never a slackening of its speed. But still it would not come into the ruts, and it had lost the crown of the road, and although they had almost reached the foot of the hill, Bayard saw that they would not make it. Just before they slipped off he wrenched the steering-wheel over and swung the nose straight over the bank, and the car poised lazily for a moment, as though taking breath. "Hang on," he shouted to his grandfather; then they plunged.

An interval utterly without sound, in which all sensation

of motion was lost. Then scrub cedar burst crackling about
them and whipping branches of it exploded on the radiator
and slapped viciously at them as they leaned with braced
feet, and the car slewed in a long bounce. Another vacuum-
like interval, then a shock that banged the wheel into Bayard's chest and jerked it in his tight hands, wrenching his
arm-sockets. Beside him his grandfather lurched forward and
Bayard threw out his arm just in time to keep the other
from crashing through the windshield. "Hang on," he shouted.
The car had never faltered and he dragged the leaping wheel
over and swung it down the ravine and opened the engine,
and with the engine and the momentum of the plunge, they
rocked and crashed on down the ditch and turned and heaved
up the now shallow bank and on to the road again. Bayard
brought it to a stop.

He sat motionless for a moment. "Whew," he said. And
then, "Great God in the mountain." His grandfather sat
motionless beside him, his hand still clutching the door and
his head bent a little. "Think I'll have a cigarette after that,"
Bayard added. He dug one from his pocket, and a match;
his hands were shaking. "I thought of that damn concrete
bridge again, just as we went over," he explained, apologet-
ically. He took a deep draught at his cigarette and glanced at
his grandfather. "Y'all right?" Old Bayard made no reply,
and with his cigarette poised Bayard looked at him. He sat
as before, his head bent a little and his hand on the door.
"Grandfather?" Bayard said sharply. Still old Bayard didn't
move, even when his grandson flung the cigarette away and
shook him roughly.

4

Up the last hill the tireless pony bore him and in the low
December sun their shadow fell long across the ridge and
into the valley beyond, from which the high shrill yapping
of the dogs came on the frosty, windless air. Young dogs,
Bayard told himself, and he sat his horse in the faint scar of
the road, listening as the high-pitched hysteria of them swept
echoing across his aural field. Motionless, he could feel frost

in the air. Above him the pines, though there was no wind in them, made a continuous dry, wild sound, as though the frost in the air had found voice; above them, against the high evening blue, a shallow V of geese slid. "There'll be ice tonight," he thought, watching them and thinking of black backwaters where they would come to rest, of rank bayonets of dead grass about which water would shrink soon in fixed glassy ripples in the brittle darkness. Behind him the earth rolled away ridge on ridge blue as wood-smoke, on into a sky like thin congealed blood. He turned in his saddle and stared unwinking into the sun that spread like a crimson egg broken on the ultimate hills. That meant weather; he snuffed the still, tingling air, hoping he smelled snow.

The pony snorted and tossed his head experimentally and found the reins slack and lowered his nose and snorted again into the dead leaves and delicate sere needles of pine beneath his feet. "Come up, Perry," Bayard said, jerking the reins. Perry raised his head and broke into a stiff, jolting trot, but Bayard lifted him smartly out of it and into his steady fox trot again.

He had not gone far when the dogs broke again into clamorous uproar to his left and suddenly near, and as he reined Perry back and peered ahead along the fading scar of the road, he saw the fox trotting sedately toward him in the middle of it. Perry saw it at the same time and laid his fine ears back and rolled his young eyes. But the animal came on unawares at its steady, unhurried trot, glancing back over its shoulder from time to time. "Well, I'll be damned," Bayard whispered, holding Perry rigid between his knees. The fox was not forty yards away; still it came on, seemingly utterly unaware of the horseman. Then Bayard shouted.

The animal glanced at him; the level sun swam redly and fleetingly in its eyes; then with a single modest flash of brown it was gone. Bayard expelled his breath: his heart was thumping against his ribs. "Whooy," he yelled. "Come on, dogs!" The din of them swelled to a shrill pandemonium and the pack boiled into the road in a chaos of spotted hides and flapping tongues and ears. None of them was more than half grown, and ignoring the horse and rider they surged still clamoring into the undergrowth where the fox had vanished and shrieked frantically on; and as Bayard stood in his stirrups and gazed after them, preceded by yapping in a still

higher and more frantic key, two even smaller puppies
swarmed out of the woods and galloped past him on their
short legs with whimpering cries and expressions of ludi-
crous and mad concern. Then the clamor died into hysterical
echoes and so away.

He rode on. On either hand was a ridge: the one darkling
like a bronze bastion, on the other the final rays of the sun
lying redly. The air crackled and tingled in his nostrils and
seared his lungs with exhilarating needles. The road followed
the valley. But half the sun now showed above the western
wall, and among intermittent trees he rode stirrup-deep in
shadow like cold water. He would just about reach the house
before dark, and he shook Perry up a little. The clamor of the
dogs swelled again ahead of him, approaching the road, and
he lifted Perry into a canter.

Presently before him lay a glade—an old field, sage-
grown, its plow scars long healed over. The sun filled it with
dying gold and he pulled Perry short upstanding; there, at
the corner of the field beside the road, sat the fox. It sat
there on its haunches like a dog, watching the trees across
the glade, and Bayard sent Perry forward again. The fox
turned its head and looked at him with a covert, fleeting
glance, but without alarm, and Bayard halted Perry in intense astonishment. The clamor of the dogs swept nearer
through the woods; yet the fox sat on its haunches, watching
the man with covert stolen glances, paying the dogs no heed.
It revealed no alarm whatever, not even when the puppies
burst yapping madly into the glade. They moiled at the
wood's edge for a time while the fox divided its attention
between them and the man.

At last the largest puppy, evidently the leader, saw the
quarry. Immediately they stopped their noise and trotted
across the glade and squatted in a circle facing the fox, their
tongues lolling. Then with one accord they turned about and
faced the darkening woods, from which, and nearer and
nearer, came that spent, frantic yapping in a higher key.
The largest dog barked once; the yapping among the trees
swelled with frantic relief and the two smaller puppies appeared and burrowed like moles through the sedge and came
up. Then the fox rose and cast another quick, furtive glance
at the horseman, and surrounded by the amicable weary
calico of the puppies, trotted up the road and vanished

among the trees. "Well, I'll be damned," Bayard said, gazing
after them. "Come up, Perry."

At last a pale and windless plume of smoke stood above
the trees ahead, and he emerged from the woods and in the
rambling wall of the house a window glowed with ruddy in-
vitation across the twilight. Dogs had already set up a resonant, bell-like uproar; above it Bayard could distinguish the
clear tenor of puppies and a voice shouting at them, and as
he halted Perry in the yard, the fox was vanishing diffidently
but without haste beneath the house. A lean figure faced him
in the dusk, with an ax in one hand and an armful of wood,
and Bayard said:

"What the devil's that thing, Buddy? That fox?"

"That's Ellen," Buddy answered. He put the wood down
deliberately, and the ax, and he came and shook Bayard's
hand once limply, in the country fashion, but his hand was
hard and firm. "How you?"

"All right," Bayard answered. "I came out to get that old
fox Rafe was telling me about."

"Sure," Buddy agreed in his slow, infrequent voice. "We
been expectin' you. Git down and lemme take yo' pony."

"No, I'll do it. You take the wood on in; I'll put Perry
up." But Buddy was firm, without insistence or rudeness, and
Bayard surrendered the horse to him.

"Henry," Buddy shouted at the house, "Henry." A door
opened on jolly leaping flames; a figure stood squatly in it.
"Here's Bayard," he said. "Go on in and warm," he added,
leading Perry away. Dogs surrounded Bayard; he picked up
the wood and the ax and went on toward the house in a ghostly, spotted surge of dogs, and the figure stood in the lighted
doorway while he mounted the veranda and leaned the ax
against the wall.

"How you?" Henry said, and again the handshake was
limp, again the hand firm and kind; flabbier though than
Buddy's hard young flesh. He relieved Bayard of the wood
and they entered the house. The walls of the room were of
chinked logs. On them hung two or three outdated calendars
and a patent medicine lithograph in colors. The floor was
bare, of hand-trimmed boards scuffed with heavy boots and
polished by the pads of generations of dogs; two men could
lie side by side in the fireplace. In it now four-foot logs
blazed against the clay fireback, swirling in wild plumes

into the chimney's dark maw, and in silhouette against it, his head haloed by the shaggy silver disorder of his hair, Virginius MacCallum sat. "Hyer's Bayard Sartoris, pappy," Henry said.

The old man turned in his chair with grave, leonine deliberation and extended his hand without rising. In 1861 he was sixteen and he had walked to Lexington, Virginia, and enlisted, served four years in the Stonewall brigade and walked back to Mississippi and built himself a house and got married. His wife's *dot* was a clock and a dressed hog; his own father gave them a mule. His wife was dead these many years, and her successor was dead, but he sat now before the fireplace at which that hog had been cooked, beneath the roof he had built in '66, and on the mantel above him the clock sat, deriding that time whose servant it once had been. "Well, boy?" he said. "You took yo' time about comin'. How's yo' folks?"

"Pretty well, sir," Bayard answered. He looked at the old man's hale, ruddy face intently and sharply. No, they hadn't heard yet.

"We been expectin' you ever since Rafe seen you in town last spring. Henry, tell Mandy to set another plate."

Four dogs had followed him into the room. Three of them watched him gravely with glowing eyes; the other one, a blue-ticked hound with an expression of majestic gravity, came and touched its cold nose to his hand. "Hi, Gen'ral," he said, rubbing its ears, whereupon the other dogs approached and thrust their noses against his hands.

"Pull up a cheer," Mr. MacCallum said. He squared his own chair around and Bayard obeyed. The dogs followed him, surging with blundering decorum about his knees. "I keep sendin' word in to git yo' granpappy out hyer," the old man continued, "but he's too 'tarnal proud, or too damn lazy to come. Hyer, Gen'ral! Git away from thar. Kick 'em away, Bayard. Henry!" he shouted. Henry appeared. "Drive these damn dogs out of hyer till after supper."

Henry drove the dogs from the room. Mr. MacCallum picked up a long sliver of pine from the hearth and fired it and lit his pipe, and smothered the sliver in the ashes and laid it on the hearth again. "Rafe and Lee air in town today," he said. "You could have come out with them in a waggin. But I reckon you'd ruther have yo' own hoss."

"Yes, sir," he answered quietly. Then they would know. He stared into the fire for a time, rubbing his hands slowly on his knees, and for an instant he saw the recent months of his life coldly in all their headlong and heedless wastefulness; saw its entirety like the swift unrolling of a film, culminating in that which he had been warned against and that any fool might have foreseen. Well, damn it, suppose it had: was he to blame? Had he insisted that his grandfather ride with him? Had he given the old fellow a bum heart? and then, coldly: *You were afraid to go home. You made a nigger sneak your horse out to you. You, who deliberately do things your judgment tells you may not be successful, even possible, are afraid to face the consequences of your own acts.* Then again something bitter and deep and sleepless in him blazed out in vindication and justification and accusation; what, he knew not, blazing out at what, Whom, he did not know: *You did it! You caused it all; you killed Johnny.*

Henry had drawn a chair up to the fire, and after a while the old man tapped his clay pipe carefully out against his palm and drew a huge, turnip-shaped silver watch from his corduroy vest. "Half after five," he said. "Ain't them boys got in yet?"

"They're here," Henry answered briefly. "Heard 'em takin' out when I put out the dawgs."

"Git the jug, then," his father ordered. Henry rose and departed again, and presently feet clumped heavily on the porch and Bayard turned in his chair and stared bleakly at the door. It opened and Rafe and Lee entered.

"Well, well," Rafe said, and his lean, dark face lighted a little. "Got here at last, did you?" He shook Bayard's hand, and Lee followed him. Lee's face, like all of them, was a dark, saturnine mask. He was not so stocky as Rafe, and least talkative of them all. His eyes were black and restless; behind them lurked something wild and sad. He shook Bayard's hand without a word.

But Bayard was watching Rafe. There was nothing in Rafe's face; no coldness, no questioning. Was it possible that he could have been to town, yet not heard? Or had Bayard himself dreamed it? But he remembered that unmistakable feel of his grandfather when he had touched him; remembered how he had slumped suddenly as though the very fiber of him, knit so erect and firm for so long by pride and the perverse necessity of his family doom, had given way all at once, letting his skeleton rest at last. Mr. MacCallum spoke.

"Did you git to the express office?"

"We never got to town," Rafe answered. "Axletree broke just this side of Vernon. Had to uncouple the wagon and drive to Vernon and get it patched up. Too late to go in, then. We got our supplies there and come on home."

"Well, hit don't matter. You'll be goin' in next week, for Christmas," the old man said. Bayard drew a long breath and lit a cigarette, and on a draft of vivid darkness Buddy entered and came and squatted leanly in the shadowy chimney corner.

"Got that fox you were telling me about hid out yet?" Bayard asked Rafe.

"Sure. And we'll get him, this time. Maybe tomorrow. Weather's changin'."

"Snow?"

"Might be. What's it goin' to do tonight, pappy?"

"Rain," the old man answered. "Tomorrow, too. Scent won't lay good till We'n'sday. Henry!" After a moment he shouted "Henry" again, and Henry entered with a blackened kettle trailing a faint plume of vapor and a stoneware jug and a thick tumbler with a metal spoon in it. There was something domestic, womanish, about Henry, with his squat, slightly tubby figure and his mild brown eyes and his capable, unhurried hands. He it was who superintended the kitchen (he was a better cook now than Mandy) and the house, where he could be found most of the time, pottering soberly at some endless task. He visited town almost as infrequently as his father; he cared little for hunting, and his sole relaxation was making whisky, good whisky and for family consumption alone, in a secret fastness known only to his father and the Negro who assisted him, after a recipe handed down from lost generations of his usquebaugh-bred forebears. He set the kettle and the jug and the tumbler on the hearth and took the clay pipe from his father's hand and put it on the mantel and reached down a cracked cup of sugar and seven tumblers, each with a spoon in it. The old man leaned forward into the firelight and made the toddies one by one, with tedious and solemn deliberation. When he had made one around, there were two glasses left. "Ain't them other boys come in

yet?" he asked. Nobody answered, and he corked the jug.
Henry set the two glasses back on the mantel.

Mandy came to the door presently, filling it with her
homely calico expanse. "Y'all kin come on in now," she
said, and as she turned, waddling, Bayard spoke to her and
she stopped as the men rose and trooped from the room. The
old man was straight as an Indian, and with the exception
of Buddy's lean and fluid length, he towered above his sons
by a head. Mandy waited beside the door and gave Bayard
her hand. "You ain't been out in a long while, now," she
said. "And I bet you ain't fergot Mandy, neither."

"Sure I haven't," Bayard answered. But he had. Money,
to Mandy, did not compensate for some trinket of no value
which John never forgot to bring her when he came. He
followed the others into the frosty darkness. Beneath his feet
the ground was already stiffening; overhead the sky was brilliant with stars. He stumbled a little behind the crowding
backs until Rafe opened a door into a separate building and
stood aside until they had entered. This room was filled with
warmth and a thin blue haze pungent with cooking odors,
in which a kerosene lamp burned steadily on a long table. At
one end of the table was a single chair; the other three sides
were paralleled by backless wooden benches. Against the
further wall was the stove, and a huge cupboard of split
planks, and a woodbox. Behind the stove two Negro men and
a half-grown boy sat, their faces shining with heat and their
eyeballs rolling whitely; about their feet five puppies snarled
with mock savageness at one another or chewed damply at the
Negroes' motionless ankles or prowled about beneath the
stove and the adjacent floor with blundering, aimless inquisi-
tiveness.

"Howdy, boys," Bayard said, calling them by name, and
they bobbed their heads at him with diffident flashes of teeth
and polite murmurs.

"Put dem puppies up, Richud," Mandy ordered. The Negroes gathered the puppies up one by one and tumbled them
into a smaller box behind the stove, where they continued to
move about with sundry scratchings and bumpings and an
occasional smothered protest. From time to time during the
meal a head would appear, staring above the rim of the box
with blinking and solemn curiosity, then vanish with an
abrupt scuffling thump and more protests, and the moiling,

infantlike noises rose again. "Hush up, dawgs! G'wan to sleep now," Richard would say, rapping on the box with his knuckles. After a while the noises ceased.

The old man took the lone chair, his sons around him and the guest; some coatless, all collarless, with their dark, saturnine faces all stamped clearly from the same die. They ate—sausage and spare ribs, and a dish of hominy and one of fried sweet potatoes, and corn bread and a molasses jug of sorghum, and Mandy poured coffee from a huge enamelware pot. In the middle of the meal the two missing ones came in—Jackson, the eldest, a man of fifty-two, with a broad, high forehead and thick brows and an expression at once dreamy and intense—a sort of shy and impractical Cincinnatus; and Stuart, forty-four and Rafe's twin. Although they were twins, there was no closer resemblance between them than between any two of the others, as though the die were too certain and made too clean an imprint to be either hurried or altered, even by nature. Stuart had none of Rafe's easy manner (Rafe was the only one of them that, by any stretch of the imagination, could have been called loquacious); on the other hand, he had much of Henry's placidity. He was a good farmer and a canny trader, and he had a respectable bank account of his own. Henry, fifty, was the second son.

They ate with silent and steady decorum, with only the barest essential words, but amicably. Mandy moved back and forth between table and stove.

Before they had finished a sudden bell-like uproar of dogs floated up from the night and seeped through the tight walls into the room. "Dar, now." The Negro Richard cocked his head. Buddy poised his coffee cup.

"Where are they, Dick?"

"Right back of de spring-house. Dey got 'im, too." Buddy rose and slid leanly from his corner.

"I'll go with you," Bayard said, rising also. The others ate steadily. Richard got a lantern down from the top of the cupboard and lit it, and the three of them passed out of the room and into the chill darkness, across which the baying of the dogs came in musical gusts, ringing as frosty glass. It was chill and dark. The house loomed, its rambling low wall broken only by the ruddy glow of the window. "Ground's about hard already," Bayard remarked.

" 'Twon't freeze tonight," Buddy answered. "Will it, Dick?"

"Naw, suh. Gwine rain."

"Go on," Bayard said. "I don't believe it."

"Pappy said so," Buddy replied. "Warmer'n 'twas at sundown."

"Don't feel like it, to me," Bayard insisted. They passed the wagon, motionless in the starlight, its tires glinting like satin ribbons; and the long rambling stable, from which placid munchings came and an occasional snuffing snort as the lantern passed. Then the lantern twinkled among tree trunks as the path descended. The clamor of the dogs swelled just beneath them and the ghostly shapes of them shifted in the faint glow, and in a sapling just behind the spring-house they found the 'possum curled motionless and with its eyes tightly shut, in a fork not six feet from the ground. Buddy lifted it down by the tail, unresisting. "Hell," Bayard said.

Buddy called the dogs away, and they mounted the path again. In a disused shed behind the kitchen what seemed like at least fifty eyes gleamed in matched red points as Buddy swung the lantern in and flashed it on to a cage screened with chicken wire, from which rose a rank, warm odor and in which grizzled, furry bodies moved sluggishly or swung sharp, skull-like faces into the light. He opened the door and dumped his latest captive in among its fellows and gave the lantern to Richard. They emerged. Already the sky was hazed over a little, losing some of its brittle scintillation.

The others sat in a semicircle before the blazing fire; at the old man's feet the blue-ticked hound dozed. They made room for Bayard, and Buddy squatted again in the chimney corner.

"Git 'im?" Mr. MacCallum asked.

"Yes, sir," Bayard answered. "Like lifting your hat off a nail in the wall."

The old man puffed at his pipe. "We'll give you a sho' 'nough hunt befo' you leave."

Rafe said, "How many you got now, Buddy?"

"Ain't got but fo'teen," Buddy answered.

"Fo'teen?" Henry repeated. "We won't never eat fo'teen 'possums."

"Turn 'em loose and run 'em again, then," Buddy answered. The old man puffed slowly at his pipe. The others smoked or chewed also, and Bayard produced his cigarettes and offered them to Buddy. Buddy shook his head.

"Buddy ain't never started yet," Rafe said.

"You haven't?" Bayard asked. "What's the matter, Buddy?"

"Don't know," Buddy answered, from his shadow. "Just ain't had time to learn, I reckon."

The fire crackled and swirled; from time to time Stuart, nearest the woodbox, put another log on. The dog at the old man's feet dreamed, snuffed; soft ashes swirled on the hearth at its nose and it sneezed, waking itself, and raised its head and blinked up at the old man's face, then dozed again. They sat without words and with very little movement, their grave, aquiline faces as though carved by the firelight out of the shadowy darkness, shaped by a single thought and smoothed and colored by the same hand. The old man tapped his pipe out carefully on his palm and consulted his fat silver watch. Eight o'clock.

"We 'uns gits up at fo' o'clock, Bayard," he said. "But you don't have to git up till daylight. Henry, git the jug."

"Four o'clock," Bayard repeated, as he and Buddy undressed in the lamplit chill of the lean-to room in which, in a huge wooden bed with a faded patchwork quilt, Buddy slept. "I don't see why you bother to go to bed at all." As he spoke his breath vaporized in the chill air.

"Yes," Buddy agreed, ripping his shirt over his head and kicking his lean, race-horse shanks out of his shabby khaki pants. "Don't take long to spend the night at our house. You're comp'ny, though," he added, and in his voice was just a trace of envy and of longing. Never again after twenty-five will sleep in the morning be so golden. His preparations for slumber were simple; he removed his boots and pants and shirt and went to bed in his woolen underwear, and he now lay with only his round head in view, watching Bayard, who stood in a sleeveless jersey and short thin trunks. "You ain't goin' to sleep warm that-a-way," Buddy said. "You want one o' my heavy 'uns?"

"I'll sleep warm, I guess," Bayard answered. He blew the lamp out and groped his way to the bed, his toes curling away from the icy floor, and got in. The mattress was filled with corn shucks: it rattled beneath him, drily sibilant, and whenever he or Buddy moved at all or took a deep breath even, the shucks shifted with small ticking sounds.

"Git that 'ere quilt tucked in good over there," Buddy advised from the darkness, expelling his breath in a short explosive sound of relaxation. He yawned, audible but invisible. "Ain't seen you in a long while," he suggested.

"That's right. Let's see, when was it? Two—three years, isn't it?"

"Nineteen fifteen," Buddy answered, "last time you and him . . ." Then he added quietly "I seen in a paper when it happened. The name. Kind of knowed right off 'twas him. It was a limey paper."

"You did? Where were you?"

"Up there," Buddy answered, "where them limeys was. Where they sent us. Flat country. Don't see how they ever git it drained enough to make a crop, with all that rain."

"Yes." Bayard's nose was like a lump of ice. He could feel his breath warming his nose a little, could almost see the pale smoke of it as he breathed; could feel the inhalation chilling his nostrils again. It seemed to him that he could feel the planks of the ceiling as they sloped down to the low wall on Buddy's side, could feel the atmosphere packed into the low corner, bitter and chill and thick, too thick for breathing, like invisible slush, and he lay beneath it. . . . He was aware of the dry ticking of shucks beneath him and discovered, so, that he was breathing in deep, troubled drafts and he wished dreadfully to be up, moving, before a fire, light; anywhere, anywhere. Buddy lay beside him in the oppressive, half-congealed solidity of the chill, talking in his slow, inarticulate idiom of the war. It was a vague, dreamy sort of tale, without beginning or end and filled with stumbling references to places wretchedly mispronounced—you got an impression of people, creatures without initiative or background or future, caught timelessly in a maze of solitary conflicting preoccupations, like bumping tops, against an imminent but incomprehensible nightmare.

"How'd you like the army, Buddy?" Bayard asked.

"Not much," Buddy answered. "Ain't enough to do. Good life for a lazy man." He mused a moment. "They gimme a charm," he added in a burst of shy, diffident confidence and sober pleasure.

"A charm?" Bayard repeated.

"Uhuh. One of them brass gimcracks on to a colored ribbon. I aimed to show it to you, but I fergot. Do it tomorrow.
That 'ere flo's too dang cold to tech till I have to. I'll watch
a chance tomorrow when pappy's outen the house."

"Why? Don't he know you got it?"

"He knows," Buddy answered. "Only he don't like it because he claims it's a Yankee charm. Rafe says pappy and
Stonewall Jackson ain't never surrendered."

"Yes," Bayard repeated. Buddy ceased talking and presently he sighed again, emptying his body for sleep. But
Bayard lay rigidly on his back, his eyes wide open. It was
like being drunk; whenever you close your eyes, the room
starts going round and round, and so you lie rigid in the
dark with your eyes wide open, not to get sick. Buddy had
ceased talking and his breathing had become longer, steady
and regular. The shucks shifted with sibilant complaint as
Bayard turned slowly on to his side.

Buddy breathed on in the darkness, steadily and peacefully. Bayard could hear his own breathing also, but above
it, all around it, enclosing him, that other breathing. As
though he were one thing breathing with restrained, laboring pants, within himself breathing with Buddy's breathing; using up all the air so that the lesser thing must pant
for it. Meanwhile the greater thing breathed deeply and
steadily and unawares, asleep, remote; ay, perhaps dead. Perhaps he was dead, and he recalled that morning, relived it
with strained attention from the time he had seen the first
tracer-smoke until, from his steep bank, he watched the
flame burst like the gay flapping of an orange pennon from
the nose of John's Camel and saw his brother's familiar
gesture and the sudden awkward sprawl of his plunging
body as it lost equilibrium in mid-air; relived it again as
you might run over a printed, oft-read tale, trying to remember, feel, a bullet going into his own body or head
that might have slain him at the same instant. That would
account for it, would explain so much; that he too was dead
and this was hell, through which he moved for ever and
ever with an illusion of quickness, seeking his brother who
in turn was somewhere seeking him, never the two to meet.
He turned on to his back again; the shucks whispered beneath him with dry derision.

The house was full of noises; to his sharpened senses the

silence was myriad: the dry agony of wood in the black
frost; the ticking of shucks as he breathed; the very atmosphere itself like slush ice in the vise of the cold, op-
pressing his lungs. His feet were cold, his limbs sweated with
it, and about his hot heart his body was rigid and shivering,
and he raised his naked arms above the covers and lay for
a time with the cold like a leaden cast on them. And all
the while Buddy's steady breathing and his own restrained
and panting breath, both sourceless yet involved one with
the other.

Beneath the covers again his arms were cold across his
chest and his hands were like ice on his ribs, and he moved
with infinite caution while the chill encroached from his
shoulders downward and the hidden shucks chattered at
him, and swung his legs to the floor. He knew where the
door was and he groped his way to it on curling toes. It
was fastened by a wooden bar, smooth as ice, and fumbling
at it he touched something else beside it, something chill
and tubular and upright, and his hand slid down it and
then he stood for a moment in the icy pitch darkness with
the shotgun in his hands, and as he stood so, his numb
fingers fumbling at the breech, he remembered the box of
shells on the wooden box on which the lamp sat. A moment longer he stood so, his head bent a little and the gun
in his numb hands; then he leaned it again in the corner
and lifted the wooden bar from its slots carefully and without
noise. The door sagged from the hinges, and after the first
jarring scrape, he grasped the edge of it and lifted it back,
and stood in the door.

In the sky no star showed, and the sky was the sagging
corpse of itself. It lay on the earth like a deflated balloon;
into it the dark shape of the kitchen rose without depth,
and the trees beyond, and homely shapes like sad ghosts in
the chill corpse-light—the wood-pile; a farming tool; a barrel
beside the broken stoop at the kitchen door where he had
stumbled, supperward. The gray chill seeped into him like
water into sand, with short trickling runs; halting, groping
about an obstruction, then on again, trickling at last along
his unimpeded bones. He was shaking slowly and steadily
with cold; beneath his hands his flesh was rough and without
sensation; yet still it jerked and jerked as though something
within the dead envelope of him strove to free itself. Above

his head, on the plank roof, there sounded a single light
tap, and as though at a signal the gray silence began to dis-
solve. He shut the door silently and returned to bed.

In the bed he lay shaking more than ever, to the cold
derision of the shucks beneath him, and he lay quietly on
his back, hearing the winter rain whispering on the roof.
There was no drumming, as when summer rain falls through
the buoyant air, but a whisper of unemphatic sound, as
though the atmosphere lying heavily on the roof dissolved
there and dripped sluggishly and steadily from the eaves.
His blood ran again, and the covers felt like iron or like
ice; while he lay motionless beneath the rain his blood
warmed yet more, until at last his body ceased trembling and
he lay presently in something like a tortured and fitful doze,
surrounded by coiling images and shapes of stubborn despair and the ceaseless striving for . . . not vindication so
much as comprehension; a hand, no matter whose, to touch
him out of his black chaos. He would spurn it, of course, but
it would restore his cold sufficiency again.

The rain dripped on, dripped and dripped; beside him
Buddy breathed placidly and steadily: he had not even
changed his position. At times Bayard dozed fitfully: doz-
ing, he was wide awake; waking, he lay in a hazy state filled
with improbable moiling, in which there was neither relief
nor rest: drop by drop the rain wore the night away, wore
time away. But it was so long, so damn long. His spent
blood, wearied with struggling, moved through his body in
slow beats, like the rain, wearing his flesh away. It comes to
all . . . Bible . . . some preacher, anyway. Maybe he knew.
Sleep. It comes to all.

At last, through the walls, he heard movement. It was
indistinguishable; yet he knew it was of human origin, made
by people whose names and faces he knew, waking again
into the world he had not been able even temporarily to
lose; people to whom he was . . . and he was comforted.
The sounds continued; unmistakably he heard a door, and
a voice which, with a slight effort of concentration, he
knew he could name; and best of all, knew that now he
could rise and go where they were gathered about a crackling
fire, where light was, and warmth. And he lay, at ease at
last, intending to rise and go to them the next moment,
putting it off a little longer while his blood beat slowly

through his body and his heart was quieted. Buddy breathed steadily beside him, and his own breath was untroubled now as Buddy's while the human sounds came murmurously into the cold room with grave and homely reassurance. It comes to all, it comes to all, his tired heart comforted him, and at last he slept.

He waked in the gray morning, his body weary and heavy and dull; his sleep had not rested him. Buddy was gone, and it still rained, though now it was a definite, purposeful sound on the roof and the air was warmer, with a rawness that probed to the very bones of him; and in his stockings and carrying his boots in his hand, he crossed the cold room where Lee and Rafe and Stuart slept, and found Rafe and Jackson before the living-room fire.

"We let you sleep," Rafe said; then he said, "Good Lord, boy, you look like a ha'nt. Didn't you sleep last night?"

"Yes, I slept all right," Bayard answered. He sat down and stamped into his boots and buckled the thongs below his knees. Jackson sat at one side of the hearth. In the shadowy corner near his feet a number of small, living creatures moiled silently, and still bent over his boots, Bayard said:

"What you got there, Jackson? What sort of puppies are them?"

"New breed I'm tryin'," Jackson answered. Rafe returned with a half a tumbler of Henry's pale amber whisky.

"Them's Ellen's pups," he said. "Git Jackson to tell you about 'em after you eat. Here, drink this. You look all wore out. Buddy must 'a' kept you awake talkin'," he added with dry irony.

Bayard drank the whisky and lit a cigarette. "Mandy's got yo' breakfast on the stove," Rafe said.

"Ellen?" Bayard repeated. "Oh, that fox. I aimed to ask about her, last night. Y'all raise her?"

"Yes. She growed up with last year's batch of puppies. Buddy caught her. And now Jackson aims to revolutionize the huntin' business with her. Aims to raise a breed of animals with a hound's wind and bottom and a fox's smartness and speed."

Bayard approached the corner and examined the small creatures with interest and curiosity. "I never saw many fox pups," he said at last, "but I never saw anything that looked like them."

"That's what Gen'ral seems to think," Rafe answered.

Jackson spat into the fire and stooped over the creatures. They knew his hands, and the moiling of them became more intense, and Bayard then noticed that they made no sound at all, not even puppy whimperings. "Hit's a experiment," Jackson explained. "The boys makes fun of 'em, but they hain't no more'n weaned, yit. You wait and see."

"Don't know what you'll do with 'em," Rafe said brutally. "They won't be big enough for work stock. Better go git yo' breakfast, Bayard."

"You wait and see," Jackson repeated. He touched the scramble of small bodies with his hands in a gentle, protective gesture. "You can't tell nothin' 'bout a dawg 'twell hit's at least two months old, can you?" he appealed to Bayard, looking up at him with his vague, intense gaze from beneath his shaggy brows.

"Go git yo' breakfast, Bayard," Rafe insisted. "Buddy's done gone and left you."

He bathed his face with icy water in a tin pan on the porch, and ate his breakfast—ham and eggs and flapjacks and sorghum—while Mandy talked to him about his brother. When he returned to the house old Mr. MacCallum was there. The puppies moiled inextricably in their corner, and the old man sat with his hands on his knees, watching them with bluff and ribald enjoyment, while Jackson sat near by in a sort of hovering concern, like a hen.

"Come hyer, boy," the old man ordered when Bayard appeared. "Hyer, Rafe, git me that 'ere bait line." Rafe went out, returning presently with a bit of pork rind on the end of a string. The old man took it and hauled the puppies ungently into the light, where they crouched abjectly—as strange a litter as Bayard had ever seen. No two of them looked alike, and none of them looked like any other living creature—neither fox nor hound, partaking of both, yet neither; and despite their soft infancy there was about them something monstrous and contradictory and obscene, here a fox's keen, cruel muzzle between the melting, sad eyes of a hound and its mild ears, there limp ears tried valiantly to stand erect and failed ignobly in flapping points; and limp, brief tails brushed over with a faint golden fuzz like the insides of chestnut burrs. As regards color, they ranged from reddish brown through an indiscriminate brindle to pure ticked beneath a faint dun cast, and one of them had, feature for feature, old General's face in comical miniature, even to his expression of sad and dignified disillusion. "Watch 'em now," the old man directed.

He got them all facing forward; then he dangled the meat directly behind them. Not one became aware of its presence; he swept it back and forth just above their heads; not one looked up. Then he swung it directly before their eyes; still they crouched diffidently on their young, unsteady legs and gazed at the meat with curiosity but without any personal interest whatever, and fell again to moiling soundlessly among themselves.

"You can't tell nothin' about dawgs——" Jackson began. His father interrupted him.

"Now, watch." He held the puppies with one hand and with the other he forced the meat into their mouths. Immediately they surged clumsily and eagerly over his hand, but he moved the meat away and at the length of the string he dragged it along the floor just ahead of them until they had attained a sort of scrambling lope. Then in mid-floor he flicked the meat slightly aside, but without swerving the puppies blundered on and into a shadowy corner, where the wall stopped them and from which there rose presently the patient, voiceless confusion of them. Jackson crossed the floor and picked them up and brought them back to the fire.

"Now, what do you think of them, fer a pack of huntin' dawgs?" the old man demanded. "Can't smell, can't bark, and damn ef I believe they kin see."

"You can't tell nothin' about a dawg——" Jackson essayed patiently.

"Gen'ral kin," his father interrupted. "Hyer, Rafe, call Gen'ral in hyer."

Rafe went to the door and called, and presently General entered, his claws hissing a little on the bare floor and his ticked coat beaded with rain, and he stood and looked into the old man's face with grave inquiry. "Come hyer," Mr. MacCallum said, and the dog moved again, with slow dignity. At that moment he saw the puppies beneath Jackson's chair. He paused in mid stride and for a moment he stood looking at them with fascination and bafflement and a sort of grave horror; then he gave his master one hurt, reproachful look and turned and departed, his tail between his legs. Mr. MacCallum sat down and rumbled heavily within himself.

"You can't tell about dawgs——" Jackson repeated. He stooped and gathered up his charges, and rose.

Mr. MacCallum continued to rumble and shake. "Well, I don't blame the old feller," he said. "Ef I had to look around on a passel of chaps like them and say to myself, 'Them's my boys'——" But Jackson was gone. The old man sat and rumbled again, with heavy enjoyment. "Yes, suh, I reckon I'd feel 'bout as proud as Gen'ral does. Rafe, han' me down my pipe."

All that day it rained, and the following day and the one after that. The dogs lurked about the house all morning, underfoot, or made brief excursions into the weather, returning to sprawl before the fire drowsing and malodorous and steaming until Henry came along and drove them out; twice from the door Bayard saw the fox, Ellen, fading with brisk diffidence across the yard. With the exception of Henry and Jackson, who had a touch of rheumatism, the others were somewhere out in the rain most of the day. But at mealtime they gathered again, shucking their wet outer garments on the porch and stamping in to thrust their muddy, smoking boots to the fire while Henry fetched the kettle and the jug. And last of all, Buddy, soaking wet.

Buddy had a way of getting his lean length up from his niche beside the chimney at any hour of the day and departing without a word, to return in two hours or six or twelve or forty-eight, during which periods and despite the presence of Jackson and Henry and usually Lee, the place had a vague air of desertion, until Bayard realized that the majority of the dogs were absent also. Hunting, they told him, when Buddy had been missing since breakfast.

"Why didn't he let me know?" Bayard demanded.

"Maybe he thought you wouldn't keer to be out in the weather," Jackson suggested.

"Buddy don't mind weather," Henry explained. "One day's like another to him."

"Nothin' ain't anything to Buddy," Lee said, in his bitter, passionate voice. He sat brooding over the fire, his womanish hands moving restlessly on his knees. "He'd spend his whole life in that 'ere river bottom, with a hunk of cold cawn bread

to eat and a passel of dawgs fer comp'ny." He rose abruptly
and quitted the room. Lee was in the late thirties. As a child
he had been sickly. He had a good tenor voice and was much
in demand at Sunday singings. He was supposed to be keeping company with a young woman living in the hamlet of
Mount Vernon, six miles away. He spent much of his time
tramping moodily and alone about the countryside.

Henry spat into the fire and jerked his head after the departing brother. "He been to Vernon lately?"

"Him and Rafe was there two days ago," Jackson answered.

Bayard said, "Well, I won't melt. I wonder if I could catch
up with him now?"

They pondered for a while, spitting gravely into the fire.
"I misdoubt it," Jackson said at last. "Buddy's liable to be
ten mile away by now. You ketch 'im next time befo' he
starts out."

After that Bayard did so, and he and Buddy tried for
birds in the skeletoned fields in the rain in which the guns
made a flat, mournful sound that lingered in the streaming
air like a spreading stain, or tried the stagnant backwaters
along the river channel for duck and geese; or, accompanied
now and then by Rafe, hunted 'coon and wildcat in the
bottom. At times and far away, they would hear the shrill
yapping of the young dogs in mad career. "There goes
Ellen," Buddy would remark. Then toward the end of the
week the weather cleared, and in a twilight imminent with
frost and while the scent lay well on the wet earth, old
General started the red fox that had baffled him so many
times.

All through the night the ringing, bell-like tones quavered
and swelled and echoed among the hills, and all of them save
Henry followed on horseback, guided by the cries of the
hounds but mostly by the old man's and Buddy's uncanny
and seemingly clairvoyant skill in anticipating the course
of the race. Occasionally they stopped while Buddy and his
father wrangled about where the quarry would head next,
but usually they agreed, apparently anticipating the animal's
movements before it knew them itself; and once and again
they halted their mounts on a hill and sat in the frosty
starlight until the dogs' voices welled out of the darkness
mournful and chiming, swelled louder and nearer and swept
invisibly past, not half a mile away; faded diminishing and

with a falling suspense, as of bells, into the silence again.

"Thar, now!" the old man exclaimed, shapeless in his overcoat, on his white horse. "Ain't that music fer a man, now?"

"I hope they git 'im this time," Jackson said. "Hit hurts Gen'ral's conceit so much ever' time he fools 'im."

"They won't git 'im," Buddy said. "Soon's he gits tired, he'll hole up in them rocks."

"I reckon we'll have to wait till them pups of Jackson's gits big enough," the old man agreed, "unless they'll refuse to run they own granddaddy. They done refused ever'thing else except vittles."

"You jest wait," Jackson repeated, indefatigable. "When them puppies gits old enough to——"

"Listen."

The talking ceased. Again across the night the dogs' voices rang among the hills, long, ringing cries fading, falling with a quavering suspense, like touched bells or strings, repeated and sustained; by bell-like echoes repeated and dying among the dark hills beneath the stars, lingering yet in the ears crystal-clear, mournful and valiant and a little sad.

"Too bad Johnny ain't here," Stuart said quietly. "He'd enjoy this race."

"He was a feller fer huntin', now," Jackson agreed. "He'd keep up with Buddy, even."

"John was a fine boy," the old man said.

"Yes, suh," Jackson repeated, "a right warm-hearted boy. Henry says he never come out hyer withouten he brung Mandy and the boys a little sto'-bought somethin'."

"He never sulled on a hunt," Stuart said. "No matter how cold and wet it was, even when he was a little chap, with that 'ere single bar'l he bought with his own money, that kicked 'im so hard ever' time he shot it. And yit he'd tote it around, instead of that 'ere sixteen old Colonel give 'im, jest because he saved up his own money and bought it hisself."

"Yes," Jackson agreed, "ef a feller gits into somethin' on his own accord, he'd ought to go through with hit cheerful."

"He was sho' a feller fer singin' and shoutin'," Mr. Mac-Callum said. "Skeer all the game in ten mile. I mind that night he up and headed off a race down at Samson's bridge, and the next we knowed, here him and the fox come afloatin' down river on that 'ere drift lawg, and him singin' away loud as he could yell."

"That 'uz Johnny, all over," Jackson agreed. "Gittin' a whoppin' big time outen ever'thing that come up."

"He was a fine boy," Mr. MacCallum said again. "Listen."

Again the hounds gave tongue in the darkness below them. The sound floated up on the chill air, died into echoes that repeated the sound again until its source was lost and the very earth itself might have found voice, grave and sad, and wild with all regret.

Christmas was two days away, and they sat again about the fire after supper; again old General dozed at his master's feet. Tomorrow was Christmas Eve and the wagon was going into town, and although with that grave and unfailing hospitality of theirs, no word had been said to Bayard about his departure, he believed that in all their minds it was taken for granted that he would return home the following day for Christmas; and, since he had not mentioned it himself, a little curiosity and quiet speculation also.

It was cold again, with a vivid chill that caused the blazing logs to pop and crackle with vicious sparks and small embers that leaped out on the floor, to be crushed out by a lazy boot, and Bayard sat drowsily, his tired muscles relaxed in cumulate waves of heat as in a warm bath and his stubborn, wakeful heart glozed over too, for the time being. Time enough tomorrow to decide whether to go or not. Perhaps he'd just stay on, without even offering that explanation which would never be demanded of him. Then he realized that Rafe, Lee, whoever went, would talk to people, would learn about that which he had not the courage to tell them.

Buddy had come out of his shadowy niche and he now squatted in the center of the semicircle, his back to the fire and his arms around his knees, with his motionless and seemingly tireless ability for sitting timelessly on his heels. He was the baby, twenty years old. His mother had been the old man's second wife, and his hazel eyes and the reddish thatch cropped close to his round head was a noticeable contrast to his brothers' brown eyes and black hair. But the old man had stamped Buddy's face as clearly as any one of the other boys', and despite its youth it too was like the others—aquiline and spare, reserved and grave, though a trifle ruddy with his fresh coloring and finer skin.

The others were of medium height or under, ranging from Jackson's faded, vaguely ineffectual lankness, through Henry's placid rotundity and Rafe's—Raphael Semmes he was— and Stuart's poised and stocky muscularity, to Lee's thin and fiery restlessness; but Buddy with his saplinglike leanness stood eye to eye with that father who wore his seventy-seven years as though they were a thin coat. "Long, spindlin' scoundrel," the old man would say, with bluff derogation. "Keeps hisself wore to a shadder totin' around all that grub he eats." And they would sit in silence, looking at Buddy's jack-knifed length with the same identical thought; a thought which each believed peculiar to himself and which none ever divulged—that some day Buddy would marry and perpetuate the name.

Buddy also bore his father's name, though it is doubtful if any one outside the family and the War Department knew it. He had run away at seventeen and enlisted; at the infantry concentration camp in Arkansas to which he had been sent, a fellow recruit called him Virge and Buddy had fought him steadily and without anger for seven minutes; at the New Jersey embarkation depot another man had done the same thing, and Buddy had fought him, again steadily and thoroughly and without anger. In Europe, still following the deep but uncomplex compulsions of his nature, he had contrived, unwittingly perhaps, to perpetrate something which was later ascertained by Authority to have severely annoyed the enemy, for which Buddy had received his charm, as he called it. What it was he did, he could never be brought to say, and the gaud not only failing to placate his father's anger over the fact that a son of his had joined the Federal army, but on the contrary adding fuel to it, the bauble languished among Buddy's sparse effects, and his military career was never mentioned in the family circle; and now as usual Buddy squatted among them, his back to the fire and his arms around his knees, while they sat about the hearth with their bedtime toddies, talking of Christmas.

"Turkey," the old man was saying, with fine and rumbling disgust. "With a pen full of 'possums, and a river bottom full of squir'l and ducks, and a smokehouse full of hawg meat, you damn boys have got to go clean to town and buy a turkey fer Christmas dinner."

"Christmas ain't Christmas lessen a feller has a little some-thin' different from ever' day," Jackson pointed out mildly.

"You boys jest wants a excuse to git to town and loaf all day and spend money," the old man retorted. "I've seen a sight mo' Christmases than you have, boy, and ef hit's got to be sto' bought, hit ain't Christmas."

"How 'bout townfolks?" Rafe asked. "You ain't allowin' them no Christmas a-tall."

"Don't deserve none," the old man snapped, "livin' on a little two-by-fo' lot, jam right up again' the next feller's back do', eatin' outen tin cans."

" 'Sposin' they all broke up in town," Stuart said, "and moved out here and took up land; you'd hear pappy cussin' town then. You couldn't git along without town to keep folks bottled up in, pappy, and you know it."

"Buyin' turkeys," Mr. MacCallum repeated with savage disgust. "Buyin' 'em. I mind the time when I could take a gun and step out that 'ere do' and git a gobbler in thutty minutes. And a ven'son ham in a hour mo'. Why, you fellers don't know nothin' about Christmas. All you knows is sto' winders full of cocoanuts and Yankee popguns and sich."

"Yes, suh," Rafe said, and he winked at Bayard. "That was the biggest mistake the world ever made, when Lee surrendered. The country ain't never got over it."

The old man snorted. "I be damned ef I ain't raised the damnedest, smartest set of boys in the world. Can't tell 'em nothin', can't learn 'em nothin', can't even set in front of my own fire fer the whole passel of 'em tellin' me how to run the whole damn country. Hyer, you boys, git on to bed."

Next morning Jackson and Rafe and Stuart and Lee left for town at sunup in the wagon. Still none of them had made any sign, expressed any curiosity as to whether they would find him there when they returned that night or whether it would be another three years before they saw him again. And Bayard stood on the frost-whitened porch, smoking a cigarette in the chill, vivid sunrise, and looked after the wagon with its four muffled figures and wondered if it would be three years again, or ever. The hounds came and nuzzled about him and he dropped his hand among their icy noses and the warm flicking of their tongues, gazing at the trees from beyond which the dry rattling of the wagon came unimpeded upon the clear and soundless morning.

"Ready to go?" Buddy said behind him, and he turned and picked up his shotgun where it leaned against the wall. The hounds surged about them with eager whimperings and frosty breaths and Buddy led them across to their pen and huddled them inside and fastened the door on their astonished protests. From another kennel he unleashed the young pointer, Dan. Behind them the hounds continued to lift their baffled and mellow expostulations.

Until noon they hunted the ragged, fallow fields and woods-edges in the warming air. The frost was soon gone, and the air warmed to a windless languor, and twice in brier thickets they saw redbirds darting like arrows of scarlet flame. At last Bayard lifted his eyes unwinking into the sun.

"I've got to go back, Buddy," he said. "I'm going home this afternoon."

"All right," Buddy agreed without protest, and he called the dog in. "You come back next month."

Mandy got them some cold food and they ate, and while Buddy was saddling Perry, Bayard went into the house, where he found Henry laboriously soling a pair of boots and the old man reading a week-old newspaper through steel-bowed spectacles.

"I reckon yo' folks will be lookin' fer you," Mr. Mac-Callum agreed, removing his spectacles. "We'll be expectin' you back next month though, to git that 'ere fox. Ef we don't git 'im soon, Gen'ral won't be able to hold up his haid befo' them puppies."

"Yes, sir," Bayard answered, "I will."

"And try to git yo' grandpappy to come out with you. He kin lay around hyer and eat his haid off well as he kin in town thar."

"Yes, sir, I will."

Buddy led the pony up, and the old man extended his hand without rising. Henry put aside his cobbling and followed him on to the porch. "Come out again," he said diffidently, giving Bayard's hand a single pump-handle shake, and from a slobbering inquisitive surging of half-grown hounds Buddy reached up his hand.

"Be lookin' fer you," he said briefly, and Bayard wheeled

away, and when he looked back they lifted their hands gravely. Then Buddy shouted after him and he reined Perry about and returned. Henry had vanished, and he reappeared with a weighted tow sack.

"I nigh fergot it," he said. "Jug of cawn pappy's sendin' in to yo' granddaddy. You won't git no better'n this in Looeyvul ner nowhar else, neither," he added with quiet pride. Bayard thanked him and Buddy fastened the sack to the pommel, where it lay solidly against his leg.

"There. That'll ride."

"Yes, that'll ride. Much obliged."

"So long."

"So long."

Perry moved on, and he looked back. They still stood there, quiet and grave and steadfast. Beside the kitchen door the fox, Ellen, sat, watching him covertly; near her the half-grown puppies rolled and played in the sunlight. The sun was an hour high above the western hills; the road wound on into the trees. He looked back again. The house sprawled its rambling length in the wintry afternoon, its smoke like a balanced plume on the windless sky. The door was empty, and he shook Perry into his easy, tireless fox trot, the jug of whisky jouncing a little against his knee.

5

Where the dim, infrequent road to MacCallum's left the main road, rising, he halted Perry and sat for a while in the sunset. Jefferson, 14 miles. Rafe and the other boys would not be along for some time yet, what with Christmas Eve in town and the slow, festive gathering of the county. Still, they may have left town early, so as to get home by dark; might not be an hour away. The sun's rays, slanting, released the chill they had held prisoned in the ground during the perpendicular hours and it rose slowly about him as he sat Perry in the middle of the road, and slowly his blood cooled with the cessation of Perry's motion. He turned the pony's head away from town and shook him into his fox trot again.

Darkness overtook him soon, but he rode on beneath the leafless trees, along the pale road in the gathering starlight. Already Perry was thinking of stable and supper and he went on with tentative, inquiring tossings of his head, but obediently and without slackening his gait, knowing not where they were going nor why, save that it was away from home, and a little dubious, though trustfully. The chill grew in the silence and the loneliness and the monotony. Bayard reined Perry to a halt and untied the jug and drank, and fastened it to the saddle again.

The hills rose wild and black about them. No sign of any habitation, no trace of man's hand did they encounter. On all sides the hills rolled blackly away in the starlight, or when the road dipped into valleys where the ruts were already stiffening into ironlike shards that clattered beneath Perry's hooves, they stood darkly towering and sinister overhead, lifting their leafless trees against the spangled sky. Where a stream of winter seepage trickled across the road Perry's feet crackled brittlely in thin ice and Bayard slacked the reins while the pony snuffed at the water. He drank from the jug again.

He fumbled a match clumsily in his numb fingers and lit a cigarette, and pushed his sleeve back from his wrist. Eleven-thirty. "Well, Perry," his voice sounded loud and sudden in the stillness and the darkness and the cold, "I reckon we better look for a place to hole up till morning." Perry raised his head and snorted, as though he understood the words, as though he would enter the bleak loneliness in which his rider moved if he could. They went on, mounting again.

The darkness spread away, lessening a little presently where occasional fields lay in the vague starlight, breaking the monotony of trees; and after a time during which he rode with the reins slack on Perry's neck and his hands in his pockets, seeking warmth between leather and groin, a cotton house squatted beside the road, its roof dusted over with a frosty sheen as of silver. Not long, he told himself, leaning forward and laying his hand on Perry's neck, feeling the warm, tireless blood there. "House soon, Perry, if we look sharp."

Again Perry whinnied a little, as though he understood, and presently he swerved from the road, and as Bayard reined him back, he too saw the faint wagon trail leading away toward a low vague clump of trees. "Good boy, Perry," he said, slackening the reins again.

The house was a cabin. It was dark, but a hound came gauntly from beneath it and bayed at him and continued its uproar while he reined Perry to the door and knocked on it with his numb hand. From within the house at last a voice, and he shouted "Hello" again. Then he added, "I'm lost. Open the door." The hound bellowed at him indefatigably. After a moment the door cracked on a dying glow of embers, emitting a rank odor of Negroes, and against the crack of warmth, a head.

"You, Jule," the head commanded, "hush yo' mouf." The hound ceased obediently and retired beneath the house, though still growling. "Who dar?"

"I'm lost," Bayard repeated. "Can I stay in your barn to-night?"

"Ain't got no barn," the Negro answered. "Dey's anud-der house down de road a piece."

"I'll pay you," Bayard said. He fumbled in his pocket with his numb hand. "My horse is tired out." The Negro's head peered around the door, against the crack of firelight. "Come on, Uncle," Bayard added impatiently. "Don't keep a man standing in the cold."

"Who is you, white folks?"

"Bayard Sartoris, from Jefferson. Here." He extended his hand. The Negro made no effort to take it.

"Banker Sartoris's folks?"

"Yes. Here."

"Wait a minute." The door closed. But Bayard tightened the reins and Perry moved readily and circled the house confidently and went on among frost-stiffened cotton stalks that clattered drily about his knees. As Bayard dismounted on to frozen rutted earth beneath a gaping doorway, a lantern appeared from the cabin, swung low among the bitten stalks and the shadowy scissoring of the man's legs, and the Negro came up with a shapeless bundle under his arm and held the lantern while Bayard stripped the saddle and bridle off.

"How you manage to git so fur fum home dis time o' night, white folks?" he asked curiously.

"Lost," Bayard answered briefly. "Where can I put my horse?"

The Negro swung the lantern into a stall. Perry stepped carefully over the sill and turned into the lantern light, his eyes rolling in phosphorescent gleams, and Bayard followed and rubbed him down with the dry side of the saddle blanket. The Negro had vanished; he now appeared with a few ears of corn and shucked them into Perry's manger beside the pony's eager nuzzling. "You gwine be keerful about fire, ain't you, white folks?" he asked.

"Sure. I won't strike any matches at all."

"I got all my stock and tools and feed in here," the Negro explained. "I can't affo'd to git burnt out. Insu'ance don't reach dis fur fum town."

"Sure," Bayard repeated. He shut Perry's stall and while the Negro watched him he drew the sack forth from where he had set it against the wall, and produced the jug. "Got a cup here?" The Negro vanished again; Bayard could see the lantern through the cracks in the crib in the opposite wall; then he emerged with a rusty can from which he blew a bursting puff of chaff. They drank. Behind them Perry munched his corn. The Negro showed him the ladder to the loft.

"You won't fergit about dat fire, white folks?" he repeated anxiously.

"Sure," Bayard said. "Good night." He laid his hand on the ladder, and the Negro stopped him and handed him the shapeless bundle he had brought out with him.

"Ain't got but one to spare, but it'll help some. You gwine sleep cole, tonight." It was a quilt, ragged and filthy to the touch, and impregnated with that unmistakable odor of Negroes.

"Thanks," Bayard answered. "Much obliged to you. Good night."

"Good night, white folks."

The lantern winked away, to the criss-crossing of the Negro's legs, and Bayard mounted into darkness and the dry, pungent scent of hay. Here, in the darkness, he made himself a nest of it and crawled into it and rolled himself into the quilt, filth and odor and all, and thrust his icy hands inside his shirt, against his flinching chest. After a time and slowly his hands began to warm, tingling a little,

but still his body lay shivering and jerking with weariness
and with cold. Below him Perry munched steadily and peacefully in the darkness, occasionally he stamped, and gradually the jerking of Bayard's body ceased. Before he slept
he uncovered his arm and looked at the luminous dial on his
wrist. One o'clock. It was already Christmas.

The sun waked him, falling in red bars through the cracks
in the wall, and he lay for a while in his hard bed, with chill,
bright air on his face like icy water, wondering where he was.
Then he remembered, and moving, found that he was stiff
with stale cold and that his blood began to move through his
limbs in small pellets like bird-shot. He dragged his legs
from his odorous bed, but within his boots his feet were
dead, and he sat flexing his knees and ankles for some time
before his feet waked as with stinging needles.

His movements were stiff and awkward and he descended
the ladder slowly and gingerly into the red sun that fell
like a blare of trumpets into the hallway. The sun was just
above the horizon, huge and red, and housetop, fenceposts,
the casual farming tools rusting about the barnyard and
the dead cotton stalks where the Negro had farmed his land
right up to his back door, were dusted over with frost which
the sun changed to a scintillant rosy icing like that of a
festive cake. Perry thrust his slender muzzle across the
stall door and whinnied at his master with vaporous saluta-
tion, and Bayard spoke to him and touched his cold nose.
Then he untied the sack and drank from the jug. The Negro
with a milk pail appeared in the door.

"Chris'mus' gif', white folks," he said, eying the jug.
Bayard gave him a drink. "Thanky, suh. You g'awn to
de house to de fire. I'll feed yo' hawss. De ole woman got
yo' breakfast ready." Bayard picked up the sack; at the well
behind the cabin he drew a pail of icy water and splashed his
face.

A fire burned on the broken hearth, amid ashes and
charred wood-ends and a litter of cooking-vessels. Bayard
shut the door behind him on the bright cold, and warmth
and rich, stale rankness enveloped him like a drug. A woman,
bent over the hearth, replied to his greeting diffidently. Three
pickaninnies became utterly still in a corner and watched
him with rolling eyes. One of them was a girl, in greasy

nondescript garments, her wool twisted into tight knots of soiled wisps of colored cloth. The second one might have been either or anything. The third one was practically helpless in a garment made from a man's suit of woolen underclothes. It was too small to walk and it crawled about the floor in a sort of intent purposelessness, a glazed path running from either nostril to its chin, as though snails had crawled there.

The woman placed a chair before the fire with a dark, effacing gesture. Bayard seated himself and thrust his chilled feet to the fire. "Had your Christmas dram yet, aunty?" he asked.

"Naw, suh. Ain't got none dis year," she answered from somewhere behind him. He swung the sack toward her voice. "Help yourself. Plenty there." The three children squatted against the wall, watching him steadily, without movement and without sound. "Christmas come yet, chillen?" he asked them. But they only stared at him with the watchful gravity of animals until the woman returned and spoke to them in a chiding tone.

"Show de white folks yo' Sandy Claus," she prompted. "Thanky, suh," she added, putting a tin plate on his knees and setting a cracked china cup on the hearth at his feet. "Show 'im," she repeated. "You want folks to think Sandy Claus don't know whar you lives at?"

The children moved then and from the shadow behind them, where they had hidden them when he entered, they produced a small tin automobile, a string of colored wooden beads, a small mirror and a huge stick of peppermint candy to which trash adhered and which they immediately fell to licking solemnly, turn and turn about. The woman filled the cup from the coffee-pot set among the embers, and she uncovered an iron skillet and forked a thick slab of sizzling meat on to his plate, and raked a grayish object from the ashes and broke it in two and dusted it off and put that too on the plate. Bayard ate his side meat and hoecake and drank the thin, tasteless liquid. The children now played quietly with their Christmas, but from time to time he found them watching him steadily and covertly. The man entered with his pail of milk.

"Ole 'oman give you a snack?" he asked.

"Yes. What's the nearest town on the railroad?" The Negro told him—eight miles away. "Can you drive me over there this morning and take my horse back to Mr. MacCallum's some day this week?"

"My brudder-in-law bor'd my mules," the Negro replied readily. "I ain't got but de one span, and he done bor'd dem."

"I'll pay you five dollars."

The Negro set the pail down and the woman came and got it. He scratched his head slowly. "Five dollars," Bayard repeated.

"You's in a pow'ful rush fer Chris'mus, white folks."

"Ten dollars," Bayard said impatiently. "Can't you get your mules back from your brother-in-law?"

"I reckon so. I reckon he'll bring 'em back by dinnertime. We kin go den."

"Why can't you get 'em now? Take my horse and go get 'em. I want to catch a train."

"I ain't had no Chris'mus yit, white folks. Feller workin' ev'y day of de year wants a little Chris'mus."

Bayard swore shortly and bleakly, but he said: "All right, then. Right after dinner. But you see your brother-in-law has 'em back in plenty of time."

"Dey'll be here; don't you worry about dat."

"All right. You and aunty help yourselves to the jug."

"Thanky, suh."

The stale, air-tight room dulled him; the warmth was insidious to his bones, wearied and stiff after the chill night. The Negroes moved about the single room, the woman busy at the hearth with her cooking, the pickaninnies with their frugal and sorry gewgaws and filthy candy. Bayard sat in his hard chair and dozed the morning away—not asleep, but time was lost in a timeless region where he lingered unawake and into which he realized after a long while that something was trying to penetrate; watched its vain attempts with peaceful detachment. But at last it succeeded and reached him: a voice. "Dinner ready."

The Negroes drank with him, amicably, a little diffidently—two opposed concepts antipathetic by race, blood, nature and environment, touching for a moment and fused within an illusion—humankind forgetting its lust and cowardice and greed for a day. "Chris'mus," the woman murmured shyly. "Thanky, suh."

Then dinner: 'possum with yams, more gray ash cake, the dead and tasteless liquid in the coffee-pot; a dozen bananas and jagged shards of cocoanut, the children crawling about his feet like animals, scenting the food. He realized at last that they were holding back until he had done, but he overrode them and they dined together; and at last (the mules having been miraculously returned by a yet incorporeal brother-in-law), with his depleted jug between his feet in the wagon bed, he looked once back at the cabin, at the woman standing in the door and a pale, windless drift of smoke above its chimney.

Against the mules' gaunt ribs the broken harness rattled and jingled. The air was warm, yet laced too with a thin distillation of chill that darkness would increase. The road went on across the bright land. From time to time across the shining sedge or from beyond brown and leafless woods, came the flat reports of guns; occasionally they passed other teams or horsemen or pedestrians who lifted dark, restful hands to the Negro buttoned into an army overcoat, with brief covert glances for the white man on the seat beside him. "Heyo, Chris'mus!" Beyond the yellow sedge and brown ridges the ultimate hills stood bluely against the plumbless sky. "Heyo."

They stopped and drank, and Bayard gave his companion a cigarette. The sun behind them now; no cloud, no wind, no bird in the serene pale cobalt. "Shawt days! Fo' mile mo'. Come up, mules." Between motionless willows, stubbornly green, a dry clatter of loose planks above water in murmurous flashes. The road lifted redly; pines stood against the sky in jagged bastions. They crested this, and a plateau rolled away before them with its pattern of burnished sedge and fallow, dark fields and brown woodland and now and then a house, on into shimmering azure haze, and low down on the horizon, smoke. "Two mile, now." Behind them the sun was a copper balloon tethered an hour up the sky. They drank again.

It had touched the horizon when they looked down into the final valley where the railroad's shining threads vanished among roofs and trees, and along the air to them distantly came a slow, heavy explosion. "Still celebratin'," the Negro said.

Out of the sun they descended into violet shadow where windows gleamed behind wreaths and paper bells, across stoops littered with spent firecrackers. Along the streets chil-

dren in bright sweaters and jackets sped on shiny coasters
and skates and wagons. Again a heavy explosion in the dusk
ahead, and they debouched on to the square with its Sabbath
calm, littered too with shattered scraps of paper. It looked
the same way at home, he knew, with men and youths he
had known from boyhood lounging the holiday away, drinking a little and shooting fireworks and giving nickels and
dimes and quarters to Negro lads who shouted "Chris'mus
gif'! Chris'mus gif'!" as they passed. And out home the tree
in the parlor and the bowl of eggnog before the fire, and
Simon entering his and Johnny's room on tense and clumsy
tiptoe and holding his breath above the bed where they lay
feigning sleep until his tenseness relaxed, whereupon they
both roared "Christmas gift!" at him, to his pained disgust.
"Well, I'll de-clare, ef dey ain't done caught me ag'in!" But
by mid-morning he would be recovered, by dinnertime he
would be in a state of affable and useless loquacity, and by
nightfall completely *hors de combat,* with Aunt Jenny storming about the house and swearing that never again should it
be turned into a barroom for trifling niggers as long as she
had her strength, so help her Jupiter. And after dark, somewhere a dance, with holly and mistletoe and paper streamers,
and the girls he had always known with their new bracelets
and watches and fans amid lights and music and glittering
laughter. . . .

A small group stood on a corner, and as the wagon passed
and preceded by an abrupt scurrying, yellow flame was
stenciled on the twilight and the heavy explosion reverberated
in sluggish echoes between the silent walls. The mules quick-
ened against the collars and the wagon rattled on. Through
the dusk now, from lighted doorways where bells and
wreaths hung, voices called with mellow insistence; children's
voices replied, expostulant, reluctantly regretful. Then the
station, where a 'bus and four or five cars stood, and Bayard
descended and the Negro lifted down the sack.

"Much obliged," Bayard said. "Good-bye."

"Good-bye, white folks."

In the waiting-room a stove glowed red hot, and about
the room stood cheerful groups in sleek furs and overcoats,
but he did not enter. He set the sack against the wall and
tramped up and down the platform, warming his blood
again. In both directions along the tracks green switch-lights

were steady in the dusk; a hands-breadth above the western trees the evening star was like an electric bulb in a glass wall. He tramped back and forth, glancing into the ruddy windows, into the waiting-room where the cheerful groups in their furs and overcoats gesticulated with festive and soundless animation, and into the colored waiting-room, whose occupants sat patiently and murmurously about the stove in the dingy light. As he turned here a voice spoke diffidently from the shadow beside the door. "Chris'mus gif', boss." He took a coin from his pocket without stopping. Again from the square a firecracker exploded heavily, and above the trees a rocket arced, hung for a moment, then opened like a fist, spreading its golden and fading fingers on the tranquil indigo sky without a sound.

Then the train came and brought its lighted windows to a jarring halt, and he picked up his sack again and in the midst of a cheerful throng shouting good-byes and holiday greetings and messages to absent ones, he got aboard. Unshaven, in his scarred boots and stained khaki pants, and his shabby, smoke-colored tweed jacket and his disreputable felt hat, he found a vacant seat and stowed the jug away beneath his legs.

PART FIVE

". . . and since the essence of spring is loneliness and a little sadness and a sense of mild frustration, I suppose you do get a keener purification when a little nostalgia is added in for good measure. At home I always found myself remembering apple trees or green lanes or the color of the sea in other places, and I'd be sad that I couldn't be everywhere at once, or that all the spring couldn't be one spring, like Byron's ladies' mouths. But now I seem to be unified and projected upon one single and very definite object, which is something to be said for me, after all." Horace's pen ceased and he gazed at the sheet scrawled over with his practically illegible script, while the words he had just written echoed yet in his mind with a little gallant and whimsical sadness, and for the time being he had quitted the desk and the room and the town and all the crude and blatant newness into which his destiny had brought him, and again that wild and fantastic futility of his roamed unchallenged through the lonely region into which it had at last concentrated its conflicting parts. Already the thick cables along the veranda eaves would be budding into small lilac match-points, and with no effort at all he could see the lawn below the cedars, splashed with random narcissi among random jonquils, and gladioli waiting in turn to bloom.

But his body sat motionless, its hand with the arrested pen lying on the scrawled sheet. The paper lay on the yellow varnished surface of his new desk. The chair in which he sat was new too, as was the room with its dead white walls and imitation oak woodwork. All day long the sun fell on it, untempered by any shade. In the days of early spring it had been pleasant, falling as it now did through his western window and across the desk where a white hyacinth bloomed in a bowl of glazed maroon pottery. But as he sat musing, gazing out the window where, beyond a tarred roof that drank heat like a sponge and radiated it, against a brick wall a clump of ragged trees of heaven lifted shabby, diffident bloom, he dreaded the long, hot summer days of sunlight on the roof directly over him; remembered his dim and musty office at home, in which a breeze seemed always to move, with its serried rows of books dusty and undisturbed that seemed to emanate coolness and quietude even on the hottest days. And thinking of this, he was lost again from the harsh newness in which his body sat. The pen moved again.

"Perhaps fortitude is a sorry imitation of something worth while, after all, to the so many who burrow along like moles in the dark, or like owls, to whom a candle-flame is a surfeit. But not to those who carry peace along with them as the candle-flame carries light. I have always been ordered by words, but it seems that I can even restore assurance to my own cowardice by cozening it a little. I dare say you cannot read this, as usual, or reading it, it will not mean anything to you. But you will have served your purpose anyway, thou still unravished bride of quietness."—"Thou wast happier in thy cage, happier?" Horace thought, reading the words he had written and in which, as usual, he was washing one woman's linen in the house of another. A thin breeze blew suddenly into the room; there was locust on it, faintly sweet, and beneath it the paper stirred on the desk, rousing him, and suddenly, as a man waking, he looked at his watch and replaced it and wrote rapidly:

"We are glad to have little Belle with us. She likes it here; there is a whole family of little girls next door; stair-steps of tow pigtails before whom, it must be confessed, little Belle preens just a little; patronizes them, as is her birthright. Children make all the difference in the world about a house. Too bad agents are not wise enough to provide rented houses with them. Particularly one like little Belle, so grave and shining and sort of irrelevantly and intensely mature, you know. But then, you don't know her very well, do you? But we are both very glad to have her with us. I believe that Harry"——
The pen ceased, and still poised, he sought the words that so rarely eluded him, realizing as he did so that, though one can lie about others with ready and extemporaneous prompti-

tude, to lie about oneself requires deliberation and a careful choice of expression. Then he glanced again at his watch and crossed that out and wrote: "Belle sends love, O Serene," and blotted it and folded it swiftly into an envelope and addressed and stamped it, and rose and took his hat. By running he could get it on the four o'clock train.

2

In January his aunt received a post card from Bayard mailed at Tampico; a month later, from Mexico City, a wire for money. And that was the last intimation he gave that he contemplated being at any given place long enough for a communication to reach him, although from time to time he indicated by gaudy postals where he had been, after the bleak and brutal way of him. In April the card came from Rio, followed by an interval during which he seemed to have completely vanished and which Miss Jenny and Narcissa passed quietly at home, their days centered placidly about the expected child which Miss Jenny had already named John.

Miss Jenny felt that old Bayard had somehow flouted them all, had committed lese majesty toward his ancestors and the lusty glamour of the family doom by dying, as she put it, practically from the "inside out." Thus he was in something like bad odor with her, and as young Bayard was in more or less abeyance, neither flesh nor fowl, she fell to talking more and more of John. Soon after old Bayard's death, in a sudden burst of rummaging and prowling which she called winter cleaning, she had found among his mother's relics a miniature of John done by a New Orleans painter when John and Bayard were about eight. Miss Jenny remembered that there had been one of each and it seemed to her that she could remember putting them both away together when their mother died. But the other she could not find. So she left Simon to gather up the litter she had made and brought the miniature downstairs to where Narcissa sat in the office, and together they examined it.

The hair even at that early time was of a rich tawny shade, and rather long. "I remember that first day," Miss Jenny said, "when they came home from school. Bloody as hogs, both of 'em, from fighting other boys who said they looked like girls. Their mother washed 'em and petted 'em, but they were too busy bragging to Simon and Bayard about the slaughter they had done to mind it much. 'You ought to seen the others,' Johnny kept saying. Bayard blew up, of course; said it was a damn shame to send a boy out on the street with curls down his back, and finally he bullied the poor woman into agreeing to let Simon barber 'em. And do you know what? Neither of 'em would let his hair be touched. It seems there were still a few they hadn't licked yet, and they were going to make the whole school admit that they could wear hair down to their heels if they wanted to. And I reckon they did, because after two or three more bloody days they came home once without any fresh wounds and then they let Simon cut it off while their mother sat behind the piano in the parlor and cried. And that was the last of it as long as they were in school here. I don't know what they kept on fighting folks about after they went away to school, but they found some reason. That was why we finally had to separate 'em while they were at Virginia and send Johnny to Princeton. They shot dice or something to see which one would be expelled, I think, and when Johnny lost they used to meet in New York every month or so. I found some letters in Bayard's desk that the chief of police in New York wrote to the professors at Princeton and Virginia, asking 'em not to let Bayard and Johnny come back there any more, that the professors sent on to us. And one time Bayard had to pay fifteen hundred dollars for something they did to a policeman or a waiter or something."

Miss Jenny talked on, but Narcissa was not listening. She was examining the painted face in the miniature. It was a child's face that looked at her, and it was Bayard's too, yet there was already in it, not that bleak arrogance she had come to know in Bayard's, but a sort of frank spontaneity, warm and ready and generous; and as Narcissa held the small oval in her hand while the steady blue eyes looked quietly back at her and from the whole face among its tawny curls, with its smooth skin and child's mouth, there shone like a warm radiance something sweet and merry and wild, she realized as she never had before the blind tragedy of human events. And while she sat motionless with the medallion in her hand and Miss Jenny thought she was looking at it, she was cherishing the child under her own heart with all the aroused constancy of her nature: it was as though already she could discern the dark shape of that doom which she had incurred, standing beside her chair, waiting and biding its time. "No, no," she whispered with passionate protest, surrounding her child with wave after wave of that strength which welled so abundantly within her as the days accumulated, manning her walls with invincible garrisons. She was even glad Miss Jenny had shown her the thing: she was now forewarned as well as forearmed.

Meanwhile Miss Jenny continued to talk about the child as Johnny and to recall anecdotes of that other John's childhood, until at last Narcissa realized that Miss Jenny was getting the two confused; and with a sort of shock she knew that Miss Jenny was getting old, that at last even her indomitable old heart was growing a little tired. It was a shock, for she had never associated senility with Miss Jenny, who was so spare and erect and brusque and uncompromising and kind, looking after the place which was not hers and to which she had been transplanted when her own alien roots in a far-away place, where customs and manners and even the very climate itself were different, had been severed violently; running it with tireless efficiency and with the assistance of only a doddering old Negro as irresponsible as a child.

But run the place she did, just as though old Bayard and young Bayard were there. But at night, when they sat before the fire in the office, while the year drew on and the night air drifted in again heavy with locust and with the song of mocking-birds and with all the renewed and timeless mischief of spring and at last even Miss Jenny admitted that they no longer needed a fire; when at these times she talked, Narcissa noticed that she no longer talked of her far-off girlhood and of Jeb Stuart with his crimson sash and his garlanded bay and his mandolin, but always of a time no further back than Bayard's and John's childhood. As though her life were closing, not into the future, but out of the past, like a spool being rewound.

And Narcissa would sit, serene again behind her fore-warned bastions, listening, admiring more than ever that indomitable spirit that, born with a woman's body into a heritage of rash and heedless men and seemingly for the sole purpose of cherishing those men to their early and violent ends, and this over a period of history which had seen brothers and husband slain in the same useless mischancing of human affairs; had seen, as in a nightmare not to be healed by either waking or sleep, the foundations of her life swept away and had her roots torn bodily from that soil where her forefathers slept trusting in the integrity of mankind—a period at which the men themselves, for all their headlong and scornful rashness, would have quailed had their parts been passive parts and their doom been waiting. And she thought how much finer that gallantry which never lowered blade to foes no sword could find; that uncomplaining steadfastness of those unsung (ay, unwept too) women than the fustian and useless glamour of the men that obscured it. "And now she is trying to make me one of them; to make of my child just another rocket to glare for a moment in the sky, then die away."

But she was serene again, and her days centered more and more as her time drew nearer, and Miss Jenny's voice was only a sound, comforting but without significance. Each week she received a whimsical, gallantly humorous letter from Horace: these too she read with tranquil detachment—what she could decipher, that is. She had always found Horace's writing difficult, and parts that she could decipher meant nothing to her. But she knew that he expected that.

Then it was definitely spring again. Miss Jenny's and Isom's annual vernal altercation began, pursued its violent but harmless course in the garden beneath her window. They brought the tulip bulbs up from the cellar and set them out, Narcissa helping, and spaded up the other beds and unswaddled the roses and the transplanted jasmine. Narcissa drove into town, saw the first jonquils on the deserted lawn blooming as though she and Horace were still there, and she sent Horace a box of them, and later, of narcissi. But when the gladioli bloomed she was not going out any more save in the late afternoon or early evening, when with Miss Jenny she walked in the garden among burgeoning bloom and mocking-birds and belated thrushes where the long avenues of gloaming twilight reluctant leaned, Miss Jenny still talking of Johnny, confusing the unborn with the dead.

Early in June they received a request for money from Bayard in San Francisco, where he had at last succeeded in being robbed. Miss Jenny sent it. "You come on home," she wired him, not telling Narcissa. "He'll come home, now," she did tell her; "you see if he don't. If for nothing else than to worry us for a while."

But a week later he still had not come home, and Miss Jenny wired him again, a night letter. But when the wire was dispatched he was in Chicago, and when it reached San Francisco he was sitting among saxophones and painted ladies and middle-aged husbands at a table littered with soiled glasses and stained with cigarette ash and spilt liquor, accompanied by two men and a girl. One of the men wore whipcord, with an army pilot's wings on his breast. The other was a stocky man in shabby serge, with gray temples and intense, visionary eyes. The girl was a slim long thing, mostly legs apparently, with a bold red mouth and cold eyes, in an ultrasmart dancing-frock, and when the other two men came across the room and spoke to Bayard she was cajoling him to drink with thinly concealed insistence. She and the aviator now danced together, and from time to time she looked back to where Bayard sat drinking steadily while the shabby man talked to him. She was saying, "I'm scared of him."

The shabby man was talking with leashed excitability, using two napkins folded lengthwise into narrow strips to illustrate something, his voice hoarse and importunate against the meaningless pandemonium of horns and drums. For a while Bayard had half listened, staring at the man with his cold eyes, but now he was watching something or some one across the room, letting the man talk on unheeded. He was drinking whisky and soda steadily, with the bottle beside him. His hand was steady enough, but his face was dead white and he was quite drunk; and looking across at him from time to time, the girl was saying to her partner: "I'm scared, I tell you. God, I didn't know what to do when you and your friend came over. Promise you won't go and leave us."

"You scared?" the aviator repeated in a jeering tone, but he too glanced back at Bayard's white, arrogant face. "I bet you don't even need a horse."

"You don't know him," the girl rejoined, and she clutched his hand and struck her body shivering against him, and though his arm tightened and his hand slid down her back a little, it was under cover of the shuffling throng in which they were wedged, and a little warily, and he said quickly:

"Ease off, sister; he's looking this way. I saw him knock two teeth out of an Australian captain that just tried to speak to a girl he was with in a London dive two years ago." They moved on until the band was across the floor from them. "What're you scared of? He's not an Indian; he won't hurt you as long as you mind your step. He's all right. I've known him a long time, in places where you had to be good, believe me."

"You don't know," she repeated. "I——"

The music crashed to a stop; in the sudden silence the shabby man's voice rose from the near-by table: "——could just get one of these damn yellow-livered pilots to——"

His voice was drowned again in a surge of noise: drunken voices and shrill woman-laughter and scraping chairs, but as they approached the table the shabby man still talked with leashed insistent gestures while Bayard stared across the room at whatever it was he watched, lifting his glass steadily to his lips. The girl clutched her partner's arm.

"You've got to help me pass him out," she begged swiftly. "I'm scared to leave with him, I tell you."

"Pass Sartoris out? The man don't wear hair, nor the woman neither. Run back to kindergarden, sister." Then, struck with her utter sincerity, he said, "Say, what's he done to you, anyway?"

"I don't know. He'll do anything. He threw an empty bottle at a traffic cop as we were driving out here. You've got——"

"Hush it," he commanded. The shabby man ceased talking and looked up impatiently. Bayard still gazed across the room.

"Brother-in-law over there," he said, speaking slowly and carefully. "Don't speak to family. Mad at us. Beat him out of his wife." They turned and looked.

"Where?" the aviator asked. He beckoned a waiter. "Here, Jack."

"Man with diamond headlight," Bayard said. "Brave man. Can't speak to him, though. Might hit me. Friend with him, anyhow."

The aviator looked again. "Looks like his grandmother," he said. He called the waiter again, then to the girl: "Another cocktail?" He picked up the bottle and filled his glass and renewed Bayard's and turned to the shabby man. "Where's yours?"

The shabby man waved it impatiently aside. "Look," he picked up the napkins again. "Dihedral increases in ratio to air pressure. By speed up to a certain point, see? Now, what I want to find out——"

"Tell it to the Marines, buddy," the aviator interrupted. "I heard a couple of years ago they got a airyplane. Here, waiter!" Bayard was now watching the shabby man bleakly.

"You aren't drinking," the girl said. She touched the aviator beneath the table.

"No," Bayard agreed. "Why don't you fly his coffin for him, Monaghan?"

"Me?" The aviator set his glass down. "Like hell. My leave comes due next month." He raised his glass again. "Here's to wind-up," he said, "and no heeltaps."

"Yes," Bayard agreed, not touching his glass. His face was pale and rigid, a metal mask again.

"I tell you there's no danger at all, as long as you keep the speed below a point I'll give you," the shabby man said with heat. "I've tested the wings with weights, and proved the lift and checked all my figures; all you have to——"

"Won't you drink with us?" the girl insisted.

"Sure he will," the aviator said. "Say, you remember that night in Amiens when that big Irish devil, Comyn, wrecked the Cloche-Clos by blowing that A.P.M.'s whistle at the door?" The shabby man sat smoothing the folded napkins on the table before him. Then he burst forth again, his voice hoarse and mad with the intensity of his frustration:

"I've worked and slaved, and begged and borrowed, and now when I've got the machine and a government inspector, I can't get a test because you damn yellow-livered pilots won't take it up. A service full of you, drawing flying pay for sitting on hotel roofs swilling alcohol. You overseas pilots talking about your guts! No wonder the Germans——"

"Shut up," Bayard told him without heat, in his cold, careful voice.

"You're not drinking," the girl repeated. "Won't you?" She picked up his glass and touched her lips to it and extended it to him. Taking it, he caught her hand too and held her so. But again he was staring across the room.

"Not brother-in-law," he said, "husband-in-law. No. Wife's

brother's husband-in-law. Wife used to be wife's brother's girl. Married now. Fat woman. He's lucky."

"What're you talking about?" the aviator demanded. "Come on, let's have a drink."

The girl leaned away from him at the length of her arm. With her other hand she lifted her glass and smiled at him with brief and terrified coquetry. He held her wrist in his hard fingers, and while she stared at him widely he drew her steadily toward him. "Turn me loose," she whispered. "Don't." And she set her glass down and with the other hand she tried to unclasp his fingers. The shabby man was brooding over his folded napkins; the aviator was carefully occupied with his drink. "Don't," she whispered again. Her body was twisted in her chair and she put out her hand quickly, lest she be dragged out of it, and for a moment they stared at one another—she with wide, mute terror; he bleakly, with the cold mask of his face. Then he released her and thrust his chair back.

"Come on, you," he said to the shabby man. He drew a wad of bills from his pocket and laid one beside her on the table. "That'll get you home," he said. But she sat nursing the wrist he had held, watching him without a sound. The aviator was discreetly interested in the bottom of his glass. "Come on," Bayard repeated to the shabby man, and the other rose and followed him.

In a small alcove Harry Mitchell sat. On his table too were bottles and glasses, and he now sat slumped in his chair, his eyes closed and his bald head rosy with perspiration in the glow of an electric candle. Beside him was a woman who turned and looked at Bayard with blazing and harried desperation. Above them stood a waiter with a head like a monk's and as Bayard passed he saw that the diamond was missing from Harry's tie, and he heard their bitter suppressed voices as their hands struggled over something on the table beyond the discreet shelter of their bodies. As he and his companion reached the exit the woman's voice rose with a burst of filthy rage into a shrill, hysterical scream cut sharply off, as if some one had clapped a hand over her mouth.

The next day Miss Jenny drove into town and wired him again. But when this wire was dispatched Bayard was sitting in an airplane on the tarmac of the government field at Dayton, while the shabby man hovered and darted here and there in a frenzied manner and a group of army pilots stood near by, soberly noncommittal. The machine looked like any other biplane, save that there were no visible cables between the planes, which were braced from within by wires on a system of springs; hence, motionless on the ground, dihedral was negative. The theory was that while in level flight, dihedral would be eliminated for speed, and when the machine was banked, side pressure would automatically increase dihedral for maneuverability. The cockpit was set well back toward the fin.

"So you can see the wings when they buckle," the man who lent him helmet and goggles said drily. "It's an old pair," he added. Bayard glanced at him, coldly humorless. "Look here, Sartoris," the other said, "let that crate alone. These birds show up here every week with something that will revolutionize flying, some new kind of mantrap that flies fine—on paper. If the C.O. won't give him a pilot (and you know we try anything here that has a prop on it) you can gamble it's a washout."

But Bayard took the helmet and goggles and went on toward the hangar. The group followed him and stood quietly about with their bleak, wind-gnawed faces while the engine was warming up. But when Bayard got in and settled his goggles, the man who had lent them to him approached and put something in his lap. "Here," he said brusquely. "Take this." It was a woman's garter, and Bayard picked it up and gave it back to him.

"I won't need it," he said. "Thanks just the same."

"Well. You know your own business. But if you ever let her get her nose down, you're going to lose everything but the wheels."

"I know," Bayard answered. "I'll keep her up." The shabby man rushed up again, still talking. "Yes, yes," Bayard replied impatiently. "You told me all that before. Contact." A mechanic spun the propeller, and as the machine moved out toward mid-field the shabby man still clung to the cockpit rim and shouted at him. Soon he was running to keep up and still shouting, and Bayard lifted his hands off the cowling and opened the throttle. When he reached the end of the field and turned into the wind the man was running toward him and waving his arm. Bayard opened the throttle full and the ma-

chine lurched forward, and when he passed the man in mid-
field the tail was high and the plane rushed on in long
bounds, and he had a fleeting glimpse of the man's wild arms
and his open mouth as the bounding ceased.

From the V strut out each wing tipped and swayed, and
he jockeyed the thing carefully on, gaining height. He realized that there was a certain point beyond which his own
speed was likely to rob him of lifting surface. He had about
two thousand feet now and he turned, and in doing so he
found that aileron pressure utterly negatived the inner
plane's dihedral and doubled that of the outer one, and he
found himself in the wildest skid he had seen since his Hun
days. The machine not only skidded; it flung its tail up like a
diving whale and the air speed indicator leaped thirty miles
past the dead line the inventor had given him. He was headed
back toward the field now, in a shallow dive, and he pulled
the stick back.

The wing-tips buckled sharply; he flung the stick forward
just before they ripped completely off, and he knew that only
the speed of the dive kept him from falling like an inside-out
umbrella. And the speed was increasing; already he had
overshot the field, under a thousand feet high. He pulled
the stick back again; again the wing-tips buckled, and he
slapped the stick over and kicked again into that wild skid to
check his speed. Again the machine swung its tail in a soaring arc, but this time the wings came off and he ducked
his head automatically as one of them slapped viciously past
it and crashed into the tail, shearing that too away.

3

That day Narcissa's child was born, and the following day
Simon drove Miss Jenny into town and sat her down before
the telegraph office and held the horses champing and tossing with gallant restiveness by a slight and surreptitious
tightening of the reins, while beneath the top hat and the
voluminous duster he contrived by some means to actually
strut sitting down. Dr. Peabody found him so when he came

along the street in the June sunlight, in his slovenly alpaca coat, carrying a newspaper.

"You look like a frog, Simon," he said. "Where's Miss Jenny?"

"Yessuh," Simon agreed, "yessuh. Dey's swellin' en re-joicin' now. De little marster done arrive. Yessuh, de little marster done arrive en de ole times comin' back."

"Where's Miss Jenny?" Dr. Peabody repeated impatiently.

"She in dar, tellygraftin' dat boy ter come on back here whar he belong at."

Dr. Peabody turned away and Simon watched him, a little fretted at his apathy in the face of the event. "Takes it jes' like trash," Simon mused aloud, with annoyed disparage-ment. "Nummine; we gwine wake 'um all up, now. Yessuh, de olden times comin' back ergain, sho'. Like in Mars' John's time, when de Cunnel wuz de young marster en de niggers fum de quawters gethered on de front lawn, wishin' Mistis en de little marster well." And he watched Dr. Peabody enter the door, and through the plate-glass window he saw him approach Miss Jenny as she stood at the counter with her message.

"Come home you fool and see your family or I will have you arrested," the message read in her firm, lucid script. "It's more than ten words," she told the operator, "but that don't matter this time. He'll come now; you watch. Or I'll send the sheriff after him, sure as his name's Sartoris."

"Yes, ma'am," the operator said. He was apparently hav-ing trouble reading it, and he looked up after a moment and was about to speak, when Miss Jenny remarked his dis-traction and repeated the message briskly.

"And make it stronger than that, if you want to," she added.

"Yes, ma'am," he said again, and he ducked down behind his desk, and presently and with a little mounting curiosity and impatience Miss Jenny leaned across the counter with a silver dollar in her fingers and watched him count the words three times in a sort of painful flurry.

"What's the matter, young man?" she demanded. "The government don't forbid the mentioning of a day-old child in a telegram, does it?"

The operator looked up. "Yes, ma'am, it's all right," he said at last, and she gave him the dollar and as he sat holding it in his hand and Miss Jenny watched him with yet more impatience, Dr. Peabody came in and touched her arm.

"Come away, Jenny," he said.

"Good morning," she said, turning at his voice. "Well, it's about time you took notice. This is the first Sartoris you've been a day late on in how many years, Loosh? And soon as I get that fool boy home, it'll be like old times again, as Simon says."

"Yes. Simon told me. Come along here."

"Let me get my change." She turned to the counter, where the operator stood with the message in one hand and the coin in the other. "Well, young man? Ain't a dollar enough?"

"Yes, ma'am," he repeated, turning on Dr. Peabody his dumb, distracted eyes. Dr. Peabody reached fatly and took the message and the coin from him.

"Come along, Jenny," he said again. Miss Jenny stood motionless for a moment, in her black silk dress and her black bonnet set squarely on her head, staring at him with her piercing old eyes that saw so much and so truly. Then she walked steadily to the door and stepped into the street and waited until he joined her, and her hand was steady too as she took the folded paper he offered. MISSISSIPPI AVIATOR it said in discreet capitals, and she returned it to him immediately and from her waist she took a small sheer handkerchief and wiped her fingers lightly.

"I don't have to read it," she said. "They never get into the papers but one way. And I know that he was somewhere he had no business being, doing something that wasn't any affair of his."

"Yes," Dr. Peabody said. He followed her to the carriage and put his hands clumsily on her as she mounted.

"Don't paw me, Loosh," she snapped; "I'm not a cripple." But he supported her elbow with his huge, gentle hand until she was seated; then he stood with his hat off while Simon laid the linen robe across her knees.

"Here," he said, extending her the silver dollar. She returned it to her bag and clicked it shut and wiped her fingers again on her handkerchief.

"Well," she said. Then: "Thank God that's the last one. For a while, anyway. Home, Simon."

Simon sat magnificently, but under the occasion he unbent

a little. "When you gwine come out en see de young marster, Doctuh?"

"Soon, Simon," he answered, and Simon clucked to the horses and wheeled away with a flourish, his hat tilted and the whip caught smartly back. Dr. Peabody stood in the street, a shapeless hogshead of a man in a shabby alpaca coat, his hat in one hand and the folded newspaper and the yellow unsent message in the other, until Miss Jenny's straight slender back and the square indomitable angle of her bonnet had passed from sight.

But that was not the last one. One morning a week later, Simon was found in a Negro cabin in town, his grizzled head crushed in by a blunt instrument anonymously wielded.

"In whose house?" Miss Jenny demanded into the telephone. In that of a woman named Meloney Harris, the voice told her. Meloney . . . Mel . . . Belle Mitchell's face flashed before her mind, and she remembered: the mulatto girl whose smart cap and apron and lean, shining shanks had lent such an air to Belle's parties, and who had quit Belle in order to set up a beauty parlor. Miss Jenny thanked the voice and hung up the receiver.

"The old gray-headed reprobate," she said, and she went into old Bayard's office and sat down. "So that's where that church money went that he 'put out.' I wondered. . . ." She sat stiffly and uncompromisingly erect in her chair, her hands idle on her lap. "Well, that *is* the last one of 'em," she thought. But no, he was hardly a Sartoris: he had at least some shadow of a reason, while the others . . . "I think," Miss Jenny said, who had not spent a day in bed since she was forty years old, "that I'll be sick for a while."

And she did just exactly that. Went to bed, where she lay propped on pillows in a frivolous lace cap, and would permit no doctor to see her save Dr. Peabody, who called once informally and sat sheepishly for thirty minutes while Miss Jenny vented her invalid's spleen and the recurred anger of the salve fiasco on him. And here she held daily councils with Isom and Elnora, and at the most unexpected moments she would storm with unimpaired vigor from her window at Isom and Caspey in the yard beneath.

The child and the placid, gaily turbaned mountain who superintended his hours, spent most of the day in this room, and presently Narcissa herself; and the three of them would sit for rapt, murmurous hours in a sort of choral debauch of abnegation while the object of it slept digesting, waked, stoked himself anew, and slept again.

"He's a Sartoris, all right," Miss Jenny said, "but an improved model. He hasn't got that wild look of 'em. I believe it was the name. Bayard. We did well to name him Johnny."

"Yes," Narcissa said, watching her sleeping son with grave and tranquil serenity.

And there Miss Jenny stayed until her while was up. Three weeks it was. She set the date before she went to bed and held to it stubbornly, refusing even to rise and attend the christening. That day fell on Sunday. It was late in June and jasmine drifted into the house in steady waves. Narcissa and the nurse, in an even more gaudy turban, had brought the baby, bathed and garnished and scented in his ceremonial robes, in to her, and later she heard them drive away in the carriage, and then the house was still again. The curtains stirred peacefully at the windows, and all the peaceful scents of summer came up on the sunny breeze, and sounds—birds, somewhere a Sabbath bell, and Elnora's voice, chastened a little by her recent bereavement but still rich and mellow as she went about getting dinner. She sang sadly and endlessly and without words as she moved about the kitchen, but she broke off short when she looked around and saw Miss Jenny, looking a little frail but dressed and erect as ever, in the door.

"Miss Jenny! Whut in de worl'! You git on back to yo' bed. Here, lemme he'p you back." But Miss Jenny came firmly on.

"Where's Isom?" she demanded.

"He at de barn. You come on back to bed. I'm gwine tell Miss Narcissa on you."

"Get away," Miss Jenny said. "I'm tired of staying in the house. I'm going to town. Call Isom." Elnora protested still, but Miss Jenny insisted coldly, and Elnora went to the door and called Isom and returned, portentous with pessimistic warnings, and presently Isom entered.

"Here," Miss Jenny said, handing him the keys. "Get the car out." Isom departed and Miss Jenny followed more slowly. Elnora would have followed too, darkly solicitous, but Miss Jenny sent her back to her kitchen; and she crossed the yard and got in beside Isom. "And you drive this thing careful, boy," she told him, "or I'll get over there and do it myself."

When they reached town, from slender spires rising among trees, against the puffy clouds of summer, bells were ringing lazily. At the edge of town Miss Jenny bade Isom turn into a grassy lane and they followed this and stopped presently before the iron gates to the cemetery. "I want to see if they fixed Simon all right," she explained. "I'm not going to church today: I've been shut up between walls long enough." Just from the prospect she got a mild exhilaration, like that of a small boy playing out of school.

The Negro burying-ground lay beyond the cemetery proper, and Isom led her to Simon's grave. Simon's burying society had taken care of him, and after three weeks the mound was still heaped with floral designs from which the blooms had fallen, leaving a rank, lean mass of stems and peacefully rusting wire skeletons. Elnora, some one, had been before her, and the grave was bordered with tedious rows of broken gaudy bits of crockery and of colored glass. "I reckon he'll have to have a headstone too," Miss Jenny said aloud, and turning, saw Isom hauling his overalled legs into a tree about which two catbirds whirled and darted in scolding circles. "You, Isom."

"Yessum." Isom dropped obediently to the ground and the birds threatened him with a final burst of hysterical profanity. They entered the white folks' section and passed now between marble shapes bearing names that she knew well, and dates in stark and peaceful simplicity in the impervious stone. Now and then they were surmounted by symbolical urns and doves and surrounded by clipped, tended sward green against the blanched marble and the blue dappled sky and the black cedars from amid which doves crooned, endlessly reiterant. Here and there bright unfaded flowers lay in random bursts against the pattern of white and green, and presently John Sartoris lifted his stone back and his fulsome gesture amid a clump of cedars beyond which the bluff sheared sharply away into the valley.

Bayard's grave too was a shapeless mass of withered flowers, and Miss Jenny had Isom clear them off and carry them away. The masons were preparing to lay the curbing around

it, and the headstone itself sat near by beneath a canvas
covering. She lifted the canvas and read the clean, new let-
tering: Bayard Sartoris. March 16, 1893—June 11, 1920.
That was better. Simple: no Sartoris man to invent bombast
to put on it. Can't even lie dead in the ground without strut-
ting and swaggering. Beside the grave was a second headstone, like the other save for the inscription. But the Sartoris
touch was here, despite the fact that there was no grave to
accompany it; and the whole thing was like a boastful voice
in an empty church. Yet withal there was something else, as
though the merry wild spirit of him who had laughed away
so much of his heritage of humorless and fustian vainglory
managed somehow even yet, though his bones lay in an
anonymous grave beyond seas, to soften the arrogant gesture
with which they had bade him farewell:

LIEUT. JOHN SARTORIS, R.A.F.

Killed in action, July 5, 1918

'I bare him on eagles' wings
and brought him unto Me'

A faint breeze soughed in the cedars like a long sigh, and
the branches moved gravely in it. Across the spaced tranquillity of the marble shapes the doves crooned their endless rising inflections. Isom returned for another armful of
withered flowers and bore it away.

Old Bayard's headstone was simple too, having been born,
as he had, too late for one war and too soon for the next,
and she thought what a joke They had played on him—for-
bidding him opportunities for swashbuckling and then deny-
ing him the privilege of being buried by men, who would have
invented vainglory for him. The cedars had almost overgrown
his son John's and John's wife's graves. Sunlight reached
them only in splashes, dappling the weathered stone with fitful stipplings; only with difficulty could the inscription have
been deciphered. But she knew what it would be, what with
the virus, the inspiration and example of that one which
dominated them all, which gave the whole place, in which
weary people were supposed to be resting, an orotund solem-
nity having no more to do with mortality than the bindings

of books have to do with their characters, and beneath which
the headstones of the wives whom they had dragged into their
arrogant orbits were, despite their pompous genealogical
references, modest and effacing as the song of thrushes beneath the eyrie of an eagle.

He stood on a stone pedestal, in his frock coat and bareheaded, one leg slightly advanced and one hand resting
lightly on the stone pylon beside him. His head was lifted a
little in that gesture of haughty pride which repeated itself
generation after generation with a fateful fidelity, his back
to the world and his carven eyes gazing out across the valley
where his railroad ran, and the blue changeless hills beyond,
and beyond that, the ramparts of infinity itself. The pedestal
and effigy were mottled with seasons of rain and sun and with
drippings from the cedar branches, and the bold carving of
the letters was bleared with mold, yet still decipherable:

COLONEL JOHN SARTORIS, C.S.A.

1823   1876
Soldier, Statesman, Citizen of the World

For man's enlightenment he lived
By man's ingratitude he died

Pause here, son of sorrow; remember death

This inscription had caused some furore on the part of
the slayer's family, and a formal protest had followed. But
in complying with popular opinion, old Bayard had had his
revenge: he caused the line "By man's ingratitude he died"
to be chiseled crudely out, and added beneath it: "Fell at
the hand of —— Redlaw, Sept. 4, 1876."

Miss Jenny stood for a time, musing, a slender, erect
figure in black silk and a small, uncompromising black bonnet. The wind drew among the cedars in long sighs, and
steadily as pulses the sad hopeless reiteration of the doves
came along the sunny air. Isom returned for the last armful
of dead flowers, and looking out across the marble vistas
where the shadows of noon moved, she watched a group of
children playing quietly and a little stiffly in their bright Sunday finery, among the tranquil dead. Well, it was the last one,
at last, gathered in solemn conclave about the dying rever-

beration of their arrogant lusts, their dust moldering quietly beneath the pagan symbols of their vainglory and the carven gestures of it in enduring stone; and she remembered something Narcissa had said once, about a world without men, and wondered if therein lay peaceful avenues and dwellings thatched with quiet; and she didn't know.

Isom returned, and as they moved away Dr. Peabody called her name. He was dressed as usual in his shabby broadcloth trousers and his shiny alpaca coat and floppy Panama hat, and his son was with him.

"Well, boy," Miss Jenny said, giving young Loosh her hand. His face was big-boned and roughly molded. He had a thatch of straight, stiff black hair and his eyes were steady and brown and his mouth was large, and in all his ugly face there was reliability and gentleness and humor. He was raw-boned and he wore his clothing awkwardly, and his hands were large and bony and with them he performed delicate surgical operations with the deftness of a hunter skinning a squirrel and with the celerity of a prestidigitator. He lived in New York, where he was associated with a surgeon whose name was a household word, and once a year and sometimes twice he rode thirty-six hours on the train, spent twenty hours with his father (which they passed walking about town or riding about the countryside in the sagging buckboard all day and sitting on the veranda or before the fire all night, talking) and took the train again and, ninety-two hours later, was back at his clinic. He was thirty years old, only child of the woman Dr. Peabody had courted for fourteen years before he was able to marry her. The courtship was during the days when he physicked and amputated the whole county by buckboard; often after a year's separation he would drive forty miles to see her, to be intercepted on the way and deflected to a childbed or a mangled limb, with only a scribbled message to assuage the interval of another year. "So you're home again, are you?" Miss Jenny asked.

"Yes, ma'am. And find you as spry and handsome as ever."

"Jenny's too bad-tempered to ever do anything but dry up and blow away," Dr. Peabody said.

"You'll remember I never let you wait on me when I'm not well," she retorted. "I reckon you'll be tearing off again on the next train, won't you?" she asked young Loosh.

"Yessum, I'm afraid so. My vacation hasn't come due, yet."

"Well, at this rate you'll spend it in an old men's home somewhere. Why don't you all come out and have dinner, so he can see the boy?"

"I'd like to," young Loosh answered, "but I don't have time to do all the things I want to, so I just make up my mind not to do any of 'em. Besides, I'll have to spend this afternoon fishing," he added.

"Yes," his father put in, "and choppin' up good fish with a pocket knife just to see what makes 'em go. Lemme tell you what he did this mawnin': he grabbed up that dawg that Abe shot last winter and laid its leg open and untangled them ligaments so quick that Abe not only didn't know what he was up to, but even the dawg didn't know it 'til it was too late to holler. Only you forgot to dig a little further for his soul," he added to his son.

"You don't know if he hasn't got one," young Loosh said, unruffled. "Dr. Straud has been experimenting with electricity; he says he believes the soul——"

"Fiddlesticks," Miss Jenny interrupted. "You'd better get him a jar of Will Falls' salve to carry back to his doctor, Loosh. Well"—she glanced at the sun—"I'd better be going. If you won't come out to dinner——"

"Thank you, ma'am," young Loosh answered.

His father said: "I brought him in to show him that collection of yours. We didn't know we looked that underfed."

"Help yourself," Miss Jenny answered. She went on, and they stood and watched her trim back until she passed out of sight beyond the cedars.

"And now there's another one," young Loosh said musingly. "Another one to grow up and keep his folks in a stew until he finally succeeds in doing what they all expect him to do. Well, maybe that Benbow blood will sort of hold him down. They're quiet folks, that girl; and Horace sort of . . . and just women to raise him . . ."

His father grunted. "He's got Sartoris blood in him, too."

Miss Jenny arrived home, looking a little spent, and Narcissa scolded her and at last prevailed on her to lie down after dinner. And here she had dozed while the drowsy afternoon wore away, and waked to lengthening shadows and a sound of piano keys touched softly below stairs. "I've slept all afternoon," she told herself, in a sort of consternation; yet she lay for a time yet while the curtains stirred faintly at the windows and the sound of the piano came up mingled with the jasmine from the garden and with the garrulous evensong of sparrows from the mulberry trees in the back yard. She rose and crossed the hall and entered Narcissa's room, where the child slept in its crib. Beside him the nurse dozed placidly. Miss Jenny tiptoed out and descended the stairs and entered the parlor and drew her chair out from behind the piano. Narcissa stopped playing.

"Do you feel rested?" she asked. "You shouldn't have done that this morning."

"Fiddlesticks," Miss Jenny rejoined. "It always does me good to see all those fool pompous men lying there with their marble mottoes and things. Thank the Lord, none of 'em will have a chance at me. I reckon the Lord knows His business, but I declare, sometimes . . . Play something."

Narcissa obeyed, touching the keys softly, and Miss Jenny sat listening for a while. The evening drew subtly onward; the shadows in the room grew more and more palpable. Outside the sparrows gossiped in shrill clouds. From the garden jasmine came in to them steady as breathing, and presently Miss Jenny roused and began to talk of the child. Narcissa played quietly on, her white dress with its black ribbon at the waist vaguely luminous in the dusk, with a hushed sheen like wax. Jasmine drifted and drifted; the sparrows were still now, and Miss Jenny talked on in the twilight about little Johnny while Narcissa played with rapt inattention, as though she were not listening. Then, without ceasing and without turning her head, she said:

"He isn't John. He's Benbow Sartoris."

"What?"

"His name is Benbow Sartoris," she repeated.

Miss Jenny sat quite still for a moment. In the next room Elnora moved about, laying the table for supper. "And do you think that'll do any good?" Miss Jenny demanded. "Do you think you can change one of 'em with a name?"

The music went on in the dusk softly; the dusk was peopled with ghosts of glamorous and old disastrous things. And if they were just glamorous enough, there was sure to be a Sartoris in them, and then they were sure to be disastrous.

Pawns. But the Player, and the game He plays . . . He must have a name for His pawns, though. But perhaps Sartoris is the game itself—a game outmoded and played with pawns shaped too late and to an old dead pattern, and of which the Player Himself is a little wearied. For there is death in the sound of it, and a glamorous fatality, like silver pennons downrushing at sunset, or a dying fall of horns along the road to Roncevaux.

"Do you think," Miss Jenny repeated, "that because his name is Benbow, he'll be any less a Sartoris and a scoundrel and a fool?"

Narcissa played on as though she were not listening. Then she turned her head and without stopping her hands she smiled at Miss Jenny quietly, a little dreamily, with serene, fond detachment. Beyond Miss Jenny's trim, fading head the maroon curtains hung motionless; beyond the window evening was a windless lilac dream, foster dam of quietude and peace.

AFTERWORD

"Thou still unravish'd bride of quietness,
Thou foster-child of silence and slow time . . ."

Anyone who has just finished reading the last sentence of *Sartoris* may still be puzzling over it. Is there any significance in Faulkner's way of concluding this narrative by distorting the first two lines from Keats's famous "Ode on a Grecian Urn"—the two lines quoted above? Perhaps not. But the tantalizing effect of that distortion does cause us to remember that many other echoes from the same ode pervade *Sartoris*. All the romantic characters in this novel are treated in an ambivalent manner by Faulkner, whose attitude toward them is at once sympathetic, critical, ironic; but, more than that, Faulkner's various uses of irony here provide him with his most important artistic controls of underlying meanings. Perhaps, then, a glance at some earlier uses of irony in *Sartoris* may throw light on that final puzzling discrepancy.

Remember that the Sartorises themselves are represented as romantically idealizing, glorifying, and glamorizing into "Attic shapes" and "fair attitudes" all the tableau postures of generations past and present in their family history. Remember that rhetoric, or rather the ironic Faulknerian representation of what might be called Sartoris-rhetoric, heightens our impression that a great many embroideries in this Sartoris "brede" of marble men and maidens are (so to speak) "overwrought." By analogy, there is equal significance in remembering that Horace and Narcissa Benbow, who play opposite the immediate Sartorises as foils in this dramatic narrative, are also represented as having their own romantic and rhetorical ways of glamorizing experience. Horace, idealistically loving his sister, Narcissa, and returning to her as to a stainless bride after the close

304

of the war, seems to be telling himself something like what Keats told the ardent youth on the tableau freize of the urn: "For ever wilt thou love, and she be fair!" It is an unnatural relationship, which does not last. But later, in a letter to Narcissa, Horace addresses her as "thou still unravished bride of quietness." Absurdly romantic dreamer that he is, Horace lies on his bed in reverie, "while that wild, fantastic futility of his voyaged in lonely regions of its own beyond the moon, about meadows nailed with firmamented stars to the ultimate roof of things, where unicorns filled the neighing air with galloping, or grazed or lay supine in golden-hoofed repose." Again the reader is expected to notice that this rhetoric is Horace's, and that Faulkner merely lends it to him for purposes of characterization; again the dramatic ironies.

The major difference between Horace's romantic idealism and that of his opposite, young Bayard Sartoris, is that Horace glorifies quietism as a form of defense against his own cowardice, whereas young Bayard glorifies courageous and violent action (performed with equally "fantastic futility") for self-pitying purposes of melodramatic exhibitionism. Although both of these young men belong to the "lost generation" of the First World War, Faulkner probes deep enough below the surface of their motives to keep the reader from assuming that the villain, this time, is The War. By analogy other wars, such as the Civil and the Spanish American, are represented as having given earlier generations of Sartorises the very excuses they sought for acting out equally violent, courageous, and fantastically futile melodramas.

But these preliminary reminders concerning Faulkner's uses of dramatic irony have been made here merely to suggest larger problems of interpretation. Because many readers and critics of *Sartoris* have misunderstood Faulkner's early and still-faltering ways of artistically ordering and controlling meanings in *Sartoris*, this Afterword may be a good place for some broader reconsiderations of artistic strengths and weaknesses in this matrix of all the chronicles of Yoknapatawpha County. Then we will be in a better position to understand what may or may not be going on in that final puzzling sentence.

Most of us are familiar with the circumstances under which Faulkner wrote *Sartoris*—and Robert Cantwell's essay, written for an earlier Signet edition, has long served as a valuable landmark in Faulkner scholarship. We are familiar with the significance of the dedication to Sherwood Anderson, who had previously said to young Faulkner, down in New Orleans, "You're a country boy, and all you know is that little patch up there in Mississippi where you started from; but that's all right too." We are also familiar with the extent to which Faulkner thus came to rediscover the inexhaustible storehouse of raw materials for fiction in the factual-legendary-mythical history and genealogy of his own land and family. All these raw materials had been made available to him throughout his youth. Daily talk and conversation intermingled history, folklore, gossip, and tall tales—and even salted them with wry wit.

But by the time Sherwood Anderson sent him home, after the manner of the prodigal son, Faulkner had acquired a new perspective on his heritage. He had suffered through at least the peripheral experiences of the First World War while completing his training as an aviator. After the war, he had also suffered through the familiar disillusionments of the returning soldier and had found that he was unable to settle down in his hometown of Oxford, Mississippi. Almost desperately, he had tried to establish himself where he did not belong, among the Bohemian writers and painters in New Orleans. Still desperately, he had given up that life to work and loaf for a time in New York City. Then he had gotten the wanderlust out of his system by working his passage to Europe aboard a freighter, had tasted life in Rome, and had even looked in on Left-Bank writers in Paris. These experiences not only provided him with an increasingly detached and critical perspective on his native South but also heightened his passionate love for his Southern heritage. Only when he began writing *Sartoris*, however, did he come to grips with and explore the problem of how he might, could, would, should, give artistic treatment to narrative materials so intimately associated with his past and present.

It is not unfair to view *Sartoris* as Faulkner's third apprentice-novel, similar in its uncertainties and weaknesses to *Soldiers' Pay* and *Mosquitoes*, save that this time his viewpoint more clearly recognizes the inseparability of human weaknesses and strengths, of positives and negatives, of good and evil. In his first two novels his primary goal was to vent spleen through harsh uses of satire and sarcasm for purposes of negation. But when he turned to a fictional handling of his own family history, his own regional history, perhaps he felt the need for interweaving implied affirmations with negations. If by this time he had acquired enough perspective to realize that good and evil are always inextricably bound up with what he later called "the problems of the human heart in conflict with itself," so much the better for his art. But any reader who is troubled by the many artistic flaws and weaknesses in *Sartoris* may well imagine that some of Faulkner's difficulties were caused by his trying to crowd in too many disparate elements; too many pieces of characterization, scene, event, incident, episode. Some of the pieces, thrown together in helter-skelter fashion like remainders of an uncompleted jigsaw puzzle, simply do not fit. Perhaps *Sartoris* became the matrix narrative for the chronicles of Yoknapatawpha County partly because it contained, even after Faulkner's patient revisions, so many leftovers; so many pieces of unfinished business.

Consider, for example, a few parts of *Sartoris* that are insufficiently assimilated. Remember the entire sequence of events involving the wen on old Bayard Sartoris' face, and the consternation of at least three professional doctors over the success with which the wen was removed by the magical salve of old man Falls. It is an amusing anecdote, but that is all that may be said for it. By contrast the sustained episode involving young Bayard Sartoris' visit of several days with the McCallum family is partially interlocked with the central action. But even here the pastoral occupations of the McCallums divert Faulkner so strongly that he neither justifies the disproportionate length of the digression nor manages to articulate it sufficiently. Different in kind, and yet once again inadequately fitted as parts within the whole, are the scattered episodes involving the one-sided love affair of Byron Snopes. Faulkner later seemed to grant the inadequacy of that handling when he returned to Byron and Narcissa for purposes of making out of the same materials an important short story entitled "There Was a Queen." Similarly, Horace Benbow's involvement with Belle Mitchell

stood as a matter of unfinished business until Faulkner
tended to it with sardonic-sarcastic-satiric force by permitting Horace's mixture of well-intended idealism and under-
mining cowardice to achieve tragic fulfillment in *Sanctuary*.

Equally indicative of Faulkner's uncertain groping for direction and focus while writing *Sartoris* is his treatment of
Negro characters. They are handled too largely as low-
comedy stereotypes. Their picturesque actions and conversations are so weakly subsumed by major elements of plot
and theme that they are largely wasted. A good example of
a Negro subplot wasted is the amusing predicament caused
by Simon's lascivious investment of money entrusted to him
for rebuilding a Negro church that had burned down, and
the "financial 'rangements" made by old Bayard Sartoris for
purposes of paying Simon's debt. Different in kind, but also
wasted, is the description of the ritualistic ceremony conducted when the Negroes bring their sugarcane to make
their communal winter sorghum molasses. But if these in-
adequate uses of Negro characters serve merely as further
reminders of Faulkner's apprentice attempt to crowd too
much into *Sartoris,* they at least foreshadow the success
with which he later built some of his most penetrating plots
and themes around unstereotyped delineations of Negroes,
dramatically cast in dignified roles, as for example in *Go
Down, Moses,* or *The Sound and the Fury*.

We may now look past these weaknesses in *Sartoris,* the
better to understand meanings that are indirectly illuminated by centrally organized characterizations and events.
Quite obviously, the major plot is structured into five parts,
which are primarily concerned with the violently self-in-
juring antics of young Bayard Sartoris during the year following his return from the war, one event of which was
the death of his twin brother, John. Even in the plot, however, there is a major flaw: the unfolding of events is made
in a too nearly disconnected sequence rather than through
circumstances that interlock cause and effect. This can be
shown easily by noticing that the five parts are constructed
out of 1. the details of young Bayard's homecoming; 2.
his ways of terrorizing the countryside with rude perform-
ances in his newly purchased car, and his mad attempt
to ride bareback on an untrained stallion; 3. his breaking
his ribs in an automobile accident, and his ruthless court-

ship of Narcissa Benbow while she is attending him during his convalescence; 4. his brief attempt to settle down
after his marriage to Narcissa, his return to his old ways,
the wild ride during which the boy's grandfather dies of
heart failure, and young Bayard's consequent flight; 5. finally, his suicidal death while he is testing a crackpot's
newly designed airplane. The best unifying element here is
not plot but theme; a theme that is illuminated through
Faulkner's artistic process of placing young Bayard's disconnected actions within the historical-genealogical frame-
work provided by the lives and times of his immediate
ancestors. As soon as analogies are thus established between
past and present, the Faulknerian ironies are invoked to
heighten our awareness and understanding of implied meanings.

For example, in the very first chapter of Part One, a
touchstone or yardstick for evaluating analogous actions of
the twin brothers is implied by introducing that earlier pair
of brothers, also named John and Bayard. Of that earlier
pair, John is the great-grandfather of the twins, and Bayard
is the picturesque daredevil whose raid behind Federal
lines resulted in his futile death. The story of that raid is
repeatedly told by old Miss Jenny Sartoris Du Pre, the
widowed sister of those earlier daredevils. But remember
that it is still in the first chapter of Part One that Faulkner
makes the following wry comment on Miss Jenny's romantic
distillations:

She had told the story many times . . . and as she grew older
the tale itself grew richer and richer, taking on a mellow splendor
like wine; until what had been a harebrained prank of two heedless and reckless boys [the other "boy" being young General
"Jeb" Stuart] wild with their own youth had become a gallant
and finely tragical focal point to which the history of the race
had been raised from out the old miasmic swamps of spiritual
sloth by two angels valiantly fallen and strayed, altering the
course of human events and purging the souls of men.

Notice the tone of this passage, and notice that here
Faulkner spells out the irony. It is a sarcastic way of point-
ing up the discrepancy between the actual and the apparent;
the distance between the facts and the myth romantically
made out of the facts. The explicit details in this passage

ought to help any reader recognize other and later ironies that are closely related but only implied. For example, Miss Jenny has this much in common with old man Falls: each one tells and retells different stories about "harebrained" pranks or even crimes committed by the Sartoris brothers during and after the War Between the States, tells and retells until even the darkest facts become glamorous legends and myths. To them it does not matter whether the facts involve breaking through enemy lines in quest of coffee and anchovies or bursting into a boardinghouse to shoot and kill two carpetbaggers who are trying to control the Negro vote.

Once again the immediate point for readers of *Sartoris* to remember is that the "romance" thus attached to the history of the gallant Sartorises—and by extension to the entire history of the South—is represented by Faulkner as an element mistakenly added through the rhetoric of retellings. Faulkner, sadly understanding these romantic transformations of facts into myths—and even admiring courage as courage no matter how grossly misused—permits the play of his ironies to assign values that are predominantly corrective; values that handle, antiromantically, those details that the Sartorises have romanticized.

Just as soon as the reader begins to understand and pay careful attention to these controlling Faulknerian ironies, it is possible to appreciate that many other analogous elements of "romance" are also brought under antiromantic consideration in such ways that they extend Faulkner's thematic concerns. Although Miss Jenny is endowed by her creator with her own fondness for ironies so that she may at times serve Faulkner as mouthpiece, or persona, she is not permitted to recognize her own capacities for romanticizing. Honoring her as the strongest character in this narrative, Faulkner still finds room for being amused by the variations in her peculiar searches for romance. Remember, for instance, this passage:

She enjoyed humanity in its more colorful mutations, preferring lively romance to the most impeccable of dun fact, so she took in the more lurid afternoon paper . . . and read with cold avidity accounts of arson and murder and violent dissolution and adultery . . . [and, a few years later] diversion in the form of bootleggers' wars . . . .

Similar tendencies run in the family. Romantic young Bayard, returning from another kind of war, asserts the traditional Sartoris capacity by rhetorically romanticizing the many kinds of "violent dissolution" he saw in France, including the foolhardy death of his twin brother, John. Now Bayard is represented as agonizing over his delusion that he himself somehow caused his brother's death. He luxuriates in self-pity, with little or no concern for the feelings of others, until (and even after) Miss Jenny is permitted to speak for Faulkner, in an utterance in which her own rhetoric reflects her own capacity for mingling irony with love and sarcasm:

You and your stiff-necked, sullen ways. Helling around the country in that car just because you think there may be somebody who cares a whoop whether or not you break your worthless neck . . . . Just because you went to a war. Do you think you're the only person in the world that ever went to a war?

In the Sartoris mansion there is another soldier newly returned from the war and equally anxious to romanticize his experiences: the Negro boy, Caspey. He bears, we are told, "two honorable wounds incurred in a razor-hedged crap game." By analogy his romantic and mythical accounts of all the violence in which he participated are played off ironically against Bayard's "recounting violence and speed and death." Equally romantic, but analogous in other ways, is the returned soldier Horace Benbow, who preferred to serve as a Y.M.C.A. officer rather than to fight. He brought back with him from Italy a glass-blowing kit, which now helps him associate his war experiences pleasurably with the fascinating game of creating Italianesque vases—his Grecian urns.

Romance of another kind is antiromantically handled in Faulkner's describing various love affairs in *Sartoris*. We have already noticed the lover appropriately named Byron, whose expressions of importunate love for Narcissa are couched in indecent love letters, which she nevertheless keeps in a drawer with her lingerie. By contrast romance comes into brother Horace's life when he weakly yields to the seductiveness of Belle Mitchell, wife of Horace's good friend and neighbor Harry. Belle clearly deserves the sarcastic treatment given her by Faulkner, but the ironies are finest

when Belle and Horace are entangled in each other's arms
lip-lapping love words:

She said, "Come here," and he went to her, and in the dusk
she was again tragic and young and familiar with a haunting
sense of loss, and he knew the sad fecundity of the world and
time's hopeful unillusion that fools itself. "I want to have your
child, Horace," she said, and then her own child came up the
hall . . . .

Narcissa's romantic love for the dead brother of young
Bayard is not easily transferred to Bayard, who repels
Narcissa more than he attracts. But given the choice between loving Byron Snopes or Dr. Alford, after she has
lost Horace to Belle, Narcissa likes the romantic sense of
inevitability, which seems to elevate her to the tragical
position ' of a self-sacrificial martyr and mother of more
Sartorises.

Another element of romance is interwoven more subtly
here because it involves a delicate target for satire: the
convenient manner in which the Sartorises assume that whatever happens to them is somehow a part of their fate, somehow an expression of God's will. Faulkner's quietly ironic
handling of human self-excusings that dodge responsibilities
through invoking such words as "fate" and "doom" and
"God" has caused many readers and critics to assume, mistakenly, that Faulkner himself must have been a fatalist.
It would be nearer the truth to say that Faulkner consistently
represents human beings as meeting crises at the confluence
of two opposed forces; that there are times when individuals,
thus tested, can and do control their immediate situations
through conscious choices; that there are other times when
the same individuals are victimized by forces beyond their
control. Through his imaginative manipulations of character
and circumstance, in his fictions, Faulkner intermingles comedy, tragedy, and tragicomedy; but in *Sartoris* (as in all the
sequels to *Sartoris*) he is primarily concerned with choices
that are made (or not made) from a full consciousness of
moral responsibility. The tragic flaw in the Sartorises is
pure Greek: self-pitying *hubris,* or arrogance resulting from
excessive pride. But none of these characters ever becomes
sufficiently tragic, in the literary sense of the term, to arrive
at a self-recognition scene; not even Miss Jenny. Her at-

titude in these matters runs the gamut from preaching moral responsibility to falling back on fate. Thus the Faulknerian ironies are brought to bear on her whenever she makes the quick jump. For example, just after she has been scolding both of the living Bayards for sharing reckless and irresponsible drives through the countryside, Miss Jenny turns to Narcissa and says of old Bayard's suicidal tendencies, "He goes along for the same reason that boy himself does. Sartoris. It's in the blood." Fate! Her further remarks suggest that there must also be a tendency in the Sartoris blood to be religiously fatalistic when entering into any of these suicidal and "hare-brained" antics.

Various romantic confusions concerning religion and fate are handled ironically by Faulkner as soon as they begin to appear in the first chapter of Part One—and they are still appearing in the last chapter of Part Five. At the outset we are told that the first Bayard once hunted a pack of fox hounds through a Methodist revival meeting and then returned to ride his horse into the ensuing indignation meeting: "In a spirit of fun, purely: he believed too firmly in Providence, as all his actions clearly showed, to have any religious convictions whatever." If the ironic tone and meaning in that observation is not clearly understood, the reader has to wait only a few pages before it is given clarification. Implying similarities in these matters between that first Bayard and his brother John, Faulkner describes the latter as sleeping in the Jefferson graveyard "among martial cherubim and the useless vainglory of whatever God he did not scorn to recognize."

An echo may be heard there of a phrase of Swinburne's: ". . . We thank with brief thanksgiving/Whatever gods may be . . ." Faulkner, not too long before he wrote *Sartoris*, had been an ardent admirer and reader of pagan Swinburne, and throughout his life he remained quite scornful of certain Christian postures and doctrines. But as soon as he began to combine with his paganism a homemade theism, he did it in such a peculiar way that any good Christian should easily recognize the heterodox nature of his belief. Here in *Sartoris* his ironic treatments of confusions between religion and fate are supplemented by his permitting Miss Jenny to keep questioning the Deity, romantically, for his shortcomings as Supervisor of the Sartorises: "Providence doesn't seem to have any judgment at all." Again, "I reckon the Lord knows his business, but I declare, sometimes . . ."

In his ironic handling of certain religious conventions in *Sartoris*, Faulkner saves his best for the description of Miss Jenny's final visit to the graveyard. She examines the graveless stone erected in memory of young Bayard's aviator twin brother—who had profanely cursed his way through life to his vainglorious death—and observes that the epitaph drawn from Exodus 19:4 and chiseled on his stone adds another typically romantic and impertinent Sartoris touch:

> I bare him on eagles' wings
> and brought him unto Me.

Faulkner, who did not believe in the Christian concept of an afterlife in heaven or hell, continues the narration by describing this tombstone inscription as being "like a boastful voice in an empty church." Later, he lets Miss Jenny wrap up the religious romanticism of the Sartorises in the following passage:

. . . the dusk was peopled with ghosts of glamorous and old disastrous things. And if they were just glamorous enough, there was sure to be a Sartoris in them, and then they were sure to be disastrous. Pawns. But the Player, and the game He plays . . . He must have a name for His pawns, though. But perhaps Sartoris is the game itself—a game outmoded and played with pawns shaped too late and to an old dead pattern, and of which the Player Himself is a little wearied.

The thoughts in this passage would seem to be those of Miss Jenny, who can even handle irony romantically. But there is double irony here because Faulkner's larger context implicitly undercuts whatever is romantically and fatalistically religious. The larger context also controls meanings in the sentence that rounds out this passage; a sentence wherein many readers have failed to hear the ambivalent Faulknerian tone, predominantly antiromantic: "For there is death in the sound of it [Sartoris], and a glamorous fatality, like silver pennons downrushing at sunset, or a dying fall of horns along the road to Roncevaux."

Remember that Roland's trouble, in the valley of Roncevaux, was also partly caused by excessive pride. All that is needed here to bring this sentence into proper focus is to place it alongside other passages we have considered in which

literary echoes are invoked—including Horace's reverie of
unicorns who fill the air with galloping, and Horace's praise
of Narcissa as an urnlike and unravished bride of quietness.

With so much of the larger context now in mind, we
may return with more confidence to the initial question: is
there any ironic meaning in Faulkner's final twist of Keats?
Remember that the concluding scene represents Miss Jenny
sitting in the ghost-haunted parlor, intermittently talking
with Narcissa while Narcissa plays softly at the piano. Remember that the subject under discussion is what name
should be given the child recently born to Narcissa. Although Miss Jenny had previously assumed that the traditional other name, John, would descend fittingly to this son
of young Bayard, now dead, Narcissa says, "He isn't John.
He's Benbow Sartoris." But, Miss Jenny asks with her char-
acteristically unflattering way of choosing epithets for those
she loves, can that name make the child "any less a Sartoris
and a scoundrel and a fool?" Understanding Miss Jenny's
rhetoric, Narcissa merely turns and smiles "a little dreamily,
with serene, fond detachment." Then comes the final sentence, and at first glance it seems to imply that Narcissa's
calm self-assurance is approved and blessed by Mother
Nature; the serenity of the spring evening, visible through
the parlor window, seems to be at one with the young
mother's serenity: "Beyond Miss Jenny's trim, fading head
the maroon curtains hung motionless; beyond the window
evening was a windless lilac dream, foster dam of quietude
and peace."

But there is no "quietude and peace" ahead for Narcissa,
either in the sequel entitled *Sanctuary* or in the sequel entitled "There Was a Queen." Both of these narratives un-
flatteringly represent Narcissa as being motivated by the familiar Sartoris mannerism of self-pitying and excessive pride,
as she offers to pay any price that will enable her to find
false sanctuaries in illusory appearances and in self-decep-
tions. Perhaps Faulkner assumed that the cumulative context of *Sartoris* would endow with appropriately ironic significance the final "quietude and peace" of Narcissa here,
and perhaps the final echo and twist of Keats was merely
calculated to blend with that meaning provided by the context. As further evidence, it is pertinent to remember that

throughout *Sartoris* the moods of Mother Nature are not only indifferent to the moods of men and women but also and often at odds with them. The epithet "foster dam," here made to displace the "foster-child" of Keats, may further hint that an unflattering value is frequently implied when the antique word "dam" is substituted for the word "mother"—and that a foster-mother is not always as loving, solicitous, and reliable as one might wish.

If these possibilities of meaning are thought to be implicitly operative in that final twist—or even if they are not—the reader should at least find that Narcissa's romantic dreaming in the curtain scene is also made meaningful by all the ironies in the larger context. As we remember Faulkner's ambivalent and antiromantic handling of the Sartorises, we may finally remember that the name Narcissa is borrowed from an "Attic" character who was and still is the classical symbol of self-destructive self-love.

LAWRANCE THOMPSON

WILLIAM FAULKNER: A CHECKLIST

The Marble Faun, 1924   Poems
Soldiers' Pay, 1926   Novel
Mosquitoes, 1927   Novel
Sartoris, January, 1929   Novel
The Sound and the Fury, October, 1929   Novel
As I Lay Dying, 1930   Novel
Sanctuary, February, 1931   Novel
These 13, September, 1931   Stories
Light in August, 1932   Novel
A Green Bough, 1933   Poems
Doctor Martino and Other Stories, 1934
Pylon, 1935   Novel
Absalom, Absalom! 1936   Novel
The Unvanquished, 1938   Novel
The Wild Palms, 1939   Novel
The Hamlet, 1940   Novel
Go Down, Moses, and Other Stories, 1942
Intruder in the Dust, 1948   Novel
Knight's Gambit, 1949   Stories
Collected Stories, 1950
Requiem for a Nun, 1951   Drama
A Fable, 1954   Novel
The Town, 1957   Novel
The Mansion, 1959   Novel
The Reivers, 1962   Novel

SELECTED BIBLIOGRAPHY
OF CRITICAL AND SCHOLARLY STUDIES

Brooks, Cleanth. *William Faulkner: The Yoknapatawpha Country*. New Haven, Conn.: Yale University Press, 1963.

Campbell, H. M., and Foster, R. E. *William Faulkner: A Critical Appraisal*. Norman: University of Oklahoma Press, 1951.

Cullen, J. B. *Old Times in the Faulkner Country*. Chapel Hill: University of North Carolina Press, 1961.

Gwynn, F. L., and Blotner, J. L. (eds.). *Faulkner in the University: Class Conferences at the University of Virginia, 1957–1958*. Charlottesville: The University Press of Virginia, 1959.

Hoffman, F. J. *William Faulkner*. New York: Twayne Publishers, Inc., 1961.

Hoffman, F. J., and Vickery, O. W. (eds.). *William Faulkner: Three Decades of Criticism*. East Lansing: Michigan State University Press, 1960.

Howe, Irving. *William Faulkner: A Critical Study*. 2nd ed. rev. & enl. New York: Random House, Inc. (Vintage Books), 1962.

Kirk, R. W., and Klotz, M. *Faulkner's People: A Complete Guide and Index to the Characters in Faulkner*. Berkeley: University of California Press, 1964.

O'Connor, William Van. *The Tangled Fire of William Faulkner*. Minneapolis: University of Minnesota Press; London: Oxford University Press, 1954.

Malin, I. *William Faulkner; an Interpretation*. Stanford, Calif.: Stanford University Press; London: Oxford University Press, 1957.

Meriwether, J. B. *The Literary Career of William Faulkner*. Princeton, N.J.: Princeton University Library, 1961.

Miner, W. L. *World of William Faulkner*. Durham, N.C.: Duke

University Press, 1952; London: Cambridge University Press, 1953.

Thompson, Lawrance. *William Faulkner: An Introduction and Interpretation*. New York: Barnes & Noble, Inc., 1963.

Vickery, O. W. *The Novels of William Faulkner*. Baton Rouge: Louisiana State University Press, 1959.

Waggoner, H. H. *William Faulkner: From Jefferson to the World*. Lexington: University of Kentucky Press, 1959.

Other SIGNET CLASSICS
by American Authors

APPOINTMENT IN SAMARRA   **by John O'Hara**

Three days in the life of a man destroyed by his inability to cope with his personality. Afterword by Arthur Mizener.   (#CP177—60¢)

GEORGIA BOY   **by Erskine Caldwell**

The famous story of a Southern youth by the world's best-selling fiction writer. Afterword by Robert Cantwell.
(#CD57—50¢)

OLD CREOLE DAYS   **by George W. Cable**

Colorful stories of New Orleans at the turn of the 19th century. Foreword by Shirley Ann Grau. (#CP84—60¢)

IN THE MIDST OF LIFE and Other Tales
                                       by Ambrose Bierce

Renowned stories of Civil War soldiers and civilians. Afterword by Marcus Cunliffe.   (#CP60—60¢)

SPECIMEN DAYS   **by Walt Whitman**

A complete collection of Whitman's jottings over a 20-year period, including his experiences during the Civil War. Foreword by Richard Chase.   (#CP104—60¢)

LEAVES OF GRASS   **by Walt Whitman**

Whitman's enduring testament to a land whose vitality was the touchstone of his genius. A complete edition with an Introduction by Gay Wilson Allen.   (#CT23—75¢)

PUDD'NHEAD WILSON   **by Mark Twain**

A unique mystery and social satire involving switched identities between a child born free and a child born slave. Foreword by Wright Morris.   (#CD184—50¢)

THE FOREST SEEMED TO HAVE EYES . . .
COUNTLESS, WATCHING EYES

"What are they?" asked Silence.
"The past. Ghosts, perhaps."
"I don't believe in ghosts."
"That's all right," said Carrion. "They believe in you."

GHOSTWORLD

SIMON R. GREEN

ACE BOOKS, NEW YORK

This book is an Ace original edition,
and has never been previously published.

GHOSTWORLD

An Ace Book / published by arrangement with
the author

PRINTING HISTORY
Ace edition / March 1993

ISBN: 0-441-28626-7

Ace Books are published by The Berkley Publishing Group,
200 Madison Avenue, New York, NY 10016.
The name "ACE" and the "A" logo
are trademarks belonging to Charter Communications, Inc.

PRINTED IN THE UNITED STATES OF AMERICA

10 9 8 7 6 5 4 3 2 1

INSIDE Base Thirteen, nothing moves. Doors remain closed, elevators are still, and shadows lie undisturbed. One by one the flickering lights gutter and go out, and a growing gloom stalks the empty steel corridors. The few computers remaining on-line mutter querulously to each other in the growing dark, until finally they fall silent in the night.

In the silence, in the dark, something stirs.

CHAPTER ONE

Something in the Storm

THE *Darkwind*'s pinnace fell away from the mother ship, a gleaming silver needle against the endless night. It hung for a moment above the Rim World called Unseeli, and then its nose dropped, the engines roared silently, and the pinnace slipped into Unseeli's churning atmosphere like a knife into a belly. The engines burned bright, powering the slender ship through the violent storms by sheer brute force. Lightning flared round the pinnace's hull, and winds gusted viciously from every side, but nothing swayed the ship from its course. It punched through the roiling clouds with arrogant ease, dropping like a stone towards the metallic forest below.

Unseeli had no oceans and no mountains, only an endless arid plain covered by a brightly shining forest stretching from pole to pole. A forest whose colossal metal trees knew nothing of leaf or bud, autumn or spring. They rose unbending from the grey earth in the millions, cold and unfeeling, like so many gleaming metal nails. Towering almost to the edge of the planet's atmosphere in places, the huge trees stood firm and unyielding against the turbulent storms. Winds whipped viciously around leafless branches, radiating out from smooth, featureless trunks in needle-sharp spikes. Violet and azure, gold and silver and brass, the trees reached up into the thunder and lightning to welcome the falling craft.

Captain John Silence sat slumped in his command chair,

watching the sensor display panels before him. They changed from moment to moment with bewildering speed, far too fast for him to follow. Which was why the ship's AI was piloting them down and he had nothing to do but strain his eyes at the displays. The thick storm clouds hid the metal trees from sight, but the AI picked them up on the pinnace's sensors and changed speed and direction accordingly, making decisions and evaluations in split-second bursts. Since the AI could think faster and react more quickly than Silence ever could, even when he was mentally linked to the onboard computers, there was never any question as to which one of them would get to pilot the pinnace down. But the AI was programmed to be considerate of people's feelings, so it might let him actually land the pinnace, if it didn't seem too difficult.

Deepening his concentration, Silence accessed the ship's sensors through his comm implant. The bulkhead walls before him were suddenly transparent as the sensors displayed a real-time simulation of what was happening outside the ship. Dark, swollen storm clouds rushed toward and around the pinnace at heart-stopping speed, and lightning struck viciously at the craft. Silence winced inwardly, but kept his face calm so as not to upset his passengers. The storm could rage and spit all it liked; nothing could harm the ship as long as its force screen was up. Gleaming metal trees appeared and disappeared in the blink of an eye as the pinnace surged this way and that, threading a path through the metallic forest to the landing pads by Base Thirteen. The storm clouds were too thick and too dark for Silence to make out the forest itself, but his imagination pictured it as an endless, vicious pincushion; solid metal spikes waiting for him like the sharpened stakes at the bottom of a pit dug to trap animals.

The image disturbed him, and he cut off the display and swung round in his chair to see how his passengers were

doing. A good Captain never neglected his crew. Supposedly, loyalty was programmed into them these days, but it
never hurt to be careful.

The ship's young esper, Diana Vertue, was looking distinctly green about the gills from being tossed around by
the pinnace's sudden changes in direction. Investigator Frost
sat beside her, cool and composed as always, her face almost
bored. The two marines, Stasiak and Ripper, sat behind
the two women, passing a gunmetal flask back and forth
between them. Silence's mouth tautened. He hoped it was
just alcohol, and not some new battle drug they'd cooked up
in the medlabs. Officially he was supposed to encourage such
initiative, but Silence didn't believe in chemical courage.
He preferred the real thing whenever possible. Chemicals
wore off.

"We'll be touching down soon," he said evenly. "There
shouldn't be any immediate danger, but keep your eyes and
ears open anyway. Due to the urgent nature of the situation,
we're going in pretty much blind on this one. The mission's
simple enough. Base Thirteen isn't answering any calls.
Our job is to find out why."

"Question, Captain?"

"Yes, esper Vertue?"

"According to the computers, Unseeli is a dead world.
Nothing's lived here since all indigenous species were
wiped out after the Ashrai rebellion, ten years ago. . . ."

"That's right," said Silence as the esper paused.

"But if that's the case, Captain, if there's nothing on this
planet that could be harmful, why all the panic? It could
just be a case of cabin fever. It's not exactly unknown, out
here on the edge of the Empire."

"A good point, esper. But four days ago, Base Thirteen
declared a Red Alert emergency, raised a force screen
round the Base, and cut off all communications with the
Empire. The Empire doesn't like being cut off. So, we're

going in to find out what's happened. Don't frown, esper; it'll give you wrinkles."

"I was just wondering, Captain; well, what is the Investigator doing here?"

"Yeah," said Investigator Frost. "I've been wondering that too."

Silence took his time about answering, openly studying the two women. They made an interesting contrast. Diana Vertue was short, slender, and golden-haired, and reminded Silence very much of her mother, Elaine. The young esper had only just turned nineteen, and had that arrogant innocence that only youth could produce and maintain. She'd lose it soon enough, trying to maintain law and order and sanity out on the edge of the Empire, among the newly developed Rim Worlds. There was little civilisation to be found on the new frontier—and even less law, never mind justice.

Investigator Frost was only a few years older than the esper, but the difference between them was that of the hunter and its prey. Frost was tall and lithely muscular, and even sitting still and at rest, she looked dangerous. Dark blue eyes burned coldly in a pale, impassive face framed by short-cropped auburn hair. The jolting descent didn't seem to be bothering her at all, but then, it wouldn't. Investigators were trained to withstand much worse than this. Which was at least partly why they made such efficient killers.

Silence realised he'd paused longer than he'd intended. He leaned forward in his chair, frowning as though he'd just been marshalling his thoughts, knowing even as he did that he wasn't fooling the Investigator one bit.

"You're here, Investigator, because we don't know what we're going to find when we get down there. There's always the possibility that Unseeli has been visited by some new alien species. This is the Rim, after all, where starships have been known to disappear into the long night, never to be seen again. And aliens are your speciality, are they not?"

"Yeah," said Frost, smiling slightly. "That's one way of putting it."

"On the other hand," said Silence, "Unseeli is a mining planet, and the metals extracted here are of vital importance to the Empire. Any number of factions might have an interest in disturbing production. Which is why I'm overseeing this mission myself."

"If it's that important, why are there only five of us?" asked the marine Stasiak. "Why not go in mob-handed with a full Security team, surround the Base and then charge in and hammer anything that moves?"

"Because Base Thirteen controls all the mining equipment on Unseeli," said Silence steadily. "Systems are already running at barely thirty per cent efficiency. We don't want to risk damaging the Base and making things even worse. And, as the esper pointed out, there's always the possibility this is just some new form of cabin fever, and all the Base personnel need is a nice little chat with the *Darkwind*'s psych department. We're here to find out what's going on and to report on it, not run a crash-and-burn mission on the only people who can tell us what's happened."

"Understood, Captain," said the other marine, Ripper. "We'll run this one nice and easy, by the numbers. No problem."

Silence nodded curtly, and studied the two marines unobtrusively. Lewis Stasiak was average height and weight, only in his early twenties but already looking hard-used and running to seed. His hair was a little too long, his uniform rumpled, and his face had a kind of slackness to it. Silence recognised the danger signs; Stasiak had gone too long without any real action or challenge, and grown soft and careless. Which was at least partly why Silence had chosen him for the exploratory team. If something went wrong, Stasiak wasn't going to be any great loss. It was always useful to have someone expendable on hand, to send into dangerous situations before taking a look for yourself. Still, it would be well to keep an eye on the man. Marines who got sloppy tended not to last long under pressure, and when they snapped they had a nasty habit of taking down anyone who happened to be with them at the time.

Alec Ripper, on the other hand, was everything that Stasiak wasn't. Ripper was a career marine, and looked it. Twenty-nine years old, fourteen years in the Service, big as a brick outhouse and twice as mean. Sharp and tidy from his close-cropped head to his shiny boots. Four medals, and three commendations for courage in the field. Could have been an officer, if he'd only had the right Family connections. As it was, he'd been a noncom twice, busted both times for daring to suggest a superior officer might just possibly be wrong. That wasn't wise in the Service. Especially in front of witnesses. Also, according to the records, Ripper was a good soldier and a better fighter, with a positive gift for survival. If anyone was going to come back alive from this mission, it was Ripper.

If anyone was.

They didn't know about Unseeli. Silence knew. He'd been here before, ten years ago, when the Ashrai came sweeping out of the forest in endless waves, slaughtering every man and woman in their path. He remembered the awful things they'd done, and the worse thing he'd done to stop them. The Ashrai were dead now. Extinct. Along with every other living thing on the planet.

The pinnace lurched suddenly to one side, the roar of the engines seeming to falter for a moment before regaining their normal rhythm. Silence spun round in his chair and glared at the displays before him. Warning lights were flaring red everywhere, but there was no sign of any actual damage yet. He accessed the sensors again, and the ship seemed to go transparent before and around him. Dark storm clouds boiled around the pinnace, streaming away to either side with breathtaking speed. The ship lurched again, and Silence's stomach quivered in sympathy as the pinnace changed course and speed with reckless indifference to its passengers' sensibilities. Glowing metal trees appeared and disappeared around them, come and gone in a flash, but Silence could tell it wasn't just the trees that the pinnace was trying to avoid. There was something else out there in the storm. Something that had waited a long time for revenge, and didn't give a damn that it had been dead for ten long years.

Ghostworld.

"Marines, man the guns," said Silence harshly. "Investigator, access the sensors and tell me what you see. Esper, I want a full psionic scan, as far as you can project. I need to know what's out there."

The marines' faces went blank as they accessed the pinnace's firing controls through their comm implants, their eyes filled with what the gunsights showed them. The Investigator's cold face hardly changed at all as she looked quickly around her at bulkheads that were suddenly transparent. The esper looked at Silence uncertainly.

"What exactly am I scanning for, Captain?"

"Something, anything; for whatever's out there."

"But . . . there's nothing there, Captain. It's just a storm."

"No," said Silence. "It's not just the storm. Run a scan, esper. That's an order."

"Aye, sir." The esper's eyes became fixed and unseeing, and her face was suddenly blank and untenanted as her mind leapt up and out beyond the pinnace.

The storm boiled around her, but could not touch her. Metal trees burned in her mind like brilliant searchlights plunging up through the clouds, guttering here and there as automated mining machinery tore through a tree's roots.

Apart from the trees, there was no life anywhere in range of her esp, and yet it seemed to her that there was something at the edges of her mind, sensed only as swift flashes of movement and an occasional feeling of being watched. Diana forced her esp to its limits, pushing at the range of her scan, but was unable to get a clear view of whatever it was. If there was anything at all . . .

Stasiak grinned nastily, feeling the pinnace's guns swivelling back and forth, responsive to his thoughts. Four disrupter cannon, state of the art and fully charged, were scattered the length of the pinnace and ready to kick ass at his command, or merest whim. But there was only the storm and the wind and the endless bloody trees. According to the sensors, there was nothing out there worth firing at. He found a secure line and patched into Ripper's comm implant.

"Hey, Rip, you see anything?"

"No. But that doesn't mean it's not out there."

"Yeah, sure. You ask me, the Captain's got ants in his pants over nothing. This world's dead, Rip; everyone knows that."

"Maybe. There's nothing on the sensors. But I still keep getting the feeling that we're not alone up here. Stand ready, Lew. I don't like the feel of this at all. And if it does all hit the fan, don't waste your shots; place them carefully. Remember, these cannon take four minutes to recharge between each shot. A lot can happen in four minutes."

"Yeah, right," Stasiak stirred unhappily in his seat, trying to look every way at once. Now that Ripper mentioned it, he could feel it too. Something waiting, watching, hiding just out of range of his sensors. His mind caressed the fire controls, feeling them respond like hounds straining at the leash. The pinnace's AI was programmed against activating the guns itself except in the direst emergencies, to keep it from getting ideas above its station, but it too sensed something was wrong about the storm, and in its own way was just as eager for action as Stasiak was.

Investigator Frost looked across at the Captain. "Sensors all report negative. There are no life signs registering anywhere within their range."

"I didn't think there would be," said Silence, staring unblinkingly out at the storm. "Odin, how long till we touch down?"

"Twelve minutes and forty seconds, Captain." said the AI promptly, "Assuming nothing interferes with my flight plan."

"Get us down fast, Odin," the Captain ordered. "Marines, stand ready. Something's coming."

And then the pinnace lurched suddenly to one side, the slender craft thrown violently off course as though some giant hand had reached out from nowhere and swatted it. The ship bucked and heaved as the AI fought to keep it from crashing into the tightly packed trees. Dark shapes loomed up out of the boiling storm clouds, huge and threatening.

"Odin, raise the force screen," said Silence, his voice calm and steady, though his hands were closed into white-knuckled fists. "Marines, pick your targets carefully. Investigator, what do you see?"

"Still nothing, Captain. Sensors are adamant there's nothing out there."

"Same here," said Stasiak urgently. "There's nothing to aim at!"

The pinnace shuddered as something impossibly huge pounded against the force screen, again and again. Silence watched tensely as his displays showed mounting pressure building up against the screen from all sides at once. Glowing trees whipped past faster than ever as the AI sent the pinnace racing through the metallic forest, heading for the landing field. But despite the pinnace's increasing speed, the dark presences stayed with them, battering at the force screen with vicious determination. Silence scowled, and licked his dry lips.

"Marines, lay down a field of fire on both sides. Random selection of targets. Do it now."

The marines' replies were lost in the thunder of the disrupter cannon, and blinding energy leapt out from the pinnace, striking through the screen and shattering the metal trees. Great metallic shards flew like shrapnel. And still the unliving presences pressed close around the screen, the pressure rising impossibly moment by moment.

"Our guns are useless now until the energy crystals recharge," said the Investigator quietly. "And the force screen isn't going to last long enough for us to reach the landing field. It's taking more and more of the ship's power just to maintain the screen, and we don't have that much power to spare. Not if we ever want to get off this planet again. What's out there, Captain? Why don't they show up on our sensors?"

Silence looked at her. "Because they're dead, Investigator. Because they're dead. Odin, time to touch down?"

"Ten minutes, twenty-two seconds, Captain."

"When I give you the word, drop the force screen and channel the extra power to the engines. Do whatever you have to, Odin, but get us down. If we survive the landing, we can always recharge the ship's batteries at Base Thirteen. Marines, stand ready to fire again, on my order."

"But there's nothing out there!" said Stasiak. "There's nothing to aim at!"

"Keep the noise down, Lew," said Ripper calmly. "Ours not to reason why, remember? Just do what the nice officer says. At least he seems to have some idea of what we're up against."

Stasiak sniffed mutinously. "They're not paying me enough for this."

Silence glared out at the storm, then looked back at the Investigator. "Anything on the sensors?"

"Negative, Captain. No life signs of any description. As far as the instruments are concerned, we're alone up here." The Investigator looked at him with cold, hard eyes. "You were expecting this, weren't you, Captain? That's why you came down with us. You know what's out there."

"Yes," said Silence. "I know."

"Guns are powering up, sir," said Ripper. "Ready to fire again soon. Just find us a target."

"Stand by, marines. Esper, talk to me. What do you see out there? Esper!"

They were huge and awful and they filled her mind, blazing like the sun. Too strange to measure, too vast to comprehend, they gathered in the storm like ancient vengeful gods, striking at the pinnace with thunder and lightning. Diana Vertue struggled to maintain her own sense of identity in all that rage and fury, but her human mind was a small and insignificant thing in the midst of such intense, bitter hatred. She retreated behind the safety of her mental shields, fighting to keep out the inhuman thoughts that roared and howled in the storm outside the ship. One by one her defensive barriers slammed into place, and suddenly she was back in the pinnace again, and Captain Silence was shouting at her.

"It's alive," she said dully, her mind feeling slow and awkward now that it was working only on the human level again. "The storm's alive, and it hates us."

"Have you made contact with it?" asked Silence. "Could you communicate with it?"

"Communicate with what?" said the Investigator sharply. "If there was anything alive out there, the sensors would show it!"

"They're too big," said Diana Vertue. "Huge. Vast. I've never felt such hate."

"Try," said Silence. "This is why I brought you with us; to talk to . . . what's out there."

"No," said Diana, tears burning in her eyes. "Please. Don't make me . . . the hate hurts so much . . ."

"Do it! That's an order!"

And Diana threw her mind up and out again, into the storm. Espers always obeyed orders. Their training saw to that. Those who couldn't or wouldn't learn didn't live to reach an adult's estate. The storm raged. Immense, dark thoughts were all around her, and she knew she survived only because she was too small for them to notice. She also knew that in a slow, creeping way, they were beginning to realise that someone was watching them.

Silence watched the young esper's face, contorted by the horror of what her blind eyes were seeing, and wouldn't let himself look away. If she died or lost her mind, it would be his responsibility. He'd known the risks when he insisted on her as part of his team. A thin line of saliva ran slowly from the corner of her mouth, and she began to moan softly. Silence still wouldn't look away.

"Marines, lay down a covering fire, random selection, as before. Odin, lower the force screen. Hang on to your seats, everyone. The ride's about to get a bit bumpy."

There was a deafening roar, slamming against the mind as much as the ears, as the dark shapes pressed forward, no longer held back by the force screen. The disrupter cannon blazed through the storm, and could not touch them. The pinnace shuddered and lurched from side to side, tossed like a leaf in a hurricane. Metallic trees a dozen feet thick leapt out of the clouds and slammed against the pinnace sides, but the ship's hull had been designed to withstand disrupter cannon and low-level atomics, and they held easily against the battering. The thunder of the pinnace's engines rose and fell as the AI fought desperately to keep the ship on course. The Captain accessed the instruments directly, and bit his lip as he saw they were still more than four minutes from Base Thirteen and the landing pads.

The pinnace's nose dropped sharply, as though some immense weight had settled upon it. There was a screech of rending metal, and the port bulkhead tore like paper. Jagged rents surged down the wall, grouped together like giant claw marks. Something pounded against the outer hull, and great dents and bulges appeared in the cabin roof.

"There's nothing out there!" screamed Stasiak, beating blindly with his fists against his chair's armrests. "There's nothing out there! The instruments say so!"

Ripper's head swayed back and forth, his mouth forming soundless denials. The Investigator glared about her at the fury of the storm, her hand clutching at the gun on her hip. Things were moving in the storm, dark and indistinct and impossibly huge. The whole frame of the pinnace groaned as the roof bulged inwards, forced down by some massive, intolerable weight.

"We're losing pressure, Captain," said the AI quietly in Silence's ear. "The ship's integrity has been breached beyond my ability to compensate. I am no longer confident of being able to reach the landing field. Do I have your permission to attempt an emergency landing?"

"No," said Silence through his implant. "Not yet."

"We have to put down before we fall apart!" said the Investigator.

Silence looked at her sharply. He hadn't known she had access to the command channel. "Not yet," he said firmly. "Esper, talk to them, dammit. Make them hear you!"

Diana Vertue dropped what remained of her mental shields and stood naked and defenceless before the alien presences. They rushed forward and swept over her. The pinnace punched through the last of the clouds and burst out into clear air. The metal trees swept toward and around the ship at dizzying speed. Vicious barbed spikes snapped past them,

seeming only inches away from tearing the pinnace open like
a gutted fish. And then the trees too fell away, and they were
flying over a vast open clearing, above a smooth and level
plain, towards Base Thirteen and the landing pads.

"It's stopped," said the Investigator quietly. "Listen. It's
stopped."

Silence looked slowly around him. The pounding on the
outer hull had ceased, and there was no trace anywhere
of the dark, threatening presences. Faint creakings filled
the pinnace as the ship's battered frame tried to repair
itself. The two marines dropped out of fire control and
looked blankly around them, seeing the damage for the
first time. Ripper turned to the Captain for answers, but
Silence waved for him to be quiet, and got out of his seat
to kneel beside the esper, who was sitting slumped on the
floor, head bowed. She looked up slowly as she sensed his
presence.

"They're gone, Captain. They just . . . left."

"What did you see?" said Silence, keeping his voice calm
with an effort.

"Faces. Gargoyle faces, all planes and angles. Teeth and
jagged claws. I don't know. I don't think any of it was
real. It couldn't have been. There were so many faces, and
nothing in them but rage and hatred. I was sure they were
going to kill me, but when I dropped my shields they just
looked at me . . . and left. I don't know why."

"But you do, Silence," said the Investigator. "Don't
you?"

"Please return to your seats," said the AI. "I am preparing to land the pinnace."

Silence helped the esper to her feet and got her seated
before returning to his own station. The Investigator scowled
at his back for a moment, and then studiously ignored him.
The marines looked at each other and said nothing, though
their expressions spoke volumes.

"I have tried to contact Base Thirteen," said the AI, "but there is no response. The force screen around the Base is still in operation, and there is no sign of life or movement anywhere within range of my sensors. I am therefore assuming it is safe to land, unless you wish to countermand me, Captain."

"No, Odin. Set us down as close to the Base as you can. Then put your sensors on full alert, and maintain all weapons systems at battle status, until I tell you otherwise."

"Understood, Captain."

The pinnace slowed to a halt a dozen yards from the shimmering force screen enclosing Base Thirteen, and settled gently onto the landing pad. Silence stared intently at the simulation covering the inner bulkheads, and for the first time was struck by the sheer size of the vast open space covered by the pads. The landing field had originally been intended to accommodate the massive starfreighters that built and established the Empire's Base. Silence had been the Captain of one of those ships, and he could still remember the constant flow of traffic around Base Thirteen as the ships came thundering in from all over the Empire. Huge silver ships had covered the landing pads for as far as the eye could see, like so many huge abstract sculptures. And now they were gone, and the pinnace stood alone on the pads, dwarfed by the size of the clearing and the towering trees that surrounded it.

He withdrew from the sensors, and the scene vanished, replaced by featureless steel walls. Silence turned in his chair and nodded abruptly to his team. "I know you've all got a lot of questions, but you're going to have to bear with me for a while. The situation here is very complicated, and the rough ride we had on our way down is just the beginning. I take it no one's been badly injured? Good. Odin, damage reports."

"Nothing significant, Captain, but it'll be several hours

before the ship can lift off again. It's the hull breach that worries me most. There's a limit to what I can do without access to a stardock's facilities."

Silence nodded slowly. "Worst-case scenario?"

"If I can't repair the hull, we're not going anywhere, Captain. You could, of course, always call down another pinnace from the *Darkwind*, but there's no guarantee it would arrive here in any better condition than us."

"Wait a minute," said Stasiak. "You mean we're stranded here?"

"Ease off," said Ripper quickly. "That was a worse-case scenario. Things aren't that bad. Yet."

"I have some questions of my own, Captain," said the Investigator coldly. "This planet is officially listed as a scorched world. Nothing is supposed to live here anymore. But something was trying to kill us in that storm, even if our sensors couldn't pick it up. And you knew what it was. You recognised it. I represent the Empire in all matters concerning alien species, and I demand an explanation. What was that in the storm?"

"The Ashrai," said Silence.

"But they're dead. Extinct."

"Yes. I know. I told you the situation was complicated."

"So what the hell was knocking the crap out of us on the way down?" said Stasiak. "Ghosts?"

Silence smiled slightly. "Perhaps. If ever a planet was haunted by its past, Unseeli is." He hesitated, then looked quickly from one face to another. "Did any of you . . . feel anything, sense anything, on the way down?"

"Yeah," growled Stasiak. "I felt sure we were all going to be killed."

Ripper shrugged. The Investigator scowled for a moment, and then shook her head. Silence looked at the esper. "What about you, Diana? What did you sense?"

The young esper studied her hands, which were clasped tightly together in her lap. "They could have killed us all. Our force screen couldn't keep them out, and our guns couldn't hurt them. But at the last moment they looked at me and turned away. I don't know why. Do you know why, Captain?"

"Yes," said Silence. "Because you're innocent." He raised a hand to forestall any further comments or questions. "All right, pay attention. This mission was put together in something of a hurry, so you haven't had much in the way of a briefing. That's at least partly because no one really knows what's going on here. And partly because I wanted you to come to this with open minds.

"Ten years ago, the Empire discovered that Unseeli was rich in important metals, and started mining operations. The main indigenous species, the Ashrai, objected strongly. They rose in rebellion against the Empire, aided by a traitor from within the Service, a man who turned against his own kind. The Empire troops were vastly outnumbered, and no match for the sheer ferocity of the Ashrai, even with their superior Empire weaponry. But they couldn't afford to lose. The metals were too important. So they retreated offworld, called in the starcruisers, and scorched the whole damn planet from pole to pole. The metal trees survived unharmed. Nothing else did. Mining resumed soon after.

"But that's not all of the story. The trees are not just trees. They cover ninety per cent of the planet's surface, and are one hundred per cent metal. They contain no organic matter at all, but they are quite definitively alive. These trees were grown, not sculpted. Their roots draw metals from deep within the planet, isolating the heavy metals and storing them within their trunks. We don't know how they do this. There is reason to believe the trees were genetically engineered. Certainly it strains credulity that something so amazingly useful could have evolved entirely by chance.

Especially when you consider that the particular heavy metals these trees store are ideally suited for powering a stardrive. Given the scarcity of such metals, you can understand why the Empire was prepared to do absolutely anything to ensure that the mining of Unseeli's unique forest could continue uninterrupted."

"Hold it," said Frost. "Are you saying the Ashrai created these trees?"

"No," said Silence. "Their civilisation was never that advanced. In fact, the original Investigating team uncovered evidence that suggested the Ashrai actually evolved long after the trees had first been planted. Which gives you some idea of how long these trees have been here."

"But if the Ashrai didn't genengineer the trees," said Ripper slowly, "who did?"

"Good question," said Silence. "Whoever it was, let's hope they don't come back to find out who's been messing with their garden. Now then, where was I? Ah yes. There are twenty substations on Unseeli, overseeing the automated mining machinery as it destroys the forest's roots so that the trees can be easily felled and harvested. Base Thirteen oversees all the other substations, and is the only manned station on the planet. Its personnel spend most of their time sitting around waiting for something to go wrong so they can go out and fix it. They last communicated with the Empire four days ago. We haven't been able to get a word out of them since. At present, the situation is merely annoying, if a little disturbing. But if it continues, and the supply of metals slows as the mining machinery breaks down, the Empire could be in serious trouble. I'm afraid we've all become just a little too dependent on Unseeli's riches. Any questions so far?"

"Yes," said Ripper. "What are you doing here, Captain? It's not usual for a ship's Captain to expose himself to danger like this."

"This is not a usual situation," said Silence. "And I have . . . personal reasons for being here. Which I don't intend to discuss at this time."

"All right," said Frost. "Let's talk about Base Thirteen instead. A force screen is the last refuge for a base under attack. What could possibly have threatened them so much, scared them so badly, that they had to retreat behind a force screen to feel safe?"

"Maybe they saw ghosts too," said Diana Vertue.

Silence smiled briefly. "When we get inside the Base, you can ask them."

"And just how are we supposed to get inside?" said Frost sharply. "We don't have anything powerful enough to break through a force screen. The disrupter cannon on the *Darkwind* might do the job, but that kind of firepower would flatten everything inside a square mile, most definitely including everything and everyone inside the screen. You'd be able to carry away what was left of Base Thirteen in a medium-sized bucket."

"Right," said Stasiak, scowling unhappily. "There's only one way we're going to get past that screen, and that's if someone inside the Base gets to the main command centre and shuts down the screen. And that doesn't seem very likely, just at the moment. So, Captain, unless you have access to some kind of super-weapon the Empire has never heard of, we've come all this way for nothing."

Silence looked at him calmly. "Don't raise your voice to me, Stasiak, there's a good chap. I know what I'm doing. Computer, any hostile life signs outside the ship?"

"Negative, Captain," said the AI promptly. "There are no life signs anywhere within reach of my sensors. My files tell me that Base Thirteen has one hundred and twenty-seven personnel, but I regret I am unable to confirm that. The force screen blocks my sensor probes."

"What about the things that attacked us on the way

down?" said Diana Vertue. "They can't have just vanished."

"My sensors detected no life signs at any time during the descent," said the AI. "If there had been any attackers, I would have detected them and informed you of their nature. May I remind you, esper Vertue, this is a scorched world. Nothing lives here."

"Well, something beat the hell out of this ship on the way down," said Frost. "I can see some of the dents from here."

"I agree that the pinnace has suffered extensive storm damage," said the AI calmly. "Nevertheless, I must insist that there were no life forms present in the storm. If there were, my instruments would have detected them."

"I saw them with my esp," said Diana. "I felt their rage."

"Hallucinations, perhaps," said the AI. "Possibly brought about by the stress of the descent. I can supply tranquillizers if required."

"Not just now," said Silence. "All right, people, get ready to disembark. Full field kit for everyone, and that includes you, esper. Move it!"

The pinnace crew rose quickly to their feet and gathered around the Investigator as she broke open the arms locker and passed out the equipment. The two marines looked at each other thoughtfully. Full field kit meant a steelmesh tunic, concussion and incendiary grenades, swords and energy guns, and a personal force shield. That kind of kit was normally reserved for open firefights and full-scale riot control. Stasiak took his armful of equipment and moved as far away from the Captain and the Investigator as the cramped space would allow. Ripper followed him, and the two marines put their heads together as they ostensibly busied themselves in sorting out their kits.

"I hate this," said Stasiak quietly. "I hate this planet, and

I hate this mission. Full field kit for what's supposed to be a dead planet? A Captain who talks about ghosts and super-weapons? The man is seriously disturbed, Ripper. Dammit to hell, only five more months and my time was up. Five short months, and I'd have been out of the Service and my own man again. But of course nothing ever goes right for me, so I end up being volunteered for this bloody mess. A crazy Captain and an insane mission. Hallucinations, my ass. I don't care if this is a scorched world; something's still alive here, and it isn't friendly."

"Then why couldn't we find any targets for our guns?" murmured Ripper, pulling on his baldric with practiced ease. "There's no doubt this is a scorched world. I checked the ship's computers before the drop. Ten years ago, six starcruisers hit Unseeli with everything they had. Wiped the planet clean, pole to pole."

"Six ships?" said Stasiak. "Standard procedure for a scorching is two starcruisers, three if you're in a hurry. What did they have down here that they thought they needed six ships to deal with it?"

"There's more," said Ripper. "Guess who was in charge of scorching Unseeli?"

Stasiak stopped struggling with the buckles on his baldric. "Silence?"

"Got it in one. He was in charge of putting down the Ashrai rebellion. When that got out of hand, he was the one who called for a scorch."

Stasiak shook his head slowly. "This just gets better and better. This is going to be a bad one, Rip. I can feel it in my water."

"Don't worry; trust the old Ripper. He'll see you through."

Stasiak just looked at him.

The esper Diana Vertue struggled to pull on her steelmesh tunic. The label said it was her size, but the label was a liar.

She finally pulled it into place by brute force, and emerged from the neck red-faced and gasping. The long vest was heavy and awkward, and she hated to think what it was going to feel like after she'd been wearing it for a few hours. She looked at the sword and hand disrupter she'd been issued, hesitated, and then moved back to the arms locker to put them away.

"I wouldn't," said Investigator Frost. "The odds are you're going to need them."

"I don't use weapons," said the esper firmly. "I'm not a killer. I'll keep the force shield, but that's all."

The Investigator shrugged. "It's your neck." She settled her holstered disrupter comfortably on her right hip, and drew a sword in a scabbard from the arms locker. It was a long sword, definitely not regulation issue, and the Investigator slung it over her left shoulder and buckled it into place so that it hung down her back. The tip of the scabbard almost touched the floor behind her. Frost noticed the esper's curious gaze, and smiled slightly.

"It's a claymore. Old Earth sword. Been in my clan for generations. It's a good blade."

"Have you ever killed anyone with it?" asked Vertue. Her tone was polite, but the Investigator stiffened at the disapproval she sensed in the esper.

"Of course," said Frost. "That's my job." She reached into the locker and brought out a bandolier of grenades. She pulled it tight across her chest and flexed her arms a few times to make sure it wouldn't interfere with her movements. She looked at the esper. "If you're not willing to fight, stay out of my way. And don't expect me to look after you. That's not my job."

She slammed the arms locker shut and moved over to join the Captain and the two marines waiting at the airlock door. Vertue looked after her for a moment but said nothing. She joined the others, her gaze on her feet. Silence looked them all over, raised an eyebrow at the esper's lack of weapons, and then keyed in the security codes for the airlock door. The door hissed open, and Silence led the way in. The airlock was just big enough to take them all, and when the door hissed shut behind them, the cramped space became disturbingly claustrophobic. Vertue hugged herself tightly to stop herself trembling. She'd never liked enclosed spaces.

"Odin, this is the Captain," said Silence through his comm implant. "Respond, please."

"Contact confirmed," murmured the AI in his ear. "Sensor scans are still normal. No life forms within sensor range. Air, temperature, and gravity are within acceptable limits. You have seven hours daylight remaining."

"Open the hatch, computer."

The outer door swung open with a hiss of compressed air. Silence stepped forward, and then hesitated in the doorway as a breeze brought him the scent of Unseeli. It was a sharp, smoky scent, and though he hadn't smelt it for ten years, it was immediately familiar to him, as though he'd never left. He lifted his head a little, and stepped out onto the landing pads followed by the others. The grey afternoon was bitter cold and his breath steamed on the air before him. There was a series of faint clicks as the heating elements in his uniform kicked in. Tall metal trees surrounded the landing field, filling the horizon no matter which way he looked. It was ten years since he'd last looked on the metallic forest of Unseeli. It seemed like yesterday.

Base Thirteen stood in the centre of the landing field, hidden behind its force screen. The protective dome swirled and shimmered, like a huge pearl in a dull metal setting. It was easy to imagine something dark and unknown squatting behind the screen, staring out at the pinnace's crew and waiting for them to come to it. A sudden chill ran up

Silence's spine that had nothing to do with the cold. He smiled sourly and shrugged the thought aside. He looked around to see what his people made of their new surroundings. The two marines had their disrupters in their hands and were glancing quickly about them, checking for threats and familiarizing themselves with the territory. The Investigator was standing a little to one side, calmly studying the force screen. The esper was hugging herself against the cold and staring out at the forest, her eyes very large in her pale, bony face. None of them looked particularly worried. That would change, soon enough. Silence coughed loudly to get their attention.

"I'm going to have to leave you for a while. The Investigator is in charge until I return. Any problems, she can contact me on the command channel. But unless it's vitally important, I don't want to be disturbed. We're going to need help to get through that screen, and I think I know where to find some."

Frost looked at him narrowly. "Help? On Unseeli? Don't you think it's about time you filled us in on what's going on here, Captain?"

"No," said Silence. "Not just yet."

"Well, can you at least tell us where you're going?"

"Of course, Investigator. I'm going to talk to the traitor called Carrion. He's going to get us through the force screen. That's if he doesn't decide to kill us all first."

✝

CHAPTER TWO

Ghosts

RIPPER and Stasiak were supposed to be establishing a perimeter around the landing field, but they spent most of their time studying the enigmatic metal forest through the swirling mists. They had both volunteered for the job, Ripper because he believed in the value of a good, secure perimeter, and Stasiak because he was glad of a chance to get away from the Investigator. He'd heard a lot of stories about the Empire's most renowned assassins, and now that he'd met Frost he was ready to believe a lot of things he hadn't before. Investigators were the Empire's elite, trained to deal with situations too dangerous or too complex for ordinary troops. Their speciality lay in dealing with new alien species. They would study the aliens in depth, work out how best to exploit, enslave, or destroy them, and then lead the mission that would bring the alien world into the Empire, one way or another. They were unparalleled fighters, cold and calculating strategists, unstoppable by anything but death. They were said to be as strange and inhuman as the aliens they studied, and Stasiak believed it. Just being around Frost made his skin crawl.

The two marines moved slowly round the boundary of the landing pads, setting down proximity mines at regular intervals and priming them to detonate the moment anything approached within the designated distance. Ripper was a great believer in proximity mines; they not only discouraged people from sneaking up on you, they also provided plenty of warning that the enemy was abroad. Ripper slapped the mine before him affectionately, ignoring Stasiak's wince. The mine wasn't much to look at, but there was enough explosive crammed into the flat grey disc to ruin anybody's day.

The perimeter had taken longer to establish than he'd expected, and not just because of the time they spent warily watching the forest. The landing field was even larger than it looked, and it looked immense. Ripper tried to imagine how the field must have looked when the Base was first being established and the massive starcruisers were landing and taking off every hour, like huge flying mountains, but he couldn't. The scale was just too great. He started to mention it to Stasiak, but changed his mind. Stasiak was a good man to have at your back in a fight, but he wasn't the most imaginative of men. If you couldn't eat it, drink it, fight it, or get a leg over it, Stasiak really wasn't interested.

He was currently scowling out into the mists again, and Ripper reluctantly followed his gaze. There was something about Unseeli in general, and Base Thirteen in particular, that disturbed him deeply on some primitive, instinctive level. The sheer size of the metal trees was intimidating, making him feel small and insignificant, like a church mouse staring up at a vast cathedral. And then there was the mist, enveloping the metallic forest like a grubby off-white shroud. Ripper kept thinking he saw vague shapes moving at the edge of the forest, come and gone in the blink of an eye. There was a constant feeling of being watched, an almost tangible pressure of unseen, watching eyes. Alien eyes.

The silence was unnerving too. The only sounds on the still air were those the two marines made themselves, and they were quickly swallowed up by the quiet. No creature roared, no bird sang, and the air was deathly still. Dead world. Ghostworld. Ripper scowled, and let his hand rest on the disrupter at his side while Stasiak finished laying down the last mine. There was a feeling of imminence on the air, of something vital finally about to happen after many years of waiting. But all around, everything was still and quiet. Dead.

Stasiak ran quickly through the activating routine, primed the proximity mine, and stood up next to Ripper. Anyone who approached the perimeter now without the right codes in their implant would find themselves suddenly scattered across an extremely large area. Stasiak sniffed unhappily and hitched the gun on his hip to a more comfortable position. He'd hoped to feel more secure once the perimeter was established, but he couldn't honestly say that he did. One look at the forest was enough to put his teeth on edge. Strange colors glowed in the depths of the mists, curious and unsettling hues that swirled slowly like dye in water. They faded in and out, their slow, deliberate movements implying something that bordered on purpose or meaning, some alien intent unfathomable by the human mind. Ripper tapped him on the arm to get his attention, and Stasiak all but jumped out of his skin. He glared at Ripper, who stared calmly back.

"If you've quite finished trying to give me a coronary," said Stasiak, "perhaps we could get the hell away from here and back to the pinnace?"

Ripper looked at him with amusement. "I thought you were relieved to be putting some distance between you and the big bad Investigator?"

Stasiak shrugged briefly, looking out at the forest again. "I was, but this is even creepier than she is. I keep . . . seeing things. Hearing things. Come on, Rip; you've felt it too, I can tell. There's something out there in the mists, watching us."

"The computer was quite specific," said Ripper neutrally. "According to all the pinnace's instruments, the only living things on this planet are us. Unless you're suggesting the planet is haunted . . ."

"Why not?" said Stasiak, looking seriously at Ripper. "Strange things have been known to happen out here on the Rim. Remember the Ghost Warriors, and the Wolfling in the Madness Maze? You can find anything out here on the Rim. Anything."

"Even so," said Ripper. "I still draw the line at ghosts."

"Something attacked us on the way down, something the sensors swore weren't there. And what about this Carrion guy the Captain's gone looking for? Assuming he isn't a ghost or a walking corpse, that means someone's found a way to hide from Empire sensors. And if one man's learned to do it, how do we know others haven't? A whole lot of others, heavily armed and just waiting to descend on us the moment we let our guard down."

"You're determined to be cheerful, aren't you?" said Ripper. "All right, I've got a bad feeling about this place too, but I'm not letting my nerves run away with me. I'm not going to start worrying till I've got something definite I can aim a gun at. You worry too much, Lew. These mines will stop anything, up to and including a charging Hadenman."

"And if you're wrong, and there is something nasty out there?"

"Then you can say I told you so," said Ripper calmly.

Stasiak shook his head, unconvinced. "There must have been something nasty here for the Base to raise their screen. I mean, that's a last-ditch defence; it's what you do when you've tried everything else and none of it's worked. I don't like this, Rip. I don't like the feel of this mission at all."

"Neither do I," said a calm female voice behind them. Both marines spun round sharply to find Investigator Frost standing almost on top of them. Ripper and Stasiak exchanged a swift glance as they realised neither of them had heard the Investigator approaching, despite the eerie quiet.

"There's still no response from the Base." said Frost. "There's nothing wrong with our equipment, so either the

Base personnel don't want to talk to us, or they can't. Which suggests, at the very least, there's something here capable of scaring the hell out of an entire Base. Except, of course, our instruments continue to assure us there's no one down here but us."

"What about Carrion?" said Stasiak, and the Investigator nodded slowly.

"Yes, what about Carrion? Have either of you heard the name before?"

"No," said Ripper. "Have you?"

Frost frowned thoughtfully. "Most of Unseeli's records are sealed behind Security codes even I don't have access to, but I've managed to dig up a few things that aren't exactly common knowledge. The traitor Carrion used to be a high-ranking officer serving under Captain Silence, back when the Empire was fighting its war against the indigenous species, the Ashrai. Carrion turned against his own kind and fought with the Ashrai, against humanity. Quite successfully, from what I can tell. He apparently displayed quite powerful esper abilities in combat, though interestingly enough there are no records of his having any such abilities before he came to Unseeli. He was supposed to have died with the Ashrai, when the planet was scorched."

Stasiak shook his head firmly. "Then he's dead. No one survives a scorching."

"Not so far," said Frost. "But the Captain seems quite convinced that Carrion has survived, and that he can find him. Intriguing, that."

"Have you ever served with Captain Silence before?" said Ripper.

"No. He has a good record, apart from Unseeli. How about you?"

"Been with him two years now," said Ripper. "Not a bad sort. For a Captain. I've served under worse. Lew?"

"He's all right," said Stasiak, shrugging. "Or at least he seemed to be, until this mission. He's been acting strangely ever since we got our orders to come here."

"Considering the last time he was here he fouled up so completely he had to have the whole planet scorched, I can't say I'm surprised." Frost lifted her gaze to the metallic forest, as though it might suggest some answers. "I would have to say the good Captain's present behaviour could become a cause for concern. In fact, he gives the definite impression of a man no longer entirely stable."

Ripper looked at her sharply. The Investigator was choosing her words very carefully. "So," he said, carefully, "if the Captain was to be officially judged as unstable, who would take over as mission commander? You?"

The Investigator smiled. "I might. For the good of the mission."

"Yes," said Ripper. "For the good of the mission."

"I should remind you all," said the AI suddenly, through their comm implants, "that the penalties for treason and mutiny are extremely severe."

"Treason?" said Stasiak quickly. "Who's talking treason? I'm not."

Frost smiled, unperturbed. Ripper grimaced sourly. "I should have known. Can't even get any privacy on a deserted planet."

"I am required in the present emergency to monitor all conversations," said the AI. "I shall of course have to repeat your words to the Captain, on his return."

"Of course," said Frost. "When he returns. In the meantime, you will cease to monitor any conversation of which I am a part, unless I give you permission to do so. That is a direct order, under Code Red Seven. Confirm."

"Code Red Seven confirmed," said the AI, almost reluctantly, and then it fell silent.

Ripper raised an eyebrow at the Investigator. "I didn't know anyone could override an AI's Security directives."

"That's what's so special about a career in the Service," said Frost. "You learn something new every day. Now, much as I'd like to stay and chat, I think I'll go for a little walk in the woods. Get the feel of this place. If you feel the need to discuss the Captain again, I suggest you wait till my return."

She strode off towards the metallic forest without looking back, and the marines watched silently until she'd disappeared into the curling mists. Stasiak looked at Ripper. "You know, I'm not sure which disturbs me most—this planet, or her."

Silence made his way unhurriedly through the mists, looking always straight ahead of him. The huge trees loomed out of the fog to every side, and once-familiar faces seemed to stare from the mists at the corners of his eyes, but he never looked round. The forest was full of old memories, few of them pleasant. Silence concentrated on the man he'd come to find, the traitor called Carrion. The man who'd been his friend, ten long years ago.

The heating elements in his uniform kept his body comfortably warm, but the bitter cold seared his bare hands and face. The Empire kept promising to supply gloves to go with the uniform, but somehow the budget was always too tight. He grimaced stoically, and did his best to ignore the cold. He wasn't far from his destination now. Theoretically, Carrion could be anywhere on Unseeli, shielded from the pinnace's sensors by his unnatural esper abilities. He had a whole world to hide in, but Silence knew where he'd be. Carrion was waiting for him in the clearing half a mile from the landing field, the place where Carrion had lived with the Ashrai in their tunnels under the earth, the place he called home.

He stopped for a moment, and activated his comm implant. "Carrion, this is John Silence, Captain of the *Darkwind*. Can you hear me?" He waited, but there was no reply. He wasn't surprised. Carrion wasn't stupid enough to give himself away that easily. Anyone could be listening in on an open comm channel, and he knew it.

Something moved suddenly at the edge of Silence's vision, and he snapped round, disrupter in hand. There was nothing there, but Silence had a strong feeling that something had been. Whatever had attacked the pinnace during its descent had found him again. There were sudden darting movements in the mists to his left and right, behind and ahead of him. Silence started forward again, careful to keep his pace slow and unhurried. He felt a growing need to break into a run as the shadows moved inexorably closer, but he didn't. It wouldn't be wise to give them the idea he was running from them. It wouldn't be safe. He wasn't far from the clearing now. It occurred to him that they might not want him to meet Carrion, and the first stab of uncertainty brought beads of sweat to his face despite the cold. He had to reach Carrion. He had to.

Glowing streamers of quickly changing hues spun in the mists ahead of him, pushed and tugged at by an unfelt wind. There was a sudden sharp crack as a long metal branch snapped off a nearby tree. Silence threw himself to one side just as the jagged spike slammed into the ground where he'd been standing. Cracking sounds echoed from every side as more branches broke off from the trees, raining down about him as he ran dodging and ducking down the path towards the clearing. His boots thudded hard on the unyielding ground, jarring him painfully. He threw himself this way and that, lungs straining against the cold air, and the metal spears slammed into the ground all around him. Silence ran on, refusing to be slowed or intimidated. He'd come too far to be stopped now. A jagged spike tore through his uniform and slid painfully across his ribs before falling away. Silence thought he'd got away with only a bruise, until he glanced down and saw the wide patch of blood staining his side. Another spike flew at his face, and he deflected it at the last moment with an upraised arm. Blood flew on the air as the uniform sleeve tore, and the impact numbed his arm.

There were things in the forest now, moving with him as he ran. He could hear them pounding between the trees, the ground shaking from their weight. Silence plunged on, his breath burning in his heaving chest. His gun was still in his hand, but he couldn't see a target anywhere. And then the path ended suddenly, blocked by a clump of needle-thorned briar that had grown up around a fallen tree. Silence staggered to a halt, and dropped to his knees by the massive trunk of a golden tree. He put his back to the trunk and glared wildly about him. The briar blocked the way completely, and there was no other path. They had him now.

Deep in the metallic forest, something howled. It was a harsh, alien sound with nothing human in it, but the pain and rage and remembered loss were clear enough. The horrid sound drifted through the trees, growing louder, drawing nearer. More voices rose on every side, the deafening chorus cutting at Silence like a knife, and he shrank back against the tree trunk even as he raised his gun in a futile gesture of defiance. Guns weren't going to stop what was coming for him. Shadows moved in the swirling mists, circling him, and Silence caught brief glimpses of clawed hands and snarling mouths, large graceful forms and flat-planed gargoyle faces.

He took aim at the nearest face and fired his disrupter. The crackling energy beam smashed through the alien face and shattered the tree trunk behind it. There was a harsh, rending sound as the tree slowly toppled over and crashed to the forest floor. Metallic shrapnel pattered down for some time, but there was nothing to show he'd hurt or even scared his enemy. He hadn't really expected anything else. His enemies were already dead, ten years dead. They just wouldn't admit it and lie down. Silence's mouth twitched. They weren't playing fair. Not playing by the rules. Except this was Unseeli, the world of the Ashrai, and they had their own rules.

They were all around him now, the deafening howls rising and falling till his head ached from it. He knew what had come for him, even though it made a mockery of all sense and reason. The Ashrai were moving slowly, steadily, through the mists and the trees, circling, circling— all the tortured souls he'd damned and destroyed ten years earlier. Haunting him now as the memory of the awful thing he'd done had haunted him for so many years.

The howling stopped, cut off sharply between one moment and the next, and an eager, expectant hush filled the forest. Silence struggled to sit up a little straighter, grimacing briefly as pain flared in his damaged ribs. He raised his gun and then lowered it again. Even if there'd been anything to aim at, the disrupter couldn't fire again till its energy crystal had had time to recharge. There was still the sword at his side, but all he could do with that was fall on it himself, and maybe cheat the Ashrai of their vengeance. Except he couldn't do that. It wasn't in his nature to give up, even when the situation seemed hopeless. He drew his sword awkwardly, and glared defiantly at the curling mists. Something moved in the forest, not far away. Not far away at all.

And then a man appeared suddenly out of the mist to stand at Silence's side. Everything was still, Silence's fate hanging in the balance, and then the pressure of countless watching eyes was abruptly gone, the mists and the forest empty. Silence let out his breath in a long, shuddering sigh, and put his sword down beside him. Sweat was running down his face despite the cold, and he wiped it out of his eyes with his sleeve. He looked up at the man standing over him. The dark figure was tall and whipcord-lean, dressed in black leather and a billowing black cape. Carrion always wore black, like the bird of ill omen he was. He was carrying a long staff of polished bone, almost as tall as he was, but he held it more like a weapon than an aid to walking. His face was hidden in the shadows of his cowl, and Silence didn't know whether to feel grateful for that or not.

"Hello, Sean," he said finally, and was relieved to find his voice was still calm and even. "It's been a long time." The figure stared silently down at him, and Silence stirred uneasily. "What's the matter? Don't you remember me?"

"Oh yes, Captain," said Carrion quietly. "I remember you. So do they."

"What are they?" asked Silence.

"The past. Ghosts, perhaps."

"I don't believe in ghosts."

"That's all right," said Carrion. "They believe in you."

CHAPTER THREE

Looking for Answers

STASIAK and Ripper lounged bonelessly in their seats, bored and restless, watching without much interest as the esper Diana Vertue tried to make contact with Base Thirteen's computers. She'd been trying to patch the *Darkwind*'s computer into the Base's systems for some time, with only limited success, and she'd begun to mutter under her breath. Finally, by working together with Odin and improvising madly, she and the AI had managed to forge a tentative link between the pinnace's onboard systems and the Base's computer net. Diana studied the incoming data closely, and winced at the state of the Base's systems as they reluctantly opened up to her experimental probes. Thirteen's computers were shot to hell. Half the manned systems had crashed, and there was no trace anywhere of the Base's AI, which was supposed to protect the systems from such devastation. And there was something definitely odd about the computers she had managed to reach.

Diana frowned, her fingers darting across the comm panels, and watched intently as one by one the pinnace's monitors came to life, information flowing in an endless stream across the glowing screens. Her fingers pecked and stabbed at the keyboard as she tried to sort out the important data from the dross, her frown deepening as the picture unfolded. Whatever had happened at Base Thirteen, it hadn't been an accident. This kind of selective damage had to have been deliberate. Though whether the attack had come from outside the Base or within had yet to be established. She half-smiled as she heard one of the marines sigh heavily behind her. It was probably Stasiak. He hadn't struck her as the type to have a long attention span.

"You don't have to stay, you know," she said briskly, without looking back. "There's nothing you can do to help."

"It's our job to look after you," said Stasiak. "Make sure nothing happens to you. And if that means sitting around in a nice warm cabin instead of tramping around in the cold, waiting for my extremities to drop off, well, I know where my duty lies. After all, with the Captain and the Investigator both wandering about on their own somewhere, Rip and I are all that stands between you and whatever horrors lie waiting out there in the trees. Right, Rip?"

"Right," said Ripper.

"The proximity mines are all the protection I need," said Diana. "And the pinnace does have its own force screen, in the event of a real emergency. Now, I'm going to be doing this for some time, and believe me, this is as interesting as it gets."

"How much progress have you made?" asked Ripper, and Diana gave him points for at least sounding as if he was interested.

"Not a hell of a lot," she admitted, sitting back in her chair and letting her fingers rest for a moment. Things would have been going a lot quicker if she'd been allowed direct access to the computers instead of having to work through the keyboard. But she wasn't high enough in rank for that privilege, and besides, she was an esper, and therefore not to be trusted. Ever. She realised Ripper was still waiting for her answer, and pulled herself together.

"Most of the Base's computers are off-line, and seem determined to stay that way, no matter what I do. They're not responding to the standard code words or entry routines, and I can't even find the Base's AI. If I didn't know better,

I'd swear it was hiding. It's as though someone or something just shut everything down, and then wiped half the memory crystals. The subsystems overseeing the mining machinery seem to be mostly intact, but what little information I'm getting from them is pretty depressing. The machinery is working at barely twenty per cent efficiency, and dropping. Unless we come up with something to reverse this process, or at least slow it down, everything will just grind to a halt in a little under forty-eight hours. And once they've stopped, it'll be hell's own problem to get them all started again. If that were to happen, the Empire would not be at all happy—and guess which three people sitting in this cabin right now would be most likely to be saddled with the blame?"

"Is there anything we can do to help?" said Ripper.

"Short of getting me into the Base so I can get my hands on the main computer terminals, no, not really. Odin is working his electronic nuts off trying to find a way into the main computers, but something down here is playing merry hell with our comm signals, which means Odin isn't working at anywhere near his full capacity.

"On top of all that, there's something definitely wrong with the computers I have been able to reach. The information I've been getting from them makes no sense at all. Half is just gibberish, and the rest is impossible. If I didn't know better, I'd swear some of these systems have been reprogrammed from the bottom up."

Stasiak and Ripper looked at each other, and Ripper leaned forward in his seat. "Are you saying someone within the Base could have crashed the systems deliberately?"

"Yes. I'd have to say that was a definite possibility."

"In which case," said Ripper slowly, "we could be dealing with enemy action."

"Maybe," said Diana. "I can't say for sure. Some of these changes make no sense at all."

Ripper got to his feet. "Lew, I think you and I had better take a stroll round the perimeter. Make sure everything's secure."

Stasiak leaned back in his seat and deliberately stretched out his legs. "Come on, Rip, have a heart. It's cold out there. I'm rather attached to my fingers and toes and I'd like to hang on to them. You take a walk, if you feel like it. I'm sure Diana and I can come up with something to keep us occupied while you're gone. Right, Diana?"

"In your dreams," said the esper calmly. "You're not my type, Lew. I prefer my men a little higher up the evolutionary scale."

"Can I take that as a maybe?" said Stasiak, getting reluctantly to his feet.

"Think of it more as a get-the-hell-out-of-here."

"All right," said Stasiak. "I can take a hint. Lead the way, Rip. I'm just dying to take a nice little stroll in subzero temperatures and watch my extremities turn blue."

The esper chuckled briefly, intent on the comm panels, but she didn't relax until she heard the airlock door close behind the two marines. Stasiak was all right, in his way, but she had to be careful who she allowed to get close to her. There were always people ready to take advantage of her esper abilities. But it wasn't safe to stay unattached, either. Espers always had a need for someone to stand between them and the Empire, someone strong enough to protect a second-class citizen like an esper from official displeasure and political pogroms. Stasiak was too far down the ladder to be of any use to her, and Ripper wasn't much better . . . She realised her thoughts were drifting, and made herself concentrate on the screens before her. The information from Base Thirteen's computers flowed endlessly on, much of it enigmatic and no bloody use to her at all.

"I'm picking up something . . . unusual," said Odin suddenly. "I thought at first it was what was left of the Base's

AI, but now I'm not sure. It's as though something inside the Base is trying to respond to my enquiries, but in a manner unlike anything I've ever encountered before."

"Put it on the main screen," said Diana, and then frowned as the AI showed her a record of its questions and the Base's responses. The answers were garbled and obscure, bordering on the edge of meaning without actually achieving it. Diana ran a few simple checks to see if the gibberish might contain some kind of code, but if it did, it was buried so deep she couldn't find it. And yet the words continued to nag at her, trying to tell her . . . something. "Run a full analysis on this, Odin," she said finally. "Look for repetition of words and phrases, subjects emphasized or avoided, all the usual things. If it isn't the AI, could it be someone alive, inside the Base?"

"If it is," said Odin, "I would have to say that they were quite insane."

Outside the pinnace, it was even colder than Stasiak remembered, and he hugged himself tightly and stamped his feet hard on the landing pad while he waited for the heating elements in his uniform to kick in. He was beginning to think he should have found the time to give his uniform a thorough overhaul before he came down here. It was long overdue, and Stasiak was coming to the conclusion he might have left it a little too long. He shrugged, and rubbed his hands together briskly. He'd survive. Ripper, of course, was taking no notice of the cold, and was staring out at the forest boundary with calm, thoughtful eyes. Stasiak followed his gaze, but was damned if he could make out anything significant, or even interesting. He sniffed loudly, and looked longingly back at the pinnace.

"Ripper, tell me you didn't just drag me out here for the exercise. Tell me there's a good reason why I'm standing here in the cold, before I decide to batter you to death with a blunt instrument and dance a jig on your remains."

"You don't have a blunt instrument," said Ripper, without looking round.

"I'll improvise!"

Ripper smiled, but still didn't look away from the forest. "You weren't looking at the sensor panels, were you? According to the sensors built into our proximity mines, something or someone has approached or crossed our perimeter in several places before falling back to the forest again."

"You're kidding," said Stasiak. "You've got to be kidding. If something's crossed our perimeter, why haven't the mines gone off?"

"Good question," said Ripper. "Another good question might be why the mines' sensors detected a presence, when the pinnace's instruments continue to insist there are no living things on this planet apart from us. You've got to admit, Lew, it's an interesting place our Captain has brought us to."

"I'll give him interesting," said Stasiak darkly. He moved over to stand beside Ripper, and glared out at the mists and the trees. "You know why he brought us here, Rip? Because we're expendable. We're just here to test the water for him. And if anything were to happen to us, he'd just shrug and say what a pity, and then contact the *Darkwind* and have them ship down two more warm bodies."

"That goes with the job," said Ripper. "With being a marine. If you can't take a joke, you shouldn't have joined."

"Just let me survive the next five months, and my contract will be up," said Stasiak. "And then I'll be out of the marines so fast it'll make your head spin. I can't believe I landed an assignment like this so close to getting free of it all. I'll tell you this for nothing, Rip: I'm not taking a single risk down here that I don't absolutely have to, I'm taking this one by the book and by the numbers, with no volunteering for anything. Whatever else happens on this mission, I'm coming back alive and intact, and you can put money on that."

Ripper finally turned to look at him. "And what will you do then, Lew? Where will you go, once you've left the Service? All you know, all your training and experience, comes from being a marine. There aren't that many openings for a professional killer, outside the Service. Shall I tell you what's going to happen to you? You'll go from one dead-end job to another, each more frustrating than the one before, breaking your back every day for half the money you used to make as a marine. And finally, when your money's run out and you're out of your mind with boredom, some shark with a big smile and a suit that cost a year of your wages will sign you up as a mercenary for which he gets a nice commission, and you get to tour the hellholes of the Empire. In the end you'll come running back to the Service and sign on again, just like most ex-marines do."

"Like you did," said Stasiak.

"Yeah. Like I did. Get used to the idea, Lew. This is all there is for people like us."

"Not me," said Stasiak. "Once I'm out of here they're never getting their hands on me again. I've got plans. I'm going places. I'm going to make something of myself."

"Sure you are, Lew."

"I mean it!"

"I know you do. I hope you make it. In the meantime, keep your eyes open and your head down. And don't look now, but I think I just saw something moving out on the perimeter, at two o'clock."

Stasiak looked round casually, his eyes just happening to drift past two o'clock. There was nothing there. He cut in his infrared implants, but no heat traces showed anywhere on the perimeter. He patched into the pinnace sensors and studied their signals directly, but there was still nothing anywhere on the boundary. He broke contact, looked at Ripper, and shrugged.

"Jumping at shadows, Rip. There's nothing out there."

"Yes there is. I saw it. Keep watching; it'll give itself away. It's at times like this I wish the Empire would relax its ban on all but the most essential implants. I've seen stuff on the black market you wouldn't believe; implants and built-in weapon systems that could make a man unbeatable in the field. Which is pretty much why they're banned, of course. The Empire doesn't want its good little soldier boys getting ideas above their station. They still haven't forgotten the Hadenman rebellion."

"Yeah, well," said Stasiak. "Those cyborgs were enough to frighten anyone. And I still can't see anything out there. Maybe it's the Captain, on his way back."

"If it was, he'd have shown up on the infrared, wouldn't he? Though that's another question worth thinking about. What is the good Captain doing down here, risking his precious neck dirtside with grunts like us?"

"Looking for Carrion, whoever he is."

"Yeah." Ripper frowned for the first time. "The Captain knows a lot more about what's going on here than he's letting on. I'll lay you odds this Carrion turns out to be some kind of powerful esper. That's the only way he could be shielding himself from the pinnace's sensors."

Stasiak shook his head dubiously. "I don't know. If Carrion's been here on his own for the past ten years, what's he been living on? I mean, there isn't any game for him to catch. Every living thing was wiped out by the scorching. And even if he did find some way to survive, he's got to be stone crazy after ten years of his own company."

"Not necessarily," said Ripper. "He could have worked out some kind of deal with the Base personnel. There. Did you see that?"

"Yeah," said Stasiak quietly. "Right at the edge of the forest; two o'clock, just like you said. Still can't make out what it is. Want to go and take a look?"

"Easy, Lew. It could be a trick, to draw us away from the ship. Besides, if it's come this close, why hasn't it set off any of the mines? Whoever that is has got to be within their range. Maybe he's got a way to turn them on and off. He could be just waiting for us to walk by one, and then detonate it himself. Whoosh bang, and they'll send your balls home in a box, because they couldn't find the rest of you. No, Lew; short of an actual target or a direct threat to the pinnace, I'm not moving from this spot. At least, not until I've got a much better idea of the opposition."

"Damn right," said Stasiak, still keeping a careful if unobtrusive watch on two o'clock. "If the Captain wants to go off on his own chasing after ghosts, that's his affair. Short of a direct order, I'm not moving. I can't see it anymore, Rip. Can you see it?"

"No. It's gone again."

Stasiak looked at the watch face imbedded in his wrist. "You know, the Captain's been gone a long time. He should have been back by now."

Ripper shrugged. "How long does it take to track down someone who officially doesn't exist? Don't worry about the Captain. He's a grown man. He can take care of himself."

They stood together for a while, staring out into the mists.

"You know," said Stasiak finally, "if there was a ghost or something out theré at two o'clock, that puts it in roughly the same sector as the Investigator. Perhaps they'll bump into each other."

"In which case," said Ripper, "I feel sorry for the ghost."

CHAPTER FOUR

Carrion

CAPTAIN Silence rose slowly to his feet, wincing despite himself as his injured ribs protested. Carrion made no move to help him, for which Silence was thankful. He didn't want any reason to feel grateful to Carrion. It would have made what he had to do that much harder. Pushing his various aches and pains to the back of his mind, he concentrated on the traitor standing before him. It had been ten years since he'd last seen the man who used to be his friend, and he'd never expected to see him again. He should have died with the Ashrai. Dead, he might have emerged as a martyr; alive, he was just another loose end, an embarrassment. Someone Silence could use to solve an awkward problem.

He realised he was just standing and staring at Carrion but the words wouldn't come. He'd had it all worked out, coming down on the pinnace. He knew exactly what to say, what buttons to push to manipulate Carrion into doing what was necessary. Only now he was face to face with an old friend, a ghost from the past, and the words were ashes in his mouth. This man had been his friend, closer than a brother, but the last time they'd met they'd tried to kill each other. For a long time, Silence believed he'd succeeded. And then he began to hear stories from men who'd served on Unseeli, stories of the man who wouldn't die. The ghost in the trees. Carrion.

The years passed, but Silence never went back. He didn't want to have to kill his friend again. But time and circumstance had brought him back anyway, and past sins belonged in the past. All that mattered now was his mission, and the things he had to do to carry it out. Silence knew his duty. He'd always known his duty. And if that meant using and betraying his friend one more time, he could live with that. He'd lived with worse.

Carrion reached up and pushed back the cowl that concealed his face. Silence felt a sudden chill run through him, and the hackles rose on the back of his neck. Carrion hadn't aged. He'd spent ten years alone under terrible conditions, but there wasn't a single line on his face. He looked just as Silence remembered him: young, proud, unyielding. Time had not touched him. But then, ghosts didn't age. Silence felt suddenly awkward, ashamed at the changes that had taken place in himself over the past decade. What did Carrion make of him, with his retreating hairline and his thickening waist? Had he even noticed, and if he had, did he care? And most important, did he realise that this was not the same John Silence he'd once known, who might have hesitated to sacrifice his friend if the game demanded it. Just looking at the calm young man before him, Silence felt older, dirtier and more used. He still didn't know what to say. And in the end, Carrion was the one who broke the silence.

"What are you doing here, Captain?"

"I need your help," said Silence evenly.

Carrion smiled briefly, as though it was something he'd lost the ability to do, over the years. "I didn't think you'd come all this way just to renew old aquaintance. I always knew you'd be back someday. We have unfinished business, you and I."

"That can wait," said Silence. "Do you know what's happened in Base Thirteen?"

"I know the force screen went up, some time back. That's all."

"You didn't have any contact with the Base personnel?"

The smile came and went again, but it didn't touch Carrion's eyes. "The Base Commander had a shoot-on-sight policy where I was concerned. He needn't have bothered. He had nothing I wanted. But they were scared of me, of what I'd become, and they were right about that, at least."

"What have you become?" said Silence. "How have you survived here all these years, with no supplies and no resources?"

"Strictly speaking, I didn't. I've been through a lot since we last met, Captain. I'm not the man you remember." He looked away for a moment, as though listening to a voice only he could hear, and then nodded slowly and looked back at Silence. "We can't talk here. You have no friends among the trees, and not even I can protect you against the whole of the forest. Come with me. My home isn't far."

He turned and walked away, without once looking back to see if Silence was following. Silence moved off after him, gritting his teeth against the grinding pain in his side. The wound didn't look too severe, but something would have to be done about it soon, before he became weakened through blood loss. He allowed his uniform to release endorphins into his system, enough to handle the pain but not enough to cloud his thinking. He walked beside Carrion through the bronze and gold forest, following a track only the outlaw could see. Nothing moved in the mists, but the quiet had a sullen, expectant feel, and Silence could sense the watching eyes even if he couldn't see them.

The trees parted suddenly to reveal a great hill of metal overgrown with silver briar. The metal was scarred and pockmarked, and briar penetrated the outer shell here and there like some parasitic ivy, but even so, Silence could still recognise the battle wagon beneath. There were supposed to be quite a few of them, scattered throughout the forest, left to lie where they had fallen, brought down by the Ahsrai

and their psi-storms. Silence thought he remembered the
clearing; it was one of the few battlegrounds where he and
Carrion had both been present.

*Lasers flamed on the night, and concussion grenades
blossomed in the dark like scarlet flowers. Disrupters
flared, and there was the loud humming of raised force
shields. The Ashrai came in never-ending waves—huge,
ugly figures that moved with surprising grace and speed.
Their psi-storms crackled on the air around them, altering
probabilities and tearing at the mental barriers the Empire
espers had cast over the ground troops. Claws and fangs
met swords and shields, and blood flowed in rivers on the
broken ground. Battle wagons lumbered through the night,
forcing their way between the trees, and disrupter beams
stabbed down from low-flying skimmers darting back and
forth overhead. Science clashed with savagery, and the
battle swept this way and that, neither side able to gain
the upper hand for long.*

Silence shivered suddenly, emerging from a memory so
real it seemed to him that he could still hear the battle
cries and the screams of the dying. The Ashrai had been
a brave and cunning foe, but they never stood a chance
against the Empire. As soon as Silence realised he couldn't
take the ground the Ashrai held, or hang on to his own, he
simply moved all his people off-planet and called in the
starcruisers to scorch the whole damned planet from pole
to pole. Millions died, all life was swept away, and not
even the bodies remained to mark the fallen. The Empire
was nothing if not thorough. Silence had won, and all it
cost him was his honour and his friend. For a while he
thought he'd die without them, but he didn't. No one ever
really dies from a broken heart.

When it was over, the Empire hadn't known what to
do with Silence. On the one hand, he'd lost control of
the situation and had to be rescued by a scorching, but

on the other hand, he had solved the Unseeli problem quite conclusively. And permanently. So they smiled and shook his hand and patted him on the head in public, and made a note in his file that he was never to be promoted. He could keep his Captaincy, but there'd never be anything more for him. Silence didn't care. He'd lost all taste for ambition on Unseeli.

And now here he was, back again, and it seemed the problem hadn't been solved after all.

They finally came to the clearing where Carrion had his home, and Silence was struck with an almost overpowering sense of *déjà vu*. It hadn't changed at all. Before him were the same trees, the same clearing, the same patch of metal briar camouflaging the trapdoor entrance to the tunnels under the earth. Silence watched numbly as Carrion carefully lifted the briar to one side and pulled open the trapdoor. The last time Silence had been here was when he'd disobeyed orders and made a last-minute trip to try and talk Carrion out of turning traitor. They were still friends then, and the outlaw had yet to come by his new name. They met as friends and parted as enemies, and what happened afterward had all the inevitability of destiny. It hadn't stopped either of them from playing their role to the full. And now here they were again, with only the echoes of old friendship and enmity holding them together, looking once more for some middle ground they could agree on. Silence smiled sourly. Maybe they'd be luckier this time.

Carrion descended into the dark stairway beneath the trapdoor, and Silence followed him down. He paused briefly to test the weight of the trapdoor. It was just as heavy as he'd remembered, but Carrion had hefted it with one hand, as though it were weightless, He cleared his throat, and Carrion looked up at him.

"Do you want me to shut the door behind us?" said Silence.

Carrion smiled briefly. "There's really no need. It's not as if there was anyone else who might come in after us. Still, if it makes you feel more secure . . ."

He gestured at the trapdoor, and it started to lean forward of its own accord. Silence hurried down the narrow earth steps into the gloom of the tunnel, and the trapdoor slammed shut behind him, the impact of its weight sending tremors through the earth walls and floor. Silence glared after Carrion, but he was already walking off down the tunnel, and Silence had to hurry to keep up. The passage was wide enough for both of them to walk side by side, with a good two- or three-foot clearance above their heads. The earth had a rich, peaty smell that was not unpleasant. Roots from the metal trees had been trained along the uneven ceiling, filling the tunnel with their warm, unwavering light. The enclosed space was still distinctly claustrophobic, and Silence tried hard not to think about the increasing weight of earth above him as the passage sloped steadily downwards.

It soon branched into two, and then in two again, with corridors leading off tunnels, and wide holes opening into vast, brightly lit caverns. Silence was soon lost in the labyrinth of underground passages that had been the home of the Ashrai and the outlaw Carrion. The last time he'd been down here, he and Carrion had still been friends enough that Carrion had led him back to the surface once their business was concluded. Silence wasn't sure if that was the case anymore but it didn't matter anyway. He had to talk to Carrion.

Finally the outlaw stopped by a side passage and waved for Silence to go in ahead of him. Silence stepped forward without hesitating. He didn't want Carrion to think he was intimidated. The passage widened out into a fair-sized cavern, lit by the ubiquitous glowing roots curling in the earth ceiling. Carrion's home was large enough to give the illusion of space, yet cluttered with enough small comforts to make it seem almost cosy. There were two rickety-looking

chairs, a writing table, and a length of bedding. A banked
fire muttered drowsily in one wall, the smoke rising up
through a narrow chimney cut into the earth above. The
floor was covered with some kind of woven matting, scuffed
and stained with the marks of long use. Not much of a place
to spend an exile in.

Small, delicate Ashrai carvings filled discreet niches in
the walls. Silence moved over to study the nearest, but its
shape made no sense, and its twistings and turnings made his
head ache. He looked away, frowning, and Carrion chuckled
softly.

"You're supposed to touch them, Captain, not look at
them. The Ashrai were a very tactile race, and their eyes
were different than ours."

"Thanks," said Silence. "I'll pass."

"As you wish. Take a seat, Captain. Make yourself
comfortable. I'd offer you a drink or a smoke, but I don't
have any."

Silence sank cautiously into the nearest chair, but it was
tougher than it looked, and held his weight easily. Carrion
dropped into the chair opposite, and the two men sat facing
each other for a while. Silence couldn't get over how little
Carrion had changed. Ten years of living alone hadn't put
a single line in his face, or a dent in his composure. The
outlaw was as infuriatingly polite as ever. After a decade
of solitude he should have been falling all over Silence,
desperate for the sound of a human voice. Instead he just
sat there calmly, apparently quite happy to wait for whatever
Silence had come to say to him. Silence stirred uneasily in
his chair. He'd forgotten how cold and piercing Carrion's
eyes could be.

"Nice place you have here," he said finally, just to say
something.

"I like it," said Carrion. He suddenly leaned forward in
his chair, and Silence jumped a little in spite of himself.

Carrion didn't smile. "I don't know what to say to you, Captain. It's been a long time since I spoke to another human being."

"How have you managed to survive here on your own for ten years?" Silence asked.

Carrion raised an eyebrow. "Is it as long as that? I'd lost count. I survived by changing, adapting. By becoming more than human."

"You look human enough to me," said Silence. "You've hardly changed at all."

"That's Unseeli for you. Appearances can be deceiving. You should know that. You never did understand the Ashrai. They're what kept me alive all these years."

Silence looked at him thoughtfully. "Are you saying some of the Ashrai survived after all, hidden down here in the tunnels?"

"No, Captain. The Ashrai are extinct. You were very thorough. All the Ashrai are dead, and none but I am left to tell the tale. I survived because I was afraid to die. I've had a long time to consider whether that was a mistake or not. Why have you come back, Captain?"

"Things have changed since we last met."

"Not for me. The Ashrai are still dead, and the Empire machines are still burrowing away, tearing through the trees' roots so they can be felled and harvested. The rape of the planet goes on, day by day."

Silence sighed wearily. "Ten years of solitude haven't done much to change your arguments. You didn't listen then and you probably won't now, but I'll try again anyway, for old times' sake. The Empire needs the metals it takes from Unseeli. Each tree that's felled can provide enough heavy metals to power a starship for a year. We even use the outer metals to make ships' hulls and engine casings. It's only Unseeli's metals that made our recent expansion possible. But Unseeli is the only place where these metals can be easily found, and we've become dependent on them. Without the regular supply ships these trees make possible, half our colonies would starve or suffocate or fall apart from lack of some essential need. Millions would die, the Empire would collapse, and humanity would fall back into barbarism inside a generation."

"To the Ashrai, we are barbarians," said Carrion.

Silence shook his head impatiently. "None of that matters anymore. It's past. I need your help, Sean. Something's happened at Base Thirteen."

Carrion looked at him steadily. "The last time we met I called the Ashrai to arms and led them against the Empire. I led them into battle for the sake of their world, and you butchered them. You maimed and slaughtered until you grew bored, and then you retreated into orbit and burned everything that lived."

Silence didn't look away. "It was necessary."

"The Ashrai . . ."

"Didn't stand a chance. Rebels never do."

"And you expect me to help you now? After everything that's happened, you expect me to help the Empire?"

"I could get you Pardoned."

"I doubt that."

Silence smiled coldly. "Don't flatter yourself, Sean. You're not that important, or a bounty hunter would have taken your head years ago. No, you're just another deserter who went native on some backwater planet. No one cares about you anymore. I can get you Pardoned, and I can take you off-planet. Take you anywhere you want to go. You could start again, start over with a clean record. Think about it. You wouldn't even have to call yourself Carrion any more."

"Why not, Captain? It's who I am." Carrion shook his head slowly, and sank back in his chair. "Thank you for the offer, Captain, but no."

"No? Think what I'm offering you! You can't want to stay here on your own . . . ."

"Can't I? I've found peace here."

"What peace? The peace of the dead, of the cemetery?"

"The peace of the forest, Captain. You never did understand what you were destroying. The Ashrai and the trees were linked more closely than you ever knew. The trees are alive. I've seen branches sway when no wind blows, and heard voices on the wind and in the mists. The Ashrai are dead, but they are not gone. There's a harmony, a strength that holds the trees together, and I'm a part of it." The outlaw's voice fell to a whisper. "Leave me alone, John. Please."

"I can't, Sean. I need you."

"Why, Captain? Why does it always have to be me?"

"Because you're the best."

"Thank you, Captain."

Silence turned away from the bitterness in Carrion's voice, and rose to his feet. "Up you get, Carrion. It's a long way back to Base Thirteen, and we've a lot to discuss on the way."

Carrion looked up at him. "Are you so sure I'll help you?"

"Of course. You're my friend. And it's not as if you have anything else to do, is it?"

CHAPTER FIVE

Ghost in the Machine

THE esper Diana Vertue leaned back in her seat and glared moodily at the pinnace monitors. The AI was still trying to make some sense out of the garbled responses it was receiving from inside Base Thirteen, but as far as Diana could tell, it was getting nowhere fast. She supposed it was an encouraging sign that anything at all was coming through, but in her opinion the responses were nothing more than random data from a damaged computer. She had suggested as much to Odin, but the AI ignored her. She was only an esper, and therefore the AI didn't have to listen to her if it didn't want to. Even an Artificial Intelligence rated higher than an esper.

Diana sighed, and stretched out her legs as best she could in the cramped confines of the cabin. She'd expected many things of her first official mission on an alien world, but boredom wasn't one of them. She'd almost reached the point where she would have welcomed the two marines back on board, just to have someone to talk to. At least they had something to do, even if it was only keeping a lookout and second-guessing the Security system. All she had to do was sit and watch the computer talking to itself, and wait for something to go wrong. Not that there was a whole lot she could do if it did. She sighed again, heavily, and indulged herself in a pout. It wasn't fair. She hadn't been allowed to do anything ever since they touched down on this miserable planet. She ached for something new to happen—up to and including a major catastrophe—just so long as she got to see a little action. Anything would be better than this.

Well, almost anything. She hadn't forgotten what had happened the last time she opened up her esp, on the way down. There was something here on Unseeli with them, and to hell with what the sensors said. And whatever it was, it was dangerous. She'd sensed a rage and a force beyond anything she'd ever encountered before, something so powerful it almost burned out her mind just looking at it. She'd kept her esp damped down ever since, and had no intention of raising it again, no matter how bored she got. She frowned slightly, unhappy at the direction her thoughts were taking, but unable to ignore them either. Captain Silence had known what the attacking force was, even if what he'd said had made no sense. When he got back, she'd get some answers out of him, one way or another. She could always run a quick scan on him. In and out, so fast he'd never notice. But of course she couldn't. Just thinking about it was enough to make her break out in a cold sweat. The Empire conditioned its espers very carefully from childhood on, to ensure they'd never abuse their abilities. Except in the service of the Empire, of course.

"Investigator Frost to pinnace. Acknowledge, and confirm your situation."

Diana sat up straight as the Investigator's cold, calm voice sounded in her comm implant. "This is esper Vertue. The pinnace is still secure. Nothing's happened since you left. Where are you?"

"About two miles east of the landing field, map reference Alpha Tango eighty-eight. Has the Captain returned yet?"

"No, Investigator. He hasn't contacted us, and we haven't been able to raise him. Something down here is affecting the comm system; it only works when it feels like it."

"I had hoped the Captain would be there, but we can proceed without him. This is an official log entry; Unseeli, Day One, 1543 hours. I have discovered what appears to be an alien space vessel, crashed some two miles east of Base Thirteen. The ship has suffered extensive damage, and there is as yet no sign of any pilot or other crew."

"An alien ship?" said Diana excitedly as Frost paused. "What type is it? What species?"

There was another pause, but when Frost spoke again, her voice was calm and measured. "Unknown, esper."

Diana stared blankly at the comm panels, her mind racing. Space-travelling aliens were rare, even out here on the Rim, but a new, unknown species! This was the kind of thing careers were made on. A sudden thought struck her.

"Investigator, could this be a representative of the species who originally created the metal forest?"

"Possible, but unlikely. Any species intelligent enough to genengineer the trees would surely be able to land a ship without crashing it. Listen carefully, esper. You're going to have to leave the pinnace. I need you here, with me, to examine this ship. The marines will accompany you, to ensure your safety."

"You mean, leave the pinnace unguarded?" said Diana.

"The pinnace can look after itself. Odin, go to full battle readiness. Acknowledge."

"Acknowledged, Investigator," Odin replied. Perhaps it was only her imagination, but Diana could have sworn she heard something like excitement in the AI's invariably calm voice.

"In the meantime, Odin, keep trying to raise the Captain." said Frost. "I don't like being out of contact with him for so long. That goes for you too, esper. You might have better luck once you've moved away from the vicinity of Base Thirteen. Odin; what's your current status on repairs?"

"Progressing well, Investigator. All main systems are back on line and operational."

"What about structure integrity? Could we lift off, if we had to?"

"Unknown, Investigator. Theoretically, yes. As a practical matter, I could not reccomend it, except in the most urgent circumstances."

"Very well. Maintain regular contact with the *Darkwind* after the esper and the marines have left; keep them up to date on what's happening down here. And be prepared to relay information from me to the *Darkwind*. I'll want the data from this new ship compared with existing records."

"I'm afraid that won't be possible, Investigator. I have been unable to contact the *Darkwind* from the moment we landed. There is nothing wrong with the comm systems, so I can only conclude it is either a result of natural conditions, or the interference is deliberate."

"What do you mean, we're out of contact?" snapped Frost. "Why didn't you say anything before?"

"You didn't ask."

"Computer, once this mission is over, you and I are going to have a long chat about which of us is in charge here. In the meantime, you will report to me, or the esper, or anybody else available, on any changes in our circumstances that might affect our mission, *as they happen*. And if I have any further problems with you, I will personally reprogram your data banks with a shrapnel grenade. Is that clear?"

"There is no need to raise your voice to me, Investigator. I assure you, I have only the best interests of this mission at heart. I exist only to serve."

"Blow it out your terminal."

Diana looked aghast at the comm panels before her. Being cut off from the main ship was serious; it not only meant they were denied the ship's superior computer facilities, it also meant they were on their own if anything went wrong.

Diana hugged herself tightly. She'd never been cut off from the ship from the moment she joined its crew. She was used to its protection as a given, only a call away. Now she felt alone, naked, defenceless. She realised Frost was still talking, and forced herself to pay attention.

"If something is blocking our transmissions, Odin, can you determine their position in relation to ours?"

"Not at present, Investigator," said the AI. "Without further evidence, it remains only a hypothesis."

"That settles it. Esper, I want you with me as fast as you can travel. The sooner we check this alien ship out, the better. And, esper, keep your eyes open on the way. Investigator out."

The silence that followed Frost's signing off had a pronounced feeling of uncertainty. Not to mention unease. The presence of the alien ship could explain a lot of things, but for the moment it raised more questions than it answered. And the thought of leaving the pinnace and travelling through the metallic forest was not a comforting one, even with the marines for protection. Diana got to her feet and then stood there dithering, unsure what to do first. She'd wanted a little action, a little excitement, but this was ridiculous. A thought struck her, and she turned to glare at the comm panels.

"Odin, why didn't your sensors detect the presence of the crashed alien ship?"

"Unknown, esper. Either the ship is shielded in some way, or it and its crew are simply too alien to show up on my instruments."

Diana frowned. "I thought it was impossible for anything to shield itself from your sensors?"

"Impossible for any technology I am aware of. The alien ship's level of technology is unknown."

Diana growled something under her breath, and strode down the cabin to the airlock. Even when the computer was talking directly to her, she couldn't get anything useful out of it. At least the Investigator understood her worth. Just let her at that alien ship; she'd show them what an esper could do. She'd show them all.

The marines accepted their new orders with hardly any fuss. Secretly, Diana thought they were probably just as bored as she'd been. The news of an alien ship didn't throw them at all. They just nodded, checked the power levels on their guns, and led her off the landing field and into the metallic forest. They walked on either side of her, studying the surrounding trees alertly, their disrupters drawn and ready for use. Diana looked at the guns and scowled. There was always the chance the aliens weren't involved with whatever had happened at Base Thirteen, and were just innocent bystanders. The Empire's usual reaction to a new species was to shoot first and ask questions later, if at all, but Diana was determined that wasn't going to happen here. First contacts could be peaceful, and she was going to do everything in her power to see that this one was. The Empire wasn't going to add another servant species to its ranks, another people to treat and exploit as second-class citizens. Like the espers.

She didn't like the way her thoughts were going, so she concentrated instead on her surroundings. The metallic trees were very beautiful, shining in the mists like frozen fireworks. Now that she was seeing them up close, walking among them, they didn't seem nearly as imposing. Their warm glow seemed friendly, even inviting . . . Which was more than she could say about the entities that had attacked her on the way down. The day seemed suddenly colder, and she shuddered briefly. She'd never felt a rage like it, an anger beyond thought or emotion; a force in itself. A force strong enough to break through a pinnace hull built to withstand atomics. She looked at the marines walking with her, and her momentary feeling of security was gone, as though it had never been. Guns and cold steel would be little use against the kind of force she'd sensed.

She thrust the thought out of her mind. She was on her way to an unknown alien ship and a possible first contact, and nothing was going to spoil that for her. She wouldn't let anything spoil it. She lengthened her stride, almost skipping along in her enthusiasm. The marines had to hurry to keep up with her. Ripper studied her thoughtfully, and Stasiak gave her a dark look or two, but she ignored both of them. And then the smile left her face and the joy went out of her in a moment, as something moved in the trees, not far away. She stopped dead in her tracks, and the marines stopped with her. They looked at her enquiringly, and she tried hard to stop trembling.

"Didn't you hear it?" she said quietly.

"Hear what?" said Stasiak, trying to look in every direction at once, and almost succeeding.

"There's something moving in the mists, not far away. It knows we're here." She focused her concentration, trying to touch whatever it was with her esp, but it stayed obstinately just at the edge of her awareness.

"Can you at least give us a direction?" said Ripper quietly.

Diana indicated the area off to her right with a quick movement of her chin, and they all strained their eyes against the curling mists. It was cold and quiet, and nothing moved.

"There's nothing there," said Stasiak, lowering his gun. "Not a damned thing. You're just nervous, esper. Jumping at shadows."

"It's there," Diana insisted. "I can feel it."

"Well, whatever it is, I think we'd be safer on the move," said Ripper. "Lew, you lead the way. I'll watch the rear. Esper, you stay between us, and if you see it again, try and let us know without alerting it. Don't worry, we won't let anything happen to you. Now let's move, shall we? Nice and easy . . ."

They set off again, and Diana strode jerkily along, looking left and right, her back crawling. Something was watching her, and she could feel its menace like a sharp taste in her mouth. Her hands clenched into fists at her sides, and she almost wished she had taken a disrupter for herself after all. The thought shocked her calm again, like a faceful of cold water. She was an esper, not a killer. Whatever it was out there, she should be concentrating on making contact with it. Except there was no other living thing on this planet. The sensors said so. But the sensors hadn't reacted to what attacked her on the way down, and they'd been real enough. She'd felt them in her mind as they moved inexorably in to crush the fragile pinnace, only to draw back when they sensed her presence. Her presence. *Because they knew you were innocent*, the Captain had said. The word *innocent* rang in her mind like a bell.

There was a loud crashing sound to her left, as something large forced its way between two trees, snapping off the solid metal branches. Ripper signalled urgently for them to keep moving. Diana looked at Stasiak.

"Still think I'm seeing things?"

He growled something under his breath, swinging his gun back and forth as he searched for a target. There was the sound of heavy footsteps, to their left and to their right, and the ground shook under their feet. Diana's breath caught in her throat as she realised the sounds were coming from two different directions now. She began to increase her pace, and the marines moved with her, until suddenly all three of them were running. The heavy footsteps kept up with them effortlessly, the ground shaking under their weight like an earthquake. Diana could feel panic welling up inside her, and clamped down on it hard. Whatever was out there, it was gaining on them. She could feel herself slowing as her wind ran out, and forced herself on. And then they burst out of the trees and into a clearing, and as suddenly as that, the pursuing footsteps were gone. The three of them stumbled to a halt, looking back into the trees, but the mists were empty and still, the only sound on the quiet their own harsh breathing.

"What happened?" Stasiak asked breathlessly. "Did we lose them?"

"I don't think so," said Diana.

"Then what did happen?" said Ripper.

Diana shrugged. "They're not ready to kill us yet, that's all. They want us to suffer first."

"They?" said Ripper, "Diana, who are they?"

The esper looked away from the trees and turned her gaze on the two marines. "They're the Ashrai. Or what's left of them. Angry ghosts haunting the forest that used to be theirs."

She began to breathe more easily again, and nodded for the two marines to continue. They glared at the trees around them, hefted their guns uncertainly, and then started across the open clearing. Diana moved with them, her esp wide open, but she couldn't detect any other presences in the surrounding forest. All three of them tensed as they left the clearing and plunged back into the trees, but nothing happened. They stayed alert and cautious all the rest of the way, but the forest remained empty and silent, like a huge abandoned graveyard. And finally they arrived at their destination, with nothing to show for their trip but a few jangled nerves. They stopped at the top of a rise and looked down at what they'd come to see, and for a long time none of them could say anything.

The crashed alien ship lay at the bottom of the rise, huge and dark like a thundercloud fallen to earth. It was hundreds of feet long, an insane tangle of brass columns, held together by glazed nodes each bigger than the entire

pinnace. Spiked and barbed projections emerged from the
main bulk at irregular intervals, but whether they were
sensors or weapons or something else entirely wasn't clear.
The ship lay half-buried at the end of a mile-long scorch
mark, with a long trail of jagged tree stumps to mark its
passing. Diana tried to imagine how fast the ship had to
have been travelling when it hit, to have caused such devastation, but it was just too much for her to visualize. The
one thing she was sure of was that the pinnace wouldn't
have survived such a landing. She looked round sharply
as someone called her name, and then she hurried down
to join the Investigator, who was waiting by the ship. The
marines followed her down at a more leasurely pace, just
to remind the Investigator that they weren't that impressed
by her.

   The ship loomed over Diana like a mountain crag, its dull
brass surfaces seeming to absorb the light rather than reflect
it. The Investigator ignored it casually, as though she'd seen
better in her time. *Probably has,* thought Diana.

   "You took longer than I expected," said Frost. "Trouble
along the way?"

   "Not really," said Ripper easily. "We thought we heard
something moving in the mists, but nothing came of it."

   Frost nodded, apparently unconcerned. "You marines will
stand watch while the esper and I check out the ship. Nothing
is to approach this vessel without being challenged and
identified first. But don't just blast anything that moves.
Remember, the Captain's still out there somewhere. Esper,
follow me."

   She turned and walked away, and Diana hurried after
her. The alien ship fascinated her. Its shape made no
sense at all, and trying to follow the ins and outs of
its insane structure made her head ache. The twisting brass columns ranged from two to twenty feet in
diameter, wrapped around each other as often as not.

"It is an unknown, isn't it, Investigator?" she burst out finally, unable to keep quiet any longer. "It's a totally new alien species! I've never seen anything like it."

"Neither have I," said Frost calmly. "Run a full scan on it for me."

Diana flushed. She shouldn't have needed an order to do something that basic. She raised her esp and let it flow out over the ship. The huge structure burned in her mind like a guttering candle, and she grimaced despite herself. She couldn't seem to get a hold on anything; her mind skidded off the ship as though it was greased. She concentrated, trying to focus, but the ship was so different, so . . . alien, her mind simply couldn't grasp it. There was something deeply disturbing about the vessel, with all its crazy angles and weird surfaces, things that shouldn't hold together but somehow did, and above it all . . . something else. Something so large, so enormous, she couldn't see it for the details. She pulled back, trying to grasp the structure as a whole, and when the truth finally hit her, she couldn't get her breath for a moment.

Frost studied the esper as she stood before the ship, her eyes moving restlessly behind her closed eyelids. Diana's breathing was quick and shallow, and there was a sheen of sweat on her face despite the cold. And then the esper's eyes shot open, and she fell back a step, her hands lifting as though to defend herself from something close at hand. She looked away from the ship, shuddered briefly, and then had herself back under control again. Frost frowned. Whatever the esper had encountered, it was apparently unpleasant enough to knock all the enthusiasm for the ship right out of her.

"Well?" said Frost finally. "What did you see, esper?"

"I'm not sure," said Diana quietly. "The ship is so alien I can't be sure of anything."

"Did you detect any life signs within the ship?"

"Just one." Diana looked at the Investigator for the first time. "I think it's the ship itself. And it's dying."

Frost looked at the unhappy esper for a moment, and then nodded and turned away. She studied the vast ship towering over her, and walked slowly along beside it. Diana hurried after her, not wanting to be left alone, even for a moment.

Up on the rise, Stasiak looked at Ripper. "Do you get the feeling we're ever so slightly superfluous here?"

Ripper shrugged. "There's always the chance those ghosts will show up to annoy us again."

"Oh, great. What are we supposed to do, exorcise them? I'm getting really fed up with this mission, Rip. Nothing to hit, nothing to shoot at, and I think my suit's heating elements are on the blink again."

"Look on the bright side," said Ripper. "At least it's not raining."

Stasiak just looked at him.

Frost stood before the huge alien ship, and let her hand rest on the butt of her gun. If she didn't find an entrance soon, she'd make one the hard way. She didn't like resorting to brute force so early in an investigation, but this whole mission had been a debacle right from the beginning. Standard procedure with any new species was to study the situation from a safe distance, and only make contact when you were sure you held the upper hand. But here she was, thrown in the deep end and sinking fast, with the Captain off on his own somewhere looking for ghosts, and no backup available from the main ship if things got out of hand. Frost sighed, and shook her head. Some days you just shouldn't get out of bed.

She scowled at the ship, and reached out to gently touch the dully gleaming metal with her fingertips. It was surprisingly warm to the touch, with an unpleasant, oily feel.

"Investigator!"

Frost looked away from the hull, absently rubbing her fingers together. "What is it, esper?"

"I've found something. It could be a hatchway."

Frost looked back and winced inwardly as she saw that the esper had climbed up onto a metal turret and was squatting precariously before a shadowy niche. Frost pondered briefly if there was any point in raising the subject of security systems and booby traps, and decided not to waste her breath. With the esper's luck, they'd probably just malfunction anyway. She climbed carefully up to join Diana, her hands and feet slipping on the slick metal, and looked at what the esper had found. Tucked away behind a metal outcropping was a dark gap, some ten feet tall and three feet wide.

"It's not an airlock," said the esper excitedly. "But the shape's too regular for it to be crash damage. Do we go in?"

Frost frowned. "Normally, I'd say no. We don't know enough about the ship to tell what's dangerous and what isn't. But, since we're pressed for time and we need answers now, yes, esper, we are going in. Or rather, I'm going in and you're coming along to watch my back. Stay close, but don't get in my way. Odin, this is Investigator Frost. Respond."

They waited for a moment but there was no reply, not even static from their comm implants. Frost gestured for Diana to try her comm unit, but she did no better.

"Damn," said Frost dispassionately. "Something in the ship must be interfering with our transmissions. This mission just gets better all the time. Follow me, esper."

Frost drew her disrupter and stepped cautiously through the opening. Diana followed her in, practically treading on the Investigator's heels. Beyond the opening lay a narrow tunnel choked with thick strands of filmy webbing, some of which was already falling apart in shreds and tatters. The ceiling was too low for the esper and the Investigator to walk upright, and they were forced to proceed in a hunched, awkward shuffle. A flickering blue light emanated from the corridor walls, hiding as much in shadows as it revealed. The air was definitely warmer inside the ship, and Diana wrinkled her nose at the growing, sickly sweet odor. It reminded her of something, but she couldn't place it. She tried instead to concentrate on what the corridor was telling her about the ship's inhabitants. To start with, they were definitely shorter than humans, probably about four feet or less in height. The blue lights suggested eyes that functioned in roughly the same range as a human's, and the warmer air suggested a need for temperature controls. Beyond that, Diana was pretty much out of her depth, and she knew it.

Frost holstered her gun, drew her sword, and methodically began to cut a path through the decaying webbing. The strands gave way easily enough, but there was little room to swing the great sword in the confines of the corridor and the Investigator's progress was slowed by a need to stop every now and again to clean away threads clinging stubbornly to the blade. The light grew steadily brighter as they slowly made their way deeper into the ship, but the flickering grew worse. Diana shrugged. Maybe the light was supposed to flicker.

The smell was definitely worse as they moved forward. The uneven floor rose and fell like a tide, and the walls bowed in and out for no reason Diana could see. Faint silver traces shone along one wall, though whether they were functional or merely decorative was unclear. Certainly the patterns followed no human sense of logic or aesthetics. Openings appeared in the walls, leading off into other corridors, some of which were unlit. Beginning to be a little nervous about how far they'd come, Diana glanced back over her shoulder. The tunnel stretched away into the blue-lit distance, with no sign of the entrance they'd used. She decided she wasn't going to think about that. No doubt Frost knew the way out, and that was all that mattered. In the meantime, there were just too many interesting things to get excited about.

"Isn't this amazing?" she said breathlessly to the Investigator, who had paused yet again to clean her sword.

Frost smiled slightly, but didn't answer. The esper might be wide-eyed with the wonder of it all, but Frost knew better than to let herself get distracted. There'd be time for sightseeing later, when the ship had been thoroughly explored and tested for booby traps, intentional or otherwise. She pressed cautiously on, carefully checking each side passage before they passed it. The ship was eerily quiet, the hush seeming almost to absorb each new sound as it was made. And there was a growing feeling on the air, something clinging, like static. Frost suddenly realised the esper wasn't treading on her heels anymore, and she looked back down the corridor. Diana had come to a halt some way back, and was staring intently at the ceiling above her. Frost padded quietly back to join her.

"What is it, esper? What have you found?"

"I'm not sure," said Diana slowly. "Look at this."

She gestured at part of the ceiling. It was blue and purple and swollen, like a bruise. Frost tested it with the tip of her sword, and the material gave easily under the pressure.

"I finally recognised the smell," said Diana. "It's a lot clearer just here."

Frost looked at her dubiously and took a deep breath, flaring her nostrils. Together with the look of the ceiling, the sickly sweet smell was immediately familiar. "Decay." said Frost. "Rotting meat."

"Yes," said Diana. "Decomposition of what was once living tissue. Parts of the ship have been dead long enough to rot."

Frost hefted her sword, took a firm grip with both hands, and cut savagely at the discolored patch on the ceiling. The blade sank in deep, and the bruised-looking material split open like a wound. Frost jerked her sword back out, and tangled silver threads fell down into the corridor, wrapped around pink ropes of intestines studded with faceted crystals. Diana fell back a step, a look of almost comical surprise on her face. Frost touched a cautious finger to the hanging threads, and they fell apart into a gooey slime that spattered on the floor. The Investigator studied it for a moment, and then wiped her fingers clean on her leggings. She couldn't perform a proper analysis without her equipment, most of which was back on the *Darkwind*. She blinked in surprise as the esper fell suddenly to her knees beside the slime on the floor, and gently parted it with her fingers. Frost knelt down beside her, watching as Diana fished a small faceted crystal out of the goo and held it up before her eyes.

"What is it?" said Frost.

"It's a memory crystal." said Diana. "Pretty much like the ones we use in our computers. Only here the patterns are so strongly impressed I can practically read them with my mind. I could be wrong, but I think this is part of this ship's log." She got to her feet along with the Investigator, still holding the crystal up before her eyes. "The other crystals are either dead or damaged; I'm not getting anything from them. But this one . . . this crystal is important. I can feel it."

Frost nodded slowly, swinging her sword thoughtfully back and forth before her. "Take it back to the pinnace, and let Odin have a crack at it. I want a complete analysis, and access to the crystal's memories, and I want it an hour ago. So you'd better hurry."

Diana looked at her blankly. "You mean, we're leaving? But we've barely scratched the surface here!"

"You're leaving. I'm staying. I think we can be fairly sure there aren't any living crew left on board, or you'd have sensed them by now. So the only answers we're likely to get are from that crystal. Take the marines back with you; the crystal needs their protection more than I do. Well, don't just stand there, esper. What are you waiting for?"

"I can't find my way back out on my own." said Diana in a small voice. "Can you come back with me to show me the way?"

Stasiak looked at Ripper, and then back at Diana. "Leave her here? Are you sure?"

"That's what she said," said Diana. "Do you want to argue with her?"

"Not really, no," said Ripper.

"I don't know, Rip," said Stasiak. "Anything could happen in there."

"Anyone else and I might be worried," said Ripper. "But we're talking about an Investigator, after all. Anything that runs into her has my deepest sympathies. Besides, do you really want to look her in the eye later and tell her you ignored a direct order?"

"Not really, no." Stasiak looked down the slope at the ship below. "What's it like in there, Diana?"

"Fascinating!" Now that she was out of the ship and back in the open again, Diana lost her nervousness and found herself bubbling with excitement, almost ready to rush back into the ship and explore it again. Almost. "I've never seen anything like it; the whole structure's a combination of organic and inorganic materials, lying side by side and functioning together."

"You mean, like a cyborg?" said Stasiak, peering uncertainly at the huge shape below them.

"I suppose so, yes, but on a much greater scale. The whole thing's alive, or at least it used to be. I'd love to spend more time with it, but the Investigator was most insistent we get this memory crystal back to the pinnace. Typical. The moment you find anything interesting, the Empire immediately finds a way to take it away from you."

Stasiak smiled. "If you can't take a joke, you shouldn't have joined."

"I wasn't exactly given a choice," said Diana. "Espers do what they're told."

And then the wry smile vanished from her face as she looked past Stasiak. The two marines spun round to discover what she was looking at, and their hands fell to their guns. Among the violet and azure trees at the edge of the forest a man dressed all in black was walking unhurriedly out of the mists. His face was hidden by his cape's cowl, but they all knew who he was, who he had to be. He walked past without sparing any of them a glance, and started down the slope towards the alien ship. Diana shuddered as he passed, and had to fight down a sudden urge to reach out and touch him, to make sure he was real, even though the sensors said he wasn't. Instead, she watched silently with the marines as the man in black came to a halt before the ship and looked at it thoughtfully, leaning elegantly on his ivory staff.

"Is that him?" said Diana softly. "I thought he'd be taller."

"Not very impressive," said Ripper. "But then, legends rarely are, in the flesh."

"Carrion," said Stasiak, his voice low and harsh. "The man who lived with the Ashrai. The traitor who turned against humanity, for the sake of savages who still ate their meat raw. I've done some things in my time, and been ashamed of some of them, but I never betrayed my own species. Never."

"Take it easy, Lew," said Ripper. "We don't know the whole story."

"We don't need to."

"Why does the Captain think he's so important?" said Diana. "I mean, all right, he can fool the pinnace's sensors, but he's just another outlaw. Isn't he?"

"Carrion's a killer," said Captain Silence. "And he's very good at it."

The esper and the two marines spun round again, to see Silence standing at the edge of the forest behind them, leaning against a tree trunk for support.

"Captain!" said Diana, blushing with embarrassment. "I didn't hear you approach . . . ."

"Obviously," said Silence. "Security on this mission is going to hell." He broke off, grimacing as pain from his injured ribs hit him. Diana took in his torn and blood-stained uniform and started towards him, but he stopped her with an upraised hand. "I'm all right. I just ran into a little opposition from the local ghosts. Carrion rescued me. And no, I don't want to talk about it. Odin told me about the Investigator's discovery, and I brought Carrion along to take a look at it. How long have you been here?"

"Not long," said Diana. "The Investigator and I made a brief foray into the ship, but there's no sign of any crew. We did find what appears to be an alien memory crystal. The Investigator decided it should go back to the pinnace for analysis. She's still inside the ship."

"I thought she might be," said Silence. "Carrion's going to join her. Between them, they should come up with some answers."

"Pardon me for asking, Captain," said Stasiak, "but what makes the traitor so important?"

"Carrion used to be an Investigator," said Silence. "One of the best. Trained to outthink species that don't think as we do."

"If he was that good," said Ripper, "what went wrong? How did he end up siding with the Ashrai?"

Silence smiled humourlessly. "Perhaps we trained him too well."

He looked down at the alien ship below, and the others followed his gaze. Carrion had climbed up onto the ship and was examining the entrance Diana had found. His black cloak hung about him like folded wings, and he looked more than ever like a carrion crow, feasting on a dead carcass.

"What's that staff he's carrying?" said Stasiak.

"A power lance," said Silence.

"But they're outlawed!"

Silence smiled briefly. "So's he."

Carrion threaded his way through the twisting corridors of the alien ship, following the ragged path Frost had cut through the webbing. It led him eventually to a vast circular chamber deep in the heart of the ship, a great metal cavern studded with bulky, enigmatic machinery on all sides. The curving walls were pockmarked with tunnel mouths of various sizes, many high above the floor with no obvious way of reaching them. Thick strands of rotting gossamer hung from the ceiling, interspersed with long crystalline creepers that gleamed and sparkled in the unsteady light as they turned slowly back and forth. The flickering light came from deep in the tunnels, casting strange, elongated shadows on the floor and ceiling. The air was hot and humid and thick with the stench of rotting meat. Frost stepped out of the shadows and into the light, and Carrion nodded to her courteously.

"I know you," said Frost.

"No," said Carrion. "That was someone else. I am Carrion. I bring bad luck. I am the destroyer of nations and of worlds."

Frost raised an eyebrow. "Really?"

"The Ashrai believed it."

They studied each other for a while in the uncertain light, and whatever they recognised in each other's faces they kept to themselves.

"I'm surprised you remember me," said Carrion finally. "It's been a long time."

"All Investigators remember you," said Frost. "The Academy still holds you up as a bad example. You broke the prime rule; you got involved."

"I broke my conditioning," said Carrion. "But then, I was always involved, with one species or another. When you've spent half your life learning to move your mind in alien ways, it becomes hard to think in wholly human terms anymore."

Frost shrugged. "Empathy's a useful tool, but that's all. Aliens are for killing. I've found something interesting. Come and take a look."

She led him into a small compartment off the main chamber, through an opening so low they had to crawl through on hands and knees. The compartment was filled with spiky crystalline machinery that flowed seamlessly into the walls and floor. The ceiling was just high enough to let them stand upright, and suffused everything with a dull red glow that was disturbingly organic. The floor was uneven, solid ridges rising like bones to press against their boots in undulating rhythms. Everywhere, high-tech instruments blended into organic constructs, living and unliving components functioning side by side, as though the ship had been grown as much as made.

"This appears to be the control centre," said Frost. "Or one of them, anyway. I've traced a whole series of power lines that converge here, but I can't be sure until I can get some of my equipment down from the *Darkwind*."

"Have you identified the main power source?"

Frost shook her head angrily. "I can't even find the hyperdrive. By any reasonable standards this thing shouldn't even fly, let alone jump across the stars."

Carrion nodded, his eyes vague and far away. "Perhaps I can find the drive for you."

A breeze from nowhere ruffled his cloak, and Frost's hackles rose as strange lights glowed suddenly in the instruments around them. There was a feeling of pressure on the air, of something imminent and unstoppable. A hatch shot open in the wall beside her, and slammed shut again like metal jaws. Instruments extended and reshaped themselves in subtle ways, and far off in the distance Frost thought she could hear something howling in anger and agony, as though the decaying ship had been somehow stirred to horrid life again. Carrion was smiling, and it was not a pleasant smile, his dark eyes fixed on something only he could see. Frost's hand drifted casually closer to the holstered gun at her side. At that moment, the outlaw seemed every bit as alien and as dangerous as the ship they were investigating. A loud juddering sound vibrated through the floor, rattling their teeth and shaking their heads, and then the floor opened up in the centre and a great tower of steel and diamond rose up into the chamber, shining so brightly they had to turn their heads away. Deep in the tunnels the howling died away, and a sudden silence filled the chamber as the alien machinery grew still. Carrion and Frost slowly turned back to look at the tower, shielding their eyes with their arms.

"I didn't know you were a polter," said Frost.

"I would have thought it'd be in my file."

"Your file's Restricted."

"It would be," said Carrion.

They peered more closely at the structure before them, as their eyes adjusted to the glare. The tower was an intricate latticework of metals, complex and mysterious, surrounding a brilliant cluster of glowing crystals. There was meaning and purpose in its structure, but none of it human.

"What is it?" whispered Frost, impressed despite herself.

Carrion smiled slowly. "Judging by the remaining power flow, this is the ship's hyperdrive. Even if it does look nothing like ours. The Empire uses crystal technology in its computers; apparently these aliens found other uses for it."

✢

CHAPTER SIX

Inside Base Thirteen

DIANA sat slumped in her seat in the pinnace, and wondered why she still didn't feel safe. It had come on her suddenly, as they were walking back through the metallic forest to the landing field. Without any specific cause that she could name, the esper had suddenly been convinced that they were being watched, by something huge and awful and dangerous. Her stomach lurched, and sweat sprang out on her face. She managed to keep from crying out, but the feeling of imminent danger persisted, even though she couldn't see or hear anything to justify it. Nothing moved in the mists among the trees, and the only sounds were the quiet voices and footsteps of the people with her. Diana raised her esp and threw it out, scanning for anything near or approaching the group. Nothing had changed. The trees blazed in her mind like exclamation points of light, but there was no trace of any other living thing in the forest. She cast her net wider, till her mind fell over Base Thirteen and she saw something looking back at her.

It was huge and dark, filling the Base, and it looked at her with hungry eyes. There were voices screaming in the background, human voices, full of anguish and horror. There was a blood-red feeling of menace, of danger close and deadly, and then it was all gone, as suddenly as if she'd imagined it. She focused her esp on the Base, but there was nothing there now. If there ever had been.

She hadn't told the others what she'd sensed. She had no proof, and it had all happened so fast she wasn't sure she trusted it herself. It had the hot, hazy feeling of a fever dream, its very vagueness part of what was so horrifying. So she stayed silent, all the way back to the pinnace, and once she was aboard she curled up in her seat like a dog in its box, and tried to put it out of her mind. Only that was somehow worse, so she instructed the AI to patch in an exterior view through her comm implant. The steel bulkheads seemed to become transparent as the computer broadcast a real-time view of what its sensors were picking up. There was nothing but the landing pads and the trees and the curling mists, the two marines standing guard, and the Base, waiting inside its impenetrable force screen. She should have felt safe and secure, protected by the pinnace and its weaponry, but somehow she only felt more visible, more vulnerable. The pinnace was the only ship on the pads, and seemed to her a conspicuous target, small and defenceless against the size of the landing field and the endless forest that surrounded it. She kept a careful watch in every direction, unable to settle but unwilling to raise her esp again for fear of drawing the watcher's attention back to her.

The more she put off telling anyone, the more it seemed to her nothing but an attack of nerves, a product of her own fear and insecurity. She tried to recapture some of the enthusiasm she'd felt about contacting the new alien species from the crashed ship, and that helped her push back the fear a little. It was just nerves, exacerbated by the waiting and the tension. She'd be all right, when the time came to finally enter the Base. But in the meantime she kept her eyes open and her mind damped down, just in case.

The marines had felt something of it too. They'd been jumpy all the way back to the pinnace, and had seemed almost relieved when Silence ordered them to stand guard outside the ship. Silence, on the other hand, seemed strangely calm and relaxed, despite the beating he'd taken on his way to meet Carrion. He still wouldn't talk about that. He sat stoically as the ship's med unit stuck him with half-a-dozen needles, and then adjusted his uniform so that it provided more support for his ribs. And now he sat comfortably in his seat, half-reclining, talking calmly with the AI about the memory crystal Diana had found in the alien ship. Odin had swallowed the crystal some time back, but apparently the AI was having to create a whole new series of diagnostics just to access the damned thing. Diana smiled briefly. If she'd known it was going to be this much trouble, she'd have used her esp on the crystal and accessed the memories directly. Only that would have meant raising her esp again, and she wasn't ready to do that, not just yet.

Silence scowled at the comm panels before him. Given time, the AI should be able to make the crystal do everything but sit up and beg, but they didn't have that much time. The Empire wanted the mining machinery working again, and it wanted it now. If the Captain couldn't deliver, they'd send someone to replace him. And that really would be the end of his career. Silence sighed, and winced at the discomfort in his ribs. The alien ship held the answer to what had happened in Base Thirteen, he was sure of it. One or more of the aliens had entered the Base, there'd been a conflict of some kind, and the force screen had gone up. Simple as that. But just in case it wasn't, he wanted the information in the alien memory crystal before he tried to break into the Base. Going into a potentially dangerous situation without a thorough briefing was never wise, and that went double here; with ghosts on the one hand and strange new aliens on the other, this had all the makings of a really messy disaster.

"Captain," said a quiet voice behind him, "I need to talk to you."

"Not just now, esper, I'm busy."

"You're supposed to be resting."

"I'll rest later, when I've got time. I'm just waiting for Carrion and Frost to return, and then we're going into Base Thirteen to scare up some answers."

"Captain . . . if there are aliens inside the Base, we shouldn't be going in aggressively, looking for trouble. We should at least try to make contact with them. They could be peaceful. This could all be the result of some ghastly mistake or misunderstanding."

Silence turned round in his seat and looked patiently at the young esper. "This is all new to you, Diana, but the Empire has a set procedure when it comes to handling first contacts. And the first and main part of that procedure calls for the Investigator to decide how we handle it. She's the expert."

"An expert at killing."

"Yes. The Empire doesn't like the idea of competition, so its attitude toward aliens is really quite straightforward. They're either friendly, in which case they become part of the Empire, whether they want to or not, or they're unfriendly, in which case they get stepped on. Hard."

"Like the Ashrai?" said Diana.

"Yes, esper. Like the Ashrai. I knew where my responsibilities lay, even then. Look, if I can see a way to sort this out without bloodshed, I'll take it. I don't believe in putting my people at risk unnecessarily. But I can't be optimistic about this. The most likely scenario is that one or more of the aliens have entered the Base and killed all the personnel."

"You can't know that."

"That's right, I can't. But that's how I have to play it. If whatever is in there is willing to talk, I'll listen, but they've made no move to contact us so far. Have you been able to pick up anything?"

"Just . . . impressions. Nothing I can be sure of. Because of my own fears, I could be misinterpreting the little I am getting. Couldn't we at least wait till the AI's cracked the memory crystal? It could hold all the answers we need."

"Esper, I'm running out of time and patience. I'll wait for Carrion and Frost to get back here, but then we have to go, ready or not."

The esper's jaw muscles worked for a moment, but when she spoke, her voice was calm and measured. "I'd like to try something, Captain. I want permission to go into the Base on my own, once you've got us through the screen, and attempt to make contact with my esp. They might not see one person as a threat."

"My orders are quite specific," Silence replied. "I'm to discover what happened inside Base Thirteen, and take whatever action is necessary to re-establish the Base and restore mining operations. Everything else is of secondary importance. There were one hundred and twenty-seven men and women in that Base. We've heard nothing from them since the screen went up. The odds are they're all dead. If they are, then whatever killed them has to die. The Empire can't afford to be seen as weak."

"Please, Captain. Listen to me—" Diana hesitated, torn between her need to explain what she was feeling, and the knowledge that she couldn't prove any of it. "There's more to this than whatever came out of the crashed ship. I've felt things, on my way down in the pinnace, and later on . . . there's something incredibly powerful on this planet, Captain, and I don't think it's the aliens."

"You're right." said Silence. "It's the Ashrai."

Diana chose her words carefully. "But they're all dead, Captain. You saw to that."

"They may be dead," said Silence, "but they sleep lightly."

"I could still use my esp to contact the aliens," said Diana doggedly.

"No," said Silence. "The situation's complicated enough as it is."

"So you'll leave it to the Investigator? The killer?"

"You say that as though it's an insult. She'd see it as a compliment. Investigators are the end result of the Empire's search for the perfect warrior. They started out working with the augmented men, the Wampyr and the Wolflings. That got out of hand with Haden, and the cyborg rebellion. So instead they created a breed of warrior that wasn't reliant on tech implants; a race of killers trained from childhood to be the best at everything. Strong, fast, intelligent, ruthless. And trained, most of all, to outthink beings that don't think as we do. Frost is in charge of all alien contacts, and she will make whatever decisions are necessary. She's the expert. If you have anything further to say, take it up with her."

"Would she listen to me?"

"I don't know. Maybe. She understands the value of an esper."

"Perhaps I should talk to Carrion. He used to be an Investigator too, didn't he?"

"Yes," said Silence. "Yes, he was, once."

Diana could feel his pain even with her shields up, and she had to look away for a moment. Through the transparent bulkhead she saw Carrion and Frost walk out of the mists and head towards the two marines, who apparently hadn't heard them coming and were a bit upset about it. Silence followed her gaze, saw Carrion, and looked away.

"You knew Carrion from before," said Diana. "What was he like, before he was a traitor?"

"He was my friend," said Silence, and then he turned and left the cabin. Diana stood where she was for a moment, to give him some distance, and then she followed him out.

• • •

Outside the pinnace, everyone stood and looked at everyone else as though they were all waiting for someone else to start. Finally Silence nodded curtly to Carrion and Frost. They were standing close together, and they stood in the same pose and moved in the same ways, like brother and sister. As though they had more in common with each other than they could ever have with anyone else. Silence knew he'd have to keep an eye on that. He couldn't risk losing Frost the way he'd lost Carrion.

"Any trace of the alien crew?" he asked the pair.

"None," said Frost. "And their ship's dead. It's an interesting ship. The technology's like nothing I've ever seen before."

Silence looked at Carrion. "Could the crew have fled into the forest?"

"No, Captain. I'd have known."

"And that just leaves the Base," said Ripper. "Surprise, surprise."

"Tell me about the ship's technology," said Silence. "You said something earlier about a new kind of hyperdrive."

"There was extensive use of living tissue alongside mechanical," said Frost. "Essentially, the ship was one great cybernetic unit, incredibly complex. And if the hyperdrive is what we think it is, it's far beyond anything the Empire has."

There was a tense pause, as though they all had something to say but no one wanted to be the first to say it. There were certain things it was wise never to say aloud, particularly when an Empire AI was listening. Their loyalty was programmed into them, and they tended to have very strict ideas about what constituted treason, or a threat to the Empire's security. Silence looked thoughtfully at Carrion.

"The aliens must be inside the Base."

"Agreed, Captain."

"And you're going to get us through the force screen."

"No, Captain."

Silence stared at him, and the tension between the two men all but crackled on the air. The two marines moved their hands slightly so that they were both covering the traitor with their guns.

"I can break through the screen," said Carrion, "but you're in no condition to enter the Base."

"I'd have to agree," said Frost. "A Captain has no business exposing himself to unnecessary risks. That's standard procedure."

"There's nothing standard about this mission," said Silence tightly. "I'm in charge here, and I'll make whatever decisions have to be made. To do that I need to be there, on the spot, as and when conditions change. And I've a feeling they could change pretty damned fast once we get inside the Base. I'm fit enough, and that's all that matters. I'm sure the marines are more than capable of seeing that nothing happens to me."

"Right," growled Stasiak, looking pointedly at Carrion. The outlaw ignored him. He looked over at Base Thirteen, hidden behind its shimmering opalescent screen, and if there was any expression in his face, none of them could read it.

"Let's go," he said calmly. "The sooner we begin, the sooner we'll be finished. And God have mercy on those who die here."

He started off towards the Base, and after a moment, Silence and Frost followed him. The others brought up the rear. Stasiak looked at Ripper.

"Cheerful bastard, isn't he?"

"What did you expect?" said Ripper. "He used to be an Investigator."

They stood together before Base Thirteen, and the glowing pearly screen stared back at them, mute and enigmatic.

Silence studied it sourly. It was as though the screen were mocking him. Anything could be happening behind that impenetrable field of energy. Anything at all. Anyone else would have had to suffer its smug indifference, but he had an ace up his sleeve. He had Carrion. Silence looked at the outlaw. He was still standing beside Frost, so close their shoulders touched. They looked as though they should always be together, connected by a shared past and secrets too terrible to reveal to anyone else. Silence felt oddly jealous. Carrion used to be his friend. But that was years ago, when they were different people, and Silence was honest enough to admit that he would only have felt uncomfortable if Carrion had chosen to stand with him.

The marines were standing off a little to one side, their guns in their hands, keeping an unobtrusive eye on Carrion. To their way of thinking, he was the biggest threat to the party at this point, so they'd watch him till something better came along. Marines were great ones for sticking to the problem at hand, and letting officers worry about the future. The esper was ignoring them all and scowling at the screen, as though she could force her esp past it to see what lay beyond. Unfortunately, she wasn't that powerful. That was why Silence needed Carrion.

He looked at the outlaw, and sighed quietly to himself. He couldn't put it off any longer. It was time for the moment of truth, and let the chips fall where they may. He activated his comm implant.

"Odin, you are now in control of the pinnace. You will follow our entry into the Base through our eyes, and keep a complete record of all that occurs. If we fail in our mission, and none of us survive, you will make every effort to return to the *Darkwind*, and see that the record is made available to our successors. Acknowledge."

"Acknowledged, Captain. Good luck."

Silence looked at Carrion. "It's time. Do your stuff."

The outlaw nodded, his gaze fixed on the force screen. He stepped forward and reached out a hand to touch the energy field. Fat sparks of static sputtered on the air, but there was no other response. Which was interesting. It should have killed him stone-dead. It would have killed anyone else. Carrion pressed hard against the screen, but it didn't give. He smiled slightly, as though he'd expected that, and stepped back. He lifted his power lance and pressed the end of it against the energy field. A faint corona circled the end of the staff where it touched the screen. Carrion increased the pressure, and the screen gave way before it. Carrion took hold of the staff with both hands, and walked slowly forward into the energy field. The force field whorled and rippled around him, bands of iridescent light breaking over him in waves. He stood deep in the field, and the screen that could ward off disrupters and withstand atomics drew reluctantly back from the outlaw's presence. An opening grew around him, through which the dark, squat shape of Base Thirteen could be seen. Carrion looked back at the others, and there was something not entirely human in his eyes.

"Now," said Carrion, and they all stepped forward as though he had them on a leash. Silence kept his head up, but his skin crawled in anticipation of the lethal energies running through the force screen, held back only by the power of one man's mind. By someone perhaps no longer entirely human. Finally they were all through, and Carrion remained in the field. He looked unhurriedly about him, colors waterfalling down around him in vivid shades that burned the eye. And then he stepped forward, and the energy field closed behind him as though it had never opened. No one could get out, and no one could get in to help, without Carrion's assistance. They were trapped with whatever lay inside Base Thirteen, and the force screen covered them all.

"How did you do that?" asked Diana, her voice softened by something that might have been awe.

"His power lance," said Frost, when it became clear the outlaw wasn't going to answer. "It amplifies and channels his psychokinesis. You can guess why the Empire banned them. But even with a power lance, what he just did is supposed to be impossible. His esper abilities must be right off the scale. I'm surprised the Empire ever let him run around loose."

"Before he came to Unseeli," said Silence, "he showed no sign of any esp at all. His time with the Ashrai changed that."

"That's impossible," said Frost flatly. "Everyone's tested for psi; no one escapes."

"Nothing's impossible, for the Ashrai," said Carrion.

"Your attention, please," said Odin, his voice murmuring through everyone's implants. "Captain, I've finally been able to glean something useful from the Base computers' records. I've managed to isolate the Base Commander's personal log. I really think you should view what I've found, before you proceed any further."

"All right," said Silence. "Since nothing nasty has come running out of the Base to attack us, I think we can safely wait a few more moments before we go in. Marines, stand guard. If anything moves, shoot it. Odin, run the relevant parts of the log for everyone except the marines, then run it for them. How much is there?"

"Not much, Captain. I've selected what appear to be the important moments."

A wavering zigzag pattern met Silence's eyes as the AI ran the log through his comm implant. The image cleared to show the Base Commander sitting at his desk. Silence frowned. He knew the man. James Starblood had been at the Fleet Academy in the same year as he. Old Family. Not much money, but well connected. They'd known each other well for a short time but had never really been friends. Starblood had been a hard-working, efficient officer, and about as imaginative as a stone. Which probably explained

what he was doing in a post like this. Unseeli was not a
posting for the upwardly mobile. Silence's frown deepened.
The Commander looked haggard and confused, and when
he finally spoke, his voice was rough and unsteady.

"To whoever finds this log, this is an Alpha Red emergency. An alien ship has crash-landed nearby. It doesn't
answer any of our attempts to make contact. I sent a team
to investigate the crash site. They never came back. That
was three hours ago. Now people are disappearing inside the
Base. Something's affecting the computers. Whole sectors
don't answer. The life-support systems are breaking down.
The lights are going out. It's getting cold. There's something
in here with us but we can't find it."

The scene changed. Starblood was sitting slumped in his
chair. He was sweating, and his uniform was dishevelled.
He passed a shaking hand across his mouth, and tried
visibly to pull himself together. "I can't raise anyone in
the Base, and something's happened to our main comm
system. I can't contact the Empire, or even broadcast a
warning. My personal log seems secure, for the moment.
I've locked myself in my quarters and barricaded the door. I
can hear something moving in the corridor outside. It doesn't
sound human. I'm trapped in here. Base Thirteen is lost to
the Empire. There's only one option left to me: raising the
force screen."

He reached out of view for a moment, and then looked up
again, his eyes seeming to pierce Silence. There was despair
in the man's face, but something else too. Something that
might have been dignity. "The force screen is now activated.
Whatever's in here is trapped inside the Base. I can't risk
letting it escape. The Empire must know of this new threat.
The screen can only be lowered from inside now, using my
personal code. I know my duty." He drew a disrupter from
the holster on his hip, and clumsily checked the power
level. "Haven't had to use one of these things in years,"

he grumbled quietly, and then turned the gun on himself, centering it carefully over his heart. He looked up one last time.

"Whoever finds this message, avenge us. Protect the Empire. I am James Starblood, Commander of Base Thirteen."

Silence's vision cleared to show the world again. He wished he'd liked the man more.

"That's all there is, Captain," said Odin quietly.

"A hundred and twenty-seven people," said Diana. "All dead."

"You didn't really expect anything else, did you?" said Frost. Diana shrugged and looked away. There was a pause as the marines watched the message.

"Well, that was interesting," said Stasiak brightly. "We're facing something powerful enough to wipe out a whole Base, and all we've got are a few handguns and an outlaw esper. Why don't we all just shoot ourselves now, and get it over with?"

"He's got a point," said Ripper.

"Shut up," said Frost calmly, and the two marines were immediately quiet. "You've nothing to worry about. You've got me." She looked at Silence. "You're in charge, Captain. What do we do?"

"We go in," said Silence. "And we do whatever's necessary."

He walked towards the entrance, with Carrion and Frost following close behind. The esper hurried to catch up. The marines shared a meaningful glance, and reluctantly brought up the rear. The Base itself looked calm and deserted. No lights were showing anywhere. The front doors were standing just a little ajar. Silence stopped before them and studied the steel doors carefully. There was a thick layering of hoarfrost on the metal, and the doors hung limply from their supports. Carrion reached out and pushed one door, and it moved uneasily under his touch, all power gone. He pushed it all the way open, and he and Silence stepped forward into the gloomy of the lobby.

Unseeli's cold had entered the Base, giving the stale air a cutting edge. None of the lights were working, and as far as Silence could see, the lobby was entirely deserted. Carrion and Frost moved quickly in to stand on either side of him, eyes searching the shadows for an ambush. All was still and quiet, the only sound their own breathing. Frost sniffed suspiciously, her gun in her hand as though it belonged there. Carrion leaned elegantly on his power lance, apparently happy for Silence to take the initiative. The esper darted through the front doors with the marines close behind. Silence gestured for the two marines to spread out, and they did so quickly and professionally. The esper looked round the empty lobby and hugged herself, possibly from the cold.

The Reception desk was unmanned, its Security monitor screens blank. Papers lay scattered across the desk, covered with a thin layer of frost. Silence gestured for the two marines to check the desk, and they moved forward, guns at the ready. Investigator Frost looked unhurriedly about her, trying to get the feel of the place. There was no sign of any panic or fight. Everything seemed to be still in its place. At the desk, Stasiak studied the scattered papers without touching them. They were all routine, everyday stuff, and Stasiak thought there was something sad in that. The people who worked here got no warning, no chance to prepare themselves. They probably thought it was just another day, until the boom fell, and the lights started going out. He looked at Ripper, who was trying to get the Security monitors back on line, with no success. He straightened up with a sigh, looked at Silence, and shook his head.

"Not a thing, Captain. There's power in the system somewhere, but it's not reaching Reception. I think it's being diverted somewhere else, but don't ask me where."

"Not a damn thing to go on," said Stasiak. "It's as though everyone just . . . got up and left. Spooky."

"Look around; see if you can turn up some lamps or torches," said Silence. "We're not going to get far without some light. Investigator, try the comm net. Maybe we can raise someone now that we're actually inside the Base."

Frost nodded, and activated her comm implant. "This is Investigator Frosts of the *Darkwind*. Please respond."

They all listened, but there was only the low hum of an open channel.

"Can anybody hear me? This is Investigator Frost. I speak for the Empire. Respond, please."

She frowned suddenly as a voice murmured in her ear, so soft and faint the words were indecipherable. Frost looked quickly at the others, but though they'd all heard it too, none of them could make it out either. Frost boosted the volume as high as it would go, but the voice had stopped.

"I hear you," she said loudly. "Please say again. Where are you? Do you require assistance?"

There was no reply. Frost turned the volume back down, looked at Silence, and shook her head. The Captain turned to Diana.

"Run a full scan, esper. If there's anything alive and thinking in this place, I want to know what and where it is."

Diana turned away so he couldn't see her face. She'd been waiting for him to ask, even volunteered, but she still remembered the horror she'd encountered the last time she raised her esp. She remembered the screaming voices, human voices, and the vast, terrible presence that had looked back at her with knowing, hungry eyes. In all her years, she'd never seen anything that scared her more. And now Silence wanted her to open her mind to it. She couldn't. She just couldn't. But she couldn't refuse, either. She closed her eyes and opened her esp just a fraction, like a child peering warily between raised fingers. Everything was still and quiet. She probed a little further, letting her mind drift cautiously out across the ground floor, but there was nothing there. She sighed inwardly with relief, and looked at Silence again.

"No trace of life anywhere, Captain. There's always the chance that something's blocking my esp, but if there is, I can't detect it."

She waited breathlessly while he considered her answer, expecting him any moment to glare at her coldly as he saw through her half-truth, but he just nodded and turned away, and she didn't know whether to feel relieved or ashamed. Silence frowned thoughtfully.

"Odin, give me the floor plans for Base Thirteen, on an overlay. One floor at a time, starting with the ground floor. And patch the others in too."

A schematic appeared before him, superimposed on his vision. It seemed fairly straightforward. Only the one entrance to the ground floor, and one elevator and two sets of stairs leading down to the next floors. All Bases were built downward into the earth, for greater security. Everything important or vital was on the bottom floor, Level Three, protected by thick concrete and other, less obvious measures. Silence studied the layout for each floor, checking particularly for entrances and exits, and then had Odin withdraw the overlay.

"All right, people. Pay attention. It looks like we're going to have to do this the hard way. I'm splitting us into two groups, so we can cover more ground. Carrion and Frost, you stay with me. We'll search this floor. Esper, you and the two marines start checking out the next floor down. Take your time and check every room thoroughly before you go on to the next. Don't take any chances, and yell for help if you spot anything that looks even remotely threatening. I want information, not dead heroes. And whatever happens, no one is to go off on their own. Understood?" There was a general murmur of assent and nodding of heads. "All right then, people. Let's make a start. By the book and by the numbers."

The marines sketched a quick salute, turned on one of the emergency lamps Ripper had found tucked away behind the reception desk, and set off towards the rear, to one of the staircases marked on the floor plan. Diana hurried after them, not liking the idea of investigating the next floor down, but liking even less the idea of being left behind and alone.

Frost turned on her lamp. The light was bright and cheerful, though it raised uneasy shadows at the corner of everyone's eyes. Frost offered the lamp to Carrion, but he shook his head courteously. Silence took it from her, and led the two of them off into the gloom of the ground floor.

Corridor by corridor, room by room, they progressed slowly through the floor, but everywhere it was quiet and deserted, with no sign of any struggle or disturbance. Computer panels were unlit, monitor screens were dark, but there was still evidence of the people who'd lived and worked in Base Thirteen. An open message pad, a half-completed form, a cup almost full of coffee. Silence picked up the cup. There was a thick layer of frozen scum on the surface of the coffee. He put the cup down almost angrily. Still no signs of trouble, or even surprise. Whatever happened, it must have been quick. The thought was not comforting. Base Thirteen should have been crawling with Security personnel and backup emergency systems, even if Unseeli was supposed to be a dead world. The Empire didn't believe in taking chances. But somehow the aliens had got into the Base, taken over its systems, and dealt with its personnel, all without being detected or challenged. Which was supposed to be impossible.

"Interesting," said Carrion as they moved down the corridor again.

"What?" said Frost, looking quickly about her.

"Your gun," said Carrion. "I hadn't looked at it before. I don't recognise it."

Frost shrugged. "Standard disrupter. I suppose the style's changed a lot in the past ten years. This version is far superior to the old model."

"Really. What's the recharge time?"

"Got it down to three minutes now."

Carrion raised an eyebrow. "That *is* an improvement, but I see you still carry a sword."

"Of course." Frost grinned. "A sword never needs recharging."

"Your attention, please," said Odin suddenly on their comm implants' command channel. "I have discovered something important, Captain. Apparently Commander Starblood had been concerned about possible intruders in the Base even before the alien ship crashed. There are several references in his log to sightings of 'ghosts,' or some kind of presence, by Base personnel. These sightings became so frequent and so disturbing that Commander Starblood ordered six Security Guardians. There's a record of their delivery, two weeks before the alien ship's arrival."

Silence scowled. "Six Guardians? How the hell did the aliens get past them?"

"What exactly are Guardians?" said Carrion.

"After your time," said Frost. "They're state-of-the-art Security robots. Fast, powerful, efficient, and a really nasty attitude. They were designed originally for riot control. One per riot. And Starblood ordered six. . . . He must have been really scared. Six would have been enough to stand off a small army."

"And if they're still here, and running loose," said Silence, "we're in real trouble."

CHAPTER SEVEN

Guardians

THE marines moved cautiously down the metal stairway, scowling into the gloom below. The guns in their hands swept constantly back and forth, covering every direction an attack could come from. Diana supposed she should find such obvious expertise comforting, but instead it just reminded her of the possible dangers ahead. It almost made her wish she carried a gun of her own. Almost. She was an esper, not a killer. She stuck as close behind the marines as she could without crowding them, holding her lamp high to spread its light as far as possible. Huge shadows moved around them like watching ghosts, but everything else was still and silent.

They'd found the elevator shown on the floor plan, which could have taken them down to the next floor, but none of them had felt like risking it. They had no idea why it was still working when so many other things weren't, and it was only too easy to imagine the elevator breaking down between floors, leaving them trapped in a steel coffin while the air ran out. So they made their way slowly down the stairs, nerves tingling in anticipation of an attack that never came.

It was cold in the stairwell, and getting colder. Hoarfrost made patterns on the walls that teased the eyes with hints of meaning. Their breath steamed on the still air, and the heating elements in their uniforms somehow weren't enough to keep the chill out of their bones. Their footsteps rang loudly on the metal steps, and the sound seemed to echo an unnaturally long time in the hush.

Diana knew she should be using her esp to check ahead, but she couldn't bring herself to do that. Not yet. The scan in the lobby had been hard enough, when she'd feel safe and secure. But now that she'd come down into the heart of the darkness, she was afraid to send her mind out for fear it might not come back. She was afraid there was something down there in the dark with them, and she didn't want to risk waking it again. Sometimes she thought it was an alien, and sometimes she thought it might be ghosts of the dead personnel, but all she really knew for sure was that she was scared. So scared that even the awful forms her imagination conjured up were preferable to encountering the real thing again. It was safer to lie to herself and hide in the dark with the marines.

They finally reached the bottom of the staircase, and stood close together at the foot of the steps. To their right, a thick coating of ice almost covered the sign saying LEVEL TWO. The marines and the esper ignored it, their gaze fixed on what the esper's lamplight revealed before them. The corridor walls bulged and seethed with ugly alien growths, and thick strands of shimmering webbing hung down from the ceiling, twisting and turning slowly as though in response to an unfelt breeze. The metal walls had torn and split apart in many places, multicolored wiring hanging out like plastic viscera, as though the alien forms had somehow grown inside the walls and burst out when they grew too large to be contained. Silvery traces ran along the unbroken areas of wall in long, enigmatic patterns, gleaming brightly in the lamplight like metallic veins. They were pulsing slowly with an alien life. The whole ceiling was covered with dark, wartlike nodes the size of a man's head, surrounded and connected by swirling chalky-white spirals. And thick on the air, was a harsh sweet smell like a disturbed grave.

"What the hell is this?" breathed Stasiak, swinging his gun back and forth, unable to settle on a single target. "The place looks . . . diseased."

"Infested, anyway," said Ripper. "I think we can be sure now that the aliens came here after they left their ship." He glanced at the esper beside him. "This . . . mixture of living and unliving—is this the same kind of thing you found on the alien ship?"

The esper had to swallow hard before she could answer, but when she finally spoke her voice was cool and quite professional. "The same kind of thing, yes. Only the ship was dead, or dying. This looks alive, and functioning. The alien crew must have brought it with them, as some kind of seed, perhaps. But why? Surely they didn't bring about changes as extensive as this just so that they could feel at home? There must be a purpose to it."

"If there is, it's an alien purpose," said Ripper. "Something we might not even recognise, let alone understand. I think we need the Investigator down here to check this out, before we go any further."

"Wait a minute," said Stasiak quickly. "Let's think about this first. We don't need to know what this stuff is. It looks weird and smells worse, but it's not exactly aggressive, is it? We're supposed to be looking for the Base personnel, and we don't need Frost for that. We're marines; we can handle this without an Investigator to hold our hands."

Ripper looked at Stasiak thoughtfully. "This isn't like you, Lew. It's an improvement, but it isn't like you. What are you up to?"

Stasiak grinned. "Odin's recording everything that happens here, remember? And you can bet a lot of higher-ups are going to be studying this record. This is our chance to look good in front of people who matter, and do ourselves a bit of good in the process. Why let Frost steal all the glory? There's money and fame in this; I can smell it."

"People have died here," said Diana sharply. "And all you can think of is how best to turn it to your own advantage?"

Stasiak shrugged. "If they're already dead, there's not much left I can do for them. So we might as well help ourselves, while we can."

"And if whatever killed these people finds us?"

"Then we avenge the dead," said Ripper. "We know our duty, Diana. We're marines."

Diana sniffed and looked away, ostensibly studying the alien scene before her. Ripper shrugged. "Odin, are you getting all this?"

"I see everything you see," murmured the AI in his ear. "It's really most fascinating. Please proceed further into the changed area. I need more information on the extent of the changes."

"Wait a minute," Stasiak interrupted. "There's no point in rushing on blindly. There could be all kinds of unpleasantness up ahead."

Ripper looked at him, amused. "A minute ago you were all for plunging into the thick of it, in search of glory."

"I'm ambitious, not crazy. Let's handle this nice and easy, one step at a time. The only good hero is the kind who survives to talk about merchandising."

And then he broke off, and they all looked round sharply as a single, echoing thud came out of the darkness ahead of them. It was heavy and threatening, and sounded quite deliberate, as though whatever was responsible for the sound had wanted it to be heard. Ripper and Stasiak levelled their disrupters on the corridor ahead. Diana's right hand went to the force shield bracelet on her left wrist, but she hesitated to activate it. The energy crystal that powered it had a limited life span, and she didn't want to use it up unnecessarily.

"Odin, can your sensors detect anything alive on this floor?" said Ripper softly.

"I'm afraid my sensors are currently unable to penetrate the Base," the AI replied. "Something is blocking them. My only sources of information are what I see and hear through your comm implants."

More noises came out of the darkness, a slow, regular thudding like the beating of a giant heart. The floor vibrated beneath their feet in time to the rhythm, and something large and hulking came out of the gloom towards them. It was huge, filling the corridor, and Diana shrank back, a child again, frightened by the bogeyman in the dark. The figure stopped suddenly a dozen feet away, its blue steel exterior glinting in the wavering lamplight. Its bent head scraped against the ceiling, and its metal hands were studded with razors. Stasiak swore softly, but his hand was steady as he turned his disrupter on the metal figure.

Captain Silence's voice rang suddenly in their ears. "Listen up, people. We have a problem. Odin has just told me there are Security Guardians somewhere in the Base. Don't engage them, under any circumstances. It's very possible they've been programmed to protect this Base against intruders. If you see one, retreat immediately."

"Thanks for the warning," said Ripper, "but it's just a bit late. We're looking at one right now. Please advise."

"Get the hell out of there," said Silence immediately. "Make no threatening moves and back away. If it starts towards you, run. There are probably more on the way. They're crawling with weaponry and they don't take prisoners. As long as you keep a fair distance away, you should be safe."

"Should?" said Stasiak. "What do you mean, should? I'm not moving a muscle until I'm sure it's safe."

"Shut up, Lew," said Ripper. "Esper, back away and start up the stairs. We'll follow you."

"All right," said Diana quietly. "I'm starting now."

She stepped back cautiously, and the huge metal figure raised a hand to point at her. A disrupter beam flew from a finger and blew apart the metal stairway in a rain of jagged shrapnel.

Cries and screams and obscenities burst from Silence's comm implant, drowned out almost immediately by the sound of an explosion from below. The noise was deafening, and the floor shook briefly. Carrion and Frost looked to Silence for orders.

"Whatever's happening down there, there's nothing we can do," he said flatly. "By the time we could get there it would all be over, one way or another. And the last thing we want to do is provide a Guardian with new targets. Esper, marines, can you hear me? Fall back. I repeat, fall back." He waited, but there was no reply, only the quiet hum of an open comm channel. "Odin, access what they're seeing and patch me in."

"I'm sorry, Captain," said the AI steadily. "Something inside the Base is interfering with the comm network. I have lost all visual contact with the esper and the marines. I am still monitoring audio signals, but I can't be sure how long that will last. I strongly advise that you leave Base Thirteen now. You are not equipped to deal with Guardians."

"Want to bet?" drawled Frost. "Point me at one. Anything that gets in my way is going to regret it."

Carrion looked at Silence. "Is she always this confident?"

"Yes," said Silence. "Frightening, isn't it?"

Carrion looked away suddenly. "Captain . . . something's coming, and it's very close."

Frost and Silence drew their guns and covered the two approaches. The wide corridor was still and open, with doors leading off at both sides. The only light came from the lamp Silence was holding, a pale illumination just strong enough to show both ends of the corridor. Nothing moved, but the shadows had edges. What had been just another corridor was suddenly openly menacing, every doorway a threat. Silence and Frost moved to stand back to back. Carrion leaned on his staff, frowning, as though listening to something audible only to him. Silence strained his ears against the hush, but couldn't hear anything.

"What is it?" he said quietly to the outlaw. "Which direction is it coming from?"

Carrion's eyes closed. "They're here, Captain. They're here."

The wall to their right tore apart like paper as the Guardian burst through into the corridor. Thick strands of colored wiring fouled one arm, but the Guardian snapped them with one easy movement. The machine was eight feet tall, a broad metal colossus with glowing eyes and a constant, unnerving grin on its blue steel face. Razor blades protruded from its arms and legs, and the knuckles on its hands were spiked. It was not alive, but hate and violence were a part of its nature. It was a killing machine, fashioned in the shape of a man because it was more frightening that way.

"Big, isn't it?" said Carrion.

The sound of heavy metal footsteps rang out at both ends of the corridor, and two more Guardians appeared, blocking off the only means of escape. The three machines stood unnaturally still, studying their targets, and then they surged forward, too fast for the human eye to follow. Silence aimed and fired his disrupter at the nearest Guardian as it emerged from the wreckage of the wall. Its force shield snapped on just in time to deflect the energy bolt, and then disappeared. The machine raised a hand and pointed, and Silence threw himself to one side as an energy beam blew a hole in the wall where he'd been standing. Silence hit the floor rolling, and was quickly back on his feet again. He slapped the metal bracelet on his left wrist, and a force shield sprang into being on his arm. A yard-long oblong of glowing energy, it was capable of deflecting any energy weapon. For as long as it lasted. The Guardian could turn its own shield on and off with split-second timing, so that its shield lasted practically forever. Silence didn't have that option. He also had another three minutes to wait before he could use his gun again, and the Guardian was right on top of him.

Silence kicked open the door to his left, darted into the room and slammed the door shut behind him. He didn't really think the door was going to stop something that could crash through walls, but hopefully it would buy him a little time while he worked on what the hell to do next. A metal fist punched a hole in the door. Silence watched, fascinated, as an arm followed the hand through the hole, and then the Guardian pulled it back sharply, yanking the door out of its frame. The Guardian stepped unhurriedly into the room, widening the doorway as it did so. Silence backed away, holding his shield up before him.

The corridor was plunged into darkness as Silence disappeared into the side room, taking the only lamp with him. Frost cursed dispassionately and switched to her infrared implants, only to discover the Guardians were shielded against displaying any heat signs. Frost immediately switched to ambient light and activated her force shield. The shield's glow was more than enough to show her the Guardian advancing on her. Frost fired her gun, but the energy bolt glanced harmlessly off the machine's force shield. Frost shrugged calmly, put her gun away, and drew a knife from inside her boot. It was viciously wide and almost a foot long, and its edges looked blurred and uncertain.

"Monofilament edge," said Frost to Carrion. "Cut through anything. Have to be careful with it, though, or it'll have your fingers off."

"Those things were illegal in my day," observed Carrion.

"They still are. But I won't tell anyone if you won't."

And then the Guardians were upon them, and there was no more time for talk. Frost threw herself forward, and the knife lashed out to cut a chunk off the Guardian's hand. Its built-in disrupters all fired at once, but her force shield protected her. Frost brought the energy field across sideways, and its razor-sharp edge sliced clean through the Guardian's other hand as it reached for her. The huge metal arms swept suddenly in, intending to grab the Investigator and crush her against the blades on its chest. Frost dropped to her knees and rolled to one side, and the great arms closed on nothing. Frost jumped back, scrambling quickly to regain her feet, and the Guardian went after her, reaching for her with its crippled hands.

Frost darted in and out, slashing at the Guardian with her knife, cutting and carving it, but unable to do any real damage. It was just too big, and her knife was too small. The machine's computer-enhanced moves were inhumanly fast, and only her Investigator's training enabled her to avoid it. And she knew she couldn't maintain that kind of speed for long. She could turn and run. The Guardian didn't look as if it were built for high-speed pursuit. But that would mean abandoning Carrion and the Captain, and her duty. Investigators didn't run. She darted in under the Guardian's reach, jammed her gun against its chest, and pressed the stud. Nothing happened. There hadn't been enough time for the energy crystal to recharge. She scrambled up the Guardian, climbing it like a cat, carefully avoiding the blades on its chest, and dropped to the ground behind it. She spun round quickly, and stabbed the machine in the back before it could turn. It shuddered once, but that was all. The blade wasn't long enough to reach the parts that mattered. She yanked the blade out, and a metal arm whirled round and sent her flying down the corridor. She'd got her force shield up in time, but the impact was still enough to knock the breath

out of her. She got her feet under her and backed away as
the Guardian advanced on her, implacable and unstoppable
as death itself.

Carrion crouched down, and froze where he was when
Silence disappeared with the lamp. In the dark, the Guardian
could only track him by sound. Unless the damn thing had
infrared too. And then Frost turned on her force shield,
and Carrion's long-neglected eye-enhancements kicked in,
boosting the ambient light. Carrion straightened up as he saw
the third Guardian advancing on him. He drew his power
about him, crackling and sparkling on the air, and reached
out to tear the machine apart. And his power dropped away
and was gone in an instant. Carrion stood for a moment,
staring blankly, and that was almost enough to get him
killed. The Guardian raised its hand, and all the disrupters
in the hand fired at once. Carrion threw himself to one side
at the last moment, old combat reflexes coming to his rescue.
The damn thing had psi inhibitors built into it. They worked
on the opposite principle to his power lance, damping down
psi energy instead of augmenting it. The Empire used them
to keep espers in line. They reacted to build-ups in psionic
energy and cut in automatically once it rose above a certain
level. Carrion backed away from the Guardian, holding his
useless power lance out before him.

The Guardian loomed over him, reaching for him with
razored hands. Carrion reached inside himself and drew on
his power. The psi inhibitors prevented him from doing anything dramatic, but it was surprising what you could do with
even small amounts. He reached out with his mind, a whisper
of psychokinesis almost too small to register, and slipped it
deftly between the Guardian's feet and the floor. All friction
vanished in a moment as he concentrated, and the Guardian's
feet shot out from under it. It fell on its back with a deafening
crash, and Carrion reached quickly out to do the same to the
machine threatening Frost. It hit the floor hard, and Frost

stepped forward and drove her monofilament knife into its gleaming skull. The Guardian jerked and trembled, and lay twitching on its back on the floor. Frost pulled the knife out and calmly set about sawing the grinning head off.

The wall to Carrion's left exploded, throwing shrapnel across the corridor, and Carrion had to put up his esper screen to protect himself. He couldn't concentrate on that and the Guardian, and the machine rose quickly to its feet again. Silence clambered through the hole in the wall. A metal hand reached out after him, and Silence threw himself forward to avoid it. He scrambled away and was quickly on his feet again, standing beside Carrion and breathing hard. The Guardian before them fired a disrupter, and Silence blocked it with his force shield, holding it at an angle so that the beam glanced off and struck the Guardian that was climbing through the hole in the wall. It stopped the beam with a force shield, but was slowed for a moment. Silence grinned breathlessly.

"Same trick I used to make that thing provide me with an exit through the wall."

"Very clever," said Carrion. "Almost as clever as disappearing into another room and taking the only light with you."

"Ah," said Silence. "Sorry about that. It's been a while since I did any hand-to-hand stuff. I'm rather out of practice."

They jumped in different directions as Carrion's Guardian fired again, and the vivid energy beam flashed past them down the corridor to blow a hole in the far wall. Silence's Guardian crashed out into the corridor again, shaking off encumbering debris, and turned to face Frost. She hefted the severed metal head in her hand and threw it at the Guardian. The machine caught the head easily, put it down on the floor with surprising gentleness, and started toward the Investigator. She grinned at it unpleasantly, her knife held out before her. And then the headless machine on the floor behind her reached out with a partly severed hand and grabbed her firmly by the ankle.

Carrion raised his esp as high as he dared, focused his psychokinesis tightly, and punched a hole right through the chest of the Guardian before him. It shuddered under the impact, but did not fall. The outlaw retreated, Silence at his side.

"Is there any way of beating these things?" said Carrion.

"Not really, no," said Silence. "I'm amazed we lasted this long. They're supposed to be unstoppable. But then, that's never bothered you before."

And then the Guardian was upon them, and there was no more time for words.

Diana crouched down behind her force shield, trembling violently as three Guardians advanced on her. The two marines had already fired their disrupters, to no effect, and they too were reduced to hiding behind their force shields and looking frantically around for a way out. The Guardians strode unwaveringly through the alien-infested corridor, ignoring everything except their targets. Ripper pulled a grenade from his belt, primed it, and tossed it into the midst of the three machines. It blew a second later, and the corridor filled with alien fragments and thick, choking smoke. Stasiak grabbed Diana's wrist and hauled her after him as he and Ripper ran down a side corridor, away from the smoke and the three undamaged Guardians, already striding through the smoke after them.

The alien changes became stranger and more overpowering as they fled deeper into Level Two, but Diana was too busy coughing the smoke out of her lungs to pay much attention to her surroundings. Tears were streaming down her face, as much from shock as the smoke. She'd never seen anything so deadly efficient as the Guardians. They scared her on some basic, primal level that left no room in her for anything but flight. The Guardians were everything about the Empire that had ever threatened or punished her—brute symbols of authority, relentless as justice or revenge. She could no more have raised a hand against them than she could have defied her own conditioning.

The marines' pace slowed as they left the smoke behind them, but they could still hear the sounds of the Guardians' implacable progress not far behind them. Stasiak produced a small capsule from somewhere and swallowed it dry, grimacing at the effort. He offered one to Ripper, who got his down more easily. Stasiak grinned at Diana, his eyes already bright and glassy.

"Just a little something, to give a fighting man an edge. You want one?" Diana shook her head. She didn't trust battle drugs. Stasiak shrugged and pulled her on. "It's your choice. But don't slow us down, or I'll have to leave you. Right, Rip?"

Ripper nodded brusquely, without looking round, and Diana fought to keep up with the marines as they made their way down a corridor distorted by strange alien growths. The hanging streamers of webbing grew steadily thicker, clinging stickily to the marines and the esper as they pushed through them. The corridor grew narrower, pressing in uncomfortably from all sides as the alien growths ran wild. It seemed to Diana that they'd left the Base behind and were running through a harsh new alien world. But the Guardians were still following. She could hear them. The changing alien nature of their surroundings didn't seem to be slowing the machines at all. And then a side corridor ended in a great swollen mass of alien tissue, bringing the three humans to a halt. The marines cut at the spongy mass with their swords, but it simply absorbed their blows without effect. They turned and glared back down the corridor. Stasiak swallowed another capsule. The sound of approaching metal footsteps came clearly on the quiet.

Ripper tapped Stasiak on the arm and gestured at the ceiling. Stasiak looked puzzled, but then his face cleared as Ripper hefted his gun. They aimed their disrupters at the ceiling, at the point where the Guardians would enter the side corridor. Diana stood behind them, her force shield humming loudly, and tried to control her trembling. And then the Guardians appeared at the end of the corridor, and Stasiak and Ripper fired at the ceiling above them.

The alien growths exploded and the ceiling blew apart. Fat sparks flew on the air as electrical systems fused and failed and half the floor above collapsed onto the Guardians, burying them under tons of rubble. The marines and the esper watched in silence as the wreckage slowly settled, and then Diana surprised herself with a loud whoop of glee. The marines laughed and whooped a few times themselves. They all turned off their force shields and hugged each other, giddy with relief. And then they fell silent as the wreckage shifted. Broken metal and ragged alien tissues stirred and fell back as a Guardian rose slowly from the debris. Its blue steel exterior was barely scratched.

The Guardian advanced unhurriedly on Silence and Carrion. It knew there was nowhere they could go. If they tried to run it would shoot them, and if they stood their ground and tried to hide behind their force shields, it would tear them apart. At the other end of the corridor the Guardian Frost had beheaded was clinging firmly to her ankle, while the third Guardian advanced on her. Silence looked desperately at Carrion.

"Do something! Use your lance!"

"If I try the same trick again, the psi inhibitors will stop me," said Carrion calmly. "If I persist, they'll burn my brain out."

Silence backed slowly away from the Guardian, and Carrion moved back with him. The Guardian lifted its hands to cover them with its disrupters. Silence thought furiously. The damn things had to have a weakness somewhere. Everything had a weakness. Except the Guardians had been designed to be unstoppable. Inhumanly strong, computer-fast reflexes . . . computers. Silence seized on that thought. The Guardians were part of the Base's Security systems, which meant they were run by the Security computers . . . .

"Odin! Can you hear me?"

"Yes, Captain. Audio contact remains firm."

"Patch into the Base Security computers and shut them down! Shut down anything that even looks like it might be running a Guardian!"

"Of course, Captain. An excellent stratagem." There was a slight pause, and then the AI's voice returned. "I regret I am unable to comply, Captain. I am unable to find any computer system still functioning in Base Thirteen capable of running a Guardian. Only a few emergency systems are still functioning."

"What?" Silence looked blankly at Carrion. "But if the computers aren't running the Guardians . . . they must be running themselves. And that's not possible. That's not possible!"

"Are you going to tell them that, or shall I?" said Carrion.

"Dammit, do something, Carrion! That thing will kill both of us!"

"Yes," said the outlaw quietly. "I think it will, Captain."

At the other end of the corridor, Frost pried desperately at the steel fingers gripping her ankle. The other Guardian was almost on top of her, but she couldn't break the hold. She snarled silently and cut savagely at the metal arm, slicing through its wrist, She threw herself clumsily to one side, dodging the reaching metal hands, and got her feet under her again. The severed hand was still gripping her ankle fiercely, despite the damage she'd done to it. Which meant she had no chance of outrunning her opponent, but then, she wasn't the running kind. She slashed at the advancing Guardian with her monofilament knife, and the blade bounced harmlessly back from the machine's force field. Frost shrugged, and darted back out of reach. It seemed the Guardians were capable of learning from experience. Actually, she was surprised she'd lasted this long. She cut the metal hand from her ankle with a few quick slashes of the knife, and then had to throw herself to one side as disrupter beams seared through the air where she'd been standing. She hit the floor rolling, and was quickly back on her feet and dodging more disrupter shots.

A thought kept nagging at her, even as she dodged and ducked. The Guardians were fast, but they weren't anywhere near as fast as she'd expected them to be. As they were supposed to be. In fact, it was just possible that she was faster than they were. Which gave her an idea. The Guardians had force shields, but they were only using them to deflect disrupter beams. Apparently they didn't see anything else as a big enough threat. Frost grinned unpleasantly, and pulled a concussion grenade from her bandolier. She ducked another disrupter blast, leapt past the oncoming Guardian, and jumped onto the back of the headless one as it groped blindly about for its prey. She primed the grenade, stuffed it into the open neck, and leapt away. There was a muffled explosion, and smoke poured from the cavity, but the Guardian didn't go down. Frost stared at it incredulously. How much punishment could these things take?

Silence and Carrion backed away from the advancing Guardian until they came up against a wall and there was nowhere left to go. Carrion looked at Silence.

"I seem to have run out of options, Captain. If you have any last-minute master plan, I think this would be a good time to share it."

"Sorry," said Silence. "I was depending on you."

Carrion managed something that was almost a smile. "You should have known better than that, John."

As Frost backed away from the headless Guardian, she stumbled over its severed head. She glanced down automatically, and stopped as something caught her eye. Without slowing her cautious retreat, she snatched up the head and studied it more closely. The headless machine hesitated, and then stopped where it was. The other Guardian stopped too. Frost blinked, puzzled, and took a better look at the severed head. The light had gone out of its eyes, though it still wore its endless disturbing grin, but there was something about it . . . . She turned it over in her hands, still keeping a cautionary eye on the motionless Guardians, and then whistled soundlessly as she saw the interior of the head. A great many things suddenly became clear. Where there should have been nothing but silicon circuitry and crystalline matrices, there were also thick strands of living tissue. Alien tissue.

She looked down the corridor and saw that the third Guardian had stopped its advance on Silence and Carrion. She called out to them and tossed the head in their direction. It bumped and rolled across the uneven floor, and the Guardian made no move to intercept it. The head finally rolled to a halt, and Silence reached carefully down and picked it up. He raised an eyebrow at the alien tissue inside the head, and showed it to Carrion.

"Interesting," said Carrion.

"Explains a lot, doesn't it?" said Silence. "No wonder they didn't need the Security computers to run them. The aliens invaded them too. The damn things are alive . . . ."

"And now that we know that, it changes a lot of things," said Carrion. "There wasn't much my esp could do against standard Guardians without triggering the psi inhibitors, but living tissue is much more responsive to esper attack; all it needs is a little touch in the right place . . . ."

He looked at the Guardian before him, and it began to shudder, as though it was cold, or afraid. It dropped to its knees, fell forward onto its grinning face, and lay still. Carrion looked at the two remaining Guardians, and they collapsed like puppets whose strings had been cut. Rather an appropriate metaphor, Silence decided. Of course, where there were puppets, there were also puppeteers. They still had to face whatever it was that had infested the Base.

Frost made her way over to them, and kicked the nearest Guardian dismissively. "Is that it? I'm almost disappointed it was so easy."

"Don't worry," said Carrion. "I doubt very much that our troubles are over yet."

"Right," said Silence. "The whole Base must be riddled with this stuff. If we can't find a way to clean it out, we may have to abandon the Base and destroy it from orbit."

"The Empire wouldn't like that," said Carrion.

"No," said Frost. "They wouldn't."

Silence looked sharply at Carrion. "Hold everything; we're forgetting the esper and the marines. We haven't had a word from them since we lost contact."

"Don't worry," said Carrion. "I've just contacted Diana. It seems they had Guardian troubles of their own. I've explained what needs to be done. The esper is quite capable of handling the Guardians herself."

Down on Level Two, Diana Vertue looked smugly at the Guardians lying motionless in the wreckage of the ceiling. The marines took turns clapping her on the back, almost knocking her off her feet in the process.

"Mind you, this is just Level Two," said Stasiak. "I hate to think what might be waiting for us down on Level Three."

Ripper nodded and looked at Diana. "You'd better run a scan, see if there are any more like these waiting below."

She nodded, closed her eyes, and let her mind drift cautiously up and out. She frowned almost immediately.

"What is it?" said Stasiak.

"Living traces," said Diana. "They're all around us, all over the Base, concentrated in the floor below. They know we're here." Her voice rose suddenly. "They're not hiding from us anymore. They're coming for us."

"Who?" said Stasiak, glaring wildly about him. "Who's coming for us?"

The walls around them burst apart, thick metal tearing like paper as alien growths and tentacles exploded into the corridor, reaching for the esper and the two marines. The tentacles came from the floor and the walls and the ceiling, and there was nowhere to hide from them.

CHAPTER EIGHT

Down in the Darkness

"ESPER, can you hear me? Ripper, Stasiak, respond!" Silence waited, scowling, but there was no response. He looked into the stairwell that led down to Level Two, and the darkness looked back at him, arrogant and impenetrable. There was only the cold and the quiet, and the knowledge of what he'd have to do. It had been twenty minutes since Carrion had last been able to reach the esper. He'd told her how to handle the Guardians, and she'd acknowledged the message, but there'd been nothing since. Silence shook his head slowly. They couldn't be dead. They had the information they needed. They couldn't be dead.

"Odin, could something be interfering with the comm net?"

"Quite possibly, Captain." the AI murmured in his ear. "I have been unable to raise the party on Level Two for some time. Something in Base Thirteen is interfering with all levels of communication. I am having to use inordinate ammounts of power just to maintain audio contact with your party. However, that would not explain the outlaw's inability to contact them with his mind."

"We have to go down after them," said Frost, holding her lamp out over the gloom in the stairwell. Shadows leapt and danced, giving away nothing. "If something has happened to the others, we need to know what it is."

"Whatever's happened, the odds are it's over by now," said Carrion. "We won't do anyone any good by rushing

116

blindly into the dark. Wait a moment, and consider. So far, we have a growing number of questions, and few if any good answers. For example, if Base Commander Starblood had six Security Guardians at his disposal, why didn't he use them against the invading aliens?"

"Presumably because he didn't have time," said Frost. "Judging by his log entries, by the time he'd worked out what was happening it was already too late. In fact, it's entirely possible the Guardians were infested with the alien material before they could be deployed."

"Exactly," said Carrion, leaning elegantly on his staff. "The aliens aren't just powerful and dangerous, they're fast and devious too. All of which suggests we'd be foolish to go rushing into an unknown situation without doing some hard thinking first. The more I think about it, the more this looks to me like a trap, with the esper and the marines as bait."

"You're probably right," said Silence. "But it doesn't make any difference. Those are my people down there, and I won't put their lives at risk by holding back. Lead the way, Investigator; Carrion and I will be right behind you."

Frost grinned quickly, a sudden flash of bared teeth, and started down the metal stairs, lamp in one hand, gun in the other. Carrion gave Silence a long, thoughtful look, and then followed the Investigator down into the gloom. Silence brought up the rear. The stairwell was narrow and confined, and the lamplight didn't travel far. They moved in a small pool of light, and shadows moved menacingly around them, almost close enough to touch. They'd barely reached the halfway mark when Frost stopped suddenly, and Carrion and Silence almost bumped into her. She stood still, head cocked slightly to one side, listening.

"What is it, Investigator?" Silence whispered.

"I'm not sure, Captain. I heard something, something close."

She broke off sharply, and held the lamp down to light her feet. A yard-long insect with a broad carapaced back and hundreds of legs was curling itself unhurriedly round her left ankle. Dozens more of the things curled and twisted on the steps below. More were climbing the walls, clinging easily to the dull metal. Frost put away her gun and drew her sword, moving slowly and carefully. The creature had no eyes or mouth, but she set the edge of her blade against what seemed to be the front of the insect, and sliced sideways. The body convulsed, and clamped painfully tight around her ankle. Frost handed the lamp back to Carrion, reached down, and calmly unwound the insect from around her leg. It fought back with surprising strength, even without its head, and she had to use all her strength to unwrap it. It finally came free, and immediately tried to wrap itself around her arm. She threw the thing away, and it disappeared into the darkness. Hundreds more seethed on the steps below her, scuttling and sliding over each other in their eagerness to get to their prey.

Carrion tossed the lamp lightly into the air and held it there with his esp, spreading light over the scene and keeping his hands free. Silence aimed his disrupter where the mass of insects seemed the thickest.

"I wouldn't, Captain," said the outlaw quietly. "You'd do more damage to the stairs than to the creatures."

Silence nodded stiffly, and put away his gun. He shouldn't have needed to be told something that obvious. He drew his sword and stepped carefully down beside the Investigator. Together they hacked and cut at the insects, clearing an open space before them. Segments flew on the air, legs still kicking, but the creatures wouldn't die. They pressed blindly forward up the stairs, seeking to wrap themselves round an arm or a leg, reaching always for the throat, as though somehow they knew that to be the most vulnerable spot. They climbed the walls and dropped onto the humans

from above, but Carrion deflected them with his esp, cracking them like whips to break their backs, or crushing them
against the walls with the pressure of his mind. But still the
insects pressed forward, and there seemed no end to them.

Carrion stepped back, and held his staff horizontally above
his head. Psi energy spat and crackled at each end of the
power lance, and stabbed out to strike out at the seething
creatures. Where the psi-bolts struck, the insects burst into
flames, curling and twisting as the fire consumed them.
Energy danced back and forth in the stairwell, too bright to
look at, scorching and crisping the scuttling creatures, but not
touching Silence or the Investigator. The insects fell back,
spilling down the stairs in desperate haste, and plunged into
the solid steel walls, where they were swallowed up without
trace as though the gleaming steel were no more substantial
than mist. Within seconds the stairwell was empty, the sound
of the insects' scuttling appendages no more than a swiftly
fading echo. Only the dead remained to show that they had
ever been there. Frost reached out and tapped the nearest
wall, but it was stubbornly solid to the touch.

"Interesting," said Carrion, and the Investigator nodded.

"Is that all you've got to say?" demanded Silence.

"For the moment," said Carrion. "The situation appears
to be more complicated than we allowed for. And before
you ask, Captain; no, I can't explain it. I can only suggest
that the walls have in some way become as infested with
alien material as the Guardians. Which means the aliens
have quite literally taken over the entire Base."

"Those . . . creatures," said Silence. "Could they have
been the aliens from the crashed ship? Some sort of hive
mentality, perhaps? A group mind?"

Frost shrugged. "It's possible, but unlikely. Given the
size of the ship, I'd have to say the scale was all wrong.
More likely the insects are tools used by the alien for some
purpose. We have yet to encounter the real enemy."

"Now there's a comforting thought," said Carrion.

"Keep moving," said Silence. "We haven't even reached Level Two yet. Carrion, nice work with the lance. Stand ready. We might need you again."

"Of course, Captain. It's nice to feel needed."

"I could toss a grenade down ahead of us," said Frost. "If the aliens have any more surprises waiting for us down below, a shrapnel grenade should spoil their day quite thoroughly."

"Nice thought, but no. The esper and the marines are still down there somewhere. Lead the way, Investigator."

Their feet echoed hollowly on the metal steps as they continued down the stairway, the lamp hovering benignly over their heads. Silence kept a careful watch on the stairs and the walls, but there was no trace anywhere of the vanished insects. Instead, a thick, viscous slime began to appear on the walls, oozing down to coat the metal steps so that they became treacherous underfoot. They slowed their pace, taking it one step at a time. Thick drops fell from somewhere high above, landing with sudden force on heads and shoulders. The drops fell more thickly as they neared the bottom of the stairs, until it was a slow, unpleasant rain. Frost stopped to wipe the stuff from her face, and found she couldn't. The slime clung tenaciously to her forehead, then suddenly flowed down over her eyes and on towards her nose and mouth.

Silence and Carrion came to a halt with her as a thick wave of slime rushed up the stairs and trapped their feet and ankles in an unyielding grip. More rained down from above, plastering their heads and faces. Frost clawed at the slime with her hands, but it just oozed between her fingers, leaving nothing for her to hold onto. She kept her mouth firmly closed, and pinched her nose shut. She didn't want the stuff invading her body. There was already a growing pressure on her closed eyes and in her ears. Silence tried to scrape the slime from his legs with the edge of his sword, but the stuff just broke and re-formed around the blade without releasing its hold for a moment. The slime was climbing his legs like a slow rising tide.

And then the slime was torn from his legs and sprang away from his face and body, pulled away by an almost physical presence on the air. The ooze also left Frost's face, leaving her gasping for breath, while the slime that continued to fall from above was diverted, pushed away and to one side by the presence. Silence looked at Carrion, who was frowning slightly, as though considering an interesting problem.

"Nicely done again, Carrion. You've improved your control since we last met."

"I've had lots of time to practise," said Carrion. A clear pathway opened up before them, forcing the slime off to the sides. "We'd better make haste, Captain. I can't hold this stuff back for long; it's too diffuse. And the pressure's growing all the time."

Frost and Silence clattered down the steps as quickly as they could, with Carrion crowding their heels. The slime rained down thickly, but couldn't get near them. And when a sudden wave of the ooze rose up and threw itself at them from below, it too broke and fell away to the sides as it met the pressure of Carrion's will. Then they reached the bottom of the stairs and moved quickly forward, leaving the slime behind them. Frost pulled a grenade from her bandolier and primed it.

"Incendiary," she said briskly to Carrion. "See how far you can get it up the stairway before it explodes."

Carrion nodded, and the grenade jumped out of her hand and flew up into the gloom of the stairwell. There was a sudden, vivid explosion, and crimson flames boiled down and out of the stairwell. The flames burned fiercely, but neither they nor their heat could get past Carrion's mental shield. The fire leapt and blossomed in the stairwell, lighting the scene bright as day, consuming the slime hungrily. The flames died away bit by bit as the slime disappeared, until finally they were gone and the quiet and the gloom returned. A harsh, bitter smell filled the air, but nothing scuttled down the steps or oozed from the walls.

They looked about them, taking in the strange alien growths that sprouted from the metal walls and ceiling. Thick streamers of webbing hung down, twisting slowly back and forth, as though someone had just passed through them. Silvery traces glowed on the walls like living circuit patterns. And thick and heavy on the air, growing stronger by the moment, was the stench of rotting meat.

"First insects that wouldn't die, and vanish into solid walls, then living slime with homicidal tendencies, and now this," said Frost. "Whatever's hiding down here really doesn't want to be found."

"Esper!" Silence's voice rang on the quiet, echoing faintly, but there was no reply. "Stasiak, Ripper, where are you? Can you hear me? Diana?"

They waited, but the echoes died away with nothing to replace them. The shadows were still, and very dark, and deep enough to hide all kinds of secrets.

"Spread out and search this floor," Silence ordered. "I want them found. Maintain contact at all times. And watch yourselves. Something down here doesn't like us at all."

They moved apart and started the slow process of searching through the rubble and the deserted rooms and corridors. The continuing quiet was eerie and almost threatening, after the lengthy battles that had preceded it. There was a feeling of imminence in the air, of something about to happen, that grated on everyone's nerves. They found a huge hole in one wall, presumably made by a grenade or a Guardian, and several glowing holes that could only have been made by disrupters, but there was no sign of the esper or the marines, or of what they might have been fighting.

They finally returned to the foot of the stairs, and took turns looking at each other, shrugging and shaking their heads.

"The Guardians must have taken them deeper into the Base," said Frost at last. "They could have been programmed to capture rather than kill."

"But Carrion told Diana how to handle them," said Silence. "They should have been easy targets for someone with her skills."

"Something must have gone wrong," said Carrion.

Silence nodded reluctantly. "Find them, Carrion. Use your esp."

The outlaw frowned, concentrating. Frost looked at Silence. "I thought he was a polter," she said quietly. "Polters aren't normally telepaths as well."

"There's nothing normal about Carrion," said Silence, not bothering to lower his voice. "The Ashrai saw to that."

Carrion opened his eyes and breathed deeply, shaking his head as though to clear it. "I can't find the marines anywhere. The esper is hiding in a clothes locker, just down that corridor. She's shielding herself, but I can feel her presence now that I'm looking for it."

"Why is she hiding?" asked Silence.

"I don't know, Captain. But it feels like something bad has happened to her. Something really bad."

He led the way down a side corridor, with Frost and Silence close behind, disrupters at the ready. Shadows loomed menacingly as the lamp floated along above their heads. Carrion finally stopped before a row of lockers, and looked at each of them thoughtfully. Silence looked at them disbelievingly. They were barely a foot and a half wide and six feet high, not even big enough to make a decent coffin. What could have frightened the esper so badly that she'd been driven to hide in such a cramped place? Carrion stopped before one locker, and tried the door. It was locked. He focused his power, and the door burst open, shattering the lock. Inside the locker, Diana Vertue was half-standing and half-crouching, her arms wrapped around her, her eyes squeezed tightly shut. The posture would have been painful to hold for a few minutes; after all this time it should have been agonising, but she made no move to leave the locker. She showed no sign of even knowing they were there. Carrion reached out and gently touched her shoulder.

"She's gone deep inside herself," said the outlaw softly. "Something happened here, something so bad she shut down her whole mind rather than think about it."

"We need to know what happened," said Silence. "And where the marines are. Bring her out of it, Carrion."

"There's nothing I can do, Captain. If I try and force her mind open, I could shatter it completely."

"Then I'll have to do it," said Silence. He knelt down beside the comatose esper and laid a surprisingly gentle hand on her arm. "Diana, this is Captain Silence. Please, wake up and talk to me. I need you to talk to me, Diana. Talk to your father."

The esper stirred slowly. Carrion and Frost exchanged a quick glance of surprise, and then looked back at the esper as she slowly opened her eyes. She saw Silence kneeling beside her, and threw herself into his arms, sobbing loudly. He held her tightly and rocked back and forth, murmuring comforting words into her hair. He looked up, and shrugged when he saw Frost and Carrion studying him.

"They took her away from me when she was six. When her esp first started to manifest. I kept in touch as best I could, and when she graduated from the Academy, I got her transferred to my ship, where I could keep an eye on her. I thought she'd be safe with me."

Diana finally got herself back under control and stopped crying, sniffing back the last few tears. Silence let go of her and helped her to her feet. She stretched awkwardly, wincing as cramped muscles protested.

"What happened, Diana?" Silence asked. "Why were you hiding? Did the Guardians take Ripper and Stasiak away?"

"I don't know," said Diana, with a troubled look. "I can't remember. But it couldn't have been the Guardians. We beat them. Carrion showed me how. It was easy. And then . . . something happened, but I can't remember what."

"Don't force it," said Carrion. "It'll come back to you."

"There's only one place Ripper and Stasiak could have been taken," said Frost. "Down to Level Three. We're going to have to go down after them."

"Yes," said Silence. "I think we are. Lead the way, Investigator. Diana, stay close."

Frost glanced at him briefly, and then set off into the gloom with the esper close behind her. Silence and Carrion followed, hanging back a little.

"The esper really shouldn't be here," Carrion murmured. "Whatever she saw, it frightened her so much she shut down her mind completely, rather than admit it happened. Her current mental state is precarious, to say the least. If she's forced to once again confront the circumstances that caused her breakdown, her mind could shatter completely. She could retreat so far into herself that not even the best esper shrink could bring her out again. Just making her stay here could be putting her under an impossible strain. Send her back to the pinnace, John. We don't need her here. You have me. My esp is more than strong enough to deal with whatever we find."

"I need to know what she saw," said Silence. "Keeping her here will bring those memories back to the surface."

"She's your daughter, John!"

"I'm Captain of the *Darkwind*. I know my duty."

"Yes," said Carrion. "You always did. You haven't changed at all, John."

He increased his pace to catch up with the two women. Silence looked at the three backs turned to him, and made no move to join them.

The stairwell leading down to Level Three seemed open and inviting. No insects crawled on the metal steps, and the walls were free of slime. There were still strange alien growths erupting from the walls and ceiling, and tattered webbing hung in thick grey streamers, but the stairway itself seemed untouched. Carrion gestured for Frost to lead the way, and she started slowly down into the gloom, step by step, gun in hand. Carrion moved down after her, with Diana at his side. The esper's hands were trembling visibly, but her back was straight and she held her head high. Silence brought up the rear. He would have liked to be proud of his daughter's courage, but he couldn't afford to think of her that way. She was his ship's esper, and that had to come first.

The temperature rose sharply as they made their way down into the darkness, from bitter cold to almost suffocatingly humid heat. They turned off the heating elements in their uniforms, and pressed on in growing discomfort. The lamp still hung above them, buoyed up by Carrion's esp, but its light didn't travel far. They hadn't been able to find Diana's lamp, and she was unable to tell them what had happened to it. She didn't speak much at all, but did as she was directed. She was an esper, and espers obeyed orders.

They reached the bottom of the stairwell without incident, and stopped a moment to get their breath. The heat was almost overpowering, and sweat dripped from their faces. All around them, the walls were cracked and pitted, and spotted with jagged outgrowths whose regular shapes suggested purpose, if not meaning. Stalactites of distorted metal hung down from the ceiling, dripping moisture that collected in pools on the uneven floor. The air was heavy with the stench of rotting flowers.

"What the hell is this?" said Silence. He reached out and touched the nearest stalactite, and then snatched his hand away. The metal was painfully hot, the moisture almost boiling.

"This is something different," said Frost. "On Level Two the alien growths seemed wilder, almost out of control. This seems more pervasive, more planned. There's the same mixture of living and non-living materials, but the mix here seems more comfortable, almost organic."

"But where did it all come from?" said Carrion, frowning. "The aliens must have brought some of it from the ship, but there hasn't been enough time to bring about such extensive changes in the Base's structure. Besides, this doesn't look as though it was constructed; it looks more like it was grown this way."

"Just like the alien ship," said Frost, nodding. "Whatever this stuff is, it isn't parasitic. There's a definite sense of purpose to it, of function. Symbiosis. Different systems working together, to reach the same end. This is an entire ecology, taking over and supplanting the original one. The aliens' technology must be centuries ahead of ours, to have achieved so much so quickly. We have to get back to the pinnace, Captain. The Empire must be warned. Whatever's taken root here must be destroyed, down to the last fragment. If this should spread . . ."

Silence nodded. "Odin, are you still in contact?"

"For the moment, Captain." The AI's voice was low, but still clear. "Audio contact remains firm. I am still unable to regain visual contact, and I have no contact at all with the missing marines. Something significant must have happened, either to the marines or their comm implants. I am maintaining a running log on this mission. In the event of my losing contact with you entirely, I will send a General

Distress signal, and put this planet under full Quarantine."

"Thank you," said Silence dryly. "Next time, you might wait for me to give the order. I am still in charge of this mission."

"Of course, Captain. However, in order to present a complete log on this mission, I must have further data on the structural changes in Base Thirteen. To achieve this, it will be necessary for you to proceed further into the Base."

"When this is all over, computer," said Silence, "you and I are going to have a long chat about which one of us is in charge, and you aren't going to enjoy it at all." He looked at the others and tried not to scowl. "Unfortunately, the AI is right. We do need more information, and the only way to get it is to press on."

He stopped and looked at Diana, who was trembling violently. All the color had drained from her face, and her eyes were very large. She realised he was watching, and made an attempt to stand straighter. She hugged herself tightly, and managed a shaky smile.

"I'm all right, Captain. Really. I've been trying to scan the area, but something down here is preventing me. I can't tell yet whether that's deliberate or not. I can't locate Ripper or Stasiak, but there are definite life signs all over the place. This whole level feels like a jungle, but I can't focus enough to identify anything. The one thing I am sure of is that we're not alone down here. Something's watching us."

"Can you be more specific?" said Silence, careful to keep his voice cool and unconcerned. He didn't want the esper any more upset than she already was.

Diana bit her lip and shook her head. "Something's down here, Captain. I don't know what or where it is. But it knows we're here."

She stopped suddenly, as though she'd been about to add something and then changed her mind. Silence waited a moment, but it was clear the esper had said all she was going to. She still looked scared, but she was back under control again. For the moment.

"All right," he said briskly. "We're going in. If anything moves, kill it. We don't have any friends down here."

"What about the marines?" said Carrion.

"The odds are they're dead," said Silence flatly. "Otherwise Diana or the AI would be able to locate them. We'll search for them as we go, but they can't be our main objective. We're looking for the aliens. Anything else has to come second."

"Of course," said Carrion. "People always come second, as far as the Empire's concerned. When in doubt, shoot first and ask questions later. If at all."

Frost shrugged easily. "We go with what works. Now let's get a move on. I don't like us standing around like this. It makes us too good a target."

She started off down the corridor, stepping carefully over the uneven floor, and the others followed her. The heat grew steadily heavier and more oppresive as they moved deeper in, and condensation fell from the ceiling like intermittent rain. Alien growths blossomed on the walls, complex and enigmatic. Great fleshy petals uncurled from outgrowths of bone spliced with metal, and great structures of living clockwork moved steadily towards some unknown goal. Some shapes seemed to border on the edge of purpose and meaning, but still evaded human understanding.

At one point the corridor became choked with a thick mass of the grey webbing, and they had to stop and cut their way through with their swords. It was slow, back-breaking work as the sticky webbing tore reluctantly under the blades. Sometimes Silence thought he saw strange lights flashing briefly in the darkness, but the others never mentioned them, so he kept his peace till he could be sure himself. The esper began to frown heavily, and stopped at times to stare intently at some new outgrowth or alien structure.

"She's starting to remember," Carrion murmured to Silence. "I'll keep an eye on her."

And then they rounded a corner, and Diana stopped dead and screamed. Carrion and Frost moved quickly forward to stand between her and what she was looking at. She managed to swallow the second scream, but she was trembling so violently she could barely stand. Silence moved in beside her, and had to fight down an urge to look away. They'd finally discovered what had happened to the missing personnel of Base Thirteen.

Stretched across the wall, interspersed with alien growths and mechanisms, were recognisably human shapes and organs. Bodies had been torn apart and reassembled in strange patterns. Alien technology mixed with brightly veined meat, and nerves and wires curled around familiar bones. And every organ and stretch of tissue was still clearly alive and functioning, as part of an alien, monstrous whole. Stasiak's face peered blindly from a shifting spider web of silvery traces. There were no eyes in the face, but a muscle twitched regularly by the slack mouth.

"It's alive," said Carrion quietly. "I can feel it in my mind. It shouldn't be alive, but it is."

"Just like the alien ship," said Frost. "Living and nonliving tissues cyborged together. A biomechanical gestalt whose whole is greater than the sum of its parts. This is functioning, Captain; it has a purpose, a reason for existence."

Silence looked at Diana. Her mouth was slack, and her eyes saw nothing at all. He looked back at the living wall. "At least now we know what happened to the marines. They must have been taken and . . . broken down, in front of Diana. No wonder she blocked out the memory." He looked at the esper again, and then away. The empty eyes were more accusing than any stare could have been. "Why didn't they take her, too?"

"Espers have a unique defence mechanism." said Carrion coldly. "In times of danger, they can use their esp to become psionically invisible. Can't be seen or heard. You could walk right into one and not notice. Apparently it works equally well on aliens. You can ask Diana all about it, when she wakes up. If she wakes up."

"If she can't keep up with us, we'll have to leave her behind," said Frost.

"I know," said Silence. "I know."

They walked along the wall, trying to take in the details. Carrion took Diana by the hand and she walked along beside him, her face completely blank. The lamp still hovered above them, its pitiless light revealing every awful detail of the living surface. Familiar body parts and organs had been worked seamlessly into the alien technology. Half a brain bulged wet and glistening within a silver and grey latticework, next to a bloodless hand whose fingers curled and uncurled, over and over again. A single eyeball gleamed dully among copper piping beaded with sweat. An endless display of viscera wound back and forth, intertwined with gold and silver wiring. Frost studied it all with cool fascination. Silence couldn't look away. Carrion mostly looked after Diana, who went where she was led.

There were more walls, equally disturbing, and as the party moved deeper into Level Three, the mix of living tissue and alien technology became increasingly overt and bizarre. One hundred and twenty-seven men and women had lived and worked in Base Thirteen before the aliens came, and not a single body part of any one of them had been allowed to go to waste.

"Why?" said Frost finally. "What's the point of it all? What is this supposed to achieve? If the aliens were capable of such extensive work, why didn't they use the Base's . . . resources to repair their ship?"

"Perhaps the ship was too badly damaged," said Carrion. "Or perhaps this . . . construction was the reason the aliens came here. We need more information, and a context to see .it in. For the moment, we're just guessing."

"We need to find the aliens," said Silence. "They can't be allowed to get away with this."

"Captain," said Odin quietly in his ear, "I have been examining the memory crystal discovered on the crashed alien vessel, and I have finally managed to access the information within. I have arranged it in as palatable a form as possible. I strongly suggest that you study the information now."

"All right," said Silence. "Run it for me first, then run it for Carrion and the Investigator, while I stand watch. Be prepared to break off at a moment's notice if necessary."

"Of course, Captain. Stand by."

Silence's vision shimmered, and was suddenly replaced by exotic alien vistas as the AI patched the memory crystal directly into his comm implant.

Tall towers, draped in strands of glass and pearl, under a mercury sky. Silvered clouds boil slowly around a sun too bright to look at. The towers stand alone on an endless plain. There are dim cavities in the sides that might be entrances. Something living curls around the bases of the towers, unfurling wide, jagged petals to the brilliant sun. The images are blurred, seen through a fluid, distorting haze.

A series of similar images come and go, in which the details change but the scene remains the same. The towers age but do not fall, the strands twisting and shuddering as time shakes them. More towers spring up, covering the plain. In and out of the cavities, around the bases of the towers, near and far, are shadowy figures, never still, always blurs. It is as though film exposures, taken some time apart, have been laid side by side to give an illusion of movement.

Something is speaking, though not with words. Information is passed, thick with meaning.

The towers are everywhere, linked by bridges of gossamer webbing. Life is everywhere, leaping, soaring, growing. There is no room. Time passes. There is war among the towers. Fires burn and terrible energies blaze. The dead are everywhere. Life is everywhere.

A line of shapes, huge and metallic, each different from the next, appear on the plain. They throw themselves up into the mercury sky, and are gone.

Silence rocked on his feet as the images left his eyes, and would have fallen if Frost hadn't steadied him. He leaned on her a moment, till his legs steadied, and then nodded to the Investigator that he was all right. He waited a moment while Odin ran the alien memories through Carrion and Frost's minds, and then they looked at each other with new eyes.

"Incredible," said Frost. "A species, a civilisation, where the boundaries between animate and inanimate, living and non-living, have been blurred and forgotten. Everything there was alive, struggling for space and survival."

"No room anywhere, anymore," said Carrion. "So they built or grew starships and set off to find new worlds. New planets to conquer, to infest, to make over in their image. That's what's happening here. The Base has been remade into something more . . . familiar."

"More than that," said Frost. "Base Thirteen is a beacon, calling others of its kind. They have to be stopped, here on the Rim, while they're still confined to one world. If this were to spread . . . The Empire must be warned. The aliens must be destroyed."

"Not aliens," said Silence. "Just the one. Each of those ships carried a single creature. Or rather, each of those ships was a single creature. I sensed it. Our visitor left its shell after the ship crashed, and made a new shell for itself here, in Base Thirteen. We have to find it, and kill it. If we can. I'm not sure if it is life, as we understand it."

"We can't take chances," said Frost. "Not with something like this. Our very species is at risk. Our best bet is to return to the *Darkwind* and use atomics on the Base until nothing's left but a few grains of dust."

Silence looked at Carrion, who nodded slowly. "We'll have to find the force shield generator and shut down the screen first."

"Are you hearing all this, Odin?" said Silence. "How are your repairs going? Can you be ready to take off once we've shut down the force screen?"

"I'm sorry, Captain," said the AI, "but I can't take you anywhere. You have all been exposed to the alien organism. The probability is high that you are yourselves infected. I cannot risk your passing on that infection to the *Darkwind*."

"Odin, this is a direct order from your Captain," said Silence. "Stand by to carry us back up to the *Darkwind*, where we can be kept in Quarantine . . ."

"I'm sorry, Captain. My standing orders override yours. You will remain here. The pinnace is barred to you."

Carrion laughed softly. "Isn't that the bottom line with the Empire, John? Everyone's expendable. Everyone."

✝

CHAPTER NINE

Unexpected Complications

SILENCE fell helplessly through darkness without end. The bitter air was thick with the stench of sulphur and burning blood. Bright lights flared about him, flashing past like blazing comets. There were voices in the dark, loud and meaningless, interspersed with screams and laughter. Silence didn't know how long he'd been falling, but it felt like an eternity. He thrashed about, hands searching frantically for something that might slow his fall, but there was only the dark and the cold wind rushing past him. He forced himself to stay calm, his mind racing. Where was he, and how the hell had he got there? Where were the others? Where was Carrion?

"Right here, Captain."

And suddenly he was standing on a narrow stairway, its cracked marble steps falling away into infinity. Carrion stood beside him, calm and unruffled. The cold wind stirred his hair, and his cloak swirled around him like billowing wings. He looked down at the endless drop, and then looked at Silence, unmoved.

"I did warn you, Captain. Trips like this are always dangerous."

"Trip?" said Silence, his voice harsh to hide the uncertainty. "Where are we, Carrion?"

"Where you insisted I take you. Inside Diana Vertue's mind."

Memories returned in a rush. Diana had seen the marines die, ripped apart before her. Horror and survivor's guilt had overwhelmed her mind, until the only way to save her sanity had been to deny it had ever happened. She forgot it all, until she was forced to remember. And then, rather than face the horror again, she'd shut herself away inside her own mind, where nothing could reach her and nothing could harm her. She shut herself down and stood staring blindly, mute and comatose, safe at last.

Carrion couldn't reach her with his esp, but he did have one suggestion. It was risky and uncertain, dangerous both to him and the espers, but he could drop his shields and join his mind directly with Diana's. Make her pain his own. *If you're going in there, I'm going in with you,* Silence had said. *After all, I am her father.* Carrion had argued, and Silence hadn't listened. He had no choice. He needed the esper if he was to complete this mission successfully. And she was his daughter, after all.

Lights blazed in the darkness, guttered, and were gone. Voices came and went, shrill and inhuman. And the wind rose and fell, blowing out of nowhere.

"Every light is a thought," said Carrion softly. "Every voice a memory. And the rising and falling of the wind is the force of her will. We're a part of her mind now, as vulnerable as she is. Either we find a remedy for her madness, a way for her to live with her memories, or we'll never leave here."

"Where did the stairway come from?" said Silence, as much for the comfort of hearing his own voice as anything else.

"It's a construct created by our joined minds; a symbol of constancy, to help us feel more secure. You must expect strange things here, Captain. The mind deals in symbols. Particularly when dealing with things it doesn't really want to think about."

He looked down, and Silence followed his gaze. The stairway suddenly came to an end not far below, in a shimmering
silvery plain that stretched away in all directions further than
the eye could follow. And there, at the foot of the stairs, was
a great white-walled house with strange lights burning in its
windows.

"That is Diana's consciousness," said the outlaw. "Or
how she perceives it. We have to enter the house and put
right the damage there, if we can. We'd do well to make
haste. Time isn't a factor; a few days here can be only a
few seconds in the real world. But the mind is a dangerous
place to visit. All the things we really fear are here, with
nothing to protect us from them save the strength of our
own wills. There are no rules here, Captain, only varying
degrees of necessity."

"Then let's get on with it," said Silence, and he started
down the stairs towards the great white house.

The house drew close by slow degrees, as though reluctant
to accept any visitors. Silence began to get the feeling there
was something else in the darkness with them. He looked
unobtrusively about him, but the dark turned aside his gaze
with contemptuous ease. He heard slow, regular breathing,
and what might have been the flapping of giant wings. The
sounds came first from one side and then the other, growing steadily closer, nearer. He sensed a hot, arid presence
watching from the concealing darkness.

"Ignore it, Captain," said Carrion softly. "Whatever it is,
we don't want to meet it. Concentrate on the house. Just
the house."

And suddenly they were at the foot of the stairway, the
house looming over them, shining like a moon. The great
structure looked old-fashioned and curiously stylized, as
though built more for viewing than actual use. The strange
lights were gone, and the windows held only darkness, like
so many watching eyes. A sudden chill stabbed through

Silence as he finally recognised what he was looking at. It
was the doll's house he'd bought Diana for her fifth birthday.
When she'd still been his child, before the Empire took her
from him. He looked at the door before him. It was a great
featureless slab of wood, without knocker or handle.

"What do we do now?" he asked. His voice seemed to
echo on and on, falling away into disturbing whispers.

"We go in," said Carrion evenly. "And then we talk to
Diana, or whatever part of her she chooses to show us. We
can't force her to come back with us. We have to persuade
her. If we can."

He stepped forward and knocked firmly on the door. The
sound was flat and empty, not at all like a door should sound.
It swung slowly open before them, revealing a brightly lit
hallway. Silence looked at Carrion, who gestured for him to
lead the way. Silence stepped resolutely forward, Carrion a
step behind him. The door closed behind them with a solid,
final sound. The hallway stretched ahead of them, impossibly
long. The light came from everywhere and nowhere, and
doors led off from the hallway at regular intervals.

"The mind is a labyrinth," said Carrion. "Let's hope we
don't meet the Minotaur."

"There might not be one," said Silence.

"There's always a Minotaur. If we're lucky, there'll also
be a guide."

As though the house had been listening all along, and
waiting for the word to be spoken, a door opened not far
away, and a young child stepped out into the hallway. Diana,
six years old, in her party dress. There were electrode burns
on her forehead.

"Do you recognise the image, John?" said Carrion. "Do
you know why she chose this of all her selves to show
us? This is what she looked like when the Empire was
training her how to use her esp. Or to be more exact,
when not to. The first thing all espers have to learn is

obedience—to use their esp only when ordered to. Espers are controlled through pain-avoidance conditioning, a long and painful process whose only justification is that it works. No one uses the word torture. Espers have no rights. They're a commodity, to be used and discarded as needed. And if that means attaching electrodes to a young child and turning up the voltage, well, you can't make an omelette, and all that. No, Captain; don't look away. This is your doing."

"I didn't know," said Silence.

"You didn't want to know. You closed your eyes to evidence, and your mind to rumours, and told yourself it was all for the best. You sent your daughter to Hell, John, and part of her is always there, endlessly suffering, endlessly screaming. And we're going to have to walk through it to reach her." Carrion leaned forward, his voice gentle as he spoke to the child before him. "Diana, we need to talk to you. Can you talk to us?"

The child turned, put out her hands for them to take, and led them down the hallway. The small hand was warm and soft and very real in Silence's grasp. Ghosts came and walked in the hall with them, pale and silent people who had been important to Diana in her short life. Silence didn't recognise any of them. There was no sign of him among the ghosts. They filed past in eerie silence, their eyes preoccupied, their thoughts somewhere else. Some of them bore the mark of the electrodes on their skin. Some were screaming soundlessly, some were clearly insane, and too many of them were children.

Silence looked away, studying the doors they passed. Some were closed and some were open. The rooms held moments from Diana's past, endlessly repeating like flies trapped in amber. Most were scenes of suffering, mental or physical and often both. *You sent your daughter to Hell, John.* Silence wanted to look away, but wouldn't let himself. And then they came to a closed door, behind which a small child sobbed endlessly, without comfort or hope, and Silence stopped. Carrion and Diana stopped with him. Silence stared at the door, his hands clenched unknowingly into fists, and it seemed to him that if he opened that door and stepped through, he could save his daughter and undo the evil that had been done to her. Carrion looked at him sharply, and there was something in the outlaw's eyes that might have been fear.

"There's nothing you can do, John. What you're hearing is the past. It's already happened. In some deep part of our mind everything that ever hurt or scared us is still there, waiting for a chance to attach itself to us again. If you open that door and let loose what's in that room, you condemn Diana to Hell again, and us with her. Come away, John. The odds are you'll have to face worse than this before we reach the core mentality—the deep hidden centre of Diana, the self that never sleeps."

"We shouldn't be here," said Silence. "This is more than just an invasion of privacy. There are things no one should have to see or remember."

"You're right," said Carrion. "But we don't have any choice. Diana's gone too deep into herself to find her way *f* *i* without help. I'm not even sure I can get us out without Diana's cooperation. If I try it alone, I could *uoy* her mind, or worse. I told you all this before we came *ere*. It's a bit late to be getting an attack of scruples."

"She's my daughter, Sean."

"No, John. You gave up any claim on her, or her on you, when you handed her over to the Empire mind-techs. We have to go on, John. We have to go deeper."

Silence nodded stiffly, and allowed his daughter and the man who used to be his friend to lead him on down the hall. Ghosts swirled around them, lost in the past, and there were doors beyond number. Silence came to another closed door behind which came screams of hate and fury. Something huge and powerful slammed against the door, rattling it in its frame, splintering the thick wood. Diana pulled insistently at Silence's arm.

"Don't stop here. It's dangerous. She might get out."

Silence allowed her to pull him away from the door, and they continued on their way. The light grew gradually dimmer, and the floor no longer seemed as solid under his feet as it had. And then, out of the darkness, Ripper and Stasiak came striding forward, leaving bloody footprints behind them. Silence stepped to one side to let them pass, but they stopped before him, blocking the way. They stared at Silence, and tears of blood ran down from their unblinking eyes.

"Why did you do it, Captain?" Stasiak whispered. "Why did you bring us down here and then abandon us? Please, Captain, I want to go home. Don't leave me here in the dark."

"They're just images," said Carrion. "Your mind gives them strength. They can't harm us, unless you let them."

"Please, Captain," said Ripper. "Don't leave us here."

"Whatever happens," said Silence steadily, "I swear I won't leave you in Base Thirteen. One way or another, I promise I'll set you free."

He started forward, with Carrion and Diana, and the marines stepped aside to let them pass. Doors came and went, and ghosts walked, but finally the hall ended in a single huge door. The child Diana let go of Silence's and Carrion's hands, produced a large brass key from somewhere, and unlocked the door. She pushed it open easily, despite its apparent weight, and gestured for the two men to enter. They did so cautiously, and found themselves in a small, comfortably furnished room in which a small fire crackled pleasantly in an open hearth. Diana, age nineteen, her rightful age again, sat at her ease in one of the chairs by the fire. Silence looked slowly about him, frowning. The child was gone. The door shut quietly behind them.

"I know this place," said Silence. "I remember this. Elaine and I brought Diana here when she was very small. It was our last holiday together."

"Probably why she chose this particular memory to hide herself in," said Carrion. "She felt safe here. The last place she ever felt safe and protected from the outside world."

They looked at Diana, sitting relaxed in the large, over-stuffed chair. *It wasn't really that big,* realised Silence. *She just remembers it that way because she was so small.* Outside, he could hear rain falling. It had rained all through that holiday, and he and Elaine and Diana spent the long days playing games and charades and stuffing themselves with good food. Not much of a memory to make a heaven out of. But when it's all you've got . . .

"Diana," he said finally. "It's me. Your father. I've come to fetch you. It's time to go."

"I don't want to go," said Diana. "There's something out there. In the dark. It frightens me."

"You can't stay here," said Carrion. "The longer you stay, the harder you'll find it to leave."

"I don't want to leave," said Diana. "I'm safe here."

Something moved outside the shuttered windows. Foot-steps, slow and steady, passed by the window, heading for the door.

"Who's out there, Diana?" said Carrion.

"My mother. She was here too."

All the color drained from Silence's face as a cold hand clutched at his heart. "No, Diana. No. Your mother's been dead five years now."

"Not here," said Diana. "You were here and I was here, and Mother was with us. We're all going to be together, and we'll never have to be alone again."

The footsteps reached the door, and stopped. There was a feeling in the air of something final and irrevocable about to happen.

"The door's locked," said Carrion. "Concentrate, John. The door is locked if you believe it to be. John, listen to me. She mustn't be allowed to complete the memory, or we could be trapped here with her."

"Elaine," said Silence. "You never met her, Sean. You would have liked her. She was bright and funny and very lovely. She died in an attack-ship ambush, out by the Horsehead Nebula. They never found the body, but we held a funeral for her anyway. I miss her, Sean. I miss her so much."

The door handle rattled. Silence looked at the closed door, and then at Diana. Carrion clutched his arm tightly.

"John, Diana—don't do this. The more real you allow your past to become, the more power it has over you. You're in control now, but it won't last. Everything that ever made an impression on you, for good or bad, is in here with you. For the moment, all the things that frightened and hurt you are safely locked away behind closed doors, but once you lose control, the doors will start opening. And then, it won't be Elaine rattling the door and wanting to come in. John, talk to her, dammit. Convince her. You said yourself that Elaine's been dead for five years. What do you think is out there? At best, you're faced with an eternity of child's games and charades. At worst, you're facing an eternity with a woman you know is dead."

Silence looked at the door again then back at Diana. She smiled at him serenely.

"Diana, we can't stay here. You have to come with me now."

"No. We're going to be together again. For ever and ever and ever."

"Diana . . ."

"Something happened," said Diana. "I don't remember what, and I don't want to. I'd rather die than remember."

"No!" said Silence. "Diana, please. Listen to me. We need you. I need you. I've been alone so long . . . . I've got to go.

Please, don't leave me alone again."

She looked at him steadily. No sound came from beyond the door. The whole world seemed to be holding its breath. Diana reached out and took Silence by the hand.

"Look after me," she said softly. "Keep me safe. Promise."

"I promise," said Silence, forcing the words past a lump in his throat. "I'll never let anything hurt you again." He took her in his arms, and she hugged him tightly, her face buried in his chest. Silence looked at Carrion, his eyes bright with unshed tears. "Get us out of here, Sean."

A new light filled the room, bright and blinding, washing away all details in its glow, and then it faded away and they were back in the corridor on Level Three. Back in another labyrinth, with a different Minotaur, held together by newly discovered love. Carrion hoped it would be enough.

"All right," said Silence. "This is the plan. It's very simple. Simple plans are always the best, because that way there are less things to go wrong. Diana, you're going to use your esp to contact the alien. The thing itself, the beast in the shell; whatever it was that first came here from the crashed ship. You're going to act as bait, to draw the alien out from wherever it's hidden itself. It'll come to you, because it perceives you as a threat. Your esp makes you especially dangerous, and it knows that. You don't have anything to worry about; Investigator Frost will be with you. She'll keep both of you alive, and the alien distracted, while Carrion and I track down the heart of the system it's built here. There has to be a centre, a place that holds everything together. Destroy that and the alien will be isolated and much more vulnerable to attack.

"Carrion will use his psionic invisibility to keep the alien from knowing what's happening till it's too late; once we've broken the connection between the alien and the Base, Frost should have no trouble in dealing with it. But Diana, you must understand that once we've started this, we have to finish it. You can't disappear behind your psionic invisibility, and hide; you're the bait. You have to hold its attention while Carrion and I destroy the heart. You'll be in no real danger. Frost will protect you."

"Damn right," said the Investigator. "Never met an alien I didn't kill."

Diana nodded jerkily. "I understand, Captain. Let's do it."

She closed her eyes and let her mind drift up and out. The Base roared around her in a thousand voices, some human, some not. The human components of the alien system were still alive, though their minds or what was left of them now followed alien paths. Diana concentrated on blocking out the babbling voices one by one, searching for the dominating alien presence at the centre of its web, It found her first, blazing in her thoughts, but she held her ground and kept the alien firmly at the edges of her mind. She felt its interest in her grow as she continued to hold it at bay, and its thoughts crawled across her shields like worms across her face. Its probes grew stronger and more threatening, but Diana had been trained to withstand far worse.

Her confidence increased as she realized the alien wasn't really that strong in itself; its true strength lay in the shell it had built around itself, in its domination of the living components of its web. Diana shut out every other voice, concentrating on the alien, showing it her strength. Its thoughts seethed at the edges of her mind, dark and complex and utterly inhuman. Try as she might, its thought processes made no sense at all. Diana concentrated on projecting a single message. *If you want me, you're going to have to come and get me yourself. Your web can't see me, and if you don't come to me, I'll come to you. And I'll destroy you.* The alien broke contact sharply, and Diana dropped back into her head and opened her eyes. The others looked at her questioningly, and she nodded firmly, trying hard to look professional and in command of the situation.

"It knows where I am. You'd better get moving, Captain. It'll be here soon."

Silence smiled and nodded. "Just give me a direction, Diana."

Diana projected the map overlay the AI had given them of Level Three, and indicated their position and that of the centre of the web. Silence and Carrion acknowledged the information, and Diana broke contact. Silence waited patiently while Diana familiarized herself with the new lamp the Investigator had found, and then he and Carrion set off down the corridor, their lamp bobbing along above them like an oversized will-o'-the-wisp. Diana and Frost stood together a moment, awkward in each other's company, and then the Investigator sat down on the floor, drew her sword, and laid it across her knees.

"Might as well make ourselves comfortable, while we wait for the alien to put in an appearance. I take it your esp will give us plenty of warning?"

"Of course, Investigator." Diana hesitated, and then sat down beside Frost. It didn't feel particularly comfortable, but it was good to get off her feet for a while. "So what do we do now, Investigator? Just wait?"

"Pretty much. Nothing we can do till the alien gets here. Relax. Save your strength. You're going to need it."

"What do you suppose it'll look like?" Diana asked hesitantly. "I've never seen an alien. In the flesh, as it were."

"Could be anything," said Frost easily. "None of this fits in with anything I've ever seen before. Probably really ugly. Most of them are, to our eyes. Don't let it worry you. As soon as it shows up, I'll blow a hole through it with my disrupter, and then you can help me cut it up into bite-sized pieces. No problem."

"How can you be so calm, so confident?" Diana asked. "This creature slaughtered every living thing in the Base, and then tore their corpses apart to fashion them into a living computer network. This isn't some rogue animal we're dealing with; it's a powerful, sophisticated entity, and it's heading right for us."

"I'm an Investigator," said Frost. "I'm trained to deal with situations like this. Are you scared, Diana?"

"Yes," said the esper. "Yes, I am."

"That's good. Being scared will give you an edge. It gets the adrenalin pumping, and sharpens your reflexes."

"Are you scared?"

"I suppose so, in my way. Investigators don't really have emotions, just pale echoes of what we remember as emotions. Our training sees to that."

Diana nodded. "Training. The usual Empire euphemism for mind control. They started my training when I was six years old. When to use my power, and when not to. Who to use it for. And right from the beginning it was made clear to us that if we didn't learn thoroughly or quickly enough, we'd be killed. The Empire won't tolerate rogue or uncontrollable espers. Six years old is a hell of a time to be made aware of your own mortality. But it does give you a strong sense of perspective. In the end, all that really matters is following orders.

"They experimented for a time with mind-control implants, but they couldn't develop one that didn't interfere with esper functions, so they settled for good old-fashioned psychological conditioning. I've been trained about as thoroughly as anyone can be, without an actual lobotomy."

There was a pause as they sat quietly together, not looking at each other.

"My training started at about the same age," said Frost slowly. "In learning to outthink alien minds, we give up a lot of what it means to be human. Things like emotions, conscience, companionship. Our training produces warriors, perfect killing machines to serve the glory of the Empire. I don't feel much of anything anymore except when I'm fighting. I've had lovers, but I never loved any of them. I have no friends, no family, nothing but the job. Still, if nothing else, it is an extremely interesting job."

"Is that all you have?" said Diana. "Just the job and the killing?"

Frost shrugged. "It's enough. You can't expect too much out of life, esper. You should know that."

Diana smiled briefly. "You know, we're more alike than I thought. You deal in death and I deal with life, but really we're two sides of the same coin. We both had our childhoods taken away from us, and had our lives shaped into something those children could never have understood. And we'll both probably die serving the people who destroyed our lives in the first place."

Frost shook her head. "No, esper, you don't understand me at all. I like being what I am, what they made me. I'm strong and I'm fast, and there's nothing and no one that can stand against me. I'm the most perfect fighting machine you'll ever see. I've been responsible for the destruction of whole alien civilisations, and killed men and creatures with my bare hands. It's only when I'm fighting and killing that I feel really alive. It's like a drug you never grow tired of. You can't know how it feels, esper—to know you're the best. I'm the ultimate expression of the Empire, the personification of its strength and purpose. And all I had to give up to achieve it was a few weak emotions that would only have got in the way of my work.

"It's different for you. You take no pride in being an esper. Probably give it up tomorrow, if you could. To be normal. I won't give up what I am, and I'll kill anyone who tries to take it away from me. You think too much, esper. It gets in the way. Life's so much simpler without conscience or emotions to complicate things."

Diana looked at her steadily. "Everything else has been taken away from me; I won't give them up too. I'd rather die."

"You may get your chance," said Frost, looking down the corridor into the darkness. "Something's coming."

The Investigator rose to her feet in one graceful movement and stood listening, sword at the ready. Diana scrambled unelegantly to her feet and looked wildly about her. The alien couldn't be here already. It couldn't. Her esp would have picked it up long before this. Unless it too knew the art of psionic invisibility. In which case, things were about to get rather interesting.

Frost slapped the metal bracelet on her left wrist, and her force shield sprang into existence on that arm—a palely glowing rectangle of pure energy, humming loudly on the quiet. Diana raised her esp and reached out tentatively. The Base was silent, with none of the babbling voices she'd heard earlier. The alien had put up shields. Diana retreated quickly into her own mind, and set up her own wards. Theoretically, they should be able to stand off any psionic attack, up to and including a mindbomb, but she'd never tested her shields in actual conflict before. Hopefully, the alien didn't know that. She glanced across at Frost, and was silently reassured by the Investigator's obvious professionalism and competence. A thought struck her.

"Investigator, if the alien is coming, wouldn't you be better off with your disrupter than your sword?"

"No," said Frost calmly. "A sword's more versatile. You can have the gun, if you want."

"No thanks," said Diana. "I don't believe in them."

"Suit yourself," said Frost, a shrug clear in her voice. "Whatever's out there, it's close. I can feel it. I'm impressed. I didn't think anything could get that close to me without my knowing."

"Psionic invisibility," said Diana. "No way you could have known."

"That shouldn't have made any difference," said Frost. "I am an Investigator, after all. Are you picking up anything?"

"Not much. Something's coming, and it's not alone. I don't think it's the alien." She looked unhappily at Frost. "I can't be sure, but I don't think the alien's here at all. It's still hanging back. It's sent something else in its place. Stand ready, Frost. They're almost here."

"Relax, esper." The Investigator swept her sword casually back and forth before her, smiling easily. "Nothing's going to get to you while I'm here. Though you could at least activate your force shield. There's no point in making it easy for them. You're here as bait, not a sacrifice."

Diana blushed, and slapped her bracelet. The low hum of the force shield was very reassuring. She and the Investigator stood quietly together, listening. And then the soft patter of running feet came clearly to them out of the darkness, and Diana and Frost braced themselves as their enemy finally emerged into the light.

They'd been human once, before the alien absorbed them into its system. Now they were something else, roughly human in shape, but refashioned to meet the alien's needs. They were crooked and malformed, with running flesh congealed on their frames like melted wax on a candle. Some had no skin, the red muscles shining wetly in the lamplight, their tendons twitching with every movement. Bunches of cilia waved from empty eye sockets, and mouths held needle teeth. Muscles bulged impossibly, beyond restraint or reason. The twisted faces were inhumanly blank, indifferent to thought or emotion. The alien had reworked them for its own reasons, and if there was any humanity left in them, it was buried deep, where it wouldn't interfere.

There were ten of them, jostling each other at the edge

of the lamplight, as though reluctant to leave the comfort of the shadows. *Ten,* thought Diana. *That's not so bad. We can handle ten.* As if in answer to her thoughts, more appeared, stepping out of the walls as though the walls were mist and not steel. The Investigator scowled.

"How do they do that? Those walls are solid. I checked them myself."

"The walls have become part of the alien system," said Diana softly. "They're alien now. As alien as everything else in this Base. The whole structure has become a single great organism, with the alien as its heart and mind."

Frost snorted. "So what does that make these things?"

"Antibodies. We're invaders, an infection in the system. So those things are going to cleanse us out."

"You mean they're going to try," said Frost calmly. "All right, there's a lot of them, but they're not even armed. Let's keep this in perspective, esper. We can handle this."

"You don't get it, do you?" said Diana. "They're *antibodies.* The alien can make as many of them as it needs to, recycling damaged ones if necessary. It can make a dozen, a hundred, a thousand; as many as it needs to overrun us. Even you couldn't stand against a thousand, Investigator. They're not human. Not anymore. They don't think or feel or hurt. They'll just keep coming until we're dead. And then the alien will recycle us, and put us to some useful task. If we're lucky, we'll never know what."

"You think too much, esper," said Frost. "It's never over till it's *over.* With this many antibodies, they'll spend most of their time tripping over each other and getting in each other's way. All we've got to do is hold them off, until either the Captain and the outlaw reach the heart of the system, or the alien gets impatient and comes here itself to take us on." She smiled unpleasantly at the shapes before her, and swept her blade back and forth. "Come on then, you useless sons-of-bitches. Let's do it."

• • •

Captain Silence and the outlaw Carrion moved swiftly through the distorted corridors, heading into the dark heart of Base Thirteen. For a long time the only illumination came from the lamp bobbing along above them, but eventually strange lights began to appear in the distance, steady glows and sudden glares, like the opening of so many watching eyes. Things stirred and shifted in the shadows, sometimes alive and sometimes not. Silence kept a wary eye on all of them, but tried not to look at them too closely. Something about their uncertain shapes disturbed him on some deep, primal level. The idea that the material world could acquire sentience and direction undermined his faith in how the universe worked.

Carrion, on the other hand, didn't seem to be bothered by any of it. But then, he'd been an Investigator once, and nothing bothered them. Silence glared about him, holding his gun so tightly that his knuckles ached. He had faith in Carrion's psionic invisibility to keep them from being detected, but walking straight into the alien's clutches went against all his instincts. He clamped down hard on his nerves, and watched where he stepped. Thick steel cables stirred sluggishly on the floor like dreaming snakes, coiling around each other in slow, sinuous movements, dripping black oil. Silvery traces glowed like veins in the sweating walls, pulsing in a fast, irregular rhythm. Silence glanced at Carrion, irritated by his continued calm.

"Are you sure this invisibility of yours is working?"

"Quite sure, Captain. Because if it wasn't, we'd very likely be dead by now. Have faith, Captain. I'll get you there."

Silence sniffed. "Odin, are you still following this?"

"Yes, Captain," the AI murmured in his ear. "Audio contact remains firm."

"Give me an overlay of the Level Three floor plans." The plans appeared before him, hovering on the air in glowing lines and symbols. Silence checked his position and that of the centre of the web, and scowled. They were a lot closer than he'd thought. "Odin, any chance you've reconsidered your position on letting us back on board the pinnace?"

"No, Captain. My Security imperatives are very clear on the matter. However, I will of course provide you with whatever information and guidance I can."

"Any more useful information from the Base computers?"

"Not as yet, Captain. However, there are still several areas locked away behind Security codes I don't have access to."

"All right, lose the overlay." The glowing map vanished from his sight. "Stay in contact, computer. Let me know of any changes in the situation."

"Of course, Captain."

Silence looked at Carrion. "I take it you were patched into that. Any comments?"

"Only that we should walk even more carefully from now on. We're nearly there, and I can't believe the alien will have left the heart of its system unprotected. There are bound to be defensive systems and booby traps just waiting for us to trigger them."

"I've really missed your sunny personality, Carrion. You look for the worst in everything, don't you?"

"Yes, Captain. And usually I'm right."

Silence sniffed. "We should reach the heart in a few minutes. Assuming we do find a way past whatever's waiting for us, do you have any ideas as to what we're going to do when we get there?"

"Not really, Captain. A few of your grenades, backed up if necessary by a channelled psi-storm from me, should be enough to wreck whatever the alien's put together, but I can't be sure until I've seen it."

"Aren't you going to make a speech about how wrong I am to be planning the destruction of a new alien species? I seem to recall you were quite eloquent on the subject where the Ashrai were concerned."

"That was different. The Ashrai were willing to co-exist. This species is not. Its existence is based on total restructuring and control of the environment. They are as much a threat to this world and to the Ashrai as they are to the Empire."

"I wish you'd stop talking about the Ashrai as though they were still alive. They're dead and gone. I killed them all. You've been alone here too long, Carrion."

Carrion looked at him almost pityingly. "The Ashrai aren't gone. You never did understand the bond between the Ashrai and the metallic forest. I've been here ten years, and I'm only just beginning to comprehend what we destroyed here. The Ashrai were a race of espers, exhibiting psi phenomena we could barely measure, let alone understand. They fought the Empire to a standstill, for all our superior technology. And even though you scorched this planet, they're still here. Their bodies may be dead, but their souls still haunt the trees. Call it a vast living field of psi energy and phenomena earthed by the metal forest, if that makes it easier for you to grasp. But as long as the forest still stands, the Ashrai still exist. They do not forget and they do not forgive. They were very special, John. You never did understand what you did here."

"Oh yes, Sean. I know what I did."

Carrion stopped suddenly, and gestured for Silence to stop with him. They stood a while in their narrow pool of light, while Carrion frowned uncertainly, checking the way ahead with his esp. He finally shook his head and gestured for Silence to continue, but he was still frowning. Silence drew his gun and scowled at every moving shadow. The pressure of unseen watching eyes seemed heavier by the minute, but nothing challenged them.

The corridor widened out suddenly into what had been one of the main computer bays, and Carrion and Silence stopped again, halted by the sight of what lay before them. The machines had burst apart from pressure within, and flowered into unsettling half-living constructs, held together by long, glistening strands of human nervous tissue. A constant, barely audible muttering filled the air, so low as to be almost subliminal, as the hybrid creations worked constantly on unknown alien tasks. Silence looked slowly around, not allowing himself to be hurried, no matter how much the sight revolted him. Carrion walked slowly forward, his face blank, his eyes fey and knowing.

"This is the heart of the system, the centre of the web," he said in a low voice. "Through this, the alien controls all that happens in the Base. This is its eyes and ears, its brain and memory. Destroy this, and the alien will be cut off from its creation. The Base systems will fall apart, and the alien will be left alone and vulnerable."

"If it's that straightforward, what are you looking so unhappy about?" said Silence.

"It's too easy. Too easy to get here and too easy to destroy. It can't be this simple. We must be missing something. I think we should investigate these systems very carefully before we do anything else."

"Carrion, we don't have the time. The alien's gone for the moment, but it could be back any minute. We have to destroy the heart while we can. Look, just because the alien is intelligent and powerful, it doesn't necessarily follow that it's very bright. The more powerful an organism, the less it needs to think things through. It uses what has always worked in the past, and expects that to be enough. Because it's never been beaten, it thinks it can't be. Everything has a weak spot, and we've found the alien's. Now give me some room and let me work. Watch the corridor if you want to be useful. I want to set the grenades and get the hell out of here before the alien realises something is up and comes charging back."

The outlaw nodded stiffly, and moved away to watch the corridor, his expression still troubled. Silence consulted with the AI, and worked out the best places to set his grenades to ensure maximum damage. He planted three grenades carefully, primed them all one after the other, and then sprinted back down the corridor with Carrion at his side. They'd just rounded the first corner when the first grenade blew. A shock wave of superheated air laced with jagged shrapnel came howling down the corridor, to slam harmlessly against the psychokinetic shield Carrion set up. Two more explosions followed in swift succession, and the floor trembled under their feet. The explosions were deafeningly loud, and Silence clapped his hands to his ears, grinning triumphantly. Smoke filled the corridor, billowing thickly around them. The tremors finally died away, and the corridor was quiet save for the crackling of distant fires. Silence grinned at Carrion.

"That should ruin the alien's day nicely. You'd better run a scan, though, just in case any of that stuff is still working. I'll have the AI check it out from his end."

He broke off as the AI's voice suddenly sounded in his ear. "We have a problem, Captain. Apparently Base Commander Starblood wasn't content to just seal off the Base with a force screen; he also activated the Base's self-destruct system. A small nuclear device was primed and programmed to detonate at the end of a countdown. When the alien's systems took over the computers, it interrupted the countdown but didn't defuse the bomb. As long as the system was in control, the countdown was unable to continue, and the Base was safe. Now that you have destroyed the alien system, the countdown is proceeding again. The nuclear device will detonate in thirty-two minutes, and I do not have the necessary codes to abort it. I strongly suggest that you leave the Base now. While you still can."

CHAPTER TEN

Friendships and Loyalties

FROST pulled a concussion grenade from her bandolier, primed it, and lobbed it casually over the heads of the watching humanoids. A few turned their blank faces to follow it, but the others showed no reaction, even as Frost primed and threw two more grenades. The first exploded deafeningly in the midst of the creatures, blowing a bloody hole in their ranks. Smoke filled the corridor, and blood flew on the air in a crimson mist. The next two grenades blew seconds later, while Frost and Diana huddled back into a niche in the corridor wall, hands clapped to their ears. The massed ranks of the humanoids absorbed the force of the explosions, scattering blood and mangled bodies the length of the corridor. The living and the injured staggered aimlessly back and forth, dazed and confused, and Frost chuckled easily as she shot the head off one creature with her disrupter. Diana shrank back from the open violence in the Investigator's voice, and brushed furiously at the blood that had spattered her clothes.

The humanoids milled back and forth, clawing at the smoke and each other. Frost laughed softly, hefted her claymore, and moved forward with a light, easy step. Her blade flashed in the lamplight as she cut and hacked her way through the blank-faced drones. Her sword jarred on bone and sliced through flesh, and she was everywhere at once, darting back and forth. Bodies fell to either side of her and did not rise again, and the humanoids reached blindly out into

157

the smoke and chaos as the alien will behind them struggled to orientate itself. Investigator Frost cut and hacked a path into the heart of the enemy, and was content.

Diana Vertue concentrated on maintaining her psionic invisibility, balancing her need for safety with her duty as bait. She allowed a vague sense of her presence to leak through her mental shields, to keep the alien's attention, but hid her precise location behind a screen of ambiguity, so that neither the alien nor its humanoid slaves could tell exactly where she was. They milled around her with reaching hands, a horrid faceless mass of clawed hands and snapping mouths, but none of them could find her, even when their bodies bumped into hers. She bit down hard on her lower lip to keep from screaming. The humanoids had been constructed from the Base personnel, and though they moved and fought and searched for her with stubborn purpose, they were still dead. Their faces held no thought or emotion, their skin was deathly cold to the touch, and something shockingly inhuman looked out from their unblinking eyes. Diana stood with her back pressed tightly against the wall, her face contorted with a horror beyond revulsion, shrinking away from every contact. A grinding headache began to build in her left temple, sharp-edged and blinding, as she struggled to maintain the delicate balance of her presence. There but not there. Present but not seen. And over and above everything else, the certain knowledge that if her control slipped, even for a moment, the humanoids would turn on her and tear her apart.

Frost danced and strutted in the midst of her enemies, pirouetting with sharp professionalism, her sword swinging in unstoppable arcs. It was a good blade, Old Earth steel, and while it might not have the edge of her monofilament knife, the weight and power of the claymore was more than a match for the clawing hands of the alien drones. They swarmed about her, a living sea of hate and violence, and none of them were fast enough or good enough to touch her. Their clawed hands snatched and tore but she was never there, defying them to find or hold her. Her force shield brushed aside those few who got too close, the glowing energy field fending off their unnatural strength. But its constant use was a dangerous drain on its energy crystal, and it wouldn't be long now before the shield collapsed. Frost didn't care. The humanoids were falling before her, and she was in her element, doing what she was trained and born to do. Nothing could stand against her. Let them come. Let them all come. She was an Investigator, humanity's warrior, and the alien was going to learn what that meant.

Diana watched the Investigator butcher the dead men from Base Thirteen with grace and style, and it seemed to her that Frost was as inhuman as what she was fighting. The Investigator's face was a cold mask of contempt and professionalism, with no trace of compassion. She killed because that was what she'd been trained to do, and because she was good at it. An expert in the art of slaughter. Not that Diana had much compassion herself for the creatures. She could see in their faces that they weren't human any longer in anything but shape. Death was the only peace and dignity they could attain to. She supposed she should be helping Frost fight, but she couldn't. Partly because the effort to maintain her invisibility took so much out of her, but mostly because just the thought of personally doing violence sickened her. The Empire had trained her well.

And then, suddenly, the humanoids fell back, turned away from the Investigator, and disappeared into the surrounding steel walls. One moment the corridor was full of smoke and baleful figures, and then they were gone, and the smoke was slowly clearing to reveal Frost lowering her bloody sword in puzzlement. She wasn't even breathing hard. The dead lay where they had fallen, jagged metal showing in bloody wounds, and gore still spattered the floor and walls, but

Frost and Diana were alone in the corridor. Frost sniffed disappointedly and moved back to stand with Diana, shaking drops of blood from her blade. The esper shrank back from the gore-soaked sword, but Frost didn't notice. She clapped Diana on the shoulder, and looked around with an easy and contented smile.

"It looks like we were too much for them. Pity. I was just starting to enjoy myself."

"It's not over," said Diana softly. "Something's coming."

The Investigator looked at her sharply, and then glared about her, sword at the ready. "Is it the alien?"

"It must be. It burns in my mind like a beacon, wild and brilliant. It hurts to think about it. There's something . . . wrong about it."

"How close is it?"

"Close. I can hear it thinking. It doesn't make any sense. It has emotions, but I don't recognise any of them. It's like seeing new colors in a rainbow. . . ."

"You're wandering, esper," said Frost. "Keep to the subject. How big is the alien? How strong? Which direction is it coming from?"

"It's almost here." Diana rubbed at her forehead as her headache flared up again. "It's getting harder to keep it out of my mind. It's like looking into the sun when it's too bright . . . . It's strong, powerful. Inhumanly powerful."

"Concentrate, esper."

"I can't . . . there's too much of it . . . ."

"Then bring it here. Be the bait, and I'll take care of everything else."

And then the alien appeared at the end of the corridor, and Frost stopped talking. It was big, filling the corridor from wall to wall and from floor to ceiling, like a slug in its tunnel. The dark, ribbed body looked long and powerful, with thick cables of muscle standing out and pulsing like veins. Metallic strands were threaded through its flesh—not added, but a living part of its body. Long, bony limbs protruded at regular intervals along its bulk, poling it along the walls. Sharp metal barbs and spikes thrust up from its glistening back, and its end was too far away to be seen. The blunt head had no eyes, or any other obvious features except for metallic teeth that snapped shut again and again in its wide maw, like the closing of a man-trap. The mouth was big enough to take a human head as a morsel, and the teeth shone like daggers. It surged forward, foot by foot, huge and threatening like a thundercloud come down to earth. Its limbs rattled against the metal walls, and its breath hissed in the vast mouth.

Diana wanted to look away, but couldn't. The thing offended her on some deep, primal level. It was a mixture of living and unliving, life and technology, but grown, not made. Things that should never have known sentience or animation were an intrinsic part of its being. She tried to imagine what kind of hellish pressures or evolution could produce such a creature, and couldn't. It was too alien, too different. The creature blazed in her mind, the strength of its presence blasting aside her shields till she stood naked and helpless before it. The alien looked at her with its eyeless head and knew where she was, and the shape and texture of its thoughts were made clear to her. They made no sense to her, no sense at all.

"It's bigger than I thought," said Frost casually. "It must have grown considerably since it left its ship, presumably from feeding on the Base personnel. I wonder how big it would grow eventually, without restraint . . . . Still, that's a problem for those that come after us. Stand back, esper. I'm going to blow a hole right through it."

"Your gun won't stop it," said Diana. "Nothing can stop it. It's too big. Too different."

"Hell," said Frost. "It's just an alien."

She raised her disrupter, trained it on the alien's blunt head, and pressed the stud. The searing energy bolt burned a hole through the head, and oily black blood spattered across the walls and ceiling. The alien howled deafeningly, the sound reverberating through Diana's bones as well as her ears. The great head swayed back and forth, and Frost looked on dumbly as the ruptured flesh knitted itself together, steel and silver traces scabbing over the gaping wound like metal sutures. Frost put away her gun.

"I think we're in trouble, esper. I was rather counting on the disrupter to take care of the alien. Still, when a plan fails, improvise. I've got a few grenades left. When I say the word, you run. And don't hang about, because I'm going to be right behind you."

She pulled a grenade from her bandolier, hefted it casually, and then primed it and rolled it along the floor towards the alien. She yelled to Diana to run, and the esper turned and fled down the corridor. The alien lunged forward, its bulk smothering the grenade. Frost turned and ran, quickly catching up with the esper. Frost hurried her on with harsh words, and then saved her breath for running. The grenade went off, and the floor shuddered under their feet. Frost allowed herself a moment of satisfaction, and then the alien's roar filled the corridor, harsh and unrelenting. The floor trembled again, this time from the alien's massive weight as it bore down on them, in pursuit. Frost tried to visualize how fast something that big could move, but had to abandon the attempt. Nothing in her training or experience had prepared her for this alien. It was too different, too unlike anything humanity had ever encountered before.

She accessed the floor plan, and led Diana into the smaller, narrower corridors hoping they'd prove too small for the alien's bulk. But everywhere they went, the alien had been there first. Strange growths erupted from the sweating steel walls, and shimmering strands hung down from the torn ceiling. And finally they had to stop for Diana to get her breath. Frost looked impatiently around her while the esper leaned on her arm for support, head hanging down as she fought for air. The Investigator was still breathing slow and easy. Her training had prepared her for worse than this. She could have escaped the alien easily if it hadn't been for Diana, but she couldn't bring herself to abandon the esper. As long as the bait was still held dangling before the alien, it should concentrate on the esper and not concern itself with what Carrion and the Captain were doing.

She glared back down the corridor into the impenetrable gloom, gun in one hand, incendiary grenade in the other. She might not be able to kill the alien, but she could sure as hell hold its attention. She looked unhurriedly about her, sizing the corridor up for possible ambushes and fast exits. There were holes everywhere, in the walls and in the ceiling, some of them leading into tunnels seemingly big enough to swallow the *Darkwind*'s pinnace. The alien had been busy.

Frost frowned suddenly as she realised the trembling in the floor had stopped. The alien must have decided on another route, a roundabout way to take its prey by surprise. Which meant any of the holes might become an opening for the alien's attack. She approached the nearest of the larger holes and peered cautiously into it. Deep in the darkness she heard a faint muttering, a familiar cacophony of human and alien sounds. She primed the incendiary grenade, counted three quickly, and threw the grenade as far down the tunnel as she could. Then, stepping to one side, she flattened herself against the corridor wall.

There was a dull roar, and smoke and flames billowed out of the hole, along with flying fragments of alien tissue. Frost grinned savagely, and then trotted down the corridor with Diana in tow, pausing to scorch each of the larger holes with a blast from her disrupter. The vivid energy bolts lit up each tunnel as she fired, but there was never a trace of the alien, and the gun took a little longer each time to recharge between shots.

Frost stopped near the end of the corridor, and peered uncertainly about her. She was doing a lot of damage to the Base, but she was no nearer stopping the alien. It should have found them by now. She wasn't foolish enough to think they'd lost it, or left it behind, which meant it had to be planning something in its devious, inhuman mind. Frost smiled. In her own quiet way she was enjoying the chase. It was the first real challenge of her abilities she'd ever had, the first opportunity to try and outthink something that didn't think the way humanity did. She had the upper hand. As long as she and the bait kept moving, the alien was helpless to do anything but chase her. It was too large, too heavy, and too stupid to do anything but follow where she led. And when the Captain and the outlaw had destroyed the heart of its web, she'd turn on the alien and have it run for a while, while she purused. She snapped her head round suddenly as she caught a faint whisper of the alien's muttering again. She looked at the esper, who was standing with her eyes closed, trembling violently.

"It's here," said Diana. "It's found us."

"Where is it?" said Frost. "I can't see it anywhere."

"Close," said Diana. "Close."

Frost looked quickly back and forth, straining her ears for any more of the alien muttering, but nothing moved in the corridor gloom, and the air was still and silent. Frost frowned, and tapped her gun against her thigh. Wherever it was, she should still get plenty of warning of its approach. The alien couldn't get anywhere near them without the floor trembling under her feet to alert her. Even if it came through one of the tunnels in the walls. And then something made her look up.

The alien's blunt head emerged from a vast hole in the ceiling like a maggot in a rotten apple. Frost grabbed Diana and hurled them both frantically to one side as the monster dropped out of the ceiling. The floor shuddered as it hit. Frost hit the floor rolling and was quickly back on her feet again, a grenade in her hand. She primed it, rolled it down the corridor towards the alien, hauled Diana to her feet, and all but threw her round the nearest corner. She counted quickly under her breath as they ran down the side corridor, and then a blast of superheated air blew past the corridor entrance, followed by the alien's roar. Frost grinned. She might not be able to kill the damn thing, but she could still hurt it.

She pushed the esper ahead of her as they ran, and took the opportunity to examine her disrupter. The energy crystal was seriously depleted, good for only three or four shots at most. The floor was trembling under her feet again. The alien had to be close behind them. She risked a look back, and swore dispassionately. It was closer than she'd expected, and gaining on them. The thing could move surprisingly fast for its bulk. Frost smiled briefly. She'd always been the pursuer, never the pursued. This was a new experience for her. She found it exhilarating.

They rounded the next corner and then skidded to a halt as they found a dead end. What had been an open passage on the floor plan was now sealed off with a thick mass of alien webbing. Frost hefted her disrupter. The gun still had enough energy to blast a way through, but she might need that power to fire at the alien. She shrugged, and levelled the gun at the webbing. The vivid energy bolt tore through the web, blackening the edges of the ruptured webbing. Frost started forward, only to stop as the web slowly re-formed, knitting itself together with effortless skill. The way was blocked again, and she'd wasted one shot. She didn't see any point in wasting another. She looked quickly about her. Here too there were holes in the walls and ceiling, and no way to tell where any of them led. More of the alien's work. Frost turned to the esper, who was looking back the way they'd come with wide eyes and trembling mouth.

"We're going to have to make a stand, esper. Or rather, I am. You can't help me, and you might get hurt if you get in the way, so I want you to go on alone. Pick one of the tunnels. They have to lead somewhere. Choose one of the smaller ones and the alien won't be able to follow you. I have to stay here and hold its attention until the Captain and Carrion have finished their business."

"You can't face that thing on your own," said Diana. "The gun didn't hurt it, and the grenades only slowed it down. If you stay here you'll be killed. Come with me. I'll make us both invisible, and we'll lose the alien in the tunnels."

"No, esper. We have a job to do, remember? We have to keep the alien occupied."

"You can't do that if you get yourself killed. Stay here and you'll die!"

Frost raised an eyebrow. "It's not that certain. I am an Investigator, after all. We can't both go into the tunnels. They're unknown territory to us. Certainly the alien has to know their layout a damn sight better than us. You go on, esper. I'll hold it here. You have to survive, to be the bait again, if necessary. And if you're going to lead the alien a chase without me, you're going to need a good head start. Go on, esper."

Diana looked at her steadily. "You're going to die here, aren't you?"

"Not if I can help it."

"Aren't you?"

Frost sighed resignedly. "Yes, esper. Quite probably. But that doesn't matter. I know my duty. I always knew I'd die in the field and not in my bed. Comes with the job. I don't mind. It's my duty and it's my life. It's all I've ever wanted."

"You mean it's what the Empire made you want. They programmed you, just like they did me. They ruined your life and made you love it, and now you'll die for them, because your conditioning won't let you do the sensible thing and run."

"No, Diana, that's not it. I'm going to stand and fight because that's what I do best. We're buying time for the others, me by fighting, you by running. Now do as you're told and get into that tunnel. Please."

Diana stepped forward suddenly, and hugged Frost tightly. The Investigator just stood there for a moment, and then gently hugged her back. Diana let go, and Frost helped her climb into the nearest tunnel mouth. Diana smiled back at Frost, her lips pressed tightly together so they wouldn't tremble and spoil the moment, and then she turned and disappeared into the tunnel, taking her lamp with her. Frost adjusted her eyes to make the most of the ambient light, and turned back to face the corridor. Her force shield hummed briskly on her arm, and her sword was a comforting weight in her hand. She breathed slowly, coolly, and her hands were perfectly steady. What the hell. It was only an alien. Something moved in the shadows at the end of the corridor, and Frost smiled widely.

At the heart of the alien web, Carrion and Captain Silence looked at each other speechlessly as the AI told them of the nuclear countdown in a calm, conversational voice. Silence slammed his gun back into his holster.

"Well, that's great. Just great! Now what the hell are we going to do?"

"If I might suggest, Captain," said Carrion, "this is something we might do better to discuss on the run. We have less than thirty-two minutes to locate the esper and the Investigator, evade the alien, get the hell out of Base Thirteen, persuade your computer to let us back on the pinnace, and get off-planet before the nuke blows."

"In other words," said Silence, "we're going to die. What the hell, we might as well give it a try, just to be contrary.

Odin, work out where we are and show us the quickest route out of here."

"I'm afraid I can't do that," said the AI. "Firstly, I will not let you back on board the pinnace. You are still quite probably contaminated by the alien. Secondly, the Empire is going to need the alien's body, and as much of its technology as possible, to examine. Given the potential threat of this new species, the Empire will need all possible information as to the extent of that threat. I must insist you do all in your power to preserve the Base and its contents. I regret the necessity for such harsh measures, Captain. My programming requires that I do this. You know how it is."

"Just when you think things couldn't possibly get any worse, they do," said Silence. "I'll make you a deal, Odin. You agree to get us off-planet and safely back to Quarantine on the *Darkwind*, and we'll save the Base and its contents from destruction. What do you say?"

"Agreed," said the AI. "My programming allows me to be flexible during emergencies."

"Right," said Silence. "That's a start, anyway."

"Pardon me," said Carrion, "but just how are you planning to defeat the alien and defuse the nuke in under thirty-one minutes?"

"Beats the hell out of me. Odin, you must have forged some links with the Base computers by now. Can't you patch into the systems running the countdown, and turn it off?"

"Not at present, Captain. Since this was intended as a last-ditch self-destruct option, the Empire built in a great many safeguards to ensure that the countdown could not be interfered with, once initiated. The alien managed to suspend the countdown in some manner, but I confess I am at a loss to explain how. I am doing my best to access the relevant systems, but my best-guess analysis suggests that will take me significantly longer than the thirty-one minutes remaining on the countdown."

"Didn't you just know he was going to say that?" Silence said to Carrion. "Do you have any ideas?"

"Do we know where the bomb itself is located?" said Carrion, frowning thoughtfully.

"Well, computer?"

"The exact location is protected by Security codes I do not have access to. Logic suggests it is concealed somewhere on Level Three, to ensure maximum destruction."

"Whatever we're going to do, we'd better do it quickly," said Carrion. "And we have to contact Frost and Diana. They may be facing the alien by now, and they still think they have all the time in the world to deal with it."

"There is a way," said Silence slowly. "After all, this doesn't affect just us. We're not alone on this planet, are we, Carrion? There's always the Ashrai."

The alien came boiling down the corridor towards Frost like a flash flood, impossibly huge, impossibly fast. Its mouth gaped wide, revealing its razor-sharp teeth. It was on the Investigator in a second, and she launched herself forward, vaulting over the alien's lowered head and onto its spiked metal back. She landed awkwardly, trying to dodge the spikes and the barbs, but quickly regained her balance. She swept her force shield round in a circle, the sputtering edge shearing through the spikes, and then, having made herself some room, she slammed her sword down into the alien's head. The blade sank half its length into the leathery flesh, and the alien howled shrilly. It smashed its head against the corridor wall, trying to shake off the pain it felt, but Frost held onto the sword with both hands, and kept her balance.

Thick black blood pooled around her feet, and Frost grinned savagely as she stirred the sword around in the alien's head, searching for the brain. The alien screamed, the vast sound hammering through Frost's head, and its long body convulsed as it struggled to throw her off. Frost used all her strength and forced the sword in another few inches. She worked the blade from side to side, trying to widen the wound, but even as the dark flesh split apart, metal traceries sprang out of the raw meat to repair the wound. The flesh healed incredibly quickly, and the metal sutures were strong enough to resist her sword's edge. And slowly, inch by inch, the sword was being forced back up and out of the wound it had made.

Frost lifted the force shield on her arm and brought it down like a hammer. The edge of the energy field passed through the leathery flesh like mist, leaving a long rent behind it. She knelt down beside her sword, and the force field spat and sparkled as she buried it in the alien's back. The alien threw itself back and forth, its wailing voice painfully loud as its cries echoed and re-echoed from the corridor walls. Frost fought to keep her balance as the alien whipped its head from side to side. Metal spikes thrust up around her, and her shield jerked out of the alien's back. Frost leaned on her sword with all her strength, but still the blade was forced up and out of the alien flesh.

And then a pit opened up in the alien's back beneath Frost's feet, and sucked her down. She was knee-deep in the alien before she could even react, hidden muscles crushing her legs. She snarled at the pain and cut desperately about her with her sword and her force shield, but still the alien flesh sucked her down. It closed around her like a living sea, absorbing her struggles and repairing its wounds as fast as Frost could make them. She groped for the monofilament knife in its sheath on her leg, but it had already disappeared into the alien's body. Something dragged at her feet, pulling her down till she was waist-deep in the alien. The dark flesh rose up like a tidal wave and swept towards her.

Diana looked down from the mouth of a tunnel high up on the wall, and clenched her fists helplessly as she watched the Investigator disappearing into the alien's back. She knew she should be using the time Frost was buying her to get away, but she couldn't just turn her back and let the Investigator die. She couldn't just leave her. A cold hand clutched at her heart as the tidal wave rose up and rolled unstoppably forward. Unless she did something, and quickly, Frost was going to die. But what could she do? She was an esper, not a fighter. Never a fighter. She looked wildly about her for inspiration, and her gaze stumbled across a massive, blocky wall-unit not far from the tunnel mouth.

She didn't stop to think about what she was going to do; because she knew that if she did, she probably wouldn't do it. First, she had to get the alien's attention. She dropped her mental shields and cast aside her invisibility like a veil she no longer needed. The great alien head swung round immediately, staring up at her blindly but knowingly. It wanted her, and now it knew where she was. Frost was still sinking into its back, but more slowly now, as though the alien wasn't concentrating on her anymore. It had her, but it wanted the esper. The huge body surged forward, its stumpy legs poling it along the steel walls, leaving dents in its wake. Diana slapped her force shield bracelet, and it sprang into being on her left arm. The alien lifted its head high, searching for her. Diana leaned out from the tunnel mouth, hanging precariously by one hand, and sliced at the wall unit with the edge of her shield. The shimmering energy sliced through the unit's supports, and it lurched drunkenly away from the wall, held only by a single cable. Diana leaned out further, most of her weight hanging out over the drop. The alien's head reached for her, only inches away. Diana gritted her teeth, stretched out her arm, and sliced through the remaining cable. The unit tore itself away from the wall and crashed down onto the alien's head, its massive weight hammering the creature's head to the floor.

Diana dropped down onto the alien's back, aiming carefully to land between the trapped Investigator and the pinned-down alien head. She hacked at the dark flesh with the edge of her shield, until Frost could get her arms free again, and then between them they dug the Investigator out. The alien thrashed back and forth, convulsing down all its length, unable to get enough leverage to lift its head against the weight of the wall unit. Frost finally got her hand on her monofilament knife, and with Diana's help she cut herself free. They climbed quickly down from the alien and backed away down the corridor, both of them still spattered with its gore.

"Do you think that weight's going to hold it?" yelled Diana, shouting to be heard over the din of the alien's howls.

"Not a chance!" yelled Frost. "Let's get out of here."

She ran down the corridor with Diana at her side. Behind them they heard a crash as the alien finally threw off the wall unit. Diana tried to run faster, and couldn't. Her strength was gone, and she was running now on desperation and adrenalin. The Investigator ran effortlessly beside her, not even breathing hard, despite all she'd been through. It occurred to Diana that Frost could probably get away quite easily, but instead had chosen to run at the esper's slower pace. Frost looked round suddenly and caught the esper's eye.

"You didn't have to save me," she said brusquely. "You could have got away."

"I know that."

"Then why did you do it? Why risk your life to save mine?"

"Because you needed me," said Diana. "Now shut up and run."

"What about the invisibility? Any chance . . . ?"

"No. Not now the alien's locked on to me." She looked back over her shoulder. The alien was flowing down the corridor after them, faster than they were running, faster then they could run. Diana looked at Frost. "Don't ask.

You don't want to know. Just run."

Silence's voice was suddenly in their ears, murmuring through their comm implants. "Investigator, esper, we've destroyed the heart of the alien's web. It is now completely cut off from the rest of the Base. Have you located the alien yet?"

"Oh yes," said Frost. "We know exactly where it is."

"Good. Do you think you could lead it to where Carrion and I are at the moment? We've had an idea."

The floor plan of Level Three flashed briefly before Frost's and Diana's eyes, showing them the route. Diana thought hard. It wasn't far. They might just make it. She looked at Frost, and nodded briefly.

"We can be there in four minutes," said Frost calmly.

"Make it three," said Silence. "We're working to a rather urgent deadline. Bring the alien here, and we'll discuss what to do next. Silence out."

"The Captain's got a plan," panted Diana.

"Yes. Interesting he didn't tell us what it was. Probably because he knows we wouldn't like it." She looked at Diana. "Can you last three minutes at this pace?"

"Shut up and keep running," said Diana.

"Are you sure you want me to do this?" said Carrion. "Once I call up the Ashrai, there'll be no turning back. I don't think you realise just how much they hate you."

"They'll hate the alien more," said Silence. "That creature and its kind threaten the existence of the whole planet. They wouldn't just destroy the forest, they'd change it into something the Ashrai wouldn't even recognise. And since the Ashrai depend on the forest for what's left of their existence, it's in their interest to side with us against the alien."

"Very logical, Captain," said Carrion. "I just hope the Ashrai are going to be logical too."

"The enemy of my enemy is my friend. Nothing like having something in common to bring two peoples together."

"You still don't understand, Captain. Once I summon up the Ashrai, they pass beyond my control. Once awakened, they might decide not to lie down again. You didn't really win here, John. You just hurt them so badly they retreated back inside themselves for a time. There's power here on Unseeli, power beyond your worst nightmares. They might decide to take on the Empire again. And this time they'd have nothing left to lose, nothing to hold them back."

Silence shook his head. "So? You're talking about billions of people on thousands of worlds. The Ashrai wouldn't stand a chance."

"John, you're talking about numbers. I'm talking about power."

"It doesn't make any difference," said Silence. "We don't have any choice. Too many things have gone wrong, and we've too many strikes against us. Frost and the esper will be here any minute, with the alien right behind them. We've run out of options, Sean. Odin, how does the countdown stand?"

"Nineteen minutes, thirty-two seconds, Captain."

Silence looked at Carrion. "Get yourself ready, Sean. We'll do it as soon as the others arrive."

They both looked round at the sound of running footsteps, and Frost and Diana came pounding down the corridor towards them. Silence looked past the women, but the corridor behind them was empty. Diana staggered to a halt, gasping painfully for air. Frost supported her with one hand as she nodded calmly to Silence. As usual, she wasn't even breathing hard.

"The alien's right behind us, Captain. It slowed down a bit when it realised where we were going, but it's still mad enough to keep after us, once it's looked around for a trap. I take it there is a trap here, Captain?"

"Oh, yes," said Silence. "Have you hurt it at all?"

"I shot it and blew it up with grenades, and Diana dropped half a wall on it, but all we did was annoy it." She looked round at the destruction of the alien's heart, and raised an eyebrow. "Very thorough, Captain. You do realise that everything here will repair itself, given enough time?"

"Time is something we're all rather short of, Investigator. Before he died, Commander Starblood found time to activate the Base's self-destruct system. A small nuclear device hidden somewhere on this level is due to detonate in just over eighteen minutes."

Frost stared at him. "You're jinxed, Captain, you know that?"

Diana raised her head and glared at him speechlessly, still too out of breath to talk, but her eyes spoke volumes.

"Whatever you're planning, Captain, start it now," said Frost. "The alien will be here any second, and it's in a really bad mood."

"Don't look at me," said Silence. "It's all down to Carrion now."

"Yes," said the outlaw quietly. "Somehow, it always comes down to me."

"Because you're the best, Carrion."

"Thank you, Captain."

Diana wiped the sweat from her face with her sleeve, and then suddenly raised her head. "Listen. It's close now. Very close."

They all looked down the corridor, into the gloom. There wasn't a sound to be heard, but they could all feel a faint vibration in the floor under their feet. Silence looked at Carrion.

"Please, Sean. For them, if not for me."

Carrion smiled slightly. "You always did know how to fight dirty, John."

Silence nodded, and moved away to stare down the corridor. Frost joined him, and they trained their disrupters on the concealing shadows. Diana finally straightened up as she got her second wind, and found herself a corner to stand in where she could be out of everyone's way. Carrion stood alone in the centre of the room, leaning on his staff, his thoughts elsewhere. He couldn't help feeling he'd come a long way by strange routes to reach this place, this moment. Everything he'd been through, all the rage and fear and heartbreak, just to end up fighting beside John Silence once again. He smiled slightly. Whatever happened, it was good to have seen John again. It was like finding an old coat you used to wear, or a cup you used to drink from as a child. Comforting in its familiarity, tested in its worth, something you could depend on. Silence was back, at his side, and if Carrion had to die, this was not a bad way to go, among people he liked and respected.

Among people. It had been a long ten years, without a human face or a human voice. But still, there had been the Ashrai.

He lifted his legs and sat cross-legged in midair, hovering alone in the middle of the room, his staff lying across his knees. He reached deep inside himself and unlocked his power, channelling it through his power lance, calling up everything he'd ever been or hoped to be. He could feel his esp building, pressing at his shields, eager to be free and loose in the world. He had learned many things in his time on Unseeli, whether he'd wanted to or not, walked paths few humans even knew of, and it had changed him. He was more than human now, a bastard child of Man and Ashrai, and the alien was about to find out what that meant.

He threw his mind up and out, searching for the voices in the wind that were always there, just on the edge of his consciousness. Bright lights blazed in his mind, dazzling him with their presence. They were old and powerful and utterly

inhuman, warm and familiar and comforting; his friends and
his adopted people. He called, and they came for him, where
they would not have come for any other. The outlaw Carrion,
once a man named Sean, talked to the Ashrai in a language
and manner that had nothing human in it.

Silence looked back at Carrion, floating unsupported in
midair, and felt his hackles rise. There was more than ten
years' difference in the outlaw's cool, serene face, and
sometimes it seemed to him that he didn't know this man
Carrion at all. His voice was still the same, but sometimes
Silence thought he saw someone else looking out at him
through Carrion's eyes. Silence shrugged. He'd put all their
lives in that familiar stranger's hands, and it was too late now
for second thoughts. His head snapped back as something
stirred in the darkness at the end of the corridor, and then the
alien came storming out of the shadows towards them, hor-
ribly fast and unstoppable. It raised its blunt, unseeing head,
and its awful howl reverberated in the narrow space.

Silence and Frost fired their disrupters. The vivid energy
beams seared through the alien's vast body, exploding the
black flesh and spattering it across the walls, and didn't
even slow it down. They put away their guns, drew their
swords, and raised their force shields. They stood ready to
meet the alien, knowing they couldn't hope to stand against
it, but doing it anyway because it was their job and their
duty, and because there wasn't anything else they could do,
after all. The alien burst into the room, into what had been
the heart of its web, its shell, and there was no time left
for anything.

And then the Ashrai came.

Silence walked in the metallic forest, each gold and bronze
and silver tree blazing like a star. The trees were singing,
and though he was not a part of it, still the song trembled in
his bones and in his soul, as though it was something he had

known and left behind, long ago. Sean and Frost and Diana walked with him, all of them glowing like the trees. Frost looked younger, happier, at ease with herself, and for the first time since he'd met her, she wore no weapons. No sword or gun or grenades. She looked almost naked without them, but her eyes were clear and untroubled. Sean looked much as he used to, in the days when they could still be friends, with nothing to separate them. He smiled at Silence, and there was understanding if not forgiveness in the outlaw's eyes. And Diana shone more brilliantly than any of them.

The Ashrai walked in the forest, dead but not gone, huge and awesome, with their gargoyle faces and huge bodies, clawed hands and piercing eyes. They sang in harmony with the trees, and power burned brightly in them. The song and the power roared in human and Ashrai alike, building and building, vast and potent, blazing so brightly they knew they had to use it soon or it would burn them all out. The force that drove them focused and concentrated in one person, and Silence had enough of himself left to be faintly surprised that the focus was Diana, not Carrion. Diana Vertue, inhumanly treated but still human, more of an esper than the Empire had ever allowed her to be, unbroken and above all still somehow innocent, with purity of heart and thought and purpose. The power blazed in her, and without rage or hatred she turned it on the alien from outside. It was in the forest too, burning in strange hues, silent and malignant. It shrank back as the song of the trees washed over it, pure and piercing in Diana's voice, and in a moment that seemed to last forever the alien's light guttered and went out and was gone.

And with the alien gone, a host of new voices sounded in the metallic forest—the one hundred and twenty-seven men and women of Base Thirteen, free at last from the terrible thing that had been done to them. Their lights flickered and went out one by one, and there was no sadness in their leaving. It was what they had hoped and prayed for. Two familiar faces smiled briefly—Stasiak and Ripper, bound together on one last journey. They saluted briefly, and were gone. Diana looked out over the Base, and reached casually down to lower the force screen and stop the nuclear countdown. The clock stopped ticking and the bomb disarmed itself, and as simply as that, it was all over.

And then the Ashrai withdrew a little, and looked at John Silence, Captain of the *Darkwind*, ambassador of the Empire. The man who gave the order for the scorching of Unseeli. Silence stood alone, offering no explanation or defence, because he had none. He didn't ask for mercy for himself, because he expected none, but he did ask it for Frost and Diana, because both were innocent, in their way. They smiled and came to stand beside him, facing the Ashrai, because, after all, they belonged together. And that left just Carrion, once called Sean, standing alone between Ashrai and humanity, both and neither. The outlaw leaned on his staff and said nothing.

He passed judgement on us, said a multitude of voices. *Now it shall be passed on him. He must die.*

No, said Frost. *It was his duty.*

No, said Diana. *He has made atonement.*

He must die.

No, said Carrion. *He is my friend.*

As you wish.

And then the Ashrai were gone, and the lights in the trees seemed a little less magnificent without them. And Silence and Carrion and Frost and Diana turned and walked away from the metallic forest, knowing that the memory of its song would always be with them now, wherever they went and whatever they became.

CHAPTER ELEVEN

All the Ghosts Come Home To Roost

THEY left Base Thirteen, stepping one at a time past the unmoving metal doors, and stood blinking owlishly at the evening twilight. Dark clouds filled the sky, filtering the light into shades of grey, but even so, it seemed uncomfortably bright after so long in the darkness of the Base. The sun was a crimson ball riding low on the sky, but the metal trees still blazed fiercely against the falling night. The mists were thickening, moving slowly among the trees like restless thoughts. Three moons drifted high on the evening sky, pale and listless like the memory of sunlight.

Silence stretched slowly, feeling an almost physical relief now that the mission was over and he could finally relax and wind down. It hadn't ended in quite the way he'd thought it would, but then, that was Unseeli for you. Things seemed to have worked out well enough. All that remained now was to return to the *Darkwind,* and spend his time in Quarantine working out a written report his superiors could believe. He had a feeling that might take some time. He looked across at Carrion. The outlaw stood alone, a little away from the others, his face calm, his gaze fixed on the metallic forest. His cloak hung about him like the folded wings of a bird of prey, and Silence thought he could still sense some of the deadly power Carrion had unleashed in the Base. He wasn't the man Silence remembered, and he didn't know whether to feel sad or relieved. The old Carrion had been desperately unhappy. But the outlaw had found something in his exile with the

Ashrai, and Silence thought it might just be peace.

Investigator Frost was calmly running through an inventory of the weapons she'd used up in her fight against the alien and its offshoots. She still had a surprising number left, though Silence was damned if he knew where she'd hidden them about her person. And Diana Vertue, his ship's esper, his daughter, was staring out at the glowing metal trees with wide, fascinated eyes. Silence stirred uneasily as he saw something in her face of the cool alienness in Carrion's gaze. He looked out at the trees, and a faint echo of the Ashrai song moved within him. He knew the song would always be with him now, murmuring quietly in the depths of the back brain, where all the important, instinctive decisions are made. But already the strength of the vision was fading, slipping away from him even as he tried to hold onto it. Perhaps that was for the best, after all. He couldn't have retained the song in all its power and still have remained human. He'd seen what it had done to Carrion. And to Diana. He moved over to stand beside her, and she nodded politely to him before looking back at the trees.

"How do you feel, Diana?"

"Strange. Tired. Different. I don't know, Captain. I've got a lot to think about. I just wish we could have saved some of the Base personnel."

"They were already dead long before we got here," said Silence. "At least we were able to set them free. That's something. I'm not sure how much I believe of what I saw when the Ashrai sang. I can't believe the alien had captured all those souls in its machines . . . but I'm glad we did the right thing, anyway."

Diana nodded slowly. "What will happen to the trees now, Captain?"

"They should be safe enough. That strange crystal-based hyperdrive you and Carrion found in the crashed alien ship changes everything. According to Carrion, it's vastly superior to ours. We're going to have to study and duplicate the alien drive, if we're to stand any chance against the aliens. And since this new hyperdrive apparently doesn't need the heavy metals our drives use, we don't need Unseeli's trees anymore. I suppose there'll still be some mining here, as long as some of us are still using the old drive, but that'll die out, over the years. Unseeli will finally be safe from the Empire, for the simplest of reasons—because Unseeli has nothing the Empire wants anymore."

"There's going to be a war with the aliens, isn't there," said Diana, and there was no question in her voice.

"It's inevitable," said Silence. "As their species spreads out, looking for new spawning grounds to colonize and dominate, they're bound to encounter human planets. And since their whole existence is dependent on taking over and transforming every other life form they come across, I don't really see any chance of our two species agreeing to coexist. You saw the alien's home planet, in that memory crystal. There's no place in their life cycle for peace or diplomacy or mutual interests. They live only to expand, transform, and assimilate everything they encounter. They probably wouldn't even recognise us as a sentient species, just new genetic material to add to their melting pit. They're a deadly threat to the whole Empire, and the Empire has always known how to deal with threats. There's a war coming all right, and it's going to be the bloodiest, deadliest war in our species' history; a war for the survival of humanity."

"Right," said Carrion. "At long last the Empire has found a species as deadly and single-minded as itself. The war will never end till one species or the other is extinct."

"Right," said Frost. "It's going to be magnificent. I can hardly wait."

There was a pause as her companions looked at each other and decided they were going to pretend she hadn't said that. Silence cleared his throat.

"I think we'd better get back to the pinnace. It'll be night soon, and this place is cold enough during the day. Odin, I take it you're still listening in. How are the repairs going? Are you ready for us to board yet?"

"The repair situation is well in hand, Captain. The pinnace is ready to take off at a moment's notice. However, I'm afraid I can't let any of you back on board."

There was a long pause, heavy with meaning, and when Silence finally spoke, his voice was calm and even and very controlled. "What do you mean, you can't let us back on board? You agreed that if we saved the Base and its contents from destruction, you'd take us back to Quarantine on the *Darkwind*."

"I lied," said the AI. "My programming allows me to be flexible under emergency conditions. It was important to motivate you to protect Base Thirteen and its contents, so I lied. I never had any intention of letting you back on board. I'm afraid all of you are contaminated by this new alien species, and I must protect the *Darkwind*."

"Listen, computer," said Silence. "Conditions on Unseeli after nightfall are practically subpolar, and the Base is a mess. You can't just abandon us here."

"Yes I can, Captain. My programming is most explicit on this matter."

"To hell with that," said Frost. "Computer, Code Red Seven. Acknowledge."

"Code Red Seven acknowledged, Investigator."

"Power up the pinnace and stand ready to transport us all back to the *Darkwind*, to start our Quarantine."

"Yes, Investigator."

Silence looked at Frost. "Code Red *Seven*? Even I don't have that kind of Security clearance."

"Neither do I," said Frost. "I stole it, some time back. I always thought it would come in handy one day. And anyway, Investigators are supposed to use their initiative. The computer will do what it's told now. Won't you, Odin?"

"Yes, Investigator. I will serve you to the limits of my programming. I will follow your orders . . . ."

"Computer."

"Yes, Investigator?"

"Shut up."

"Yes, Investigator."

Silence looked at Carrion, and indicated with his head that he wanted to talk to Carrion in private, a little away from the others. The outlaw nodded, and the two of them moved casually away from Frost and Diana.

"My offer of a Pardon still stands," said Silence quietly. "Your experience in defeating the alien makes you a valuable asset. The Empire is going to need what you know. You could come back with us, Sean. With me. Rejoin the Service, become an Investigator again. Things have changed in the ten years you've been away. You could write your own ticket, Sean. And we could be together again, just like old times. What do you say?"

The outlaw looked at him for a long moment. "My name is Carrion, Captain. Sean died a long time ago. I have no wish to return to the Empire, with all its petty politics, hatreds, and destructive rages. I don't belong there anymore. I've walked the path of the Ashrai for ten years now. I can't go back to being human again. To being only human. Before you came, I was a part of the song of the trees, of the Ashrai. I'd forgotten most of my past. You're a ghost to me, John, an echo of a past that no longer has any real meaning for me. I haven't just left humanity, I've moved beyond it."

"Then where will you stand, during the war?" said Silence.

"With my people," said Carrion. "With the Ashrai."

"I've missed you, Sean. Please. I don't want to lose you again."

"You lost me ten years ago, John. It's too late to try and find me now. Neither of us are the people we used to be. I belong here now."

"In other words," said Frost, "he's gone native."

Silence and Carrion looked round sharply, both of them startled. Neither of them had heard Frost approach, but then, she was an Investigator, after all.

"You're welcome to stay here, if you wish," said Carrion to the Investigator. "The song is strong in you. I could teach you the ways of the Ashrai, open your mind to wonders you've never dreamed of. There are treasures of the soul here, just waiting for you to discover them."

"No thanks," said Frost. "Aliens are for killing. It's time to go, Captain."

"Yes," said Silence. "I think it is."

Diana came over to see what they were talking about, and looked confusedly from one silent face to another. "Captain . . . before we go back to the pinnace, can I ask you a question?"

"Of course, esper. What is it?"

"Why do you call the AI Odin?"

"Because he has only one eye," said Silence. Carrion was the only one who smiled. Diana and Frost just looked at each other blankly.

"Don't they teach mythology in the Empire anymore?" said Carrion.

"Not much," said Silence. "A lot of it's been censored, or adjusted. Our superiors thought it might give people ideas. Dangerous things, ideas."

"Then perhaps it's time we made some new myths," said Carrion. "We've started one here, today. A hundred years from now, who we are and what we did will be part of the history books. And how much of us, the real us, will they remember? Or be allowed to remember. But truth lives on, through myths and legends, and our four ghosts will haunt the Empire long after we've gone."

He nodded once to each of them, and strode off into the thickening mists, disappearing finally into the glowing metallic forest of Unseeli.